EDGAR
RICE
BURROUGHS

TARZAN
OF THE
APES

BARNES & NOBLE
NEW YORK

Barnes & Noble, Inc.
122 Fifth Avenue
New York, NY 10011

ISBN: 978-1-4351-6143-6

Cover illustration by Nancy Stahl
Cover design by Patrice Kaplan
Endpaper ©ZiaMary/depositphotos

Manufactured in China

1 3 5 7 9 10 8 6 4 2

Contents

Introduction

Edgar Rice Burroughs' *Tarzan of the Apes* first appeared in the pulp magazine *All-Story* in October 1912. It made an even bigger impact than the author's first novel, *A Princess of Mars*, which had been serialized earlier that year. Indeed, it made a bigger impact than any other novel ever to appear in the pulps. Tarzan became one of the great heroes of twentieth-century fiction, a household name. Tarzan not only made Burroughs rich but eventually convinced the authorities of his hometown to change its name to Tarzana in his honor.

Tarzan owed his great success to his remarkable dual nature. He was a paragon of civilized nobility. Tarzan is a hereditary peer, after all, but that merely confirms his consummate gentility. Yet Tarzan is also of natural nobility, having all the qualifications of an ideal king of the jungle. He was by no means the first feral child to figure in fiction. Many of his predecessors had been inspired by ideas of natural virtue derived from Jean-Jacques Rousseau's thesis that most of the evils afflicting mankind are not the result of heredity but of the perverting effects of civilization. Tarzan, however, easily outshines the rest, proving to be far more charismatic than any rival.

The combination of innocence and strength that made Tarzan so perfect as a hybrid of nature and civilization owed a great deal to Burroughs' principal talent as a writer of popular fiction. Burroughs took daydream fantasies to extremes no writer had reached before, pushing narrative plausibility to new limits. Considered rationally, the myth of Tarzan is completely lacking in realism; his Africa bears no resemblance to the actual Africa and his jungle bears no resemblance to a real jungle—but these are irrelevant quibbles. *Tarzan of the Apes* is not a realistic novel, but it is a great Romance, part of a tradition that goes back at least as far as the Middle Ages. Burroughs brought that tradition into the twentieth century with an unparalleled zest.

The exploration of the heart of Africa made rapid progress in the nineteenth century, when Africa became an important focus of adventure story fiction. Jules Verne, one of the great pioneers of nineteenth-century adventure fiction, set his first novel there, as did H. Rider Haggard, who became Verne's most successful successor. Haggard followed Verne's example in many of his works, writing novels as realistic as possible in the context of contemporary knowledge. Haggard also exploited the Romantic possibilities of Africa in *King Solomon's Mines* and *She*. Burroughs came along at a time when many critics thought the Romantic tradition might be outdated and ripe for replacement—but vulgar realists have been thinking that since the thirteenth century.

Burroughs demonstrated yet again that there is something in the Romantic tradition that offers a deep and fundamental appeal to the human imagination. The key to winning the affection of a large number of readers, Burroughs realized, is to use the Romantic tradition in a manner that fits the demands of the day. Tarzan does so by appealing to the frustrations of conformity that we all feel in living in a complex society. Yet Burroughs does so not by simply writing a fantasy in which his hero "gets away from all that," but by defining a fantasy in which getting away becomes a redemptive process. Tarzan does not merely live an ideal existence in his symbolic jungle, but he also carries the skills learned there into his social intercourse with the damaged products of civilization.

In a way, *Tarzan of the Apes* contained the entirety of the modern hero-myth. But once it became clear that sequels were commercially necessary, Burroughs attacked the problem with typical gusto. *The Return of Tarzan* and *The Beasts of Tarzan* elaborate the mythical schema cleverly. They both involve Tarzan much more extensively in civilized life and give him two things every hero of series fiction needs: a nemesis and a hostage to fortune. The second and third novels in this omnibus complete another phase of the story, not only by exploring Tarzan's dealings with his archvillain, Nikolas Rokoff, but also by bringing his relationship with Jane Porter through stormy waters to a satisfactory haven of stability. The second and third novels also reiterate the celebratory core of the myth in describing Tarzan's homecomings, when he is able to cast off the shackles of civilization and liberate his fundamental self in its ideal context.

Tarzan soon expanded out of the pulp magazines, not merely into hardcover books—where Burroughs was so successful he was able to start his own publishing company—but also into movies and comic books. Burroughs' new audiences probably never went back to the originals. In a way, that is a shame, because comic strips and movies are both stripped-down media obliged to simplify and streamline far more than prose. The movie Tarzans, in particular, are two-dimensional cut-outs of the Tarzan novels written when the author still had all his narrative energy. Burroughs hated the movie Tarzans, which he considered to be travesties. He even went to the trouble of writing a boisterous comedy—*Tarzan and the Lion Man*—in which Tarzan applies to play himself onscreen and is rejected because he is not the right type.

Movies, of course, represent a different fictional world with its own conventions and myths. Perhaps it is unfair to make a direct comparison, but it remains the case that the best Tarzan—and the only authentic one—is the one found in these pages: a masterpiece of the imagination to compare with the heroes of Greek mythology and medieval Romance. Perhaps, being only human, Tarzan could not win a fight against a demigod like Hercules or a gifted extraterrestrial like Superman, but that does not make him any less remarkable. It surely entitles Tarzan to a more intimate place in the secret chamber of the human heart where the resonant string of Romance resides.

BRIAN STABLEFORD

Brian Stableford is the author of more than seventy-five books, including fifty novels and short-fiction collections and the definitive critical studies *Glorious Perversity: The Decline and Fall of Literary Decadence, Scientific Romance in Britain: 1890–1950*, and *The Sociology of Science Fiction*.

TARZAN
of the
APES

The Adventures of Lord Greystoke:
Book One

CONTENTS

I

OUT TO SEA

 had this story from one who had no business to tell it to me, or to any other. I may credit the seductive influence of an old vintage upon the narrator for the beginning of it, and my own skeptical incredulity during the days that followed for the balance of the strange tale.

When my convivial host discovered that he had told me so much, and that I was prone to doubtfulness, his foolish pride assumed the task the old vintage had commenced, and so he unearthed written evidence in the form of musty manuscript, and dry official records of the British Colonial Office to support many of the salient features of his remarkable narrative.

I do not say the story is true, for I did not witness the happenings which it portrays, but the fact that in the telling of it to you I have taken fictitious names for the principal characters quite sufficiently evidences the sincerity of my own belief that it *may* be true.

The yellow, mildewed pages of the diary of a man long dead, and the records of the Colonial Office dovetail perfectly with the narrative of my convivial host, and so I give you the story as I painstakingly pieced it out from these several various agencies.

If you do not find it credible you will at least be as one with me in acknowledging that it is unique, remarkable, and interesting.

From the records of the Colonial Office and from the dead man's diary we learn that a certain young English nobleman, whom we shall call John Clayton, Lord Greystoke, was commissioned to make a peculiarly delicate investigation of conditions in a British West Coast African Colony from whose simple native inhabitants another European power was known to be recruiting soldiers for its native army, which it used solely for the forcible collection of rubber and ivory from the savage tribes along the Congo and the Aruwimi.

The natives of the British Colony complained that many of their young men were enticed away through the medium of fair and glowing promises, but that few if any ever returned to their families.

The Englishmen in Africa went even further, saying that these poor blacks were held in virtual slavery, since after their terms of enlistment expired their ignorance was imposed upon by their white officers, and they were told that they had yet several years to serve.

And so the Colonial Office appointed John Clayton to a new post in British West Africa, but his confidential instructions centered on a thorough investigation of the unfair treatment of black British subjects by the officers of a friendly European power. Why he was sent, is, however, of little moment to this story, for he never made an investigation, nor, in fact, did he ever reach his destination.

Clayton was the type of Englishman that one likes best to associate with the noblest monuments of historic achievement upon a thousand victorious battlefields—a strong, virile man—mentally, morally, and physically.

In stature he was above the average height; his eyes were gray, his features regular and strong; his carriage that of perfect, robust health influenced by his years of army training.

Political ambition had caused him to seek transference from the army to the Colonial Office and so we find him, still young, entrusted with a delicate and important commission in the service of the Queen.

When he received this appointment he was both elated and appalled. The preferment seemed to him in the nature of a well-merited reward for painstaking and intelligent service, and as a stepping stone to posts of greater importance and responsibility; but, on the other hand, he had been married to the Hon. Alice Rutherford for scarce a three months, and it was the thought of taking this fair young girl into the dangers and isolation of tropical Africa that appalled him.

For her sake he would have refused the appointment, but she would not have it so. Instead she insisted that he accept, and, indeed, take her with him.

There were mothers and brothers and sisters, and aunts and cousins to express various opinions on the subject, but as to what they severally advised history is silent.

We know only that on a bright May morning in 1888, John, Lord Greystoke, and Lady Alice sailed from Dover on their way to Africa.

A month later they arrived at Freetown where they chartered a small sailing vessel, the *Fuwalda*, which was to bear them to their final destination.

And here John, Lord Greystoke, and Lady Alice, his wife, vanished from the eyes and from the knowledge of men.

Two months after they weighed anchor and cleared from the port of Freetown a half dozen British war vessels were scouring the south Atlantic for trace of them or their little vessel, and it was almost immediately that the wreckage was found upon the shores of St. Helena which convinced the world that the *Fuwalda* had gone down with all on board, and hence the search was stopped ere it had scarce begun; though hope lingered in longing hearts for many years.

The *Fuwalda*, a barkentine of about one hundred tons, was a vessel of the type often seen in coastwise trade in the far southern Atlantic, their crews composed of the offscourings of the sea—unhanged murderers and cutthroats of every race and every nation.

The *Fuwalda* was no exception to the rule. Her officers were swarthy bullies, hating and hated by their crew. The captain, while a competent seaman, was a brute in his treatment of his men. He knew, or at least he used, but two arguments in his dealings with them—a belaying pin and a revolver—nor is it likely that the motley aggregation he signed would have understood aught else.

So it was that from the second day out from Freetown John Clayton and his young wife witnessed scenes upon the deck of the *Fuwalda* such as they had believed were never enacted outside the covers of printed stories of the sea.

It was on the morning of the second day that the first link was forged in what was destined to form a chain of circumstances ending in a life for one then unborn such as has never been paralleled in the history of man.

Two sailors were washing down the decks of the *Fuwalda*, the first mate was on duty, and the captain had stopped to speak with John Clayton and Lady Alice.

The men were working backwards toward the little party who were facing away from the sailors. Closer and closer they came, until one of them was directly behind the captain. In another moment he would have passed by and this strange narrative would never have been recorded.

But just that instant the officer turned to leave Lord and Lady Greystoke, and, as he did so, tripped against the sailor and sprawled headlong upon the deck, overturning the water-pail so that he was drenched in its dirty contents.

For an instant the scene was ludicrous; but only for an instant. With a volley of awful oaths, his face suffused with the scarlet of mortification and rage, the captain regained his feet, and with a terrific blow felled the sailor to the deck.

The man was small and rather old, so that the brutality of the act was thus accentuated. The other seaman, however, was neither old nor small—a huge bear of a man, with fierce black mustachios, and a great bull neck set between massive shoulders.

As he saw his mate go down he crouched, and, with a low snarl, sprang upon the captain crushing him to his knees with a single mighty blow.

From scarlet the officer's face went white, for this was mutiny; and mutiny he had met and subdued before in his brutal career. Without waiting to rise he whipped a revolver from his pocket, firing point blank at the great mountain of muscle towering before him; but, quick as he was, John Clayton was almost as quick, so that the bullet which was intended for the sailor's heart lodged in the sailor's leg instead, for Lord Greystoke had struck down the captain's arm as he had seen the weapon flash in the sun.

Words passed between Clayton and the captain, the former making it plain that he was disgusted with the brutality displayed toward the crew, nor would he countenance anything further of the kind while he and Lady Greystoke remained passengers.

The captain was on the point of making an angry reply, but, thinking better of it, turned on his heel and black and scowling, strode aft.

He did not care to antagonize an English official, for the Queen's mighty arm wielded a punitive instrument which he could appreciate, and which he feared—England's far-reaching navy.

The two sailors picked themselves up, the older man assisting his wounded comrade to rise. The big fellow, who was known among his mates as Black Michael, tried his leg gingerly, and, finding that it bore his weight, turned to Clayton with a word of gruff thanks.

Though the fellow's tone was surly, his words were evidently well meant. Ere he had scarce finished his little speech he had turned and was limping off toward the forecastle with the very apparent intention of forestalling any further conversation.

They did not see him again for several days, nor did the captain accord them more than the surliest of grunts when he was forced to speak to them.

They took their meals in his cabin, as they had before the unfortunate occurrence; but the captain was careful to see that his duties never permitted him to eat at the same time.

The other officers were coarse, illiterate fellows, but little above the villainous crew they bullied, and were only too glad to avoid social intercourse with the polished English noble and his lady, so that the Claytons were left very much to themselves.

This in itself accorded perfectly with their desires, but it also rather isolated them from the life of the little ship so that they were unable to keep in touch with the daily happenings which were to culminate so soon in bloody tragedy.

There was in the whole atmosphere of the craft that undefinable something which presages disaster. Outwardly, to the knowledge of the Claytons, all went on as before upon the little vessel; but that there was an undertow leading them toward some unknown danger both felt, though they did not speak of it to each other.

On the second day after the wounding of Black Michael, Clayton came on deck just in time to see the limp body of one of the crew being carried below by four of his fellows while the first mate, a heavy belaying pin in his hand, stood glowering at the little party of sullen sailors.

Clayton asked no questions—he did not need to—and the following day, as the great lines of a British battleship grew out of the distant horizon, he half determined to demand that he and Lady Alice be put aboard her, for his fears were steadily increasing that nothing but harm could result from remaining on the lowering, sullen *Fuwalda*.

Toward noon they were within speaking distance of the British vessel, but when Clayton had nearly decided to ask the captain to put them aboard her, the obvious ridiculousness of such a request became suddenly apparent. What reason could he give the officer commanding her majesty's ship for desiring to go back in the direction from which he had just come!

What if he told them that two insubordinate seamen had been roughly handled by their officers? They would but laugh in their sleeves and attribute his reason for wishing to leave the ship to but one thing—cowardice.

John Clayton, Lord Greystoke, did not ask to be transferred to the British man-of-war. Late in the afternoon he saw her upper works fade below the far horizon, but not before he learned that which confirmed his greatest fears, and caused him to curse the false pride which had restrained him from seeking safety for his young wife a few short hours before, when safety was within reach—a safety which was now gone forever.

It was mid-afternoon that brought the little old sailor, who had been felled by the captain a few days before, to where Clayton and his wife stood by the ship's side watching the ever diminishing outlines of the great battleship. The old fellow was polishing brasses, and as he came edging along until close to Clayton he said, in an undertone:

"'Ell's to pay, sir, on this 'ere craft, an' mark my word for it, sir. 'Ell's to pay."

"What do you mean, my good fellow?" asked Clayton.

"Wy, hasn't ye seen wats goin' on? Hasn't ye 'eard that devil's spawn of a capting an' is mates knockin' the bloomin' lights outen 'arf the crew?

"Two busted 'eads yeste'day, an' three to-day. Black Michael's as good as new agin an' 'e's not the bully to stand fer it, not 'e; an' mark my word for it, sir."

"You mean, my man, that the crew contemplates mutiny?" asked Clayton.

"Mutiny!" exclaimed the old fellow. "Mutiny! They means murder, sir, an' mark my word for it, sir."

"When?"

"Hit's comin', sir; hit's comin' but I'm not a-sayin' wen, an' I've said too damned much now, but ye was a good sort t'other day an' I thought it no more'n right to warn ye. But keep a still tongue in yer 'ead an' when ye 'ear shootin' git below an' stay there.

"That's all, only keep a still tongue in yer 'ead, or they'll put a pill between yer ribs, an' mark my word for it, sir," and the old fellow went on with his polishing, which carried him away from where the Claytons were standing.

"Deuced cheerful outlook, Alice," said Clayton.

"You should warn the captain at once, John. Possibly the trouble may yet be averted," she said.

"I suppose I should, but yet from purely selfish motives I am almost prompted to 'keep a still tongue in my 'ead.' Whatever they do now they will spare us in recognition of my stand for this fellow Black Michael, but should they find that I had betrayed them there would be no mercy shown us, Alice."

"You have but one duty, John, and that lies in the interest of vested authority. If you do not warn the captain you are as much a party to whatever follows as though you had helped to plot and carry it out with your own head and hands."

"You do not understand, dear," replied Clayton. "It is of you I am thinking—there lies my first duty. The captain has brought this condition upon himself, so why then should I risk subjecting my wife to unthinkable horrors in a probably futile attempt to save him from his own brutal folly? You have no conception, dear, of what would follow were this pack of cutthroats to gain control of the *Fuwalda*."

"Duty is duty, John, and no amount of sophistries may change it. I would be a poor wife for an English lord were I to be responsible for his shirking a plain duty. I realize the danger which must follow, but I can face it with you."

"Have it as you will then, Alice," he answered, smiling. "Maybe we are borrowing trouble. While I do not like the looks of things on board this ship, they may not be so bad after all, for it is possible that the 'Ancient Mariner' was but voicing the desires of his wicked old heart rather than speaking of real facts.

"Mutiny on the high sea may have been common a hundred years ago, but in this good year 1888 it is the least likely of happenings.

"But there goes the captain to his cabin now. If I am going to warn him I might as well get the beastly job over for I have little stomach to talk with the brute at all."

So saying he strolled carelessly in the direction of the companionway through which the captain had passed, and a moment later was knocking at his door.

"Come in," growled the deep tones of that surly officer.

And when Clayton had entered, and closed the door behind him: "Well?"

"I have come to report the gist of a conversation I heard to-day, because I feel that, while there may be nothing to it, it is as well that you be forearmed. In short, the men contemplate mutiny and murder."

"It's a lie!" roared the captain. "And if you have been interfering again with the discipline of this ship, or meddling in affairs that don't concern you you can take the consequences, and be damned. I don't care whether you are an English lord or not. I'm captain of this here ship, and from now on you keep your meddling nose out of my business."

The captain had worked himself up to such a frenzy of rage that he was fairly purple of face, and he shrieked the last words at the top of his voice, emphasizing his remarks by a loud thumping of the table with one huge fist, and shaking the other in Clayton's face.

Greystoke never turned a hair, but stood eying the excited man with level gaze.

"Captain Billings," he drawled finally, "if you will pardon my candor, I might remark that you are something of an ass."

Whereupon he turned and left the captain with the same indifferent ease that was habitual with him, and which was more surely calculated to raise the ire of a man of Billings' class than a torrent of invective.

So, whereas the captain might easily have been brought to regret his hasty speech had Clayton attempted to conciliate him, his temper was now irrevocably set in the mold in which Clayton had left it, and the last chance of their working together for their common good was gone.

"Well, Alice," said Clayton, as he rejoined his wife, "I might have saved my breath. The fellow proved most ungrateful. Fairly jumped at me like a mad dog.

"He and his blasted old ship may hang, for aught I care; and until we are safely off the thing I shall spend my energies in looking after our own welfare. And I rather fancy the first step to that end should be to go to our cabin and look over my revolvers. I am sorry now that we packed the larger guns and the ammunition with the stuff below."

They found their quarters in a bad state of disorder. Clothing from their open boxes and bags strewed the little apartment, and even their beds had been torn to pieces.

"Evidently someone was more anxious about our belongings than we," said Clayton. "Let's have a look around, Alice, and see what's missing."

A thorough search revealed the fact that nothing had been taken but Clayton's two revolvers and the small supply of ammunition he had saved out for them.

"Those are the very things I most wish they had left us," said Clayton, "and the fact that they wished for them and them alone is most sinister."

"What are we to do, John?" asked his wife. "Perhaps you were right in that our best chance lies in maintaining a neutral position.

"If the officers are able to prevent a mutiny, we have nothing to fear, while if the mutineers are victorious our one slim hope lies in not having attempted to thwart or antagonize them."

"Right you are, Alice. We'll keep in the middle of the road."

As they started to straighten up their cabin, Clayton and his wife simultaneously noticed the corner of a piece of paper protruding from beneath the door of their quarters. As Clayton stooped to reach for it he was amazed to see it move further into the room, and then he realized that it was being pushed inward by someone from without.

Quickly and silently he stepped toward the door, but, as he reached for the knob to throw it open, his wife's hand fell upon his wrist.

"No, John," she whispered. "They do not wish to be seen, and so we cannot afford to see them. Do not forget that we are keeping to the middle of the road."

Clayton smiled and dropped his hand to his side. Thus they stood watching the little bit of white paper until it finally remained at rest upon the floor just inside the door.

"Then Clayton stooped and picked it up. It was a bit of grimy, white paper roughly folded into a ragged square. Opening it they found a crude message printed almost illegibly, and with many evidences of an unaccustomed task.

Translated, it was a warning to the Claytons to refrain from reporting the loss of the revolvers, or from repeating what the old sailor had told them—to refrain on pain of death.

"I rather imagine we'll be good," said Clayton with a rueful smile. "About all we can do is to sit tight and wait for whatever may come."

II

THE SAVAGE HOME

Nor did they have long to wait, for the next morning as Clayton was emerging on deck for his accustomed walk before breakfast, a shot rang out, and then another, and another.

The sight which met his eyes confirmed his worst fears. Facing the little knot of officers was the entire motley crew of the *Fuwalda*, and at their head stood Black Michael.

At the first volley from the officers the men ran for shelter, and from points of vantage behind masts, wheel-house and cabin they returned the fire of the five men who represented the hated authority of the ship.

Two of their number had gone down before the captain's revolver. They lay where they had fallen between the combatants. But then the first mate lunged forward upon his face, and at a cry of command from Black Michael the mutineers charged the remaining four. The crew had been able to muster but six firearms, so most of them were armed with boat hooks, axes, hatchets and crowbars.

The captain had emptied his revolver and was reloading as the charge was made. The second mate's gun had jammed, and so there were but two weapons opposed to the mutineers as they bore down upon the officers, who now started to give back before the infuriated rush of their men.

Both sides were cursing and swearing in a frightful manner, which, together with the reports of the firearms and the screams and groans of the wounded, turned the deck of the *Fuwalda* to the likeness of a mad-house.

Before the officers had taken a dozen backward steps the men were upon them. An ax in the hands of a burly Negro cleft the captain from forehead to chin, and an instant later the others were down: dead or wounded from dozens of blows and bullet wounds.

Short and grisly had been the work of the mutineers of the *Fuwalda*, and through it all John Clayton had stood leaning carelessly beside the companionway puffing meditatively upon his pipe as though he had been but watching an indifferent cricket match.

As the last officer went down he thought it was time that he returned to his wife lest some members of the crew find her alone below.

Though outwardly calm and indifferent, Clayton was inwardly apprehensive and wrought up, for he feared for his wife's safety at the hands of these ignorant, half-brutes into whose hands fate had so remorselessly thrown them.

As he turned to descend the ladder he was surprised to see his wife standing on the steps almost at his side.

"How long have you been here, Alice?"

"Since the beginning," she replied. "How awful, John. Oh, how awful! What can we hope for at the hands of such as those?"

"Breakfast, I hope," he answered, smiling bravely in an attempt to allay her fears.

"At least," he added, "I'm going to ask them. Come with me, Alice. We must not let them think we expect any but courteous treatment."

The men had by this time surrounded the dead and wounded officers, and without either partiality or compassion proceeded to throw both living and dead over the sides of the vessel. With equal heartlessness they disposed of their own dead and dying.

Presently one of the crew spied the approaching Claytons, and with a cry of: "Here's two more for the fishes," rushed toward them with uplifted ax.

But Black Michael was even quicker, so that the fellow went down with a bullet in his back before he had taken a half dozen steps.

With a loud roar, Black Michael attracted the attention of the others, and, pointing to Lord and Lady Greystoke, cried:

"These here are my friends, and they are to be left alone. D'ye understand?

"I'm captain of this ship now, an' what I says goes," he added, turning to Clayton. "Just keep to yourselves, and nobody'll harm ye," and he looked threateningly on his fellows.

The Claytons heeded Black Michael's instructions so well that they saw but little of the crew and knew nothing of the plans the men were making.

Occasionally they heard faint echoes of brawls and quarrelling among the mutineers, and on two occasions the vicious bark of firearms rang out on the still air. But Black Michael was a fit leader for this band of cutthroats, and, withal held them in fair subjection to his rule.

On the fifth day following the murder of the ship's officers, land was sighted by the lookout. Whether island or mainland, Black Michael did not know, but he announced to Clayton that if investigation showed that the place was habitable he and Lady Greystoke were to be put ashore with their belongings.

"You'll be all right there for a few months," he explained, "and by that time we'll have been able to make an inhabited coast somewhere and scatter a bit. Then I'll see that yer gover'ment's notified where you be an' they'll soon send a man-o'war to fetch ye off.

"It would be a hard matter to land you in civilization without a lot o' questions being asked, an' none o' us here has any very convincin' answers up our sleeves."

Clayton remonstrated against the inhumanity of landing them

upon an unknown shore to be left to the mercies of savage beasts, and, possibly, still more savage men.

But his words were of no avail, and only tended to anger Black Michael, so he was forced to desist and make the best he could of a bad situation.

About three o'clock in the afternoon they came about off a beautiful wooded shore opposite the mouth of what appeared to be a landlocked harbor.

Black Michael sent a small boat filled with men to sound the entrance in an effort to determine if the *Fuwalda* could be safely worked through the entrance.

In about an hour they returned and reported deep water through the passage as well as far into the little basin.

Before dark the barkentine lay peacefully at anchor upon the bosom of the still, mirror-like surface of the harbor.

The surrounding shores were beautiful with semitropical verdure, while in the distance the country rose from the ocean in hill and tableland, almost uniformly clothed by primeval forest.

No signs of habitation were visible, but that the land might easily support human life was evidenced by the abundant bird and animal life of which the watchers on the *Fuwalda's* deck caught occasional glimpses, as well as by the shimmer of a little river which emptied into the harbor, insuring fresh water in plenitude.

As darkness settled upon the earth, Clayton and Lady Alice still stood by the ship's rail in silent contemplation of their future abode. From the dark shadows of the mighty forest came the wild calls of savage beasts—the deep roar of the lion, and, occasionally, the shrill scream of a panther.

The woman shrank closer to the man in terror-stricken anticipation of the horrors lying in wait for them in the awful blackness of the nights to come, when they should be alone upon that wild and lonely shore.

Later in the evening Black Michael joined them long enough to instruct them to make their preparations for landing on the morrow. They tried to persuade him to take them to some more hospitable coast near enough to civilization so that they might hope to fall into friendly hands. But no pleas, or threats, or promises of reward could move him.

"I am the only man aboard who would not rather see ye both safely dead, and, while I know that's the sensible way to make sure of our own necks, yet Black Michael's not the man to forget a favor. Ye saved my life once, and in return I'm goin' to spare yours, but that's all I can do.

"The men won't stand for any more, and if we don't get ye landed pretty quick they may even change their minds about giving ye that much show. I'll put all yer stuff ashore with ye as well as cookin' utensils an' some old sails for tents, an' enough grub to last ye until ye can find fruit and game.

"With yer guns for protection, ye ought to be able to live here easy enough until help comes. When I get safely hid away I'll see to it that the British gover'ment learns about where ye be; for the life of me I couldn't tell 'em exactly where, for I don't know myself. But they'll find ye all right."

After he had left them they went silently below, each wrapped in gloomy forebodings.

Clayton did not believe that Black Michael had the slightest intention of notifying the British government of their whereabouts, nor was he any too sure but that some treachery was contemplated for the following day when they should be on shore with the sailors who would have to accompany them with their belongings.

Once out of Black Michael's sight any of the men might strike them down, and still leave Black Michael's conscience clear.

And even should they escape that fate was it not but to be faced with far graver dangers? Alone, he might hope to survive for years; for he was a strong, athletic man.

But what of Alice, and that other little life so soon to be launched amidst the hardships and grave dangers of a primeval world?

The man shuddered as he meditated upon the awful gravity, the fearful helplessness, of their situation. But it was a merciful Providence which prevented him from foreseeing the hideous reality which awaited them in the grim depths of that gloomy wood.

Early next morning their numerous chests and boxes were hoisted on deck and lowered to waiting small boats for transportation to shore.

There was a great quantity and variety of stuff, as the Claytons had expected a possible five to eight years' residence in their new home. Thus, in addition to the many necessities they had brought, there were also many luxuries.

Black Michael was determined that nothing belonging to the Claytons should be left on board. Whether out of compassion for them, or in furtherance of his own self-interests, it would be difficult to say.

There was no question but that the presence of property of a missing British official upon a suspicious vessel would have been a difficult thing to explain in any civilized port in the world.

So zealous was he in his efforts to carry out his intentions that he insisted upon the return of Clayton's revolvers to him by the sailors in whose possession they were.

Into the small boats were also loaded salt meats and biscuit, with a small supply of potatoes and beans, matches, and cooking vessels, a chest of tools, and the old sails which Black Michael had promised them.

As though himself fearing the very thing which Clayton had suspected, Black Michael accompanied them to shore, and was the last to leave them when the small boats, having filled the ship's casks with fresh water, were pushed out toward the waiting *Fuwalda.*

As the boats moved slowly over the smooth waters of the bay, Clayton and his wife stood silently watching their departure—in the breasts of both a feeling of impending disaster and utter hopelessness.

And behind them, over the edge of a low ridge, other eyes watched—close set, wicked eyes, gleaming beneath shaggy brows.

As the *Fuwalda* passed through the narrow entrance to the harbor and out of sight behind a projecting point, Lady Alice threw her arms about Clayton's neck and burst into uncontrolled sobs.

Bravely had she faced the dangers of the mutiny; with heroic fortitude she had looked into the terrible future; but now that the horror of absolute solitude was upon them, her overwrought nerves gave way, and the reaction came.

He did not attempt to check her tears. It were better that nature have her way in relieving these long-pent emotions, and it was many minutes before the girl—little more than a child she was—could again gain mastery of herself.

"Oh, John," she cried at last, "the horror of it. What are we to do? What are we to do?"

"There is but one thing to do, Alice," and he spoke as quietly as though they were sitting in their snug living room at home, "and that is work. Work must be our salvation. We must not give ourselves time to think, for in that direction lies madness.

"We must work and wait. I am sure that relief will come, and come quickly, when once it is apparent that the *Fuwalda* has been lost, even though Black Michael does not keep his word to us."

"But John, if it were only you and I," she sobbed, "we could endure it I know; but—"

"Yes, dear," he answered, gently, "I have been thinking of that, also; but we must face it, as we must face whatever comes, bravely and with the utmost confidence in our ability to cope with circumstances whatever they may be.

"Hundreds of thousands of years ago our ancestors of the dim and distant past faced the same problems which we must face, possibly in these same primeval forests. That we are here today evidences their victory.

"What they did may we not do? And even better, for are we not armed with ages of superior knowledge, and have we not the means of protection, defense, and sustenance which science has given us, but of which they were totally ignorant? What they accomplished, Alice, with instruments and weapons of stone and bone, surely that may we accomplish also."

"Ah, John, I wish that I might be a man with a man's philosophy, but I am but a woman, seeing with my heart rather than my head, and all that I can see is too horrible, too unthinkable to put into words.

"I only hope you are right, John. I will do my best to be a brave primeval woman, a fit mate for the primeval man."

Clayton's first thought was to arrange a sleeping shelter for the night; something which might serve to protect them from prowling beasts of prey.

He opened the box containing his rifles and ammunition, that they might both be armed against possible attack while at work, and then together they sought a location for their first night's sleeping place.

A hundred yards from the beach was a little level spot, fairly free of trees; here they decided eventually to build a permanent house, but for the time being they both thought it best to construct a little platform in the trees out of reach of the larger of the savage beasts in whose realm they were.

To this end Clayton selected four trees which formed a rectangle about eight feet square, and cutting long branches from other trees he constructed a framework around them, about ten feet from the ground, fastening the ends of the branches securely to the trees by means of rope, a quantity of which Black Michael had furnished him from the hold of the *Fuwalda*.

Across this framework Clayton placed other smaller branches quite close together. This platform he paved with the huge fronds of elephant's ear which grew in profusion about them, and over the fronds he laid a great sail folded into several thicknesses.

Seven feet higher he constructed a similar, though lighter platform to serve as roof, and from the sides of this he suspended the balance of his sailcloth for walls.

When completed he had a rather snug little nest, to which he carried their blankets and some of the lighter luggage.

It was now late in the afternoon, and the balance of the daylight hours were devoted to the building of a rude ladder by means of which Lady Alice could mount to her new home.

All during the day the forest about them had been filled with excited birds of brilliant plumage, and dancing, chattering monkeys, who watched these new arrivals and their wonderful nest building operations with every mark of keenest interest and fascination.

Notwithstanding that both Clayton and his wife kept a sharp lookout they saw nothing of larger animals, though on two occasions they had seen their little simian neighbors come screaming and chattering from the near-by ridge, casting frightened glances back over their little shoulders, and evincing as plainly as though by speech that they were fleeing some terrible thing which lay concealed there.

Just before dusk Clayton finished his ladder, and, filling a great basin with water from the near-by stream, the two mounted to the comparative safety of their aerial chamber.

As it was quite warm, Clayton had left the side curtains thrown back over the roof, and as they sat, like Turks, upon their blankets, Lady Alice, straining her eyes into the darkening shadows of the wood, suddenly reached out and grasped Clayton's arms.

"John," she whispered, "look! What is it, a man?"

As Clayton turned his eyes in the direction she indicated, he saw silhouetted dimly against the shadows beyond, a great figure standing upright upon the ridge.

For a moment it stood as though listening and then turned slowly, and melted into the shadows of the jungle.

"What is it, John?"

"I do not know, Alice," he answered gravely, "it is too dark to see so far, and it may have been but a shadow cast by the rising moon."

"No, John, if it was not a man it was some huge and grotesque mockery of man. Oh, I am afraid."

He gathered her in his arms, whispering words of courage and love into her ears.

Soon after, he lowered the curtain walls, tying them securely to the trees so that, except for a little opening toward the beach, they were entirely enclosed.

As it was now pitch dark within their tiny aerie they lay down upon their blankets to try to gain, through sleep, a brief respite of forgetfulness.

Clayton lay facing the opening at the front, a rifle and a brace of revolvers at his hand.

Scarcely had they closed their eyes than the terrifying cry of a panther rang out from the jungle behind them. Closer and closer it came until they could hear the great beast directly beneath them. For an hour or more they heard it sniffing and clawing at the trees which supported their platform, but at last it roamed away across the beach, where Clayton could see it clearly in the brilliant moonlight—a great, handsome beast, the largest he had ever seen.

During the long hours of darkness they caught but fitful snatches of sleep, for the night noises of a great jungle teeming with myriad animal life kept their overwrought nerves on edge, so that a hundred times they were startled to wakefulness by piercing screams, or the stealthy moving of great bodies beneath them.

III

LIFE AND DEATH

orning found them but little, if at all refreshed, though it was with a feeling of intense relief that they saw the day dawn.

As soon as they had made their meager breakfast of salt pork, coffee and biscuit, Clayton commenced work upon their house, for he realized that they could hope for no safety and no peace of mind at night until four strong walls effectually barred the jungle life from them.

The task was an arduous one and required the better part of a month, though he built but one small room. He constructed his cabin of small logs about six inches in diameter, stopping the chinks with clay which he found at the depth of a few feet beneath the surface soil.

At one end he built a fireplace of small stones from the beach. These also he set in clay and when the house had been entirely completed he applied a coating of the clay to the entire outside surface to the thickness of four inches.

In the window opening he set small branches about an inch in diameter both vertically and horizontally, and so woven that they formed a substantial grating that could withstand the strength of a powerful animal. Thus they obtained air and proper ventilation without fear of lessening the safety of their cabin.

The A-shaped roof was thatched with small branches laid close together and over these long jungle grass and palm fronds, with a final coating of clay.

The door he built of pieces of the packing-boxes which had held their belongings, nailing one piece upon another, the grain of contiguous layers running transversely, until he had a solid body some three inches thick and of such great strength that they were both moved to laughter as they gazed upon it.

Here the greatest difficulty confronted Clayton, for he had no means whereby to hang his massive door now that he had built it. After two days' work, however, he succeeded in fashioning two massive hardwood hinges, and with these he hung the door so that it opened and closed easily.

The stuccoing and other final touches were added after they moved into the house, which they had done as soon as the roof was on, piling their boxes before the door at night and thus having a comparatively safe and comfortable habitation.

The building of a bed, chairs, table, and shelves was a relatively easy matter, so that by the end of the second month they were well settled, and, but for the constant dread of attack by wild beasts and the ever growing loneliness, they were not uncomfortable or unhappy.

At night great beasts snarled and roared about their tiny cabin, but, so accustomed may one become to oft repeated noises, that soon they paid little attention to them, sleeping soundly the whole night through.

Thrice had they caught fleeting glimpses of great man-like figures like that of the first night, but never at sufficiently close range to know positively whether the half-seen forms were those of man or brute.

The brilliant birds and the little monkeys had become accustomed to their new acquaintances, and as they had evidently never seen human beings before they presently, after their first fright had worn off, approached closer and closer, impelled by that strange curiosity which dominates the wild creatures of the forest and the jungle and the plain, so that within the first month several of the birds had gone so far as even to accept morsels of food from the friendly hands of the Claytons.

One afternoon, while Clayton was working upon an addition to their cabin, for he contemplated building several more rooms, a number of their grotesque little friends came shrieking and scolding through the trees from the direction of the ridge. Ever as they fled they cast fearful glances back of them, and finally they stopped near Clayton jabbering excitedly to him as though to warn him of approaching danger.

At last he saw it, the thing the little monkeys so feared—the man-brute of which the Claytons had caught occasional fleeting glimpses.

It was approaching through the jungle in a semi-erect position, now and then placing the backs of its closed fists upon the ground—a great anthropoid ape, and, as it advanced, it emitted deep guttural growls and an occasional low barking sound.

Clayton was at some distance from the cabin, having come to fell a particularly perfect tree for his building operations. Grown careless from months of continued safety, during which time he had seen no dangerous animals during the daylight hours, he had left his rifles and revolvers all within the little cabin, and now that he saw the great ape crashing through the underbrush directly toward him, and from a direction which practically cut him off from escape, he felt a vague little shiver play up and down his spine.

He knew that, armed only with an ax, his chances with this ferocious monster were small indeed—and Alice; O God, he thought, what will become of Alice?

There was yet a slight chance of reaching the cabin. He turned and ran toward it, shouting an alarm to his wife to run in and close the great door in case the ape cut off his retreat.

Lady Greystoke had been sitting a little way from the cabin, and when she heard his cry she looked up to see the ape springing with almost incredible swiftness, for so large and awkward an animal, in an effort to head off Clayton.

With a low cry she sprang toward the cabin, and, as she entered, gave a backward glance which filled her soul with terror, for the brute had intercepted her husband, who now stood at bay grasping his ax with both hands ready to swing it upon the infuriated animal when he should make his final charge.

"Close and bolt the door, Alice," cried Clayton. "I can finish this fellow with my ax."

But he knew he was facing a horrible death, and so did she.

The ape was a great bull, weighing probably three hundred pounds. His nasty, close-set eyes gleamed hatred from beneath his shaggy brows, while his great canine fangs were bared in a horrid snarl as he paused a moment before his prey.

Over the brute's shoulder Clayton could see the doorway of his cabin, not twenty paces distant, and a great wave of horror and fear swept over him as he saw his young wife emerge, armed with one of his rifles.

She had always been afraid of firearms, and would never touch them, but now she rushed toward the ape with the fearlessness of a lioness protecting its young.

"Back, Alice," shouted Clayton, "for God's sake, go back."

But she would not heed, and just then the ape charged, so that Clayton could say no more.

The man swung his ax with all his mighty strength, but the powerful brute seized it in those terrible hands, and tearing it from Clayton's grasp hurled it far to one side.

With an ugly snarl he closed upon his defenseless victim, but ere his fangs had reached the throat they thirsted for, there was a sharp report and a bullet entered the ape's back between his shoulders.

Throwing Clayton to the ground the beast turned upon his new enemy. There before him stood the terrified girl vainly trying to fire another bullet into the animal's body; but she did not understand the mechanism of the firearm, and the hammer fell futilely upon an empty cartridge.

Almost simultaneously Clayton regained his feet, and without thought of the utter hopelessness of it, he rushed forward to drag the ape from his wife's prostrate form.

With little or no effort he succeeded, and the great bulk rolled inertly upon the turf before him—the ape was dead. The bullet had done its work.

A hasty examination of his wife revealed no marks upon her, and Clayton decided that the huge brute had died the instant he had sprung toward Alice.

Gently he lifted his wife's still unconscious form, and bore her to the little cabin, but it was fully two hours before she regained consciousness.

Her first words filled Clayton with vague apprehension. For some time after regaining her senses, Alice gazed wonderingly about the interior of the little cabin, and then, with a satisfied sigh, said:

"O, John, it is so good to be really home! I have had an awful dream, dear. I thought we were no longer in London, but in some horrible place where great beasts attacked us."

"There, there, Alice," he said, stroking her forehead, "try to sleep again, and do not worry your head about bad dreams."

That night a little son was born in the tiny cabin beside the primeval forest, while a leopard screamed before the door, and the deep notes of a lion's roar sounded from beyond the ridge.

Lady Greystoke never recovered from the shock of the great ape's attack, and, though she lived for a year after her baby was born, she was never again outside the cabin, nor did she ever fully realize that she was not in England.

Sometimes she would question Clayton as to the strange noises of the nights; the absence of servants and friends, and the strange rudeness of the furnishings within her room, but, though he made no effort to deceive her, never could she grasp the meaning of it all.

In other ways she was quite rational, and the joy and happiness she took in the possession of her little son and the constant attentions of her husband made that year a very happy one for her, the happiest of her young life.

That it would have been beset by worries and apprehension had she been in full command of her mental faculties Clayton well knew; so that while he suffered terribly to see her so, there were times when he was almost glad, for her sake, that she could not understand.

Long since had he given up any hope of rescue, except through accident. With unremitting zeal he had worked to beautify the interior of the cabin.

Skins of lion and panther covered the floor. Cupboards and bookcases lined the walls. Odd vases made by his own hand from the clay of the region held beautiful tropical flowers. Curtains of grass and bamboo covered the windows, and, most arduous task of all, with his meager assortment of tools he had fashioned lumber to neatly seal the walls and ceiling and lay a smooth floor within the cabin.

That he had been able to turn his hands at all to such unaccustomed labor was a source of mild wonder to him. But he loved the work because it was for her and the tiny life that had come to cheer them, though adding a hundredfold to his responsibilities and to the terribleness of their situation.

During the year that followed, Clayton was several times attacked by the great apes which now seemed to continually infest the vicinity of the cabin; but as he never again ventured outside without both rifle and revolvers he had little fear of the huge beasts.

He had strengthened the window protections and fitted a unique wooden lock to the cabin door, so that when he hunted for game and fruits, as it was constantly necessary for him to do to insure sustenance, he had no fear that any animal could break into the little home.

At first he shot much of the game from the cabin windows, but toward the end the animals learned to fear the strange lair from whence issued the terrifying thunder of his rifle.

In his leisure Clayton read, often aloud to his wife, from the store of books he had brought for their new home. Among these were many for little children—picture books, primers, readers—for they had known that their little child would be old enough for such before they might hope to return to England.

At other times Clayton wrote in his diary, which he had always been accustomed to keep in French, and in which he recorded the details of their strange life. This book he kept locked in a little metal box.

A year from the day her little son was born Lady Alice passed quietly away in the night. So peaceful was her end that it was hours before Clayton could awake to a realization that his wife was dead.

The horror of the situation came to him very slowly, and it is doubtful that he ever fully realized the enormity of his sorrow and the fearful responsibility that had devolved upon him with the care of that wee thing, his son, still a nursing babe.

The last entry in his diary was made the morning following her death, and there he recites the sad details in a matter-of-fact way that adds to the pathos of it; for it breathes a tired apathy born of long sorrow and hopelessness, which even this cruel blow could scarcely awake to further suffering:

My little son is crying for nourishment—O Alice, Alice, what shall I do?

And as John Clayton wrote the last words his hand was destined ever to pen, he dropped his head wearily upon his outstretched arms where they rested upon the table he had built for her who lay still and cold in the bed beside him.

For a long time no sound broke the deathlike stillness of the jungle midday save the piteous wailing of the tiny man-child.

IV

THE APES

n the forest of the table-land a mile back from the ocean old Kerchak the Ape was on a rampage of rage among his people.

The younger and lighter members of his tribe scampered to the higher branches of the great trees to escape his wrath; risking their lives upon branches that scarce supported their weight rather than face old Kerchak in one of his fits of uncontrolled anger.

The other males scattered in all directions, but not before the infuriated brute had felt the vertebra of one snap between his great, foaming jaws.

A luckless young female slipped from an insecure hold upon a high branch and came crashing to the ground almost at Kerchak's feet.

With a wild scream he was upon her, tearing a great piece from her side with his mighty teeth, and striking her viciously upon her head and shoulders with a broken tree limb until her skull was crushed to a jelly.

And then he spied Kala, who, returning from a search for food with her young babe, was ignorant of the state of the mighty male's temper until suddenly the shrill warnings of her fellows caused her to scamper madly for safety.

But Kerchak was close upon her, so close that he had almost grasped her ankle had she not made a furious leap far into space from one tree to another——a perilous chance which apes seldom if ever take, unless so closely pursued by danger that there is no alternative.

She made the leap successfully, but as she grasped the limb of the further tree the sudden jar loosened the hold of the tiny babe where it clung frantically to her neck, and she saw the little thing hurled, turning and twisting, to the ground thirty feet below.

With a low cry of dismay Kala rushed headlong to its side, thoughtless now of the danger from Kerchak; but when she gathered the wee, mangled form to her bosom life had left it.

With low moans, she sat cuddling the body to her; nor did Kerchak attempt to molest her. With the death of the babe his fit of demoniacal rage passed as suddenly as it had seized him.

Kerchak was a huge king ape, weighing perhaps three hundred and fifty pounds. His forehead was extremely low and receding, his eyes bloodshot, small and close set to his coarse, flat nose; his ears large and thin, but smaller than most of his kind.

His awful temper and his mighty strength made him supreme among the little tribe into which he had been born some twenty years before.

Now that he was in his prime, there was no simian in all the mighty forest through which he roved that dared contest his right to rule, nor did the other and larger animals molest him.

Old Tantor, the elephant, alone of all the wild savage life, feared him not——and he alone did Kerchak fear. When Tantor trumpeted, the great ape scurried with his fellows high among the trees of the second terrace.

The tribe of anthropoids over which Kerchak ruled with an iron hand and bared fangs, numbered some six or eight families, each family consisting of an adult male with his females and their young, numbering in all some sixty or seventy apes.

Kala was the youngest mate of a male called Tublat, meaning broken nose, and the child she had seen dashed to death was her first; for she was but nine or ten years old.

Notwithstanding her youth, she was large and powerful—a splendid, clean-limbed animal, with a round, high forehead, which denoted more intelligence than most of her kind possessed. So, also, she had a great capacity for mother love and mother sorrow.

But she was still an ape, a huge, fierce, terrible beast of a species closely allied to the gorilla, yet more intelligent; which, with the strength of their cousin, made her kind the most fearsome of those awe-inspiring progenitors of man.

When the tribe saw that Kerchak's rage had ceased they came slowly down from their arboreal retreats and pursued again the various occupations which he had interrupted.

The young played and frolicked about among the trees and bushes. Some of the adults lay prone upon the soft mat of dead and decaying vegetation which covered the ground, while others turned over pieces of fallen branches and clods of earth in search of the small bugs and reptiles which formed a part of their food.

Others, again, searched the surrounding trees for fruit, nuts, small birds, and eggs.

They had passed an hour or so thus when Kerchak called them together, and, with a word of command to them to follow him, set off toward the sea.

They traveled for the most part upon the ground, where it was open, following the path of the great elephants whose comings and goings break the only roads through those tangled mazes of bush, vine, creeper, and tree. When they walked it was with a rolling, awkward motion, placing the knuckles of their closed hands upon the ground and swinging their ungainly bodies forward.

But when the way was through the lower trees they moved more swiftly, swinging from branch to branch with the agility of their smaller cousins, the monkeys. And all the way Kala carried her little dead baby hugged closely to her breast.

It was shortly after noon when they reached a ridge overlooking the beach where below them lay the tiny cottage which was Kerchak's goal.

He had seen many of his kind go to their deaths before the loud noise made by the little black stick in the hands of the strange white ape who lived in that wonderful lair, and Kerchak had made up his brute mind to own that death-dealing contrivance, and to explore the interior of the mysterious den.

He wanted, very, very much, to feel his teeth sink into the neck of the queer animal that he had learned to hate and fear, and because of this, he came often with his tribe to reconnoiter, waiting for a time when the white ape should be off his guard.

Of late they had quit attacking, or even showing themselves; for every time they had done so in the past the little stick had roared out its terrible message of death to some member of the tribe.

Today there was no sign of the man about, and from where they watched they could see that the cabin door was open. Slowly, cautiously, and noiselessly they crept through the jungle toward the little cabin.

There were no growls, no fierce screams of rage—the little black stick had taught them to come quietly lest they awaken it.

On, on they came until Kerchak himself slunk stealthily to the very door and peered within. Behind him were two males, and then Kala, closely straining the little dead form to her breast.

Inside the den they saw the strange white ape lying half across a table, his head buried in his arms; and on the bed lay a figure covered by a sailcloth, while from a tiny rustic cradle came the plaintive wailing of a babe.

Noiselessly Kerchak entered, crouching for the charge; and then John Clayton rose with a sudden start and faced them.

The sight that met his eyes must have frozen him with horror, for there, within the door, stood three great bull apes, while behind them crowded many more; how many he never knew, for his revolvers were hanging on the far wall beside his rifle, and Kerchak was charging.

When the king ape released the limp form which had been John Clayton, Lord Greystoke, he turned his attention toward the little cradle; but Kala was there before him, and when he would have grasped the child she snatched it herself, and before he could intercept her she had bolted through the door and taken refuge in a high tree.

As she took up the little live baby of Alice Clayton she dropped the dead body of her own into the empty cradle; for the wail of the living had answered the call of universal motherhood within her wild breast which the dead could not still.

High up among the branches of a mighty tree she hugged the shrieking infant to her bosom, and soon the instinct that was as dominant in this fierce female as it had been in the breast of his tender and beautiful mother—the instinct of mother love—reached out to the tiny man-child's half-formed understanding, and he became quiet.

Then hunger closed the gap between them, and the son of an English lord and an English lady nursed at the breast of Kala, the great ape.

In the meantime the beasts within the cabin were warily examining the contents of this strange lair.

Once satisfied that Clayton was dead, Kerchak turned his attention to the thing which lay upon the bed, covered by a piece of sailcloth.

Gingerly he lifted one corner of the shroud, but when he saw the body of the woman beneath he tore the cloth roughly from her form and seized the still, white throat in his huge, hairy hands.

A moment he let his fingers sink deep into the cold flesh, and then, realizing that she was already dead, he turned from her, to examine the contents of the room; nor did he again molest the body of either Lady Alice or Sir John.

The rifle hanging upon the wall caught his first attention; it was for this strange, death-dealing thunder-stick that he had yearned for months; but now that it was within his grasp he scarcely had the temerity to seize it.

Cautiously he approached the thing, ready to flee precipitately should it speak in its deep roaring tones, as he had heard it speak before, the last words to those of his kind who, through ignorance or rashness, had attacked the wonderful white ape that had borne it.

Deep in the beast's intelligence was something which assured him that the thunder-stick was only dangerous when in the hands of one who could manipulate it, but yet it was several minutes ere he could bring himself to touch it.

Instead, he walked back and forth along the floor before it, turning his head so that never once did his eyes leave the object of his desire.

Using his long arms as a man uses crutches, and rolling his huge carcass from side to side with each stride, the great king ape paced to and fro, uttering deep growls, occasionally punctuated with the ear-piercing scream, than which there is no more terrifying noise in all the jungle.

Presently he halted before the rifle. Slowly he raised a huge hand until it almost touched the shining barrel, only to withdraw it once more and continue his hurried pacing.

It was as though the great brute by this show of fearlessness, and through the medium of his wild voice, was endeavoring to bolster up his courage to the point which would permit him to take the rifle in his hand.

Again he stopped, and this time succeeded in forcing his reluctant hand to the cold steel, only to snatch it away almost immediately and resume his restless beat.

Time after time this strange ceremony was repeated, but on each occasion with increased confidence, until, finally, the rifle was torn from its hook and lay in the grasp of the great brute.

Finding that it harmed him not, Kerchak began to examine it closely. He felt of it from end to end, peered down the black depths of the muzzle, fingered the sights, the breech, the stock, and finally the trigger.

During all these operations the apes who had entered sat huddled near the door watching their chief, while those outside strained and crowded to catch a glimpse of what transpired within.

Suddenly Kerchak's finger closed upon the trigger. There was a deafening roar in the little room and the apes at and beyond the door fell over one another in their wild anxiety to escape.

Kerchak was equally frightened, so frightened, in fact, that he quite forgot to throw aside the author of that fearful noise, but bolted for the door with it tightly clutched in one hand.

As he passed through the opening, the front sight of the rifle caught upon the edge of the inswung door with sufficient force to close it tightly after the fleeing ape.

When Kerchak came to a halt a short distance from the cabin and discovered that he still held the rifle, he dropped it as he might have dropped a red hot iron, nor did he again attempt to recover it—the noise was too much for his brute nerves; but he was now quite convinced that the terrible stick was quite harmless by itself if left alone.

It was an hour before the apes could again bring themselves to approach the cabin to continue their investigations, and when they finally did so, they found to their chagrin that the door was closed and so securely fastened that they could not force it.

The cleverly constructed latch which Clayton had made for the door had sprung as Kerchak passed out; nor could the apes find means of ingress through the heavily barred windows.

After roaming about the vicinity for a short time, they started back for the deeper forests and the higher land from whence they had come.

Kala had not once come to earth with her little adopted babe, but now Kerchak called to her to descend with the rest, and as there was no note of anger in his voice she dropped lightly from branch to branch and joined the others on their homeward march.

Those of the apes who attempted to examine Kala's strange baby were repulsed with bared fangs and low menacing growls, accompanied by words of warning from Kala.

When they assured her that they meant the child no harm she permitted them to come close, but would not allow them to touch her charge.

It was as though she knew that her baby was frail and delicate and feared lest the rough hands of her fellows might injure the little thing.

Another thing she did, and which made traveling an onerous trial for her. Remembering the death of her own little one, she clung desperately to the new babe, with one hand, whenever they were upon the march.

The other young rode upon their mothers' backs; their little arms tightly clasping the hairy necks before them, while their legs were locked beneath their mothers' armpits.

Not so with Kala; she held the small form of the little Lord Greystoke tightly to her breast, where the dainty hands clutched the long black hair which covered that portion of her body. She had seen one child fall from her back to a terrible death, and she would take no further chances with this.

V

THE WHITE APE

 enderly Kala nursed her little waif, wondering silently why it did not gain strength and agility as did the little apes of other mothers. It was nearly a year from the time the little fellow came into her possession before he would walk alone, and as for climbing—my, but how stupid he was!

Kala sometimes talked with the older females about her young hopeful, but none of them could understand how a child could be so slow and backward in learning to care for itself. Why, it could not even find food alone, and more than twelve moons had passed since Kala had come upon it.

Had they known that the child had seen thirteen moons before it had come into Kala's possession they would have considered its case as absolutely hopeless, for the little apes of their own tribe were as far advanced in two or three moons as was this little stranger after twenty-five.

Tublat, Kala's husband, was sorely vexed, and but for the female's careful watching would have put the child out of the way.

"He will never be a great ape," he argued. "Always will you have to carry him and protect him. What good will he be to the tribe? None; only a burden.

"Let us leave him quietly sleeping among the tall grasses, that you may bear other and stronger apes to guard us in our old age."

41

"Never, Broken Nose," replied Kala. "If I must carry him forever, so be it."

And then Tublat went to Kerchak to urge him to use his authority with Kala, and force her to give up little Tarzan, which was the name they had given to the tiny Lord Greystoke, and which meant "White-Skin."

But when Kerchak spoke to her about it Kala threatened to run away from the tribe if they did not leave her in peace with the child; and as this is one of the inalienable rights of the jungle folk, if they be dissatisfied among their own people, they bothered her no more, for Kala was a fine clean-limbed young female, and they did not wish to lose her.

As Tarzan grew he made more rapid strides, so that by the time he was ten years old he was an excellent climber, and on the ground could do many wonderful things which were beyond the powers of his little brothers and sisters.

In many ways did he differ from them, and they often marveled at his superior cunning, but in strength and size he was deficient; for at ten the great anthropoids were fully grown, some of them towering over six feet in height, while little Tarzan was still but a half-grown boy.

Yet such a boy!

From early childhood he had used his hands to swing from branch to branch after the manner of his giant mother, and as he grew older he spent hour upon hour daily speeding through the tree tops with his brothers and sisters.

He could spring twenty feet across space at the dizzy heights of the forest top, and grasp with unerring precision, and without apparent jar, a limb waving wildly in the path of an approaching tornado.

He could drop twenty feet at a stretch from limb to limb in rapid descent to the ground, or he could gain the utmost pinnacle of the loftiest tropical giant with the ease and swiftness of a squirrel.

Though but ten years old he was fully as strong as the average man of thirty, and far more agile than the most practiced athlete ever becomes. And day by day his strength was increasing.

His life among these fierce apes had been happy; for his recollection held no other life, nor did he know that there existed within the universe aught else than his little forest and the wild jungle animals with which he was familiar.

He was nearly ten before he commenced to realize that a great difference existed between himself and his fellows. His little body, burned brown by exposure, suddenly caused him feelings of intense shame, for he realized that it was entirely hairless, like some low snake, or other reptile.

He attempted to obviate this by plastering himself from head to foot with mud, but this dried and fell off. Besides it felt so uncomfortable that he quickly decided that he preferred the shame to the discomfort.

In the higher land which his tribe frequented was a little lake, and it was here that Tarzan first saw his face in the clear, still waters of its bosom.

It was on a sultry day of the dry season that he and one of his cousins had gone down to the bank to drink. As they leaned over, both little faces were mirrored on the placid pool; the fierce and terrible features of the ape beside those of the aristocratic scion of an old English house.

Tarzan was appalled. It had been bad enough to be hairless, but to own such a countenance! He wondered that the other apes could look at him at all.

That tiny slit of a mouth and those puny white teeth! How they looked beside the mighty lips and powerful fangs of his more fortunate brothers!

And the little pinched nose of his; so thin was it that it looked half starved. He turned red as he compared it with the beautiful broad nostrils of his companion. Such a generous nose! Why it spread half across his face! It certainly must be fine to be so handsome, thought poor little Tarzan.

But when he saw his own eyes; ah, that was the final blow—a brown spot, a gray circle and then blank whiteness! Frightful! not even the snakes had such hideous eyes as he.

So intent was he upon this personal appraisement of his features that he did not hear the parting of the tall grass behind him as a great body pushed itself stealthily through the jungle; nor did his companion, the ape, hear either, for he was drinking and the noise of his sucking lips and gurgles of satisfaction drowned the quiet approach of the intruder.

Not thirty paces behind the two she crouched—Sabor, the huge lioness—lashing her tail. Cautiously she moved a great padded paw forward, noiselessly placing it before she lifted the next. Thus she advanced; her belly low, almost touching the surface of the ground—a great cat preparing to spring upon its prey.

Now she was within ten feet of the two unsuspecting little playfellows—carefully she drew her hind feet well up beneath her body, the great muscles rolling under the beautiful skin.

So low she was crouching now that she seemed flattened to the earth except for the upward bend of the glossy back as it gathered for the spring.

No longer the tail lashed—quiet and straight behind her it lay.

An instant she paused thus, as though turned to stone, and then, with an awful scream, she sprang.

Sabor, the lioness, was a wise hunter. To one less wise the wild alarm of her fierce cry as she sprang would have seemed a foolish thing, for could she not more surely have fallen upon her victims had she but quietly leaped without that loud shriek?

But Sabor knew well the wondrous quickness of the jungle folk and their almost unbelievable powers of hearing. To them the sudden scraping of one blade of grass across another was as effectual a warning as her loudest cry, and Sabor knew that she could not make that mighty leap without a little noise.

Her wild scream was not a warning. It was voiced to freeze her poor victims in a paralysis of terror for the tiny fraction of an instant which would suffice for her mighty claws to sink into their soft flesh and hold them beyond hope of escape.

So far as the ape was concerned, Sabor reasoned correctly. The little fellow crouched trembling just an instant, but that instant was quite long enough to prove his undoing.

Not so, however, with Tarzan, the man-child. His life amidst the dangers of the jungle had taught him to meet emergencies with self-confidence, and his higher intelligence resulted in a quickness of mental action far beyond the powers of the apes.

So the scream of Sabor, the lioness, galvanized the brain and muscles of little Tarzan into instant action.

Before him lay the deep waters of the little lake, behind him certain death; a cruel death beneath tearing claws and rending fangs.

Tarzan had always hated water except as a medium for quenching his thirst. He hated it because he connected it with the chill and discomfort of the torrential rains, and he feared it for the thunder and lightning and wind which accompanied them.

The deep waters of the lake he had been taught by his wild mother to avoid, and further, had he not seen little Neeta sink beneath its quiet surface only a few short weeks before never to return to the tribe?

But of the two evils his quick mind chose the lesser ere the first note of Sabor's scream had scarce broken the quiet of the jungle, and before the great beast had covered half her leap Tarzan felt the chill waters close above his head.

He could not swim, and the water was very deep; but still he lost no particle of that self-confidence and resourcefulness which were the badges of his superior being.

Rapidly he moved his hands and feet in an attempt to scramble upward, and, possibly more by chance than design, he fell into the stroke that a dog uses when swimming, so that within a few seconds his nose was above water and he found that he could keep it there by continuing his strokes, and also make progress through the water.

He was much surprised and pleased with this new acquirement which had been so suddenly thrust upon him, but he had no time for thinking much upon it.

He was now swimming parallel to the bank and there he saw the cruel beast that would have seized him crouching upon the still form of his little playmate.

The lioness was intently watching Tarzan, evidently expecting him to return to shore, but this the boy had no intention of doing.

Instead he raised his voice in the call of distress common to his tribe, adding to it the warning which would prevent would-be rescuers from running into the clutches of Sabor.

Almost immediately there came an answer from the distance, and presently forty or fifty great apes swung rapidly and majestically through the trees toward the scene of tragedy.

In the lead was Kala, for she had recognized the tones of her best beloved, and with her was the mother of the little ape who lay dead beneath cruel Sabor.

Though more powerful and better equipped for fighting than the apes, the lioness had no desire to meet these enraged adults, and with a snarl of hatred she sprang quickly into the brush and disappeared.

Tarzan now swam to shore and clambered quickly upon dry land. The feeling of freshness and exhilaration which the cool waters had imparted to him, filled his little being with grateful surprise, and ever after he lost no opportunity to take a daily plunge in lake or stream or ocean when it was possible to do so.

For a long time Kala could not accustom herself to the sight; for though her people could swim when forced to it, they did not like to enter water, and never did so voluntarily.

The adventure with the lioness gave Tarzan food for pleasurable memories, for it was such affairs which broke the monotony of his daily life—otherwise but a dull round of searching for food, eating, and sleeping.

The tribe to which he belonged roamed a tract extending, roughly, twenty-five miles along the seacoast and some fifty miles inland. This they traversed almost continually, occasionally remaining for months in one locality; but as they moved through the trees with great speed they often covered the territory in a very few days.

Much depended upon food supply, climatic conditions, and the prevalence of animals of the more dangerous species; though Kerchak often led them on long marches for no other reason than that he had tired of remaining in the same place.

At night they slept where darkness overtook them, lying upon the ground, and sometimes covering their heads, and more seldom their bodies, with the great leaves of the elephant's ear. Two or three might lie cuddled in each other's arms for additional warmth if the night were chill, and thus Tarzan had slept in Kala's arms nightly for all these years.

That the huge, fierce brute loved this child of another race is beyond question, and he, too, gave to the great, hairy beast all the affection that would have belonged to his fair young mother had she lived.

When he was disobedient she cuffed him, it is true, but she was never cruel to him, and was more often caressing him than chastising him.

Tublat, her mate, always hated Tarzan, and on several occasions had come near ending his youthful career.

Tarzan on his part never lost an opportunity to show that he fully reciprocated his foster father's sentiments, and whenever he could safely annoy him or make faces at him or hurl insults upon him from the safety of his mother's arms, or the slender branches of the higher trees, he did so.

His superior intelligence and cunning permitted him to invent a thousand diabolical tricks to add to the burdens of Tublat's life.

Early in his boyhood he had learned to form ropes by twisting and tying long grasses together, and with these he was forever tripping Tublat or attempting to hang him from some overhanging branch.

By constant playing and experimenting with these he learned to tie rude knots, and make sliding nooses; and with these he and the younger apes amused themselves. What Tarzan did they tried to do also, but he alone originated and became proficient.

One day while playing thus Tarzan had thrown his rope at one of his fleeing companions, retaining the other end in his grasp. By accident the noose fell squarely about the running ape's neck, bringing him to a sudden and surprising halt.

Ah, here was a new game, a fine game, thought Tarzan, and immediately he attempted to repeat the trick. And thus, by painstaking and continued practice, he learned the art of roping.

Now, indeed, was the life of Tublat a living nightmare. In sleep, upon the march, night or day, he never knew when that quiet noose would slip about his neck and nearly choke the life out of him.

Kala punished, Tublat swore dire vengeance, and old Kerchak took notice and warned and threatened; but all to no avail.

Tarzan defied them all, and the thin, strong noose continued to settle about Tublat's neck whenever he least expected it.

The other apes derived unlimited amusement from Tublat's discomfiture, for Broken Nose was a disagreeable old fellow, whom no one liked, anyway.

In Tarzan's clever little mind many thoughts revolved, and back of these was his divine power of reason.

If he could catch his fellow apes with his long arm of many grasses, why not Sabor, the lioness?

It was the germ of a thought, which, however, was destined to mull around in his conscious and subconscious mind until it resulted in magnificent achievement.

But that came in later years.

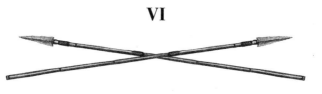

VI

JUNGLE BATTLES

he wanderings of the tribe brought them often near the closed and silent cabin by the little land-locked harbor. To Tarzan this was always a source of never-ending mystery and pleasure.

He would peek into the curtained windows, or, climbing upon the roof, peer down the black depths of the chimney in vain endeavor to solve the unknown wonders that lay within those strong walls.

His child-like imagination pictured wonderful creatures within, and the very impossibility of forcing entrance added a thousandfold to his desire to do so.

He could clamber about the roof and windows for hours attempting to discover means of ingress, but to the door he paid little attention, for this was apparently as solid as the walls.

It was in the next visit to the vicinity, following the adventure with old Sabor, that, as he approached the cabin, Tarzan noticed that from a distance the door appeared to be an independent part of the wall in which it was set, and for the first time it occurred to him that this might prove the means of entrance which had so long eluded him.

He was alone, as was often the case when he visited the cabin, for the apes had no love for it; the story of the thunder-stick having lost nothing in the telling during these ten years had quite surrounded the white man's deserted abode with an atmosphere of weirdness and terror for the simians.

The story of his own connection with the cabin had never been told him. The language of the apes had so few words that they could talk but little of what they had seen in the cabin, having no words to accurately describe either the strange people or their belongings, and so, long before Tarzan was old enough to understand, the subject had been forgotten by the tribe.

Only in a dim, vague way had Kala explained to him that his father had been a strange white ape, but he did not know that Kala was not his own mother.

On this day, then, he went directly to the door and spent hours examining it and fussing with the hinges, the knob and the latch. Finally he stumbled upon the right combination, and the door swung creakingly open before his astonished eyes.

For some minutes he did not dare venture within, but finally, as his eyes became accustomed to the dim light of the interior he slowly and cautiously entered.

In the middle of the floor lay a skeleton, every vestige of flesh gone from the bones to which still clung the mildewed and moldered remnants of what had once been clothing. Upon the bed lay a similar gruesome thing, but smaller, while in a tiny cradle near-by was a third, a wee mite of a skeleton.

To none of these evidences of a fearful tragedy of a long dead day did little Tarzan give but passing heed. His wild jungle life had inured him to the sight of dead and dying animals, and had he known that he was looking upon the remains of his own father and mother he would have been no more greatly moved.

The furnishings and other contents of the room it was which riveted his attention. He examined many things minutely—strange tools and weapons, books, paper, clothing—what little had withstood the ravages of time in the humid atmosphere of the jungle coast.

He opened chests and cupboards; such as did not baffle his small experience, and in these he found the contents much better preserved.

Among other things he found a sharp hunting knife, on the keen blade of which he immediately proceeded to cut his finger. Undaunted he continued his experiments, finding that he could hack and hew splinters of wood from the table and chairs with this new toy.

For a long time this amused him, but finally tiring he continued his explorations. In a cupboard filled with books he came across one with brightly colored pictures—it was a child's illustrated alphabet—

A is for Archer
Who shoots with a bow.
B is for Boy,
His first name is Joe.

The pictures interested him greatly.

There were many apes with faces similar to his own, and further over in the book he found, under "M," some little monkeys such as he saw daily flitting through the trees of his primeval forest. But nowhere was pictured any of his own people; in all the book was none that resembled Kerchak, or Tublat, or Kala.

At first he tried to pick the little figures from the leaves, but he soon saw that they were not real, though he knew not what they might be, nor had he any words to describe them.

The boats, and trains, and cows and horses were quite meaningless to him, but not quite so baffling as the odd little figures which appeared beneath and between the colored pictures—some strange kind of bug he thought they might be, for many of them had legs though nowhere could he find one with eyes and a mouth. It was his first introduction to the letters of the alphabet, and he was over ten years old.

Of course he had never before seen print, or ever had spoken with any living thing which had the remotest idea that such a thing as a written language existed, nor ever had he seen anyone reading.

So what wonder that the little boy was quite at a loss to guess the meaning of these strange figures.

Near the middle of the book he found his old enemy, Sabor, the lioness, and further on, coiled Histah, the snake.

Oh, it was most engrossing! Never before in all his ten years had he enjoyed anything so much. So absorbed was he that he did not note the approaching dusk, until it was quite upon him and the figures were blurred.

He put the book back in the cupboard and closed the door, for he did not wish anyone else to find and destroy his treasure, and as he went out into the gathering darkness he closed the great door of the cabin behind him as it had been before he discovered the secret of its lock, but before he left he had noticed the hunting knife lying where he had thrown it upon the floor, and this he picked up and took with him to show to his fellows.

He had taken scarce a dozen steps toward the jungle when a great form rose up before him from the shadows of a low bush. At first he thought it was one of his own people but in another instant he realized that it was Bolgani, the huge gorilla.

So close was he that there was no chance for flight and little Tarzan knew that he must stand and fight for his life; for these great beasts were the deadly enemies of his tribe, and neither one nor the other ever asked or gave quarter.

Had Tarzan been a full-grown bull ape of the species of his tribe he would have been more than a match for the gorilla, but being only a little English boy, though enormously muscular for such, he stood no chance against his cruel antagonist. In his veins, though, flowed the blood of the best of a race of mighty fighters, and back of this was the training of his short lifetime among the fierce brutes of the jungle.

He knew no fear, as we know it; his little heart beat the faster but from the excitement and exhilaration of adventure. Had the opportunity presented itself he would have escaped, but solely because his judgment told him he was no match for the great thing which confronted him. And since reason showed him that successful flight was impossible he met the gorilla squarely and bravely without a tremor of a single muscle, or any sign of panic.

In fact he met the brute midway in its charge, striking its huge body with his closed fists and as futilely as he had been a fly attacking an elephant. But in one hand he still clutched the knife he had found in the cabin of his father, and as the brute, striking and biting, closed upon him the boy accidentally turned the point toward the hairy breast. As the knife sank deep into its body the gorilla shrieked in pain and rage.

But the boy had learned in that brief second a use for his sharp and shining toy, so that, as the tearing, striking beast dragged him to earth he plunged the blade repeatedly and to the hilt into its breast.

The gorilla, fighting after the manner of its kind, struck terrific blows with its open hand, and tore the flesh at the boy's throat and chest with its mighty tusks.

For a moment they rolled upon the ground in the fierce frenzy of combat. More and more weakly the torn and bleeding arm struck home with the long sharp blade, then the little figure stiffened with a spasmodic jerk, and Tarzan, the young Lord Greystoke, rolled unconscious upon the dead and decaying vegetation which carpeted his jungle home.

A mile back in the forest the tribe had heard the fierce challenge of the gorilla, and, as was his custom when any danger threatened, Kerchak called his people together, partly for mutual protection against a common enemy, since this gorilla might be but one of a party of several, and also to see that all members of the tribe were accounted for.

It was soon discovered that Tarzan was missing, and Tublat was strongly opposed to sending assistance. Kerchak himself had no liking for the strange little waif, so he listened to Tublat, and, finally, with a shrug of his shoulders, turned back to the pile of leaves on which he had made his bed.

But Kala was of a different mind; in fact, she had not waited but to learn that Tarzan was absent ere she was fairly flying through the matted branches toward the point from which the cries of the gorilla were still plainly audible.

Darkness had now fallen, and an early moon was sending its faint light to cast strange, grotesque shadows among the dense foliage of the forest.

Here and there the brilliant rays penetrated to earth, but for the most part they only served to accentuate the Stygian blackness of the jungle's depths.

Like some huge phantom, Kala swung noiselessly from tree to tree; now running nimbly along a great branch, now swinging through space at the end of another, only to grasp that of a farther tree in her rapid progress toward the scene of the tragedy her knowledge of jungle life told her was being enacted a short distance before her.

The cries of the gorilla proclaimed that it was in mortal combat with some other denizen of the fierce wood. Suddenly these cries ceased, and the silence of death reigned throughout the jungle.

Kala could not understand, for the voice of Bolgani had at last been raised in the agony of suffering and death, but no sound had come to her by which she possibly could determine the nature of his antagonist.

That her little Tarzan could destroy a great bull gorilla she knew to be improbable, and so, as she neared the spot from which the sounds of the struggle had come, she moved more warily and at last slowly and with extreme caution she traversed the lowest branches, peering eagerly into the moon-splashed blackness for a sign of the combatants.

Presently she came upon them, lying in a little open space full under the brilliant light of the moon—little Tarzan's torn and bloody form, and beside it a great bull gorilla, stone dead.

With a low cry Kala rushed to Tarzan's side, and gathering the poor, blood-covered body to her breast, listened for a sign of life. Faintly she heard it—the weak beating of the little heart.

Tenderly she bore him back through the inky jungle to where the tribe lay, and for many days and nights she sat guard beside him, bringing him food and water, and brushing the flies and other insects from his cruel wounds.

Of medicine or surgery the poor thing knew nothing. She could but lick the wounds, and thus she kept them cleansed, that healing nature might the more quickly do her work.

At first Tarzan would eat nothing, but rolled and tossed in a wild delirium of fever. All he craved was water, and this she brought him in the only way she could, bearing it in her own mouth.

No human mother could have shown more unselfish and sacrificing devotion than did this poor, wild brute for the little orphaned waif whom fate had thrown into her keeping.

At last the fever abated and the boy commenced to mend. No word of complaint passed his tight set lips, though the pain of his wounds was excruciating.

A portion of his chest was laid bare to the ribs, three of which had been broken by the mighty blows of the gorilla. One arm was nearly severed by the giant fangs, and a great piece had been torn from his neck, exposing his jugular vein, which the cruel jaws had missed but by a miracle.

With the stoicism of the brutes who had raised him he endured his suffering quietly, preferring to crawl away from the others and lie huddled in some clump of tall grasses rather than to show his misery before their eyes.

Kala, alone, he was glad to have with him, but now that he was better she was gone longer at a time, in search of food; for the devoted animal had scarcely eaten enough to support her own life while Tarzan had been so low, and was in consequence, reduced to a mere shadow of her former self.

VII

THE LIGHT OF KNOWLEDGE

fter what seemed an eternity to the little sufferer he was able to walk once more, and from then on his recovery was so rapid that in another month he was as strong and active as ever.

During his convalescence he had gone over in his mind many times the battle with the gorilla, and his first thought was to recover the wonderful little weapon which had transformed him from a hopelessly outclassed weakling to the superior of the mighty terror of the jungle.

Also, he was anxious to return to the cabin and continue his investigations of its wondrous contents.

So, early one morning, he set forth alone upon his quest. After a little search he located the clean-picked bones of his late adversary, and close by, partly buried beneath the fallen leaves, he found the knife, now red with rust from its exposure to the dampness of the ground and from the dried blood of the gorilla.

He did not like the change in its former bright and gleaming surface; but it was still a formidable weapon, and one which he meant to use to advantage whenever the opportunity presented itself. He had in mind that no more would he run from the wanton attacks of old Tublat.

In another moment he was at the cabin, and after a short time had again thrown the latch and entered. His first concern was to learn the mechanism of the lock, and this he did by examining it closely while the door was open, so that he could learn precisely what caused it to hold the door, and by what means it released at his touch.

He found that he could close and lock the door from within, and this he did so that there would be no chance of his being molested while at his investigation.

He commenced a systematic search of the cabin; but his attention was soon riveted by the books which seemed to exert a strange and powerful influence over him, so that he could scarce attend to aught else for the lure of the wondrous puzzle which their purpose presented to him.

Among the other books were a primer, some child's readers, numerous picture books, and a great dictionary. All of these he examined, but the pictures caught his fancy most, though the strange little bugs which covered the pages where there were no pictures excited his wonder and deepest thought.

Squatting upon his haunches on the table top in the cabin his father had built—his smooth, brown, naked little body bent over the book which rested in his strong slender hands, and his great shock of long, black hair falling about his well-shaped head and bright, intelligent eyes—Tarzan of the apes, little primitive man, presented a picture filled, at once, with pathos and with promise—an allegorical figure of the primordial groping through the black night of ignorance toward the light of learning.

His little face was tense in study, for he had partially grasped, in a hazy, nebulous way, the rudiments of a thought which was destined to prove the key and the solution to the puzzling problem of the strange little bugs.

In his hands was a primer opened at a picture of a little ape similar to himself, but covered, except for hands and face, with strange, colored fur, for such he thought the jacket and trousers to be. Beneath the picture were three little bugs—

BOY

And now he had discovered in the text upon the page that these three were repeated many times in the same sequence.

Another fact he learned—that there were comparatively few individual bugs; but these were repeated many times, occasionally alone, but more often in company with others.

Slowly he turned the pages, scanning the pictures and the text for a repetition of the combination b-o-y. Presently he found it beneath a picture of another little ape and a strange animal which went upon four legs like the jackal and resembled him not a little. Beneath this picture the bugs appeared as:

A BOY AND A DOG

There they were, the three little bugs which always accompanied the little ape.

And so he progressed very, very slowly, for it was a hard and laborious task which he had set himself without knowing it—a task which might seem to you or me impossible—learning to read without having the slightest knowledge of letters or written language, or the faintest idea that such things existed.

He did not accomplish it in a day, or in a week, or in a month, or in a year; but slowly, very slowly, he learned after he had grasped the possibilities which lay in those little bugs, so that by the time he was fifteen he knew the various combinations of letters which stood for every pictured figure in the little primer and in one or two of the picture books.

Of the meaning and use of the articles and conjunctions, verbs and adverbs and pronouns he had but the faintest conception.

One day when he was about twelve he found a number of lead pencils in a hitherto undiscovered drawer beneath the table, and in scratching upon the table top with one of them he was delighted to discover the black line it left behind it.

He worked so assiduously with this new toy that the table top was soon a mass of scrawly loops and irregular lines and his pencil-point worn down to the wood. Then he took another pencil, but this time he had a definite object in view.

He would attempt to reproduce some of the little bugs that scrambled over the pages of his books.

It was a difficult task, for he held the pencil as one would grasp the hilt of a dagger, which does not add greatly to ease in writing or to the legibility of the results.

But he persevered for months, at such times as he was able to come to the cabin, until at last by repeated experimenting he found a position in which to hold the pencil that best permitted him to guide and control it, so that at last he could roughly reproduce any of the little bugs.

Thus he made a beginning of writing.

Copying the bugs taught him another thing—their number; and though he could not count as we understand it, yet he had an idea of quantity, the base of his calculations being the number of fingers upon one of his hands.

His search through the various books convinced him that he had discovered all the different kinds of bugs most often repeated in combination, and these he arranged in proper order with great ease because of the frequency with which he had perused the fascinating alphabet picture book.

His education progressed; but his greatest finds were in the inexhaustible storehouse of the huge illustrated dictionary, for he learned more through the medium of pictures than text, even after he had grasped the significance of the bugs.

When he discovered the arrangement of words in alphabetical order he delighted in searching for and finding the combinations with which he was familiar, and the words which followed them, their definitions, led him still further into the mazes of erudition.

By the time he was seventeen he had learned to read the simple, child's primer and had fully realized the true and wonderful purpose of the little bugs.

No longer did he feel shame for his hairless body or his human features, for now his reason told him that he was of a different race from his wild and hairy companions. He was a M-A-N, they were A-P-E-S, and the little apes which scurried through the forest top were M-O-N-K-E-Y-S. He knew, too, that old Sabor was a L-I-O-N-E-S-S, and Histah a S-N-A-K-E, and Tantor an E-L-E-P-H-A-N-T. And so he learned to read.

From then on his progress was rapid. With the help of the great dictionary and the active intelligence of a healthy mind endowed by inheritance with more than ordinary reasoning powers he shrewdly guessed at much which he could not really understand, and more often than not his guesses were close to the mark of truth.

There were many breaks in his education, caused by the migratory habits of his tribe, but even when removed from his books his active brain continued to search out the mysteries of his fascinating avocation.

Pieces of bark and flat leaves and even smooth stretches of bare earth provided him with copy books whereon to scratch with the point of his hunting knife the lessons he was learning.

Nor did he neglect the sterner duties of life while following the bent of his inclination toward the solving of the mystery of his library.

He practiced with his rope and played with his sharp knife, which he had learned to keep keen by whetting upon flat stones.

The tribe had grown larger since Tarzan had come among them, for under the leadership of Kerchak they had been able to frighten the other tribes from their part of the jungle so that they had plenty to eat and little or no loss from predatory incursions of neighbors.

Hence the younger males as they became adult found it more comfortable to take mates from their own tribe, or if they captured one of another tribe to bring her back to Kerchak's band and live in amity with him rather than attempt to set up new establishments of their own, or fight with the redoubtable Kerchak for supremacy at home.

Occasionally one more ferocious than his fellows would attempt this latter alternative, but none had come yet who could wrest the palm of victory from the fierce and brutal ape.

Tarzan held a peculiar position in the tribe. They seemed to consider him one of them and yet in some way different. The older males either ignored him entirely or else hated him so vindictively that but for his wondrous agility and speed and the fierce protection of the huge Kala he would have been dispatched at an early age.

Tublat was his most consistent enemy, but it was through Tublat that, when he was about thirteen, the persecution of his enemies suddenly ceased and he was left severely alone, except on the occasions when one of them ran amuck in the throes of one of those strange, wild fits of insane rage which attacks the males of many of the fiercer animals of the jungle. Then none was safe.

On the day that Tarzan established his right to respect, the tribe was gathered about a small natural amphitheater which the jungle had left free from its entangling vines and creepers in a hollow among some low hills.

The open space was almost circular in shape. Upon every hand rose the mighty giants of the untouched forest, with the matted undergrowth banked so closely between the huge trunks that the only opening into the little, level arena was through the upper branches of the trees.

Here, safe from interruption, the tribe often gathered. In the center of the amphitheater was one of those strange earthen drums which the anthropoids build for the queer rites the sounds of which men have heard in the fastnesses of the jungle, but which none has ever witnessed.

Many travelers have seen the drums of the great apes, and some have heard the sounds of their beating and the noise of the wild, weird revelry of these first lords of the jungle, but Tarzan, Lord Greystoke, is, doubtless, the only human being who ever joined in the fierce, mad, intoxicating revel of the Dum-Dum.

From this primitive function has arisen, unquestionably, all the forms and ceremonials of modern church and state, for through all the countless ages, back beyond the uttermost ramparts of a dawning humanity our fierce, hairy forebears danced out the rites of the Dum-Dum to the sound of their earthen drums, beneath the bright light of a tropical moon in the depth of a mighty jungle which stands unchanged today as it stood on that long forgotten night in the dim, unthinkable vistas of the long dead past when our first shaggy ancestor swung from a swaying bough and dropped lightly upon the soft turf of the first meeting place.

On the day that Tarzan won his emancipation from the persecution that had followed him remorselessly for twelve of his thirteen years of life, the tribe, now a full hundred strong, trooped silently through the lower terrace of the jungle trees and dropped noiselessly upon the floor of the amphitheater.

The rites of the Dum-Dum marked important events in the life of the tribe—a victory, the capture of a prisoner, the killing of some large fierce denizen of the jungle, the death or accession of a king, and were conducted with set ceremonialism.

Today it was the killing of a giant ape, a member of another tribe, and as the people of Kerchak entered the arena two mighty bulls were seen bearing the body of the vanquished between them.

They laid their burden before the earthen drum and then squatted there beside it as guards, while the other members of the community curled themselves in grassy nooks to sleep until the rising moon should give the signal for the commencement of their savage orgy.

For hours absolute quiet reigned in the little clearing, except as it was broken by the discordant notes of brilliantly feathered parrots, or the screeching and twittering of the thousand jungle birds flitting ceaselessly amongst the vivid orchids and flamboyant blossoms which festooned the myriad, moss-covered branches of the forest kings.

At length as darkness settled upon the jungle the apes

commenced to bestir themselves, and soon they formed a great circle about the earthen drum. The females and young squatted in a thin line at the outer periphery of the circle, while just in front of them ranged the adult males. Before the drum sat three old females, each armed with a knotted branch fifteen or eighteen inches in length.

Slowly and softly they began tapping upon the resounding surface of the drum as the first faint rays of the ascending moon silvered the encircling tree tops.

As the light in the amphitheater increased the females augmented the frequency and force of their blows until presently a wild, rhythmic din pervaded the great jungle for miles in every direction. Huge, fierce brutes stopped in their hunting, with up-pricked ears and raised heads, to listen to the dull booming that betokened the Dum-Dum of the apes.

Occasionally one would raise his shrill scream or thunderous roar in answering challenge to the savage din of the anthropoids, but none came near to investigate or attack, for the great apes, assembled in all the power of their numbers, filled the breasts of their jungle neighbors with deep respect.

As the din of the drum rose to almost deafening volume Kerchak sprang into the open space between the squatting males and the drummers.

Standing erect he threw his head far back and looking full into the eye of the rising moon he beat upon his breast with his great hairy paws and emitted his fearful roaring shriek.

One—twice—thrice that terrifying cry rang out across the teeming solitude of that unspeakably quick, yet unthinkably dead, world.

Then, crouching, Kerchak slunk noiselessly around the open circle, veering far away from the dead body lying before the altar-drum, but, as he passed, keeping his little, fierce, wicked, red eyes upon the corpse.

Another male then sprang into the arena, and, repeating the horrid cries of his king, followed stealthily in his wake. Another and another followed in quick succession until the jungle reverberated with the now almost ceaseless notes of their bloodthirsty screams.

It was the challenge and the hunt.

When all the adult males had joined in the thin line of circling dancers the attack commenced.

Kerchak, seizing a huge club from the pile which lay at hand for the purpose, rushed furiously upon the dead ape, dealing the corpse a terrific blow, at the same time emitting the growls and snarls of combat. The din of the drum was now increased, as well as the frequency of the blows, and the warriors, as each approached the victim of the hunt and delivered his bludgeon blow, joined in the mad whirl of the Death Dance.

Tarzan was one of the wild, leaping horde. His brown, sweat-streaked, muscular body, glistening in the moonlight, shone supple and graceful among the uncouth, awkward, hairy brutes about him.

None was more stealthy in the mimic hunt, none more ferocious than he in the wild ferocity of the attack, none who leaped so high into the air in the Dance of Death.

As the noise and rapidity of the drumbeats increased the dancers apparently became intoxicated with the wild rhythm and the savage yells. Their leaps and bounds increased, their bared fangs dripped saliva, and their lips and breasts were flecked with foam.

For half an hour the weird dance went on, until, at a sign from Kerchak, the noise of the drums ceased, the female drummers scampering hurriedly through the line of dancers toward the outer rim of squatting spectators. Then, as one, the males rushed headlong upon the thing which their terrific blows had reduced to a mass of hairy pulp.

Flesh seldom came to their jaws in satisfying quantities, so a fit finale to their wild revel was a taste of fresh killed meat, and it was to the purpose of devouring their late enemy that they now turned their attention.

Great fangs sunk into the carcass tearing away huge hunks, the mightiest of the apes obtaining the choicest morsels, while the weaker circled the outer edge of the fighting, snarling pack awaiting their chance to dodge in and snatch a dropped tidbit or filch a remaining bone before all was gone.

Tarzan, more than the apes, craved and needed flesh. Descended from a race of meat eaters, never in his life, he thought, had he once satisfied his appetite for animal food; and so now his agile little body wormed its way far into the mass of struggling, rending apes in an endeavor to obtain a share which his strength would have been unequal to the task of winning for him.

At his side hung the hunting knife of his unknown father in a sheath self-fashioned in copy of one he had seen among the pictures of his treasure-books.

At last he reached the fast disappearing feast and with his sharp knife slashed off a more generous portion than he had hoped for, an entire hairy forearm, where it protruded from beneath the feet of the mighty Kerchak, who was so busily engaged in perpetuating the royal prerogative of gluttony that he failed to note the act of *lèsemajesté*.

So little Tarzan wriggled out from beneath the struggling mass, clutching his grisly prize close to his breast.

Among those circling futilely the outskirts of the banqueters was old Tublat. He had been among the first at the feast, but had retreated with a goodly share to eat in quiet, and was now forcing his way back for more.

So it was that he spied Tarzan as the boy emerged from the clawing, pushing throng with that hairy forearm hugged firmly to his body.

Tublat's little, close-set, bloodshot, pig-eyes shot wicked gleams of hate as they fell upon the object of his loathing. In them, too, was greed for the toothsome dainty the boy carried.

But Tarzan saw his arch enemy as quickly, and divining what the great beast would do he leaped nimbly away toward the females and the young, hoping to hide himself among them. Tublat, however, was close upon his heels, so that he had no opportunity to seek a place of concealment, but saw that he would be put to it to escape at all.

Swiftly he sped toward the surrounding trees and with an agile bound gained a lower limb with one hand, and then, transferring his burden to his teeth, he climbed rapidly upward, closely followed by Tublat.

Up, up he went to the waving pinnacle of a lofty monarch of the forest where his heavy pursuer dared not follow him. There he perched, hurling taunts and insults at the raging, foaming beast fifty feet below him.

And then Tublat went mad.

With horrifying screams and roars he rushed to the ground, among the females and young, sinking his great fangs into a dozen tiny necks and tearing great pieces from the backs and breasts of the females who fell into his clutches.

In the brilliant moonlight Tarzan witnessed the whole mad carnival of rage. He saw the females and the young scamper to the safety of the trees. Then the great bulls in the center of the arena felt the mighty fangs of their demented fellow, and with one accord they melted into the black shadows of the overhanging forest.

There was but one in the amphitheater beside Tublat, a belated female running swiftly toward the tree where Tarzan perched, and close behind her came the awful Tublat.

It was Kala, and as quickly as Tarzan saw that Tublat was gaining on her he dropped with the rapidity of a falling stone, from branch to branch, toward his foster mother.

Now she was beneath the overhanging limbs and close above her crouched Tarzan, waiting the outcome of the race.

She leaped into the air grasping a low-hanging branch, but almost over the head of Tublat, so nearly had he distanced her. She should have been safe now but there was a rending, tearing sound, the branch broke and precipitated her full upon the head of Tublat, knocking him to the ground.

Both were up in an instant, but as quick as they had been Tarzan had been quicker, so that the infuriated bull found himself facing the man-child who stood between him and Kala.

Nothing could have suited the fierce beast better, and with a roar of triumph he leaped upon the little Lord Greystoke. But his fangs never closed in that nut brown flesh.

A muscular hand shot out and grasped the hairy throat, and another plunged a keen hunting knife a dozen times into the broad breast. Like lightning the blows fell, and only ceased when Tarzan felt the limp form crumple beneath him.

As the body rolled to the ground Tarzan of the Apes placed his foot upon the neck of his lifelong enemy and, raising his eyes to the full moon, threw back his fierce young head and voiced the wild and terrible cry of his people.

One by one the tribe swung down from their arboreal retreats and formed a circle about Tarzan and his vanquished foe. When they had all come Tarzan turned toward them.

"I am Tarzan," he cried. "I am a great killer. Let all respect Tarzan of the Apes and Kala, his mother. There be none among you as mighty as Tarzan. Let his enemies beware."

Looking full into the wicked, red eyes of Kerchak, the young Lord Greystoke beat upon his mighty breast and screamed out once more his shrill cry of defiance.

VIII

THE TREE-TOP HUNTER

he morning after the Dum-Dum the tribe started slowly back through the forest toward the coast.

The body of Tublat lay where it had fallen, for the people of Kerchak do not eat their own dead.

The march was but a leisurely search for food. Cabbage palm and gray plum, pisang and scitamine they found in abundance, with wild pineapple, and occasionally small mammals, birds, eggs, reptiles, and insects. The nuts they cracked between their powerful jaws, or, if too hard, broke by pounding between stones.

Once old Sabor, crossing their path, sent them scurrying to the safety of the higher branches, for if she respected their number and their sharp fangs, they on their part held her cruel and mighty ferocity in equal esteem.

Upon a low-hanging branch sat Tarzan directly above the majestic, supple body as it forged silently through the thick jungle. He hurled a pineapple at the ancient enemy of his people. The great beast stopped and, turning, eyed the taunting figure above her.

With an angry lash of her tail she bared her yellow fangs, curling her great lips in a hideous snarl that wrinkled her bristling snout in serried ridges and closed her wicked eyes to two narrow slits of rage and hatred.

With back-laid ears she looked straight into the eyes of Tarzan of the Apes and sounded her fierce, shrill challenge.

And from the safety of his overhanging limb the ape-child sent back the fearsome answer of his kind.

For a moment the two eyed each other in silence, and then the great cat turned into the jungle, which swallowed her as the ocean engulfs a tossed pebble.

But into the mind of Tarzan a great plan sprang. He had killed the fierce Tublat, so was he not therefore a mighty fighter? Now would he track down the crafty Sabor and slay her likewise. He would be a mighty hunter, also.

At the bottom of his little English heart beat the great desire to cover his nakedness with *clothes* for he had learned from his picture books that all men were so covered, while *monkeys* and *apes* and every other living thing went naked.

Clothes therefore, must be truly a badge of greatness; the insignia of the superiority of *man* over all other animals, for surely there could be no other reason for wearing the hideous things.

Many moons ago, when he had been much smaller, he had desired the skin of Sabor, the lioness, or Numa, the lion, or Sheeta, the leopard to cover his hairless body that he might no longer resemble hideous Histah, the snake; but now he was proud of his sleek skin for it betokened his descent from a mighty race, and the conflicting desires to go naked in prideful proof of his ancestry, or to conform to the customs of his own kind and wear hideous and uncomfortable apparel found first one and then the other in the ascendency.

As the tribe continued their slow way through the forest after the passing of Sabor, Tarzan's head was filled with his great scheme for slaying his enemy, and for many days thereafter he thought of little else.

On this day, however, he presently had other and more immediate interests to attract his attention.

Suddenly it became as midnight; the noises of the jungle ceased; the trees stood motionless as though in paralyzed expectancy of some great and imminent disaster. All nature waited—but not for long.

Faintly, from a distance, came a low, sad moaning. Nearer and nearer it approached, mounting louder and louder in volume.

The great trees bent in unison as though pressed earthward by a mighty hand. Farther and farther toward the ground they inclined, and still there was no sound save the deep and awesome moaning of the wind.

Then, suddenly, the jungle giants whipped back, lashing their mighty tops in angry and deafening protest. A vivid and blinding light flashed from the whirling, inky clouds above. The deep cannonade of roaring thunder belched forth its fearsome challenge. The deluge came—all hell broke loose upon the jungle.

The tribe shivering from the cold rain, huddled at the bases of great trees. The lightning, darting and flashing through the blackness, showed wildly waving branches, whipping streamers and bending trunks.

Now and again some ancient patriarch of the woods, rent by a flashing bolt, would crash in a thousand pieces among the surrounding trees, carrying down numberless branches and many smaller neighbors to add to the tangled confusion of the tropical jungle.

Branches, great and small, torn away by the ferocity of the tornado, hurtled through the wildly waving verdure, carrying death and destruction to countless unhappy denizens of the thickly peopled world below.

For hours the fury of the storm continued without surcease, and still the tribe huddled close in shivering fear. In constant danger from falling trunks and branches and paralyzed by the vivid flashing of lightning and the bellowing of thunder they crouched in pitiful misery until the storm passed.

The end was as sudden as the beginning. The wind ceased, the sun shone forth—nature smiled once more.

The dripping leaves and branches, and the moist petals of gorgeous flowers glistened in the splendor of the returning day. And, so—as Nature forgot, her children forgot also. Busy life went on as it had been before the darkness and the fright.

But to Tarzan a dawning light had come to explain the mystery of *clothes*. How snug he would have been beneath the heavy coat of Sabor! And so was added a further incentive to the adventure.

For several months the tribe hovered near the beach where stood Tarzan's cabin, and his studies took up the greater portion of his time, but always when journeying through the forest he kept his rope in readiness, and many were the smaller animals that fell into the snare of the quick thrown noose.

Once it fell about the short neck of Horta, the boar, and his mad lunge for freedom toppled Tarzan from the overhanging limb where he had lain in wait and from whence he had launched his sinuous coil.

The mighty tusker turned at the sound of his falling body, and, seeing only the easy prey of a young ape, he lowered his head and charged madly at the surprised youth.

Tarzan, happily, was uninjured by the fall, alighting catlike upon all fours far outspread to take up the shock. He was on his feet in an instant and, leaping with the agility of the monkey he was, he gained the safety of a low limb as Horta, the boar, rushed futilely beneath.

Thus it was that Tarzan learned by experience the limitations as well as the possibilities of his strange weapon.

He lost a long rope on this occasion, but he knew that had it been Sabor who had thus dragged him from his perch the outcome might have been very different, for he would have lost his life, doubtless, into the bargain.

It took him many days to braid a new rope, but when, finally, it was done he went forth purposely to hunt, and lie in wait among the dense foliage of a great branch right above the well-beaten trail that led to water.

Several small animals passed unharmed beneath him. He did not want such insignificant game. It would take a strong animal to test the efficacy of his new scheme.

At last came she whom Tarzan sought, with lithe sinews rolling beneath shimmering hide; fat and glossy came Sabor, the lioness.

Her great padded feet fell soft and noiseless on the narrow trail. Her head was high in ever alert attention; her long tail moved slowly in sinuous and graceful undulations.

Nearer and nearer she came to where Tarzan of the Apes crouched upon his limb, the coils of his long rope poised ready in his hand.

Like a thing of bronze, motionless as death, sat Tarzan. Sabor passed beneath. One stride beyond she took—a second, a third, and then the silent coil shot out above her.

For an instant the spreading noose hung above her head like a great snake, and then, as she looked upward to detect the origin of the swishing sound of the rope, it settled about her neck. With a quick jerk Tarzan snapped the noose tight about the glossy throat, and then he dropped the rope and clung to his support with both hands.

Sabor was trapped.

With a bound the startled beast turned into the jungle, but Tarzan was not to lose another rope through the same cause as the first. He had learned from experience. The lioness had taken but half her second bound when she felt the rope tighten about her neck; her body turned completely over in the air and she fell with a heavy crash upon her back. Tarzan had fastened the end of the rope securely to the trunk of the great tree on which he sat.

Thus far his plan had worked to perfection, but when he grasped the rope, bracing himself behind a crotch of two mighty branches, he found that dragging the mighty, struggling, clawing, biting, screaming mass of iron-muscled fury up to the tree and hanging her was a very different proposition.

The weight of old Sabor was immense, and when she braced her huge paws nothing less than Tantor, the elephant, himself, could have budged her.

The lioness was now back in the path where she could see the author of the indignity which had been placed upon her. Screaming with rage she suddenly charged, leaping high into the air toward Tarzan, but when her huge body struck the limb on which Tarzan had been, Tarzan was no longer there.

Instead he perched lightly upon a smaller branch twenty feet above the raging captive. For a moment Sabor hung half across the branch, while Tarzan mocked, and hurled twigs and branches at her unprotected face.

Presently the beast dropped to the earth again and Tarzan came quickly to seize the rope, but Sabor had now found that it was only a slender cord that held her, and grasping it in her huge jaws severed it before Tarzan could tighten the strangling noose a second time.

Tarzan was much hurt. His well-laid plan had come to naught, so he sat there screaming at the roaring creature beneath him and making mocking grimaces at it.

Sabor paced back and forth beneath the tree for hours; four times she crouched and sprang at the dancing sprite above her, but might as well have clutched at the illusive wind that murmured through the tree tops.

At last Tarzan tired of the sport, and with a parting roar of challenge and a well-aimed ripe fruit that spread soft and sticky over the snarling face of his enemy, he swung rapidly through the trees, a hundred feet above the ground, and in a short time was among the members of his tribe.

Here he recounted the details of his adventure, with swelling chest and so considerable swagger that he quite impressed even his bitterest enemies, while Kala fairly danced for joy and pride.

IX

MAN AND MAN

arzan of the Apes lived on in his wild, jungle existence with little change for several years, only that he grew stronger and wiser, and learned from his books more and more of the strange worlds which lay somewhere outside his primeval forest.

To him life was never monotonous or stale. There was always Pisah, the fish, to be caught in the many streams and the little lakes, and Sabor, with her ferocious cousins to keep one ever on the alert and give zest to every instant that one spent upon the ground.

Often they hunted him, and more often he hunted them, but though they never quite reached him with those cruel, sharp claws of theirs, yet there were times when one could scarce have passed a thick leaf between their talons and his smooth hide.

Quick was Sabor, the lioness, and quick were Numa and Sheeta, but Tarzan of the Apes was lightning.

With Tantor, the elephant, he made friends. How? Ask not. But this is known to the denizens of the jungle, that on many moonlight nights Tarzan of the Apes and Tantor, the elephant, walked together, and where the way was clear Tarzan rode, perched high upon Tantor's mighty back.

Many days during these years he spent in the cabin of his father, where still lay, untouched, the bones of his parents and the skeleton of Kala's baby. At eighteen he read fluently and understood nearly all he read in the many and varied volumes on the shelves.

Also could he write, with printed letters, rapidly and plainly, but script he had not mastered, for though there were several copy books among his treasure, there was so little written English in the cabin that he saw no use for bothering with this other form of writing, though he could read it, laboriously.

Thus, at eighteen, we find him, an English lordling, who could speak no English, and yet who could read and write his native language. Never had he seen a human being other than himself, for the little area traversed by his tribe was watered by no greater river to bring down the savage natives of the interior.

High hills shut it off on three sides, the ocean on the fourth. It was alive with lions and leopards and poisonous snakes. Its untouched mazes of matted jungle had as yet invited no hardy pioneer from the human beasts beyond its frontier.

But as Tarzan of the Apes sat one day in the cabin of his father delving into the mysteries of a new book, the ancient security of his jungle was broken forever.

At the far eastern confine a strange cavalcade strung, in single file, over the brow of a low hill.

In advance were fifty black warriors armed with slender wooden spears with ends hard baked over slow fires, and long bows and poisoned arrows. On their backs were oval shields, in their noses huge rings, while from the kinky wool of their heads protruded tufts of gay feathers.

Across their foreheads were tattooed three parallel lines of color, and on each breast three concentric circles. Their yellow teeth were filed to sharp points, and their great protruding lips added still further to the low and bestial brutishness of their appearance.

Following them were several hundred women and children, the former bearing upon their heads great burdens of cooking pots, household utensils and ivory. In the rear were a hundred warriors, similar in all respects to the advance guard.

That they more greatly feared an attack from the rear than whatever unknown enemies lurked in their advance was evidenced by the formation of the column; and such was the fact, for they were fleeing from the white man's soldiers who had so harassed them for rubber and ivory that they had turned upon their conquerors one day and massacred a white officer and a small detachment of his black troops.

For many days they had gorged themselves on meat, but eventually a stronger body of troops had come and fallen upon their village by night to revenge the death of their comrades.

That night the black soldiers of the white man had had meat a-plenty, and this little remnant of a once powerful tribe had slunk off into the gloomy jungle toward the unknown, and freedom.

But that which meant freedom and the pursuit of happiness to these savage blacks meant consternation and death to many of the wild denizens of their new home.

For three days the little cavalcade marched slowly through the heart of this unknown and untracked forest, until finally, early in the fourth day, they came upon a little spot near the banks of a small river, which seemed less thickly overgrown than any ground they had yet encountered.

Here they set to work to build a new village, and in a month a great clearing had been made, huts and palisades erected, plantains, yams and maize planted, and they had taken up their old life in their new home. Here there were no white men, no soldiers, nor any rubber or ivory to be gathered for cruel and thankless taskmasters.

Several moons passed by ere the blacks ventured far into the territory surrounding their new village. Several had already fallen prey to old Sabor, and because the jungle was so infested with these fierce and bloodthirsty cats, and with lions and leopards, the ebony warriors hesitated to trust themselves far from the safety of their palisades.

But one day, Kulonga, a son of the old king, Mbonga, wandered far into the dense mazes to the west. Warily he stepped, his slender lance ever ready, his long oval shield firmly grasped in his left hand close to his sleek ebony body.

At his back his bow, and in the quiver upon his shield many slim, straight arrows, well smeared with the thick, dark, tarry substance that rendered deadly their tiniest needle prick.

Night found Kulonga far from the palisades of his father's village, but still headed westward, and climbing into the fork of a great tree he fashioned a rude platform and curled himself for sleep.

Three miles to the west slept the tribe of Kerchak.

Early the next morning the apes were astir, moving through the jungle in search of food. Tarzan, as was his custom, prosecuted his search in the direction of the cabin so that by leisurely hunting on the way his stomach was filled by the time he reached the beach.

The apes scattered by ones, and twos, and threes in all directions, but ever within sound of a signal of alarm.

Kala had moved slowly along an elephant track toward the east, and was busily engaged in turning over rotted limbs and logs in search of succulent bugs and fungi, when the faintest shadow of a strange noise brought her to startled attention.

For fifty yards before her the trail was straight, and down this leafy tunnel she saw the stealthy advancing figure of a strange and fearful creature.

It was Kulonga.

Kala did not wait to see more, but, turning, moved rapidly back along the trail. She did not run; but, after the manner of her kind when not aroused, sought rather to avoid than to escape.

Close after her came Kulonga. Here was meat. He could make a killing and feast well this day. On he hurried, his spear poised for the throw.

At a turning of the trail he came in sight of her again upon another straight stretch. His spear hand went far back the muscles rolled, lightning-like, beneath the sleek hide. Out shot the arm, and the spear sped toward Kala.

A poor cast. It but grazed her side.

With a cry of rage and pain the she-ape turned upon her tormentor. In an instant the trees were crashing beneath the weight of her hurrying fellows, swinging rapidly toward the scene of trouble in answer to Kala's scream.

As she charged, Kulonga unslung his bow and fitted an arrow with almost unthinkable quickness. Drawing the shaft far back he drove the poisoned missile straight into the heart of the great anthropoid.

With a horrid scream Kala plunged forward upon her face before the astonished members of her tribe.

Roaring and shrieking the apes dashed toward Kulonga, but that wary savage was fleeing down the trail like a frightened antelope.

He knew something of the ferocity of these wild, hairy men, and his one desire was to put as many miles between himself and them as he possibly could.

They followed him, racing through the trees, for a long distance, but finally one by one they abandoned the chase and returned to the scene of the tragedy.

None of them had ever seen a man before, other than Tarzan, and so they wondered vaguely what strange manner of creature it might be that had invaded their jungle.

On the far beach by the little cabin Tarzan heard the faint echoes of the conflict and knowing that something was seriously amiss among the tribe he hastened rapidly toward the direction of the sound.

When he arrived he found the entire tribe gathered jabbering about the dead body of his slain mother.

Tarzan's grief and anger were unbounded. He roared out his hideous challenge time and again. He beat upon his great chest with his clenched fists, and then he fell upon the body of Kala and sobbed out the pitiful sorrowing of his lonely heart.

To lose the only creature in all his world who ever had manifested love and affection for him was the greatest tragedy he had ever known.

What though Kala was a fierce and hideous ape! To Tarzan she had been kind, she had been beautiful.

Upon her he had lavished, unknown to himself, all the reverence and respect and love that a normal English boy feels for his own mother. He had never known another, and so to Kala was given, though mutely, all that would have belonged to the fair and lovely Lady Alice had she lived.

After the first outburst of grief Tarzan controlled himself, and questioning the members of the tribe who had witnessed the killing of Kala he learned all that their meager vocabulary could convey.

It was enough, however, for his needs. It told him of a strange, hairless, black ape with feathers growing upon its head, who launched death from a slender branch, and then ran, with the fleetness of Bara, the deer, toward the rising sun.

Tarzan waited no longer, but leaping into the branches of the trees sped rapidly through the forest. He knew the windings of the elephant trail along which Kala's murderer had flown, and so he cut straight through the jungle to intercept the black warrior who was evidently following the tortuous detours of the trail.

At his side was the hunting knife of his unknown sire, and across his shoulders the coils of his own long rope. In an hour he struck the trail again, and coming to earth examined the soil minutely.

In the soft mud on the bank of a tiny rivulet he found footprints such as he alone in all the jungle had ever made, but much larger than his. His heart beat fast. Could it be that he was trailing a MAN—one of his own race?

There were two sets of imprints pointing in opposite directions. So his quarry had already passed on his return along the trail. As he examined the newer spoor a tiny particle of earth toppled from the outer edge of one of the footprints to the bottom of its shallow depression—ah, the trail was very fresh, his prey must have but scarcely passed.

Tarzan swung himself to the trees once more, and with swift noiselessness sped along high above the trail.

He had covered barely a mile when he came upon the black warrior standing in a little open space. In his hand was his slender bow to which he had fitted one of his death dealing arrows.

Opposite him across the little clearing stood Horta, the boar, with lowered head and foam flecked tucks, ready to charge.

Tarzan looked with wonder upon the strange creature beneath him—so like him in form and yet so different in face and color. His books had portrayed the *Negro*, but how different had been the dull, dead print to this sleek thing of ebony, pulsing with life.

As the man stood there with taut drawn bow Tarzan recognized him not so much the *Negro* as the *Archer* of his picture book—

A IS FOR ARCHER

How wonderful! Tarzan almost betrayed his presence in the deep excitement of his discovery.

But things were commencing to happen below him. The sinewy black arm had drawn the shaft far back; Horta, the boar, was charging, and then the black released the little poisoned arrow, and Tarzan saw it fly with the quickness of thought and lodge in the bristling neck of the boar.

Scarcely had the shaft left his bow ere Kulonga had fitted another to it, but Horta, the boar, was upon him so quickly that he had no time to discharge it. With a bound the black leaped entirely over the rushing beast and turning with incredible swiftness planted a second arrow in Horta's back.

Then Kulonga sprang into a near-by tree.

Horta wheeled to charge his enemy once more; a dozen steps he took, then he staggered and fell upon his side. For a moment his muscles stiffened and relaxed convulsively, then he lay still.

Kulonga came down from his tree.

With a knife that hung at his side he cut several large pieces from the boar's body, and in the center of the trail he built a fire, cooking and eating as much as he wanted. The rest he left where it had fallen.

Tarzan was an interested spectator. His desire to kill burned fiercely in his wild breast, but his desire to learn was even greater. He would follow this savage creature for a while and know from whence he came. He could kill him at his leisure later, when the bow and deadly arrows were laid aside.

When Kulonga had finished his repast and disappeared beyond a near turning of the path, Tarzan dropped quietly to the ground. With his knife he severed many strips of meat from Horta's carcass, but he did not cook them.

He had seen fire, but only when Ara, the lightning, had destroyed some great tree. That any creature of the jungle could produce the red-and-yellow fangs which devoured wood and left nothing but fine dust surprised Tarzan greatly, and why the black warrior had ruined his delicious repast by plunging it into the blighting heat was quite beyond him. Possibly Ara was a friend with whom the Archer was sharing his food.

But, be that as it may, Tarzan would not ruin good meat in any such foolish manner, so he gobbled down a great quantity of the raw flesh, burying the balance of the carcass beside the trail where he could find it upon his return.

And then Lord Greystoke wiped his greasy fingers upon his naked thighs and took up the trail of Kulonga, the son of Mbonga, the king; while in far-off London another Lord Greystoke, the younger brother of the real Lord Greystoke's father, sent back his chops to the club's *chef* because they were underdone, and when he had finished his repast he dipped his finger-ends into a silver bowl of scented water and dried them upon a piece of snowy damask.

All day Tarzan followed Kulonga, hovering above him in the trees like some malign spirit. Twice more he saw him hurl his arrows of destruction—once at Dango, the hyena, and again at Manu, the monkey. In each instance the animal died almost instantly, for Kulonga's poison was very fresh and very deadly.

Tarzan thought much on this wondrous method of slaying as he swung slowly along at a safe distance behind his quarry. He knew that alone the tiny prick of the arrow could not so quickly dispatch these wild things of the jungle, who were often torn and scratched and gored in a frightful manner as they fought with their jungle neighbors, yet as often recovered as not.

No, there was something mysterious connected with these tiny slivers of wood which could bring death by a mere scratch. He must look into the matter.

That night Kulonga slept in the crotch of a mighty tree and far above him crouched Tarzan of the Apes.

When Kulonga awoke he found that his bow and arrows had disappeared. The black warrior was furious and frightened, but more frightened than furious. He searched the ground below the tree, and he searched the tree above the ground; but there was no sign of either bow or arrows or of the nocturnal marauder.

Kulonga was panic-stricken. His spear he had hurled at Kala and had not recovered; and, now that his bow and arrows were gone, he was defenseless except for a single knife. His only hope lay in reaching the village of Mbonga as quickly as his legs would carry him.

That he was not far from home he was certain, so he took the trail at a rapid trot.

From a great mass of impenetrable foliage a few yards away emerged Tarzan of the Apes to swing quietly in his wake.

Kulonga's bow and arrows were securely tied high in the top of a giant tree from which a patch of bark had been removed by a sharp knife near to the ground, and a branch half cut through and left hanging about fifty feet higher up. Thus Tarzan blazed the forest trails and marked his caches.

As Kulonga continued his journey Tarzan closed on him until he traveled almost over the black's head. His rope he now held coiled in his right hand; he was almost ready for the kill.

The moment was delayed only because Tarzan was anxious to ascertain the black warrior's destination, and presently he was rewarded, for they came suddenly in view of a great clearing, at one end of which lay many strange lairs.

Tarzan was directly over Kulonga, as he made the discovery. The forest ended abruptly and beyond lay two hundred yards of planted fields between the jungle and the village.

Tarzan must act quickly or his prey would be gone; but Tarzan's life training left so little space between decision and action when an emergency confronted him that there was not even room for the shadow of a thought between.

So it was that as Kulonga emerged from the shadow of the jungle a slender coil of rope sped sinuously above him from the lowest branch of a mighty tree directly upon the edge of the fields of Mbonga, and ere the king's son had taken a half dozen steps into the clearing a quick noose tightened about his neck.

So quickly did Tarzan of the Apes drag back his prey that Kulonga's cry of alarm was throttled in his windpipe. Hand over hand Tarzan drew the struggling black until he had him hanging by his neck in mid-air; then Tarzan climbed to a larger branch drawing the still threshing victim well up into the sheltering verdure of the tree.

Here he fastened the rope securely to a stout branch, and then, descending, plunged his hunting knife into Kulonga's heart. Kala was avenged.

Tarzan examined the black minutely, for he had never seen any other human being. The knife with its sheath and belt caught his eye; he appropriated them. A copper anklet also took his fancy, and this he transferred to his own leg.

He examined and admired the tattooing on the forehead and breast. He marveled at the sharp filed teeth. He investigated and appropriated the feathered headdress, and then he prepared to get down to business, for Tarzan of the Apes was hungry, and here was meat; meat of the kill, which jungle ethics permitted him to eat.

How may we judge him, by what standards, this ape-man with the heart and head and body of an English gentleman, and the training of a wild beast?

Tublat, whom he had hated and who had hated him, he had killed in a fair fight, and yet never had the thought of eating Tublat's flesh entered his head. It could have been as revolting to him as is cannibalism to us.

But who was Kulonga that he might not be eaten as fairly as Horta, the boar, or Bara, the deer? Was he not simply another of the countless wild things of the jungle who preyed upon one another to satisfy the cravings of hunger?

Suddenly, a strange doubt stayed his hand. Had not his books taught him that he was a man? And was not The Archer a man, also?

Did men eat men? Alas, he did not know. Why, then, this hesitancy! Once more he essayed the effort, but a qualm of nausea overwhelmed him. He did not understand.

All he knew was that he could not eat the flesh of this black man, and thus hereditary instinct, ages old, usurped the functions of his untaught mind and saved him from transgressing a worldwide law of whose very existence he was ignorant.

Quickly he lowered Kulonga's body to the ground, removed the noose, and took to the trees again.

X

THE FEAR-PHANTOM

rom a lofty perch Tarzan viewed the village of thatched huts across the intervening plantation.

He saw that at one point the forest touched the village, and to this spot he made his way, lured by a fever of curiosity to behold animals of his own kind, and to learn more of their ways and view the strange lairs in which they lived.

His savage life among the fierce wild brutes of the jungle left no opening for any thought that these could be aught else than enemies. Similarity of form led him into no erroneous conception of the welcome that would be accorded him should he be discovered by these, the first of his own kind he had ever seen.

Tarzan of the Apes was no sentimentalist. He knew nothing of the brotherhood of man. All things outside his own tribe were his deadly enemies, with the few exceptions of which Tantor, the elephant, was a marked example.

And he realized all this without malice or hatred. To kill was the law of the wild world he knew. Few were his primitive pleasures, but the greatest of these was to hunt and kill, and so he accorded to others the right to cherish the same desires as he, even though he himself might be the object of their hunt.

His strange life had left him neither morose nor bloodthirsty. That he joyed in killing, and that he killed with a joyous laugh upon his handsome lips betokened no innate cruelty. He killed for food most often, but, being a man, he sometimes killed for pleasure, a thing which no other animal does; for it has remained for man alone among all creatures to kill senselessly and wantonly for the mere pleasure of inflicting suffering and death.

And when he killed for revenge, or in self-defense, he did that also without hysteria, for it was a very businesslike proceeding which admitted of no levity.

So it was that now, as he cautiously approached the village of Mbonga, he was quite prepared either to kill or be killed should he be discovered. He proceeded with unwonted stealth, for Kulonga had taught him great respect for the little sharp splinters of wood which dealt death so swiftly and unerringly.

At length he came to a great tree, heavy laden with thick foliage and loaded with pendant loops of giant creepers. From this almost impenetrable bower above the village he crouched, looking down upon the scene below him, wondering over every feature of this new, strange life.

There were naked children running and playing in the village street. There were women grinding dried plantain in crude stone mortars, while others were fashioning cakes from the powdered flour. Out in the fields he could see still other women hoeing, weeding, or gathering.

All wore strange protruding girdles of dried grass about their hips and many were loaded with brass and copper anklets, armlets and bracelets. Around many a dusky neck hung curiously coiled strands of wire, while several were further ornamented by huge nose rings.

Tarzan of the Apes looked with growing wonder at these strange creatures. Dozing in the shade he saw several men, while at the extreme outskirts of the clearing he occasionally caught glimpses of armed warriors apparently guarding the village against surprise from an attacking enemy.

He noticed that the women alone worked. Nowhere was there

evidence of a man tilling the fields or performing any of the homely duties of the village.

Finally his eyes rested upon a woman directly beneath him.

Before her was a small cauldron standing over a low fire and in it bubbled a thick, reddish, tarry mass. On one side of her lay a quantity of wooden arrows the points of which she dipped into the seething substance, then laying them upon a narrow rack of boughs which stood upon her other side.

Tarzan of the Apes was fascinated. Here was the secret of the terrible destructiveness of The Archer's tiny missiles. He noted the extreme care which the woman took that none of the matter should touch her hands, and once when a particle spattered upon one of her fingers he saw her plunge the member into a vessel of water and quickly rub the tiny stain away with a handful of leaves.

Tarzan knew nothing of poison, but his shrewd reasoning told him that it was this deadly stuff that killed, and not the little arrow, which was merely the messenger that carried it into the body of its victim.

How he should like to have more of those little death-dealing slivers. If the woman would only leave her work for an instant he could drop down, gather up a handful, and be back in the tree again before she drew three breaths.

As he was trying to think out some plan to distract her attention he heard a wild cry from across the clearing. He looked and saw a black warrior standing beneath the very tree in which he had killed the murderer of Kala an hour before.

The fellow was shouting and waving his spear above his head. Now and again he would point to something on the ground before him.

The village was in an uproar instantly. Armed men rushed from the interior of many a hut and raced madly across the clearing toward the excited sentry. After them trooped the old men, and the women and children until, in a moment, the village was deserted.

Tarzan of the Apes knew that they had found the body of his victim, but that interested him far less than the fact that no one remained in the village to prevent his taking a supply of the arrows which lay below him.

Quickly and noiselessly he dropped to the ground beside the cauldron of poison. For a moment he stood motionless, his quick, bright eyes scanning the interior of the palisade.

No one was in sight. His eyes rested upon the open doorway of a nearby hut. He would take a look within, thought Tarzan, and so, cautiously, he approached the low thatched building.

For a moment he stood without, listening intently. There was no sound, and he glided into the semi-darkness of the interior.

Weapons hung against the walls—long spears, strangely shaped knives, a couple of narrow shields. In the center of the room was a cooking pot, and at the far end a litter of dry grasses covered by woven mats which evidently served the owners as beds and bedding. Several human skulls lay upon the floor.

Tarzan of the Apes felt of each article, hefted the spears, smelled of them, for he "saw" largely through his sensitive and highly trained nostrils. He determined to own one of these long, pointed sticks, but he could not take one on this trip because of the arrows he meant to carry.

As he took each article from the walls, he placed it in a pile in the center of the room. On top of all he placed the cooking pot, inverted, and on top of this he laid one of the grinning skulls, upon which he fastened the headdress of the dead Kulonga.

Then he stood back, surveyed his work, and grinned. Tarzan of the Apes enjoyed a joke.

But now he heard, outside, the sounds of many voices, and long mournful howls, and mighty wailing. He was startled. Had he remained too long? Quickly he reached the doorway and peered down the village street toward the village gate.

The natives were not yet in sight, though he could plainly hear them approaching across the plantation. They must be very near.

Like a flash he sprang across the opening to the pile of arrows. Gathering up all he could carry under one arm, he overturned the seething cauldron with a kick, and disappeared into the foliage above just as the first of the returning natives entered the gate at the far end of the village street. Then he turned to watch the proceeding below, poised like some wild bird ready to take swift wing at the first sign of danger.

The natives filed up the street, four of them bearing the dead body of Kulonga. Behind trailed the women, uttering strange cries and weird lamentation. On they came to the portals of Kulonga's hut, the very one in which Tarzan had wrought his depredations.

Scarcely had half a dozen entered the building ere they came rushing out in wild, jabbering confusion. The others hastened to gather about. There was much excited gesticulating, pointing, and chattering; then several of the warriors approached and peered within.

Finally an old fellow with many ornaments of metal about his arms and legs, and a necklace of dried human hands depending upon his chest, entered the hut.

It was Mbonga, the king, father of Kulonga.

For a few moments all was silent. Then Mbonga emerged, a look of mingled wrath and superstitious fear writ upon his hideous countenance. He spoke a few words to the assembled warriors, and in an instant the men were flying through the little village searching minutely every hut and corner within the palisades.

Scarcely had the search commenced than the overturned cauldron was discovered, and with it the theft of the poisoned arrows. Nothing more they found, and it was a thoroughly awed and frightened group of savages which huddled around their king a few moments later.

Mbonga could explain nothing of the strange events that had taken place. The finding of the still warm body of Kulonga—on the very verge of their fields and within easy earshot of the village—knifed and stripped at the door of his father's home, was in itself sufficiently mysterious, but these last awesome discoveries within the village, within the dead Kulonga's own hut, filled their hearts with dismay, and conjured in their poor brains only the most frightful of superstitious explanations.

They stood in little groups, talking in low tones, and ever casting affrighted glances behind them from their great rolling eyes.

Tarzan of the Apes watched them for a while from his lofty perch in the great tree. There was much in their demeanor which he could not understand, for of superstition he was ignorant, and of fear of any kind he had but a vague conception.

The sun was high in the heavens. Tarzan had not broken fast this day, and it was many miles to where lay the toothsome remains of Horta the boar.

So he turned his back upon the village of Mbonga and melted away into the leafy fastness of the forest.

XI

"KING OF THE APES"

t was not yet dark when he reached the tribe, though he stopped to exhume and devour the remains of the wild boar he had cached the preceding day, and again to take Kulonga's bow and arrows from the tree top in which he had hidden them.

It was a well-laden Tarzan who dropped from the branches into the midst of the tribe of Kerchak.

With swelling chest he narrated the glories of his adventure and exhibited the spoils of conquest.

Kerchak grunted and turned away, for he was jealous of this strange member of his band. In his little evil brain he sought for some excuse to wreak his hatred upon Tarzan.

The next day Tarzan was practicing with his bow and arrows at the first gleam of dawn. At first he lost nearly every bolt he shot, but finally he learned to guide the little shafts with fair accuracy, and ere a month had passed he was no mean shot; but his proficiency had cost him nearly his entire supply of arrows.

The tribe continued to find the hunting good in the vicinity of the beach, and so Tarzan of the Apes varied his archery practice with further investigation of his father's choice though little store of books.

It was during this period that the young English lord found hidden in the back of one of the cupboards in the cabin a small metal box. The key was in the lock, and a few moments of investigation and experimentation were rewarded with the successful opening of the receptacle.

In it he found a faded photograph of a smooth faced young man, a golden locket studded with diamonds, linked to a small gold chain, a few letters and a small book.

Tarzan examined these all minutely.

The photograph he liked most of all, for the eyes were smiling, and the face was open and frank. It was his father.

The locket, too, took his fancy, and he placed the chain about his neck in imitation of the ornamentation he had seen to be so common among the black men he had visited. The brilliant stones gleamed strangely against his smooth, brown hide.

The letters he could scarcely decipher for he had learned little or nothing of script, so he put them back in the box with the photograph and turned his attention to the book.

This was almost entirely filled with fine script, but while the little bugs were all familiar to him, their arrangement and the combinations in which they occurred were strange, and entirely incomprehensible.

Tarzan had long since learned the use of the dictionary, but much to his sorrow and perplexity it proved of no avail to him in this emergency. Not a word of all that was writ in the book could he find, and so he put it back in the metal box, but with a determination to work out the mysteries of it later on.

Little did he know that this book held between its covers the key to his origin—the answer to the strange riddle of his strange life. It was the diary of John Clayton, Lord Greystoke—kept in French, as had always been his custom.

Tarzan replaced the box in the cupboard, but always thereafter he carried the features of the strong, smiling face of his father in his heart, and in his head a fixed determination to solve the mystery of the strange words in the little black book.

At present he had more important business in hand, for his supply of arrows was exhausted, and he must needs journey to the black men's village and renew it.

Early the following morning he set out, and, traveling rapidly, he came before midday to the clearing. Once more he took up his position in the great tree, and, as before, he saw the women in the fields and the village street, and the cauldron of bubbling poison directly beneath him.

For hours he lay awaiting his opportunity to drop down unseen and gather up the arrows for which he had come; but nothing now occurred to call the villagers away from their homes. The day wore on, and still Tarzan of the Apes crouched above the unsuspecting woman at the cauldron.

Presently the workers in the fields returned. The hunting warriors emerged from the forest, and when all were within the palisade the gates were closed and barred.

Many cooking pots were now in evidence about the village. Before each hut a woman presided over a boiling stew, while little cakes of plantain, and cassava puddings were to be seen on every hand.

Suddenly there came a hail from the edge of the clearing.

Tarzan looked.

It was a party of belated hunters returning from the north, and among them they half led, half carried a struggling animal.

As they approached the village the gates were thrown open to admit them, and then, as the people saw the victim of the chase, a savage cry rose to the heavens, for the quarry was a man.

As he was dragged, still resisting, into the village street, the women and children set upon him with sticks and stones, and Tarzan of the Apes, young and savage beast of the jungle, wondered at the cruel brutality of his own kind.

Sheeta, the leopard, alone of all the jungle folk, tortured his prey. The ethics of all the others meted a quick and merciful death to their victims.

Tarzan had learned from his books but scattered fragments of the ways of human beings.

When he had followed Kulonga through the forest he had expected to come to a city of strange houses on wheels, puffing clouds of black smoke from a huge tree stuck in the roof of one of them—or to a sea covered with mighty floating buildings which he had learned were called, variously, ships and boats and steamers and craft.

He had been sorely disappointed with the poor little village of the blacks, hidden away in his own jungle, and with not a single house as large as his own cabin upon the distant beach.

He saw that these people were more wicked than his own apes, and as savage and cruel as Sabor, herself. Tarzan began to hold his own kind in low esteem.

Now they had tied their poor victim to a great post near the center of the village, directly before Mbonga's hut, and here they formed a dancing, yelling circle of warriors about him, alive with flashing knives and menacing spears.

In a larger circle squatted the women, yelling and beating upon drums. It reminded Tarzan of the Dum-Dum, and so he knew what to expect. He wondered if they would spring upon their meat while it was still alive. The Apes did not do such things as that.

The circle of warriors about the cringing captive drew closer and closer to their prey as they danced in wild and savage abandon to the maddening music of the drums. Presently a spear reached out and pricked the victim. It was the signal for fifty others.

Eyes, ears, arms and legs were pierced; every inch of the poor writhing body that did not cover a vital organ became the target of the cruel lancers.

The women and children shrieked their delight.

The warriors licked their hideous lips in anticipation of the feast to come, and vied with one another in the savagery and loathsomeness of the cruel indignities with which they tortured the still conscious prisoner.

Then it was that Tarzan of the Apes saw his chance. All eyes were fixed upon the thrilling spectacle at the stake. The light of day had given place to the darkness of a moonless night, and only the fires in the immediate vicinity of the orgy had been kept alight to cast a restless glow upon the restless scene.

Gently the lithe boy dropped to the soft earth at the end of the village street. Quickly he gathered up the arrows—all of them this time, for he had brought a number of long fibers to bind them into a bundle.

Without haste he wrapped them securely, and then, ere he turned to leave, the devil of capriciousness entered his heart. He looked about for some hint of a wild prank to play upon these strange, grotesque creatures that they might be again aware of his presence among them.

Dropping his bundle of arrows at the foot of the tree, Tarzan crept among the shadows at the side of the street until he came to the same hut he had entered on the occasion of his first visit.

Inside all was darkness, but his groping hands soon found the object for which he sought, and without further delay he turned again toward the door.

He had taken but a step, however, ere his quick ear caught the sound of approaching footsteps immediately without. In another instant the figure of a woman darkened the entrance of the hut.

Tarzan drew back silently to the far wall, and his hand sought the long, keen hunting knife of his father. The woman came quickly to the center of the hut. There she paused for an instant feeling about with her hands for the thing she sought. Evidently it was not in its accustomed place, for she explored ever nearer and nearer the wall where Tarzan stood.

So close was she now that the ape-man felt the animal warmth of her naked body. Up went the hunting knife, and then the woman turned to one side and soon a guttural "ah" proclaimed that her search had at last been successful.

97

Immediately she turned and left the hut, and as she passed through the doorway Tarzan saw that she carried a cooking pot in her hand.

He followed closely after her, and as he reconnoitered from the shadows of the doorway he saw that all the women of the village were hastening to and from the various huts with pots and kettles. These they were filling with water and placing over a number of fires near the stake where the dying victim now hung, an inert and bloody mass of suffering.

Choosing a moment when none seemed near, Tarzan hastened to his bundle of arrows beneath the great tree at the end of the village street. As on the former occasion he overthrew the cauldron before leaping, sinuous and catlike, into the lower branches of the forest giant.

Silently he climbed to a great height until he found a point where he could look through a leafy opening upon the scene beneath him.

The women were now preparing the prisoner for their cooking pots, while the men stood about resting after the fatigue of their mad revel. Comparative quiet reigned in the village.

Tarzan raised aloft the thing he had pilfered from the hut, and, with aim made true by years of fruit and coconut throwing, launched it toward the group of savages.

Squarely among them it fell, striking one of the warriors full upon the head and felling him to the ground. Then it rolled among the women and stopped beside the half-butchered thing they were preparing to feast upon.

All gazed in consternation at it for an instant, and then, with one accord, broke and ran for their huts.

It was a grinning human skull which looked up at them from the ground. The dropping of the thing out of the open sky was a miracle well aimed to work upon their superstitious fears.

Thus Tarzan of the Apes left them filled with terror at this new manifestation of the presence of some unseen and unearthly evil power which lurked in the forest about their village.

Later, when they discovered the overturned cauldron, and that once more their arrows had been pilfered, it commenced to dawn upon them that they had offended some great god by placing their village in this part of the jungle without propitiating him. From then on an offering of food was daily placed below the great tree from whence the arrows had disappeared in an effort to conciliate the mighty one.

But the seed of fear was deep sown, and had he but known it, Tarzan of the Apes had laid the foundation for much future misery for himself and his tribe.

That night he slept in the forest not far from the village, and early the next morning set out slowly on his homeward march, hunting as he traveled. Only a few berries and an occasional grub worm rewarded his search, and he was half famished when, looking up from a log he had been rooting beneath, he saw Sabor, the lioness, standing in the center of the trail not twenty paces from him.

The great yellow eyes were fixed upon him with a wicked and baleful gleam, and the red tongue licked the longing lips as Sabor crouched, worming her stealthy way with belly flattened against the earth.

Tarzan did not attempt to escape. He welcomed the opportunity for which, in fact, he had been searching for days past, now that he was armed with something more than a rope of grass.

Quickly he unslung his bow and fitted a well-daubed arrow, and as Sabor sprang, the tiny missile leaped to meet her in mid-air. At the same instant Tarzan of the Apes jumped to one side, and as the great cat struck the ground beyond him another death-tipped arrow sunk deep into Sabor's loin.

With a mighty roar the beast turned and charged once more, only to be met with a third arrow full in one eye; but this time she was too close to the ape-man for the latter to sidestep the onrushing body.

Tarzan of the Apes went down beneath the great body of his enemy, but with gleaming knife drawn and striking home. For a moment they lay there, and then Tarzan realized that the inert mass lying upon him was beyond power ever again to injure man or ape.

With difficulty he wriggled from beneath the great weight, and as he stood erect and gazed down upon the trophy of his skill, a mighty wave of exultation swept over him.

With swelling breast, he placed a foot upon the body of his powerful enemy, and throwing back his fine young head, roared out the awful challenge of the victorious bull ape.

The forest echoed to the savage and triumphant paean. Birds fell still, and the larger animals and beasts of prey slunk stealthily away, for few there were of all the jungle who sought for trouble with the great anthropoids.

And in London another Lord Greystoke was speaking to *his* kind in the House of Lords, but none trembled at the sound of his soft voice.

Sabor proved unsavory eating even to Tarzan of the Apes, but hunger served as a most efficacious disguise to toughness and rank taste, and ere long, with well-filled stomach, the ape-man was ready to sleep again. First, however, he must remove the hide, for it was as much for this as for any other purpose that he had desired to destroy Sabor.

Deftly he removed the great pelt, for he had practiced often on smaller animals. When the task was finished he carried his trophy to the fork of a high tree, and there, curling himself securely in a crotch, he fell into deep and dreamless slumber.

What with loss of sleep, arduous exercise, and a full belly, Tarzan of the Apes slept the sun around, awakening about noon of the following day. He straightway repaired to the carcass of Sabor, but was angered to find the bones picked clean by other hungry denizens of the jungle.

Half an hour's leisurely progress through the forest brought to sight a young deer, and before the little creature knew that an enemy was near a tiny arrow had lodged in its neck.

So quickly the virus worked that at the end of a dozen leaps the deer plunged headlong into the undergrowth, dead. Again did Tarzan feast well, but this time he did not sleep.

Instead, he hastened on toward the point where he had left the tribe, and when he had found them proudly exhibited the skin of Sabor, the lioness.

"Look!" he cried, "Apes of Kerchak. See what Tarzan, the mighty killer, has done. Who else among you has ever killed one of Numa's people? Tarzan is mightiest amongst you for Tarzan is no ape. Tarzan is—" But here he stopped, for in the language of the anthropoids there was no word for man, and Tarzan could only write the word in English; he could not pronounce it.

The tribe had gathered about to look upon the proof of his wondrous prowess, and to listen to his words.

Only Kerchak hung back, nursing his hatred and his rage.

Suddenly something snapped in the wicked little brain of the anthropoid. With a frightful roar the great beast sprang among the assemblage.

Biting, and striking with his huge hands, he killed and maimed a dozen ere the balance could escape to the upper terraces of the forest.

Frothing and shrieking in the insanity of his fury, Kerchak looked about for the object of his greatest hatred, and there, upon a near-by limb, he saw him sitting.

"Come down, Tarzan, great killer," cried Kerchak. "Come down and feel the fangs of a greater! Do mighty fighters fly to the trees at the first approach of danger?" And then Kerchak emitted the volleying challenge of his kind.

Quietly Tarzan dropped to the ground. Breathlessly the tribe watched from their lofty perches as Kerchak, still roaring, charged the relatively puny figure.

Nearly seven feet stood Kerchak on his short legs. His enormous shoulders were bunched and rounded with huge muscles. The back of his short neck was as a single lump of iron sinew which bulged beyond the base of his skull, so that his head seemed like a small ball protruding from a huge mountain of flesh.

His back-drawn, snarling lips exposed his great fighting fangs, and his little, wicked, blood-shot eyes gleamed in horrid reflection of his madness.

Awaiting him stood Tarzan, himself a mighty muscled animal, but his six feet of height and his great rolling sinews seemed pitifully inadequate to the ordeal which awaited them.

His bow and arrows lay some distance away where he had dropped them while showing Sabor's hide to his fellow apes, so that he confronted Kerchak now with only his hunting knife and his superior intellect to offset the ferocious strength of his enemy.

As his antagonist came roaring toward him, Lord Greystoke tore his long knife from its sheath, and with an answering challenge as horrid and bloodcurdling as that of the beast he faced, rushed swiftly to meet the attack. He was too shrewd to allow those long hairy arms to encircle him, and just as their bodies were about to crash together, Tarzan of the Apes grasped one of the huge wrists of his assailant, and, springing lightly to one side, drove his knife to the hilt into Kerchak's body, below the heart.

Before he could wrench the blade free again, the bull's quick lunge to seize him in those awful arms had torn the weapon from Tarzan's grasp.

Kerchak aimed a terrific blow at the ape-man's head with the flat of his hand, a blow which, had it landed, might easily have crushed in the side of Tarzan's skull.

The man was too quick, and, ducking beneath it, himself delivered a mighty one, with clenched fist, in the pit of Kerchak's stomach.

The ape was staggered, and what with the mortal wound in his side had almost collapsed, when, with one mighty effort he rallied for an instant—just long enough to enable him to wrest his arm frcc from Tarzan's grasp and close in a terrific clinch with his wiry opponent.

Straining the ape-man close to him, his great jaws sought Tarzan's throat, but the young lord's sinewy fingers were at Kerchak's own before the cruel fangs could close on the sleek brown skin.

Thus they struggled, the one to crush out his opponent's life with those awful teeth, the other to close forever the windpipe beneath his strong grasp while he held the snarling mouth from him.

The greater strength of the ape was slowly prevailing, and the teeth of the straining beast were scarce an inch from Tarzan's throat when, with a shuddering tremor, the great body stiffened for an instant and then sank limply to the ground.

Kerchak was dead.

Withdrawing the knife that had so often rendered him master of far mightier muscles than his own, Tarzan of the Apes placed his foot upon the neck of his vanquished enemy, and once again, loud through the forest rang the fierce, wild cry of the conqueror.

And thus came the young Lord Greystoke into the kingship of the Apes.

XII

MAN'S REASON

here was one of the tribe of Tarzan who questioned his authority, and that was Terkoz, the son of Tublat, but he so feared the keen knife and the deadly arrows of his new lord that he confined the manifestation of his objections to petty disobediences and irritating mannerisms; Tarzan knew, however, that he but waited his opportunity to wrest the kingship from him by some sudden stroke of treachery, and so he was ever on his guard against surprise.

For months the life of the little band went on much as it had before, except that Tarzan's greater intelligence and his ability as a hunter were the means of providing for them more bountifully than ever before. Most of them, therefore, were more than content with the change in rulers.

Tarzan led them by night to the fields of the black men, and there, warned by their chief's superior wisdom, they ate only what they required, nor ever did they destroy what they could not eat, as is the way of Manu, the monkey, and of most apes.

So, while the blacks were wroth at the continued pilfering of their fields, they were not discouraged in their efforts to cultivate the land, as would have been the case had Tarzan permitted his people to lay waste the plantation wantonly.

During this period Tarzan paid many nocturnal visits to the village, where he often renewed his supply of arrows. He soon noticed the food always standing at the foot of the tree which was his avenue into the palisade, and after a little, he commenced to eat whatever the blacks put there.

When the awe-struck savages saw that the food disappeared overnight they were filled with consternation and dread, for it was one thing to put food out to propitiate a god or a devil, but quite another thing to have the spirit really come into the village and eat it. Such a thing was unheard of, and it clouded their superstitious minds with all manner of vague fears.

Nor was this all. The periodic disappearance of their arrows, and the strange pranks perpetrated by unseen hands, had wrought them to such a state that life had become a veritable burden in their new home, and now it was that Mbonga and his head men began to talk of abandoning the village and seeking a site farther on in the jungle.

Presently the black warriors began to strike farther and farther south into the heart of the forest when they went to hunt, looking for a site for a new village.

More often was the tribe of Tarzan disturbed by these wandering huntsmen. Now was the quiet, fierce solitude of the primeval forest broken by new, strange cries. No longer was there safety for bird or beast. Man had come.

Other animals passed up and down the jungle by day and by night—fierce, cruel beasts—but their weaker neighbors only fled from their immediate vicinity to return again when the danger was past.

With man it is different. When he comes many of the larger animals instinctively leave the district entirely, seldom if ever to return; and thus it has always been with the great anthropoids. They flee man as man flees a pestilence.

For a short time the tribe of Tarzan lingered in the vicinity of the beach because their new chief hated the thought of leaving the treasured contents of the little cabin forever. But when one day a member of the tribe discovered the blacks in great numbers on the banks of a little stream that had been their watering place for generations, and in the act of clearing a space in the jungle and erecting many huts, the apes would remain no longer; and so Tarzan led them inland for many marches to a spot as yet undefiled by the foot of a human being.

Once every moon Tarzan would go swinging rapidly back through the swaying branches to have a day with his books, and to replenish his supply of arrows. This latter task was becoming more and more difficult, for the blacks had taken to hiding their supply away at night in granaries and living huts.

This necessitated watching by day on Tarzan's part to discover where the arrows were being concealed.

Twice had he entered huts at night while the inmates lay sleeping upon their mats, and stolen the arrows from the very sides of the warriors. But this method he realized to be too fraught with danger, and so he commenced picking up solitary hunters with his long, deadly noose, stripping them of weapons and ornaments and dropping their bodies from a high tree into the village street during the still watches of the night.

These various escapades again so terrorized the blacks that, had it not been for the monthly respite between Tarzan's visits, in which they had opportunity to renew hope that each fresh incursion would prove the last, they soon would have abandoned their new village.

The blacks had not as yet come upon Tarzan's cabin on the distant beach, but the ape-man lived in constant dread that, while he was away with the tribe, they would discover and despoil his treasure. So it came that he spent more and more time in the vicinity of his father's last home, and less and less with the tribe. Presently the members of his little community began to suffer on account of his neglect, for disputes and quarrels constantly arose which only the king might settle peaceably.

At last some of the older apes spoke to Tarzan on the subject, and for a month thereafter he remained constantly with the tribe.

The duties of kingship among the anthropoids are not many or arduous.

In the afternoon comes Thaka, possibly, to complain that old Mungo has stolen his new wife. Then must Tarzan summon all before him, and if he finds that the wife prefers her new lord he commands that matters remain as they are, or possibly that Mungo give Thaka one of his daughters in exchange.

Whatever his decision, the apes accept it as final, and return to their occupations satisfied.

Then comes Tana, shrieking and holding tight her side from which blood is streaming. Gunto, her husband, has cruelly bitten her! And Gunto, summoned, says that Tana is lazy and will not bring him nuts and beetles, or scratch his back for him.

So Tarzan scolds them both and threatens Gunto with a taste of the death-bearing slivers if he abuses Tana further, and Tana, for her part, is compelled to promise better attention to her wifely duties.

And so it goes, little family differences for the most part, which, if left unsettled would result finally in greater factional strife, and the eventual dismemberment of the tribe.

But Tarzan tired of it, as he found that kingship meant the curtailment of his liberty. He longed for the little cabin and the sun-kissed sea—for the cool interior of the well-built house, and for the never-ending wonders of the many books.

As he had grown older, he found that he had grown away from his people. Their interests and his were far removed. They had not kept pace with him, nor could they understand aught of the many strange and wonderful dreams that passed through the active brain of their human king. So limited was their vocabulary that Tarzan could not even talk with them of the many new truths, and the great fields of thought that his reading had opened up before his longing eyes, or make known ambitions which stirred his soul.

Among the tribe he no longer had friends as of old. A little child may find companionship in many strange and simple creatures, but to a grown man there must be some semblance of equality in intellect as the basis for agreeable association.

Had Kala lived, Tarzan would have sacrificed all else to remain near her, but now that she was dead, and the playful friends of his childhood grown into fierce and surly brutes he felt that he much preferred the peace and solitude of his cabin to the irksome duties of leadership amongst a horde of wild beasts.

The hatred and jealousy of Terkoz, son of Tublat, did much to counteract the effect of Tarzan's desire to renounce his kingship among the apes, for, stubborn young Englishman that he was, he could not bring himself to retreat in the face of so malignant an enemy.

That Terkoz would be chosen leader in his stead he knew full well, for time and again the ferocious brute had established his claim to physical supremacy over the few bull apes who had dared resent his savage bullying.

Tarzan would have liked to subdue the ugly beast without recourse to knife or arrows. So much had his great strength and agility increased in the period following his maturity that he had come to believe that he might master the redoubtable Terkoz in a hand to hand fight were it not for the terrible advantage the anthropoid's huge fighting fangs gave him over the poorly armed Tarzan.

The entire matter was taken out of Tarzan's hands one day by force of circumstances, and his future left open to him, so that he might go or stay without any stain upon his savage escutcheon.

It happened thus:

The tribe was feeding quietly, spread over a considerable area, when a great screaming arose some distance east of where Tarzan lay upon his belly beside a limpid brook, attempting to catch an elusive fish in his quick, brown hands.

With one accord the tribe swung rapidly toward the frightened cries, and there found Terkoz holding an old female by the hair and beating her unmercifully with his great hands.

As Tarzan approached he raised his hand aloft for Terkoz to desist, for the female was not his, but belonged to a poor old ape whose fighting days were long over, and who, therefore, could not protect his family.

Terkoz knew that it was against the laws of his kind to strike this woman of another, but being a bully, he had taken advantage of the weakness of the female's husband to chastise her because she had refused to give up to him a tender young rodent she had captured.

When Terkoz saw Tarzan approaching without his arrows, he continued to belabor the poor woman in a studied effort to affront his hated chieftain.

Tarzan did not repeat his warning signal, but instead rushed bodily upon the waiting Terkoz.

Never had the ape-man fought so terrible a battle since that long-gone day when Bolgani, the great king gorilla had so horribly man-handled him ere the new-found knife had, by accident, pricked the savage heart.

Tarzan's knife on the present occasion but barely offset the gleaming fangs of Terkoz, and what little advantage the ape had over the man in brute strength was almost balanced by the latter's won-derful quickness and agility.

In the sum total of their points, however, the anthropoid had a shade the better of the battle, and had there been no other per-sonal attribute to influence the final outcome, Tarzan of the Apes, the young Lord Greystoke, would have died as he had lived—an unknown savage beast in equatorial Africa.

But there was that which had raised him far above his fellows of the jungle—that little spark which spells the whole vast difference between man and brute—Reason. This it was which saved him from death beneath the iron muscles and tearing fangs of Terkoz.

Scarcely had they fought a dozen seconds ere they were rolling upon the ground, striking, tearing and rending—two great savage beasts battling to the death.

Terkoz had a dozen knife wounds on head and breast, and Tarzan was torn and bleeding—his scalp in one place half torn from his head so that a great piece hung down over one eye, obstructing his vision.

But so far the young Englishman had been able to keep those horrible fangs from his jugular and now, as they fought less fiercely for a moment, to regain their breath, Tarzan formed a cunning plan. He would work his way to the other's back and, clinging there with tooth and nail, drive his knife home until Terkoz was no more.

The maneuver was accomplished more easily than he had hoped, for the stupid beast, not knowing what Tarzan was attempting, made no particular effort to prevent the accomplishment of the design.

But when, finally, he realized that his antagonist was fastened to him where his teeth and fists alike were useless against him, Terkoz hurled himself about upon the ground so violently that Tarzan could but cling desperately to the leaping, turning, twisting body, and ere he had struck a blow the knife was hurled from his hand by a heavy impact against the earth, and Tarzan found himself defenseless.

During the rollings and squirmings of the next few minutes, Tarzan's hold was loosened a dozen times until finally an accidental circumstance of those swift and everchanging evolutions gave him a new hold with his right hand, which he realized was absolutely unassailable.

His arm was passed beneath Terkoz's arm from behind and his hand and forearm encircled the back of Terkoz's neck. It was the half-Nelson of modern wrestling which the untaught ape-man had stumbled upon, but superior reason showed him in an instant the value of the thing he had discovered. It was the difference to him between life and death.

And so he struggled to encompass a similar hold with the left hand, and in a few moments Terkoz's bull neck was creaking beneath a full-Nelson.

There was no more lunging about now. The two lay perfectly still upon the ground, Tarzan upon Terkoz's back. Slowly the bullet head of the ape was being forced lower and lower upon his chest.

Tarzan knew what the result would be. In an instant the neck would break. Then there came to Terkoz's rescue the same thing that had put him in these sore straits—a man's reasoning power.

"If I kill him," thought Tarzan, "what advantage will it be to me? Will it not rob the tribe of a great fighter? And if Terkoz be dead, he will know nothing of my supremacy, while alive he will ever be an example to the other apes."

"*Ka-goda?*" hissed Tarzan in Terkoz's ear, which, in ape tongue, means, freely translated: "Do you surrender?"

For a moment there was no reply, and Tarzan added a few more ounces of pressure, which elicited a horrified shriek of pain from the great beast.

"*Ka-goda?*" repeated Tarzan.

"*Ka-goda!*" cried Terkoz.

"Listen," said Tarzan, easing up a trifle, but not releasing his hold. "I am Tarzan, King of the Apes, mighty hunter, mighty fighter. In all the jungle there is none so great.

"You have said: '*Ka-goda*' to me. All the tribe have heard. Quarrel no more with your king or your people, for next time I shall kill you. Do you understand?"

"*Huh*," assented Terkoz.

"And you are satisfied?"

"*Huh*," said the ape.

Tarzan let him up, and in a few minutes all were back at their vocations, as though naught had occurred to mar the tranquility of their primeval forest haunts.

But deep in the minds of the apes was rooted the conviction that Tarzan was a mighty fighter and a strange creature. Strange because he had had it in his power to kill his enemy, but had allowed him to live—unharmed.

That afternoon as the tribe came together, as was their wont before darkness settled on the jungle, Tarzan, his wounds washed in the waters of the stream, called the old males about him.

"You have seen again to-day that Tarzan of the Apes is the greatest among you," he said.

"*Huh*," they replied with one voice, "Tarzan is great."

"Tarzan," he continued, "is not an ape. He is not like his people. His ways are not their ways, and so Tarzan is going back to the lair of his own kind by the waters of the great lake which has no farther shore. You must choose another to rule you, for Tarzan will not return."

And thus young Lord Greystoke took the first step toward the goal which he had set—the finding of other white men like himself.

XIII

HIS OWN KIND

he following morning, Tarzan, lame and sore from the wounds of his battle with Terkoz, set out toward the west and the seacoast.

He traveled very slowly, sleeping in the jungle at night, and reaching his cabin late the following morning.

For several days he moved about but little, only enough to gather what fruits and nuts he required to satisfy the demands of hunger.

In ten days he was quite sound again, except for a terrible, half-healed scar, which, starting above his left eye ran across the top of his head, ending at the right ear. It was the mark left by Terkoz when he had torn the scalp away.

During his convalescence Tarzan tried to fashion a mantle from the skin of Sabor, which had lain all this time in the cabin. But he found the hide had dried as stiff as a board, and as he knew naught of tanning, he was forced to abandon his cherished plan.

Then he determined to filch what few garments he could from one of the black men of Mbonga's village, for Tarzan of the Apes had decided to mark his evolution from the lower orders in every possible manner, and nothing seemed to him a more distinguishing badge of manhood than ornaments and clothing.

To this end, therefore, he collected the various arm and leg ornaments he had taken from the black warriors who had succumbed to his swift and silent noose, and donned them all after the way he had seen them worn.

About his neck hung the golden chain from which depended the diamond encrusted locket of his mother, the Lady Alice. At his back was a quiver of arrows slung from a leathern shoulder belt, another piece of loot from some vanquished black.

About his waist was a belt of tiny strips of rawhide fashioned by himself as a support for the home-made scabbard in which hung his father's hunting knife. The long bow which had been Kulonga's hung over his left shoulder.

The young Lord Greystoke was indeed a strange and warlike figure, his mass of black hair falling to his shoulders behind and cut with his hunting knife to a rude bang upon his forehead, that it might not fall before his eyes.

His straight and perfect figure, muscled as the best of the ancient Roman gladiators must have been muscled, and yet with the soft and sinuous curves of a Greek god, told at a glance the wondrous combination of enormous strength with suppleness and speed.

A personification, was Tarzan of the Apes, of the primitive man, the hunter, the warrior.

With the noble poise of his handsome head upon those broad shoulders, and the fire of life and intelligence in those fine, clear eyes, he might readily have typified some demigod of a wild and warlike bygone people of his ancient forest.

But of these things Tarzan did not think. He was worried because he had not clothing to indicate to all the jungle folks that he was a man and not an ape, and grave doubt often entered his mind as to whether he might not yet become an ape.

Was not hair commencing to grow upon his face? All the apes had hair upon theirs but the black men were entirely hairless, with very few exceptions.

True, he had seen pictures in his books of men with great masses of hair upon lip and cheek and chin, but, nevertheless, Tarzan was afraid. Almost daily he whetted his keen knife and scraped and whittled at his young beard to eradicate this degrading emblem of apehood.

And so he learned to shave—rudely and painfully, it is true—but, nevertheless, effectively.

When he felt quite strong again, after his bloody battle with Terkoz, Tarzan set off one morning towards Mbonga's village. He was moving carelessly along a winding jungle trail, instead of making his progress through the trees, when suddenly he came face to face with a black warrior.

The look of surprise on the savage face was almost comical, and before Tarzan could unsling his bow the fellow had turned and fled down the path crying out in alarm as though to others before him.

Tarzan took to the trees in pursuit, and in a few moments came in view of the men desperately striving to escape.

There were three of them, and they were racing madly in single file through the dense undergrowth.

Tarzan easily distanced them, nor did they see his silent passage above their heads, nor note the crouching figure squatted upon a low branch ahead of them beneath which the trail led them.

Tarzan let the first two pass beneath him, but as the third came swiftly on, the quiet noose dropped about the black throat. A quick jerk drew it taut.

There was an agonized scream from the victim, and his fellows turned to see his struggling body rise as by magic slowly into the dense foliage of the trees above.

With frightened shrieks they wheeled once more and plunged on in their efforts to escape.

Tarzan dispatched his prisoner quickly and silently; removed the weapons and ornaments, and—oh, the greatest joy of all—a handsome deerskin breechcloth, which he quickly transferred to his own person.

Now indeed was he dressed as a man should be. None there was who could now doubt his high origin. How he should have liked to have returned to the tribe to parade before their envious gaze this wondrous finery.

Taking the body across his shoulder, he moved more slowly through the trees toward the little palisaded village, for he again needed arrows.

As he approached quite close to the enclosure he saw an excited group surrounding the two fugitives, who, trembling with fright and exhaustion, were scarce able to recount the uncanny details of their adventure.

Mirando, they said, who had been ahead of them a short distance, had suddenly come screaming toward them, crying that a terrible white and naked warrior was pursuing him. The three of them had hurried toward the village as rapidly as their legs would carry them.

Again Mirando's shrill cry of mortal terror had caused them to look back, and there they had seen the most horrible sight— their companion's body flying upwards into the trees, his arms and legs beating the air and his tongue protruding from his open mouth. No other sound did he utter nor was there any creature in sight about him.

The villagers were worked up into a state of fear bordering on panic, but wise old Mbonga affected to feel considerable skepticism regarding the tale, and attributed the whole fabrication to their fright in the face of some real danger.

"You tell us this great story," he said, "because you do not dare to speak the truth. You do not dare admit that when the lion sprang upon Mirando you ran away and left him. You are cowards."

Scarcely had Mbonga ceased speaking when a great crashing of branches in the trees above them caused the blacks to look up in renewed terror. The sight that met their eyes made even wise old

Mbonga shudder, for there, turning and twisting in the air, came the dead body of Mirando, to sprawl with a sickening reverberation upon the ground at their feet.

With one accord the blacks took to their heels; nor did they stop until the last of them was lost in the dense shadows of the surrounding jungle.

Again Tarzan came down into the village and renewed his supply of arrows and ate of the offering of food which the blacks had made to appease his wrath.

Before he left he carried the body of Mirando to the gate of the village, and propped it up against the palisade in such a way that the dead face seemed to be peering around the edge of the gatepost down the path which led to the jungle.

Then Tarzan returned, hunting, always hunting, to the cabin by the beach.

It took a dozen attempts on the part of the thoroughly frightened blacks to reenter their village, past the horrible, grinning face of their dead fellow, and when they found the food and arrows gone they knew, what they had only too well feared, that Mirando had seen the evil spirit of the jungle.

That now seemed to them the logical explanation. Only those who saw this terrible god of the jungle died; for was it not true that none left alive in the village had ever seen him? Therefore, those who had died at his hands must have seen him and paid the penalty with their lives.

As long as they supplied him with arrows and food he would not harm them unless they looked upon him, so it was ordered by Mbonga that in addition to the food offering there should also be laid out an offering of arrows for this Munan-go-Keewati, and this was done from then on.

If you ever chance to pass that far off African village you will still see before a tiny thatched hut, built just without the village, a little iron pot in which is a quantity of food, and beside it a quiver of well-daubed arrows.

When Tarzan came in sight of the beach where stood his cabin, a strange and unusual spectacle met his vision.

On the placid waters of the landlocked harbor floated a great ship, and on the beach a small boat was drawn up.

But, most wonderful of all, a number of white men like himself were moving about between the beach and his cabin.

Tarzan saw that in many ways they were like the men of his picture books. He crept closer through the trees until he was quite close above them.

There were ten men, swarthy, sun-tanned, villainous looking fellows. Now they had congregated by the boat and were talking in loud, angry tones, with much gesticulating and shaking of fists.

Presently one of them, a little, mean-faced, black-bearded fellow with a countenance which reminded Tarzan of Pamba, the rat, laid his hand upon the shoulder of a giant who stood next him, and with whom all the others had been arguing and quarreling.

The little man pointed inland, so that the giant was forced to turn away from the others to look in the direction indicated. As he turned, the little, mean-faced man drew a revolver from his belt and shot the giant in the back.

The big fellow threw his hands above his head, his knees bent beneath him, and without a sound he tumbled forward upon the beach, dead.

The report of the weapon, the first that Tarzan had ever heard, filled him with wonderment, but even this unaccustomed sound could not startle his healthy nerves into even a semblance of panic.

The conduct of the white strangers it was that caused him the greatest perturbation. He puckered his brows into a frown of deep thought. It was well, thought he, that he had not given way to his first impulse to rush forward and greet these white men as brothers.

They were evidently no different from the black men—no more civilized than the apes—no less cruel than Sabor.

For a moment the others stood looking at the little, mean-faced man and the giant lying dead upon the beach.

Then one of them laughed and slapped the little man upon the back. There was much more talk and gesticulating, but less quarreling.

Presently they launched the boat and all jumped into it and rowed away toward the great ship, where Tarzan could see other figures moving about upon the deck.

When they had clambered aboard, Tarzan dropped to earth behind a great tree and crept to his cabin, keeping it always between himself and the ship.

Slipping in at the door he found that everything had been ransacked. His books and pencils strewed the floor. His weapons and shields and other little store of treasures were littered about.

As he saw what had been done a great wave of anger surged through him, and the new made scar upon his forehead stood suddenly out, a bar of inflamed crimson against his tawny hide.

Quickly he ran to the cupboard and searched in the far recess of the lower shelf. Ah! He breathed a sigh of relief as he drew out the little tin box, and, opening it, found his greatest treasures undisturbed.

The photograph of the smiling, strong-faced young man, and the little black puzzle book were safe.

What was that?

His quick ear had caught a faint but unfamiliar sound.

Running to the window Tarzan looked toward the harbor, and there he saw that a boat was being lowered from the great ship beside the one already in the water. Soon he saw many people clambering over the sides of the larger vessel and dropping into the boats. They were coming back in full force.

For a moment longer Tarzan watched while a number of boxes and bundles were lowered into the waiting boats, then, as they shoved off from the ship's side, the ape-man snatched up a piece of paper, and with a pencil printed on it for a few moments until it bore several lines of strong, well-made, almost letter-perfect characters.

This notice he stuck upon the door with a small sharp splinter of wood. Then gathering up his precious tin box, his arrows, and as many bows and spears as he could carry, he hastened through the door and disappeared into the forest.

When the two boats were beached upon the silvery sand it was a strange assortment of humanity that clambered ashore.

Some twenty souls in all there were, fifteen of them rough and villainous appearing seamen.

The others of the party were of different stamp.

One was an elderly man, with white hair and large rimmed spectacles. His slightly stooped shoulders were draped in an ill-fitting, though immaculate, frock coat, and a shiny silk hat added to the incongruity of his garb in an African jungle.

The second member of the party to land was a tall young man in white ducks, while directly behind came another elderly man with a very high forehead and a fussy, excitable manner.

After these came a huge Negress clothed like Solomon as to colors. Her great eyes rolled in evident terror, first toward the jungle and then toward the cursing band of sailors who were removing the bales and boxes from the boats.

The last member of the party to disembark was a girl of about nineteen, and it was the young man who stood at the boat's prow to lift her high and dry upon land. She gave him a brave and pretty smile of thanks, but no words passed between them.

In silence the party advanced toward the cabin. It was evident that whatever their intentions, all had been decided upon before they left the ship; and so they came to the door, the sailors carrying the boxes and bales, followed by the five who were of so different a class.

The men put down their burdens, and then one caught sight of the notice which Tarzan had posted.

"Ho, mates!" he cried. "What's here? This sign was not posted an hour ago or I'll eat the cook."

The others gathered about, craning their necks over the shoulders of those before them, but as few of them could read at all, and then only after the most laborious fashion, one finally turned to the little old man of the top hat and frock coat.

"Hi, perfesser," he called, "step for'rd and read the bloomin' notis."

Thus addressed, the old man came slowly to where the sailors stood, followed by the other members of his party. Adjusting his spectacles he looked for a moment at the placard and then, turning away, strolled off muttering to himself: "Most remarkable—most remarkable!"

"Hi, old fossil," cried the man who had first called on him for assistance, "did je think we wanted of you to read the bloomin' notis to yourself? Come back here and read it out loud, you old barnacle."

The old man stopped and, turning back, said: "Oh, yes, my dear sir, a thousand pardons. It was quite thoughtless of me, yes—very thoughtless. Most remarkable—most remarkable!"

Again he faced the notice and read it through, and doubtless would have turned off again to ruminate upon it had not the sailor grasped him roughly by the collar and howled into his ear.

"Read it out loud, you blithering old idiot."

"Ah, yes indeed, yes indeed," replied the professor softly, and adjusting his spectacles once more he read aloud:

> THIS IS THE HOUSE OF TARZAN, THE KILLER OF
> BEASTS AND MANY BLACKMEN. DO NOT HARM THE
> THINGS WHICH ARE TARZAN'S. TARZAN WATCHES.
>
> TARZAN OF THE APES.

"Who the devil is Tarzan?" cried the sailor who had before spoken.

"He evidently speaks English," said the young man.

"But what does 'Tarzan of the Apes' mean?" cried the girl.

"I do not know, Miss Porter," replied the young man, "unless we have discovered a runaway simian from the London Zoo who has brought back a European education to his jungle home. What do you make of it, Professor Porter?" he added, turning to the old man.

Professor Archimedes Q. Porter adjusted his spectacles.

"Ah, yes, indeed; yes indeed—most remarkable, most remarkable!" said the professor; "but I can add nothing further to what I have already remarked in elucidation of this truly momentous occurrence," and the professor turned slowly in the direction of the jungle.

"But, papa," cried the girl, "you haven't said anything about it yet."

"Tut, tut, child; tut, tut," responded Professor Porter, in a kindly and indulgent tone, "do not trouble your pretty head with such weighty and abstruse problems," and again he wandered slowly off in still another direction, his eyes bent upon the ground at his feet, his hands clasped behind him beneath the flowing tails of his coat.

"I reckon the daffy old bounder don't know no more'n we do about it," growled the rat-faced sailor.

"Keep a civil tongue in your head," cried the young man, his face paling in anger, at the insulting tone of the sailor. "You've murdered our officers and robbed us. We are absolutely in your power, but you'll treat Professor Porter and Miss Porter with respect or I'll break that vile neck of yours with my bare hands—guns or no guns," and the young fellow stepped so close to the rat-faced sailor that the latter, though he bore two revolvers and a villainous looking knife in his belt, slunk back abashed.

"You damned coward," cried the young man. "You'd never dare shoot a man until his back was turned. You don't dare shoot me even then," and he deliberately turned his back full upon the sailor and walked nonchalantly away as if to put him to the test.

The sailor's hand crept slyly to the butt of one of his revolvers; his wicked eyes glared vengefully at the retreating form of the young Englishman. The gaze of his fellows was upon him, but still he hesitated. At heart he was even a greater coward than Mr. William Cecil Clayton had imagined.

Two keen eyes had watched every move of the party from the foliage of a nearby tree. Tarzan had seen the surprise caused by his notice, and while he could understand nothing of the spoken language of these strange people their gestures and facial expressions told him much.

The act of the little rat-faced sailor in killing one of his comrades had aroused a strong dislike in Tarzan, and now that he saw him quarreling with the fine-looking young man his animosity was still further stirred.

Tarzan had never seen the effects of a firearm before, though his books had taught him something of them, but when he saw the rat-faced one fingering the butt of his revolver he thought of the scene he had witnessed so short a time before, and naturally expected to see the young man murdered as had been the huge sailor earlier in the day.

So Tarzan fitted a poisoned arrow to his bow and drew a bead upon the rat-faced sailor, but the foliage was so thick that he soon saw the arrow would be deflected by the leaves or some small branch, and instead he launched a heavy spear from his lofty perch.

Clayton had taken but a dozen steps. The rat-faced sailor had half drawn his revolver; the other sailors stood watching the scene intently.

Professor Porter had already disappeared into the jungle, whither he was being followed by the fussy Samuel T. Philander, his secretary and assistant.

Esmeralda, the Negress, was busy sorting her mistress' baggage from the pile of bales and boxes beside the cabin, and Miss Porter had turned away to follow Clayton, when something caused her to turn again toward the sailor.

And then three things happened almost simultaneously. The sailor jerked out his weapon and leveled it at Clayton's back, Miss Porter screamed a warning, and a long, metal-shod spear shot like a bolt from above and passed entirely through the right shoulder of the rat-faced man.

The revolver exploded harmlessly in the air, and the seaman crumpled up with a scream of pain and terror.

Clayton turned and rushed back toward the scene. The sailors stood in a frightened group, with drawn weapons, peering into the jungle. The wounded man writhed and shrieked upon the ground.

Clayton, unseen by any, picked up the fallen revolver and slipped it inside his shirt, then he joined the sailors in gazing, mystified, into the jungle.

"Who could it have been?" whispered Jane Porter, and the young man turned to see her standing, wide-eyed and wondering, close beside him.

"I dare say Tarzan of the Apes is watching us all right," he answered, in a dubious tone. "I wonder, now, who that spear was intended for. If for Snipes, then our ape friend is a friend indeed.

"By jove, where are your father and Mr. Philander? There's someone or something in that jungle, and it's armed, whatever it is. Ho! Professor! Mr. Philander!" young Clayton shouted. There was no response.

"What's to be done, Miss Porter?" continued the young man, his face clouded by a frown of worry and indecision.

"I can't leave you here alone with these cutthroats, and you certainly can't venture into the jungle with me; yet someone must go in search of your father. He is more than apt to wandering off aimlessly, regardless of danger or direction, and Mr. Philander is only a trifle less impractical than he. You will pardon my bluntness, but our lives are all in jeopardy here, and when we get your father back something must be done to impress upon him the dangers to which he exposes you as well as himself by his absent-mindedness."

"I quite agree with you," replied the girl, "and I am not offended at all. Dear old papa would sacrifice his life for me without an instant's hesitation, provided one could keep his mind on so frivolous a matter for an entire instant. There is only one way to keep him in safety, and that is to chain him to a tree. The poor dear is *so* impractical."

"I have it!" suddenly exclaimed Clayton. "You can use a revolver, can't you?"

"Yes. Why?"

"I have one. With it you and Esmeralda will be comparatively safe in this cabin while I am searching for your father and Mr. Philander. Come, call the woman and I will hurry on. They can't have gone far."

Jane did as he suggested and when he saw the door close safely behind them Clayton turned toward the jungle.

Some of the sailors were drawing the spear from their wounded comrade and, as Clayton approached, he asked if he could borrow a revolver from one of them while he searched the jungle for the professor.

The rat-faced one, finding he was not dead, had regained his composure, and with a volley of oaths directed at Clayton refused in the name of his fellows to allow the young man any firearms.

This man, Snipes, had assumed the role of chief since he had killed their former leader, and so little time had elapsed that none of his companions had as yet questioned his authority.

Clayton's only response was a shrug of the shoulders, but as he left them he picked up the spear which had transfixed Snipes, and thus primitively armed, the son of the then Lord Greystoke strode into the dense jungle.

Every few moments he called aloud the names of the wanderers. The watchers in the cabin by the beach heard the sound of his voice growing ever fainter and fainter, until at last it was swallowed up by the myriad noises of the primeval wood.

When Professor Archimedes Q. Porter and his assistant, Samuel T. Philander, after much insistence on the part of the latter, had finally turned their steps toward camp, they were as completely lost in the wild and tangled labyrinth of the matted jungle as two human beings well could be, though they did not know it.

It was by the merest caprice of fortune that they headed toward the west coast of Africa, instead of toward Zanzibar on the opposite side of the dark continent.

When in a short time they reached the beach, only to find no camp in sight, Philander was positive that they were north of their proper destination, while, as a matter of fact they were about two hundred yards south of it.

It never occurred to either of these impractical theorists to call aloud on the chance of attracting their friends' attention. Instead, with all the assurance that deductive reasoning from a wrong premise induces in one, Mr. Samuel T. Philander grasped Professor Archimedes Q. Porter firmly by the arm and hurried the weakly protesting old gentleman off in the direction of Cape Town, fifteen hundred miles to the south.

When Jane and Esmeralda found themselves safely behind the cabin door the Negress's first thought was to barricade the portal from the inside. With this idea in mind she turned to search for some means of putting it into execution; but her first view of the interior of the cabin brought a shriek of terror to her lips, and like a frightened child the huge woman ran to bury her face on her mistress' shoulder.

Jane, turning at the cry, saw the cause of it lying prone upon the floor before them—the whitened skeleton of a man. A further glance revealed a second skeleton upon the bed.

126

"What horrible place are we in?" murmured the awe-struck girl. But there was no panic in her fright.

At last, disengaging herself from the frantic clutch of the still shrieking Esmeralda, Jane crossed the room to look into the little cradle, knowing what she should see there even before the tiny skeleton disclosed itself in all its pitiful and pathetic frailty.

What an awful tragedy these poor mute bones proclaimed! The girl shuddered at thought of the eventualities which might lie before herself and her friends in this ill-fated cabin, the haunt of mysterious, perhaps hostile, beings.

Quickly, with an impatient stamp of her little foot, she endeavored to shake off the gloomy forebodings, and turning to Esmeralda bade her cease her wailing.

"Stop, Esmeralda, stop it this minute!" she cried. "You are only making it worse."

She ended lamely, a little quiver in her own voice as she thought of the three men, upon whom she depended for protection, wandering in the depth of that awful forest.

Soon the girl found that the door was equipped with a heavy wooden bar upon the inside, and after several efforts the combined strength of the two enabled them to slip it into place, the first time in twenty years.

Then they sat down upon a bench with their arms about one another, and waited.

XIV

AT THE MERCY
OF THE JUNGLE

fter Clayton had plunged into the jungle, the sailors—mutineers of the *Arrow*—fell into a discussion of their next step; but on one point all were agreed—that they should hasten to put off to the anchored *Arrow*, where they could at least be safe from the spears of their unseen foe. And so, while Jane Porter and Esmeralda were barricading themselves within the cabin, the cowardly crew of cutthroats were pulling rapidly for their ship in the two boats that had brought them ashore.

So much had Tarzan seen that day that his head was in a whirl of wonder. But the most wonderful sight of all, to him, was the face of the beautiful white girl.

Here at last was one of his own kind; of that he was positive. And the young man and the two old men; they, too, were much as he had pictured his own people to be.

But doubtless they were as ferocious and cruel as other men he had seen. The fact that they alone of all the party were unarmed might account for the fact that they had killed no one. They might be very different if provided with weapons.

Tarzan had seen the young man pick up the fallen revolver of the wounded Snipes and hide it away in his breast; and he had also seen him slip it cautiously to the girl as she entered the cabin door.

He did not understand anything of the motives behind all that he had seen; but, somehow, intuitively he liked the young man and the two old men, and for the girl he had a strange longing which he scarcely understood. As for the big black woman, she was evidently connected in some way to the girl, and so he liked her, also.

For the sailors, and especially Snipes, he had developed a great hatred. He knew by their threatening gestures and by the expression upon their evil faces that they were enemies of the others of the party, and so he decided to watch closely.

Tarzan wondered why the men had gone into the jungle, nor did it ever occur to him that one could become lost in that maze of undergrowth which to him was as simple as is the main street of your own home town to you.

When he saw the sailors row away toward the ship, and knew that the girl and her companion were safe in his cabin, Tarzan decided to follow the young man into the jungle and learn what his errand might be. He swung off rapidly in the direction taken by Clayton, and in a short time heard faintly in the distance the now only occasional calls of the Englishman to his friends.

Presently Tarzan came up with the white man, who, almost fagged, was leaning against a tree wiping the perspiration from his forehead. The ape-man, hiding safe behind a screen of foliage, sat watching this new specimen of his own race intently.

At intervals Clayton called aloud and finally it came to Tarzan that he was searching for the old man.

Tarzan was on the point of going off to look for them himself, when he caught the yellow glint of a sleek hide moving cautiously through the jungle toward Clayton.

It was Sheeta, the leopard. Now, Tarzan heard the soft bending of grasses and wondered why the young white man was not warned. Could it be he had failed to note the loud warning? Never before had Tarzan known Sheeta to be so clumsy.

No, the white man did not hear. Sheeta was crouching for the spring, and then, shrill and horrible, there rose from the stillness of the jungle the awful cry of the challenging ape, and Sheeta turned, crashing into the underbrush.

Clayton came to his feet with a start. His blood ran cold. Never in all his life had so fearful a sound smote upon his ears. He was no coward; but if ever man felt the icy fingers of fear upon his heart, William Cecil Clayton, eldest son of Lord Greystoke of England, did that day in the fastness of the African jungle.

The noise of some great body crashing through the underbrush so close beside him, and the sound of that bloodcurdling shriek from above, tested Clayton's courage to the limit; but he could not know that it was to that very voice he owed his life, nor that the creature who hurled it forth was his own cousin—the real Lord Greystoke.

The afternoon was drawing to a close, and Clayton, disheartened and discouraged, was in a terrible quandary as to the proper course to pursue; whether to keep on in search of Professor Porter, at the almost certain risk of his own death in the jungle by night, or to return to the cabin where he might at least serve to protect Jane from the perils which confronted her on all sides.

He did not wish to return to camp without her father; still more, he shrank from the thought of leaving her alone and unprotected in the hands of the mutineers of the *Arrow*, or to the hundred unknown dangers of the jungle.

Possibly, too, he thought, the professor and Philander might have returned to camp. Yes, that was more than likely. At least he would return and see, before he continued what seemed to be a most fruitless quest. And so he started, stumbling back through the thick and matted underbrush in the direction that he thought the cabin lay.

To Tarzan's surprise the young man was heading further into the jungle in the general direction of Mbonga's village, and the shrewd young ape-man was convinced that he was lost.

To Tarzan this was scarcely incomprehensible; his judgment told him that no man would venture toward the village of the cruel blacks armed only with a spear which, from the awkward way in which he carried it, was evidently an unaccustomed weapon to this white man. Nor was he following the trail of the old men. That, they had crossed and left long since, though it had been fresh and plain before Tarzan's eyes.

Tarzan was perplexed. The fierce jungle would make easy prey of this unprotected stranger in a very short time if he were not guided quickly to the beach.

Yes, there was Numa, the lion, even now, stalking the white man a dozen paces to the right.

Clayton heard the great body paralleling his course, and now there rose upon the evening air the beast's thunderous roar. The man stopped with upraised spear and faced the brush from which issued the awful sound. The shadows were deepening, darkness was settling in.

God! To die here alone, beneath the fangs of wild beasts; to be torn and rended; to feel the hot breath of the brute on his face as the great paw crushed down up his breast!

For a moment all was still. Clayton stood rigid, with raised spear. Presently a faint rustling of the bush apprised him of the stealthy creeping of the thing behind. It was gathering for the spring. At last he saw it, not twenty feet away—the long, lithe, muscular body and tawny head of a huge black-maned lion.

The beast was upon its belly, moving forward very slowly. As its eyes met Clayton's it stopped, and deliberately, cautiously gathered its hind quarters behind it.

In agony the man watched, fearful to launch his spear, power-less to fly.

He heard a noise in the tree above him. Some new danger, he thought, but he dared not take his eyes from the yellow green orbs before him. There was a sharp twang as of a broken banjo-string, and at the same instant an arrow appeared in the yellow hide of the crouching lion.

With a roar of pain and anger the beast sprang; but, somehow, Clayton stumbled to one side, and as he turned again to face the infuriated king of beasts, he was appalled at the sight which confronted him. Almost simultaneously with the lion's turning to renew the attack a half-naked giant dropped from the tree above squarely on the brute's back.

With lightning speed an arm that was banded layers of iron muscle encircled the huge neck, and the great beast was raised from behind, roaring and pawing the air—raised as easily as Clayton would have lifted a pet dog.

The scene he witnessed there in the twilight depths of the African jungle was burned forever into the Englishman's brain.

The man before him was the embodiment of physical perfection and giant strength; yet it was not upon these he depended in his battle with the great cat, for mighty as were his muscles, they were as nothing by comparison with Numa's. To his agility, to his brain and to his long keen knife he owed his supremacy.

His right arm encircled the lion's neck, while the left hand plunged the knife time and again into the unprotected side behind the left shoulder. The infuriated beast, pulled up and backwards until he stood upon his hind legs, struggled impotently in this unnatural position.

Had the battle been of a few seconds' longer duration the outcome might have been different, but it was all accomplished so quickly that the lion had scarce time to recover from the confusion of its surprise ere it sank lifeless to the ground.

Then the strange figure which had vanquished it stood erect upon the carcass, and throwing back the wild and handsome head, gave out the fearsome cry which a few moments earlier had so startled Clayton.

Before him he saw the figure of a young man, naked except for a loin cloth and a few barbaric ornaments about arms and legs; on the breast a priceless diamond locket gleaming against a smooth brown skin.

The hunting knife had been returned to its homely sheath, and the man was gathering up his bow and quiver from where he had tossed them when he leaped to attack the lion.

Clayton spoke to the stranger in English, thanking him for his brave rescue and complimenting him on the wondrous strength and dexterity he had displayed, but the only answer was a steady stare and a faint shrug of the mighty shoulders, which might betoken either disparagement of the service rendered, or ignorance of Clayton's language.

When the bow and quiver had been slung to his back the wild man, for such Clayton now thought him, once more drew his knife and deftly carved a dozen large strips of meat from the lion's carcass. Then, squatting upon his haunches, he proceeded to eat, first motioning Clayton to join him.

The strong white teeth sank into the raw and dripping flesh in apparent relish of the meal, but Clayton could not bring himself to share the uncooked meat with his strange host; instead he watched him, and presently there dawned upon him the conviction that this was Tarzan of the Apes, whose notice he had seen posted upon the cabin door that morning.

If so he must speak English.

Again Clayton attempted speech with the ape-man; but the replies, now vocal, were in a strange tongue, which resembled the chattering of monkeys mingled with the growling of some wild beast.

No, this could not be Tarzan of the Apes, for it was very evident that he was an utter stranger to English.

When Tarzan had completed his repast he rose and, pointing a very different direction from that which Clayton had been pursuing, started off through the jungle toward the point he had indicated.

Clayton, bewildered and confused, hesitated to follow him, for he thought he was but being led more deeply into the mazes of the forest; but the ape-man, seeing him disinclined to follow, returned, and, grasping him by the coat, dragged him along until he was convinced that Clayton understood what was required of him. Then he left him to follow voluntarily.

The Englishman, finally concluding that he was a prisoner, saw no alternative open but to accompany his captor, and thus they traveled slowly through the jungle while the sable mantle of the impenetrable forest night fell about them, and the stealthy footfalls of padded paws mingled with the breaking of twigs and the wild calls of the savage life that Clayton felt closing in upon him.

Suddenly Clayton heard the faint report of a firearm—a single shot, and then silence.

In the cabin by the beach two thoroughly terrified women clung to each other as they crouched upon the low bench in the gathering darkness.

The Negress sobbed hysterically, bemoaning the evil day that had witnessed her departure from her dear Maryland, while the white girl, dry eyed and outwardly calm, was torn by inward fears and forebodings. She feared not more for herself than for the three men whom she knew to be wandering in the abysmal depths of the savage jungle, from which she now heard issuing the almost incessant shrieks and roars, barkings and growlings of its terrifying and fearsome denizens as they sought their prey.

And now there came the sound of a heavy body brushing against the side of the cabin. She could hear the great padded paws upon the ground outside. For an instant, all was silence; even the bedlam of the forest died to a faint murmur. Then she distinctly heard the beast outside sniffing at the door, not two feet from where she crouched. Instinctively the girl shuddered, and shrank closer to the black woman.

"Hush!" she whispered. "Hush, Esmeralda," for the woman's sobs and groans seemed to have attracted the thing that stalked there just beyond the thin wall.

A gentle scratching sound was heard on the door. The brute tried to force an entrance; but presently this ceased, and again she heard the great pads creeping stealthily around the cabin. Again they stopped—beneath the window on which the terrified eyes of the girl now glued themselves.

"God!" she murmured, for now, silhouetted against the moonlit sky beyond, she saw framed in the tiny square of the latticed window the head of a huge lioness. The gleaming eyes were fixed upon her in intent ferocity.

"Look, Esmeralda!" she whispered. "For God's sake, what shall we do? Look! Quick! The window!"

Esmeralda, cowering still closer to her mistress, took one frightened glance toward the little square of moonlight, just as the lioness emitted a low, savage snarl.

The sight that met the poor woman's eyes was too much for the already overstrung nerves.

"Oh, Gaberelle!" she shrieked, and slid to the floor an inert and senseless mass.

For what seemed an eternity the great brute stood with its forepaws upon the sill, glaring into the little room. Presently it tried the strength of the lattice with its great talons.

The girl had almost ceased to breathe, when, to her relief, the head disappeared and she heard the brute's footsteps leaving the window. But now they came to the door again, and once more the scratching commenced; this time with increasing force until the great beast was tearing at the massive panels in a perfect frenzy of eagerness to seize its defenseless victims.

Could Jane have known the immense strength of that door, built piece by piece, she would have felt less fear of the lioness reaching her by this avenue.

Little did John Clayton imagine when he fashioned that crude but mighty portal that one day, twenty years later, it would shield a fair American girl, then unborn, from the teeth and talons of a man-eater.

For fully twenty minutes the brute alternately sniffed and tore at the door, occasionally giving voice to a wild, savage cry of baffled rage. At length, however, she gave up the attempt, and Jane heard her returning toward the window, beneath which she paused for an instant, and then launched her great weight against the timeworn lattice.

The girl heard the wooden rods groan beneath the impact; but they held, and the huge body dropped back to the ground below.

Again and again the lioness repeated these tactics, until finally the horrified prisoner within saw a portion of the lattice give way, and in an instant one great paw and the head of the animal were thrust within the room.

Slowly the powerful neck and shoulders spread the bars apart, and the lithe body protruded farther and farther into the room.

As in a trance, the girl rose, her hand upon her breast, wide eyes staring horror-stricken into the snarling face of the beast scarce ten feet from her. At her feet lay the prostrate form of the Negress. If she could but arouse her, their combined efforts might possibly avail to beat back the fierce and bloodthirsty intruder.

Jane stooped to grasp the black woman by the shoulder. Roughly she shook her.

"Esmeralda! Esmeralda!" she cried. "Help me, or we are lost."

Esmeralda opened her eyes. The first object they encountered was the dripping fangs of the hungry lioness.

With a horrified scream the poor woman rose to her hands and knees, and in this position scurried across the room, shrieking: "O Gaberelle! O Gaberelle!" at the top of her lungs.

Esmeralda weighed some two hundred and eighty pounds, and her extreme haste, added to her extreme corpulency, produced a most amazing result when Esmeralda elected to travel on all fours.

For a moment the lioness remained quiet with intense gaze directed upon the flitting Esmeralda, whose goal appeared to be the cupboard, into which she attempted to propel her huge bulk; but as the shelves were but nine or ten inches apart, she only succeeded in getting her head in; whereupon, with a final screech, which paled the jungle noises into insignificance, she fainted once again.

With the subsidence of Esmeralda the lioness renewed her efforts to wriggle her huge bulk through the weakening lattice.

The girl, standing pale and rigid against the farther wall, sought with ever-increasing terror for some loophole of escape. Suddenly her hand, tight-pressed against her bosom, felt the hard outline of the revolver that Clayton had left with her earlier in the day.

Quickly she snatched it from its hiding-place, and, leveling it full at the lioness's face, pulled the trigger.

There was a flash of flame, the roar of the discharge, and an answering roar of pain and anger from the beast.

Jane Porter saw the great form disappear from the window, and then she, too, fainted, the revolver falling at her side.

But Sabor was not killed. The bullet had but inflicted a painful wound in one of the great shoulders. It was the surprise at the blinding flash and the deafening roar that had caused her hasty but temporary retreat.

In another instant she was back at the lattice, and with renewed fury was clawing at the aperture, but with lessened effect, since the wounded member was almost useless.

She saw her prey—the two women—lying senseless upon the floor. There was no longer any resistance to be overcome. Her meat lay before her, and Sabor had only to worm her way through the lattice to claim it.

Slowly she forced her great bulk, inch by inch, through the opening. Now her head was through, now one great forearm and shoulder.

Carefully she drew up the wounded member to insinuate it gently beyond the tight pressing bars.

A moment more and both shoulders through, the long, sinuous body and the narrow hips would glide quickly after.

It was on this sight that Jane Porter again opened her eyes.

XV

THE FOREST GOD

hen Clayton heard the report of the firearm he fell into an agony of fear and apprehension. He knew that one of the sailors might be the author of it; but the fact that he had left the revolver with Jane, together with the overwrought condition of his nerves, made him morbidly positive that she was threatened with some great danger. Perhaps even now she was attempting to defend herself against some savage man or beast.

What were the thoughts of his strange captor or guide Clayton could only vaguely conjecture; but that he had heard the shot, and was in some manner affected by it was quite evident, for he quickened his pace so appreciably that Clayton, stumbling blindly in his wake, was down a dozen times in as many minutes in a vain effort to keep pace with him, and soon was left hopelessly behind.

Fearing that he would again be irretrievably lost, he called aloud to the wild man ahead of him, and in a moment had the satisfaction of seeing him drop lightly to his side from the branches above.

For a moment Tarzan looked at the young man closely, as though undecided as to just what was best to do; then, stooping down before Clayton, he motioned him to grasp him about the neck, and, with the white man upon his back, Tarzan took to the trees.

The next few minutes the young Englishman never forgot. High into bending and swaying branches he was borne with what seemed to him incredible swiftness, while Tarzan chafed at the slowness of his progress.

From one lofty branch the agile creature swung with Clayton through a dizzy arc to a neighboring tree; then for a hundred yards maybe the sure feet threaded a maze of interwoven limbs, balancing like a tightrope walker high above the black depths of verdure beneath.

From the first sensation of chilling fear Clayton passed to one of keen admiration and envy of those giant muscles and that wondrous instinct or knowledge which guided this forest god through the inky blackness of the night as easily and safely as Clayton would have strolled a London street at high noon.

Occasionally they would enter a spot where the foliage above was less dense, and the bright rays of the moon lit up before Clayton's wondering eyes the strange path they were traversing.

At such times the man fairly caught his breath at sight of the horrid depths below them, for Tarzan took the easiest way, which often led over a hundred feet above the earth.

And yet with all his seeming speed, Tarzan was in reality feeling his way with comparative slowness, searching constantly for limbs of adequate strength for the maintenance of this double weight.

Presently they came to the clearing before the beach. Tarzan's quick ears had heard the strange sounds of Sabor's efforts to force her way through the lattice, and it seemed to Clayton that they dropped a straight hundred feet to earth, so quickly did Tarzan descend. Yet when they struck the ground it was with scarce a jar; and as Clayton released his hold on the ape-man he saw him dart like a squirrel for the opposite side of the cabin.

The Englishman sprang quickly after him just in time to see the hind quarters of some huge animal about to disappear through the window of the cabin.

As Jane opened her eyes to a realization of the imminent peril which threatened her, her brave young heart gave up at last its final vestige of hope. But then to her surprise she saw the huge animal being slowly drawn back through the window, and in the moonlight beyond she saw the heads and shoulders of two men.

As Clayton rounded the corner of the cabin to behold the animal disappearing within, it was also to see the ape-man seize the long tail in both hands, and, bracing himself with his feet against the side of the cabin, throw all his mighty strength into the effort to draw the beast out of the interior.

Clayton was quick to lend a hand, but the ape-man jabbered to him in a commanding and peremptory tone something which Clayton knew to be orders, though he could not understand them.

At last, under their combined efforts, the great body was slowly dragged farther and farther outside the window, and then there came to Clayton's mind a dawning conception of the rash bravery of his companion's act.

For a naked man to drag a shrieking, clawing man-eater forth from a window by the tail to save a strange white girl, was indeed the last word in heroism.

Insofar as Clayton was concerned it was a very different matter, since the girl was not only of his own kind and race, but was the one woman in all the world whom he loved.

Though he knew that the lioness would make short work of both of them, he pulled with a will to keep it from Jane Porter. And then he recalled the battle between this man and the great, black-maned lion which he had witnessed a short time before, and he commenced to feel more assurance.

Tarzan was still issuing orders which Clayton could not understand.

He was trying to tell the stupid white man to plunge his poisoned arrows into Sabor's back and sides, and to reach the savage heart with the long, thin hunting knife that hung at Tarzan's hip; but the man would not understand, and Tarzan did not dare release his hold to do the things himself, for he knew that the puny white man never could hold mighty Sabor alone, for an instant.

Slowly the lioness was emerging from the window. At last her shoulders were out.

And then Clayton saw an incredible thing. Tarzan, racking his brains for some means to cope single-handed with the infuriated beast, had suddenly recalled his battle with Terkoz; and as the great shoulders came clear of the window, so that the lioness hung upon the sill only by her forepaws, Tarzan suddenly released his hold upon the brute.

With the quickness of a striking rattler he launched himself full upon Sabor's back, his strong young arms seeking and gaining a full-Nelson upon the beast, as he had learned it that other day during his bloody, wrestling victory over Terkoz.

With a roar the lioness turned completely over upon her back, falling full upon her enemy; but the black-haired giant only closed tighter his hold.

Pawing and tearing at earth and air, Sabor rolled and threw herself this way and that in an effort to dislodge this strange antagonist; but ever tighter and tighter drew the iron bands that were forcing her head lower and lower upon her tawny breast.

Higher crept the steel forearms of the ape-man about the back of Sabor's neck. Weaker and weaker became the lioness's efforts.

At last Clayton saw the immense muscles of Tarzan's shoulders and biceps leap into corded knots beneath the silver moonlight. There was a long sustained and supreme effort on the ape-man's part—and the vertebrae of Sabor's neck parted with a sharp snap.

In an instant Tarzan was upon his feet, and for the second time that day Clayton heard the bull ape's savage roar of victory. Then he heard Jane's agonized cry:

"Cecil—Mr. Clayton! Oh, what is it? What is it?"

Running quickly to the cabin door, Clayton called out that all was right, and shouted to her to open the door. As quickly as she could she raised the great bar and fairly dragged Clayton within.

"What was that awful noise?" she whispered, shrinking close to him.

"It was the cry of the kill from the throat of the man who has just saved your life, Miss Porter. Wait, I will fetch him so you may thank him."

The frightened girl would not be left alone, so she accompanied Clayton to the side of the cabin where lay the dead body of the lioness.

Tarzan of the Apes was gone.

Clayton called several times, but there was no reply, and so the two returned to the greater safety of the interior.

"What a frightful sound!" cried Jane, "I shudder at the mere thought of it. Do not tell me that a human throat voiced that hideous and fearsome shriek."

"But it did, Miss Porter," replied Clayton; "or at least if not a human throat that of a forest god."

And then he told her of his experiences with this strange creature—of how twice the wild man had saved his life—of the wondrous strength, and agility, and bravery—of the brown skin and the handsome face.

"I cannot make it out at all," he concluded. "At first I thought he might be Tarzan of the Apes; but he neither speaks nor understands English, so that theory is untenable."

"Well, whatever he may be," cried the girl, "we owe him our lives, and may God bless him and keep him in safety in his wild and savage jungle!"

"Amen," said Clayton, fervently.

"For the good Lord's sake, ain't I dead?"

The two turned to see Esmeralda sitting upright upon the floor, her great eyes rolling from side to side as though she could not believe their testimony as to her whereabouts.

And now, for Jane Porter, the reaction came, and she threw herself upon the bench, sobbing with hysterical laughter.

XVI

"MOST REMARKABLE"

everal miles south of the cabin, upon a strip of sandy beach, stood two old men, arguing.

Before them stretched the broad Atlantic. At their backs was the Dark Continent. Close around them loomed the impenetrable blackness of the jungle.

Savage beasts roared and growled; noises, hideous and weird, assailed their ears. They had wandered for miles in search of their camp, but always in the wrong direction. They were as hopelessly lost as though they suddenly had been transported to another world.

At such a time, indeed, every fiber of their combined intellects must have been concentrated upon the vital question of the minute— the life-and-death question to them of retracing their steps to camp.

Samuel T. Philander was speaking.

"But, my dear professor," he was saying, "I still maintain that but for the victories of Ferdinand and Isabella over the fifteenth-century Moors in Spain the world would be today a thousand years in advance of where we now find ourselves. The Moors were essentially a tolerant, broad-minded, liberal race of agriculturists, artisans and merchants—the very type of people that has made possible such civilization as we find today in America and Europe—while the Spaniards—"

"Tut, tut, dear Mr. Philander," interrupted Professor Porter; "their religion positively precluded the possibilities you suggest.

145

Moslemism was, is, and always will be, a blight on that scientific progress which has marked—"

"Bless me! Professor," interjected Mr. Philander, who had turned his gaze toward the jungle, "there seems to be someone approaching."

Professor Archimedes Q. Porter turned in the direction indicated by the nearsighted Mr. Philander.

"Tut, tut, Mr. Philander," he chided. "How often must I urge you to seek that absolute concentration of your mental faculties which alone may permit you to bring to bear the highest powers of intellectuality upon the momentous problems which naturally fall to the lot of great minds? And now I find you guilty of a most flagrant breach of courtesy in interrupting my learned discourse to call attention to a mere quadruped of the genus *Felis*. As I was saying, Mr.—"

"Heavens, Professor, a lion?" cried Mr. Philander, straining his weak eyes toward the dim figure outlined against the dark tropical underbrush.

"Yes, yes, Mr. Philander, if you insist upon employing slang in your discourse, a 'lion.' But as I was saying—"

"Bless me, Professor," again interrupted Mr. Philander; "permit me to suggest that doubtless the Moors who were conquered in the fifteenth century will continue in that most regrettable condition for the time being at least, even though we postpone discussion of that world calamity until we may attain the enchanting view of yon *Felis carnivora* which distance proverbially is credited with lending."

In the meantime the lion had approached with quiet dignity to within ten paces of the two men, where he stood curiously watching them.

The moonlight flooded the beach, and the strange group stood out in bold relief against the yellow sand.

"Most reprehensible, most reprehensible," exclaimed Professor Porter, with a faint trace of irritation in his voice. "Never, Mr. Philander, never before in my life have I known one of these animals to be permitted to roam at large from its cage. I shall most certainly report this outrageous breach of ethics to the directors of the adjacent zoological garden."

"Quite right, Professor," agreed Mr. Philander, "and the sooner it is done the better. Let us start now."

Seizing the professor by the arm, Mr. Philander set off in the direction that would put the greatest distance between themselves and the lion.

They had proceeded but a short distance when a backward glance revealed to the horrified gaze of Mr. Philander that the lion was following them. He tightened his grip upon the protesting professor and increased his speed.

"As I was saying, Mr. Philander," repeated Professor Porter.

Mr. Philander took another hasty glance rearward. The lion also had quickened his gait, and was doggedly maintaining an unvarying distance behind them.

"He is following us!" gasped Mr. Philander, breaking into a run.

"Tut, tut, Mr. Philander," remonstrated the professor, "this unseemly haste is most unbecoming to men of letters. What will our friends think of us, who may chance to be upon the street and witness our frivolous antics? Pray let us proceed with more decorum."

Mr. Philander stole another observation astern.

The lion was bounding along in easy leaps scarce five paces behind.

Mr. Philander dropped the professor's arm, and broke into a mad orgy of speed that would have done credit to any varsity track team.

"As I was saying, Mr. Philander—" screamed Professor Porter, as, metaphorically speaking, he himself "threw her into high." He, too, had caught a fleeting backward glimpse of cruel yellow eyes and half open mouth within startling proximity of his person.

With streaming coat tails and shiny silk hat Professor Archimedes Q. Porter fled through the moonlight close upon the heels of Mr. Samuel T. Philander.

Before them a point of the jungle ran out toward a narrow promontory, and it was for the heaven of the trees he saw there that Mr.
Samuel T. Philander directed his prodigious leaps and bounds; while
from the shadows of this same spot peered two keen eyes in interested appreciation of the race.

It was Tarzan of the Apes who watched, with face a-grin, this
odd game of follow-the-leader.

He knew the two men were safe enough from attack in so far as
the lion was concerned. The very fact that Numa had foregone such
easy prey at all convinced the wise forest craft of Tarzan that Numa's
belly already was full.

The lion might stalk them until hungry again; but the chances
were that if not angered he would soon tire of the sport, and slink
away to his jungle lair.

Really, the one great danger was that one of the men might
stumble and fall, and then the yellow devil would be upon him in
a moment and the joy of the kill would be too great a temptation to
withstand.

So Tarzan swung quickly to a lower limb in line with the
approaching fugitives; and as Mr. Samuel T. Philander came panting and blowing beneath him, already too spent to struggle up to the
safety of the limb, Tarzan reached down and, grasping him by the
collar of his coat, yanked him to the limb by his side.

Another moment brought the professor within the sphere of the
friendly grip, and he, too, was drawn upward to safety just as the
baffled Numa, with a roar, leaped to recover his vanishing quarry.

For a moment the two men clung panting to the great branch,
while Tarzan squatted with his back to the stem of the tree, watching
them with mingled curiosity and amusement.

It was the professor who first broke the silence.

"I am deeply pained, Mr. Philander, that you should have evinced
such a paucity of manly courage in the presence of one of the lower

orders, and by your crass timidity have caused me to exert myself to such an unaccustomed degree in order that I might resume my discourse. As I was saying, Mr. Philander, when you interrupted me, the Moors——"

"Professor Archimedes Q. Porter," broke in Mr. Philander, in icy tones, "the time has arrived when patience becomes a crime and mayhem appears garbed in the mantle of virtue. You have accused me of cowardice. You have insinuated that you ran only to overtake me, not to escape the clutches of the lion. Have a care, Professor Archimedes Q. Porter! I am a desperate man. Goaded by long-suffering patience the worm will turn."

"Tut, tut, Mr. Philander, tut, tut!" cautioned Professor Porter; "you forget yourself."

"I forget nothing as yet, Professor Archimedes Q. Porter; but, believe me, sir, I am tottering on the verge of forgetfulness as to your exalted position in the world of science, and your gray hairs."

The professor sat in silence for a few minutes, and the darkness hid the grim smile that wreathed his wrinkled countenance. Presently he spoke.

"Look here, Skinny Philander," he said, in belligerent tones, "if you are lookin' for a scrap, peel off your coat and come on down on the ground, and I'll punch your head just as I did sixty years ago in the alley back of Porky Evans' barn."

"Ark!" gasped the astonished Mr. Philander. "Lordy, how good that sounds! When you're human, Ark, I love you; but somehow it seems as though you had forgotten how to be human for the last twenty years."

The professor reached out a thin, trembling old hand through the darkness until it found his old friend's shoulder.

"Forgive me, Skinny," he said, softly. "It hasn't been quite twenty years, and God alone knows how hard I have tried to be 'human' for Jane's sake, and yours, too, since He took my other Jane away."

Another old hand stole up from Mr. Philander's side to clasp the one that lay upon his shoulder, and no other message could better have translated the one heart to the other.

They did not speak for some minutes. The lion below them paced nervously back and forth. The third figure in the tree was hidden by the dense shadows near the stem. He, too, was silent—motionless as a graven image.

"You certainly pulled me up into this tree just in time," said the professor at last. "I want to thank you. You saved my life."

"But I didn't pull you up here, Professor," said Mr. Philander. "Bless me! The excitement of the moment quite caused me to forget that I myself was drawn up here by some outside agency—there must be someone or something in this tree with us."

"Eh?" ejaculated Professor Porter. "Are you quite positive, Mr. Philander?"

"Most positive, Professor," replied Mr. Philander, "and," he added, "I think we should thank the party. He may be sitting right next to you now, Professor."

"Eh? What's that? Tut, tut, Mr. Philander, tut, tut!" said Professor Porter, edging cautiously nearer to Mr. Philander.

Just then it occurred to Tarzan of the Apes that Numa had loitered beneath the tree for a sufficient length of time, so he raised his young head toward the heavens, and there rang out upon the terrified ears of the two old men the awful warning challenge of the anthropoid.

The two friends, huddled trembling in their precarious position on the limb, saw the great lion halt in his restless pacing as the blood-curdling cry smote his ears, and then slink quickly into the jungle, to be instantly lost to view.

"Even the lion trembles in fear," whispered Mr. Philander.

"Most remarkable, most remarkable," murmured Professor Porter, clutching frantically at Mr. Philander to regain the balance which the sudden fright had so perilously endangered. Unfortunately for them both, Mr. Philander's center of equilibrium was at that very moment hanging upon the ragged edge of nothing, so that it needed but the gentle impetus supplied by the additional weight of Professor Porter's body to topple the devoted secretary from the limb.

For a moment they swayed uncertainly, and then, with mingled and most unscholarly shrieks, they pitched headlong from the tree, locked in frenzied embrace.

It was quite some moments ere either moved, for both were positive that any such attempt would reveal so many breaks and fractures as to make further progress impossible.

At length Professor Porter made an attempt to move one leg. To his surprise, it responded to his will as in days gone by. He now drew up its mate and stretched it forth again.

"Most remarkable, most remarkable," he murmured.

"Thank God, Professor," whispered Mr. Philander, fervently, "you are not dead, then?"

"Tut, tut, Mr. Philander, tut, tut," cautioned Professor Porter, "I do not know with accuracy as yet."

With infinite solicitude Professor Porter wiggled his right arm—joy! It was intact. Breathlessly he waved his left arm above his prostrate body—it waved!

"Most remarkable, most remarkable," he said.

"To whom are you signaling, Professor?" asked Mr. Philander, in an excited tone.

Professor Porter deigned to make no response to this puerile inquiry. Instead he raised his head gently from the ground, nodding it back and forth a half dozen times.

"Most remarkable," he breathed. "It remains intact."

Mr. Philander had not moved from where he had fallen; he had not dared the attempt. How indeed could one move when one's arms and legs and back were broken?

One eye was buried in the soft loam; the other, rolling sidewise, was fixed in awe upon the strange gyrations of Professor Porter.

"How sad!" exclaimed Mr. Philander, half aloud. "Concussion of the brain, superinducing total mental aberration. How very sad indeed! and for one still so young!"

Professor Porter rolled over upon his stomach; gingerly he bowed his back until he resembled a huge tom cat in proximity to a yelping dog. Then he sat up and felt of various portions of his anatomy.

"They are all here," he exclaimed. "Most remarkable!"

Whereupon he arose, and, bending a scathing glance upon the still prostrate form of Mr. Samuel T. Philander, he said:

"Tut, tut, Mr. Philander; this is no time to indulge in slothful ease. We must be up and doing."

Mr. Philander lifted his other eye out of the mud and gazed in speechless rage at Professor Porter. Then he attempted to rise; nor could there have been any more surprised than he when his efforts were immediately crowned with marked success.

He was still bursting with rage, however, at the cruel injustice of Professor Porter's insinuation, and was on the point of rendering a tart rejoinder when his eyes fell upon a strange figure standing a few paces away, scrutinizing them intently.

Professor Porter had recovered his shiny silk hat, which he had brushed carefully upon the sleeve of his coat and replaced upon his head. When he saw Mr. Philander pointing to something behind him he turned to behold a giant, naked but for a loin cloth and a few metal ornaments, standing motionless before him.

"Good evening, sir!" said the professor, lifting his hat.

For reply the giant motioned them to follow him, and set off up the beach in the direction from which they had recently come.

"I think it the better part of discretion to follow him," said Mr. Philander.

"Tut, tut, Mr. Philander," returned the professor. "A short time since you were advancing a most logical argument in substantiation of your theory that camp lay dircctly south of us. I was skeptical, but you finally convinced me; so now I am positive that toward the south we must travel to reach our friends. Therefore I shall continue south."

"But, Professor Porter, this man may know better than either of us. He seems to be indigenous to this part of the world. Let us at least follow him for a short distance."

"Tut, tut, Mr. Philander," repeated the professor. "I am a difficult man to convince, but when once convinced my decision is unalterable. I shall continue in the proper direction, if I have to circumambulate the continent of Africa to reach my destination."

Further argument was interrupted by Tarzan, who, seeing that these strange men were not following him, had returned to their side.

Again he beckoned to them; but still they stood in argument.

Presently the ape-man lost patience with their stupid ignorance. He grasped the frightened Mr. Philander by the shoulder, and before that worthy gentleman knew whether he was being killed or merely maimed for life, Tarzan had tied one end of his rope securely about Mr. Philander's neck.

"Tut, tut, Mr. Philander," remonstrated Professor Porter; "it is most unbeseeming in you to submit to such indignities."

But scarcely were the words out of his mouth ere he, too, had been seized and securely bound by the neck with the same rope. Then Tarzan set off toward the north, leading the now thoroughly frightened professor and his secretary.

In deathly silence they proceeded for what seemed hours to the two tired and hopeless old men; but presently as they topped a little rise of ground they were overjoyed to see the cabin lying before them, not a hundred yards distant.

Here Tarzan released them, and, pointing toward the little building, vanished into the jungle beside them.

"Most remarkable, most remarkable!" gasped the professor. "But you see, Mr. Philander, that I was quite right, as usual; and but for your stubborn willfulness we should have escaped a series of most humiliating, not to say dangerous accidents. Pray allow yourself to be guided by a more mature and practical mind hereafter when in need of wise counsel."

Mr. Samuel T. Philander was too much relieved at the happy outcome to their adventure to take umbrage at the professor's cruel fling. Instead he grasped his friend's arm and hastened him forward in the direction of the cabin.

It was a much-relieved party of castaways that found itself once more united. Dawn discovered them still recounting their various adventures and speculating upon the identity of the strange guardian and protector they had found on this savage shore.

Esmeralda was positive that it was none other than an angel of the Lord, sent down especially to watch over them.

"Had you seen him devour the raw meat of the lion, Esmeralda," laughed Clayton, "you would have thought him a very material angel."

"There was nothing heavenly about his voice," said Jane Porter, with a little shudder at recollection of the awful roar which had followed the killing of the lioness.

"Nor did it precisely comport with my preconceived ideas of the dignity of divine messengers," remarked Professor Porter, "when the—ah—gentleman tied two highly respectable and erudite scholars neck to neck and dragged them through the jungle as though they had been cows."

XVII

BURIALS

s it was now quite light, the party, none of whom had eaten or slept since the previous morning, began to bestir themselves to prepare food.

The mutineers of the *Arrow* had landed a small supply of dried meats, canned soups and vegetables, crackers, flour, tea, and coffee for the five they had marooned, and these were hurriedly drawn upon to satisfy the craving of long-famished appetites.

The next task was to make the cabin habitable, and to this end it was decided to at once remove the gruesome relics of the tragedy which had taken place there on some bygone day.

Professor Porter and Mr. Philander were deeply interested in examining the skeletons. The two larger, they stated, had belonged to a male and female of one of the higher white races.

The smallest skeleton was given but passing attention, as its location, in the crib, left no doubt as to its having been the infant offspring of this unhappy couple.

As they were preparing the skeleton of the man for burial, Clayton discovered a massive ring which had evidently encircled the man's finger at the time of his death, for one of the slender bones of the hand still lay within the golden bauble.

Picking it up to examine it, Clayton gave a cry of astonishment, for the ring bore the crest of the house of Greystoke.

At the same time, Jane discovered the books in the cupboard, and on opening the fly-leaf of one of them saw the name, *John Clayton, London.* In a second book which she hurriedly examined was the single name, *Greystoke.*

"Why, Mr. Clayton," she cried, "what does this mean? Here are the names of some of your own people in these books."

"And here," he replied gravely, "is the great ring of the house of Greystoke which has been lost since my uncle, John Clayton, the former Lord Greystoke, disappeared, presumably lost at sea."

"But how do you account for these things being here, in this savage African jungle?" exclaimed the girl.

"There is but one way to account for it, Miss Porter," said Clayton. "The late Lord Greystoke was not drowned. He died here in this cabin and this poor thing upon the floor is all that is mortal of him."

"Then this must have been Lady Greystoke," said Jane reverently, indicating the poor mass of bones upon the bed.

"The beautiful Lady Alice," replied Clayton, "of whose many virtues and remarkable personal charms I often have heard my mother and father speak. Poor woman," he murmured sadly.

With deep reverence and solemnity the bodies of the late Lord and Lady Greystoke were buried beside their little African cabin, and between them was placed the tiny skeleton of the baby of Kala, the ape.

As Mr. Philander was placing the frail bones of the infant in a bit of sail cloth, he examined the skull minutely. Then he called Professor Porter to his side, and the two argued in low tones for several minutes.

"Most remarkable, most remarkable," said Professor Porter.

"Bless me," said Mr. Philander, "we must acquaint Mr. Clayton with our discovery at once."

"Tut, tut, Mr. Philander, tut, tut!" remonstrated Professor Archimedes Q. Porter. "'Let the dead past bury its dead.'"

And so the white-haired old man repeated the burial service over this strange grave, while his four companions stood with bowed and uncovered heads about him.

From the trees Tarzan of the Apes watched the solemn ceremony; but most of all he watched the sweet face and graceful figure of Jane Porter.

In his savage, untutored breast new emotions were stirring. He could not fathom them. He wondered why he felt so great an interest in these people—why he had gone to such pains to save the three men. But he did not wonder why he had torn Sabor from the tender flesh of the strange girl.

Surely the men were stupid and ridiculous and cowardly. Even Manu, the monkey, was more intelligent than they. If these were creatures of his own kind he was doubtful if his past pride in blood was warranted.

But the girl, ah—that was a different matter. He did not reason here. He knew that she was created to be protected, and that he was created to protect her.

He wondered why they had dug a great hole in the ground merely to bury dry bones. Surely there was no sense in that; no one wanted to steal dry bones.

Had there been meat upon them he could have understood, for thus alone might one keep his meat from Dango, the hyena, and the other robbers of the jungle.

When the grave had been filled with earth the little party turned back toward the cabin, and Esmeralda, still weeping copiously for the two she had never heard of before today, and who had been dead twenty years, chanced to glance toward the harbor. Instantly her tears ceased.

"Look at them low down white trash out there!" she shrilled, pointing toward the *Arrow.* "They-all's a desecrating us, right here on this here perverted island."

And, sure enough, the *Arrow* was being worked toward the open sea, slowly, through the harbor's entrance.

"They promised to leave us firearms and ammunition," said Clayton. "The merciless beasts!"

"It is the work of that fellow they call Snipes, I am sure," said Jane. "King was a scoundrel, but he had a little sense of humanity. If they had not killed him I know that he would have seen that we were properly provided for before they left us to our fate."

"I regret that they did not visit us before sailing," said Professor Porter. "I had proposed requesting them to leave the treasure with us, as I shall be a ruined man if that is lost."

Jane looked at her father sadly.

"Never mind, dear," she said. "It wouldn't have done any good, because it is solely for the treasure that they killed their officers and landed us upon this awful shore."

"Tut, tut, child, tut, tut!" replied Professor Porter. "You are a good child, but inexperienced in practical matters," and Professor Porter turned and walked slowly away toward the jungle, his hands clasped beneath his long coat tails and his eyes bent upon the ground.

His daughter watched him with a pathetic smile upon her lips, and then turning to Mr. Philander, she whispered:

"Please don't let him wander off again as he did yesterday. We depend upon you, you know, to keep a close watch upon him."

"He becomes more difficult to handle each day," replied Mr. Philander, with a sigh and a shake of his head. "I presume he is now off to report to the directors of the Zoo that one of their lions was at large last night. Oh, Miss Jane, you don't know what I have to contend with."

"Yes, I do, Mr. Philander; but while we all love him, you alone are best fitted to manage him; for, regardless of what he may say to you, he respects your great learning, and, therefore, has immense confidence in your judgment. The poor dear cannot differentiate between erudition and wisdom."

Mr. Philander, with a mildly puzzled expression on his face, turned to pursue Professor Porter, and in his mind he was revolving the question of whether he should feel complimented or aggrieved at Miss Porter's rather backhanded compliment.

Tarzan had seen the consternation depicted upon the faces of the little group as they witnessed the departure of the *Arrow*; so, as the ship was a wonderful novelty to him in addition, he determined to hasten out to the point of land at the north of the harbor's mouth and obtain a nearer view of the boat, as well as to learn, if possible, the direction of its flight.

Swinging through the trees with great speed, he reached the point only a moment after the ship had passed out of the harbor, so that he obtained an excellent view of the wonders of this strange, floating house.

There were some twenty men running hither and thither about the deck, pulling and hauling on ropes.

A light land breeze was blowing, and the ship had been worked through the harbor's mouth under scant sail, but now that they had cleared the point every available shred of canvas was being spread that she might stand out to sea as handily as possible.

Tarzan watched the graceful movements of the ship in rapt admiration, and longed to be aboard her. Presently his keen eyes caught the faintest suspicion of smoke on the far northern horizon, and he wondered over the cause of such a thing out on the great water.

About the same time the lookout on the *Arrow* must have discerned it, for in a few minutes Tarzan saw the sails being shifted and shortened. The ship came about, and presently he knew that she was beating back toward land.

A man at the bows was constantly heaving into the sea a rope to the end of which a small object was fastened. Tarzan wondered what the purpose of this action might be.

At last the ship came up directly into the wind; the anchor was lowered; down came the sails. There was great scurrying about on deck.

A boat was lowered, and in it a great chest was placed. Then a dozen sailors bent to the oars and pulled rapidly toward the point where Tarzan crouched in the branches of a tree.

In the stern of the boat, as it drew nearer, Tarzan saw the rat-faced man.

It was but a few minutes later that the boat touched the beach. The men jumped out and lifted the great chest to the sand. They were on the north side of the point so that their presence was concealed from those at the cabin.

The men argued angrily for a moment. Then the rat-faced one, with several companions, ascended the low bluff on which stood the tree that concealed Tarzan. They looked about for several minutes.

"Here is a good place," said the rat-faced sailor, indicating a spot beneath Tarzan's tree.

"It is as good as any," replied one of his companions. "If they catch us with the treasure aboard it will all be confiscated anyway. We might as well bury it here on the chance that some of us will escape the gallows to come back and enjoy it later."

The rat-faced one now called to the men who had remained at the boat, and they came slowly up the bank carrying picks and shovels.

"Hurry, you!" cried Snipes.

"Stow it!" retorted one of the men, in a surly tone. "You're no admiral, you damned shrimp."

"I'm Cap'n here, though, I'll have you to understand, you swab," shrieked Snipes, with a volley of frightful oaths.

"Steady, boys," cautioned one of the men who had not spoken before. "It ain't goin' to get us nothing by fightin' amongst ourselves."

"Right enough," replied the sailor who had resented Snipes' autocratic tones; "but it ain't a-goin' to get nobody nothin' to put on airs in this bloomin' company neither."

"You fellows dig here," said Snipes, indicating a spot beneath the tree. "And while you're diggin', Peter kin be a-makin' of a map of the location so's we kin find it again. You, Tom, and Bill, take a couple more down and fetch up the chest."

"Wot are you a-goin' to do?" asked he of the previous altercation. "Just boss?"

"Git busy there," growled Snipes. "You didn't think your Cap'n was a-goin' to dig with a shovel, did you?"

The men all looked up angrily. None of them liked Snipes, and this disagreeable show of authority since he had murdered King, the real head and ringleader of the mutineers, had only added fuel to the flames of their hatred.

"Do you mean to say that you don't intend to take a shovel, and lend a hand with this work? Your shoulder's not hurt so all-fired bad as that," said Tarrant, the sailor who had before spoken.

"Not by a damned sight," replied Snipes, fingering the butt of his revolver nervously.

"Then, by God," replied Tarrant, "if you won't take a shovel you'll take a pickax."

With the words he raised his pick above his head, and, with a mighty blow, he buried the point in Snipes' brain.

For a moment the men stood silently looking at the result of their fellow's grim humor. Then one of them spoke.

"Served the skunk jolly well right," he said.

One of the others commenced to ply his pick to the ground. The soil was soft and he threw aside the pick and grasped a shovel; then the others joined him. There was no further comment on the killing, but the men worked in a better frame of mind than they had since Snipes had assumed command.

When they had a trench of ample size to bury the chest, Tarrant suggested that they enlarge it and inter Snipes' body on top of the chest.

"It might 'elp fool any as 'appened to be diggin' 'ereabouts," he explained.

The others saw the cunning of the suggestion, and so the trench was lengthened to accommodate the corpse, and in the center a deeper hole was excavated for the box, which was first wrapped in sailcloth and then lowered to its place, which brought its top about a foot below the bottom of the grave. Earth was shovelled in and tramped down about the chest until the bottom of the grave showed level and uniform.

Two of the men rolled the rat-faced corpse unceremoniously into the grave, after first stripping it of its weapons and various other articles which the several members of the party coveted for their own.

They then filled the grave with earth and tramped upon it until it would hold no more.

The balance of the loose earth was thrown far and wide, and a mass of dead undergrowth spread in as natural a manner as possible over the new-made grave to obliterate all signs of the ground having been disturbed.

Their work done the sailors returned to the small boat, and pulled off rapidly toward the *Arrow*.

The breeze had increased considerably, and as the smoke upon the horizon was now plainly discernible in considerable volume, the mutineers lost no time in getting under full sail and bearing away toward the southwest.

Tarzan, an interested spectator of all that had taken place, sat speculating on the strange actions of these peculiar creatures.

Men were indeed more foolish and more cruel than the beasts of the jungle! How fortunate was he who lived in the peace and security of the great forest!

Tarzan wondered what the chest they had buried contained. If they did not want it why did they not merely throw it into the water? That would have been much easier.

Ah, he thought, but they do want it. They have hidden it here because they intend returning for it later.

Tarzan dropped to the ground and commenced to examine the earth about the excavation. He was looking to see if these creatures had dropped anything which he might like to own. Soon he discovered a spade hidden by the underbrush which they had laid upon the grave.

He seized it and attempted to use it as he had seen the sailors do. It was awkward work and hurt his bare feet, but he persevered until he had partially uncovered the body. This he dragged from the grave and laid to one side.

Then he continued digging until he had unearthed the chest. This also he dragged to the side of the corpse. Then he filled in the smaller hole below the grave, replaced the body and the earth around and above it, covered it over with underbrush, and returned to the chest.

Four sailors had sweated beneath the burden of its weight— Tarzan of the Apes picked it up as though it had been an empty packing case, and with the spade slung to his back by a piece of rope, carried it off into the densest part of the jungle.

He could not well negotiate the trees with his awkward burden, but he kept to the trails, and so made fairly good time.

For several hours he traveled a little north of east until he came to an impenetrable wall of matted and tangled vegetation. Then he took to the lower branches, and in another fifteen minutes he emerged into the amphitheater of the apes, where they met in council, or to celebrate the rites of the Dum-Dum.

Near the center of the clearing, and not far from the drum, or altar, he commenced to dig. This was harder work than turning up the freshly excavated earth at the grave, but Tarzan of the Apes was persevering and so he kept at his labor until he was rewarded by seeing a hole sufficiently deep to receive the chest and effectually hide it from view.

Why had he gone to all this labor without knowing the value of the contents of the chest?

Tarzan of the Apes had a man's figure and a man's brain, but he was an ape by training and environment. His brain told him that the chest contained something valuable, or the men would not have hidden it. His training had taught him to imitate whatever was new and unusual, and now the natural curiosity, which is as common to men as to apes, prompted him to open the chest and examine its contents.

But the heavy lock and massive iron bands baffled both his cunning and his immense strength, so that he was compelled to bury the chest without having his curiosity satisfied.

By the time Tarzan had hunted his way back to the vicinity of the cabin, feeding as he went, it was quite dark.

Within the little building a light was burning, for Clayton had found an unopened tin of oil which had stood intact for twenty years, a part of the supplies left with the Claytons by Black Michael. The lamps also were still useable, and thus the interior of the cabin appeared as bright as day to the astonished Tarzan.

He had often wondered at the exact purpose of the lamps. His reading and the pictures had told him what they were, but he had no idea of how they could be made to produce the wondrous sunlight that some of his pictures had portrayed them as diffusing upon all surrounding objects.

As he approached the window nearest the door he saw that the cabin had been divided into two rooms by a rough partition of boughs and sailcloth.

In the front room were the three men; the two older deep in argument, while the younger, tilted back against the wall on an improvised stool, was deeply engrossed in reading one of Tarzan's books.

Tarzan was not particularly interested in the men, however, so he sought the other window. There was the girl. How beautiful her features! How delicate her snowy skin!

She was writing at Tarzan's own table beneath the window. Upon a pile of grasses at the far side of the room lay the Negress asleep.

For an hour Tarzan feasted his eyes upon her while she wrote. How he longed to speak to her, but he dared not attempt it, for he was convinced that, like the young man, she would not understand him, and he feared, too, that he might frighten her away.

At length she arose, leaving her manuscript upon the table. She went to the bed upon which had been spread several layers of soft grasses. These she rearranged.

Then she loosened the soft mass of golden hair which crowned her head. Like a shimmering waterfall turned to burnished metal by a dying sun it fell about her oval face; in waving lines, below her waist it tumbled.

Tarzan was spellbound. Then she extinguished the lamp and all within the cabin was wrapped in Cimmerian darkness.

Still Tarzan watched. Creeping close beneath the window he waited, listening, for half an hour. At last he was rewarded by the sounds of the regular breathing within which denotes sleep.

Cautiously he intruded his hand between the meshes of the lattice until his whole arm was within the cabin. Carefully he felt upon the desk. At last he grasped the manuscript upon which Jane Porter had been writing, and as cautiously withdrew his arm and hand, holding the precious treasure.

Tarzan folded the sheets into a small parcel which he tucked into the quiver with his arrows. Then he melted away into the jungle as softly and as noiselessly as a shadow.

XVIII

THE JUNGLE TOLL

arly the following morning Tarzan awoke, and his first thought of the new day, as the last of yesterday, was of the wonderful writing which lay hidden in his quiver.

Hurriedly he brought it forth, hoping against hope that he could read what the beautiful white girl had written there the preceding evening.

At the first glance he suffered a bitter disappointment; never before had he so yearned for anything as now he did for the ability to interpret a message from that golden-haired divinity who had come so suddenly and so unexpectedly into his life.

What did it matter if the message were not intended for him? It was an expression of her thoughts, and that was sufficient for Tarzan of the Apes.

And now to be baffled by strange, uncouth characters the like of which he had never seen before! Why, they even tipped in the opposite direction from all that he had ever examined either in printed books or the difficult script of the few letters he had found.

Even the little bugs of the black book were familiar friends, though their arrangement meant nothing to him; but these bugs were new and unheard of.

For twenty minutes he pored over them, when suddenly they commenced to take familiar though distorted shapes. Ah, they were his old friends, but badly crippled.

Then he began to make out a word here and a word there. His heart leaped for joy. He could read it, and he would.

In another half hour he was progressing rapidly, and, but for an exceptional word now and again, he found it very plain sailing.

Here is what he read:

West Coast of Africa, About 10° Degrees South Latitude.
(So Mr. Clayton says.)

February 3 (?), 1909.

Dearest Hazel:

It seems foolish to write you a letter that you may never see, but I simply must tell somebody of our awful experiences since we sailed from Europe on the ill-fated Arrow.

If we never return to civilization, as now seems only too likely, this will at least prove a brief record of the events which led up to our final fate, whatever it may be.

As you know, we were supposed to have set out upon a scientific expedition to the Congo. Papa was presumed to entertain some wondrous theory of an unthinkably ancient civilization, the remains of which lay buried somewhere in the Congo valley. But after we were well under sail the truth came out.

It seems that an old bookworm who has a book and curio shop in Baltimore discovered between the leaves of a very old Spanish manuscript a letter written in 1550 detailing the adventures of a crew of mutineers of a Spanish galleon bound from Spain to South America with a vast treasure of "doubloons" and "pieces of eight," I suppose, for they certainly sound weird and piraty.

The writer had been one of the crew, and the letter was to his son, who was, at the very time the letter was written, master of a Spanish merchantman.

Many years had elapsed since the events the letter narrated had transpired, and the old man had become a respected citizen of an obscure

Spanish town, but the love of gold was still so strong upon him that he risked all to acquaint his son with the means of attaining fabulous wealth for them both.

The writer told how when but a week out from Spain the crew had mutinied and murdered every officer and man who opposed them; but they defeated their own ends by this very act, for there was none left competent to navigate a ship at sea.

They were blown hither and thither for two months, until sick and dying of scurvy, starvation, and thirst, they had been wrecked on a small islet.

The galleon was washed high upon the beach where she went to pieces; but not before the survivors, who numbered but ten souls, had rescued one of the great chests of treasure.

This they buried well up on the island, and for three years they lived there in constant hope of being rescued.

One by one they sickened and died, until only one man was left, the writer of the letter.

The men had built a boat from the wreckage of the galleon, but having no idea where the island was located they had not dared to put to sea.

When all were dead except himself, however, the awful loneliness so weighed upon the mind of the sole survivor that he could endure it no longer, and choosing to risk death upon the open sea rather than madness on the lonely isle, he set sail in his little boat after nearly a year of solitude.

Fortunately he sailed due north, and within a week was in the track of the Spanish merchantmen plying between the West Indies and Spain, and was picked up by one of these vessels homeward bound.

The story he told was merely one of shipwreck in which all but a few had perished, the balance, except himself, dying after they reached the island. He did not mention the mutiny or the chest of buried treasure.

The master of the merchantman assured him that from the position at which they had picked him up, and the prevailing winds for the past week he could have been on no other island than one of the Cape Verde group, which lie off the West Coast of Africa in about 16° or 17° north latitude.

His letter described the island minutely, as well as the location of the treasure, and was accompanied by the crudest, funniest little old map you ever saw; with trees and rocks all marked by scrawly X's to show the exact spot where the treasure had been buried.

When papa explained the real nature of the expedition, my heart sank, for I know so well how visionary and impractical the poor dear has always been that I feared that he had again been duped; especially when he told me he had paid a thousand dollars for the letter and map.

To add to my distress, I learned that he had borrowed ten thousand dollars more from Robert Canler, and had given his notes for the amount.

Mr. Canler had asked for no security, and you know, dearie, what that will mean for me if papa cannot meet them. Oh, how I detest that man!

We all tried to look on the bright side of things, but Mr. Philander, and Mr. Clayton—he joined us in London just for the adventure—both felt as skeptical as I.

Well, to make a long story short, we found the island and the treasure—a great iron-bound oak chest, wrapped in many layers of oiled sail-cloth, and as strong and firm as when it had been buried nearly two hundred years ago.

It was simply filled with gold coin, and was so heavy that four men bent underneath its weight.

The horrid thing seems to bring nothing but murder and misfortune to those who have anything to do with it, for three days after we sailed from the Cape Verde Islands our own crew mutinied and killed every one of their officers.

Oh, it was the most terrifying experience one could imagine—I cannot even write of it.

They were going to kill us too, but one of them, the leader, named King, would not let them, and so they sailed south along the coast to a lonely spot where they found a good harbor, and here they landed and have left us.

They sailed away with the treasure to-day, but Mr. Clayton says they will meet with a fate similar to the mutineers of the ancient galleon, because

King, the only man aboard who knew aught of navigation, was murdered on the beach by one of the men the day we landed.

I wish you could know Mr. Clayton; he is the dearest fellow imaginable, and unless I am mistaken he has fallen very much in love with me.

He is the only son of Lord Greystoke, and some day will inherit the title and estates. In addition, he is wealthy in his own right, but the fact that he is going to be an English Lord makes me very sad—you know what my sentiments have always been relative to American girls who married titled foreigners. Oh, if he were only a plain American gentleman!

But it isn't his fault, poor fellow, and in everything except birth he would do credit to my country, and that is the greatest compliment I know how to pay any man.

We have had the most weird experiences since we were landed here. Papa and Mr. Philander lost in the jungle, and chased by a real lion.

Mr. Clayton lost, and attacked twice by wild beasts. Esmeralda and I cornered in an old cabin by a perfectly awful man-eating lioness. Oh, it was simply "terrifical," as Esmeralda would say.

But the strangest part of it all is the wonderful creature who rescued us. I have not seen him, but Mr. Clayton and papa and Mr. Philander have, and they say that he is a perfectly god-like white man tanned to a dusky brown, with the strength of a wild elephant, the agility of a monkey, and the bravery of a lion.

He speaks no English and vanishes as quickly and as mysteriously after he has performed some valorous deed, as though he were a disembodied spirit.

Then we have another weird neighbor, who printed a beautiful sign in English and tacked it on the door of his cabin, which we have preempted, warning us to destroy none of his belongings, and signing himself "Tarzan of the Apes."

We have never seen him, though we think he is about, for one of the sailors, who was going to shoot Mr. Clayton in the back, received a spear in his shoulder from some unseen hand in the jungle.

The sailors left us but a meager supply of food, so, as we have only a single revolver with but three cartridges left in it, we do not know how we can procure meat, though Mr. Philander says that we can exist indefinitely on the wild fruit and nuts which abound in the jungle.

I am very tired now, so I shall go to my funny bed of grasses which Mr. Clayton gathered for me, but will add to this from day to day as things happen.

Lovingly,
JANE PORTER.

To Hazel Strong, Baltimore, MD

Tarzan sat in a brown study for a long time after he finished reading the letter. It was filled with so many new and wonderful things that his brain was in a whirl as he attempted to digest them all.

So they did not know that he was Tarzan of the Apes. He would tell them.

In his tree he had constructed a rude shelter of leaves and boughs, beneath which, protected from the rain, he had placed the few treasures brought from the cabin. Among these were some pencils.

He took one, and beneath Jane Porter's signature he wrote:

I am Tarzan of the Apes

He thought that would be sufficient. Later he would return the letter to the cabin.

In the matter of food, thought Tarzan, they had no need to worry—he would provide, and he did.

The next morning Jane found her missing letter in the exact spot from which it had disappeared two nights before. She was mystified; but when she saw the printed words beneath her signature, she felt a cold, clammy chill run up her spine. She showed the letter, or rather the last sheet with the signature, to Clayton.

"And to think," she said, "that uncanny thing was probably watching me all the time that I was writing—oo! It makes me shudder just to think of it."

"But he must be friendly," reassured Clayton, "for he has returned your letter, nor did he offer to harm you, and unless I am mistaken he left a very substantial memento of his friendship outside the cabin door last night, for I just found the carcass of a wild boar there as I came out."

From then on scarcely a day passed that did not bring its offering of game or other food. Sometimes it was a young deer, again a quantity of strange, cooked food—cassava cakes pilfered from the village of Mbonga—or a boar, or leopard, and once a lion.

Tarzan derived the greatest pleasure of his life in hunting meat for these strangers. It seemed to him that no pleasure on earth could compare with laboring for the welfare and protection of the beautiful white girl.

Some day he would venture into the camp in daylight and talk with these people through the medium of the little bugs which were familiar to them and to Tarzan.

But he found it difficult to overcome the timidity of the wild thing of the forest, and so day followed day without seeing a fulfillment of his good intentions.

The party in the camp, emboldened by familiarity, wandered farther and yet farther into the jungle in search of nuts and fruit.

Scarcely a day passed that did not find Professor Porter straying in his preoccupied indifference toward the jaws of death. Mr. Samuel T. Philander, never what one might call robust, was worn to the shadow of a shadow through the ceaseless worry and mental distraction resultant from his Herculean efforts to safeguard the professor.

A month passed. Tarzan had finally determined to visit the camp by daylight.

It was early afternoon. Clayton had wandered to the point at the harbor's mouth to look for passing vessels. Here he kept a great mass of wood, high piled, ready to be ignited as a signal should a steamer or a sail top the far horizon.

Professor Porter was wandering along the beach south of the camp with Mr. Philander at his elbow, urging him to turn his steps back before the two became again the sport of some savage beast.

The others gone, Jane and Esmeralda had wandered into the jungle to gather fruit, and in their search were led farther and farther from the cabin.

Tarzan waited in silence before the door of the little house until they should return. His thoughts were of the beautiful white girl. They were always of her now. He wondered if she would fear him, and the thought all but caused him to relinquish his plan.

He was rapidly becoming impatient for her return, that he might feast his eyes upon her and be near her, perhaps touch her. The ape-man knew no god, but he was as near to worshipping his divinity as mortal man ever comes to worship. While he waited he passed the time printing a message to her; whether he intended giving it to her he himself could not have told, but he took infinite pleasure in seeing his thoughts expressed in print—in which he was not so uncivilized after all. He wrote:

I am Tarzan of the Apes. I want you. I am yours. You are mine. We live here together always in my house. I will bring you the best of fruits, the tenderest deer, the finest meats that roam the jungle. I will hunt for you. I am the greatest of the jungle fighters. I will fight for you. I am the mightiest of the jungle fighters. You are Jane Porter, I saw it in your letter. When you see this you will know that it is for you and that Tarzan of the Apes loves you.

As he stood, straight as a young Indian, by the door, waiting after he had finished the message, there came to his keen ears a familiar sound. It was the passing of a great ape through the lower branches of the forest.

For an instant he listened intently, and then from the jungle came the agonized scream of a woman, and Tarzan of the Apes, dropping his first love letter upon the ground, shot like a panther into the forest.

Clayton, also, heard the scream, and Professor Porter and Mr. Philander, and in a few minutes they came panting to the cabin, calling out to each other a volley of excited questions as they approached. A glance within confirmed their worst fears.

Jane and Esmeralda were not there.

Instantly, Clayton, followed by the two old men, plunged into the jungle, calling the girl's name aloud. For half an hour they stumbled on, until Clayton, by merest chance, came upon the prostrate form of Esmeralda.

He stopped beside her, feeling for her pulse and then listening for her heartbeats. She lived. He shook her.

"Esmeralda!" he shrieked in her ear. "Esmeralda! For God's sake, where is Miss Porter? What has happened? Esmeralda!"

Slowly Esmeralda opened her eyes. She saw Clayton. She saw the jungle about her.

"Oh, Gaberelle!" she screamed, and fainted again.

By this time Professor Porter and Mr. Philander had come up.

"What shall we do, Mr. Clayton?" asked the old professor. "Where shall we look? God could not have been so cruel as to take my little girl away from me now."

"We must arouse Esmeralda first," replied Clayton. "She can tell us what has happened. Esmeralda!" he cried again, shaking the black woman roughly by the shoulder.

"O Gaberelle, I want to die!" cried the poor woman, but with eyes fast closed. "Let me die, dear Lord, don't let me see that awful face again."

"Come, come, Esmeralda," cried Clayton.

"The Lord isn't here; it's Mr. Clayton. Open your eyes."

Esmeralda did as she was bade.

"O Gaberelle! Thank the Lord," she said.

"Where's Miss Porter? What happened?" questioned Clayton.

"Ain't Miss Jane here?" cried Esmeralda, sitting up with wonderful celerity for one of her bulk. "Oh, Lord, now I remember! It must have took her away," and the Negress commenced to sob, and wail her lamentations.

"What took her away?" cried Professor Porter.

"A great big giant all covered with hair."

"A gorilla, Esmeralda?" questioned Mr. Philander, and the three men scarcely breathed as he voiced the horrible thought.

"I thought it was the devil; but I guess it must have been one of them gorilephants. Oh, my poor baby, my poor little honey," and again Esmeralda broke into uncontrollable sobbing.

Clayton immediately began to look about for tracks, but he could find nothing save a confusion of trampled grasses in the close vicinity, and his woodcraft was too meager for the translation of what he did see.

All the balance of the day they sought through the jungle; but as night drew on they were forced to give up in despair and hopelessness, for they did not even know in what direction the thing had borne Jane.

It was long after dark ere they reached the cabin, and a sad and grief-stricken party it was that sat silently within the little structure.

Professor Porter finally broke the silence. His tones were no longer those of the erudite pedant theorizing upon the abstract and the unknowable; but those of the man of action—determined, but

175

tinged also by a note of indescribable hopelessness and grief which wrung an answering pang from Clayton's heart.

"I shall lie down now," said the old man, "and try to sleep. Early tomorrow, as soon as it is light, I shall take what food I can carry and continue the search until I have found Jane. I will not return without her."

His companions did not reply at once. Each was immersed in his own sorrowful thoughts, and each knew, as did the old professor, what the last words meant—Professor Porter would never return from the jungle.

At length Clayton arose and laid his hand gently upon Professor Porter's bent old shoulder.

"I shall go with you, of course," he said.

"I knew that you would offer—that you would wish to go, Mr. Clayton; but you must not. Jane is beyond human assistance now. What was once my dear little girl shall not lie alone and friendless in the awful jungle.

"The same vines and leaves will cover us, the same rains beat upon us; and when the spirit of her mother is abroad, it will find us together in death, as it has always found us in life.

"No; it is I alone who may go, for she was my daughter—all that was left on earth for me to love."

"I shall go with you," said Clayton simply.

The old man looked up, regarding the strong, handsome face of William Cecil Clayton intently. Perhaps he read there the love that lay in the heart beneath—the love for his daughter.

He had been too preoccupied with his own scholarly thoughts in the past to consider the little occurrences, the chance words, which would have indicated to a more practical man that these young people were being drawn more and more closely to one another. Now they came back to him, one by one.

"As you wish," he said.

"You may count on me, also," said Mr. Philander.

"No, my dear old friend," said Professor Porter. "We may not all go. It would be cruelly wicked to leave poor Esmeralda here alone, and three of us would be no more successful than one.

"There be enough dead things in the cruel forest as it is. Come— let us try to sleep a little."

XIX

THE CALL
OF THE PRIMITIVE

rom the time Tarzan left the tribe of great anthro-
poids in which he had been raised, it was torn by
continual strife and discord. Terkoz proved a cruel
and capricious king, so that, one by one, many of
the older and weaker apes, upon whom he was
particularly prone to vent his brutish nature, took their families and
sought the quiet and safety of the far interior.

But at last those who remained were driven to desperation by the
continued truculence of Terkoz, and it so happened that one of them
recalled the parting admonition of Tarzan:

"If you have a chief who is cruel, do not do as the other apes do,
and attempt, any one of you, to pit yourself against him alone. But,
instead, let two or three or four of you attack him together. Then, if
you will do this, no chief will dare to be other than he should be, for
four of you can kill any chief who may ever be over you."

And the ape who recalled this wise counsel repeated it to several
of his fellows, so that when Terkoz returned to the tribe that day he
found a warm reception awaiting him.

There were no formalities. As Terkoz reached the group, five
huge, hairy beasts sprang upon him.

At heart he was an arrant coward, which is the way with bullies
among apes as well as among men; so he did not remain to fight and

die, but tore himself away from them as quickly as he could and fled into the sheltering boughs of the forest.

Two more attempts he made to rejoin the tribe, but on each occasion he was set upon and driven away. At last he gave it up, and turned, foaming with rage and hatred, into the jungle.

For several days he wandered aimlessly, nursing his spite and looking for some weak thing on which to vent his pent anger.

It was in this state of mind that the horrible, man-like beast, swinging from tree to tree, came suddenly upon two women in the jungle.

He was right above them when he discovered them. The first intimation Jane Porter had of his presence was when the great hairy body dropped to the earth beside her, and she saw the awful face and the snarling, hideous mouth thrust within a foot of her.

One piercing scream escaped her lips as the brute hand clutched her arm. Then she was dragged toward those awful fangs which yawned at her throat. But ere they touched that fair skin another mood claimed the anthropoid.

The tribe had kept his women. He must find others to replace them. This hairless white ape would be the first of his new household, and so he threw her roughly across his broad, hairy shoulders and leaped back into the trees, bearing Jane away.

Esmeralda's scream of terror had mingled once with that of Jane, and then, as was Esmeralda's manner under stress of emergency which required presence of mind, she swooned.

But Jane did not once lose consciousness. It is true that that awful face, pressing close to hers, and the stench of the foul breath beating upon her nostrils, paralyzed her with terror; but her brain was clear, and she comprehended all that transpired.

With what seemed to her marvelous rapidity the brute bore her through the forest, but still she did not cry out or struggle. The sudden advent of the ape had confused her to such an extent that she thought now that he was bearing her toward the beach.

For this reason she conserved her energies and her voice until she could see that they had approached near enough to the camp to attract the succor she craved.

She could not have known it, but she was being borne farther and farther into the impenetrable jungle.

The scream that had brought Clayton and the two older men stumbling through the undergrowth had led Tarzan of the Apes straight to where Esmeralda lay, but it was not Esmeralda in whom his interest centered, though pausing over her he saw that she was unhurt.

For a moment he scrutinized the ground below and the trees above, until the ape that was in him by virtue of training and environment, combined with the intelligence that was his by right of birth, told his wondrous woodcraft the whole story as plainly as though he had seen the thing happen with his own eyes.

And then he was gone again into the swaying trees, following the high-flung spoor which no other human eye could have detected, much less translated.

At boughs' ends, where the anthropoid swings from one tree to another, there is most to mark the trail, but least to point the direction of the quarry; for there the pressure is downward always, toward the small end of the branch, whether the ape be leaving or entering a tree. Nearer the center of the tree, where the signs of passage are fainter, the direction is plainly marked.

Here, on this branch, a caterpillar has been crushed by the fugitive's great foot, and Tarzan knows instinctively where that same foot would touch in the next stride. Here he looks to find a tiny particle of the demolished larva, ofttimes not more than a speck of moisture.

Again, a minute bit of bark has been upturned by the scraping hand, and the direction of the break indicates the direction of the passage. Or some great limb, or the stem of the tree itself has been brushed by the hairy body, and a tiny shred of hair tells him by the direction from which it is wedged beneath the bark that he is on the right trail.

Nor does he need to check his speed to catch these seemingly faint records of the fleeing beast.

To Tarzan they stand out boldly against all the myriad other scars and bruises and signs upon the leafy way. But strongest of all is the scent, for Tarzan is pursuing up the wind, and his trained nostrils are as sensitive as a hound's.

There are those who believe that the lower orders are specially endowed by nature with better olfactory nerves than man, but it is merely a matter of development.

Man's survival does not hinge so greatly upon the perfection of his senses. His power to reason has relieved them of many of their duties, and so they have, to some extent, atrophied, as have the muscles which move the ears and scalp, merely from disuse.

The muscles are there, about the ears and beneath the scalp, and so are the nerves which transmit sensations to the brain, but they are under-developed because they are not needed.

Not so with Tarzan of the Apes. From early infancy his survival had depended upon acuteness of eyesight, hearing, smell, touch, and taste far more than upon the more slowly developed organ of reason.

The least developed of all in Tarzan was the sense of taste, for he could eat luscious fruits, or raw flesh, long buried with almost equal appreciation; but in that he differed but slightly from more civilized epicures.

Almost silently the ape-man sped on in the track of Terkoz and his prey, but the sound of his approach reached the ears of the fleeing beast and spurred it on to greater speed.

Three miles were covered before Tarzan overtook them, and then Terkoz, seeing that further flight was futile, dropped to the ground in a small open glade, that he might turn and fight for his prize or be free to escape unhampered if he saw that the pursuer was more than a match for him.

He still grasped Jane in one great arm as Tarzan bounded like a leopard into the arena which nature had provided for this primeval-like battle.

When Terkoz saw that it was Tarzan who pursued him, he jumped to the conclusion that this was Tarzan's woman, since they were of the same kind—white and hairless—and so he rejoiced at this opportunity for double revenge upon his hated enemy.

To Jane the strange apparition of this god-like man was as wine to sick nerves.

From the description which Clayton and her father and Mr. Philander had given her, she knew that it must be the same wonderful creature who had saved them, and she saw in him only a protector and a friend.

But as Terkoz pushed her roughly aside to meet Tarzan's charge, and she saw the great proportions of the ape and the mighty muscles and the fierce fangs, her heart quailed. How could any vanquish such a mighty antagonist?

Like two charging bulls they came together, and like two wolves sought each other's throat. Against the long canines of the ape was pitted the thin blade of the man's knife.

Jane—her lithe, young form flattened against the trunk of a great tree, her hands tight pressed against her rising and falling bosom, and her eyes wide with mingled horror, fascination, fear, and admiration—watched the primordial ape battle with the primeval man for possession of a woman—for her.

As the great muscles of the man's back and shoulders knotted beneath the tension of his efforts, and the huge biceps and forearm held at bay those mighty tusks, the veil of centuries of civilization and culture was swept from the blurred vision of the Baltimore girl.

When the long knife drank deep a dozen times of Terkoz' heart's blood, and the great carcass rolled lifeless upon the ground, it was a primeval woman who sprang forward with outstretched arms toward the primeval man who had fought for her and won her.

And Tarzan?

He did what no red-blooded man needs lessons in doing. He took his woman in his arms and smothered her upturned, panting lips with kisses.

For a moment Jane lay there with half-closed eyes. For a moment—the first in her young life—she knew the meaning of love.

But as suddenly as the veil had been withdrawn it dropped again, and an outraged conscience suffused her face with its scarlet mantle, and a mortified woman thrust Tarzan of the Apes from her and buried her face in her hands.

Tarzan had been surprised when he had found the girl he had learned to love after a vague and abstract manner a willing prisoner in his arms. Now he was surprised that she repulsed him.

He came close to her once more and took hold of her arm. She turned upon him like a tigress, striking his great breast with her tiny hands.

Tarzan could not understand it.

A moment ago and it had been his intention to hasten Jane back to her people, but that little moment was lost now in the dim and distant past of things which were but can never be again, and with it the good intentions had gone to join the impossible.

Since then Tarzan of the Apes had felt a warm, lithe form close pressed to his. Hot, sweet breath against his cheek and mouth had fanned a new flame to life within his breast, and perfect lips had clung to his in burning kisses that had seared a deep brand into his soul—a brand which marked a new Tarzan.

Again he laid his hand upon her arm. Again she repulsed him. And then Tarzan of the Apes did just what his first ancestor would have done.

He took his woman in his arms and carried her into the jungle.

• • •

Early the following morning the four within the little cabin by the beach were awakened by the booming of a cannon. Clayton was the first to rush out, and there, beyond the harbor's mouth, he saw two vessels lying at anchor.

One was the *Arrow* and the other a small French cruiser. The sides of the latter were crowded with men gazing shoreward, and it was evident to Clayton, as to the others who had now joined him, that the gun which they had heard had been fired to attract their attention if they still remained at the cabin.

Both vessels lay at a considerable distance from shore, and it was doubtful if their glasses would locate the waving hats of the little party far in between the harbor's points.

Esmeralda had removed her red apron and was waving it frantically above her head; but Clayton, still fearing that even this might not be seen, hurried off toward the northern point where lay his signal pyre ready for the match.

It seemed an age to him, as to those who waited breathlessly behind, ere he reached the great pile of dry branches and underbrush.

As he broke from the dense wood and came in sight of the vessels again, he was filled with consternation to see that the *Arrow* was making sail and that the cruiser was already under way.

Quickly lighting the pyre in a dozen places, he hurried to the extreme point of the promontory, where he stripped off his shirt, and, tying it to a fallen branch, stood waving it back and forth above him.

But still the vessels continued to stand out; and he had given up all hope, when the great column of smoke, rising above the forest in one dense vertical shaft, attracted the attention of a lookout aboard the cruiser, and instantly a dozen glasses were leveled on the beach.

Presently Clayton saw the two ships come about again; and while

184

the *Arrow* lay drifting quietly on the ocean, the cruiser steamed slowly back toward shore.

At some distance away she stopped, and a boat was lowered and dispatched toward the beach.

As it was drawn up a young officer stepped out.

"Monsieur Clayton, I presume?" he asked.

"Thank God, you have come!" was Clayton's reply. "And it may be that it is not too late even now."

"What do you mean, Monsieur?" asked the officer.

Clayton told of the abduction of Jane Porter and the need of armed men to aid in the search for her.

"*Mon Dieu!*" exclaimed the officer, sadly. "Yesterday and it would not have been too late. Today and it may be better that the poor lady were never found. It is horrible, Monsieur. It is too horrible."

Other boats had now put off from the cruiser, and Clayton, having pointed out the harbor's entrance to the officer, entered the boat with him and its nose was turned toward the little landlocked bay, into which the other craft followed.

Soon the entire party had landed where stood Professor Porter, Mr. Philander and the weeping Esmeralda.

Among the officers in the last boats to put off from the cruiser was the commander of the vessel; and when he had heard the story of Jane's abduction, he generously called for volunteers to accompany Professor Porter and Clayton in their search.

Not an officer or a man was there of those brave and sympathetic Frenchmen who did not quickly beg leave to be one of the expedition.

The commander selected twenty men and two officers, Lieutenant D'Arnot and Lieutenant Charpentier. A boat was dispatched to the cruiser for provisions, ammunition, and carbines; the men were already armed with revolvers.

Then, to Clayton's inquiries as to how they had happened to anchor off shore and fire a signal gun, the commander, Captain

Dufranne, explained that a month before they had sighted the *Arrow* bearing south-west under considerable canvas, and that when they had signaled her to come about she had but crowded on more sail.

They had kept her hull-up until sunset, firing several shots after her, but the next morning she was nowhere to be seen. They had then continued to cruise up and down the coast for several weeks, and had about forgotten the incident of the recent chase, when, early one morning a few days before the lookout had described a vessel laboring in the trough of a heavy sea and evidently entirely out of control.

As they steamed nearer to the derelict they were surprised to note that it was the same vessel that had run from them a few weeks earlier. Her forestaysail and mizzen spanker were set as though an effort had been made to hold her head up into the wind, but the sheets had parted, and the sails were tearing to ribbons in the half gale of wind.

In the high sea that was running it was a difficult and dangerous task to attempt to put a prize crew aboard her; and as no signs of life had been seen above deck, it was decided to stand by until the wind and sea abated; but just then a figure was seen clinging to the rail and feebly waving a mute signal of despair toward them.

Immediately a boat's crew was ordered out and an attempt was successfully made to board the *Arrow*.

The sight that met the Frenchmen's eyes as they clambered over the ship's side was appalling.

A dozen dead and dying men rolled hither and thither upon the pitching deck, the living intermingled with the dead. Two of the corpses appeared to have been partially devoured as though by wolves.

The prize crew soon had the vessel under proper sail once more and the living members of the ill-starred company carried below to their hammocks.

The dead were wrapped in tarpaulins and lashed on deck to be identified by their comrades before being consigned to the deep.

None of the living was conscious when the Frenchmen reached the *Arrow*'s deck. Even the poor devil who had waved the single despairing signal of distress had lapsed into unconsciousness before he had learned whether it had availed or not.

It did not take the French officer long to learn what had caused the terrible condition aboard; for when water and brandy were sought to restore the men, it was found that there was none, nor even food of any description.

He immediately signalled to the cruiser to send water, medicine, and provisions, and another boat made the perilous trip to the *Arrow*.

When restoratives had been applied several of the men regained consciousness, and then the whole story was told. That part of it we know up to the sailing of the *Arrow* after the murder of Snipes, and the burial of his body above the treasure chest.

It seems that the pursuit by the cruiser had so terrorized the mutineers that they had continued out across the Atlantic for several days after losing her; but on discovering the meager supply of water and provisions aboard, they had turned back toward the east.

With no one on board who understood navigation, discussions soon arose as to their whereabouts; and as three days' sailing to the east did not raise land, they bore off to the north, fearing that the high north winds that had prevailed had driven them south of the southern extremity of Africa.

They kept on a north-northeasterly course for two days, when they were overtaken by a calm which lasted for nearly a week. Their water was gone, and in another day they would be without food.

Conditions changed rapidly from bad to worse. One man went mad and leaped overboard. Soon another opened his veins and drank his own blood.

When he died they threw him overboard also, though there were those among them who wanted to keep the corpse on board. Hunger was changing them from human beasts to wild beasts.

187

Two days before they had been picked up by the cruiser they had become too weak to handle the vessel, and that same day three men died. On the following morning it was seen that one of the corpses had been partially devoured.

All that day the men lay glaring at each other like beasts of prey, and the following morning two of the corpses lay almost entirely stripped of flesh.

The men were but little stronger for their ghoulish repast, for the want of water was by far the greatest agony with which they had to contend. And then the cruiser had come.

When those who could had recovered, the entire story had been told to the French commander; but the men were too ignorant to be able to tell him at just what point on the coast the professor and his party had been marooned, so the cruiser had steamed slowly along within sight of land, firing occasional signal guns and scanning every inch of the beach with glasses.

They had anchored by night so as not to neglect a particle of the shore line, and it had happened that the preceding night had brought them off the very beach where lay the little camp they sought.

The signal guns of the afternoon before had not been heard by those on shore, it was presumed, because they had doubtless been in the thick of the jungle searching for Jane Porter, where the noise of their own crashing through the underbrush would have drowned the report of a far distant gun.

By the time the two parties had narrated their several adventures, the cruiser's boat had returned with supplies and arms for the expedition.

Within a few minutes the little body of sailors and the two French officers, together with Professor Porter and Clayton, set off upon their hopeless and ill-fated quest into the untracked jungle.

XX

HEREDITY

hen Jane realized that she was being borne away a captive by the strange forest creature who had rescued her from the clutches of the ape she struggled desperately to escape, but the strong arms that held her as easily as though she had been but a dayold babe only pressed a little more tightly.

So presently she gave up the futile effort and lay quietly, looking through half-closed lids at the faces of the man who strode easily through the tangled undergrowth with her.

The face above her was one of extraordinary beauty.

A perfect type of the strongly masculine, unmarred by dissipation, or brutal or degrading passions. For, though Tarzan of the Apes was a killer of men and of beasts, he killed as the hunter kills, dispassionately, except on those rare occasions when he had killed for hate—though not the brooding, malevolent hate which marks the features of its own with hideous lines.

When Tarzan killed he more often smiled than scowled, and smiles are the foundation of beauty.

One thing the girl had noticed particularly when she had seen Tarzan rushing upon Terkoz—the vivid scarlet band upon his forehead, from above the left eye to the scalp; but now as she scanned his features she noticed that it was gone, and only a thin white line marked the spot where it had been.

As she lay more quietly in his arms Tarzan slightly relaxed his grip upon her.

Once he looked down into her eyes and smiled, and the girl had to close her own to shut out the vision of that handsome, winning face.

Presently Tarzan took to the trees, and Jane, wondering that she felt no fear, began to realize that in many respects she had never felt more secure in her whole life than now as she lay in the arms of this strong, wild creature, being borne, God alone knew where or to what fate, deeper and deeper into the savage fastness of the untamed forest.

When, with closed eyes, she commenced to speculate upon the future, and terrifying fears were conjured by a vivid imagination, she had but to raise her lids and look upon that noble face so close to hers to dissipate the last remnant of apprehension.

No, he could never harm her; of that she was convinced when she translated the fine features and the frank, brave eyes above her into the chivalry which they proclaimed.

On and on they went through what seemed to Jane a solid mass of verdure, yet ever there appeared to open before this forest god a passage, as by magic, which closed behind them as they passed.

Scarce a branch scraped against her, yet above and below, before and behind, the view presented naught but a solid mass of inextricably interwoven branches and creepers.

As Tarzan moved steadily onward his mind was occupied with many strange and new thoughts. Here was a problem the like of which he had never encountered, and he felt rather than reasoned that he must meet it as a man and not as an ape.

The free movement through the middle terrace, which was the route he had followed for the most part, had helped to cool the ardor of the first fierce passion of his new found love.

Now he discovered himself speculating upon the fate which

would have fallen to the girl had he not rescued her from Terkoz.

He knew why the ape had not killed her, and he commenced to compare his intentions with those of Terkoz.

True, it was the order of the jungle for the male to take his mate by force; but could Tarzan be guided by the laws of the beasts? Was not Tarzan a Man? But what did men do? He was puzzled; for he did not know.

He wished that he might ask the girl, and then it came to him that she had already answered him in the futile struggle she had made to escape and to repulse him.

But now they had come to their destination, and Tarzan of the Apes with Jane in his strong arms, swung lightly to the turf of the arena where the great apes held their councils and danced the wild orgy of the Dum-Dum.

Though they had come many miles, it was still but midafternoon, and the amphitheater was bathed in the half light which filtered through the maze of encircling foliage.

The green turf looked soft and cool and inviting. The myriad noises of the jungle seemed far distant and hushed to a mere echo of blurred sounds, rising and falling like the surf upon a remote shore.

A feeling of dreamy peacefulness stole over Jane as she sank down upon the grass where Tarzan had placed her, and as she looked up at his great figure towering above her, there was added a strange sense of perfect security.

As she watched him from beneath half-closed lids, Tarzan crossed the little circular clearing toward the trees upon the further side. She noted the graceful majesty of his carriage, the perfect symmetry of his magnificent figure and the poise of his well-shaped head upon his broad shoulders.

What a perfect creature! There could be naught of cruelty or baseness beneath that godlike exterior. Never, she thought had such a man strode the earth since God created the first in his own image.

With a bound Tarzan sprang into the trees and disappeared. Jane wondered where he had gone. Had he left her there to her fate in the lonely jungle?

She glanced nervously about. Every vine and bush seemed but the lurking-place of some huge and horrible beast waiting to bury gleaming fangs into her soft flesh. Every sound she magnified into the stealthy creeping of a sinuous and malignant body.

How different now that he had left her!

For a few minutes that seemed hours to the frightened girl, she sat with tense nerves waiting for the spring of the crouching thing that was to end her misery of apprehension.

She almost prayed for the cruel teeth that would give her unconsciousness and surcease from the agony of fear.

She heard a sudden, slight sound behind her. With a cry she sprang to her feet and turned to face her end.

There stood Tarzan, his arms filled with ripe and luscious fruit.

Jane reeled and would have fallen, had not Tarzan, dropping his burden, caught her in his arms. She did not lose consciousness, but she clung tightly to him, shuddering and trembling like a frightened deer.

Tarzan of the Apes stroked her soft hair and tried to comfort and quiet her as Kala had him, when, as a little ape, he had been frightened by Sabor, the lioness, or Histah, the snake.

Once he pressed his lips lightly upon her forehead, and she did not move, but closed her eyes and sighed.

She could not analyze her feelings, nor did she wish to attempt it. She was satisfied to feel the safety of those strong arms, and to leave her future to fate; for the last few hours had taught her to trust this strange wild creature of the forest as she would have trusted but few of the men of her acquaintance.

As she thought of the strangeness of it, there commenced to dawn upon her the realization that she had, possibly, learned something else which she had never really known before—love. She wondered and then she smiled.

And still smiling, she pushed Tarzan gently away; and looking at him with a half-smiling, half-quizzical expression that made her face wholly entrancing, she pointed to the fruit upon the ground, and seated herself upon the edge of the earthen drum of the anthropoids, for hunger was asserting itself.

Tarzan quickly gathered up the fruit, and, bringing it, laid it at her feet; and then he, too, sat upon the drum beside her, and with his knife opened and prepared the various fruits for her meal.

Together and in silence they ate, occasionally stealing sly glances at one another, until finally Jane broke into a merry laugh in which Tarzan joined.

"I wish you spoke English," said the girl.

Tarzan shook his head, and an expression of wistful and pathetic longing sobered his laughing eyes.

Then Jane tried speaking to him in French, and then in German; but she had to laugh at her own blundering attempt at the latter tongue.

"Anyway," she said to him in English, "you understand my German as well as they did in Berlin."

Tarzan had long since reached a decision as to what his future procedure should be. He had had time to recollect all that he had read of the ways of men and women in the books at the cabin. He would act as he imagined the men in the books would have acted were they in his place.

Again he rose and went into the trees, but first he tried to explain by means of signs that he would return shortly, and he did so well that Jane understood and was not afraid when he had gone.

Only a feeling of loneliness came over her and she watched the point where he had disappeared, with longing eyes, awaiting his return. As before, she was appraised of his presence by a soft sound behind her, and turned to see him coming across the turf with a great armful of branches.

Then he went back again into the jungle and in a few minutes reappeared with a quantity of soft grasses and ferns.

Two more trips he made until he had quite a pile of material at hand.

Then he spread the ferns and grasses upon the ground in a soft flat bed, and above it leaned many branches together so that they met a few feet over its center. Upon these he spread layers of huge leaves of the great elephant's ear, and with more branches and more leaves he closed one end of the little shelter he had built.

Then they sat down together again upon the edge of the drum and tried to talk by signs.

The magnificent diamond locket which hung about Tarzan's neck, had been a source of much wonderment to Jane. She pointed to it now, and Tarzan removed it and handed the pretty bauble to her.

She saw that it was the work of a skilled artisan and that the diamonds were of great brilliancy and superbly set, but the cutting of them denoted that they were of a former day. She noticed too that the locket opened, and, pressing the hidden clasp, she saw the two halves spring apart to reveal in either section an ivory miniature.

One was of a beautiful woman and the other might have been a likeness of the man who sat beside her, except for a subtle difference of expression that was scarcely definable.

She looked up at Tarzan to find him leaning toward her gazing on the miniatures with an expression of astonishment. He reached out his hand for the locket and took it away from her, examining the likenesses within with unmistakable signs of surprise and new interest. His manner clearly denoted that he had never before seen them, nor imagined that the locket opened.

This fact caused Jane to indulge in further speculation, and it taxed her imagination to picture how this beautiful ornament came into the possession of a wild and savage creature of the unexplored jungles of Africa.

Still more wonderful was how it contained the likeness of one who might be a brother, or, more likely, the father of this woodland demi-god who was even ignorant of the fact that the locket opened.

Tarzan was still gazing with fixity at the two faces. Presently he removed the quiver from his shoulder, and emptying the arrows upon the ground reached into the bottom of the bag-like receptacle and drew forth a flat object wrapped in many soft leaves and tied with bits of long grass.

Carefully he unwrapped it, removing layer after layer of leaves until at length he held a photograph in his hand.

Pointing to the miniature of the man within the locket he handed the photograph to Jane, holding the open locket beside it.

The photograph only served to puzzle the girl still more, for it was evidently another likeness of the same man whose picture rested in the locket beside that of the beautiful young woman.

Tarzan was looking at her with an expression of puzzled bewilderment in his eyes as she glanced up at him. He seemed to be framing a question with his lips.

The girl pointed to the photograph and then to the miniature and then to him, as though to indicate that she thought the likenesses were of him, but he only shook his head, and then shrugging his great shoulders, he took the photograph from her and having carefully rewrapped it, placed it again in the bottom of his quiver.

For a few moments he sat in silence, his eyes bent upon the ground, while Jane held the little locket in her hand, turning it over and over in an endeavor to find some further clue that might lead to the identity of its original owner.

At length a simple explanation occurred to her.

The locket had belonged to Lord Greystoke, and the likenesses were of himself and Lady Alice.

This wild creature had simply found it in the cabin by the beach. How stupid of her not to have thought of that solution before.

But to account for the strange likeness between Lord Greystoke and this forest god—that was quite beyond her, and it is not strange that she could not imagine that this naked savage was indeed an English nobleman.

At length Tarzan looked up to watch the girl as she examined the locket. He could not fathom the meaning of the faces within, but he could read the interest and fascination upon the face of the live young creature by his side.

She noticed that he was watching her and thinking that he wished his ornament again she held it out to him. He took it from her and taking the chain in his two hands he placed it about her neck, smiling at her expression of surprise at his unexpected gift.

Jane shook her head vehemently and would have removed the golden links from about her throat, but Tarzan would not let her. Taking her hands in his, when she insisted upon it, he held them tightly to prevent her.

At last she desisted and with a little laugh raised the locket to her lips.

Tarzan did not know precisely what she meant, but he guessed correctly that it was her way of acknowledging the gift, and so he rose, and taking the locket in his hand, stooped gravely like some courtier of old, and pressed his lips upon it where hers had rested.

It was a stately and gallant little compliment performed with the grace and dignity of utter unconsciousness of self. It was the hall-mark of his aristocratic birth, the natural outcropping of many generations of fine breeding, an hereditary instinct of graciousness which a lifetime of uncouth and savage training and environment could not eradicate.

It was growing dark now, and so they ate again of the fruit which was both food and drink for them; then Tarzan rose, and leading Jane to the little bower he had erected, motioned her to go within.

For the first time in hours a feeling of fear swept over her, and Tarzan felt her draw away as though shrinking from him.

Contact with this girl for half a day had left a very diferent Tarzan from the one on whom the morning's sun had risen.

Now, in every fiber of his being, heredity spoke louder than training.

He had not in one swift transition become a polished gentleman from a savage ape-man, but at last the instincts of the former predominated, and over all was the desire to please the woman he loved, and to appear well in her eyes.

So Tarzan of the Apes did the only thing he knew to assure Jane of her safety. He removed his hunting knife from its sheath and handed it to her hilt first, again motioning her into the bower.

The girl understood, and taking the long knife she entered and lay down upon the soft grasses while Tarzan of the Apes stretched himself upon the ground across the entrance.

And thus the rising sun found them in the morning.

When Jane awoke, she did not at first recall the strange events of the preceding day, and so she wondered at her odd surroundings— the little leafy bower, the soft grasses of her bed, the unfamiliar prospect from the opening at her feet.

Slowly the circumstances of her position crept one by one into her mind. And then a great wonderment arose in her heart—a mighty wave of thankfulness and gratitude that though she had been in such terrible danger, yet she was unharmed.

She moved to the entrance of the shelter to look for Tarzan. He was gone; but this time no fear assailed her for she knew that he would return.

In the grass at the entrance to her bower she saw the imprint of his body where he had lain all night to guard her. She knew that the fact that he had been there was all that had permitted her to sleep in such peaceful security.

With him near, who could entertain fear? She wondered if there was another man on earth with whom a girl could feel so safe in the heart of this savage African jungle. Even the lions and panthers had no fears for her now.

She looked up to see his lithe form drop softly from a near-by tree. As he caught her eyes upon him his face lighted with that frank and radiant smile that had won her confidence the day before.

As he approached her Jane's heart beat faster and her eyes brightened as they had never done before at the approach of any man.

He had again been gathering fruit and this he laid at the entrance of her bower. Once more they sat down together to eat.

Jane commenced to wonder what his plans were. Would he take her back to the beach or would he keep her here? Suddenly she realized that the matter did not seem to give her much concern. Could it be that she did not care!

She began to comprehend, also, that she was entirely contented sitting here by the side of this smiling giant eating delicious fruit in a sylvan paradise far within the remote depths of an African jungle—that she was contented and very happy.

She could not understand it. Her reason told her that she should be torn by wild anxieties, weighted by dread fears, cast down by gloomy forebodings; but instead, her heart was singing and she was smiling into the answering face of the man beside her.

When they had finished their breakfast Tarzan went to her bower and recovered his knife. The girl had entirely forgotten it. She realized that it was because she had forgotten the fear that prompted her to accept it.

Motioning her to follow, Tarzan walked toward the trees at the edge of the arena, and taking her in one strong arm swung to the branches above.

The girl knew that he was taking her back to her people, and she could not understand the sudden feeling of loneliness and sorrow which crept over her.

For hours they swung slowly along.

Tarzan of the Apes did not hurry. He tried to draw out the sweet pleasure of that journey with those dear arms about his neck as long as possible, and so he went far south of the direct route to the beach.

Several times they halted for brief rests, which Tarzan did not need, and at noon they stopped for an hour at a little brook, where they quenched their thirst, and ate.

So it was nearly sunset when they came to the clearing, and Tarzan, dropping to the ground beside a great tree, parted the tall jungle grass and pointed out the little cabin to her.

She took him by the hand to lead him to it, that she might tell her father that this man had saved her from death and worse than death, that he had watched over her as carefully as a mother might have done.

But again the timidity of the wild thing in the face of human habitation swept over Tarzan of the Apes. He drew back, shaking his head.

The girl came close to him, looking up with pleading eyes. Somehow she could not bear the thought of his going back into the terrible jungle alone.

Still he shook his head, and finally he drew her to him very gently and stooped to kiss her, but first he looked into her eyes and waited to learn if she were pleased, or if she would repulse him.

Just an instant the girl hesitated, and then she realized the truth, and throwing her arms about his neck she drew his face to hers and kissed him—unashamed.

"I love you—I love you," she murmured.

From far in the distance came the faint sound of many guns. Tarzan and Jane raised their heads.

From the cabin came Mr. Philander and Esmeralda.

From where Tarzan and the girl stood they could not see the two vessels lying at anchor in the harbor.

Tarzan pointed toward the sounds, touched his breast and pointed again. She understood. He was going, and something told her that it was because he thought her people were in danger.

Again he kissed her.

"Come back to me," she whispered. "I shall wait for you—always."

He was gone—and Jane turned to walk across the clearing to the cabin.

Mr. Philander was the first to see her. It was dusk and Mr. Philander was very near sighted.

"Quickly, Esmeralda!" he cried. "Let us seek safety within; it is a lioness. Bless me!"

Esmeralda did not bother to verify Mr. Philander's vision. His tone was enough. She was within the cabin and had slammed and bolted the door before he had finished pronouncing her name. The "Bless me" was startled out of Mr. Philander by the discovery that Esmeralda, in the exuberance of her haste, had fastened him upon the same side of the door as was the close-approaching lioness.

He beat furiously upon the heavy portal.

"Esmeralda! Esmeralda!" he shrieked. "Let me in. I am being devoured by a lion."

Esmeralda thought that the noise upon the door was made by the lioness in her attempts to pursue her, so, after her custom, she fainted.

Mr. Philander cast a frightened glance behind him.

Horrors! The thing was quite close now. He tried to scramble up the side of the cabin, and succeeded in catching a fleeting hold upon the thatched roof.

For a moment he hung there, clawing with his feet like a cat on a clothesline, but presently a piece of the thatch came away, and Mr. Philander, preceding it, was precipitated upon his back.

At the instant he fell a remarkable item of natural history leaped to his mind. If one feigns death lions and lionesses are supposed to ignore one, according to Mr. Philander's faulty memory.

So Mr. Philander lay as he had fallen, frozen into the horrid semblance of death. As his arms and legs had been extended stiffly upward as he came to earth upon his back the attitude of death was anything but impressive.

Jane had been watching his antics in mild-eyed surprise. Now she laughed—a little choking gurgle of a laugh; but it was enough. Mr. Philander rolled over upon his side and peered about. At length he discovered her.

"Jane!" he cried. "Jane Porter. Bless me!"

He scrambled to his feet and rushed toward her. He could not believe that it was she, and alive.

"Bless me!" Where did you come from? Where in the world have you been? How—"

"Mercy, Mr. Philander," interrupted the girl, "I can never remember so many questions."

"Well, well," said Mr. Philander. "Bless me! I am so filled with surprise and exuberant delight at seeing you safe and well again that I scarcely know what I am saying, really. But come, tell me all that has happened to you."

XXI

The Village
of Torture

s the little expedition of sailors toiled through the dense jungle searching for signs of Jane Porter, the futility of their venture became more and more apparent, but the grief of the old man and the hopeless eyes of the young Englishman prevented the kind hearted D'Arnot from turning back.

He thought that there might be a bare possibility of finding her body, or the remains of it, for he was positive that she had been devoured by some beast of prey. He deployed his men into a skirmish line from the point where Esmeralda had been found, and in this extended formation they pushed their way, sweating and panting, through the tangled vines and creepers. It was slow work. Noon found them but a few miles inland. They halted for a brief rest then, and after pushing on for a short distance further one of the men discovered a well-marked trail.

It was an old elephant track, and D'Arnot after consulting with Professor Porter and Clayton decided to follow it.

The path wound through the jungle in a northeasterly direction, and along it the column moved in single file.

Lieutenant D'Arnot was in the lead and moving at a quick pace, for the trail was comparatively open. Immediately behind him came Professor Porter, but as he could not keep pace with the younger man

202

D'Arnot was a hundred yards in advance when suddenly a half dozen black warriors arose about him.

D'Arnot gave a warning shout to his column as the blacks closed on him, but before he could draw his revolver he had been pinioned and dragged into the jungle.

His cry had alarmed the sailors and a dozen of them sprang forward past Professor Porter, running up the trail to their officer's aid.

They did not know the cause of his outcry, only that it was a warning of danger ahead. They had rushed past the spot where D'Arnot had been seized when a spear hurled from the jungle transfixed one of the men, and then a volley of arrows fell among them.

Raising their rifles they fired into the underbrush in the direction from which the missiles had come.

By this time the balance of the party had come up, and volley after volley was fired toward the concealed foe. It was these shots that Tarzan and Jane Porter had heard.

Lieutenant Charpentier, who had been bringing up the rear of the column, now came running to the scene, and on hearing the details of the ambush ordered the men to follow him, and plunged into the tangled vegetation.

In an instant they were in a hand-to-hand fight with some fifty black warriors of Mbonga's village. Arrows and bullets flew thick and fast.

Queer African knives and French gun butts mingled for a moment in savage and bloody duels, but soon the natives fled into the jungle, leaving the Frenchmen to count their losses.

Four of the twenty were dead, a dozen others were wounded, and Lieutenant D'Arnot was missing. Night was falling rapidly, and their predicament was rendered doubly worse when they could not even find the elephant trail which they had been following.

There was but one thing to do, make camp where they were until daylight. Lieutenant Charpentier ordered a clearing made and a circular abatis of underbrush constructed about the camp.

This work was not completed until long after dark, the men building a huge fire in the center of the clearing to give them light to work by.

When all was safe as possible against attack of wild beasts and savage men, Lieutenant Charpentier placed sentries about the little camp and the tired and hungry men threw themselves upon the ground to sleep.

The groans of the wounded, mingled with the roaring and growling of the great beasts which the noise and firelight had attracted, kept sleep, except in its most fitful form, from the tired eyes. It was a sad and hungry party that lay through the long night praying for dawn.

The blacks who had seized D'Arnot had not waited to participate in the fight which followed, but instead had dragged their prisoner a little way through the jungle and then struck the trail further on beyond the scene of the fighting in which their fellows were engaged.

They hurried him along, the sounds of battle growing fainter and fainter as they drew away from the contestants until there suddenly broke upon D'Arnot's vision a good-sized clearing at one end of which stood a thatched and palisaded village.

It was now dusk, but the watchers at the gate saw the approaching trio and distinguished one as a prisoner ere they reached the portals.

A cry went up within the palisade. A great throng of women and children rushed out to meet the party.

And then began for the French officer the most terrifying experience which man can encounter upon earth—the reception of a white prisoner into a village of African cannibals.

To add to the fiendishness of their cruel savagery was the poignant memory of still crueler barbarities practiced upon them and theirs by the white officers of that arch hypocrite, Leopold II of Belgium, because of whose atrocities they had fled the Congo Free State—a pitiful remnant of what once had been a mighty tribe.

They fell upon D'Arnot tooth and nail, beating him with sticks and stones and tearing at him with claw-like hands. Every vestige of clothing was torn from him, and the merciless blows fell upon his bare and quivering flesh. But not once did the Frenchman cry out in pain. He breathed a silent prayer that he be quickly delivered from his torture.

But the death he prayed for was not to be so easily had. Soon the warriors beat the women away from their prisoner. He was to be saved for nobler sport than this, and the first wave of their passion having subsided they contented themselves with crying out taunts and insults and spitting upon him.

Presently they reached the center of the village. There D'Arnot was bound securely to the great post from which no live man had ever been released.

A number of the women scattered to their several huts to fetch pots and water, while others built a row of fires on which portions of the feast were to be boiled while the balance would be slowly dried in strips for future use, as they expected the other warriors to return with many prisoners. The festivities were delayed awaiting the return of the warriors who had remained to engage in the skirmish with the white men, so that it was quite late when all were in the village, and the dance of death commenced to circle around the doomed officer.

Half fainting from pain and exhaustion, D'Arnot watched from beneath half-closed lids what seemed but the vagary of delirium, or some horrid nightmare from which he must soon awake.

The bestial faces, daubed with color—the huge mouths and flabby hanging lips—the yellow teeth, sharp filed—the rolling, demon eyes—the shining naked bodies—the cruel spears. Surely no such creatures really existed upon earth—he must indeed be dreaming.

The savage, whirling bodies circled nearer. Now a spear sprang forth and touched his arm. The sharp pain and the feel of hot, trickling blood assured him of the awful reality of his hopeless position.

Another spear and then another touched him. He closed his eyes and held his teeth firm set—he would not cry out.

He was a soldier of France, and he would teach these beasts how an officer and a gentleman died.

. . .

Tarzan of the Apes needed no interpreter to translate the story of those distant shots. With Jane Porter's kisses still warm upon his lips he was swinging with incredible rapidity through the forest trees straight toward the village of Mbonga.

He was not interested in the location of the encounter, for he judged that that would soon be over. Those who were killed he could not aid, those who escaped would not need his assistance.

It was to those who had neither been killed or escaped that he hastened. And he knew that he would find them by the great post in the center of Mbonga village.

Many times had Tarzan seen Mbonga's black raiding parties return from the northward with prisoners, and always were the same scenes enacted about that grim stake, beneath the flaring light of many fires.

He knew, too, that they seldom lost much time before consummating the fiendish purpose of their captures. He doubted that he would arrive in time to do more than avenge.

On he sped. Night had fallen and he traveled high along the upper terrace where the gorgeous tropic moon lighted the dizzy pathway through the gently undulating branches of the tree tops.

Presently he caught the reflection of a distant blaze. It lay to the right of his path. It must be the light from the camp fire the two men had built before they were attacked—Tarzan knew nothing of the presence of the sailors.

So sure was Tarzan of his jungle knowledge that he did not turn from his course, but passed the glare at a distance of a half mile. It was the camp fire of the Frenchmen.

In a few minutes more Tarzan swung into the trees above Mbonga's village. Ah, he was not quite too late! Or, was he? He could not tell. The figure at the stake was very still, yet the black warriors were but pricking it.

Tarzan knew their customs. The death blow had not been struck. He could tell almost to a minute how far the dance had gone.

In another instant Mbonga's knife would sever one of the victim's ears—that would mark the beginning of the end, for very shortly after only a writhing mass of mutilated flesh would remain.

There would still be life in it, but death then would be the only charity it craved.

The stake stood forty feet from the nearest tree. Tarzan coiled his rope. Then there rose suddenly above the fiendish cries of the dancing demons the awful challenge of the ape-man.

The dancers halted as though turned to stone.

The rope sped with singing whir high above the heads of the blacks. It was quite invisible in the flaring lights of the camp fires.

D'Arnot opened his eyes. A huge black, standing directly before him, lunged backward as though felled by an invisible hand.

Struggling and shrieking, his body, rolling from side to side, moved quickly toward the shadows beneath the trees.

The blacks, their eyes protruding in horror, watched spellbound.

Once beneath the trees, the body rose straight into the air, and as it disappeared into the foliage above, the terrified negroes, screaming with fright, broke into a mad race for the village gate.

D'Arnot was left alone.

He was a brave man, but he had felt the short hairs bristle upon the nape of his neck when that uncanny cry rose upon the air.

As the writhing body of the black soared, as though by unearthly power, into the dense foliage of the forest, D'Arnot felt an icy shiver run along his spine, as though death had risen from a dark grave and laid a cold and clammy finger on his flesh.

As D'Arnot watched the spot where the body had entered the tree he heard the sounds of movement there.

The branches swayed as though under the weight of a man's body—there was a crash and the black came sprawling to earth again,—to lie very quietly where he had fallen.

Immediately after him came a white body, but this one alighted erect.

D'Arnot saw a clean-limbed young giant emerge from the shadows into the firelight and come quickly toward him.

What could it mean? Who could it be? Some new creature of torture and destruction, doubtless.

D'Arnot waited. His eyes never left the face of the advancing man. Nor did the other's frank, clear eyes waver beneath D'Arnot's fixed gaze.

D'Arnot was reassured, but still without much hope, though he felt that that face could not mask a cruel heart.

Without a word Tarzan of the Apes cut the bonds which held the Frenchman. Weak from suffering and loss of blood, he would have fallen but for the strong arm that caught him.

He felt himself lifted from the ground. There was a sensation as of flying, and then he lost consciousness.

XXII

THE SEARCH PARTY

hen dawn broke upon the little camp of French-men in the heart of the jungle it found a sad and disheartened group.

As soon as it was light enough to see their surroundings Lieutenant Charpentier sent men in groups of three in several directions to locate the trail, and in ten minutes it was found and the expedition was hurrying back toward the beach.

It was slow work, for they bore the bodies of six dead men, two more having succumbed during the night, and several of those who were wounded required support to move even very slowly.

Charpentier had decided to return to camp for reinforcements, and then make an attempt to track down the natives and rescue D'Arnot.

It was late in the afternoon when the exhausted men reached the clearing by the beach, but for two of them the return brought so great a happiness that all their suffering and heartbreaking grief was forgotten on the instant.

As the little party emerged from the jungle the first person that Professor Porter and Cecil Clayton saw was Jane, standing by the cabin door.

With a little cry of joy and relief she ran forward to greet them, throwing her arms about her father's neck and bursting into tears for the first time since they had been cast upon this hideous and adven-turous shore.

Professor Porter strove manfully to suppress his own emotions, but the strain upon his nerves and weakened vitality were too much for him, and at length, burying his old face in the girl's shoulder, he sobbed quietly like a tired child.

Jane led him toward the cabin, and the Frenchmen turned toward the beach from which several of their fellows were advancing to meet them.

Clayton, wishing to leave father and daughter alone, joined the sailors and remained talking with the officers until their boat pulled away toward the cruiser whither Lieutenant Charpentier was bound to report the unhappy outcome of his adventure.

Then Clayton turned back slowly toward the cabin. His heart was filled with happiness. The woman he loved was safe.

He wondered by what manner of miracle she had been spared. To see her alive seemed almost unbelievable.

As he approached the cabin he saw Jane coming out. When she saw him she hurried forward to meet him.

"Jane!" he cried, "God has been good to us, indeed. Tell me how you escaped—what form Providence took to save you for—us."

He had never before called her by her given name. Forty-eight hours before it would have suffused Jane with a soft glow of pleasure to have heard that name from Clayton's lips—now it frightened her.

"Mr. Clayton," she said quietly, extending her hand, "first let me thank you for your chivalrous loyalty to my dear father. He has told me how noble and self-sacrificing you have been. How can we repay you!"

Clayton noticed that she did not return his familiar salutation, but he felt no misgivings on that score. She had been through so much. This was no time to force his love upon her, he quickly realized.

"I am already repaid," he said. "Just to see you and Professor Porter both safe, well, and together again. I do not think that I could much longer have endured the pathos of his quiet and uncomplaining grief.

"It was the saddest experience of my life, Miss Porter; and then, added to it, there was my own grief—the greatest I have ever known. But his was so hopeless—his was pitiful. It taught me that no love, not even that of a man for his wife may be so deep and terrible and self-sacrificing as the love of a father for his daughter."

The girl bowed her head. There was a question she wanted to ask, but it seemed almost sacrilegious in the face of the love of these two men and the terrible suffering they had endured while she sat laughing and happy beside a godlike creature of the forest, eating delicious fruits and looking with eyes of love into answering eyes.

But love is a strange master, and human nature is still stranger, so she asked her question.

"Where is the forest man who went to rescue you? Why did he not return?"

"I do not understand," said Clayton. "Whom do you mean?"

"He who has saved each of us—who saved me from the gorilla."

"Oh," cried Clayton, in surprise. "It was he who rescued you? You have not told me anything of your adventure, you know."

"But the wood man," she urged. "Have you not seen him? When we heard the shots in the jungle, very faint and far away, he left me. We had just reached the clearing, and he hurried off in the direction of the fighting. I know he went to aid you."

Her tone was almost pleading—her manner tense with suppressed emotion. Clayton could not but notice it, and he wondered, vaguely, why she was so deeply moved—so anxious to know the whereabouts of this strange creature.

Yet a feeling of apprehension of some impending sorrow haunted him, and in his breast, unknown to himself, was implanted the first germ of jealousy and suspicion of the ape-man, to whom he owed his life.

"We did not see him," he replied quietly. "He did not join us." And then after a moment of thoughtful pause: "Possibly he joined his

211

own tribe—the men who attacked us." He did not know why he had said it, for he did not believe it.

The girl looked at him wide eyed for a moment.

"No!" she exclaimed vehemently, much too vehemently he thought. "It could not be. They were savages."

Clayton looked puzzled.

"He is a strange, half-savage creature of the jungle, Miss Porter. We know nothing of him. He neither speaks nor understands any European tongue—and his ornaments and weapons are those of the West Coast savages."

Clayton was speaking rapidly.

"There are no other human beings than savages within hundreds of miles, Miss Porter. He must belong to the tribes which attacked us, or to some other equally savage—he may even be a cannibal."

Jane blanched.

"I will not believe it," she half whispered. "It is not true. You shall see," she said, addressing Clayton, "that he will come back and that he will prove that you are wrong. You do not know him as I do. I tell you that he is a gentleman."

Clayton was a generous and chivalrous man, but something in the girl's breathless defense of the forest man stirred him to unreasoning jealousy, so that for the instant he forgot all that they owed to this wild demi-god, and he answered her with a half sneer upon his lip.

"Possibly you are right, Miss Porter," he said, "but I do not think that any of us need worry about our carrion-eating acquaintance. The chances are that he is some half-demented castaway who will forget us more quickly, but no more surely, than we shall forget him. He is only a beast of the jungle, Miss Porter."

The girl did not answer, but she felt her heart shrivel within her.

She knew that Clayton spoke merely what he thought, and for the first time she began to analyze the structure which

supported her newfound love, and to subject its object to a critical examination.

Slowly she turned and walked back to the cabin. She tried to
imagine her wood-god by her side in the saloon of an ocean liner. She
saw him eating with his hands, tearing his food like a beast of prey,
and wiping his greasy fingers upon his thighs. She shuddered.

She saw him as she introduced him to her friends—uncouth,
illiterate—a boor; and the girl winced.

She had reached her room now, and as she sat upon the edge of
her bed of ferns and grasses, with one hand resting upon her rising
and falling bosom, she felt the hard outlines of the man's locket.

She drew it out, holding it in the palm of her hand for a moment
with tear-blurred eyes bent upon it. Then she raised it to her lips, and
crushing it there buried her face in the soft ferns, sobbing.

"Beast?" she murmured. "Then God make me a beast; for, man
or beast, I am yours."

She did not see Clayton again that day. Esmeralda brought her
supper to her, and she sent word to her father that she was suffering
from the reaction following her adventure.

The next morning Clayton left early with the relief expedition
in search of Lieutenant D'Arnot. There were two hundred armed
men this time, with ten officers and two surgeons, and provisions for
a week.

They carried bedding and hammocks, the latter for transporting
their sick and wounded.

It was a determined and angry company—a punitive expedition
as well as one of relief. They reached the sight of the skirmish of the
previous expedition shortly after noon, for they were now traveling a
known trail and no time was lost in exploring.

From there on the elephant-track led straight to Mbonga's village. It was but two o'clock when the head of the column halted upon
the edge of the clearing.

Lieutenant Charpentier, who was in command, immediately sent a portion of his force through the jungle to the opposite side of the village. Another detachment was dispatched to a point before the village gate, while he remained with the balance upon the south side of the clearing.

It was arranged that the party which was to take its position to the north, and which would be the last to gain its station should commence the assault, and that their opening volley should be the signal for a concerted rush from all sides in an attempt to carry the village by storm at the first charge.

For half an hour the men with Lieutenant Charpentier crouched in the dense foliage of the jungle, waiting the signal. To them it seemed like hours. They could see natives in the fields, and others moving in and out of the village gate.

At length the signal came—a sharp rattle of musketry, and like one man, an answering volley tore from the jungle to the west and to the south.

The natives in the field dropped their implements and broke madly for the palisade. The French bullets mowed them down, and the French sailors bounded over their prostrate bodies straight for the village gate.

So sudden and unexpected the assault had been that the whites reached the gates before the frightened natives could bar them, and in another minute the village street was filled with armed men fighting hand to hand in an inextricable tangle.

For a few moments the blacks held their ground within the entrance to the street, but the revolvers, rifles and cutlasses of the Frenchmen crumpled the native spearmen and struck down the black archers with their bows halfdrawn.

Soon the battle turned to a wild rout, and then to a grim massacre; for the French sailors had seen bits of D'Arnot's uniform upon several of the black warriors who opposed them.

They spared the children and those of the women whom they were not forced to kill in self-defense, but when at length they stopped, parting, blood covered and sweating, it was because there lived to oppose them no single warrior of all the savage village of Mbonga.

Carefully they ransacked every hut and corner of the village, but no sign of D'Arnot could they find. They questioned the prisoners by signs, and finally one of the sailors who had served in the French Congo found that he could make them understand the bastard tongue that passes for language between the whites and the more degraded tribes of the coast, but even then they could learn nothing definite regarding the fate of D'Arnot.

Only excited gestures and expressions of fear could they obtain in response to their inquiries concerning their fellow; and at last they became convinced that these were but evidences of the guilt of these demons who had slaughtered and eaten their comrade two nights before.

At length all hope left them, and they prepared to camp for the night within the village. The prisoners were herded into three huts where they were heavily guarded. Sentries were posted at the barred gates, and finally the village was wrapped in the silence of slumber, except for the wailing of the native women for their dead.

· · ·

The next morning they set out upon the return march. Their original intention had been to burn the village, but this idea was abandoned and the prisoners were left behind, weeping and moaning, but with roofs to cover them and a palisade for refuge from the beasts of the jungle.

Slowly the expedition retraced its steps of the preceding day. Ten loaded hammocks retarded its pace. In eight of them lay the more seriously wounded, while two swung beneath the weight of the dead.

Clayton and Lieutenant Charpentier brought up the rear of the column; the Englishman silent in respect for the other's grief, for D'Arnot and Charpentier had been inseparable friends since boyhood.

Clayton could not but realize that the Frenchman felt his grief the more keenly because D'Arnot's sacrifice had been so futile, since Jane had been rescued before D'Arnot had fallen into the hands of the savages, and again because the service in which he had lost his life had been outside his duty and for strangers and aliens; but when he spoke of it to Lieutenant Charpentier, the latter shook his head.

"No, Monsieur," he said, "D'Arnot would have chosen to die thus. I only grieve that I could not have died for him, or at least with him. I wish that you could have known him better, Monsieur. He was indeed an officer and a gentleman—a title conferred on many, but deserved by so few.

"He did not die futilely, for his death in the cause of a strange American girl will make us, his comrades, face our ends the more bravely, however they may come to us."

Clayton did not reply, but within him rose a new respect for Frenchmen which remained undimmed ever after.

It was quite late when they reached the cabin by the beach. A single shot before they emerged from the jungle had announced to those in camp as well as on the ship that the expedition had been too late—for it had been prearranged that when they came within a mile or two of camp one shot was to be fired to denote failure, or three for success, while two would have indicated that they had found no sign of either D'Arnot or his black captors.

So it was a solemn party that awaited their coming, and few words were spoken as the dead and wounded men were tenderly placed in boats and rowed silently toward the cruiser.

Clayton, exhausted from his five days of laborious marching through the jungle and from the effects of his two battles with the blacks, turned toward the cabin to seek a mouthful of food and then the comparative ease of his bed of grasses after two nights in the jungle.

By the cabin door stood Jane.

"The poor lieutenant?" she asked. "Did you find no trace of him?"

"We were too late, Miss Porter," he replied sadly.

"Tell me. What had happened?" she asked.

"I cannot, Miss Porter, it is too horrible."

"You do not mean that they had tortured him?" she whispered.

"We do not know what they did to him *before* they killed him," he answered, his face drawn with fatigue and the sorrow he felt for poor D'Arnot and he emphasized the word before.

"*Before* they killed him! What do you mean? They are not—? They are not—?"

She was thinking of what Clayton had said of the forest man's probable relationship to this tribe and she could not frame the awful word.

"Yes, Miss Porter, they were—cannibals," he said, almost bitterly, for to him too had suddenly come the thought of the forest man, and the strange, unaccountable jealousy he had felt two days before swept over him once more.

And then in sudden brutality that was as unlike Clayton as courteous consideration is unlike an ape, he blurted out:

"When your forest god left you he was doubtless hurrying to the feast."

He was sorry ere the words were spoken though he did not know how cruelly they had cut the girl. His regret was for his baseless disloyalty to one who had saved the lives of every member of his party, and offered harm to none.

The girl's head went high.

"There could be but one suitable reply to your assertion, Mr. Clayton," she said icily, "and I regret that I am not a man, that I might make it." She turned quickly and entered the cabin.

Clayton was an Englishman, so the girl had passed quite out of sight before he deduced what reply a man would have made.

"Upon my word," he said ruefully, "she called me a liar. And I fancy I jolly well deserved it," he added thoughtfully. "Clayton, my boy, I know you are tired out and unstrung, but that's no reason why you should make an ass of yourself. You'd better go to bed."

But before he did so he called gently to Jane upon the opposite side of the sailcloth partition, for he wished to apologize, but he might as well have addressed the Sphinx. Then he wrote upon a piece of paper and shoved it beneath the partition.

Jane saw the little note and ignored it, for she was very angry and hurt and mortified, but—she was a woman, and so eventually she picked it up and read it.

My Dear Miss Porter:

I had no reason to insinuate what I did. My only excuse is that my nerves must be unstrung—which is no excuse at all.

Please try and think that I did not say it. I am very sorry. I would not have hurt You, above all others in the world. Say that you forgive me.

WM. CECIL CLAYTON.

"He did think it or he never would have said it," reasoned the girl, "but it cannot be true—oh, I know it is not true!"

One sentence in the letter frightened her: "I would not have hurt *you* above all others in the world."

A week ago that sentence would have filled her with delight, now it depressed her.

She wished she had never met Clayton. She was sorry that she had ever seen the forest god. No, she was glad. And there was that other note she had found in the grass before the cabin the day after her return from the jungle, the love note signed by Tarzan of the Apes.

Who could be this new suitor? If he were another of the wild denizens of this terrible forest what might he not do to claim her?

"Esmeralda! Wake up," she cried.

"You make me so irritable, sleeping there peacefully when you know perfectly well that the world is filled with sorrow."

"Gaberelle!" screamed Esmeralda, sitting up. "What is it now? A hipponocerous? Where is he, Miss Jane?"

"Nonsense, Esmeralda, there is nothing. Go back to sleep. You are bad enough asleep, but you are infinitely worse awake."

"Yes honey, but what's the matter with you, precious? You acts sort of disgranulated this evening."

"Oh, Esmeralda, I'm just plain ugly to-night," said the girl. "Don't pay any attention to me—that's a dear."

"Yes, honey; now you go right to sleep. Your nerves are all on edge. What with all these ripotamuses and man eating geniuses that Mister Philander been telling about—Lord, it ain't no wonder we all get nervous prosecution."

Jane crossed the little room, laughing, and kissing the faithful woman, bid Esmeralda good night.

XXIII

BROTHER MEN

hen D'Arnot regained consciousness, he found himself lying upon a bed of soft ferns and grasses beneath a little "A" shaped shelter of boughs.

At his feet an opening looked out upon a green sward, and at a little distance beyond was the dense wall of jungle and forest.

He was very lame and sore and weak, and as full consciousness returned he felt the sharp torture of many cruel wounds and the dull aching of every bone and muscle in his body as a result of the hideous beating he had received.

Even the turning of his head caused him such excruciating agony that he lay still with closed eyes for a long time.

He tried to piece out the details of his adventure prior to the time he lost consciousness to see if they would explain his present whereabouts—he wondered if he were among friends or foes.

At length he recollected the whole hideous scene at the stake, and finally recalled the strange white figure in whose arms he had sunk into oblivion.

D'Arnot wondered what fate lay in store for him now. He could neither see nor hear any signs of life about him.

The incessant hum of the jungle—the rustling of millions of leaves—the buzz of insects—the voices of the birds and monkeys seemed blended into a strangely soothing purr, as though he lay apart, far from the myriad life whose sounds came to him only as a blurred echo.

At length he fell into a quiet slumber, nor did he awake again until afternoon.

Once more he experienced the strange sense of utter bewilderment that had marked his earlier awakening, but soon he recalled the recent past, and looking through the opening at his feet he saw the figure of a man squatting on his haunches.

The broad, muscular back was turned toward him, but, tanned though it was, D'Arnot saw that it was the back of a white man, and he thanked God.

The Frenchman called faintly. The man turned, and rising, came toward the shelter. His face was very handsome—the handsomest, thought D'Arnot, that he had ever seen.

Stooping, he crawled into the shelter beside the wounded officer, and placed a cool hand upon his forehead.

D'Arnot spoke to him in French, but the man only shook his head—sadly, it seemed to the Frenchman.

Then D'Arnot tried English, but still the man shook his head. Italian, Spanish and German brought similar discouragement.

D'Arnot knew a few words of Norwegian, Russian, Greek, and also had a smattering of the language of one of the West Coast negro tribes—the man denied them all.

After examining D'Arnot's wounds the man left the shelter and disappeared. In half an hour he was back with fruit and a hollow gourd-like vegetable filled with water.

D'Arnot drank and ate a little. He was surprised that he had no fever. Again he tried to converse with his strange nurse, but the attempt was useless.

Suddenly the man hastened from the shelter only to return a few minutes later with several pieces of bark and—wonder of wonders—a lead pencil.

Squatting beside D'Arnot he wrote for a minute on the smooth inner surface of the bark; then he handed it to the Frenchman.

D'Arnot was astonished to see, in plain print-like characters, a message in English:

I am Tarzan of the Apes. Who are you? Can you read this language?

D'Arnot seized the pencil—then he stopped. This strange man wrote English—evidently he was an Englishman.

"Yes," said D'Arnot, "I read English. I speak it also. Now we may talk. First let me thank you for all that you have done for me."

The man only shook his head and pointed to the pencil and the bark.

"*Mon Dieu!*" cried D'Arnot. "If you are English why is it then that you cannot speak English?"

And then in a flash it came to him—the man was a mute, possibly a deaf mute.

So D'Arnot wrote a message on the bark, in English.

*I am Paul d'Arnot, Lieutenant in the navy of France. I thank you
for what you have done for me. You have saved my life, and all that
I have is yours. May I ask how it is that one who writes English does
not speak it?*

Tarzan's reply filled D'Arnot with still greater wonder:

*I speak only the language of my tribe—the great apes who were Kerchak's;
and a little of the languages of Tantor, the elephant, and Numa, the lion,
and of the other folks of the jungle I understand. With a human being I
have never spoken, except once with Jane Porter, by signs. This is the first
time I have spoken with another of my kind through written words.*

D'Arnot was mystified. It seemed incredible that there lived upon earth a full-grown man who had never spoken with a fellow man, and still more preposterous that such a one could read and write.

He looked again at Tarzan's message—"except once, with Jane Porter." That was the American girl who had been carried into the jungle by a gorilla.

A sudden light commenced to dawn on D'Arnot—this then was the "gorilla." He seized the pencil and wrote:

Where is Jane Porter?

And Tarzan replied, below:

Back with her people in the cabin of Tarzan of the Apes.

She is not dead then? Where was she? What happened to her?

She is not dead. She was taken by Terkoz to be his wife; but Tarzan of the Apes took her away from Terkoz and killed him before he could harm her.

None in all the jungle may face Tarzan of the Apes in battle, and live. I am Tarzan of the Apes—mighty fighter.

D'Arnot wrote:

I am glad she is safe. It pains me to write, I will rest a while.

And then Tarzan:

Yes, rest. When you are well I shall take you back to your people.

For many days D'Arnot lay upon his bed of soft ferns. The second day a fever had come and D'Arnot thought that it meant infection and he knew that he would die.

An idea came to him. He wondered why he had not thought of it before.

He called Tarzan and indicated by signs that he would write, and when Tarzan had fetched the bark and pencil, D'Arnot wrote:

Can you go to my people and lead them here? I will write a message that you may take to them, and they will follow you.

Tarzan shook his head and taking the bark, wrote:

I had thought of that—the first day; but I dared not. The great apes come often to this spot, and if they found you here, wounded and alone, they would kill you.

D'Arnot turned on his side and closed his eyes. He did not wish to die; but he felt that he was going, for the fever was mounting higher and higher. That night he lost consciousness.

For three days he was in delirium, and Tarzan sat beside him and bathed his head and hands and washed his wounds.

On the fourth day the fever broke as suddenly as it had come, but it left D'Arnot a shadow of his former self, and very weak. Tarzan had to lift him that he might drink from the gourd.

The fever had not been the result of infection, as D'Arnot had thought, but one of those that commonly attack whites in the jungles of Africa, and either kill or leave them as suddenly as D'Arnot's had left him.

Two days later, D'Arnot was tottering about the amphitheater, Tarzan's strong arm about him to keep him from falling.

They sat beneath the shade of a great tree, and Tarzan found some smooth bark that they might converse.

D'Arnot wrote the first message:

What can I do to repay you for all that you have done for me?

And Tarzan, in reply:

Teach me to speak the language of men.

And so D'Arnot commenced at once, pointing out familiar objects and repeating their names in French, for he thought that it would be easier to teach this man his own language, since he understood it himself best of all.

It meant nothing to Tarzan, of course, for he could not tell one language from another, so when he pointed to the word man which he had printed upon a piece of bark he learned from D'Arnot that it was pronounced *homme*, and in the same way he was taught to pronounce ape, *singe* and tree, *arbre*.

He was a most eager student, and in two more days had mastered so much French that he could speak little sentences such as: "That is a tree," "this is grass," "I am hungry," and the like, but D'Arnot found that it was difficult to teach him the French construction upon a foundation of English.

The Frenchman wrote little lessons for him in English and had Tarzan repeat them in French, but as a literal translation was usually very poor French Tarzan was often confused.

D'Arnot realized now that he had made a mistake, but it seemed too late to go back and do it all over again and force Tarzan to unlearn all that he had learned, especially as they were rapidly approaching a point where they would be able to converse.

On the third day after the fever broke Tarzan wrote a message asking D'Arnot if he felt strong enough to be carried back to the cabin. Tarzan was as anxious to go as D'Arnot, for he longed to see Jane again.

It had been hard for him to remain with the Frenchman all these days for that very reason, and that he had unselfishly done so spoke more glowingly of his nobility of character than even did his rescuing the French officer from Mbonga's clutches.

D'Arnot, only too willing to attempt the journey, wrote:

But you cannot carry me all the distance through this tangled forest.

Tarzan laughed.

"*Mais oui*," he said, and D'Arnot laughed aloud to hear the phrase that he used so often glide from Tarzan's tongue.

So they set out, D'Arnot marveling as had Clayton and Jane at the wondrous strength and agility of the apeman.

Mid-afternoon brought them to the clearing, and as Tarzan dropped to earth from the branches of the last tree his heart leaped and bounded against his ribs in anticipation of seeing Jane so soon again.

No one was in sight outside the cabin, and D'Arnot was perplexed to note that neither the cruiser nor the *Arrow* was at anchor in the bay.

An atmosphere of loneliness pervaded the spot, which caught suddenly at both men as they strode toward the cabin.

Neither spoke, yet both knew before they opened the closed door what they would find beyond.

Tarzan lifted the latch and pushed the great door in upon its wooden hinges. It was as they had feared. The cabin was deserted.

The men turned and looked at one another. D'Arnot knew that his people thought him dead; but Tarzan thought only of the woman who had kissed him in love and now had fled from him while he was serving one of her people.

A great bitterness rose in his heart. He would go away, far into the jungle and join his tribe. Never would he see one of his own kind again, nor could he bear the thought of returning to the cabin. He would leave that forever behind him with the great hopes he had nursed there of finding his own race and becoming a man among men.

And the Frenchman? D'Arnot? What of him? He could get along as Tarzan had. Tarzan did not want to see him more. He wanted to get away from everything that might remind him of Jane.

As Tarzan stood upon the threshold brooding, D'Arnot had entered the cabin. Many comforts he saw that had been left behind. He recognized numerous articles from the cruiser—a camp oven, some kitchen utensils, a rifle and many rounds of ammunition, canned foods, blankets, two chairs and a cot—and several books and periodicals, mostly American.

"They must intend returning," thought D'Arnot.

He walked over to the table that John Clayton had built so many years before to serve as a desk, and on it he saw two notes addressed to Tarzan of the Apes.

One was in a strong masculine hand and was unsealed. The other, in a woman's hand, was sealed.

"Here are two messages for you, Tarzan of the Apes," cried D'Arnot, turning toward the door; but his companion was not there.

D'Arnot walked to the door and looked out. Tarzan was nowhere in sight. He called aloud but there was no response.

"*Mon Dieu!*" exclaimed D'Arnot, "he has left me. I feel it. He has gone back into his jungle and left me here alone."

And then he remembered the look on Tarzan's face when they had discovered that the cabin was empty—such a look as the hunter sees in the eyes of the wounded deer he has wantonly brought down.

The man had been hard hit—D'Arnot realized it now—but why? He could not understand.

The Frenchman looked about him. The loneliness and the horror of the place commenced to get on his nerves—already weakened by the ordeal of suffering and sickness he had passed through.

To be left here alone beside this awful jungle—never to hear a human voice or see a human face—in constant dread of savage beasts and more terribly savage men—a prey to solitude and hopelessness. It was awful.

And far to the east Tarzan of the Apes was speeding through the middle terrace back to his tribe. Never had he traveled with such reckless speed. He felt that he was running away from himself—that by hurtling through the forest like a frightened squirrel he was escaping from his own thoughts. But no matter how fast he went he found them always with him.

He passed above the sinuous body of Sabor, the lioness, going in the opposite direction—toward the cabin, thought Tarzan.

What could D'Arnot do against Sabor—or if Bolgani, the gorilla, should come upon him—or Numa, the lion, or cruel Sheeta?

Tarzan paused in his flight.

"What are you, Tarzan?" he asked aloud. "An ape or a man?"

"If you are an ape you will do as the apes would do—leave one of your kind to die in the jungle if it suited your whim to go elsewhere.

"If you are a man, you will return to protect your kind. You will not run away from one of your own people, because one of them has run away from you."

• • •

D'Arnot closed the cabin door. He was very nervous. Even brave men, and D'Arnot was a brave man, are sometimes frightened by solitude.

He loaded one of the rifles and placed it within easy reach. Then he went to the desk and took up the unsealed letter addressed to Tarzan.

Possibly it contained word that his people had but left the beach temporarily. He felt that it would be no breach of ethics to read this letter, so he took the enclosure from the envelope and read:

To Tarzan of the Apes:

We thank you for the use of your cabin, and are sorry that you did not permit us the pleasure of seeing and thanking you in person.

We have harmed nothing, but have left many things for you which may add to your comfort and safety here in your lonely home.

If you know the strange white man who saved our lives so many times, and brought us food, and if you can converse with him, thank him, also, for his kindness.

We sail within the hour, never to return; but we wish you and that other jungle friend to know that we shall always thank you for what you did for strangers on your shore, and that we should have done infinitely more to reward you both had you given us the opportunity.

Very respectfully,

WM. CECIL CLAYTON.

"'Never to return,'" muttered D'Arnot, and threw himself face downward upon the cot.

An hour later he started up listening. Something was at the door trying to enter.

D'Arnot reached for the loaded rifle and placed it to his shoulder.

Dusk was falling, and the interior of the cabin was very dark; but the man could see the latch moving from its place.

He felt his hair rising upon his scalp.

Gently the door opened until a thin crack showed something standing just beyond.

D'Arnot sighted along the blue barrel at the crack of the door— and then he pulled the trigger.

XXIV

LOST TREASURE

hen the expedition returned, following their fruitless endeavor to succor D'Arnot, Captain Dufranne was anxious to steam away as quickly as possible, and all save Jane had acquiesced.

"No," she said, determinedly, "I shall not go, nor should you, for there are two friends in that jungle who will come out of it some day expecting to find us awaiting them."

"Your officer, Captain Dufranne, is one of them, and the forest man who has saved the lives of every member of my father's party is the other."

"He left me at the edge of the jungle two days ago to hasten to the aid of my father and Mr. Clayton, as he thought, and he has stayed to rescue Lieutenant D'Arnot; of that you may be sure.

"Had he been too late to be of service to the lieutenant he would have been back before now—the fact that he is not back is suffi-cient proof to me that he is delayed because Lieutenant D'Arnot is wounded, or he has had to follow his captors further than the village which your sailors attacked."

"But poor D'Arnot's uniform and all his belongings were found in that village, Miss Porter," argued the captain, "and the natives showed great excitement when questioned as to the white man's fate."

"Yes, Captain, but they did not admit that he was dead and as for his clothes and accouterments being in their possession—why more civilized peoples than these poor savage negroes strip their prisoners of every article of value whether they intend killing them or not.

"Even the soldiers of my own dear South looted not only the living but the dead. It is strong circumstantial evidence, I will admit, but it is not positive proof."

"Possibly your forest man, himself was captured or killed by the savages," suggested Captain Dufranne.

The girl laughed.

"You do not know him," she replied, a little thrill of pride setting her nerves a-tingle at the thought that she spoke of her own.

"I admit that he would be worth waiting for, this superman of yours," laughed the captain. "I most certainly should like to see him."

"Then wait for him, my dear captain," urged the girl, "for I intend doing so."

The Frenchman would have been a very much surprised man could he have interpreted the true meaning of the girl's words.

They had been walking from the beach toward the cabin as they talked, and now they joined a little group sitting on camp stools in the shade of a great tree beside the cabin.

Professor Porter was there, and Mr. Philander and Clayton, with Lieutenant Charpentier and two of his brother officers, while Esmeralda hovered in the background, ever and anon venturing opinions and comments with the freedom of an old and much-indulged family servant.

The officers arose and saluted as their superior approached, and Clayton surrendered his camp stool to Jane.

"We were just discussing poor Paul's fate," said Captain Dufranne. "Miss Porter insists that we have no absolute proof of his death—nor have we. And on the other hand she maintains that the continued absence of your omnipotent jungle friend indicates that D'Arnot is still in need of his services, either because he is wounded, or still is a prisoner in a more distant native village."

"It has been suggested," ventured Lieutenant Charpentier, "that the wild man may have been a member of the tribe of blacks who attacked our party—that he was hastening to aid *them*—his own people."

Jane shot a quick glance at Clayton.

"It seems vastly more reasonable," said Professor Porter.

"I do not agree with you," objected Mr. Philander. "He had ample opportunity to harm us himself, or to lead his people against us. Instead, during our long residence here, he has been uniformly consistent in his role of protector and provider."

"That is true," interjected Clayton, "yet we must not overlook the fact that except for himself the only human beings within hundreds of miles are savage cannibals. He was armed precisely as are they, which indicates that he has maintained relations of some nature with them, and the fact that he is but one against possibly thousands suggests that these relations could scarcely have been other than friendly."

"It seems improbable then that he is not connected with them," remarked the captain; "possibly a member of this tribe."

"Otherwise," added another of the officers, "how could he have lived a sufficient length of time among the savage denizens of the jungle, brute and human, to have become proficient in woodcraft, or in the use of African weapons."

"You are judging him according to your own standards, gentlemen," said Jane. "An ordinary white man such as any of you—pardon me, I did not mean just that—rather, a white man above the ordinary in physique and intelligence could never, I grant you, have lived a year alone and naked in this tropical jungle; but this man not only surpasses the average white man in strength and agility, but as far transcends our trained athletes and 'strong men' as they surpass a day-old babe; and his courage and ferocity in battle are those of the wild beast."

"He has certainly won a loyal champion, Miss Porter," said

Captain Dufranne, laughing. "I am sure that there be none of us here but would willingly face death a hundred times in its most terrifying forms to deserve the tributes of one even half so loyal—or so beautiful."

"You would not wonder that I defend him," said the girl, "could you have seen him as I saw him, battling in my behalf with that huge hairy brute.

"Could you have seen him charge the monster as a bull might charge a grizzly—absolutely without sign of fear or hesitation—you would have believed him more than human.

"Could you have seen those mighty muscles knotting under the brown skin—could you have seen them force back those awful fangs—you too would have thought him invincible.

"And could you have seen the chivalrous treatment which he accorded a strange girl of a strange race, you would feel the same absolute confidence in him that I feel."

"You have won your suit, my fair pleader," cried the captain. "This court finds the defendant not guilty, and the cruiser shall wait a few days longer that he may have an opportunity to come and thank the divine Portia."

"For the Lord's sake honey," cried Esmeralda. "You all don't mean to tell *me* that you're going to stay right here in this here land of carnivable animals when you all got the opportunity to escapade on that boat? Don't you tell me *that*, honey."

"Why, Esmeralda! You should be ashamed of yourself," cried Jane. "Is this any way to show your gratitude to the man who saved your life twice?"

"Well, Miss Jane, that's all jest as you say; but that there forest man never did save us to stay here. He done save us so we all could get *away* from here. I expect he be mighty peevish when he find we ain't got no more sense than to stay right here after he done give us the chance to get away.

"I hoped I'd never have to sleep in this here geological garden another night and listen to all them lonesome noises that come out of that jumble after dark."

"I don't blame you a bit, Esmeralda," said Clayton, "and you certainly did hit it off right when you called them 'lonesome' noises. I never have been able to find the right word for them but that's it, don't you know, lonesome noises."

"You and Esmeralda had better go and live on the cruiser," said Jane, in fine scorn. "What would you think if you *had* to live all of your life in that jungle as our forest man has done?"

"I'm afraid I'd be a blooming bounder as a wild man," laughed Clayton, ruefully. "Those noises at night make the hair on my head bristle. I suppose that I should be ashamed to admit it, but it's the truth."

"I don't know about that," said Lieutenant Charpentier. "I never thought much about fear and that sort of thing—never tried to determine whether I was a coward or brave man; but the other night as we lay in the jungle there after poor D'Arnot was taken, and those jungle noises rose and fell around us I began to think that I was a coward indeed. It was not the roaring and growling of the big beasts that affected me so much as it was the stealthy noises—the ones that you heard suddenly close by and then listened vainly for a repetition of—the unaccountable sounds as of a great body moving almost noiselessly, and the knowledge that you didn't *know* how close it was, or whether it were creeping closer after you ceased to hear it? It was those noises—and the eyes.

"*Mon Dieu!* I shall see them in the dark forever—the eyes that you see, and those that you don't see, but feel—ah, they are the worst."

All were silent for a moment, and then Jane spoke.

"And he is out there," she said, in an awe-hushed whisper. "Those eyes will be glaring at him to-night, and at your comrade Lieutenant D'Arnot. Can you leave them, gentlemen, without at least rendering them the passive succor which remaining here a few days longer might insure them?"

"Tut, tut, child," said Professor Porter. "Captain Dufranne is willing to remain, and for my part I am perfectly willing, perfectly willing—as I always have been to humor your childish whims."

"We can utilize the morrow in recovering the chest, Professor," suggested Mr. Philander.

"Quite so, quite so, Mr. Philander, I had almost forgotten the treasure," exclaimed Professor Porter. "Possibly we can borrow some men from Captain Dufranne to assist us, and one of the prisoners to point out the location of the chest."

"Most assuredly, my dear Professor, we are all yours to command," said the captain.

And so it was arranged that on the next day Lieutenant Charpentier was to take a detail of ten men, and one of the mutineers of the Arrow as a guide, and unearth the treasure; and that the cruiser would remain for a full week in the little harbor. At the end of that time it was to be assumed that D'Arnot was truly dead, and that the forest man would not return while they remained. Then the two vessels were to leave with all the party.

Professor Porter did not accompany the treasure-seekers on the following day, but when he saw them returning empty-handed toward noon, he hastened forward to meet them—his usual preoccupied indifference entirely vanished, and in its place a nervous and excited manner.

"Where is the treasure?" he cried to Clayton, while yet a hundred feet separated them.

Clayton shook his head.

"Gone," he said, as he neared the professor.

"Gone! It cannot be. Who could have taken it?" cried Professor Porter.

"God only knows, Professor," replied Clayton. "We might have thought the fellow who guided us was lying about the location, but his surprise and consternation on finding no chest beneath the body of the murdered Snipes were too real to be feigned. And then our spades showed us that *something* had been buried beneath the corpse, for a hole had been there and it had been filled with loose earth."

"But who could have taken it?" repeated Professor Porter.

"Suspicion might naturally fall on the men of the cruiser," said Lieutenant Charpentier, "but for the fact that sub-lieutenant Janviers here assures me that no men have had shore leave—that none has been on shore since we anchored here except under command of an officer. I do not know that you would suspect our men, but I am glad that there is now no chance for suspicion to fall on them," he concluded.

"It would never have occurred to me to suspect the men to whom we owe so much," replied Professor Porter, graciously. "I would as soon suspect my dear Clayton here, or Mr. Philander."

The Frenchmen smiled, both officers and sailors. It was plain to see that a burden had been lifted from their minds.

"The treasure has been gone for some time," continued Clayton. "In fact the body fell apart as we lifted it, which indicates that whoever removed the treasure did so while the corpse was still fresh, for it was intact when we first uncovered it."

"There must have been several in the party," said Jane, who had joined them. "You remember that it took four men to carry it."

"By jove!" cried Clayton. "That's right. It must have been done by a party of blacks. Probably one of them saw the men bury the chest and then returned immediately after with a party of his friends, and carried it off."

"Speculation is futile," said Professor Porter sadly. "The chest is gone. We shall never see it again, nor the treasure that was in it."

Only Jane knew what the loss meant to her father, and none there knew what it meant to her.

Six days later Captain Dufranne announced that they would sail early on the morrow.

Jane would have begged for a further reprieve, had it not been that she too had begun to believe that her forest lover would return no more.

In spite of herself she began to entertain doubts and fears. The reasonableness of the arguments of these disinterested French officers commenced to convince her against her will.

That he was a cannibal she would not believe, but that he was an adopted member of some savage tribe at length seemed possible to her.

She would not admit that he could be dead. It was impossible to believe that that perfect body, so filled with triumphant life, could ever cease to harbor the vital spark—as soon believe that immortality were dust.

As Jane permitted herself to harbor these thoughts, others equally unwelcome forced themselves upon her.

If he belonged to some savage tribe he had a savage wife—a dozen of them perhaps—and wild, half-caste children. The girl shuddered, and when they told her that the cruiser would sail on the morrow she was almost glad.

It was she, though, who suggested that arms, ammunition, supplies and comforts be left behind in the cabin, ostensibly for that intangible personality who had signed himself Tarzan of the Apes, and for D'Arnot should he still be living, but really, she hoped, for her forest god—even though his feet should prove of clay.

And at the last minute she left a message for him, to be transmitted by Tarzan of the Apes.

She was the last to leave the cabin, returning on some trivial pretext after the others had started for the boat.

She kneeled down beside the bed in which she had spent so many nights, and offered up a prayer for the safety of her primeval man, and crushing his locket to her lips she murmured:

"I love you, and because I love you I believe in you. But if I did not believe, still should I love. Had you come back for me, and had there been no other way, I would have gone into the jungle with you—forever."

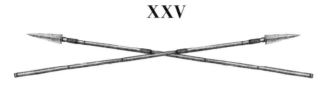

XXV

THE OUTPOST
OF THE WORLD

 ith the report of his gun D'Arnot saw the door fly open and the figure of a man pitch headlong within onto the cabin floor.

The Frenchman in his panic raised his gun to fire again into the prostrate form, but suddenly in the half dusk of the open door he saw that the man was white and in another instant realized that he had shot his friend and protector, Tarzan of the Apes.

With a cry of anguish D'Arnot sprang to the ape-man's side, and kneeling, lifted the latter's head in his arms—calling Tarzan's name aloud.

There was no response, and then D'Arnot placed his ear above the man's heart. To his joy he heard its steady beating beneath.

Carefully he lifted Tarzan to the cot, and then, after closing and bolting the door, he lighted one of the lamps and examined the wound.

The bullet had struck a glancing blow upon the skull. There was an ugly flesh wound, but no signs of a fracture of the skull.

D'Arnot breathed a sigh of relief, and went about bathing the blood from Tarzan's face.

Soon the cool water revived him, and presently he opened his eyes to look in questioning surprise at D'Arnot.

The latter had bound the wound with pieces of cloth, and as he saw that Tarzan had regained consciousness he arose and going to the table wrote a message, which he handed to the ape-man, explaining the terrible mistake he had made and how thankful he was that the wound was not more serious.

Tarzan, after reading the message, sat on the edge of the couch and laughed.

"It is nothing," he said in French, and then, his vocabulary failing him, he wrote:

You should have seen what Bolgani did to me, and Kerchak, and Terkoz, before I killed them—then you would laugh at such a little scratch.

D'Arnot handed Tarzan the two messages that had been left for him.

Tarzan read the first one through with a look of sorrow on his face. The second one he turned over and over, searching for an opening—he had never seen a sealed envelope before. At length he handed it to D'Arnot.

The Frenchman had been watching him, and knew that Tarzan was puzzled over the envelope. How strange it seemed that to a full-grown white man an envelope was a mystery. D'Arnot opened it and handed the letter back to Tarzan.

Sitting on a camp stool the ape-man spread the written sheet before him and read:

To Tarzan of the Apes:

Before I leave let me add my thanks to those of Mr. Clayton for the kindness you have shown in permitting us the use of your cabin.

That you never came to make friends with us has been a great regret to us. We should have liked so much to have seen and thanked our host.

There is another I should like to thank also, but he did not come back, though I cannot believe that he is dead.

I do not know his name. He is the great white giant who wore the diamond locket upon his breast.

If you know him and can speak his language carry my thanks to him, and tell him that I waited seven days for him to return.

Tell him, also, that in my home in America, in the city of Baltimore, there will always be a welcome for him if he cares to come.

I found a note you wrote me lying among the leaves beneath a tree near the cabin. I do not know how you learned to love me, who have never spoken to me, and I am very sorry if it is true, for I have already given my heart to another.

But know that I am always your friend,

JANE PORTER.

Tarzan sat with gaze fixed upon the floor for nearly an hour. It was evident to him from the notes that they did not know that he and Tarzan of the Apes were one and the same.

"I have given my heart to another," he repeated over and over again to himself.

Then she did not love him! How could she have pretended love, and raised him to such a pinnacle of hope only to cast him down to such utter depths of despair!

Maybe her kisses were only signs of friendship. How did he know, who knew nothing of the customs of human beings?

Suddenly he arose, and, bidding D'Arnot good night as he had learned to do, threw himself upon the couch of ferns that had been Jane Porter's.

D'Arnot extinguished the lamp, and lay down upon the cot.

For a week they did little but rest, D'Arnot coaching Tarzan in French. At the end of that time the two men could converse quite easily.

One night, as they were sitting within the cabin before retiring, Tarzan turned to D'Arnot.

"Where is America?" he said.

D'Arnot pointed toward the northwest.

"Many thousands of miles across the ocean," he replied. "Why?"

"I am going there."

D'Arnot shook his head.

"It is impossible, my friend," he said.

Tarzan rose, and, going to one of the cupboards, returned with a well-thumbed geography.

Turning to a map of the world, he said:

"I have never quite understood all this; explain it to me, please."

When D'Arnot had done so, showing him that the blue represented all the water on the earth, and the bits of other colors the continents and islands, Tarzan asked him to point out the spot where they now were.

D'Arnot did so.

"Now point out America," said Tarzan.

And as D'Arnot placed his finger upon North America, Tarzan smiled and laid his palm upon the page, spanning the great ocean that lay between the two continents.

"You see it is not so very far," he said; "scarce the width of my hand."

D'Arnot laughed. How could he make the man understand?

Then he took a pencil and made a tiny point upon the shore of Africa.

"This little mark," he said, "is many times larger upon this map than your cabin is upon the earth. Do you see now how very far it is?"

Tarzan thought for a long time.

"Do any white men live in Africa?" he asked.

"Yes."

"Where are the nearest?"

D'Arnot pointed out a spot on the shore just north of them.

"So close?" asked Tarzan, in surprise.

"Yes," said D'Arnot; "but it is not close."

"Have they big boats to cross the ocean?"

"Yes."

"We shall go there to-morrow," announced Tarzan.

Again D'Arnot smiled and shook his head.

"It is too far. We should die long before we reached them."

"Do you wish to stay here then forever?" asked Tarzan.

"No," said D'Arnot.

"Then we shall start to-morrow. I do not like it here longer. I should rather die than remain here."

"Well," answered D'Arnot, with a shrug, "I do not know, my friend, but that I also would rather die than remain here. If you go, I shall go with you."

"It is settled then," said Tarzan. "I shall start for America to-morrow."

"How will you get to America without money?" asked D'Arnot.

"What is money?" inquired Tarzan.

It took a long time to make him understand even imperfectly.

"How do men get money?" he asked at last.

"They work for it."

"Very well. I will work for it, then."

"No, my friend," returned D'Arnot, "you need not worry about money, nor need you work for it. I have enough money for two—enough for twenty. Much more than is good for one man and you shall have all you need if ever we reach civilization."

So on the following day they started north along the shore. Each man carrying a rifle and ammunition, beside bedding and some food and cooking utensils.

The latter seemed to Tarzan a most useless encumbrance, so he threw his away.

"But you must learn to eat cooked food, my friend," remonstrated D'Arnot. "No civilized men eat raw flesh."

"There will be time enough when I reach civilization," said Tarzan. "I do not like the things and they only spoil the taste of good meat."

For a month they traveled north. Sometimes finding food in plenty and again going hungry for days.

They saw no signs of natives nor were they molested by wild beasts. Their journey was a miracle of ease.

Tarzan asked questions and learned rapidly. D'Arnot taught him many of the refinements of civilization—even to the use of knife and fork; but sometimes Tarzan would drop them in disgust and grasp his food in his strong brown hands, tearing it with his molars like a wild beast.

Then D'Arnot would expostulate with him, saying:

"You must not eat like a brute, Tarzan, while I am trying to make a gentleman of you. *Mon Dieu!* Gentlemen do not thus—it is terrible."

Tarzan would grin sheepishly and pick up his knife and fork again, but at heart he hated them.

On the journey he told D'Arnot about the great chest he had seen the sailors bury; of how he had dug it up and carried it to the gathering place of the apes and buried it there.

"It must be the treasure chest of Professor Porter," said D'Arnot. "It is too bad, but of course you did not know."

Then Tarzan recalled the letter written by Jane to her friend— the one he had stolen when they first came to his cabin, and now he knew what was in the chest and what it meant to Jane.

"To-morrow we shall go back after it," he announced to D'Arnot.

"Go back?" exclaimed D'Arnot. "But, my dear fellow, we have now been three weeks upon the march. It would require three more to return to the treasure, and then, with that enormous weight which required, you say, four sailors to carry, it would be months before we had again reached this spot."

"It must be done, my friend," insisted Tarzan. "You may go on toward civilization, and I will return for the treasure. I can go very much faster alone."

"I have a better plan, Tarzan," exclaimed D'Arnot. "We shall go on together to the nearest settlement, and there we will charter a boat and sail back down the coast for the treasure and so transport it easily. That will be safer and quicker and also not require us to be separated. What do you think of that plan?"

"Very well," said Tarzan. "The treasure will be there whenever we go for it; and while I could fetch it now, and catch up with you in a moon or two, I shall feel safer for you to know that you are not alone on the trail. When I see how helpless you are, D'Arnot, I often wonder how the human race has escaped annihilation all these ages which you tell me about. Why, Sabor, single handed, could exterminate a thousand of you."

D'Arnot laughed.

"You will think more highly of your genus when you have seen its armies and navies, its great cities, and its mighty engineering works. Then you will realize that it is mind, and not muscle, that makes the human animal greater than the mighty beasts of your jungle.

"Alone and unarmed, a single man is no match for any of the larger beasts; but if ten men were together, they would combine their wits and their muscles against their savage enemies, while the beasts, being unable to reason, would never think of combining against the men. Otherwise, Tarzan of the Apes, how long would you have lasted in the savage wilderness?"

"You are right, D'Arnot," replied Tarzan, "for if Kerchak had come to Tublat's aid that night at the Dum-Dum, there would have been an end of me. But Kerchak could never think far enough ahead to take advantage of any such opportunity. Even Kala, my mother, could never plan ahead. She simply ate what she needed when she needed it, and if the supply was very scarce, even though she found plenty for several meals, she would never gather any ahead.

"I remember that she used to think it very silly of me to burden myself with extra food upon the march, though she was quite glad to eat it with me, if the way chanced to be barren of sustenance."

"Then you knew your mother, Tarzan?" asked D'Arnot, in surprise.

"Yes. She was a great, fine ape, larger than I, and weighing twice as much."

"And your father?" asked D'Arnot.

"I did not know him. Kala told me he was a white ape, and hairless like myself. I know now that he must have been a white man."

D'Arnot looked long and earnestly at his companion.

"Tarzan," he said at length, "it is impossible that the ape, Kala, was your mother. If such a thing can be, which I doubt, you would have inherited some of the characteristics of the ape, but you have not—you are pure man, and, I should say, the offspring of highly bred and intelligent parents. Have you not the slightest clue to your past?"

"Not the slightest," replied Tarzan.

"No writings in the cabin that might have told something of the lives of its original inmates?"

"I have read everything that was in the cabin with the exception of one book which I know now to be written in a language other than English. Possibly you can read it."

Tarzan fished the little black diary from the bottom of his quiver, and handed it to his companion.

D'Arnot glanced at the title page.

"It is the diary of John Clayton, Lord Greystoke, an English nobleman, and it is written in French," he said.

Then he proceeded to read the diary that had been written over twenty years before, and which recorded the details of the story which we already know—the story of adventure, hardships and sorrow of John Clayton and his wife Alice, from the day they left England until an hour before he was struck down by Kerchak.

D'Arnot read aloud. At times his voice broke, and he was forced to stop reading for the pitiful hopelessness that spoke between the lines.

Occasionally he glanced at Tarzan; but the ape-man sat upon his haunches, like a carven image, his eyes fixed upon the ground.

Only when the little babe was mentioned did the tone of the diary alter from the habitual note of despair which had crept into it by degrees after the first two months upon the shore.

Then the passages were tinged with a subdued happiness that was even sadder than the rest.

One entry showed an almost hopeful spirit.

> To-day our little boy is six months old. He is sitting in Alice's lap beside the table where I am writing—a happy, healthy, perfect child.
>
> Somehow, even against all reason, I seem to see him a grown man, taking his father's place in the world—the second John Clayton—and bringing added honors to the house of Greystoke.
>
> There—as though to give my prophecy the weight of his endorsement—he has grabbed my pen in his chubby fists and with his inkbegrimed little fingers has placed the seal of his tiny finger prints upon the page.

And there, on the margin of the page, were the partially blurred imprints of four wee fingers and the outer half of the thumb.

When D'Arnot had finished the diary the two men sat in silence for some minutes.

"Well! Tarzan of the Apes, what think you?" asked D'Arnot. "Does not this little book clear up the mystery of your parentage?

"Why man, you are Lord Greystoke."

"The book speaks of but one child," he replied. "Its little skeleton lay in the crib, where it died crying for nourishment, from the first time I entered the cabin until Professor Porter's party buried it, with its father and mother, beside the cabin.

"No, that was the babe the book speaks of—and the mystery of my origin is deeper than before, for I have thought much of late of the possibility of that cabin having been my birthplace. I am afraid that Kala spoke the truth," he concluded sadly.

D'Arnot shook his head. He was unconvinced, and in his mind had sprung the determination to prove the correctness of his theory, for he had discovered the key which alone could unlock the mystery, or consign it forever to the realms of the unfathomable.

A week later the two men came suddenly upon a clearing in the forest.

In the distance were several buildings surrounded by a strong palisade. Between them and the enclosure stretched a cultivated field in which a number of negroes were working.

The two halted at the edge of the jungle.

Tarzan fitted his bow with a poisoned arrow, but D'Arnot placed a hand upon his arm.

"What would you do, Tarzan?" he asked.

"They will try to kill us if they see us," replied Tarzan. "I prefer to be the killer."

"Maybe they are friends," suggested D'Arnot.

"They are black," was Tarzan's only reply.

And again he drew back his shaft.

"You must not, Tarzan!" cried D'Arnot. "White men do not kill wantonly. *Mon Dieu!* but you have much to learn.

"I pity the ruffian who crosses you, my wild man, when I take you to Paris. I will have my hands full keeping your neck from beneath the guillotine."

Tarzan lowered his bow and smiled.

"I do not know why I should kill the blacks back there in my jungle, yet not kill them here. Suppose Numa, the lion, should spring out upon us, I should say, then, I presume: Good morning, Monsieur Numa, how is Madame Numa; eh?"

"Wait until the blacks spring upon you," replied D'Arnot, "then you may kill them. Do not assume that men are your enemies until they prove it."

"Come," said Tarzan, "let us go and present ourselves to be killed," and he started straight across the field, his head high held and the tropical sun beating upon his smooth, brown skin.

Behind him came D'Arnot, clothed in some garments which had been discarded at the cabin by Clayton when the officers of the French cruiser had fitted him out in more presentable fashion.

Presently one of the blacks looked up, and beholding Tarzan, turned, shrieking, toward the palisade.

In an instant the air was filled with cries of terror from the fleeing gardeners, but before any had reached the palisade a white man emerged from the enclosure, rifle in hand, to discover the cause of the commotion.

What he saw brought his rifle to his shoulder, and Tarzan of the Apes would have felt cold lead once again had not D'Arnot cried loudly to the man with the leveled gun:

"Do not fire! We are friends!"

"Halt, then!" was the reply.

"Stop, Tarzan!" cried D'Arnot. "He thinks we are enemies."

Tarzan dropped into a walk, and together he and D'Arnot advanced toward the white man by the gate.

The latter eyed them in puzzled bewilderment.

"What manner of men are you?" he asked, in French.

"White men," replied D'Arnot. "We have been lost in the jungle for a long time."

The man had lowered his rifle and now advanced with outstretched hand.

"I am Father Constantine of the French Mission here," he said, "and I am glad to welcome you."

"This is Monsieur Tarzan, Father Constantine," replied D'Arnot, indicating the ape-man; and as the priest extended his hand to Tarzan, D'Arnot added: "and I am Paul D'Arnot, of the French Navy."

Father Constantine took the hand which Tarzan extended in imitation of the priest's act, while the latter took in the superb physique and handsome face in one quick, keen glance.

And thus came Tarzan of the Apes to the first outpost of civilization.

For a week they remained there, and the ape-man, keenly observant, learned much of the ways of men; meanwhile black women sewed white duck garments for himself and D'Arnot so that they might continue their journey properly clothed.

XXVI

THE HEIGHT
OF CIVILIZATION

nother month brought them to a little group of buildings at the mouth of a wide river, and there Tarzan saw many boats, and was filled with the timidity of the wild thing by the sight of many men.

Gradually he became accustomed to the strange noises and the odd ways of civilization, so that presently none might know that two short months before, this handsome Frenchman in immaculate white ducks, who laughed and chatted with the gayest of them, had been swinging naked through primeval forests to pounce upon some unwary victim, which, raw, was to fill his savage belly.

The knife and fork, so contemptuously flung aside a month before, Tarzan now manipulated as exquisitely as did the polished D'Arnot.

So apt a pupil had he been that the young Frenchman had labored assiduously to make of Tarzan of the Apes a polished gentleman in so far as nicety of manners and speech were concerned.

"God made you a gentleman at heart, my friend," D'Arnot had said; "but we want His works to show upon the exterior also."

As soon as they had reached the little port, D'Arnot had cabled his government of his safety, and requested a three-months' leave, which had been granted.

He had also cabled his bankers for funds, and the enforced wait of a month, under which both chafed, was due to their inability to charter a vessel for the return to Tarzan's jungle after the treasure.

During their stay at the coast town "Monsieur Tarzan" became the wonder of both whites and blacks because of several occurrences which to Tarzan seemed the merest of nothings.

Once a huge black, crazed by drink, had run amuck and terrorized the town, until his evil star had led him to where the black-haired French giant lolled upon the veranda of the hotel.

Mounting the broad steps, with brandished knife, the Negro made straight for a party of four men sitting at a table sipping the inevitable absinthe.

Shouting in alarm, the four took to their heels, and then the black spied Tarzan.

With a roar he charged the ape-man, while half a hundred heads peered from sheltering windows and doorways to witness the butchering of the poor Frenchman by the giant black.

Tarzan met the rush with the fighting smile that the joy of battle always brought to his lips.

As the Negro closed upon him, steel muscles gripped the black wrist of the uplifted knife-hand, and a single swift wrench left the hand dangling below a broken bone.

With the pain and surprise, the madness left the black man, and as Tarzan dropped back into his chair the fellow turned, crying with agony, and dashed wildly toward the native village.

On another occasion as Tarzan and D'Arnot sat at dinner with a number of other whites, the talk fell upon lions and lion hunting.

Opinion was divided as to the bravery of the king of beasts—some maintaining that he was an arrant coward, but all agreeing that it was with a feeling of greater security that they gripped their express rifles when the monarch of the jungle roared about a camp at night.

D'Arnot and Tarzan had agreed that his past be kept secret, and so none other than the French officer knew of the ape-man's familiarity with the beasts of the jungle.

"Monsieur Tarzan has not expressed himself," said one of the party. "A man of his prowess who has spent some time in Africa, as I understand Monsieur Tarzan has, must have had experiences with lions—yes?"

"Some," replied Tarzan, dryly. "Enough to know that each of you are right in your judgment of the characteristics of the lions—you have met. But one might as well judge all blacks by the fellow who ran amuck last week, or decide that all whites are cowards because one has met a cowardly white.

"There is as much individuality among the lower orders, gentlemen, as there is among ourselves. Today we may go out and stumble upon a lion which is over-timid—he runs away from us. To-morrow we may meet his uncle or his twin brother, and our friends wonder why we do not return from the jungle. For myself, I always assume that a lion is ferocious, and so I am never caught off my guard."

"There would be little pleasure in hunting," retorted the first speaker, "if one is afraid of the thing he hunts."

D'Arnot smiled. Tarzan afraid!

"I do not exactly understand what you mean by fear," said Tarzan. "Like lions, fear is a different thing in different men, but to me the only pleasure in the hunt is the knowledge that the hunted thing has power to harm me as much as I have to harm him. If I went out with a couple of rifles and a gun bearer, and twenty or thirty beaters, to hunt a lion, I should not feel that the lion had much chance, and so the pleasure of the hunt would be lessened in proportion to the increased safety which I felt."

"Then I am to take it that Monsieur Tarzan would prefer to go naked into the jungle, armed only with a jackknife, to kill the king of beasts," laughed the other, good naturedly, but with the merest touch of sarcasm in his tone.

"And a piece of rope," added Tarzan.

Just then the deep roar of a lion sounded from the distant jungle, as though to challenge whoever dared enter the lists with him.

"There is your opportunity, Monsieur Tarzan," bantered the Frenchman.

"I am not hungry," said Tarzan simply.

The men laughed, all but D'Arnot. He alone knew that a savage beast had spoken its simple reason through the lips of the ape-man.

"But you are afraid, just as any of us would be, to go out there naked, armed only with a knife and a piece of rope," said the banterer. "Is it not so?"

"No," replied Tarzan. "Only a fool performs any act without reason."

"Five thousand francs is a reason," said the other. "I wager you that amount you cannot bring back a lion from the jungle under the conditions we have named—naked and armed only with a knife and a piece of rope."

Tarzan glanced toward D'Arnot and nodded his head.

"Make it ten thousand," said D'Arnot.

"Done," replied the other.

Tarzan arose.

"I shall have to leave my clothes at the edge of the settlement, so that if I do not return before daylight I shall have something to wear through the streets."

"You are not going now," exclaimed the wagerer—"at night?"

"Why not?" asked Tarzan. "Numa walks abroad at night—it will be easier to find him."

"No," said the other, "I do not want your blood upon my hands. It will be foolhardy enough if you go forth by day."

"I shall go now," replied Tarzan, and went to his room for his knife and rope.

The men accompanied him to the edge of the jungle, where he left his clothes in a small storehouse.

But when he would have entered the blackness of the under-growth they tried to dissuade him; and the wagerer was most insistent of all that he abandon his foolhardy venture.

"I will accede that you have won," he said, "and the ten thousand francs are yours if you will but give up this foolish attempt, which can only end in your death."

Tarzan laughed, and in another moment the jungle had swallowed him.

The men stood silent for some moments and then slowly turned and walked back to the hotel veranda.

Tarzan had no sooner entered the jungle than he took to the trees, and it was with a feeling of exultant freedom that he swung once more through the forest branches.

This was life! Ah, how he loved it! Civilization held nothing like this in its narrow and circumscribed sphere, hemmed in by restrictions and conventionalities. Even clothes were a hindrance and a nuisance.

At last he was free. He had not realized what a prisoner he had been.

How easy it would be to circle back to the coast, and then make toward the south and his own jungle and cabin.

Now he caught the scent of Numa, for he was traveling up wind. Presently his quick ears detected the familiar sound of padded feet and the brushing of a huge, fur-clad body through the undergrowth.

Tarzan came quietly above the unsuspecting beast and silently stalked him until he came into a little patch of moonlight.

Then the quick noose settled and tightened about the tawny throat, and, as he had done it a hundred times in the past, Tarzan made fast the end to a strong branch and, while the beast fought and clawed for freedom, dropped to the ground behind him, and leaping upon the great back, plunged his long thin blade a dozen times into the fierce heart.

Then with his foot upon the carcass of Numa, he raised his voice in the awesome victory cry of his savage tribe.

For a moment Tarzan stood irresolute, swayed by conflicting emotions of loyalty to D'Arnot and a mighty lust for the freedom of his own jungle. At last the vision of a beautiful face, and the memory of warm lips crushed to his dissolved the fascinating picture he had been drawing of his old life.

The ape-man threw the warm carcass of Numa across his shoulders and took to the trees once more.

The men upon the veranda had sat for an hour, almost in silence.

They had tried ineffectually to converse on various subjects, and always the thing uppermost in the mind of each had caused the conversation to lapse.

"*Mon Dieu*," said the wagerer at length, "I can endure it no longer. I am going into the jungle with my express and bring back that mad man."

"I will go with you," said one.

"And I"—"And I"—"And I," chorused the others.

As though the suggestion had broken the spell of some horrid nightmare they hastened to their various quarters, and presently were headed toward the jungle—each one heavily armed.

"God! What was that?" suddenly cried one of the party, an Englishman, as Tarzan's savage cry came faintly to their ears.

"I heard the same thing once before," said a Belgian, "when I was in the gorilla country. My carriers said it was the cry of a great bull ape who has made a kill."

D'Arnot remembered Clayton's description of the awful roar with which Tarzan had announced his kills, and he half smiled in spite of the horror which filled him to think that the uncanny sound could have issued from a human throat—from the lips of his friend.

As the party stood finally near the edge of the jungle, debating as to the best distribution of their forces, they were startled by a low laugh near them, and turning, beheld advancing toward them a giant figure bearing a dead lion upon its broad shoulders.

Even D'Arnot was thunderstruck, for it seemed impossible that the man could have so quickly dispatched a lion with the pitiful weapons he had taken, or that alone he could have borne the huge carcass through the tangled jungle.

The men crowded about Tarzan with many questions, but his only answer was a laughing depreciation of his feat.

To Tarzan it was as though one should eulogize a butcher for his heroism in killing a cow, for Tarzan had killed so often for food and for self-preservation that the act seemed anything but remarkable to him. But he was indeed a hero in the eyes of these men—men accustomed to hunting big game.

Incidentally, he had won ten thousand francs, for D'Arnot insisted that he keep it all.

This was a very important item to Tarzan, who was just commencing to realize the power which lay beyond the little pieces of metal and paper which always changed hands when human beings rode, or ate, or slept, or clothed themselves, or drank, or worked, or played, or sheltered themselves from the rain or cold or sun.

It had become evident to Tarzan that without money one must die. D'Arnot had told him not to worry, since he had more than enough for both, but the ape-man was learning many things and one of them was that people looked down upon one who accepted money from another without giving something of equal value in exchange.

Shortly after the episode of the lion hunt, D'Arnot succeeded in chartering an ancient tub for the coastwise trip to Tarzan's land-locked harbor.

It was a happy morning for them both when the little vessel weighed anchor and made for the open sea.

The trip to the beach was uneventful, and the morning after they dropped anchor before the cabin, Tarzan, garbed once more in his jungle regalia and carrying a spade, set out alone for the amphitheater of the apes where lay the treasure.

Late the next day he returned, bearing the great chest upon his shoulder, and at sunrise the little vessel worked through the harbor's mouth and took up her northward journey.

Three weeks later Tarzan and D'Arnot were passengers on board a French steamer bound for Lyons, and after a few days in that city D'Arnot took Tarzan to Paris.

The ape-man was anxious to proceed to America, but D'Arnot insisted that he must accompany him to Paris first, nor would he divulge the nature of the urgent necessity upon which he based his demand.

One of the first things which D'Arnot accomplished after their arrival was to arrange to visit a high official of the police department, an old friend; and to take Tarzan with him.

Adroitly D'Arnot led the conversation from point to point until the policeman had explained to the interested Tarzan many of the methods in vogue for apprehending and identifying criminals.

Not the least interesting to Tarzan was the part played by finger prints in this fascinating science.

"But of what value are these imprints," asked Tarzan, "when, after a few years the lines upon the fingers are entirely changed by the wearing out of the old tissue and the growth of new?"

"The lines never change," replied the official. "From infancy to senility the fingerprints of an individual change only in size, except as injuries alter the loops and whorls. But if imprints have been taken of the thumb and four fingers of both hands one must needs lose all entirely to escape identification."

"It is marvelous," exclaimed D'Arnot. "I wonder what the lines upon my own fingers may resemble."

"We can soon see," replied the police officer, and ringing a bell he summoned an assistant to whom he issued a few directions.

The man left the room, but presently returned with a little hardwood box which he placed on his superior's desk.

"Now," said the officer, "you shall have your fingerprints in a second."

He drew from the little case a square of plate glass, a little tube of thick ink, a rubber roller, and a few snowy white cards.

Squeezing a drop of ink onto the glass, he spread it back and forth with the rubber roller until the entire surface of the glass was covered to his satisfaction with a very thin and uniform layer of ink.

"Place the four fingers of your right hand upon the glass, thus," he said to D'Arnot. "Now the thumb. That is right. Now place them in just the same position upon this card, here, no—a little to the right. We must leave room for the thumb and the fingers of the left hand. There, that's it. Now the same with the left."

"Come, Tarzan," cried D'Arnot, "let's see what your whorls look like."

Tarzan complied readily, asking many questions of the officer during the operation.

"Do fingerprints show racial characteristics?" he asked. "Could you determine, for example, solely from fingerprints whether the subject was Negro or Caucasian?"

"I think not," replied the officer.

"Could the finger prints of an ape be detected from those of a man?"

"Probably, because the ape's would be far simpler than those of the higher organism."

"But a cross between an ape and a man might show the characteristics of either progenitor?" continued Tarzan.

"Yes, I should think likely," responded the official; "but the science has not progressed sufficiently to render it exact enough in such matters. I should hate to trust its findings further than to differentiate between individuals. There it is absolute. No two people born into the world probably have ever had identical lines upon all their digits. It is very doubtful if any single fingerprint will ever be exactly duplicated by any finger other than the one which originally made it."

"Does the comparison require much time or labor?" asked D'Arnot.

"Ordinarily but a few moments, if the impressions are distinct."

D'Arnot drew a little black book from his pocket and commenced turning the pages.

Tarzan looked at the book in surprise. How did D'Arnot come to have his book?

Presently D'Arnot stopped at a page on which were five tiny little smudges.

He handed the open book to the policeman.

"Are these imprints similar to mine or Monsieur Tarzan's or can you say that they are identical with either?" The officer drew a powerful glass from his desk and examined all three specimens carefully, making notations meanwhile upon a pad of paper.

Tarzan realized now what was the meaning of their visit to the police officer.

The answer to his life's riddle lay in these tiny marks.

With tense nerves he sat leaning forward in his chair, but suddenly he relaxed and dropped back, smiling.

D'Arnot looked at him in surprise.

"You forget that for twenty years the dead body of the child who made those fingerprints lay in the cabin of his father, and that all my life I have seen it lying there," said Tarzan bitterly.

The policeman looked up in astonishment.

"Go ahead, captain, with your examination," said D'Arnot, "we will tell you the story later—provided Monsieur Tarzan is agreeable."

Tarzan nodded his head.

"But you are mad, my dear D'Arnot," he insisted. "Those little fingers are buried on the west coast of Africa."

"I do not know as to that, Tarzan," replied D'Arnot. "It is possible, but if you are not the son of John Clayton then how in heaven's name did you come into that God forsaken jungle where no white man other than John Clayton had ever set foot?"

"You forget—Kala," said Tarzan.

"I do not even consider her," replied D'Arnot.

The friends had walked to the broad window overlooking the boulevard as they talked. For some time they stood there gazing out upon the busy throng beneath, each wrapped in his own thoughts.

"It takes some time to compare finger prints," thought D'Arnot, turning to look at the police officer.

To his astonishment he saw the official leaning back in his chair hastily scanning the contents of the little black diary.

D'Arnot coughed. The policeman looked up, and, catching his eye, raised his finger to admonish silence. D'Arnot turned back to the window, and presently the police officer spoke.

"Gentlemen," he said.

Both turned toward him.

"There is evidently a great deal at stake which must hinge to a greater or lesser extent upon the absolute correctness of this comparison. I therefore ask that you leave the entire matter in my hands until Monsieur Desquerc, our expert returns. It will be but a matter of a few days."

"I had hoped to know at once," said D'Arnot. "Monsieur Tarzan sails for America tomorrow."

"I will promise that you can cable him a report within two weeks," replied the officer; "but what it will be I dare not say. There are resemblances, yet—well, we had better leave it for Monsieur Desquerc to solve."

XXVII

THE GIANT AGAIN

taxicab drew up before an old-fashioned residence upon the outskirts of Baltimore.

A man of about forty, well built and with strong, regular features, stepped out, and paying the chauffeur dismissed him.

A moment later the passenger was entering the library of the old home.

"Ah, Mr. Canler!" exclaimed an old man, rising to greet him.

"Good evening, my dear Professor," cried the man, extending a cordial hand.

"Who admitted you?" asked the professor.

"Esmeralda."

"Then she will acquaint Jane with the fact that you are here," said the old man.

"No, Professor," replied Canler, "for I came primarily to see you."

"Ah, I am honored," said Professor Porter.

"Professor," continued Robert Canler, with great deliberation, as though carefully weighing his words, "I have come this evening to speak with you about Jane."

"You know my aspirations, and you have been generous enough to approve my suit."

Professor Archimedes Q. Porter fidgeted in his armchair. The subject always made him uncomfortable. He could not understand why. Canler was a splendid match.

"But Jane," continued Canler, "I cannot understand her. She puts me off first on one ground and then another. I have always the feeling that she breathes a sigh of relief every time I bid her good-by."

"Tut, tut," said Professor Porter. "Tut, tut, Mr. Canler. Jane is a most obedient daughter. She will do precisely as I tell her."

"Then I can still count on your support?" asked Canler, a tone of relief marking his voice.

"Certainly, sir; certainly, sir," exclaimed Professor Porter. "How could you doubt it?"

"There is young Clayton, you know," suggested Canler. "He has been hanging about for months. I don't know that Jane cares for him; but beside his title they say he has inherited a very considerable estate from his father, and it might not be strange,—if he finally won her, unless—" and Canler paused.

"Tut—tut, Mr. Canler; unless—what?"

"Unless, you see fit to request that Jane and I be married at once," said Canler, slowly and distinctly.

"I have already suggested to Jane that it would be desirable," said Professor Porter sadly, "for we can no longer afford to keep up this house, and live as her associations demand."

"What was her reply?" asked Canler.

"She said she was not ready to marry anyone yet," replied Professor Porter, "and that we could go and live upon the farm in northern Wisconsin which her mother left her.

"It is a little more than self-supporting. The tenants have always made a living from it, and been able to send Jane a trifle beside, each year. She is planning on our going up there the first of the week. Philander and Mr. Clayton have already gone to get things in readiness for us."

"Clayton has gone there?" exclaimed Canler, visibly chagrined. "Why was I not told? I would gladly have gone and seen that every comfort was provided."

"Jane feels that we are already too much in your debt, Mr. Canler," said Professor Porter.

Canler was about to reply, when the sound of footsteps came from the hall without, and Jane entered the room.

"Oh, I beg your pardon!" she exclaimed, pausing on the threshold. "I thought you were alone, papa."

"It is only I, Jane," said Canler, who had risen, "won't you come in and join the family group? We were just speaking of you."

"Thank you," said Jane, entering and taking the chair Canler placed for her. "I only wanted to tell papa that Tobey is coming down from the college tomorrow to pack his books. I want you to be sure, papa, to indicate all that you can do without until fall. Please don't carry this entire library to Wisconsin, as you would have carried it to Africa, if I had not put my foot down."

"Was Tobey here?" asked Professor Porter.

"Yes, I just left him. He and Esmeralda are exchanging religious experiences on the back porch now."

"Tut, tut, I must see him at once!" cried the professor. "Excuse me just a moment, children," and the old man hastened from the room.

As soon as he was out of earshot Canler turned to Jane.

"See here, Jane," he said bluntly. "How long is this thing going on like this? You haven't refused to marry me, but you haven't promised either. I want to get the license tomorrow, so that we can be married quietly before you leave for Wisconsin. I don't care for any fuss or feathers, and I'm sure you don't either."

The girl turned cold, but she held her head bravely.

"Your father wishes it, you know," added Canler.

"Yes, I know."

She spoke scarcely above a whisper.

"Do you realize that you are buying me, Mr. Canler?" she said finally, and in a cold, level voice. "Buying me for a few paltry dollars?

Of course you do, Robert Canler, and the hope of just such a contingency was in your mind when you loaned papa the money for that hair-brained escapade, which but for a most mysterious circumstance would have been surprisingly successful.

"But you, Mr. Canler, would have been the most surprised. You had no idea that the venture would succeed. You are too good a businessman for that. And you are too good a businessman to loan money for buried treasure seeking, or to loan money without security—unless you had some special object in view.

"You knew that without security you had a greater hold on the honor of the Porters than with it. You knew the one best way to force me to marry you, without seeming to force me.

"You have never mentioned the loan. In any other man I should have thought that the prompting of a magnanimous and noble character. But you are deep, Mr. Robert Canler. I know you better than you think I know you.

"I shall certainly marry you if there is no other way, but let us understand each other once and for all."

While she spoke Robert Canler had alternately flushed and paled, and when she ceased speaking he arose, and with a cynical smile upon his strong face, said:

"You surprise me, Jane. I thought you had more self-control—more pride. Of course you are right. I am buying you, and I knew that you knew it, but I thought you would prefer to pretend that it was otherwise. I should have thought your self respect and your Porter pride would have shrunk from admitting, even to yourself, that you were a bought woman. But have it your own way, dear girl," he added lightly. "I am going to have you, and that is all that interests me."

Without a word the girl turned and left the room.

Jane was not married before she left with her father and Esmeralda for her little Wisconsin farm, and as she coldly bid Robert

Canler goodby as her train pulled out, he called to her that he would join them in a week or two.

At their destination they were met by Clayton and Mr. Philander in a huge touring car belonging to the former, and quickly whirled away through the dense northern woods toward the little farm which the girl had not visited before since childhood.

The farmhouse, which stood on a little elevation some hundred yards from the tenant house, had undergone a complete transformation during the three weeks that Clayton and Mr. Philander had been there.

The former had imported a small army of carpenters and plasterers, plumbers and painters from a distant city, and what had been but a dilapidated shell when they reached it was now a cosy little two-story house filled with every modern convenience procurable in so short a time.

"Why, Mr. Clayton, what have you done?" cried Jane Porter, her heart sinking within her as she realized the probable size of the expenditure that had been made.

"S-sh," cautioned Clayton. "Don't let your father guess. If you don't tell him he will never notice, and I simply couldn't think of him living in the terrible squalor and sordidness which Mr. Philander and I found. It was so little when I would like to do so much, Jane. For his sake, please, never mention it."

"But you know that we can't repay you," cried the girl. "Why do you want to put me under such terrible obligations?"

"Don't, Jane," said Clayton sadly. "If it had been just you, believe me, I wouldn't have done it, for I knew from the start that it would only hurt me in your eyes, but I couldn't think of that dear old man living in the hole we found here. Won't you please believe that I did it just for him and give me that little crumb of pleasure at least?"

"I do believe you, Mr. Clayton," said the girl, "because I know you are big enough and generous enough to have done it just for him—and, oh Cecil, I wish I might repay you as you deserve—as you would wish."

"Why can't you, Jane?"

"Because I love another."

"Canler?"

"No."

"But you are going to marry him. He told me as much before I left Baltimore."

The girl winced.

"I do not love him," she said, almost proudly.

"Is it because of the money, Jane?"

She nodded.

"Then am I so much less desirable than Canler? I have money enough, and far more, for every need," he said bitterly.

"I do not love you, Cecil," she said, "but I respect you. If I must disgrace myself by such a bargain with any man, I prefer that it be one I already despise. I should loathe the man to whom I sold myself without love, whomsoever he might be. You will be happier," she concluded, "alone—with my respect and friendship, than with me and my contempt."

He did not press the matter further, but if ever a man had murder in his heart it was William Cecil Clayton, Lord Greystoke, when, a week later, Robert Canler drew up before the farmhouse in his purring six cylinder.

A week passed; a tense, uneventful, but uncomfortable week for all the inmates of the little Wisconsin farmhouse.

Canler was insistent that Jane marry him at once.

At length she gave in from sheer loathing of the continued and hateful importuning.

It was agreed that on the morrow Canler was to drive to town and bring back the license and a minister.

Clayton had wanted to leave as soon as the plan was announced, but the girl's tired, hopeless look kept him. He could not desert her.

Something might happen yet, he tried to console himself by thinking. And in his heart, he knew that it would require but a tiny spark to turn his hatred for Canler into the blood lust of the killer.

Early the next morning Canler set out for town.

In the east smoke could be seen lying low over the forest, for a fire had been raging for a week not far from them, but the wind still lay in the west and no danger threatened them.

About noon Jane started off for a walk. She would not let Clayton accompany her. She wanted to be alone, she said, and he respected her wishes.

In the house Professor Porter and Mr. Philander were immersed in an absorbing discussion of some weighty scientific problem. Esmeralda dozed in the kitchen, and Clayton, heavy-eyed after a sleepless night, threw himself down upon the couch in the living room and soon dropped into a fitful slumber.

To the east the black smoke clouds rose higher into the heavens, suddenly they eddied, and then commenced to drift rapidly toward the west.

On and on they came. The inmates of the tenant house were gone, for it was market day, and none was there to see the rapid approach of the fiery demon.

Soon the flames had spanned the road to the south and cut off Canler's return. A little fluctuation of the wind now carried the path of the forest fire to the north, then blew back and the flames nearly stood still as though held in leash by some master hand.

Suddenly, out of the northeast, a great black car came careening down the road.

With a jolt it stopped before the cottage, and a black-haired giant leaped out to run up onto the porch. Without a pause he rushed into the house. On the couch lay Clayton. The man started in surprise, but with a bound was at the side of the sleeping man.

Shaking him roughly by the shoulder, he cried:

"My God, Clayton, are you all mad here? Don't you know you are nearly surrounded by fire? Where is Miss Porter?"

Clayton sprang to his feet. He did not recognize the man, but he understood the words and was upon the veranda in a bound.

"Scott!" he cried, and then, dashing back into the house, "Jane! Jane! where are you?"

In an instant Esmeralda, Professor Porter and Mr. Philander had joined the two men.

"Where is Miss Jane?" cried Clayton, seizing Esmeralda by the shoulders and shaking her roughly.

"Oh, Gaberelle, Mister Clayton, she done gone for a walk."

"Hasn't she come back yet?" and, without waiting for a reply, Clayton dashed out into the yard, followed by the others. "Which way did she go?" cried the black-haired giant of Esmeralda.

"Down that road," cried the frightened woman, pointing toward the south where a mighty wall of roaring flames shut out the view.

"Put these people in the other car," shouted the stranger to Clayton. "I saw one as I drove up—and get them out of here by the north road.

"Leave my car here. If I find Miss Porter we shall need it. If I don't, no one will need it. Do as I say," as Clayton hesitated, and then they saw the lithe figure bound away cross the clearing toward the northwest where the forest still stood, untouched by flame.

In each rose the unaccountable feeling that a great responsibility had been raised from their shoulders; a kind of implicit confidence in the power of the stranger to save Jane if she could be saved.

"Who was that?" asked Professor Porter.

"I do not know," replied Clayton. "He called me by name and he knew Jane, for he asked for her. And he called Esmeralda by name."

"There was something most startlingly familiar about him,"

exclaimed Mr. Philander, "And yet, bless me, I know I never saw him before."

"Tut, tut!" cried Professor Porter. "Most remarkable! Who could it have been, and why do I feel that Jane is safe, now that he has set out in search of her?"

"I can't tell you, Professor," said Clayton soberly, "but I know I have the same uncanny feeling."

"But come," he cried, "we must get out of here ourselves, or we shall be shut off," and the party hastened toward Clayton's car.

When Jane turned to retrace her steps homeward, she was alarmed to note how near the smoke of the forest fire seemed, and as she hastened onward her alarm became almost a panic when she perceived that the rushing flames were rapidly forcing their way between herself and the cottage.

At length she was compelled to turn into the dense thicket and attempt to force her way to the west in an effort to circle around the flames and reach the house.

In a short time the futility of her attempt became apparent and then her one hope lay in retracing her steps to the road and flying for her life to the south toward the town.

The twenty minutes that it took her to regain the road was all that had been needed to cut off her retreat as effectually as her advance had been cut off before.

A short run down the road brought her to a horrified stand, for there before her was another wall of flame. An arm of the main conflagration had shot out a half mile south of its parent to embrace this tiny strip of road in its implacable clutches.

Jane knew that it was useless again to attempt to force her way through the undergrowth.

She had tried it once, and failed. Now she realized that it would be but a matter of minutes ere the whole space between the north and the south would be a seething mass of billowing flames.

Calmly the girl kneeled down in the dust of the roadway and prayed for strength to meet her fate bravely, and for the delivery of her father and her friends from death.

Suddenly she heard her name being called aloud through the forest:

"Jane! Jane Porter!" It rang strong and clear, but in a strange voice.

"Here!" she called in reply. "Here! In the roadway!"

Then through the branches of the trees she saw a figure swinging with the speed of a squirrel.

A veering of the wind blew a cloud of smoke about them and she could no longer see the man who was speeding toward her, but suddenly she felt a great arm about her. Then she was lifted up, and she felt the rushing of the wind and the occasional brush of a branch as she was borne along.

She opened her eyes.

Far below her lay the undergrowth and the hard earth.

About her was the waving foliage of the forest.

From tree to tree swung the giant figure which bore her, and it seemed to Jane that she was living over in a dream the experience that had been hers in that far African jungle.

Oh, if it were but the same man who had borne her so swiftly through the tangled verdure on that other day! but that was impossible! Yet who else in all the world was there with the strength and agility to do what this man was now doing?

She stole a sudden glance at the face close to hers, and then she gave a little frightened gasp. It was he!

"My forest man!" she murmured, "No, I must be delerious!"

"Yes, your man, Jane Porter. Your savage, primeval man come out of the jungle to claim his mate—the woman who ran away from him," he added almost fiercely.

"I did not run away," she whispered. "I would only consent to leave when they had waited a week for you to return."

They had come to a point beyond the fire now, and he had turned back to the clearing.

Side by side they were walking toward the cottage. The wind had changed once more and the fire was burning back upon itself—another hour like that and it would be burned out.

"Why did you not return?" she asked.

"I was nursing D'Arnot. He was badly wounded."

"Ah, I knew it!" she exclaimed.

"They said you had gone to join the blacks—that they were your people."

He laughed.

"But you did not believe them, Jane?"

"No;—what shall I call you?" she asked. "What is your name?"

"I was Tarzan of the Apes when you first knew me," he said.

"Tarzan of the Apes!" she cried—"and that was your note I answered when I left?"

"Yes, whose did you think it was?"

"I did not know; only that it could not be yours, for Tarzan of the Apes had written in English, and you could not understand a word of any language."

Again he laughed.

"It is a long story, but it was I who wrote what I could not speak—and now D'Arnot has made matters worse by teaching me to speak French instead of English.

"Come," he added, "jump into my car, we must overtake your father, they are only a little way ahead."

As they drove along, he said:

"Then when you said in your note to Tarzan of the Apes that you loved another—you might have meant me?"

"I might have," she answered, simply.

"But in Baltimore—Oh, how I have searched for you—they told

me you would possibly be married by now. That a man named Canler had come up here to wed you. Is that true?"

"Yes."

"Do you love him?"

"No."

"Do you love me?"

She buried her face in her hands.

"I am promised to another. I cannot answer you, Tarzan of the Apes," she cried.

"You have answered. Now, tell me why you would marry one you do not love."

"My father owes him money."

Suddenly there came back to Tarzan the memory of the letter he had read—and the name Robert Canler and the hinted trouble which he had been unable to understand then.

He smiled.

"If your father had not lost the treasure you would not feel forced to keep your promise to this man Canler?"

"I could ask him to release me."

"And if he refused?"

"I have given my promise."

He was silent for a moment. The car was plunging along the uneven road at a reckless pace, for the fire showed threateningly at their right, and another change of the wind might sweep it on with raging fury across this one avenue of escape.

Finally they passed the danger point, and Tarzan reduced their speed.

"Suppose I should ask him?" ventured Tarzan.

"He would scarcely accede to the demand of a stranger," said the girl. "Especially one who wanted me himself."

"Terkoz did," said Tarzan, grimly.

Jane shuddered and looked fearfully up at the giant figure beside her, for she knew that he meant the great anthropoid he had killed in her defense.

"This is not the African jungle," she said. "You are no longer a savage beast. You are a gentleman, and gentlemen do not kill in cold blood."

"I am still a wild beast at heart," he said, in a low voice, as though to himself.

Again they were silent for a time.

"Jane," said the man, at length, "if you were free, would you marry me?"

She did not reply at once, but he waited patiently.

The girl was trying to collect her thoughts.

What did she know of this strange creature at her side? What did he know of himself? Who was he? Who, his parents?

Why, his very name echoed his mysterious origin and his savage life.

He had no name. Could she be happy with this jungle waif? Could she find anything in common with a husband whose life had been spent in the tree tops of an African wilderness, frolicking and fighting with fierce anthropoids; tearing his food from the quivering flank of fresh-killed prey, sinking his strong teeth into raw flesh, and tearing away his portion while his mates growled and fought about him for their share?

Could he ever rise to her social sphere? Could she bear to think of sinking to his? Would either be happy in such a horrible misalliance?

"You do not answer," he said. "Do you shrink from wounding me?"

"I do not know what answer to make," said Jane sadly. "I do not know my own mind."

"You do not love me, then?" he asked, in a level tone.

"Do not ask me. You will be happier without me. You were never meant for the formal restrictions and conventionalities of society—civilization would become irksome to you, and in a little while you would long for the freedom of your old life—a life to which I am as totally unfitted as you to mine."

"I think I understand you," he replied quietly. "I shall not urge you, for I would rather see you happy than to be happy myself. I see now that you could not be happy with—an ape."

There was just the faintest tinge of bitterness in his voice.

"Don't," she remonstrated. "Don't say that. You do not understand."

But before she could go on a sudden turn in the road brought them into the midst of a little hamlet.

Before them stood Clayton's car surrounded by the party he had brought from the cottage.

XXVIII

CONCLUSION

At the sight of Jane, cries of relief and delight broke from every lip, and as Tarzan's car stopped beside the other, Professor Porter caught his daughter in his arms.

For a moment no one noticed Tarzan, sitting silently in his seat.

Clayton was the first to remember, and, turning, held out his hand.

"How can we ever thank you?" he exclaimed. "You have saved us all. You called me by name at the cottage, but I do not seem to recall yours, though there is something very familiar about you. It is as though I had known you well under very different conditions a long time ago."

Tarzan smiled as he took the proffered hand.

"You are quite right, Monsieur Clayton," he said, in French. "You will pardon me if I do not speak to you in English. I am just learning it, and while I understand it fairly well I speak it very poorly."

"But who are you?" insisted Clayton, speaking in French this time himself.

"Tarzan of the Apes."

Clayton started back in surprise.

"By Jove!" he exclaimed. "It is true."

And Professor Porter and Mr. Philander pressed forward to add their thanks to Clayton's, and to voice their surprise and pleasure at seeing their jungle friend so far from his savage home.

The party now entered the modest little hostelry, where Clayton soon made arrangements for their entertainment.

They were sitting in the little, stuffy parlor when the distant chugging of an approaching automobile caught their attention.

Mr. Philander, who was sitting near the window, looked out as the car drew in sight, finally stopping beside the other automobiles.

"Bless me!" said Mr. Philander, a shade of annoyance in his tone. "It is Mr. Canler. I had hoped, er—I had thought or—er—how very happy we should be that he was not caught in the fire," he ended lamely.

"Tut, tut! Mr. Philander," said Professor Porter. "Tut, tut! I have often admonished my pupils to count ten before speaking. Were I you, Mr. Philander, I should count at least a thousand, and then maintain a discreet silence."

"Bless me, yes!" acquiesced Mr. Philander. "But who is the clerical appearing gentleman with him?"

Jane blanched.

Clayton moved uneasily in his chair.

Professor Porter removed his spectacles nervously, and breathed upon them, but replaced them on his nose without wiping.

The ubiquitous Esmeralda grunted.

Only Tarzan did not comprehend.

Presently Robert Canler burst into the room.

"Thank God!" he cried. "I feared the worst, until I saw your car, Clayton. I was cut off on the south road and had to go away back to town, and then strike east to this road. I thought we'd never reach the cottage."

No one seemed to enthuse much. Tarzan eyed Robert Canler as Sabor eyes her prey.

Jane glanced at him and coughed nervously.

"Mr. Canler," she said, "this is Monsieur Tarzan, an old friend."

Canler turned and extended his hand. Tarzan rose and bowed as only D'Arnot could have taught a gentleman to do it, but he did not seem to see Canler's hand.

Nor did Canler appear to notice the oversight.

"This is the Reverend Mr. Tousley, Jane," said Canler, turning to the clerical party behind him. "Mr. Tousley, Miss Porter."

Mr. Tousley bowed and beamed.

Canler introduced him to the others.

"We can have the ceremony at once, Jane," said Canler. "Then you and I can catch the midnight train in town."

Tarzan understood the plan instantly. He glanced out of half-closed eyes at Jane, but he did not move.

The girl hesitated. The room was tense with the silence of taut nerves.

All eyes turned toward Jane, awaiting her reply.

"Can't we wait a few days?" she asked. "I am all unstrung. I have been through so much today."

Canler felt the hostility that emanated from each member of the party. It made him angry.

"We have waited as long as I intend to wait," he said roughly. "You have promised to marry me. I shall be played with no longer. I have the license and here is the preacher. Come Mr. Tousley; come Jane. There are plenty of witnesses—more than enough," he added with a disagreeable inflection; and taking Jane Porter by the arm, he started to lead her toward the waiting minister.

But scarcely had he taken a single step ere a heavy hand closed upon his arm with a grip of steel.

Another hand shot to his throat and in a moment he was being shaken high above the floor, as a cat might shake a mouse.

Jane turned in horrified surprise toward Tarzan.

And, as she looked into his face, she saw the crimson band upon his forehead that she had seen that other day in far distant Africa, when Tarzan of the Apes had closed in mortal combat with the great anthropoid—Terkoz.

She knew that murder lay in that savage heart, and with a little cry of horror she sprang forward to plead with the ape-man. But her fears were more for Tarzan than for Canler. She realized the stern retribution which justice metes to the murderer.

Before she could reach them, however, Clayton had jumped to Tarzan's side and attempted to drag Canler from his grasp.

With a single sweep of one mighty arm the Englishman was hurled across the room, and then Jane laid a firm white hand upon Tarzan's wrist, and looked up into his eyes.

"For my sake," she said.

The grasp upon Canler's throat relaxed.

Tarzan looked down into the beautiful face before him.

"Do you wish this to live?" he asked in surprise.

"I do not wish him to die at your hands, my friend," she replied. "I do not wish you to become a murderer."

Tarzan removed his hand from Canler's throat.

"Do you release her from her promise?" he asked. "It is the price of your life."

Canler, gasping for breath, nodded.

"Will you go away and never molest her further?"

Again the man nodded his head, his face distorted by fear of the death that had been so close.

Tarzan released him, and Canler staggered toward the door. In another moment he was gone, and the terror-stricken preacher with him.

Tarzan turned toward Jane.

"May I speak with you for a moment, alone," he asked.

The girl nodded and started toward the door leading to the narrow veranda of the little hotel. She passed out to await Tarzan and so did not hear the conversation which followed.

"Wait," cried Professor Porter, as Tarzan was about to follow.

The professor had been stricken dumb with surprise by the rapid developments of the past few minutes.

"Before we go further, sir, I should like an explanation of the events which have just transpired. By what right, sir, did you interfere between my daughter and Mr. Canler? I had promised him her hand, sir, and regardless of our personal likes or dislikes, sir, that promise must be kept."

"I interfered, Professor Porter," replied Tarzan, "because your daughter does not love Mr. Canler—she does not wish to marry him. That is enough for me to know."

"You do not know what you have done," said Professor Porter. "Now he will doubtless refuse to marry her."

"He most certainly will," said Tarzan, emphatically.

"And further," added Tarzan, "you need not fear that your pride will suffer, Professor Porter, for you will be able to pay the Canler person what you owe him the moment you reach home."

"Tut, tut, sir!" exclaimed Professor Porter. "What do you mean, sir?"

"Your treasure has been found," said Tarzan.

"What—what is that you are saying?" cried the professor. "You are mad, man. It cannot be."

"It is, though. It was I who stole it, not knowing either its value or to whom it belonged. I saw the sailors bury it, and, ape-like, I had to dig it up and bury it again elsewhere. When D'Arnot told me what it was and what it meant to you I returned to the jungle and recovered it. It had caused so much crime and suffering and sorrow that D'Arnot thought it best not to attempt to bring the treasure itself on here, as had been my intention, so I have brought a letter of credit instead.

"Here it is, Professor Porter," and Tarzan drew an envelope from his pocket and handed it to the astonished professor, "two hundred and forty-one thousand dollars. The treasure was most carefully appraised by experts, but lest there should be any question in your mind, D'Arnot himself bought it and is holding it for you, should you prefer the treasure to the credit."

"To the already great burden of the obligations we owe you, sir," said Professor Porter, with trembling voice, "is now added this greatest of all services. You have given me the means to save my honor."

Clayton, who had left the room a moment after Canler, now returned.

"Pardon me," he said. "I think we had better try to reach town before dark and take the first train out of this forest. A native just rode by from the north, who reports that the fire is moving slowly in this direction."

This announcement broke up further conversation, and the entire party went out to the waiting automobiles.

Clayton, with Jane, the professor and Esmeralda occupied Clayton's car, while Tarzan took Mr. Philander in with him.

"Bless me!" exclaimed Mr. Philander, as the car moved off after Clayton. "Who would ever have thought it possible! The last time I saw you you were a veritable wild man, skipping about among the branches of a tropical African forest, and now you are driving me along a Wisconsin road in a French automobile. Bless me! But it is most remarkable."

"Yes," assented Tarzan, and then, after a pause, "Mr. Philander, do you recall any of the details of the finding and burying of three skeletons found in my cabin beside that African jungle?"

"Very distinctly, sir, very distinctly," replied Mr. Philander.

"Was there anything peculiar about any of those skeletons?"

Mr. Philander eyed Tarzan narrowly.

"Why do you ask?"

"It means a great deal to me to know," replied Tarzan. "Your answer may clear up a mystery. It can do no worse, at any rate, than to leave it still a mystery. I have been entertaining a theory concerning those skeletons for the past two months, and I want you to answer my question to the best of your knowledge—were the three skeletons you buried all human skeletons?"

"No," said Mr. Philander, "the smallest one, the one found in the crib, was the skeleton of an anthropoid ape."

"Thank you," said Tarzan.

In the car ahead, Jane was thinking fast and furiously. She had felt the purpose for which Tarzan had asked a few words with her, and she knew that she must be prepared to give him an answer in the very near future.

He was not the sort of person one could put off, and somehow that very thought made her wonder if she did not really fear him.

And could she love where she feared?

She realized the spell that had been upon her in the depths of that far-off jungle, but there was no spell of enchantment now in prosaic Wisconsin.

Nor did the immaculate young Frenchman appeal to the primal woman in her, as had the stalwart forest god.

Did she love him? She did not know—now.

She glanced at Clayton out of the corner of her eye. Was not here a man trained in the same school of environment in which she had been trained—a man with social position and culture such as she had been taught to consider as the prime essentials to congenial association?

Did not her best judgment point to this young English nobleman, whose love she knew to be of the sort a civilized woman should crave, as the logical mate for such as herself?

Could she love Clayton? She could see no reason why she could not. Jane was not coldly calculating by nature, but training, environment and heredity had all combined to teach her to reason even in matters of the heart.

That she had been carried off her feet by the strength of the young giant when his great arms were about her in the distant African forest, and again today, in the Wisconsin woods, seemed to her only attributable to a temporary mental reversion to type on her part—to the psychological appeal of the primeval man to the primeval woman in her nature.

If he should never touch her again, she reasoned, she would never feel attracted toward him. She had not loved him, then. It had been nothing more than a passing hallucination, super-induced by excitement and by personal contact.

Excitement would not always mark their future relations, should she marry him, and the power of personal contact eventually would be dulled by familiarity.

Again she glanced at Clayton. He was very handsome and every inch a gentleman. She should be very proud of such a husband.

And then he spoke—a minute sooner or a minute later might have made all the difference in the world to three lives—but chance stepped in and pointed out to Clayton the psychological moment.

"You are free now, Jane," he said. "Won't you say yes—I will devote my life to making you very happy."

"Yes," she whispered.

That evening in the little waiting room at the station Tarzan caught Jane alone for a moment.

"You are free now, Jane," he said, "and *I* have come across the ages out of the dim and distant past from the lair of the primeval man to claim you—for your sake I have become a civilized man—for your sake I have crossed oceans and continents—for your sake I will be whatever you will me to be. I can make you happy, Jane, in the life you know and love best. Will you marry me?"

For the first time she realized the depths of the man's love—all that he had accomplished in so short a time solely for love of her. Turning her head she buried her face in her arms.

What had she done? Because she had been afraid she might succumb to the pleas of this giant, she had burned her bridges behind her—in her groundless apprehension that she might make a terrible mistake, she had made a worse one.

And then she told him all—told him the truth word by word, without attempting to shield herself or condone her error.

"What can we do?" he asked. "You have admitted that you love me. You know that I love you; but I do not know the ethics of society by which you are governed. I shall leave the decision to you, for you know best what will be for your eventual welfare."

"I cannot tell him, Tarzan," she said. "He too, loves me, and he is a good man. I could never face you nor any other honest person if I repudiated my promise to Mr. Clayton. I shall have to keep it—and you must help me bear the burden, though we may not see each other again after tonight."

The others were entering the room now and Tarzan turned toward the little window.

But he saw nothing outside—within he saw a patch of greensward surrounded by a matted mass of gorgeous tropical plants and flowers, and, above, the waving foliage of mighty trees, and, over all, the blue of an equatorial sky.

In the center of the greensward a young woman sat upon a little mound of earth, and beside her sat a young giant. They ate pleasant fruit and looked into each other's eyes and smiled. They were very happy, and they were all alone.

His thoughts were broken in upon by the station agent who entered asking if there was a gentleman by the name of Tarzan in the party.

"I am Monsieur Tarzan," said the ape-man.

"Here is a message for you, forwarded from Baltimore; it is a cablegram from Paris."

Tarzan took the envelope and tore it open. The message was from D'Arnot.

It read:

Fingerprints prove you Greystoke. Congratulations.

D'ARNOT.

As Tarzan finished reading, Clayton entered and came toward him with extended hand.

Here was the man who had Tarzan's title, and Tarzan's estates, and was going to marry the woman whom Tarzan loved—the woman who loved Tarzan. A single word from Tarzan would make a great difference in this man's life.

It would take away his title and his lands and his castles, and—it would take them away from Jane Porter also. "I say, old man," cried Clayton, "I haven't had a chance to thank you for all you've done for us. It seems as though you had your hands full saving our lives in Africa and here.

"I'm awfully glad you came on here. We must get better acquainted. I often thought about you, you know, and the remarkable circumstances of your environment.

"If it's any of my business, how the devil did you ever get into that bally jungle?"

"I was born there," said Tarzan, quietly. "My mother was an Ape, and of course she couldn't tell me much about it. I never knew who my father was."

The Return of
TARZAN

The Adventures of Lord Greystoke:
Book Two

CONTENTS

I

The Affair
on the Liner

Magnifique!" ejaculated the Countess de Coude, beneath her breath.

"Eh?" questioned the count, turning toward his young wife. "What is it that is magnificent?" and the count bent his eyes in various directions in quest of the object of her admiration.

"Oh, nothing at all, my dear," replied the countess, a slight flush momentarily coloring her already pink cheek. "I was but recalling with admiration those stupendous skyscrapers, as they call them, of New York," and the fair countess settled herself more comfortably in her steamer chair, and resumed the magazine which "nothing at all" had caused her to let fall upon her lap.

Her husband again buried himself in his book, but not without a mild wonderment that three days out from New York his countess should suddenly have realized an admiration for the very buildings she had but recently characterized as horrid.

Presently the count put down his book. "It is very tiresome, Olga," he said. "I think that I shall hunt up some others who may be equally bored, and see if we cannot find enough for a game of cards."

"You are not very gallant, my husband," replied the young woman, smiling, "but as I am equally bored I can forgive you. Go and play at your tiresome old cards, then, if you will."

When he had gone she let her eyes wander slyly to the figure of a tall young man stretched lazily in a chair not far distant.

"*Magnifique!*" she breathed once more.

The Countess Olga de Coude was twenty. Her husband forty. She was a very faithful and loyal wife, but as she had had nothing whatever to do with the selection of a husband, it is not at all unlikely that she was not wildly and passionately in love with the one that fate and her titled Russian father had selected for her. However, simply because she was surprised into a tiny exclamation of approval at sight of a splendid young stranger it must not be inferred there from that her thoughts were in any way disloyal to her spouse. She merely admired, as she might have admired a particularly fine specimen of any species. Furthermore, the young man was unquestionably good to look at.

As her furtive glance rested upon his profile he rose to leave the deck. The Countess de Coude beckoned to a passing steward. "Who is that gentleman?" she asked.

"He is booked, madam, as Monsieur Tarzan, of Africa," replied the steward.

"Rather a large estate," thought the girl, but now her interest was still further aroused.

As Tarzan walked slowly toward the smoking-room he came unexpectedly upon two men whispering excitedly just without. He would have vouchsafed them not even a passing thought but for the strangely guilty glance that one of them shot in his direction. They reminded Tarzan of melodramatic villains he had seen at the theaters in Paris. Both were very dark, and this, in connection with the shrugs and stealthy glances that accompanied their palpable intriguing, lent still greater force to the similarity.

Tarzan entered the smoking-room, and sought a chair a little apart from the others who were there. He felt in no mood for conversation, and as he sipped his absinth he let his mind run rather sorrowfully over the past few weeks of his life. Time and again he had wondered if he had acted wisely in renouncing his birthright to a man to whom he owed nothing. It is true that he liked Clayton, but—ah, but that was not the question. It was not for William Cecil Clayton, Lord Greystoke, that he had denied his birth. It was for the woman whom both he and Clayton had loved, and whom a strange freak of fate had given to Clayton instead of to him.

That she loved him made the thing doubly difficult to bear, yet he knew that he could have done nothing less than he did do that night within the little railway station in the far Wisconsin woods. To him her happiness was the first consideration of all, and his brief experience with civilization and civilized men had taught him that without money and position life to most of them was unendurable.

Jane Porter had been born to both, and had Tarzan taken them away from her future husband it would doubtless have plunged her into a life of misery and torture. That she would have spurned Clayton once he had been stripped of both his title and his estates never for once occurred to Tarzan, for he credited to others the same honest loyalty that was so inherent a quality in himself. Nor, in this instance, had he erred. Could any one thing have further bound Jane Porter to her promise to Clayton it would have been in the nature of some such misfortune as this overtaking him.

Tarzan's thoughts drifted from the past to the future. He tried to look forward with pleasurable sensations to his return to the jungle of his birth and boyhood; the cruel, fierce jungle in which he had spent twenty of his twenty-two years. But who or what of all the myriad jungle life would there be to welcome his return? Not one. Only Tantor, the elephant, could he call friend. The others would hunt him or flee from him as had been their way in the past.

Not even the apes of his own tribe would extend the hand of fellowship to him.

If civilization had done nothing else for Tarzan of the Apes, it had to some extent taught him to crave the society of his own kind, and to feel with genuine pleasure the congenial warmth of companionship. And in the same ratio had it made any other life distasteful to him. It was difficult to imagine a world without a friend—without a living thing who spoke the new tongues which Tarzan had learned to love so well. And so it was that Tarzan looked with little relish upon the future he had mapped out for himself.

As he sat musing over his cigarette his eyes fell upon a mirror before him, and in it he saw reflected a table at which four men sat at cards. Presently one of them rose to leave, and then another approached, and Tarzan could see that he courteously offered to fill the vacant chair, that the game might not be interrupted. He was the smaller of the two whom Tarzan had seen whispering just outside the smoking-room.

It was this fact that aroused a faint spark of interest in Tarzan, and so as he speculated upon the future he watched in the mirror the reflection of the players at the table behind him. Aside from the man who had but just entered the game Tarzan knew the name of but one of the other players. It was he who sat opposite the new player, Count Raoul de Coude, whom an over-attentive steward had pointed out as one of the celebrities of the passage, describing him as a man high in the official family of the French minister of war.

Suddenly Tarzan's attention was riveted upon the picture in the glass. The other swarthy plotter had entered, and was standing behind the count's chair. Tarzan saw him turn and glance furtively about the room, but his eyes did not rest for a sufficient time upon the mirror to note the reflection of Tarzan's watchful eyes. Stealthily the man withdrew something from his pocket. Tarzan could not discern what the object was, for the man's hand covered it.

Slowly the hand approached the count, and then, very deftly, the thing that was in it was transferred to the count's pocket. The man remained standing where he could watch the Frenchman's cards.

Tarzan was puzzled, but he was all attention now, nor did he permit another detail of the incident to escape him.

The play went on for some ten minutes after this, until the count won a considerable wager from him who had last joined the game, and then Tarzan saw the fellow back of the count's chair nod his head to his confederate. Instantly the player arose and pointed a finger at the count.

"Had I known that monsieur was a professional card sharp I had not been so ready to be drawn into the game," he said.

Instantly the count and the two other players were upon their feet. De Coude's face went white.

"What do you mean, sir?" he cried. "Do you know to whom you speak?"

"I know that I speak, for the last time, to one who cheats at cards," replied the fellow.

The count leaned across the table, and struck the man full in the mouth with his open palm, and then the others closed in between them.

"There is some mistake, sir," cried one of the other players. "Why, this is Count de Coude, of France." "If I am mistaken," said the accuser, "I shall gladly apologize; but before I do so first let monsieur le count explain the extra cards which I saw him drop into his side pocket."

And then the man whom Tarzan had seen drop them there turned to sneak from the room, but to his annoyance he found the exit barred by a tall, gray-eyed stranger.

"Pardon," said the man brusquely, attempting to pass to one side.

"Wait," said Tarzan.

"But why, monsieur?" exclaimed the other petulantly. "Permit me to pass, monsieur."

"Wait," said Tarzan. "I think that there is a matter in here that you may doubtless be able to explain."

The fellow had lost his temper by this time, and with a low oath seized Tarzan to push him to one side. The ape-man but smiled as he twisted the big fellow about and, grasping him by the collar of his coat, escorted him back to the table, struggling, cursing, and striking in futile remonstrance. It was Nikolas Rokoff's first experience with the muscles that had brought their savage owner victorious through encounters with Numa, the lion, and Terkoz, the great bull ape.

The man who had accused De Coude, and the two others who had been playing, stood looking expectantly at the count. Several other passengers had drawn toward the scene of the altercation, and all awaited the denouement.

"The fellow is crazy," said the count. "Gentlemen, I implore that one of you search me."

"The accusation is ridiculous." This from one of the players.

"You have but to slip your hand in the count's coat pocket and you will see that the accusation is quite serious," insisted the accuser. And then, as the others still hesitated to do so: "Come, I shall do it myself if no other will," and he stepped forward toward the count.

"No, monsieur," said De Coude. "I will submit to a search only at the hands of a gentleman."

"It is unnecessary to search the count. The cards are in his pocket. I myself saw them placed there."

All turned in surprise toward this new speaker, to behold a very well-built young man urging a resisting captive toward them by the scruff of his neck.

"It is a conspiracy," cried De Coude angrily. "There are no cards in my coat," and with that he ran his hand into his pocket. As he did so tense silence reigned in the little group. The count went dead white, and then very slowly he withdrew his hand, and in it were three cards.

He looked at them in mute and horrified surprise, and slowly the red of mortification suffused his face. Expressions of pity and contempt tinged the features of those who looked on at the death of a man's honor.

"It is a conspiracy, monsieur." It was the gray-eyed stranger who spoke. "Gentlemen," he continued, "monsieur le count did not know that those cards were in his pocket. They were placed there without his knowledge as he sat at play. From where I sat in that chair yonder I saw the reflection of it all in the mirror before me. This person whom I just intercepted in an effort to escape placed the cards in the count's pocket."

De Coude had glanced from Tarzan to the man in his grasp.

"*Mon Dieu,* Nikolas!" he cried. "You?"

Then he turned to his accuser, and eyed him intently for a moment.

"And you, monsieur, I did not recognize you without your beard. It quite disguises you, Paulvitch. I see it all now. It is quite clear, gentlemen."

"What shall we do with them, monsieur?" asked Tarzan. "Turn them over to the captain?"

"No, my friend," said the count hastily. "It is a personal matter, and I beg that you will let it drop. It is sufficient that I have been exonerated from the charge. The less we have to do with such fellows, the better. But, monsieur, how can I thank you for the great kindness you have done me? Permit me to offer you my card, and should the time come when I may serve you, remember that I am yours to command."

Tarzan had released Rokoff, who, with his confederate, Paulvitch, had hastened from the smoking-room. Just as he was leaving, Rokoff turned to Tarzan. "Monsieur will have ample opportunity to regret his interference in the affairs of others."

Tarzan smiled, and then, bowing to the count, handed him his own card.

The count read:

M. JEAN C. TARZAN

"Monsieur Tarzan," he said, "may indeed wish that he had never befriended me, for I can assure him that he has won the enmity of two of the most unmitigated scoundrels in all Europe. Avoid them, monsieur, by all means."

"I have had more awe-inspiring enemies, my dear count," replied Tarzan with a quiet smile, "yet I am still alive and unworried. I think that neither of these two will ever find the means to harm me."

"Let us hope not, monsieur," said De Coude; "but yet it will do no harm to be on the alert, and to know that you have made at least one enemy today who never forgets and never forgives, and in whose malignant brain there are always hatching new atrocities to perpetrate upon those who have thwarted or offended him. To say that Nikolas Rokoff is a devil would be to place a wanton affront upon his satanic majesty."

That night as Tarzan entered his cabin he found a folded note upon the floor that had evidently been pushed beneath the door. He opened it and read:

M. TARZAN:

Doubtless you did not realize the gravity of your offense, or you would not have done the thing you did today. I am willing to believe that you acted in ignorance and without any intention to offend a stranger. For this reason I shall gladly permit you to offer an apology, and on receiving your assurances that you will not again interfere in affairs that do not concern you, I shall drop the matter.

Otherwise—but I am sure that you will see the wisdom of adopting the course I suggest.

Very respectfully,

NIKOLAS ROKOFF.

Tarzan permitted a grim smile to play about his lips for a moment, then he promptly dropped the matter from his mind, and went to bed.

In a nearby cabin the Countess de Coude was speaking to her husband.

"Why so grave, my dear Raoul?" she asked. "You have been as glum as could be all evening. What worries you?"

"Olga, Nikolas is on board. Did you know it?"

"Nikolas!" she exclaimed. "But it is impossible, Raoul. It cannot be. Nikolas is under arrest in Germany."

"So I thought myself until I saw him today—him and that other arch scoundrel, Paulvitch. Olga, I cannot endure his persecution much longer. No, not even for you. Sooner or later I shall turn him over to the authorities. In fact, I am half minded to explain all to the captain before we land. On a French liner it were an easy matter, Olga, permanently to settle this Nemesis of ours."

"Oh, no, Raoul!" cried the countess, sinking to her knees before him as he sat with bowed head upon a divan. "Do not do that. Remember your promise to me. Tell me, Raoul, that you will not do that. Do not even threaten him, Raoul."

De Coude took his wife's hands in his, and gazed upon her pale and troubled countenance for some time before he spoke, as though he would wrest from those beautiful eyes the real reason which prompted her to shield this man.

"Let it be as you wish, Olga," he said at length. "I cannot understand. He has forfeited all claim upon your love, loyalty, or respect. He is a menace to your life and honor, and the life and honor of your husband. I trust you may never regret championing him."

"I do not champion him, Raoul," she interrupted vehemently. "I believe that I hate him as much as you do, but—Oh, Raoul, blood is thicker than water."

"I should today have liked to sample the consistency of his," growled De Coude grimly. "The two deliberately attempted to besmirch my honor, Olga," and then he told her of all that had happened in the smoking-room. "Had it not been for this utter stranger, they had succeeded, for who would have accepted my unsupported word against the damning evidence of those cards hidden on my person? I had almost begun to doubt myself when this Monsieur Tarzan dragged your precious Nikolas before us, and explained the whole cowardly transaction."

"Monsieur Tarzan?" asked the countess, in evident surprise.

"Yes. Do you know him, Olga?"

"I have seen him. A steward pointed him out to me."

"I did not know that he was a celebrity," said the count.

Olga de Coude changed the subject. She discovered suddenly that she might find it difficult to explain just why the steward had pointed out the handsome Monsieur Tarzan to her. Perhaps she flushed the least little bit, for was not the count, her husband, gazing at her with a strangely quizzical expression. "Ah," she thought, "a guilty conscience is a most suspicious thing."

II

FORGING BONDS
OF HATE AND—?

t was not until late the following afternoon that Tarzan saw anything more of the fellow passengers into the midst of whose affairs his love of fair play had thrust him. And then he came most unexpectedly upon Rokoff and Paulvitch at a moment when of all others the two might least appreciate his company.

They were standing on deck at a point which was temporarily deserted, and as Tarzan came upon them they were in heated argument with a woman. Tarzan noted that she was richly appareled, and that her slender, well-modeled figure denoted youth; but as she was heavily veiled he could not discern her features.

The men were standing on either side of her, and the backs of all were toward Tarzan, so that he was quite close to them without their being aware of his presence. He noticed that Rokoff seemed to be threatening, the woman pleading; but they spoke in a strange tongue, and he could only guess from appearances that the girl was afraid.

Rokoff's attitude was so distinctly filled with the threat of physical violence that the ape-man paused for an instant just behind the trio, instinctively sensing an atmosphere of danger. Scarcely had he hesitated ere the man seized the woman roughly by the wrist, twisting it as though to wring a promise from her through torture. What would have happened next had Rokoff had his way we may only conjecture, since he did not have his way at all. Instead, steel fingers gripped his shoulder, and he was swung unceremoniously around, to meet the cold gray eyes of the stranger who had thwarted him on the previous day.

"*Sapristi!*" screamed the infuriated Rokoff. "What do you mean? Are you a fool that you thus again insult Nikolas Rokoff?"

"This is my answer to your note, monsieur," said Tarzan, in a low voice. And then he hurled the fellow from him with such force that Rokoff lunged sprawling against the rail.

"Name of a name!" shrieked Rokoff. "Pig, but you shall die for this," and, springing to his feet, he rushed upon Tarzan, tugging the meanwhile to draw a revolver from his hip pocket. The girl shrank back in terror.

"Nikolas!" she cried. "Do not—oh, do not do that. Quick, monsieur, fly, or he will surely kill you!" But instead of flying Tarzan advanced to meet the fellow. "Do not make a fool of yourself, monsieur," he said.

Rokoff, who was in a perfect frenzy of rage at the humiliation the stranger had put upon him, had at last succeeded in drawing the revolver. He had stopped, and now he deliberately raised it to Tarzan's breast and pulled the trigger. The hammer fell with a futile click on an empty chamber—the ape-man's hand shot out like the head of an angry python; there was a quick wrench, and the revolver sailed far out across the ship's rail, and dropped into the Atlantic.

For a moment the two men stood there facing one another. Rokoff had regained his self-possession. He was the first to speak.

"Twice now has monsieur seen fit to interfere in matters which do not concern him. Twice he has taken it upon himself to humiliate Nikolas Rokoff. The first offense was overlooked on the assumption that monsieur acted through ignorance, but this affair shall not be overlooked. If monsieur does not know who Nikolas Rokoff is, this last piece of effrontery will insure that monsieur later has good reason to remember him."

"That you are a coward and a scoundrel, monsieur," replied Tarzan, "is all that I care to know of you," and he turned to ask the girl if the man had hurt her, but she had disappeared. Then, without even a glance toward Rokoff and his companion, he continued his stroll along the deck.

Tarzan could not but wonder what manner of conspiracy was on foot, or what the scheme of the two men might be. There had been something rather familiar about the appearance of the veiled woman to whose rescue he had just come, but as he had not seen her face he could not be sure that he had ever seen her before. The only thing about her that he had particularly noticed was a ring of peculiar workmanship upon a finger of the hand that Rokoff had seized, and he determined to note the fingers of the women passengers he came upon thereafter, that he might discover the identity of her whom Rokoff was persecuting, and learn if the fellow had offered her further annoyance.

Tarzan had sought his deck chair, where he sat speculating on the numerous instances of human cruelty, selfishness, and spite that had fallen to his lot to witness since that day in the jungle four years since that his eyes had first fallen upon a human being other than himself—the sleek, black Kulonga, whose swift spear had that day found the vitals of Kala, the great she-ape, and robbed the youth, Tarzan, of the only mother he had ever known.

He recalled the murder of King by the rat-faced Snipes; the abandonment of Professor Porter and his party by the mutineers of the *Arrow*; the cruelty of the black warriors and women of Mbonga to their captives; the petty jealousies of the civil and military officers of of the West Coast colony that had afforded him his first introduction to the civilized world.

"*Mon Dieu!*" he soliloquized, "but they are all alike. Cheating, murdering, lying, fighting, and all for things that the beasts of the jungle would not deign to possess—money to purchase the effeminate pleasures of weaklings. And yet withal bound down by silly customs that make them slaves to their unhappy lot while firm in the belief that they be the lords of creation enjoying the only real pleasures of existence. In the jungle one would scarcely stand supinely aside while another took his mate. It is a silly world, an idiotic world, and Tarzan of the Apes was a fool to renounce the freedom and the happiness of his jungle to come into it."

Presently, as he sat there, the sudden feeling came over him that eyes were watching from behind, and the old instinct of the wild beast broke through the thin veneer of civilization, so that Tarzan wheeled about so quickly that the eyes of the young woman who had been surreptitiously regarding him had not even time to drop before the gray eyes of the ape-man shot an inquiring look straight into them. Then, as they fell, Tarzan saw a faint wave of crimson creep swiftly over the now half-averted face.

He smiled to himself at the result of his very uncivilized and ungallant action, for he had not lowered his own eyes when they met those of the young woman. She was very young, and equally good to look upon. Further, there was something rather familiar about her that set Tarzan to wondering where he had seen her before. He resumed his former position, and presently he was aware that she had arisen and was leaving the deck. As she passed, Tarzan turned to watch her, in the hope that he might discover a clew to satisfy his mild curiosity as to her identity.

Nor was he disappointed entirely, for as she walked away she raised one hand to the black, waving mass at the nape of her neck— the peculiarly feminine gesture that admits cognizance of appraising eyes behind her—and Tarzan saw upon a finger of this hand the ring of strange workmanship that he had seen upon the finger of the veiled woman a short time before.

So it was this beautiful young woman Rokoff had been persecuting. Tarzan wondered in a lazy sort of way whom she might be, and what relations one so lovely could have with the surly, bearded Russian.

After dinner that evening Tarzan strolled forward, where he remained until after dark, in conversation with the second officer, and when that gentleman's duties called him elsewhere Tarzan lolled lazily by the rail watching the play of the moonlight upon the gently rolling waters. He was half hidden by a davit, so that two men who approached along the deck did not see him, and as they passed Tarzan caught enough of their conversation to cause him to fall in behind them, to follow and learn what deviltry they were up to. He had recognized the voice as that of Rokoff, and had seen that his companion was Paulvitch.

Tarzan had overheard but a few words: "And if she screams you may choke her until——" But those had been enough to arouse the spirit of adventure within him, and so he kept the two men in sight as they walked, briskly now, along the deck. To the smoking-room he followed them, but they merely halted at the doorway long enough, apparently, to assure themselves that one whose whereabouts they wished to establish was within.

Then they proceeded directly to the first-class cabins upon the promenade deck. Here Tarzan found greater difficulty in escaping detection, but he managed to do so successfully. As they halted before one of the polished hardwood doors, Tarzan slipped into the shadow of a passageway not a dozen feet from them.

To their knock a woman's voice asked in French: "Who is it?"

"It is I, Olga—Nikolas," was the answer, in Rokoff's now familiar guttural. "May I come in?"

"Why do you not cease persecuting me, Nikolas?" came the voice of the woman from beyond the thin panel. "I have never harmed you."

"Come, come, Olga," urged the man, in propitiary tones; "I but ask a half dozen words with you. I shall not harm you, nor shall I enter your cabin; but I cannot shout my message through the door."

Tarzan heard the catch click as it was released from the inside. He stepped out from his hiding-place far enough to see what transpired when the door was opened, for he could not but recall the sinister words he had heard a few moments before upon the deck, "And if she screams you may choke her."

Rokoff was standing directly in front of the door. Paulvitch had flattened himself against the paneled wall of the corridor beyond. The door opened. Rokoff half entered the room, and stood with his back against the door, speaking in a low whisper to the woman, whom Tarzan could not see. Then Tarzan heard the woman's voice, level, but loud enough to distinguish her words.

"No, Nikolas," she was saying, "it is useless. Threaten as you will, I shall never accede to your demands. Leave the room, please; you have no right here. You promised not to enter."

"Very well, Olga, I shall not enter; but before I am done with you, you shall wish a thousand times that you had done at once the favor I have asked. In the end I shall win anyway, so you might as well save trouble and time for me, and disgrace for yourself and your—"

"Never, Nikolas!" interrupted the woman, and then Tarzan saw Rokoff turn and nod to Paulvitch, who sprang quickly toward the doorway of the cabin, rushing in past Rokoff, who held the door open for him. Then the latter stepped quickly out. The door closed. Tarzan heard the click of the lock as Paulvitch turned it from the inside. Rokoff remained standing before the door, with head bent, as though to catch the words of the two within. A nasty smile curled his bearded lip.

Tarzan could hear the woman's voice commanding the fellow to leave her cabin. "I shall send for my husband," she cried. "He will show you no mercy."

Paulvitch's sneering laugh came through the polished panels.

"The purser will fetch your husband, madame," said the man.

"In fact, that officer has already been notified that you are entertaining a man other than your husband behind the locked door of your cabin."

"Bah!" cried the woman. "My husband will know!"

"Most assuredly your husband will know, but the purser will not; nor will the newspaper men who shall in some mysterious way hear of it on our landing. But they will think it a fine story, and so will all your friends when they read of it at breakfast on—let me see, this is Tuesday—yes, when they read of it at breakfast next Friday morning. Nor will it detract from the interest they will all feel when they learn that the man whom madame entertained is a Russian servant—her brother's valet, to be quite exact."

"Alexis Paulvitch," came the woman's voice, cold and fearless, "you are a coward, and when I whisper a certain name in your ear you will think better of your demands upon me and your threats against me, and then you will leave my cabin quickly, nor do I think that ever again will you, at least, annoy me," and there came a moment's silence in which Tarzan could imagine the woman leaning toward the scoundrel and whispering the thing she had hinted at into his ear. Only a moment of silence, and then a startled oath from the man— the scuffling of feet—a woman's scream—and silence.

But scarcely had the cry ceased before the ape-man had leaped from his hiding-place. Rokoff started to run, but Tarzan grasped him by the collar and dragged him back. Neither spoke, for both felt instinctively that murder was being done in that room, and Tarzan was confident that Rokoff had had no intention that his confederate should go that far—he felt that the man's aims were deeper than that—deeper and even more sinister than brutal, cold-blooded murder. Without hesitating to question those within, the ape-man threw his giant shoulder against the frail panel, and in a shower of splintered wood he entered the cabin, dragging Rokoff after him. Before him, on a couch, the woman lay, and on top of her was Paulvitch, his fingers gripping the fair throat, while his victim's hands beat futilely at his face, tearing desperately at the cruel fingers that were forcing the life from her.

The noise of his entrance brought Paulvitch to his feet, where he stood glowering menacingly at Tarzan. The girl rose falteringly to a sitting posture upon the couch. One hand was at her throat, and her breath came in little gasps. Although disheveled and very pale, Tarzan recognized her as the young woman whom he had caught staring at him on deck earlier in the day.

"What is the meaning of this?" said Tarzan, turning to Rokoff, whom he intuitively singled out as the instigator of the outrage. The man remained silent, scowling. "Touch the button, please," continued the ape-man; "we will have one of the ship's officers here—this affair has gone quite far enough."

"No, no," cried the girl, coming suddenly to her feet. "Please do not do that. I am sure that there was no real intention to harm me. I angered this person, and he lost control of himself, that is all. I would not care to have the matter go further, please, monsieur," and there was such a note of pleading in her voice that Tarzan could not press the matter, though his better judgment warned him that there was something afoot here of which the proper authorities should be made cognizant.

"You wish me to do nothing, then, in the matter?" he asked.

"Nothing, please," she replied.

"You are content that these two scoundrels should continue persecuting you?"

She did not seem to know what answer to make, and looked very troubled and unhappy. Tarzan saw a malicious grin of triumph curl Rokoff's lip. The girl evidently was in fear of these two—she dared not express her real desires before them.

"Then," said Tarzan, "I shall act on my own responsibility. To you," he continued, turning to Rokoff, "and this includes your accomplice, I may say that from now on to the end of the voyage I shall take it upon myself to keep an eye on you, and should there chance to come to my notice any act of either one of you that might even remotely annoy this young woman you shall be called to account for it directly to me, nor shall the calling or the accounting be pleasant experiences for either of you.

"Now get out of here," and he grabbed Rokoff and Paulvitch each by the scruff of the neck and thrust them forcibly through the doorway, giving each an added impetus down the corridor with the toe of his boot. Then he turned back to the stateroom and the girl. She was looking at him in wide-eyed astonishment.

"And you, madame, will confer a great favor upon me if you will but let me know if either of those rascals troubles you further."

"Ah, monsieur," she answered, "I hope that you will not suffer for the kind deed you attempted. You have made a very wicked and resourceful enemy, who will stop at nothing to satisfy his hatred. You must be very careful indeed, Monsieur—"

"Pardon me, madame, my name is Tarzan."

"Monsieur Tarzan. And because I would not consent to notify the officers, do not think that I am not sincerely grateful to you for the brave and chivalrous protection you rendered me. Good night, Monsieur Tarzan. I shall never forget the debt I owe you," and, with a most winsome smile that displayed a row of perfect teeth, the girl curtsied to Tarzan, who bade her good night and made his way on deck.

It puzzled the man considerably that there should be two on board—this girl and Count de Coude—who suffered indignities at the hands of Rokoff and his companion, and yet would not permit the offenders to be brought to justice. Before he turned in that night his thoughts reverted many times to the beautiful young woman into the evidently tangled web of whose life fate had so strangely introduced him. It occurred to him that he had not learned her name. That she was married had been evidenced by the narrow gold band that encircled the third finger of her left hand. Involuntarily he wondered who the lucky man might be.

Tarzan saw nothing further of any of the actors in the little drama that he had caught a fleeting glimpse of until late in the afternoon of the last day of the voyage. Then he came suddenly face to face with the young woman as the two approached their deck chairs from opposite directions. She greeted him with a pleasant smile, speaking almost immediately of the affair he had witnessed in her cabin two nights before. It was as though she had been perturbed by a conviction that he might have construed her acquaintance with such men as Rokoff and Paulvitch as a personal reflection upon herself.

"I trust monsieur has not judged me," she said, "by the unfortunate occurrence of Tuesday evening. I have suffered much on account of it—this is the first time that I have ventured from my cabin since; I have been ashamed," she concluded simply.

"One does not judge the gazelle by the lions that attack it," replied Tarzan. "I had seen those two work before—in the smoking-room the day prior to their attack on you, if I recollect it correctly, and so, knowing their methods, I am convinced that their enmity is a sufficient guarantee of the integrity of its object. Men such as they must cleave only to the vile, hating all that is noblest and best."

"It is very kind of you to put it that way," she replied, smiling. "I have already heard of the matter of the card game. My husband told me the entire story. He spoke especially of the strength and bravery of Monsieur Tarzan, to whom he feels that he owes an immense debt of gratitude."

"Your husband?" repeated Tarzan questioningly.

"Yes. I am the Countess de Coude."

"I am already amply repaid, madame, in knowing that I have rendered a service to the wife of the Count de Coude."

"Alas, monsieur, I already am so greatly indebted to you that I may never hope to settle my own account, so pray do not add further to my obligations," and she smiled so sweetly upon him that Tarzan felt that a man might easily attempt much greater things than he had accomplished, solely for the pleasure of receiving the benediction of that smile.

He did not see her again that day, and in the rush of landing on the following morning he missed her entirely, but there had been something in the expression of her eyes as they parted on deck the previous day that haunted him. It had been almost wistful as they had spoken of the strangeness of the swift friendships of an ocean crossing, and of the equal ease with which they are broken forever.

Tarzan wondered if he should ever see her again.

III

WHAT HAPPENED IN THE RUE MAULE

 n his arrival in Paris, Tarzan had gone directly to the apartments of his old friend, D'Arnot, where the naval lieutenant had scored him roundly for his decision to renounce the title and estates that were rightly his from his father, John Clayton, the late Lord Greystoke.

"You must be mad, my friend," said D'Arnot, "thus lightly to give up not alone wealth and position, but an opportunity to prove beyond doubt to all the world that in your veins flows the noble blood of two of England's most honored houses—instead of the blood of a savage she-ape. It is incredible that they could have believed you—Miss Porter least of all.

"Why, I never did believe it, even back in the wilds of your African jungle, when you tore the raw meat of your kills with mighty jaws, like some wild beast, and wiped your greasy hands upon your thighs. Even then, before there was the slightest proof to the contrary, I knew that you were mistaken in the belief that Kala was your mother.

"And now, with your father's diary of the terrible life led by him and your mother on that wild African shore; with the account of your birth, and, final and most convincing proof of all, your own baby finger prints upon the pages of it, it seems incredible to me that you are willing to remain a nameless, penniless vagabond."

"I do not need any better name than Tarzan," replied the ape-man; "and as for remaining a penniless vagabond, I have no intention of so doing. In fact, the next, and let us hope the last, burden that I shall be forced to put upon your unselfish friendship will be the finding of employment for me."

"Pooh, pooh!" scoffed D'Arnot. "You know that I did not mean that. Have I not told you a dozen times that I have enough for twenty men, and that half of what I have is yours? And if I gave it all to you, would it represent even the tenth part of the value I place upon your friendship, my Tarzan? Would it repay the services you did me in Africa? I do not forget, my friend, that but for you and your wondrous bravery I had died at the stake in the village of Mbonga's cannibals. Nor do I forget that to your self-sacrificing devotion I owe the fact that I recovered from the terrible wounds I received at their hands—I discovered later something of what it meant to you to remain with me in the amphitheater of apes while your heart was urging you on to the coast.

"When we finally came there, and found that Miss Porter and her party had left, I commenced to realize something of what you had done for an utter stranger. Nor am I trying to repay you with money, Tarzan. It is that just at present you need money; were it sacrifice that I might offer you it were the same—my friendship must always be yours, because our tastes are similar, and I admire you. That I cannot command, but the money I can and shall."

"Well," laughed Tarzan, "we shall not quarrel over the money. I must live, and so I must have it; but I shall be more contented with something to do. You cannot show me your friendship in a more convincing manner than to find employment for me—I shall die of inactivity in a short while. As for my birthright—it is in good hands. Clayton is not guilty of robbing me of it. He truly believes that he is the real Lord Greystoke, and the chances are that he will make a better English lord than a man who was born and raised in an African jungle. You know that I am but half civilized even now. Let me see red in anger but for a moment, and all the instincts of the savage beast that I really am, submerge what little I possess of the milder ways of culture and refinement.

"And then again, had I declared myself I should have robbed the woman I love of the wealth and position that her marriage to Clayton will now insure to her. I could not have done that—could I, Paul?

"Nor is the matter of birth of great importance to me," he went on, without waiting for a reply. "Raised as I have been, I see no worth in man or beast that is not theirs by virtue of their own mental or physical prowess. And so I am as happy to think of Kala as my mother as I would be to try to picture the poor, unhappy little English girl who passed away a year after she bore me. Kala was always kind to me in her fierce and savage way. I must have nursed at her hairy breast from the time that my own mother died. She fought for me against the wild denizens of the forest, and against the savage members of our tribe, with the ferocity of real mother love.

"And I, on my part, loved her, Paul. I did not realize how much until after the cruel spear and the poisoned arrow of Mbonga's black warrior had stolen her away from me. I was still a child when that occurred, and I threw myself upon her dead body and wept out my anguish as a child might for his own mother. To you, my friend, she would have appeared a hideous and ugly creature, but to me she was beautiful—so gloriously does love transfigure its object. And so I am perfectly content to remain forever the son of Kala, the she-ape."

"I do not admire you the less for your loyalty," said D'Arnot, "but the time will come when you will be glad to claim your own. Remember what I say, and let us hope that it will be as easy then as it is now. You must bear in mind that Professor Porter and Mr. Philander are the only people in the world who can swear that the little skeleton found in the cabin with those of your father and mother was that of an infant anthropoid ape, and not the offspring of Lord and Lady Greystoke. That evidence is most important. They are both old men. They may not live many years longer. And then, did it not occur to you that once Miss Porter knew the truth she would break her engagement with Clayton? You might easily have your title, your estates, and the woman you love, Tarzan. Had you not thought of that?"

Tarzan shook his head. "You do not know her," he said. "Nothing could bind her closer to her bargain than some misfortune to Clayton. She is from an old southern family in America, and southerners pride themselves upon their loyalty."

Tarzan spent the two following weeks renewing his former brief acquaintance with Paris. In the daytime he haunted the libraries and picture galleries. He had become an omnivorous reader, and the world of possibilities that were opened to him in this seat of culture and learning fairly appalled him when he contemplated the very infinitesimal crumb of the sum total of human knowledge that a single individual might hope to acquire even after a lifetime of study and research; but he learned what he could by day, and threw himself into a search for relaxation and amusement at night. Nor did he find Paris a whit less fertile field for his nocturnal avocation.

If he smoked too many cigarettes and drank too much absinth it was because he took civilization as he found it, and did the things that he found his civilized brothers doing. The life was a new and alluring one, and in addition he had a sorrow in his breast and a great longing which he knew could never be fulfilled, and so he sought in study and in dissipation—the two extremes—to forget the past and inhibit contemplation of the future.

He was sitting in a music hall one evening, sipping his absinth and admiring the art of a certain famous Russian dancer, when he caught a passing glimpse of a pair of evil black eyes upon him. The man turned and was lost in the crowd at the exit before Tarzan could catch a good look at him, but he was confident that he had seen those eyes before and that they had been fastened on him this evening through no passing accident. He had had the uncanny feeling for some time that he was being watched, and it was in response to this animal instinct that was strong within him that he had turned suddenly and surprised the eyes in the very act of watching him.

Before he left the music hall the matter had been forgotten, nor did he notice the swarthy individual who stepped deeper into the shadows of an opposite doorway as Tarzan emerged from the brilliantly lighted amusement hall.

Had Tarzan but known it, he had been followed many times from this and other places of amusement, but seldom if ever had he been alone. Tonight D'Arnot had had another engagement, and Tarzan had come by himself.

As he turned in the direction he was accustomed to taking from this part of Paris to his apartments, the watcher across the street ran from his hiding-place and hurried on ahead at a rapid pace.

Tarzan had been wont to traverse the Rue Maule on his way home at night. Because it was very quiet and very dark it reminded him more of his beloved African jungle than did the noisy and garish streets surrounding it. If you are familiar with your Paris you will recall the narrow, forbidding precincts of the Rue Maule. If you are not, you need but ask the police about it to learn that in all Paris there is no street to which you should give a wider berth after dark.

On this night Tarzan had proceeded some two squares through the dense shadows of the squalid old tenements which line this dismal way when he was attracted by screams and cries for help from the third floor of an opposite building. The voice was a woman's. Before the echoes of her first cries had died Tarzan was bounding up the stairs and through the dark corridors to her rescue.

At the end of the corridor on the third landing a door stood slightly ajar, and from within Tarzan heard again the same appeal that had lured him from the street. Another instant found him in the center of a dimly-lighted room. An oil lamp burned upon a high, old-fashioned mantel, casting its dim rays over a dozen repulsive figures. All but one were men. The other was a woman of about thirty. Her face, marked by low passions and dissipation, might once have been lovely. She stood with one hand at her throat, crouching against the farther wall.

"Help, monsieur," she cried in a low voice as Tarzan entered the room; "they were killing me."

As Tarzan turned toward the men about him he saw the crafty, evil faces of habitual criminals. He wondered that they had made no effort to escape. A movement behind him caused him to turn. Two things his eyes saw, and one of them caused him considerable wonderment. A man was sneaking stealthily from the room, and in the brief glance that Tarzan had of him he saw that it was Rokoff. But the other thing that he saw was of more immediate interest. It was a great brute of a fellow tiptoeing upon him from behind with a huge bludgeon in his hand, and then, as the man and his confederates saw that he was discovered, there was a concerted rush upon Tarzan from all sides. Some of the men drew knives. Others picked up chairs, while the fellow with the bludgeon raised it high above his head in a mighty swing that would have crushed Tarzan's head had it ever descended upon it.

But the brain, and the agility, and the muscles that had coped with the mighty strength and cruel craftiness of Terkoz and Numa in the fastness of their savage jungle were not to be so easily subdued as these apaches of Paris had believed.

Selecting his most formidable antagonist, the fellow with the bludgeon, Tarzan charged full upon him, dodging the falling weapon, and catching the man a terrific blow on the point of the chin that felled him in his tracks.

Then he turned upon the others. This was sport. He was reveling in the joy of battle and the lust of blood. As though it had been but a brittle shell, to break at the least rough usage, the thin veneer of his civilization fell from him, and the ten burly villains found themselves penned in a small room with a wild and savage beast, against whose steel muscles their puny strength was less than futile.

At the end of the corridor without stood Rokoff, waiting the outcome of the affair. He wished to be sure that Tarzan was dead before he left, but it was not a part of his plan to be one of those within the room when the murder occurred.

The woman still stood where she had when Tarzan entered, but her face had undergone a number of changes with the few minutes which had elapsed. From the semblance of distress which it had worn when Tarzan first saw it, it had changed to one of craftiness as he had wheeled to meet the attack from behind; but the change Tarzan had not seen.

Later an expression of surprise and then one of horror super-seded the others. And who may wonder. For the immaculate gentle-man her cries had lured to what was to have been his death had been suddenly metamorphosed into a demon of revenge. Instead of soft muscles and a weak resistance, she was looking upon a veritable Hercules gone mad.

"*Mon Dieu!*" she cried; "he is a beast!" For the strong, white teeth of the ape-man had found the throat of one of his assailants, and Tarzan fought as he had learned to fight with the great bull apes of the tribe of Kerchak.

He was in a dozen places at once, leaping hither and thither about the room in sinuous bounds that reminded the woman of a panther she had seen at the zoo. Now a wrist-bone snapped in his iron grip, now a shoulder was wrenched from its socket as he forced a victim's arm backward and upward.

With shrieks of pain the men escaped into the hallway as quickly as they could; but even before the first one staggered, bleeding and broken, from the room, Rokoff had seen enough to convince him that Tarzan would not be the one to lie dead in that house this night, and so the Russian had hastened to a nearby den and telephoned the police that a man was committing murder on the third floor of Rue Maule, 27. When the officers arrived they found three men groaning on the floor, a frightened woman lying upon a filthy bed, her face buried in her arms, and what appeared to be a well-dressed young gentleman standing in the center of the room awaiting the reenforcements which he had thought the footsteps of the officers hurrying up the stairway had announced—but they were mistaken in the last; it was a wild beast that looked upon them through those narrowed lids and steel-gray eyes. With the smell of blood the last vestige of civilization had deserted Tarzan, and now he stood at bay, like a lion surrounded by hunters, awaiting the next overt act, and crouching to charge its author.

"What has happened here?" asked one of the policemen.

Tarzan explained briefly, but when he turned to the woman for confirmation of his statement he was appalled by her reply.

"He lies!" she screamed shrilly, addressing the policeman. "He came to my room while I was alone, and for no good purpose. When I repulsed him he would have killed me had not my screams attracted these gentlemen, who were passing the house at the time. He is a devil, monsieurs; alone he has all but killed ten men with his bare hands and his teeth."

So shocked was Tarzan by her ingratitude that for a moment he was struck dumb. The police were inclined to be a little skeptical, for they had had other dealings with this same lady and her lovely coterie of gentlemen friends. However, they were policemen, not judges, so they decided to place all the inmates of the room under arrest, and let another, whose business it was, separate the innocent from the guilty.

But they found that it was one thing to tell this well-dressed young man that he was under arrest, but quite another to enforce it.

"I am guilty of no offense," he said quietly. "I have but sought to defend myself. I do not know why the woman has told you what she has. She can have no enmity against me, for never until I came to this room in response to her cries for help had I seen her."

"Come, come," said one of the officers; "there are judges to listen to all that," and he advanced to lay his hand upon Tarzan's shoulder. An instant later he lay crumpled in a corner of the room, and then, as his comrades rushed in upon the ape-man, they experienced a taste of what the apaches had but recently gone through. So quickly and so roughly did he handle them that they had not even an opportunity to draw their revolvers.

During the brief fight Tarzan had noted the open window and, beyond, the stem of a tree, or a telegraph pole—he could not tell which. As the last officer went down, one of his fellows succeeded in drawing his revolver and, from where he lay on the floor, fired at Tarzan. The shot missed, and before the man could fire again Tarzan had swept the lamp from the mantel and plunged the room into darkness.

The next they saw was a lithe form spring to the sill of the open window and leap, panther-like, onto the pole across the walk. When the police gathered themselves together and reached the street their prisoner was nowhere to be seen.

They did not handle the woman and the men who had not escaped any too gently when they took them to the station; they were a very sore and humiliated detail of police. It galled them to think that it would be necessary to report that a single unarmed man had wiped the floor with the whole lot of them, and then escaped them as easily as though they had not existed.

The officer who had remained in the street swore that no one had leaped from the window or left the building from the time they entered until they had come out. His comrades thought that he lied, but they could not prove it.

When Tarzan found himself clinging to the pole outside the window, he followed his jungle instinct and looked below for enemies before he ventured down. It was well he did, for just beneath stood a policeman. Above, Tarzan saw no one, so he went up instead of down.

The top of the pole was opposite the roof of the building, so it was but the work of an instant for the muscles that had for years sent him hurtling through the treetops of his primeval forest to carry him across the little space between the pole and the roof. From one building he went to another, and so on, with much climbing, until at a cross street he discovered another pole, down which he ran to the ground.

For a square or two he ran swiftly; then he turned into a little all-night cafe and in the lavatory removed the evidences of his over-roof promenade from hands and clothes. When he emerged a few moments later it was to saunter slowly on toward his apartments.

Not far from them he came to a well-lighted boulevard which it was necessary to cross. As he stood directly beneath a brilliant arc light, waiting for a limousine that was approaching to pass him, he heard his name called in a sweet feminine voice. Looking up, he met the smiling eyes of Olga de Coude as she leaned forward upon the back seat of the machine. He bowed very low in response to her friendly greeting. When he straightened up the machine had borne her away.

"Rokoff and the Countess de Coude both in the same evening," he soliloquized; "Paris is not so large, after all."

IV

THE COUNTESS EXPLAINS

"Your Paris is more dangerous than my savage jungles, Paul," concluded Tarzan, after narrating his adventures to his friend the morning following his encounter with the apaches and police in the Rue Maule. "Why did they lure me there? Were they hungry?"

D'Arnot feigned a horrified shudder, but he laughed at the quaint suggestion.

"It is difficult to rise above the jungle standards and reason by the light of civilized ways, is it not, my friend?" he queried banteringly.

"Civilized ways, forsooth," scoffed Tarzan. "Jungle standards do not countenance wanton atrocities. There we kill for food and for self-preservation, or in the winning of mates and the protection of the young. Always, you see, in accordance with the dictates of some great natural law. But here! Faugh, your civilized man is more brutal than the brutes. He kills wantonly, and, worse than that, he utilizes a noble sentiment, the brotherhood of man, as a lure to entice his unwary victim to his doom. It was in answer to an appeal from a fellow being that I hastened to that room where the assassins lay in wait for me.

"I did not realize, I could not realize for a long time afterward, that any woman could sink to such moral depravity as that one must have to call a would-be rescuer to death. But it must have been so—the sight of Rokoff there and the woman's later repudiation of me to

322

the police make it impossible to place any other construction upon her acts. Rokoff must have known that I frequently passed through the Rue Maule. He lay in wait for me—his entire scheme worked out to the last detail, even to the woman's story in case a hitch should occur in the program such as really did happen. It is all perfectly plain to me."

"Well," said D'Arnot, "among other things, it has taught you what I have been unable to impress upon you—that the Rue Maule is a good place to avoid after dark."

"On the contrary," replied Tarzan, with a smile, "it has convinced me that it is the one worth-while street in all Paris. Never again shall I miss an opportunity to traverse it, for it has given me the first real entertainment I have had since I left Africa."

"It may give you more than you will relish even without another visit," said D'Arnot. "You are not through with the police yet, remember. I know the Paris police well enough to assure you that they will not soon forget what you did to them. Sooner or later they will get you, my dear Tarzan, and then they will lock the wild man of the woods up behind iron bars. How will you like that?"

"They will never lock Tarzan of the Apes behind iron bars," replied he, grimly.

There was something in the man's voice as he said it that caused D'Arnot to look up sharply at his friend. What he saw in the set jaw and the cold, gray eyes made the young Frenchman very apprehensive for this great child, who could recognize no law mightier than his own mighty physical prowess. He saw that something must be done to set Tarzan right with the police before another encounter was possible.

"You have much to learn, Tarzan," he said gravely. "The law of man must be respected, whether you relish it or no. Nothing but trouble can come to you and your friends should you persist in defying the police. I can explain it to them once for you, and that I shall do this very day, but hereafter you must obey the law. If its representatives say 'Come,' you must come; if they say 'Go,' you must go. Now we shall go to my great friend in the department and fix up this matter of the Rue Maule. Come!"

Together they entered the office of the police official a half hour later. He was very cordial. He remembered Tarzan from the visit the two had made him several months prior in the matter of finger prints.

When D'Arnot had concluded the narration of the events which had transpired the previous evening, a grim smile was playing about the lips of the policeman. He touched a button near his hand, and as he waited for the clerk to respond to its summons he searched through the papers on his desk for one which he finally located.

"Here, Joubon," he said as the clerk entered. "Summon these officers—have them come to me at once," and he handed the man the paper he had sought. Then he turned to Tarzan.

"You have committed a very grave offense, monsieur," he said, not unkindly, "and but for the explanation made by our good friend here I should be inclined to judge you harshly. I am, instead, about to do a rather unheard-of-thing. I have summoned the officers whom you maltreated last night. They shall hear Lieutenant D'Arnot's story, and then I shall leave it to their discretion to say whether you shall be prosecuted or not.

"You have much to learn about the ways of civilization. Things that seem strange or unnecessary to you, you must learn to accept until you are able to judge the motives behind them. The officers whom you attacked were but doing their duty. They had no discretion in the matter. Every day they risk their lives in the protection of the lives or property of others. They would do the same for you. They are very brave men, and they are deeply mortified that a single unarmed man bested and beat them.

"Make it easy for them to overlook what you did. Unless I am gravely in error you are yourself a very brave man, and brave men are proverbially magnanimous."

Further conversation was interrupted by the appearance of the four policemen. As their eyes fell on Tarzan, surprise was writ large on each countenance.

"My children," said the official, "here is the gentleman whom you met in the Rue Maule last evening. He has come voluntarily to give himself up. I wish you to listen attentively to Lieutenant D'Arnot, who will tell you a part of the story of monsieur's life. It may explain his attitude toward you of last night. Proceed, my dear lieutenant."

D'Arnot spoke to the policemen for half an hour. He told them something of Tarzan's wild jungle life. He explained the savage training that had taught him to battle like a wild beast in self-preservation. It became plain to them that the man had been guided by instinct rather than reason in his attack upon them. He had not understood their intentions. To him they had been little different from any of the various forms of life he had been accustomed to in his native jungle, where practically all were his enemies.

"Your pride has been wounded," said D'Arnot, in conclusion. "It is the fact that this man overcame you that hurts the most. But you need feel no shame. You would not make apologies for defeat had you been penned in that small room with an African lion, or with the great Gorilla of the jungles.

"And yet you were battling with muscles that have time and time again been pitted, and always victoriously, against these terrors of the dark continent. It is no disgrace to fall beneath the superhuman strength of Tarzan of the Apes."

And then, as the men stood looking first at Tarzan and then at their superior the ape-man did the one thing which was needed to erase the last remnant of animosity which they might have felt for him. With outstretched hand he advanced toward them.

"I am sorry for the mistake I made," he said simply. "Let us be friends." And that was the end of the whole matter, except that Tarzan became a subject of much conversation in the barracks of the police, and increased the number of his friends by four brave men at least.

On their return to D'Arnot's apartments the lieutenant found a letter awaiting him from an English friend, William Cecil Clayton, Lord Greystoke. The two had maintained a correspondence since the birth of their friendship on that ill-fated expedition in search of Jane Porter after her theft by Terkoz, the bull ape.

"They are to be married in London in about two months," said D'Arnot, as he completed his perusal of the letter. Tarzan did not need to be told who was meant by "they." He made no reply, but he was very quiet and thoughtful during the balance of the day.

That evening they attended the opera. Tarzan's mind was still occupied by his gloomy thoughts. He paid little or no attention to what was transpiring upon the stage. Instead he saw only the lovely vision of a beautiful American girl, and heard naught but a sad, sweet voice acknowledging that his love was returned. And she was to marry another!

He shook himself to be rid of his unwelcome thoughts, and at the same instant he felt eyes upon him. With the instinct that was his by virtue of training he looked up squarely into the eyes that were looking at him, to find that they were shining from the smiling face of Olga, Countess de Coude. As Tarzan returned her bow he was positive that there was an invitation in her look, almost a plea. The next intermission found him beside her in her box.

"I have so much wished to see you," she was saying. "It has troubled me not a little to think that after the service you rendered to both my husband and myself no adequate explanation was ever made you of what must have seemed ingratitude on our part in not taking the necessary steps to prevent a repetition of the attacks upon us by those two men."

"You wrong me," replied Tarzan. "My thoughts of you have been only the most pleasant. You must not feel that any explanation is due me. Have they annoyed you further?"

"They never cease," she replied sadly. "I feel that I must tell some one, and I do not know another who so deserves an explanation as you. You must permit me to do so. It may be of service to you, for I know Nikolas Rokoff quite well enough to be positive that you have not seen the last of him. He will find some means to be revenged upon you. What I wish to tell you may be of aid to you in combating any scheme of revenge he may harbor. I cannot tell you here, but tomorrow I shall be at home to Monsieur Tarzan at five."

"It will be an eternity until tomorrow at five," he said, as he bade her good night. From a corner of the theater Rokoff and Paulvitch saw Monsieur Tarzan in the box of the Countess de Coude, and both men smiled.

At four-thirty the following afternoon a swarthy, bearded man rang the bell at the servants' entrance of the palace of the Count de Coude. The footman who opened the door raised his eyebrows in recognition as he saw who stood without. A low conversation passed between the two.

At first the footman demurred from some proposition that the bearded one made, but an instant later something passed from the hand of the caller to the hand of the servant. Then the latter turned and led the visitor by a roundabout way to a little curtained alcove off the apartment in which the countess was wont to serve tea of an afternoon.

A half hour later Tarzan was ushered into the room, and presently his hostess entered, smiling, and with outstretched hands.

"I am so glad that you came," she said.

"Nothing could have prevented," he replied.

For a few moments they spoke of the opera, of the topics that were then occupying the attention of Paris, of the pleasure of renewing their brief acquaintance which had had its inception under such odd circumstances, and this brought them to the subject that was uppermost in the minds of both.

"You must have wondered," said the countess finally, "what the object of Rokoff's persecution could be. It is very simple. The count is intrusted with many of the vital secrets of the ministry of war. He often has in his possession papers that foreign powers would give a fortune to possess—secrets of state that their agents would commit murder and worse than murder to learn.

"There is such a matter now in his possession that would make the fame and fortune of any Russian who could divulge it to his government. Rokoff and Paulvitch are Russian spies. They will stop at nothing to procure this information. The affair on the liner—I mean the matter of the card game—was for the purpose of blackmailing the knowledge they seek from my husband.

"Had he been convicted of cheating at cards, his career would have been blighted. He would have had to leave the war department. He would have been socially ostracized. They intended to hold this club over him—the price of an avowal on their part that the count was but the victim of the plot of enemies who wished to besmirch his name was to have been the papers they seek.

"You thwarted them in this. Then they concocted the scheme whereby my reputation was to be the price, instead of the count's. When Paulvitch entered my cabin he explained it to me. If I would obtain the information for them he promised to go no farther, otherwise Rokoff, who stood without, was to notify the purser that I was entertaining a man other than my husband behind the locked doors of my cabin. He was to tell every one he met on the boat, and when we landed he was to have given the whole story to the newspaper men.

"Was it not too horrible? But I happened to know something of Monsieur Paulvitch that would send him to the gallows in Russia if it were known by the police of St. Petersburg. I dared him to carry out his plan, and then I leaned toward him and whispered a name in his ear. Like that"—and she snapped her fingers—"he flew at my throat as a madman. He would have killed me had you not interfered."

"The brutes!" muttered Tarzan.

"They are worse than that, my friend," she said.

"They are devils. I fear for you because you have gained their hatred. I wish you to be on your guard constantly. Tell me that you will, for my sake, for I should never forgive myself should you suffer through the kindness you did me."

"I do not fear them," he replied. "I have survived grimmer enemies than Rokoff and Paulvitch." He saw that she knew nothing of the occurrence in the Rue Maule, nor did he mention it, fearing that it might distress her.

"For your own safety," he continued, "why do you not turn the scoundrels over to the authorities? They should make quick work of them."

She hesitated for a moment before replying.

"There are two reasons," she said finally. "One of them it is that keeps the count from doing that very thing. The other, my real reason for fearing to expose them, I have never told—only Rokoff and I know it. I wonder," and then she paused, looking intently at him for a long time.

"And what do you wonder?" he asked, smiling.

"I was wondering why it is that I want to tell you the thing that I have not dared tell even to my husband. I believe that you would understand, and that you could tell me the right course to follow. I believe that you would not judge me too harshly."

"I fear that I should prove a very poor judge, madame," Tarzan replied, "for if you had been guilty of murder I should say that the victim should be grateful to have met so sweet a fate."

"Oh, dear, no," she expostulated; "it is not so terrible as that. But first let me tell you the reason the count has for not prosecuting these men; then, if I can hold my courage, I shall tell you the real reason that I dare not. The first is that Nikolas Rokoff is my brother. We are Russians. Nikolas has been a bad man since I can remember. He was cashiered from the Russian army, in which he held a captaincy. There was a scandal for a time, but after a while it was partially forgotten, and my father obtained a position for him in the secret service.

"There have been many terrible crimes laid at Nikolas' door, but he has always managed to escape punishment. Of late he has accomplished it by trumped-up evidence convicting his victims of treason against the czar, and the Russian police, who are always only too ready to fasten guilt of this nature upon any and all, have accepted his version and exonerated him."

"Have not his attempted crimes against you and your husband forfeited whatever rights the bonds of kinship might have accorded him?" asked Tarzan. "The fact that you are his sister has not deterred him from seeking to besmirch your honor. You owe him no loyalty, madame."

"Ah, but there is that other reason. If I owe him no loyalty though he be my brother, I cannot so easily disavow the fear I hold him in because of a certain episode in my life of which he is cognizant.

"I might as well tell you all," she resumed after a pause, "for I see that it is in my heart to tell you sooner or later. I was educated in a convent. While there I met a man whom I supposed to be a gentleman. I knew little or nothing about men and less about love. I got it into my foolish head that I loved this man, and at his urgent request I ran away with him. We were to have been married.

"I was with him just three hours. All in the daytime and in public places—railroad stations and upon a train. When we reached our destination where we were to have been married, two officers stepped up to my escort as we descended from the train, and placed him under arrest. They took me also, but when I had told my story they did not detain me, other than to send me back to the convent

330

under the care of a matron. It seemed that the man who had wooed me was no gentleman at all, but a deserter from the army as well as a fugitive from civil justice. He had a police record in nearly every country in Europe.

"The matter was hushed up by the authorities of the convent. Not even my parents knew of it. But Nikolas met the man afterward, and learned the whole story. Now he threatens to tell the count if I do not do just as he wishes me to."

Tarzan laughed. "You are still but a little girl. The story that you have told me cannot reflect in any way upon your reputation, and were you not a little girl at heart you would know it. Go to your husband tonight, and tell him the whole story, just as you have told it to me. Unless I am much mistaken he will laugh at you for your fears, and take immediate steps to put that precious brother of yours in prison where he belongs."

"I only wish that I dared," she said; "but I am afraid. I learned early to fear men. First my father, then Nikolas, then the fathers in the convent. Nearly all my friends fear their husbands—why should I not fear mine?"

"It does not seem right that women should fear men," said Tarzan, an expression of puzzlement on his face. "I am better acquainted with the jungle folk, and there it is more often the other way around, except among the black men, and they to my mind are in most ways lower in the scale than the beasts. No, I cannot understand why civilized women should fear men, the beings that are created to protect them. I should hate to think that any woman feared me."

"I do not think that any woman would fear you, my friend," said Olga de Coude softly. "I have known you but a short while, yet though it may seem foolish to say it, you are the only man I have ever known whom I think that I should never fear—it is strange, too, for you are very strong. I wondered at the ease with which you handled Nikolas and Paulvitch that night in my cabin. It was marvellous." As

Tarzan was leaving her a short time later he wondered a little at the clinging pressure of her hand at parting, and the firm insistence with which she exacted a promise from him that he would call again on the morrow.

The memory of her half-veiled eyes and perfect lips as she had stood smiling up into his face as he bade her good-by remained with him for the balance of the day. Olga de Coude was a very beautiful woman, and Tarzan of the Apes a very lonely young man, with a heart in him that was in need of the doctoring that only a woman may provide.

As the countess turned back into the room after Tarzan's departure, she found herself face to face with Nikolas Rokoff.

"How long have you been here?" she cried, shrinking away from him.

"Since before your lover came," he answered, with a nasty leer.

"Stop!" she commanded. "How dare you say such a thing to me—your sister!"

"Well, my dear Olga, if he is not your lover, accept my apologies; but it is no fault of yours that he is not. Had he one-tenth the knowledge of women that I have you would be in his arms this minute. He is a stupid fool, Olga. Why, your every word and act was an open invitation to him, and he had not the sense to see it."

The woman put her hands to her ears.

"I will not listen. You are wicked to say such things as that. No matter what you may threaten me with, you know that I am a good woman. After tonight you will not dare to annoy me, for I shall tell Raoul all. He will understand, and then, Monsieur Nikolas, beware!"

"You shall tell him nothing," said Rokoff. "I have this affair now, and with the help of one of your servants whom I may trust it will lack nothing in the telling when the time comes that the details of the sworn evidence shall be poured into your husband's ears. The other affair served its purpose well—we now have something tangible to work on, Olga. A real *affair*—and you a trusted wife. Shame, Olga," and the brute laughed.

So the countess told her count nothing, and matters were worse than they had been. From a vague fear her mind was transferred to a very tangible one. It may be, too, that conscience helped to enlarge it out of all proportion.

V

THE PLOT THAT FAILED

or a month Tarzan was a regular and very welcome devotee at the shrine of the beautiful Countess de Coude. Often he met other members of the select little coterie that dropped in for tea of an afternoon. More often Olga found devices that would give her an hour of Tarzan alone.

For a time she had been frightened by what Nikolas had insinuated. She had not thought of this big, young man as anything more than friend, but with the suggestion implanted by the evil words of her brother she had grown to speculate much upon the strange force which seemed to attract her toward the gray-eyed stranger. She did not wish to love him, nor did she wish his love.

She was much younger than her husband, and without having realized it she had been craving the haven of a friendship with one nearer her own age. Twenty is shy in exchanging confidences with forty. Tarzan was but two years her senior. He could understand her, she felt. Then he was clean and honorable and chivalrous. She was not afraid of him. That she could trust him she had felt instinctively from the first.

From a distance Rokoff had watched this growing intimacy with malicious glee. Ever since he had learned that Tarzan knew that he was a Russian spy there had been added to his hatred for the apeman a great fear that he would expose him. He was but waiting now until the moment was propitious for a master stroke. He wanted to rid himself forever of Tarzan, and at the same time reap an ample revenge for the humiliations and defeats that he had suffered at his hands.

Tarzan was nearer to contentment than he had been since the peace and tranquility of his jungle had been broken in upon by the advent of the marooned Porter party. He enjoyed the pleasant social intercourse with Olga's friends, while the friendship which had sprung up between the fair countess and himself was a source of never-ending delight. It broke in upon and dispersed his gloomy thoughts, and served as a balm to his lacerated heart.

Sometimes D'Arnot accompanied him on his visits to the De Coude home, for he had long known both Olga and the count. Occasionally De Coude dropped in, but the multitudinous affairs of his official position and the never-ending demands of politics kept him from home usually until late at night.

Rokoff spied upon Tarzan almost constantly, waiting for the time that he should call at the De Coude palace at night, but in this he was doomed to disappointment. On several occasions Tarzan accompanied the countess to her home after the opera, but he invariably left her at the entrance—much to the disgust of the lady's devoted brother.

Finding that it seemed impossible to trap Tarzan through any voluntary act of his own, Rokoff and Paulvitch put their heads together to hatch a plan that would trap the ape-man in all the circumstantial evidence of a compromising position.

For days they watched the papers as well as the movements of De Coude and Tarzan. At length they were rewarded. A morning paper made brief mention of a smoker that was to be given on the following evening by the German minister. De Coude's name was among those of the invited guests. If he attended this meant that he would be absent from his home until after midnight.

On the night of the banquet Paulvitch waited at the curb before the residence of the German minister, where he could scan the face of each guest that arrived. He had not long to wait before De Coude descended from his car and passed him. That was enough. Paulvitch hastened back to his quarters, where Rokoff awaited him. There they waited until after eleven, then Paulvitch took down the receiver of their telephone. He called a number.

"The apartments of Lieutenant D'Arnot?" he asked, when he had obtained his connection.

"A message for Monsieur Tarzan, if he will be so kind as to step to the telephone."

For a minute there was silence.

"Monsieur Tarzan?"

"Ah, yes, monsieur, this is François—in the service of the Countess de Coude. Possibly monsieur does poor François the honor to recall him—yes?

"Yes, monsieur. I have a message, an urgent message from the countess. She asks that you hasten to her at once—she is in trouble, monsieur.

"No, monsieur, poor François does not know. Shall I tell madame that monsieur will be here shortly?

"Thank you, monsieur. The good God will bless you."

Paulvitch hung up the receiver and turned to grin at Rokoff.

"It will take him thirty minutes to get there. If you reach the German minister's in fifteen, De Coude should arrive at his home in about forty-five minutes. It all depends upon whether the fool will remain fifteen minutes after he finds that a trick has been played upon him; but unless I am mistaken Olga will be loath to let him go in so short a time as that. Here is the note for De Coude. Hasten!"

Paulvitch lost no time in reaching the German minister's. At the door he handed the note to a footman. "This is for the Count de Coude. It is very urgent. You must see that it is placed in his hands at once," and he dropped a piece of silver into the willing hand of the servant. Then he returned to his quarters.

A moment later De Coude was apologizing to his host as he tore open the envelope. What he read left his face white and his hand trembling.

MONSIEUR LE COUNT DE COUDE:

One who wishes to save the honor of your name takes this means to warn you that the sanctity of your home is this minute in jeopardy.

A certain man who for months has been a constant visitor there during your absence is now with your wife. If you go at once to your countess' boudoir you will find them together.

A FRIEND.

Twenty minutes after Paulvitch had called Tarzan, Rokoff obtained a connection with Olga's private line. Her maid answered the telephone which was in the countess' boudoir.

"But madame has retired," said the maid, in answer to Rokoff's request to speak with her.

"This is a very urgent message for the countess' ears alone," replied Rokoff. "Tell her that she must arise and slip something about her and come to the telephone. I shall call up again in five minutes." Then he hung up his receiver. A moment later Paulvitch entered.

"The count has the message?" asked Rokoff.

"He should be on his way to his home by now," replied Paulvitch.

"Good! My lady will be sitting in her boudoir, very much in negligee, about now. In a minute the faithful Jacques will escort Monsieur Tarzan into her presence without announcing him. It will take a few minutes for explanations. Olga will look very alluring in the filmy creation that is her nightdress, and the clinging robe which but half conceals the charms that the former does not conceal at all. Olga will be surprised, but not displeased.

337

"If there is a drop of red blood in the man the count will break in upon a very pretty love scene in about fifteen minutes from now. I think we have planned marvelously, my dear Alexis. Let us go out and drink to the very good health of Monsieur Tarzan in some of old Plancon's unparalleled absinth; not forgetting that the Count de Coude is one of the best swordsmen in Paris, and by far the best shot in all France."

When Tarzan reached Olga's, Jacques was awaiting him at the entrance.

"This way, Monsieur," he said, and led the way up the broad, marble staircase. In another moment he had opened a door, and, drawing aside a heavy curtain, obsequiously bowed Tarzan into a dimly lighted apartment. Then Jacques vanished.

Across the room from him Tarzan saw Olga seated before a little desk on which stood her telephone. She was tapping impatiently upon the polished surface of the desk. She had not heard him enter.

"Olga," he said, "what is wrong?"

She turned toward him with a little cry of alarm.

"Jean!" she cried. "What are you doing here? Who admitted you? What does it mean?"

Tarzan was thunderstruck, but in an instant he realized a part of the truth.

"Then you did not send for me, Olga?"

"Send for you at this time of night? *Mon Dieu!* Jean, do you think that I am quite mad?"

"François telephoned me to come at once; that you were in trouble and wanted me."

"François? Who in the world is François?"

"He said that he was in your service. He spoke as though I should recall the fact."

"There is no one by that name in my employ. Some one has played a joke upon you, Jean," and Olga laughed.

"I fear that it may be a most sinister 'joke,' Olga," he replied. "There is more back of it than humor."

"What do you mean? You do not think that—"

"Where is the count?" he interrupted.

"At the German ambassador's."

"This is another move by your estimable brother. Tomorrow the count will hear of it. He will question the servants. Everything will point to—to what Rokoff wishes the count to think."

"The scoundrel!" cried Olga. She had arisen, and come close to Tarzan, where she stood looking up into his face. She was very frightened. In her eyes was an expression that the hunter sees in those of a poor, terrified doe—puzzled—questioning. She trembled, and to steady herself raised her hands to his broad shoulders. "What shall we do, Jean?" she whispered. "It is terrible. Tomorrow all Paris will read of it—he will see to that."

Her look, her attitude, her words were eloquent of the age-old appeal of defenseless woman to her natural protector—man. Tarzan took one of the warm little hands that lay on his breast in his own strong one. The act was quite involuntary, and almost equally so was the instinct of protection that threw a sheltering arm around the girl's shoulders.

The result was electrical. Never before had he been so close to her. In startled guilt they looked suddenly into each other's eyes, and where Olga de Coude should have been strong she was weak, for she crept closer into the man's arms, and clasped her own about his neck. And Tarzan of the Apes? He took the panting figure into his mighty arms, and covered the hot lips with kisses.

Raoul de Coude made hurried excuses to his host after he had read the note handed him by the ambassador's butler. Never afterward could he recall the nature of the excuses he made. Everything was quite a blur to him up to the time that he stood on the threshold of his own home. Then he became very cool, moving quietly and with caution. For some inexplicable reason Jacques had the door open before he was halfway to the steps. It did not strike him at the time as being unusual, though afterward he remarked it.

Very softly he tiptoed up the stairs and along the gallery to the door of his wife's boudoir. In his hand was a heavy walking stick—in his heart, murder.

Olga was the first to see him. With a horrified shriek she tore herself from Tarzan's arms, and the ape-man turned just in time to ward with his arm a terrific blow that De Coude had aimed at his head. Once, twice, three times the heavy stick fell with lightning rapidity, and each blow aided in the transition of the ape-man back to the primordial.

With the low, guttural snarl of the bull ape he sprang for the Frenchman. The great stick was torn from his grasp and broken in two as though it had been matchwood, to be flung aside as the now infuriated beast charged for his adversary's throat. Olga de Coude stood a horrified spectator of the terrible scene which ensued during the next brief moment, then she sprang to where Tarzan was murdering her husband—choking the life from him—shaking him as a terrier might shake a rat.

Frantically she tore at his great hands. "Mother of God!" she cried. "You are killing him, you are killing him! Oh, Jean, you are killing my husband!"

Tarzan was deaf with rage. Suddenly he hurled the body to the floor, and, placing his foot upon the upturned breast, raised his head. Then through the palace of the Count de Coude rang the awesome challenge of the bull ape that has made a kill. From cellar to attic the horrid sound searched out the servants, and left them blanched and trembling. The woman in the room sank to her knees beside the body of her husband, and prayed.

Slowly the red mist faded from before Tarzan's eyes. Things began to take form—he was regaining the perspective of civilized man. His eyes fell upon the figure of the kneeling woman. "Olga," he whispered. She looked up, expecting to see the maniacal light of murder in the eyes above her. Instead she saw sorrow and contrition.

"Oh, Jean!" she cried. "See what you have done. He was my husband. I loved him, and you have killed him."

Very gently Tarzan raised the limp form of the Count de Coude and bore it to a couch. Then he put his ear to the man's breast.

"Some brandy, Olga," he said.

She brought it, and together they forced it between his lips. Presently a faint gasp came from the white lips. The head turned, and De Coude groaned.

"He will not die," said Tarzan. "Thank God!"

"Why did you do it, Jean?" she asked.

"I do not know. He struck me, and I went mad. I have seen the apes of my tribe do the same thing. I have never told you my story, Olga. It would have been better had you known it—this might not have happened. I never saw my father. The only mother I knew was a ferocious she-ape. Until I was fifteen I had never seen a human being. I was twenty before I saw a white man. A little more than a year ago I was a naked beast of prey in an African jungle.

"Do not judge me too harshly. Two years is too short a time in which to attempt to work the change in an individual that it has taken countless ages to accomplish in the white race."

"I do not judge at all, Jean. The fault is mine. You must go now— he must not find you here when he regains consciousness. Good-by."

It was a sorrowful Tarzan who walked with bowed head from the palace of the Count de Coude.

Once outside his thoughts took definite shape, to the end that twenty minutes later he entered a police station not far from the Rue Maule. Here he soon found one of the officers with whom he had had the encounter several weeks previous. The policeman was genuinely glad to see again the man who had so roughly handled him. After a moment of conversation Tarzan asked if he had ever heard of Nikolas Rokoff or Alexis Paulvitch.

"Very often, indeed, monsieur. Each has a police record, and while there is nothing charged against them now, we make it a point to know pretty well where they may be found should the occasion demand. It is only the same precaution that we take with every known criminal. Why does monsieur ask?"

"They are known to me," replied Tarzan. "I wish to see Monsieur Rokoff on a little matter of business. If you can direct me to his lodgings I shall appreciate it."

A few minutes later he bade the policeman adieu, and, with a slip of paper in his pocket bearing a certain address in a semirespectable quarter, he walked briskly toward the nearest taxi stand.

Rokoff and Paulvitch had returned to their rooms, and were sitting talking over the probable outcome of the evening's events. They had telephoned to the offices of two of the morning papers from which they momentarily expected representatives to hear the first report of the scandal that was to stir social Paris on the morrow.

A heavy step sounded on the stairway. "Ah, but these newspaper men are prompt," exclaimed Rokoff, and as a knock fell upon the door of their room: "Enter, monsieur."

The smile of welcome froze upon the Russian's face as he looked into the hard, gray eyes of his visitor.

"Name of a name!" he shouted, springing to his feet, "What brings you here!"

"Sit down!" said Tarzan, so low that the men could barely catch the words, but in a tone that brought Rokoff to his chair, and kept Paulvitch in his.

"You know what has brought me here," he continued, in the same low tone. "It should be to kill you, but because you are Olga de Coude's brother I shall not do that—now.

"I shall give you a chance for your lives. Paulvitch does not count much—he is merely a stupid, foolish little tool, and so I shall not kill him so long as I permit you to live. Before I leave you two alive in this room you will have done two things. The first will be to write a full confession of your connection with tonight's plot—and sign it.

"The second will be to promise me upon pain of death that you will permit no word of this affair to get into the newspapers. If you do not do both, neither of you will be alive when I pass next through that doorway. Do you understand?" And, without waiting for a reply: "Make haste; there is ink before you, and paper and a pen."

Rokoff assumed a truculent air, attempting by bravado to show how little he feared Tarzan's threats. An instant later he felt the ape-man's steel fingers at his throat, and Paulvitch, who attempted to dodge them and reach the door, was lifted completely off the floor, and hurled senseless into a corner. When Rokoff commenced to blacken about the face Tarzan released his hold and shoved the fellow back into his chair. After a moment of coughing Rokoff sat sullenly glaring at the man standing opposite him. Presently Paulvitch came to himself, and limped painfully back to his chair at Tarzan's command.

"Now write," said the ape-man. "If it is necessary to handle you again I shall not be so lenient."

Rokoff picked up a pen and commenced to write.

"See that you omit no detail, and that you mention every name," cautioned Tarzan.

Presently there was a knock at the door. "Enter," said Tarzan.

A dapper young man came in. "I am from the *Matin*," he announced. "I understand that Monsieur Rokoff has a story for me."

"Then you are mistaken, monsieur," replied Tarzan. "You have no story for publication, have you, my dear Nikolas."

Rokoff looked up from his writing with an ugly scowl upon his face.

"No," he growled, "I have no story for publication—now."

"Nor ever, my dear Nikolas," and the reporter did not see the nasty light in the ape-man's eye; but Nikolas Rokoff did.

"Nor ever," he repeated hastily.

"It is too bad that monsieur has been troubled," said Tarzan, turning to the newspaper man. "I bid monsieur good evening," and he bowed the dapper young man out of the room, and closed the door in his face.

An hour later Tarzan, with a rather bulky manuscript in his coat pocket, turned at the door leading from Rokoff's room.

"Were I you I should leave France," he said, "for sooner or later I shall find an excuse to kill you that will not in any way compromise your sister."

VI

A DUEL

'Arnot was asleep when Tarzan entered their apartments after leaving Rokoff's. Tarzan did not disturb him, but the following morning he narrated the happenings of the previous evening, omitting not a single detail.

"What a fool I have been," he concluded. "De Coude and his wife were both my friends. How have I returned their friendship? Barely did I escape murdering the count. I have cast a stigma on the name of a good woman. It is very probable that I have broken up a happy home."

"Do you love Olga de Coude?" asked D'Arnot.

"Were I not positive that she does not love me I could not answer your question, Paul; but without disloyalty to her I tell you that I do not love her, nor does she love me. For an instant we were the victims of a sudden madness—it was not love—and it would have left us, unharmed, as suddenly as it had come upon us even though De Coude had not returned. As you know, I have had little experience of women. Olga de Coude is very beautiful; that, and the dim light and the seductive surroundings, and the appeal of the defenseless for protection, might have been resisted by a more civilized man, but my civilization is not even skin deep—it does not go deeper than my clothes.

"Paris is no place for me. I will but continue to stumble into more and more serious pitfalls. The man-made restrictions are irksome. I feel always that I am a prisoner. I cannot endure it, my friend, and so I think that I shall go back to my own jungle, and lead the life that God intended that I should lead when He put me there."

"Do not take it so to heart, Jean," responded D'Arnot. "You have acquitted yourself much better than most 'civilized' men would have under similar circumstances. As to leaving Paris at this time, I rather think that Raoul de Coude may be expected to have something to say on that subject before long."

Nor was D'Arnot mistaken. A week later on Monsieur Flaubert was announced about eleven in the morning, as D'Arnot and Tarzan were breakfasting. Monsieur Flaubert was an impressively polite gentleman. With many low bows he delivered Monsieur le Count de Coude's challenge to Monsieur Tarzan. Would monsieur be so very kind as to arrange to have a friend meet Monsieur Flaubert at as early an hour as convenient, that the details might be arranged to the mutual satisfaction of all concerned?

Certainly. Monsieur Tarzan would be delighted to place his interests unreservedly in the hands of his friend, Lieutenant D'Arnot. And so it was arranged that D'Arnot was to call on Monsieur Flaubert at two that afternoon, and the polite Monsieur Flaubert, with many bows, left them.

When they were again alone D'Arnot looked quizzically at Tarzan.

"Well?" he said.

"Now to my sins I must add murder, or else myself be killed," said Tarzan. "I am progressing rapidly in the ways of my civilized brothers."

"What weapons shall you select?" asked D'Arnot. "De Coude is accredited with being a master with the sword, and a splendid shot."

"I might then choose poisoned arrows at twenty paces, or spears at the same distance," laughed Tarzan. "Make it pistols, Paul."

"He will kill you, Jean."

"I have no doubt of it," replied Tarzan. "I must die some day."

"We had better make it swords," said D'Arnot. "He will be satisfied with wounding you, and there is less danger of a mortal wound."

"Pistols," said Tarzan, with finality.

D'Arnot tried to argue him out of it, but without avail, so pistols it was.

D'Arnot returned from his conference with Monsieur Flaubert shortly after four.

"It is all arranged," he said. "Everything is satisfactory. Tomorrow morning at daylight—there is a secluded spot on the road not far from Etamps. For some personal reason Monsieur Flaubert preferred it. I did not demur."

"Good!" was Tarzan's only comment. He did not refer to the matter again even indirectly. That night he wrote several letters before he retired. After sealing and addressing them he placed them all in an envelope addressed to D'Arnot. As he undressed D'Arnot heard him humming a music-hall ditty.

The Frenchman swore under his breath. He was very unhappy, for he was positive that when the sun rose the next morning it would look down upon a dead Tarzan. It grated upon him to see Tarzan so unconcerned.

"This is a most uncivilized hour for people to kill each other," remarked the ape-man when he had been routed out of a comfortable bed in the blackness of the early morning hours. He had slept well, and so it seemed that his head scarcely touched the pillow ere his man deferentially aroused him. His remark was addressed to D'Arnot, who stood fully dressed in the doorway of Tarzan's bedroom.

D'Arnot had scarcely slept at all during the night. He was nervous, and therefore inclined to be irritable.

"I presume you slept like a baby all night," he said.

Tarzan laughed. "From your tone, Paul, I infer that you rather harbor the fact against me. I could not help it, really."

"No, Jean; it is not that," replied D'Arnot, himself smiling. "But

347

you take the entire matter with such infernal indifference—it is exasperating. One would think that you were going out to shoot at a target, rather than to face one of the best shots in France."

Tarzan shrugged his shoulders. "I am going out to expiate a great wrong, Paul. A very necessary feature of the expiation is the marksmanship of my opponent. Wherefore, then, should I be dissatisfied? Have you not yourself told me that Count de Coude is a splendid marksman?"

"You mean that you hope to be killed?" exclaimed D'Arnot, in horror.

"I cannot say that I hope to be; but you must admit that there is little reason to believe that I shall not be killed."

Had D'Arnot known the thing that was in the ape-man's mind—that had been in his mind almost from the first intimation that De Coude would call him to account on the field of honor—he would have been even more horrified than he was.

In silence they entered D'Arnot's great car, and in similar silence they sped over the dim road that leads to Etamps. Each man was occupied with his own thoughts. D'Arnot's were very mournful, for he was genuinely fond of Tarzan. The great friendship which had sprung up between these two men whose lives and training had been so widely different had but been strengthened by association, for they were both men to whom the same high ideals of manhood, of personal courage, and of honor appealed with equal force. They could understand one another, and each could be proud of the friendship of the other.

Tarzan of the Apes was wrapped in thoughts of the past; pleasant memories of the happier occasions of his lost jungle life. He recalled the countless boyhood hours that he had spent cross-legged upon the table in his dead father's cabin, his little brown body bent over one of the fascinating picture books from which, unaided, he had gleaned the secret of the printed language long before the sounds of human speech fell upon his ears. A smile of contentment softened his strong face as he thought of that day of days that he had had alone with Jane Porter in the heart of his primeval forest.

Presently his reminiscences were broken in upon by the stopping of the car—they were at their destination. Tarzan's mind returned to the affairs of the moment. He knew that he was about to die, but there was no fear of death in him. To a denizen of the cruel jungle death is a commonplace. The first law of nature compels them to cling tenaciously to life—to fight for it; but it does not teach them to fear death.

D'Arnot and Tarzan were first upon the field of honor. A moment later De Coude, Monsieur Flaubert, and a third gentleman arrived. The last was introduced to D'Arnot and Tarzan; he was a physician.

D'Arnot and Monsieur Flaubert spoke together in whispers for a brief time. The Count de Coude and Tarzan stood apart at opposite sides of the field. Presently the seconds summoned them. D'Arnot and Monsieur Flaubert had examined both pistols. The two men who were to face each other a moment later stood silently while Monsieur Flaubert recited the conditions they were to observe.

They were to stand back to back. At a signal from Monsieur Flaubert they were to walk in opposite directions, their pistols hanging by their sides. When each had proceeded ten paces D'Arnot was to give the final signal—then they were to turn and fire at will until one fell, or each had expended the three shots allowed.

While Monsieur Flaubert spoke Tarzan selected a cigarette from his case, and lighted it. De Coude was the personification of coolness—was he not the best shot in France?

Presently Monsieur Flaubert nodded to D'Arnot, and each man placed his principal in position.

"Are you quite ready, gentlemen?" asked Monsieur Flaubert.

"Quite," replied De Coude.

Tarzan nodded. Monsieur Flaubert gave the signal. He and D'Arnot stepped back a few paces to be out of the line of fire as the men paced slowly apart. Six! Seven! Eight! There were tears in D'Arnot's eyes. He loved Tarzan very much. Nine! Another pace, and the poor lieutenant gave the signal he so hated to give. To him it sounded the doom of his best friend.

Quickly De Coude wheeled and fired. Tarzan gave a little start. His pistol still dangled at his side. De Coude hesitated, as though waiting to see his antagonist crumple to the ground. The Frenchman was too experienced a marksman not to know that he had scored a hit. Still Tarzan made no move to raise his pistol. De Coude fired once more, but the attitude of the ape-man—the utter indifference that was so apparent in every line of the nonchalant ease of his giant figure, and the even unruffled puffing of his cigarette—had disconcerted the best marksman in France. This time Tarzan did not start, but again De Coude knew that he had hit.

Suddenly the explanation leaped to his mind—his antagonist was coolly taking these terrible chances in the hope that he would receive no staggering wound from any of De Coude's three shots. Then he would take his own time about shooting De Coude down deliberately, coolly, and in cold blood. A little shiver ran up the Frenchman's spine. It was fiendish—diabolical. What manner of creature was this that could stand complacently with two bullets in him, waiting for the third?

And so De Coude took careful aim this time, but his nerve was gone, and he made a clean miss. Not once had Tarzan raised his pistol hand from where it hung beside his leg.

For a moment the two stood looking straight into each other's eyes. On Tarzan's face was a pathetic expression of disappointment. On De Coude's a rapidly growing expression of horror—yes, of terror.

He could endure it no longer.

"Mother of God! Monsieur—shoot!" he screamed.

But Tarzan did not raise his pistol. Instead, he advanced toward De Coude, and when D'Arnot and Monsieur Flaubert, misinterpreting his intention, would have rushed between them, he raised his left hand in a sign of remonstrance.

"Do not fear," he said to them, "I shall not harm him."

It was most unusual, but they halted. Tarzan advanced until he was quite close to De Coude.

"There must have been something wrong with monsieur's pistol," he said. "Or monsieur is unstrung. Take mine, monsieur, and try again," and Tarzan offered his pistol, butt foremost, to the astonished De Coude.

"*Mon Dieu*, monsieur!" cried the latter. "Are you mad?"

"No, my friend," replied the ape-man; "but I deserve to die. It is the only way in which I may atone for the wrong I have done a very good woman. Take my pistol and do as I bid."

"It would be murder," replied De Coude. "But what wrong did you do my wife? She swore to me that——"

"I do not mean that," said Tarzan quickly. "You saw all the wrong that passed between us. But that was enough to cast a shadow upon her name, and to ruin the happiness of a man against whom I had no enmity. The fault was all mine, and so I hoped to die for it this morning. I am disappointed that monsieur is not so wonderful a marksman as I had been led to believe."

"You say that the fault was all yours?" asked De Coude eagerly.

"All mine, monsieur. Your wife is a very pure woman. She loves only you. The fault that you saw was all mine. The thing that brought me there was no fault of either the Countess de Coude or myself. Here is a paper which will quite positively demonstrate that," and Tarzan drew from his pocket the statement Rokoff had written and signed.

De Coude took it and read. D'Arnot and Monsieur Flaubert had drawn near. They were interested spectators of this strange ending of a strange duel. None spoke until De Coude had quite finished, then he looked up at Tarzan.

"You are a very brave and chivalrous gentleman," he said. "I thank God that I did not kill you."

De Coude was a Frenchman. Frenchmen are impulsive. He threw his arms about Tarzan and embraced him. Monsieur Flaubert embraced D'Arnot. There was no one to embrace the doctor. So possibly it was pique which prompted him to interfere, and demand that he be permitted to dress Tarzan's wounds.

"This gentleman was hit once at least," he said. "Possibly thrice."

"Twice," said Tarzan. "Once in the left shoulder, and again in the left side—both flesh wounds, I think." But the doctor insisted upon stretching him upon the sward, and tinkering with him until the wounds were cleansed and the flow of blood checked.

One result of the duel was that they all rode back to Paris together in D'Arnot's car, the best of friends. De Coude was so relieved to have had this double assurance of his wife's loyalty that he felt no rancor at all toward Tarzan. It is true that the latter had assumed much more of the fault than was rightly his, but if he lied a little he may be excused, for he lied in the service of a woman, and he lied like a gentleman.

The ape-man was confined to his bed for several days. He felt that it was foolish and unnecessary, but the doctor and D'Arnot took the matter so to heart that he gave in to please them, though it made him laugh to think of it.

"It is droll," he said to D'Arnot. "To lie abed because of a pin prick! Why, when Bolgani, the king gorilla, tore me almost to pieces, while I was still but a little boy, did I have a nice soft bed to lie on? No, only the damp, rotting vegetation of the jungle. Hidden beneath some friendly bush I lay for days and weeks with only Kala to nurse me—poor, faithful Kala, who kept the insects from my wounds and warned off the beasts of prey.

"When I called for water she brought it to me in her own mouth—the only way she knew to carry it. There was no sterilized gauze, there was no antiseptic bandage—there was nothing that would not have driven our dear doctor mad to have seen. Yet I recovered—recovered to lie in bed because of a tiny scratch that one of the jungle folk would scarce realize unless it were upon the end of his nose."

But the time was soon over, and before he realized it Tarzan found himself abroad again. Several times De Coude had called, and when he found that Tarzan was anxious for employment of some nature he promised to see what could be done to find a berth for him.

It was the first day that Tarzan was permitted to go out that he received a message from De Coude requesting him to call at the count's office that afternoon.

He found De Coude awaiting him with a very pleasant welcome, and a sincere congratulation that he was once more upon his feet. Neither had ever mentioned the duel or the cause of it since that morning upon the field of honor.

"I think that I have found just the thing for you, Monsieur Tarzan," said the count. "It is a position of much trust and responsibility, which also requires considerably physical courage and prowess. I cannot imagine a man better fitted than you, my dear Monsieur Tarzan, for this very position. It will necessitate travel, and later it may lead to a very much better post—possibly in the diplomatic service.

"At first, for a short time only, you will be a special agent in the service of the ministry of war. Come, I will take you to the gentleman who will be your chief. He can explain the duties better than I, and then you will be in a position to judge if you wish to accept or no."

De Coude himself escorted Tarzan to the office of General Rochere, the chief of the bureau to which Tarzan would be attached if he accepted the position. There the count left him, after a glowing description to the general of the many attributes possessed by the ape-man which should fit him for the work of the service.

A half hour later Tarzan walked out of the office the possessor of the first position he had ever held. On the morrow he was to return for further instructions, though General Rochere had made it quite plain that Tarzan might prepare to leave Paris for an almost indefinite period, possibly on the morrow.

It was with feelings of the keenest elation that he hastened home to bear the good news to D'Arnot. At last he was to be of some value in the world. He was to earn money, and, best of all, to travel and see the world.

He could scarcely wait to get well inside D'Arnot's sitting room before he burst out with the glad tidings. D'Arnot was not so pleased.

"It seems to delight you to think that you are to leave Paris, and that we shall not see each other for months, perhaps. Tarzan, you are a most ungrateful beast!" and D'Arnot laughed.

"No, Paul; I am a little child. I have a new toy, and I am tickled to death."

And so it came that on the following day Tarzan left Paris en route for Marseilles and Oran.

VII

THE DANCING GIRL
OF SIDI AISSA

arzan's first mission did not bid fair to be either exciting or vastly important. There was a certain lieutenant of *spahis* whom the government had reason to suspect of improper relations with a great European power. This Lieutenant Gernois, who was at present stationed at Sidibel-Abbes, had recently been attached to the general staff, where certain information of great military value had come into his possession in the ordinary routine of his duties. It was this information which the government suspected the great power was bartering for with the officer.

It was at most but a vague hint dropped by a certain notorious Parisienne in a jealous mood that had caused suspicion to rest upon the lieutenant. But general staffs are jealous of their secrets, and treason so serious a thing that even a hint of it may not be safely neglected. And so it was that Tarzan had come to Algeria in the guise of an American hunter and traveler to keep a close eye upon Lieutenant Gernois.

He had looked forward with keen delight to again seeing his beloved Africa, but this northern aspect of it was so different from his tropical jungle home that he might as well have been back in Paris for all the heart thrills of homecoming that he experienced. At Oran he spent a day wandering through the narrow, crooked alleys of the

Arab quarter enjoying the strange, new sights. The next day found him at Sidi-bel-Abbes, where he presented his letters of introduction to both civil and military authorities—letters which gave no clew to the real significance of his mission.

Tarzan possessed a sufficient command of English to enable him to pass among Arabs and Frenchmen as an American, and that was all that was required of it. When he met an Englishman he spoke French in order that he might not betray himself, but occasionally talked in English to foreigners who understood that tongue, but could not note the slight imperfections of accent and pronunciation that were his.

Here he became acquainted with many of the French officers, and soon became a favorite among them. He met Gernois, whom he found to be a taciturn, dyspeptic-looking man of about forty, having little or no social intercourse with his fellows.

For a month nothing of moment occurred. Gernois apparently had no visitors, nor did he on his occasional visits to the town hold communication with any who might even by the wildest flight of imagination be construed into secret agents of a foreign power. Tarzan was beginning to hope that, after all, the rumor might have been false, when suddenly Gernois was ordered to Bou Saada in the Petit Sahara far to the south.

A company of *spahis* and three officers were to relieve another company already stationed there. Fortunately one of the officers, Captain Gerard, had become an excellent friend of Tarzan's, and so when the ape-man suggested that he should embrace the opportunity of accompanying him to Bou Saada, where he expected to find hunting, it caused not the slightest suspicion.

At Bouira the detachment detrained, and the balance of the journey was made in the saddle. As Tarzan was dickering at Bouira for a mount he caught a brief glimpse of a man in European clothes eying him from the doorway of a native coffeehouse, but as Tarzan looked the man turned and entered the little, low-ceilinged mud hut, and but for a haunting impression that there had been something familiar about the face or figure of the fellow, Tarzan gave the matter no further thought.

The march to Aumale was fatiguing to Tarzan, whose equestrian experiences hitherto had been confined to a course of riding lessons in a Parisian academy, and so it was that he quickly sought the comforts of a bed in the Hotel Grossat, while the officers and troops took up their quarters at the military post.

Although Tarzan was called early the following morning, the company of *spahis* was on the march before he had finished his breakfast. He was hurrying through his meal that the soldiers might not get too far in advance of him when he glanced through the door connecting the dining room with the bar.

To his surprise, he saw Gernois standing there in conversation with the very stranger he had seen in the coffee-house at Bouira the day previous. He could not be mistaken, for there was the same strangely familiar attitude and figure, though the man's back was toward him.

As his eyes lingered on the two, Gernois looked up and caught the intent expression on Tarzan's face. The stranger was talking in a low whisper at the time, but the French officer immediately interrupted him, and the two at once turned away and passed out of the range of Tarzan's vision.

This was the first suspicious occurrence that Tarzan had ever witnessed in connection with Gernois' actions, but he was positive that the men had left the barroom solely because Gernois had caught Tarzan's eyes upon them; then there was the persistent impression of familiarity about the stranger to further augment the ape-man's belief that here at length was something which would bear watching.

A moment later Tarzan entered the barroom, but the men had left, nor did he see aught of them in the street beyond, though he found a pretext to ride to various shops before he set out after the column which had now considerable start of him. He did not over-take them until he reached Sidi Aissa shortly after noon, where the soldiers had halted for an hour's rest. Here he found Gernois with the column, but there was no sign of the stranger.

It was market day at Sidi Aissa, and the numberless caravans of camels coming in from the desert, and the crowds of bickering Arabs in the market place, filled Tarzan with a consuming desire to remain for a day that he might see more of these sons of the desert. Thus it was that the company of *spahis* marched on that afternoon toward Bou Saada without him. He spent the hours until dark wandering about the market in company with a youthful Arab, one Abdul, who had been recommended to him by the innkeeper as a trustworthy servant and interpreter.

Here Tarzan purchased a better mount than the one he had selected at Bouira, and, entering into conversation with the stately Arab to whom the animal had belonged, learned that the seller was Kadour ben Saden, sheik of a desert tribe far south of Djelfa. Through Abdul, Tarzan invited his new acquaintance to dine with him. As the three were making their way through the crowds of marketers, cam-els, donkeys, and horses that filled the market place with a confusing babel of sounds, Abdul plucked at Tarzan's sleeve.

"Look, master, behind us," and he turned, pointing at a figure which disappeared behind a camel as Tarzan turned. "He has been following us about all afternoon," continued Abdul.

"I caught only a glimpse of an Arab in a dark-blue burnoose and white turban," replied Tarzan. "Is it he you mean?"

"Yes. I suspected him because he seems a stranger here, without other business than following us, which is not the way of the Arab who is honest, and also because he keeps the lower part of his face hidden, only his eyes showing. He must be a bad man, or he would have honest business of his own to occupy his time."

"He is on the wrong scent then, Abdul," replied Tarzan, "for no one here can have any grievance against me. This is my first visit to your country, and none knows me. He will soon discover his error, and cease to follow us."

"Unless he be bent on robbery," returned Abdul.

"Then all we can do is wait until he is ready to try his hand upon us," laughed Tarzan, "and I warrant that he will get his bellyful of robbing now that we are prepared for him," and so he dismissed the subject from his mind, though he was destined to recall it before many hours through a most unlooked-for occurrence.

Kadour ben Saden, having dined well, prepared to take leave of his host. With dignified protestations of friendship, he invited Tarzan to visit him in his wild domain, where the antelope, the stag, the boar, the panther, and the lion might still be found in sufficient numbers to tempt an ardent huntsman.

On his departure the ape-man, with Abdul, wandered again into the streets of Sidi Aissa, where he was soon attracted by the wild din of sound coming from the open doorway of one of the numerous *cafés maurus*. It was after eight, and the dancing was in full swing as Tarzan entered. The room was filled to repletion with Arabs. All were smoking, and drinking their thick, hot coffee.

Tarzan and Abdul found seats near the center of the room, though the terrific noise produced by the musicians upon their Arab drums and pipes would have rendered a seat farther from them more acceptable to the quiet-loving ape-man. A rather good-looking Ouled-Nail was dancing, and, perceiving Tarzan's European clothes, and scenting a generous gratuity, she threw her silken handkerchief upon his shoulder, to be rewarded with a franc.

When her place upon the floor had been taken by another the bright-eyed Abdul saw her in conversation with two Arabs at the far side of the room, near a side door that let upon an inner court, around the gallery of which were the rooms occupied by the girls who danced in this cafe.

At first he thought nothing of the matter, but presently he noticed from the corner of his eye one of the men nod in their direction, and the girl turn and shoot a furtive glance at Tarzan. Then the Arabs melted through the doorway into the darkness of the court.

When it came again the girl's turn to dance she hovered close to Tarzan, and for the ape-man alone were her sweetest smiles. Many an ugly scowl was cast upon the tall European by swarthy, dark-eyed sons of the desert, but neither smiles nor scowls produced any outwardly visible effect upon him. Again the girl cast her handkerchief upon his shoulder, and again was she rewarded with a franc piece. As she was sticking it upon her forehead, after the custom of her kind, she bent low toward Tarzan, whispering a quick word in his ear.

"There are two without in the court," she said quickly, in broken French, "who would harm m'sieur. At first I promised to lure you to them, but you have been kind, and I cannot do it. Go quickly, before they find that I have failed them. I think that they are very bad men."

Tarzan thanked the girl, assuring her that he would be careful, and, having finished her dance, she crossed to the little doorway and went out into the court. But Tarzan did not leave the cafe as she had urged.

For another half hour nothing unusual occurred, then a surly-looking Arab entered the cafe from the street. He stood near Tarzan, where he deliberately made insulting remarks about the European, but as they were in his native tongue Tarzan was entirely innocent of their purport until Abdul took it upon himself to enlighten him.

"This fellow is looking for trouble," warned Abdul. "He is not alone. In fact, in case of a disturbance, nearly every man here would be against you. It would be better to leave quietly, master."

"Ask the fellow what he wants," commanded Tarzan.

"He says that 'the dog of a Christian' insulted the Ouled-Nail, who belongs to him. He means trouble, m'sieur."

"Tell him that I did not insult his or any other Ouled-Nail, that I

360

wish him to go away and leave me alone. That I have no quarrel with him, nor has he any with me."

"He says," replied Abdul, after delivering this message to the Arab, "that besides being a dog yourself that you are the son of one, and that your grandmother was a hyena. Incidentally you are a liar."

The attention of those near by had now been attracted by the altercation, and the sneering laughs that followed this torrent of invective easily indicated the trend of the sympathies of the majority of the audience.

Tarzan did not like being laughed at, neither did he relish the terms applied to him by the Arab, but he showed no sign of anger as he arose from his seat upon the bench. A half smile played about his lips, but of a sudden a mighty fist shot into the face of the scowling Arab, and back of it were the terrible muscles of the ape-man.

At the instant that the man fell a half dozen fierce plainsmen sprang into the room from where they had apparently been waiting for their cue in the street before the cafe. With cries of "Kill the unbeliever!" and "Down with the dog of a Christian!" they made straight for Tarzan. A number of the younger Arabs in the audience sprang to their feet to join in the assault upon the unarmed white man. Tarzan and Abdul were rushed back toward the end of the room by the very force of numbers opposing them. The young Arab remained loyal to his master, and with drawn knife fought at his side.

With tremendous blows the ape-man felled all who came within reach of his powerful hands. He fought quietly and without a word, upon his lips the same half smile they had worn as he rose to strike down the man who had insulted him. It seemed impossible that either he or Abdul could survive the sea of wicked-looking swords and knives that surrounded them, but the very numbers of their assailants proved the best bulwark of their safety. So closely packed was the howling, cursing mob that no weapon could be wielded to advantage, and none of the Arabs dared use a firearm for fear of wounding one of his compatriots.

Finally Tarzan succeeded in seizing one of the most persistent of his attackers. With a quick wrench he disarmed the fellow, and then, holding him before them as a shield, he backed slowly beside Abdul toward the little door which led into the inner courtyard. At the threshold he paused for an instant, and, lifting the struggling Arab above his head, hurled him, as though from a catapult, full in the faces of his on-pressing fellows.

Then Tarzan and Abdul stepped into the semidarkness of the court. The frightened Ouled-Nails were crouching at the tops of the stairs which led to their respective rooms, the only light in the courtyard coming from the sickly candles which each girl had stuck with its own grease to the woodwork of her door-frame, the better to display her charms to those who might happen to traverse the dark inclosure.

Scarcely had Tarzan and Abdul emerged from the room ere a revolver spoke close at their backs from the shadows beneath one of the stairways, and as they turned to meet this new antagonist, two muffled figures sprang toward them, firing as they came. Tarzan leaped to meet these two new assailants. The foremost lay, a second later, in the trampled dirt of the court, disarmed and groaning from a broken wrist. Abdul's knife found the vitals of the second in the instant that the fellow's revolver missed fire as he held it to the faithful Arab's forehead.

The maddened horde within the cafe were now rushing out in pursuit of their quarry. The Ouled-Nails had extinguished their candles at a cry from one of their number, and the only light within the yard came feebly from the open and half-blocked door of the cafe. Tarzan had seized a sword from the man who had fallen before Abdul's knife, and now he stood waiting for the rush of men that was coming in search of them through the darkness.

Suddenly he felt a light hand upon his shoulder from behind, and a woman's voice whispering, "Quick, m'sieur; this way. Follow me."

"Come, Abdul," said Tarzan, in a low tone, to the youth; "we can be no worse off elsewhere than we are here."

The woman turned and led them up the narrow stairway that ended at the door of her quarters. Tarzan was close beside her. He saw the gold and silver bracelets upon her bare arms, the strings of gold coin that depended from her hair ornaments, and the gorgeous colors of her dress. He saw that she was a Ouled-Nail, and instinctively he knew that she was the same who had whispered the warning in his ear earlier in the evening.

As they reached the top of the stairs they could hear the angry crowd searching the yard beneath.

"Soon they will search here," whispered the girl. "They must not find you, for, though you fight with the strength of many men, they will kill you in the end. Hasten; you can drop from the farther window of my room to the street beyond. Before they discover that you are no longer in the court of the buildings you will be safe within the hotel."

But even as she spoke, several men had started up the stairway at the head of which they stood. There was a sudden cry from one of the searchers. They had been discovered. Quickly the crowd rushed for the stairway. The foremost assailant leaped quickly upward, but at the top he met the sudden sword that he had not expected—the quarry had been unarmed before.

With a cry, the man toppled back upon those behind him. Like tenpins they rolled down the stairs. The ancient and rickety structure could not withstand the strain of this unwonted weight and jarring. With a creaking and rending of breaking wood it collapsed beneath the Arabs, leaving Tarzan, Abdul, and the girl alone upon the frail platform at the top.

"Come!" cried the Ouled-Nail. "They will reach us from another stairway through the room next to mine. We have not a moment to spare."

Just as they were entering the room Abdul heard and translated a cry from the yard below for several to hasten to the street and cut off escape from that side.

"We are lost now," said the girl simply.

"We?" questioned Tarzan.

"Yes, m'sieur," she responded; "they will kill me as well. Have I not aided you?"

This put a different aspect on the matter. Tarzan had rather been enjoying the excitement and danger of the encounter. He had not for an instant supposed that either Abdul or the girl could suffer except through accident, and he had only retreated just enough to keep from being killed himself. He had had no intention of running away until he saw that he was hopelessly lost were he to remain.

Alone he could have sprung into the midst of that close-packed mob, and, laying about him after the fashion of Numa, the lion, have struck the Arabs with such consternation that escape would have been easy. Now he must think entirely of these two faithful friends.

He crossed to the window which overlooked the street. In a minute there would be enemies below. Already he could hear the mob clambering the stairway to the next quarters—they would be at the door beside him in another instant. He put a foot upon the sill and leaned out, but he did not look down. Above him, within arm's reach, was the low roof of the building. He called to the girl. She came and stood beside him. He put a great arm about her and lifted her across his shoulder.

"Wait here until I reach down for you from above," he said to Abdul. "In the meantime shove everything in the room against that door—it may delay them long enough." Then he stepped to the sill of the narrow window with the girl upon his shoulders. "Hold tight," he cautioned her. A moment later he had clambered to the roof above with the ease and dexterity of an ape. Setting the girl down, he leaned far over the roof's edge, calling softly to Abdul. The youth ran to the window.

"Your hand," whispered Tarzan. The men in the room beyond were battering at the door. With a sudden crash it fell splintering in, and at the same instant Abdul felt himself lifted like a feather onto the roof above. They were not a moment too soon, for as the men broke into the room which they had just quitted a dozen more rounded the corner in the street below and came running to a spot beneath the girl's window.

VIII

THE FIGHT IN THE DESERT

s the three squatted upon the roof above the quarters of the Ouled-Nails they heard the angry cursing of the Arabs in the room beneath. Abdul translated from time to time to Tarzan.

"They are berating those in the street below now," said Abdul, "for permitting us to escape so easily. Those in the street say that we did not come that way—that we are still within the building, and that those above, being too cowardly to attack us, are attempting to deceive them into believing that we have escaped. In a moment they will have fighting of their own to attend to if they continue their brawling."

Presently those in the building gave up the search, and returned to the cafe. A few remained in the street below, smoking and talking.

Tarzan spoke to the girl, thanking her for the sacrifice she had made for him, a total stranger.

"I liked you," she said simply. "You were unlike the others who come to the cafe. You did not speak coarsely to me—the manner in which you gave me money was not an insult."

"What shall you do after tonight?" he asked. "You cannot return to the cafe. Can you even remain with safety in Sidi Aissa?"

"Tomorrow it will be forgotten," she replied. "But I should be glad if it might be that I need never return to this or another cafe. I have not remained because I wished to; I have been a prisoner."

"A prisoner!" ejaculated Tarzan incredulously.

"A slave would be the better word," she answered. "I was stolen in the night from my father's *douar* by a band of marauders. They brought me here and sold me to the Arab who keeps this cafe. It has been nearly two years now since I saw the last of mine own people. They are very far to the south. They never come to Sidi Aissa."

"You would like to return to your people?" asked Tarzan. "Then I shall promise to see you safely so far as Bou Saada at least. There we can doubtless arrange with the commandant to send you the rest of the way."

"Oh, m'sieur," she cried, "how can I ever repay you! You cannot really mean that you will do so much for a poor Ouled-Nail. But my father can reward you, and he will, for is he not a great sheik? He is Kadour ben Saden."

"Kadour ben Saden!" ejaculated Tarzan. "Why, Kadour ben Saden is in Sidi Aissa this very night. He dined with me but a few hours since."

"My father in Sidi Aissa?" cried the amazed girl. "Allah be praised then, for I am indeed saved."

"Hssh!" cautioned Abdul. "Listen."

From below came the sound of voices, quite distinguishable upon the still night air. Tarzan could not understand the words, but Abdul and the girl translated.

"They have gone now," said the latter. "It is you they want, m'sieur. One of them said that the stranger who had offered money for your slaying lay in the house of Akmed din Soulef with a broken wrist, but that he had offered a still greater reward if some would lay in wait for you upon the road to Bou Saada and kill you."

"It is he who followed m'sieur about the market today," exclaimed Abdul. "I saw him again within the cafe—him and another; and the two went out into the inner court after talking with this girl here. It was they who attacked and fired upon us, as we came out of the cafe. Why do they wish to kill you, m'sieur?"

"I do not know," replied Tarzan, and then, after a pause: "Unless——" But he did not finish, for the thought that had come to his mind, while it seemed the only reasonable solution of the mystery, appeared at the same time quite improbable. Presently the men in the street went away. The courtyard and the cafe were deserted. Cautiously Tarzan lowered himself to the sill of the girl's window. The room was empty. He returned to the roof and let Abdul down, then he lowered the girl to the arms of the waiting Arab.

From the window Abdul dropped the short distance to the street below, while Tarzan took the girl in his arms and leaped down as he had done on so many other occasions in his own forest with a burden in his arms. A little cry of alarm was startled from the girl's lips, but Tarzan landed in the street with but an imperceptible jar, and lowered her in safety to her feet.

She clung to him for a moment.

"How strong m'sieur is, and how active," she cried. "*el aldrea*, the black lion, himself is not more so."

"I should like to meet this *el aldrea* of yours," he said. "I have heard much about him."

"And you come to the *douar* of my father you shall see him," said the girl. "He lives in a spur of the mountains north of us, and comes down from his lair at night to rob my father's *douar*. With a single blow of his mighty paw he crushes the skull of a bull, and woe betide the belated wayfarer who meets *el aldrea* abroad at night."

Without further mishap they reached the hotel. The sleepy land-lord objected strenuously to instituting a search for Kadour ben Saden until the following morning, but a piece of gold put a different aspect on the matter, so that a few moments later a servant had started to make the rounds of the lesser native hostelries where it might be expected that a desert sheik would find congenial associations. Tarzan had felt it necessary to find the girl's father that night, for fear he might start on his homeward journey too early in the morning to be intercepted.

They had waited perhaps half an hour when the messenger returned with Kadour ben Saden. The old sheik entered the room with a questioning expression upon his proud face.

"Monsieur has done me the honor to—" he commenced, and then his eyes fell upon the girl. With outstretched arms he crossed the room to meet her. "My daughter!" he cried. "Allah is merciful!" and tears dimmed the martial eyes of the old warrior.

When the story of her abduction and her final rescue had been told to Kadour ben Saden he extended his hand to Tarzan.

"All that is Kadour ben Saden's is thine, my friend, even to his life," he said very simply, but Tarzan knew that those were no idle words.

It was decided that although three of them would have to ride after practically no sleep, it would be best to make an early start in the morning, and attempt to ride all the way to Bou Saada in one day. It would have been comparatively easy for the men, but for the girl it was sure to be a fatiguing journey.

She, however, was the most anxious to undertake it, for it seemed to her that she could not quickly enough reach the family and friends from whom she had been separated for two years.

It seemed to Tarzan that he had not closed his eyes before he was awakened, and in another hour the party was on its way south toward Bou Saada. For a few miles the road was good, and they made rapid progress, but suddenly it became only a waste of sand, into which the horses sank fetlock deep at nearly every step. In addition to Tarzan, Abdul, the sheik, and his daughter were four of the wild plainsmen of the sheik's tribe who had accompanied him upon the trip to Sidi Aissa. Thus, seven guns strong, they entertained little fear of attack by day, and if all went well they should reach Bou Saada before nightfall.

A brisk wind enveloped them in the blowing sand of the desert, until Tarzan's lips were parched and cracked. What little he could see of the surrounding country was far from alluring—a vast expanse of rough country, rolling in little, barren hillocks, and tufted here and there with clumps of dreary shrub. Far to the south rose the dim lines of the Saharan Atlas range. How different, thought Tarzan, from the gorgeous Africa of his boyhood!

Abdul, always on the alert, looked backward quite as often as he did ahead. At the top of each hillock that they mounted he would draw in his horse and, turning, scan the country to the rear with utmost care. At last his scrutiny was rewarded.

"Look!" he cried. "There are six horsemen behind us."

"Your friends of last evening, no doubt, monsieur," remarked Kadour ben Saden dryly to Tarzan.

"No doubt," replied the ape-man. "I am sorry that my society should endanger the safety of your journey. At the next village I shall remain and question these gentlemen, while you ride on. There is no necessity for my being at Bou Saada tonight, and less still why you should not ride in peace."

"If you stop we shall stop," said Kadour ben Saden. "Until you are safe with your friends, or the enemy has left your trail, we shall remain with you. There is nothing more to say."

Tarzan nodded his head. He was a man of few words, and possibly it was for this reason as much as any that Kadour ben Saden had taken to him, for if there be one thing that an Arab despises it is a talkative man.

All the balance of the day Abdul caught glimpses of the horsemen in their rear. They remained always at about the same distance. During the occasional halts for rest, and at the longer halt at noon, they approached no closer.

"They are waiting for darkness," said Kadour ben Saden.

And darkness came before they reached Bou Saada. The last glimpse that Abdul had of the grim, white-robed figures that trailed them, just before dusk made it impossible to distinguish them, had made it apparent that they were rapidly closing up the distance that intervened between them and their intended quarry. He whispered this fact to Tarzan, for he did not wish to alarm the girl. The ape-man drew back beside him.

"You will ride ahead with the others, Abdul," said Tarzan. "This is my quarrel. I shall wait at the next convenient spot, and interview these fellows."

"Then Abdul shall wait at thy side," replied the young Arab, nor would any threats or commands move him from his decision.

"Very well, then," replied Tarzan. "Here is as good a place as we could wish. Here are rocks at the top of this hillock. We shall remain hidden here and give an account of ourselves to these gentlemen when they appear."

They drew in their horses and dismounted. The others riding ahead were already out of sight in the darkness. Beyond them shone the lights of Bou Saada. Tarzan removed his rifle from its boot and loosened his revolver in its holster. He ordered Abdul to withdraw behind the rocks with the horses, so that they should be shielded from the enemies' bullets should they fire. The young Arab pretended to do as he was bid, but when he had fastened the two animals securely to a low shrub he crept back to lie on his belly a few paces behind Tarzan.

The ape-man stood erect in the middle of the road, waiting. Nor did he have long to wait. The sound of galloping horses came suddenly out of the darkness below him, and a moment later he discerned the moving blotches of lighter color against the solid background of the night.

"Halt," he cried, "or we fire!"

The white figures came to a sudden stop, and for a moment there was silence. Then came the sound of a whispered council, and like ghosts the phantom riders dispersed in all directions. Again the desert lay still about him, yet it was an ominous stillness that foreboded evil.

371

Abdul raised himself to one knee. Tarzan cocked his jungle-trained ears, and presently there came to him the sound of horses walking quietly through the sand to the east of him, to the west, to the north, and to the south. They had been surrounded. Then a shot came from the direction in which he was looking, a bullet whirred through the air above his head, and he fired at the flash of the enemy's gun.

Instantly the soundless waste was torn with the quick staccato of guns upon every hand. Abdul and Tarzan fired only at the flashes—they could not yet see their foemen. Presently it became evident that the attackers were circling their position, drawing closer and closer in as they began to realize the paltry numbers of the party which opposed them.

But one came too close, for Tarzan was accustomed to using his eyes in the darkness of the jungle night, than which there is no more utter darkness this side the grave, and with a cry of pain a saddle was emptied.

"The odds are evening, Abdul," said Tarzan, with a low laugh.

But they were still far too one-sided, and when the five remaining horsemen whirled at a signal and charged full upon them it looked as if there would be a sudden ending of the battle. Both Tarzan and Abdul sprang to the shelter of the rocks, that they might keep the enemy in front of them. There was a mad clatter of galloping hoofs, a volley of shots from both sides, and the Arabs withdrew to repeat the maneuver; but there were now only four against the two.

For a few moments there came no sound from out of the surrounding blackness. Tarzan could not tell whether the Arabs, satisfied with their losses, had given up the fight, or were waiting farther along the road to waylay them as they proceeded on toward Bou Saada. But he was not left long in doubt, for now all from one direction came the sound of a new charge. But scarcely had the first gun spoken ere a dozen shots rang out behind the Arabs. There came the wild shouts of a new party to the controversy, and the pounding of the feet of many horses from down the road to Bou Saada.

The Arabs did not wait to learn the identity of the oncomers. With a parting volley as they dashed by the position which Tarzan and Abdul were holding, they plunged off along the road toward Sidi Aissa. A moment later Kadour ben Saden and his men dashed up.

The old sheik was much relieved to find that neither Tarzan nor Abdul had received a scratch. Not even had their horses been wounded. They sought out the two men who had fallen before Tarzan's shots, and, finding that both were dead, left them where they lay.

"Why did you not tell me that you contemplated ambushing those fellows?" asked the sheik in a hurt tone. "We might have had them all if the seven of us had stopped to meet them."

"Then it would have been useless to stop at all," replied Tarzan, "for had we simply ridden on toward Bou Saada they would have been upon us presently, and all could have been engaged. It was to prevent the transfer of my own quarrel to another's shoulders that Abdul and I stopped off to question them. Then there is your daughter—I could not be the cause of exposing her needlessly to the marksmanship of six men."

Kadour ben Saden shrugged his shoulders. He did not relish having been cheated out of a fight.

The little battle so close to Bou Saada had drawn out a company of soldiers. Tarzan and his party met them just outside the town. The officer in charge halted them to learn the significance of the shots.

"A handful of marauders," replied Kadour ben Saden. "They attacked two of our number who had dropped behind, but when we returned to them the fellows soon dispersed. They left two dead. None of my party was injured."

This seemed to satisfy the officer, and after taking the names of the party he marched his men on toward the scene of the skirmish to bring back the dead men for purposes of identification, if possible.

Two days later, Kadour ben Saden, with his daughter and followers, rode south through the pass below Bou Saada, bound for their
home in the far wilderness. The sheik had urged Tarzan to accompany him, and the girl had added her entreaties to those of her father;
but, though he could not explain it to them, Tarzan's duties loomed
particularly large after the happenings of the past few days, so that he
could not think of leaving his post for an instant. But he promised to
come later if it lay within his power to do so, and they had to content
themselves with that assurance.

During these two days Tarzan had spent practically all his time
with Kadour ben Saden and his daughter. He was keenly interested
in this race of stern and dignified warriors, and embraced the opportunity which their friendship offered to learn what he could of their
lives and customs. He even commenced to acquire the rudiments of
their language under the pleasant tutorage of the brown-eyed girl. It
was with real regret that he saw them depart, and he sat his horse at
the opening to the pass, as far as which he had accompanied them,
gazing after the little party as long as he could catch a glimpse of
them.

Here were people after his own heart! Their wild, rough lives,
filled with danger and hardship, appealed to this half-savage man as
nothing had appealed to him in the midst of the effeminate civilization of the great cities he had visited. Here was a life that excelled
even that of the jungle, for here he might have the society of men—
real men whom he could honor and respect, and yet be near to the
wild nature that he loved. In his head revolved an idea that when he
had completed his mission he would resign and return to live for the
remainder of his life with the tribe of Kadour ben Saden.

Then he turned his horse's head and rode slowly back to Bou Saada.

The front of the Hotel du Petit Sahara, where Tarzan stopped
in Bou Saada, is taken up with the bar, two dining-rooms, and the
kitchens. Both of the dining-rooms open directly off the bar, and one

374

of them is reserved for the use of the officers of the garrison. As you stand in the barroom you may look into either of the dining-rooms if you wish.

It was to the bar that Tarzan repaired after speeding Kadour ben Saden and his party on their way. It was yet early in the morning, for Kadour ben Saden had elected to ride far that day, so that it happened that when Tarzan returned there were guests still at breakfast.

As his casual glance wandered into the officers' dining-room, Tarzan saw something which brought a look of interest to his eyes. Lieutenant Gernois was sitting there, and as Tarzan looked a white-robed Arab approached and, bending, whispered a few words into the lieutenant's ear. Then he passed on out of the building through another door.

In itself the thing was nothing, but as the man had stooped to speak to the officer, Tarzan had caught sight of something which the accidental parting of the man's burnoose had revealed—he carried his left arm in a sling.

IX

Numa "El Adrea"

n the same day that Kadour ben Saden rode south the diligence from the north brought Tarzan a letter from D'Arnot which had been forwarded from Sidi-bel-Abbes. It opened the old wound that Tarzan would have been glad to have forgotten; yet he was not sorry that D'Arnot had written, for one at least of his subjects could never cease to interest the ape-man. Here is the letter:

MY DEAR JEAN:

Since last I wrote you I have been across to London on a matter of business. I was there but three days. The very first day I came upon an old friend of yours—quite unexpectedly—in Henrietta Street. Now you never in the world would guess whom. None other than Mr. Samuel T. Philander. But it is true. I can see your look of incredulity. Nor is this all. He insisted that I return to the hotel with him, and there I found the others—Professor Archimedes Q. Porter, Miss Porter, and that enormous black woman, Miss Porter's maid—Esmeralda, you will recall. While I was there Clayton came in. They are to be married soon, or rather sooner, for I rather suspect that we shall receive announcements almost any day. On account of his father's death it is to be a very quiet affair—only blood relatives.

While I was alone with Mr. Philander the old fellow became rather confidential. Said Miss Porter had already postponed the wedding on three different occasions. He confided that it appeared to him that she was not particularly anxious to marry Clayton at all; but this time it seems that it is quite likely to go through.

Of course they all asked after you, but I respected your wishes in the matter of your true origin, and only spoke to them of your present affairs.

Miss Porter was especially interested in everything I had to say about you, and asked many questions. I am afraid I took a rather unchivalrous delight in picturing your desire and resolve to go back eventually to your native jungle. I was sorry afterward, for it did seem to cause her real anguish to contemplate the awful dangers to which you wished to return. "And yet," she said, "I do not know. There are more unhappy fates than the grim and terrible jungle presents to Monsieur Tarzan. At least his conscience will be free from remorse. And there are moments of quiet and restfulness by day, and vistas of exquisite beauty. You may find it strange that I should say it, who experienced such terrifying experiences in that frightful forest, yet at times I long to return, for I cannot but feel that the happiest moments of my life were spent there."

There was an expression of ineffable sadness on her face as she spoke, and I could not but feel that she knew that I knew her secret, and that this was her way of transmitting to you a last tender message from a heart that might still enshrine your memory, though its possessor belonged to another.

Clayton appeared nervous and ill at ease while you were the subject of conversation. He wore a worried and harassed expression. Yet he was very kindly in his expressions of interest in you. I wonder if he suspects the truth about you?

Tennington came in with Clayton. They are great friends, you know. He is about to set out upon one of his interminable cruises in that yacht of his, and was urging the entire party to accompany him. Tried to inveigle me into it, too. Is thinking of circumnavigating Africa this time. I told him that his precious toy would take him and some of his friends to the bottom of the ocean one of these days if he didn't get it out of his head that she was a liner or a battleship.

I returned to Paris day before yesterday, and yesterday I met the Count and Countess de Coude at the races. They inquired after you. De Coude really seems quite fond of you. Doesn't appear to harbor the least ill will. Olga is as beautiful as ever, but a trifle subdued. I imagine that she learned a lesson through her acquaintance with you that will serve her in good stead during the balance of her life. It is fortunate for her, and for De Coude as well, that it was you and not another man more sophisticated.

Had you really paid court to Olga's heart I am afraid that there would have been no hope for either of you.

She asked me to tell you that Nikolas had left France. She paid him twenty thousand francs to go away, and stay. She is congratulating herself that she got rid of him before he tried to carry out a threat he recently made her that he should kill you at the first opportunity. She said that she should hate to think that her brother's blood was on your hands, for she is very fond of you, and made no bones in saying so before the count. It never for a moment seemed to occur to her that there might be any possibility of any other outcome of a meeting between you and Nikolas. The count quite agreed with her in that. He added that it would take a regiment of Rokoffs to kill you. He has a most healthy respect for your prowess.

Have been ordered back to my ship. She sails from Havre in two days under sealed orders. If you will address me in her care, the letters will find me eventually. I shall write you as soon as another opportunity presents.

Your sincere friend,

PAUL D'ARNOT.

"I fear," mused Tarzan, half aloud, "that Olga has thrown away her twenty thousand francs."

He read over that part of D'Arnot's letter several times in which he had quoted from his conversation with Jane Porter. Tarzan derived a rather pathetic happiness from it, but it was better than no happiness at all.

The following three weeks were quite uneventful. On several occasions Tarzan saw the mysterious Arab, and once again he had been exchanging words with Lieutenant Gernois; but no amount of espionage or shadowing by Tarzan revealed the Arab's lodgings, the location of which Tarzan was anxious to ascertain.

Gernois, never cordial, had kept more than ever aloof from Tarzan since the episode in the dining-room of the hotel at Aumale. His attitude on the few occasions that they had been thrown together had been distinctly hostile.

That he might keep up the appearance of the character he was playing, Tarzan spent considerable time hunting in the vicinity of Bou Saada. He would spend entire days in the foothills, ostensibly searching for gazelle, but on the few occasions that he came close enough to any of the beautiful little animals to harm them he invariably allowed them to escape without so much as taking his rifle from its boot. The ape-man could see no sport in slaughtering the most harmless and defenseless of God's creatures for the mere pleasure of killing.

In fact, Tarzan had never killed for "pleasure," nor to him was there pleasure in killing. It was the joy of righteous battle that he loved—the ecstasy of victory. And the keen and successful hunt for food in which he pitted his skill and craftiness against the skill and craftiness of another; but to come out of a town filled with food to shoot down a soft-eyed, pretty gazelle—ah, that was crueller than the deliberate and cold-blooded murder of a fellow man. Tarzan would have none of it, and so he hunted alone that none might discover the sham that he was practicing.

And once, probably because of the fact that he rode alone, he was like to have lost his life. He was riding slowly through a little ravine when a shot sounded close behind him, and a bullet passed through the cork helmet he wore. Although he turned at once and galloped rapidly to the top of the ravine, there was no sign of any enemy, nor did he see aught of another human being until he reached Bou Saada.

"Yes," he soliloquized, in recalling the occurrence, "Olga has indeed thrown away her twenty thousand francs."

That night he was Captain Gerard's guest at a little dinner.

"Your hunting has not been very fortunate?" questioned the officer.

"No," replied Tarzan; "the game hereabout is timid, nor do I care particularly about hunting game birds or antelope. I think I shall move on farther south, and have a try at some of your Algerian lions."

"Good!" exclaimed the captain. "We are marching toward Djelfa on the morrow. You shall have company that far at least. Lieutenant Gernois and I, with a hundred men, are ordered south to patrol a district in which the marauders are giving considerable trouble. Possibly we may have the pleasure of hunting the lion together—what say you?"

Tarzan was more than pleased, nor did he hesitate to say so; but the captain would have been astonished had he known the real reason of Tarzan's pleasure. Gernois was sitting opposite the ape-man. He did not seem so pleased with his captain's invitation.

"You will find lion hunting more exciting than gazelle shooting," remarked Captain Gerard, "and more dangerous."

"Even gazelle shooting has its dangers," replied Tarzan. "Especially when one goes alone. I found it so today. I also found that while the gazelle is the most timid of animals, it is not the most cowardly."

He let his glance rest only casually upon Gernois after he had spoken, for he did not wish the man to know that he was under suspicion, or surveillance, no matter what he might think. The effect of his remark upon him, however, might tend to prove his connection with, or knowledge of, certain recent happenings. Tarzan saw a dull red creep up from beneath Gernois' collar. He was satisfied, and quickly changed the subject.

When the column rode south from Bou Saada the next morning there were half a dozen Arabs bringing up the rear.

"They are not attached to the command," replied Gerard in response to Tarzan's query. "They merely accompany us on the road for companionship."

Tarzan had learned enough about Arab character since he had been in Algeria to know that this was no real motive, for the Arab is never overfond of the companionship of strangers, and especially of French soldiers. So his suspicions were aroused, and he decided to keep a sharp eye on the little party that trailed behind the column at a distance of about a quarter of a mile. But they did not come close enough even during the halts to enable him to obtain a close scrutiny of them.

He had long been convinced that there were hired assassins on his trail, nor was he in great doubt but that Rokoff was at the bottom of the plot. Whether it was to be revenge for the several occasions in the past that Tarzan had defeated the Russian's purposes and humiliated him, or was in some way connected with his mission in the Gernois affair, he could not determine. If the latter, and it seemed probable since the evidence he had had that Gernois suspected him, then he had two rather powerful enemies to contend with, for there would be many opportunities in the wilds of Algeria, for which they were bound, to dispatch a suspected enemy quietly and without attracting suspicion.

After camping at Djelfa for two days the column moved to the southwest, from whence word had come that the marauders were operating against the tribes whose *douars* were situated at the foot of the mountains.

The little band of Arabs who had accompanied them from Bou Saada had disappeared suddenly the very night that orders had been given to prepare for the morrow's march from Djelfa. Tarzan made casual inquiries among the men, but none could tell him why they had left, or in what direction they had gone. He did not like the looks of it, especially in view of the fact that he had seen Gernois in conversation with one of them some half hour after Captain Gerard had issued his instructions relative to the new move. Only Gernois and Tarzan knew the direction of the proposed march. All the soldiers knew was that they were to be prepared to break camp early the next morning. Tarzan wondered if Gernois could have revealed their destination to the Arabs.

Late that afternoon they went into camp at a little oasis in which was the *douar* of a sheik whose flocks were being stolen, and whose herdsmen were being killed. The Arabs came out of their goatskin tents, and surrounded the soldiers, asking many questions in the native tongue, for the soldiers were themselves natives. Tarzan, who, by this time, with the assistance of Abdul, had picked up quite a smattering of Arab, questioned one of the younger men who had accompanied the sheik while the latter paid his respects to Captain Gerard.

No, he had seen no party of six horsemen riding from the direction of Djelfa. There were other oases scattered about—possibly they had been journeying to one of these. Then there were the marauders in the mountains above—they often rode north to Bou Saada in small parties, and even as far as Aumale and Bouira. It might indeed have been a few marauders returning to the band from a pleasure trip to one of these cities.

Early the next morning Captain Gerard split his command in two, giving Lieutenant Gernois command of one party, while he headed the other. They were to scour the mountains upon opposite sides of the plain.

"And with which detachment will Monsieur Tarzan ride?" asked the captain. "Or maybe it is that monsieur does not care to hunt marauders?"

"Oh, I shall be delighted to go," Tarzan hastened to explain. He was wondering what excuse he could make to accompany Gernois. His embarrassment was short-lived, and was relieved from a most unexpected source. It was Gernois himself who spoke.

"If my captain will forego the pleasure of Monsieur Tarzan's company for this once, I shall esteem it an honor indeed to have monsieur ride with me today," he said, nor was his tone lacking in cordiality. In fact, Tarzan imagined that he had overdone it a trifle, but, even so, he was both astounded and pleased, hastening to express his delight at the arrangement.

And so it was that Lieutenant Gernois and Tarzan rode off side by side at the head of the little detachment of *spahis*. Gernois' cordiality was short-lived. No sooner had they ridden out of sight of Captain Gerard and his men than he lapsed once more into his accustomed taciturnity. As they advanced the ground became rougher. Steadily it ascended toward the mountains, into which they filed through a narrow canon close to noon. By the side of a little rivulet Gernois called the midday halt. Here the men prepared and ate their frugal meal, and refilled their canteens.

After an hour's rest they advanced again along the canon, until they presently came to a little valley, from which several rocky gorges diverged. Here they halted, while Gernois minutely examined the surrounding heights from the center of the depression.

"We shall separate here," he said, "several riding into each of these gorges," and then he commenced to detail his various squads and issue instructions to the non-commissioned officers who were to command them. When he had done he turned to Tarzan. "Monsieur will be so good as to remain here until we return."

Tarzan demurred, but the officer cut him short. "There may be fighting for one of these sections," he said, "and troops cannot be embarrassed by civilian noncombatants during action."

"But, my dear lieutenant," expostulated Tarzan, "I am most ready and willing to place myself under command of yourself or any of your sergeants or corporals, and to fight in the ranks as they direct. It is what I came for."

"I should be glad to think so," retorted Gernois, with a sneer he made no attempt to disguise. Then shortly: "You are under my orders, and they are that you remain here until we return. Let that end the matter," and he turned and spurred away at the head of his men. A moment later Tarzan found himself alone in the midst of a desolate mountain fastness.

The sun was hot, so he sought the shelter of a nearby tree, where he tethered his horse, and sat down upon the ground to smoke. Inwardly he swore at Gernois for the trick he had played upon him. A mean little revenge, thought Tarzan, and then suddenly it occurred to him that the man would not be such a fool as to antagonize him through a trivial annoyance of so petty a description. There must be something deeper than this behind it. With the thought he arose and removed his rifle from its boot. He looked to its loads and saw that the magazine was full. Then he inspected his revolver. After this preliminary precaution he scanned the surrounding heights and the mouths of the several gorges—he was determined that he should not be caught napping.

The sun sank lower and lower, yet there was no sign of returning *spahis*. At last the valley was submerged in shadow Tarzan was too proud to go back to camp until he had given the detachment ample time to return to the valley, which he thought was to have been their rendezvous. With the closing in of night he felt safer from attack, for he was at home in the dark. He knew that none might approach him so cautiously as to elude those alert and sensitive ears of his; then there were his eyes, too, for he could see well at night; and his nose, if they came toward him from up-wind, would apprise him of the approach of an enemy while they were still a great way off.

So he felt that he was in little danger, and thus lulled to a sense of security he fell asleep, with his back against the tree.

He must have slept for several hours, for when he was suddenly awakened by the frightened snorting and plunging of his horse the moon was shining full upon the little valley, and there, not ten paces before him, stood the grim cause of the terror of his mount.

Superb, majestic, his graceful tail extended and quivering, and his two eyes of fire riveted full upon his prey, stood Numa *el adrea*, the black lion. A little thrill of joy tingled through Tarzan's nerves. It was like meeting an old friend after years of separation. For a moment he sat rigid to enjoy the magnificent spectacle of this lord of the wilderness.

But now Numa was crouching for the spring. Very slowly Tarzan raised his gun to his shoulder. He had never killed a large animal with a gun in all his life—heretofore he had depended upon his spear, his poisoned arrows, his rope, his knife, or his bare hands. Instinctively he wished that he had his arrows and his knife—he would have felt surer with them.

Numa was lying quite flat upon the ground now, presenting only his head. Tarzan would have preferred to fire a little from one side, for he knew what terrific damage the lion could do if he lived two minutes, or even a minute after he was hit. The horse stood trembling in terror at Tarzan's back. The ape-man took a cautious step to one side—Numa but followed him with his eyes. Another step he took, and then another. Numa had not moved. Now he could aim at a point between the eye and the ear.

His finger tightened upon the trigger, and as he fired Numa sprang. At the same instant the terrified horse made a last frantic effort to escape—the tether parted, and he went careening down the canon toward the desert.

No ordinary man could have escaped those frightful claws when Numa sprang from so short a distance, but Tarzan was no ordinary man. From earliest childhood his muscles had been trained by the fierce exigencies of his existence to act with the rapidity of thought. As quick as was *el adrea*, Tarzan of the Apes was quicker, and so the great beast crashed against a tree where he had expected to feel the soft flesh of man, while Tarzan, a couple of paces to the right, pumped another bullet into him that brought him clawing and roaring to his side.

Twice more Tarzan fired in quick succession, and then *el adrea* lay still and roared no more. It was no longer Monsieur Jean Tarzan; it was Tarzan of the Apes that put a savage foot upon the body of his savage kill, and, raising his face to the full moon, lifted his mighty voice in the weird and terrible challenge of his kind—a bull ape had made his kill. And the wild things in the wild mountains stopped in their hunting, and trembled at this new and awful voice, while down in the desert the children of the wilderness came out of their goatskin tents and looked toward the mountains, wondering what new and savage scourge had come to devastate their flocks.

A half mile from the valley in which Tarzan stood, a score of white-robed figures, bearing long, wicked-looking guns, halted at the sound, and looked at one another with questioning eyes. But presently, as it was not repeated, they took up their silent, stealthy way toward the valley.

Tarzan was now confident that Gernois had no intention of returning for him, but he could not fathom the object that had prompted the officer to desert him, yet leave him free to return to camp. His horse gone, he decided that it would be foolish to remain longer in the mountains, so he set out toward the desert.

He had scarcely entered the confines of the canon when the first of the white-robed figures emerged into the valley upon the opposite side. For a moment they scanned the little depression from behind sheltering bowlders, but when they had satisfied themselves that it was empty they advanced across it. Beneath the tree at one side they came upon the body of *el adrea*. With muttered exclamations they crowded about it. Then, a moment later, they hurried down the cañon which Tarzan was threading a brief distance in advance of them. They moved cautiously and in silence, taking advantage of shelter, as men do who are stalking man.

X

THROUGH THE VALLEY OF THE SHADOW

s Tarzan walked down the wild cañon beneath the brilliant African moon the call of the jungle was strong upon him. The solitude and the savage freedom filled his heart with life and buoyancy. Again he was Tarzan of the Apes—every sense alert against the chance of surprise by some jungle enemy—yet treading lightly and with head erect, in proud consciousness of his might.

The nocturnal sounds of the mountains were new to him, yet they fell upon his ears like the soft voice of a half-forgotten love. Many he intuitively sensed—ah, there was one that was familiar indeed; the distant coughing of Sheeta, the leopard; but there was a strange note in the final wail which made him doubt. It was a panther he heard.

Presently a new sound—a soft, stealthy sound—obtruded itself among the others. No human ears other than the ape-man's would have detected it. At first he did not translate it, but finally he realized that it came from the bare feet of a number of human beings. They were behind him, and they were coming toward him quietly. He was being stalked.

In a flash he knew why he had been left in that little valley by Gernois; but there had been a hitch in the arrangements—the men had come too late. Closer and closer came the footsteps. Tarzan halted and faced them, his rifle ready in his hand. Now he caught a fleeting glimpse of a white burnoose. He called aloud in French, asking what they would of him. His reply was the flash of a long gun, and with the sound of the shot Tarzan of the Apes plunged forward upon his face.

The Arabs did not rush out immediately; instead, they waited to be sure that their victim did not rise. Then they came rapidly from their concealment, and bent over him. It was soon apparent that he was not dead. One of the men put the muzzle of his gun to the back of Tarzan's head to finish him, but another waved him aside. "If we bring him alive the reward is to be greater," explained the latter. So they bound his hands and feet, and, picking him up, placed him on the shoulders of four of their number. Then the march was resumed toward the desert. When they had come out of the mountains they turned toward the south, and about daylight came to the spot where their horses stood in care of two of their number.

From here on their progress was more rapid. Tarzan, who had regained consciousness, was tied to a spare horse, which they evidently had brought for the purpose. His wound was but a slight scratch, which had furrowed the flesh across his temple. It had stopped bleeding, but the dried and clotted blood smeared his face and clothing. He had said no word since he had fallen into the hands of these Arabs, nor had they addressed him other than to issue a few brief commands to him when the horses had been reached.

For six hours they rode rapidly across the burning desert, avoiding the oases near which their way led. About noon they came to a *douar* of about twenty tents. Here they halted, and as one of the Arabs was releasing the alfa-grass ropes which bound him to his mount they were surrounded by a mob of men, women, and children. Many of the tribe, and more especially the women, appeared to take delight in heaping insults upon the prisoner, and some had even gone so far as to throw stones at him and strike him with sticks, when an old sheik appeared and drove them away.

"Ali-ben-Ahmed tells me," he said, "that this man sat alone in the mountains and slew *el adrea*. What the business of the stranger who sent us after him may be, I know not, and what he may do with this man when we turn him over to him, I care not; but the prisoner is a brave man, and while he is in our hands he shall be treated with the respect that be due one who hunts *the lord with the large head* alone and by night—and slays him."

Tarzan had heard of the respect in which Arabs held a lion-killer, and he was not sorry that chance had played into his hands thus favorably to relieve him of the petty tortures of the tribe. Shortly after this he was taken to a goat-skin tent upon the upper side of the *douar*. There he was fed, and then, securely bound, was left lying on a piece of native carpet, alone in the tent.

He could see a guard sitting before the door of his frail prison, but when he attempted to force the stout bonds that held him he realized that any extra precaution on the part of his captors was quite unnecessary; not even his giant muscles could part those numerous strands.

Just before dusk several men approached the tent where he lay, and entered it. All were in Arab dress, but presently one of the number advanced to Tarzan's side, and as he let the folds of cloth that had hidden the lower half of his face fall away the ape-man saw the malevolent features of Nikolas Rokoff. There was a nasty smile on the bearded lips. "Ah, Monsieur Tarzan," he said, "this is indeed a pleasure. But why do you not rise and greet your guest?" Then, with an ugly oath, "Get up, you dog!" and, drawing back his booted foot, he kicked Tarzan heavily in the side. "And here is another, and another, and another," he continued, as he kicked Tarzan about the face and side. "One for each of the injuries you have done me."

The ape-man made no reply—he did not even deign to look upon the Russian again after the first glance of recognition. Finally the sheik, who had been standing a mute and frowning witness of the cowardly attack, intervened.

"Stop!" he commanded. "Kill him if you will, but I will see no brave man subjected to such indignities in my presence. I have half a mind to turn him loose, that I may see how long you would kick him then."

This threat put a sudden end to Rokoff's brutality, for he had no craving to see Tarzan loosed from his bonds while he was within reach of those powerful hands.

"Very well," he replied to the Arab; "I shall kill him presently."

"Not within the precincts of my *douar*," returned the sheik. "When he leaves here he leaves alive. What you do with him in the desert is none of my concern, but I shall not have the blood of a Frenchman on the hands of my tribe on account of another man's quarrel—they would send soldiers here and kill many of my people, and burn our tents and drive away our flocks."

"As you say," growled Rokoff. "I'll take him out into the desert below the *douar*, and dispatch him."

"You will take him a day's ride from my country," said the sheik, firmly, "and some of my children shall follow you to see that you do not disobey me—otherwise there may be two dead Frenchmen in the desert."

Rokoff shrugged. "Then I shall have to wait until the morrow—it is already dark."

"As you will," said the sheik. "But by an hour after dawn you must be gone from my *douar*. I have little liking for unbelievers, and none at all for a coward."

Rokoff would have made some kind of retort, but he checked himself, for he realized that it would require but little excuse for the old man to turn upon him. Together they left the tent. At the door Rokoff could not resist the temptation to turn and fling a parting taunt at Tarzan. "Sleep well, monsieur," he said, "and do not forget to pray well, for when you die tomorrow it will be in such agony that you will be unable to pray for blaspheming."

No one had bothered to bring Tarzan either food or water since noon, and consequently he suffered considerably from thirst. He wondered if it would be worth while to ask his guard for water, but after making two or three requests without receiving any response, he decided that it would not.

Far up in the mountains he heard a lion roar. How much safer one was, he soliloquized, in the haunts of wild beasts than in the haunts of men. Never in all his jungle life had he been more relentlessly tracked down than in the past few months of his experience among civilized men. Never had he been any nearer death.

Again the lion roared. It sounded a little nearer. Tarzan felt the old, wild impulse to reply with the challenge of his kind. His kind? He had almost forgotten that he was a man and not an ape. He tugged at his bonds. God, if he could but get them near those strong teeth of his. He felt a wild wave of madness sweep over him as his efforts to regain his liberty met with failure.

Numa was roaring almost continually now. It was quite evident that he was coming down into the desert to hunt. It was the roar of a hungry lion. Tarzan envied him, for he was free. No one would tie him with ropes and slaughter him like a sheep. It was that which galled the ape-man. He did not fear to die, no—it was the humiliation of defeat before death, without even a chance to battle for his life.

It must be near midnight, thought Tarzan. He had several hours to live. Possibly he would yet find a way to take Rokoff with him on the long journey. He could hear the savage lord of the desert quite close by now. Possibly he sought his meat from among the penned animals within the *douar*.

For a long time silence reigned, then Tarzan's trained ears caught the sound of a stealthily moving body. It came from the side of the tent nearest the mountains—the back. Nearer and nearer it came. He waited, listening intently, for it to pass. For a time there was silence without, such a terrible silence that Tarzan was surprised that he did not hear the breathing of the animal he felt sure must be crouching close to the back wall of his tent.

There! It is moving again. Closer it creeps. Tarzan turns his head in the direction of the sound. It is very dark within the tent. Slowly the back rises from the ground, forced up by the head and shoulders of a body that looks all black in the semi-darkness. Beyond is a faint glimpse of the dimly starlit desert. A grim smile plays about Tarzan's lips. At least Rokoff will be cheated. How mad he will be! And death will be more merciful than he could have hoped for at the hands of the Russian.

Now the back of the tent drops into place, and all is darkness again—whatever it is is inside the tent with him. He hears it creeping close to him—now it is beside him. He closes his eyes and waits for the mighty paw. Upon his upturned face falls the gentle touch of a soft hand groping in the dark, and then a girl's voice in a scarcely audible whisper pronounces his name.

"Yes, it is I," he whispers in reply. "But in the name of Heaven who are you?"

"The Ouled-Nail of Sisi Aissa," came the answer. While she spoke Tarzan could feel her working about his bonds. Occasionally the cold steel of a knife touched his flesh. A moment later he was free.

"Come!" she whispered.

On hands and knees he followed her out of the tent by the way she had come. She continued crawling thus flat to the ground until she reached a little patch of shrub. There she halted until he gained her side. For a moment he looked at her before he spoke.

"I cannot understand," he said at last. "Why are you here? How did you know that I was a prisoner in that tent? How does it happen that it is you who have saved me?"

She smiled. "I have come a long way tonight," she said, "and we have a long way to go before we shall be out of danger. Come; I shall tell you all about as we go."

Together they rose and set off across the desert in the direction of the mountains.

"I was not quite sure that I should ever reach you," she said at last. "*El adrea* is abroad tonight, and after I left the horses I think he winded me and was following—I was terribly frightened."

"What a brave girl," he said. "And you ran all that risk for a stranger—an alien—an unbeliever?"

She drew herself up very proudly.

"I am the daughter of the Sheik Kabour ben Saden," she answered. "I should be no fit daughter of his if I would not risk my life to save that of the man who saved mine while he yet thought that I was but a common Ouled-Nail."

"Nevertheless," he insisted, "you are a very brave girl. But how did you know that I was a prisoner back there?"

"Achmet-din-Taieb, who is my cousin on my father's side, was visiting some friends who belong to the tribe that captured you. He was at the *douar* when you were brought in. When he reached home he was telling us about the big Frenchman who had been captured by Ali-ben-Ahmed for another Frenchman who wished to kill him. From the description I knew that it must be you. My father was away. I tried to persuade some of the men to come and save you, but they would not do it, saying: 'Let the unbelievers kill one another if they wish. It is none of our affair, and if we go and interfere with Ali-ben-Ahmed's plans we shall only stir up a fight with our own people.'

"So when it was dark I came alone, riding one horse and leading another for you. They are tethered not far from here. By morning we shall be within my father's *douar*. He should be there himself by now—then let them come and try to take Kadour ben Saden's friend."

For a few moments they walked on in silence.

"We should be near the horses," she said. "It is strange that I do not see them here."

Then a moment later she stopped, with a little cry of consternation. "They are gone!" she exclaimed. "It is here that I tethered them."

Tarzan stooped to examine the ground. He found that a large shrub had been torn up by the roots. Then he found something else. There was a wry smile on his face as he rose and turned toward the girl.

"*El adrea* has been here. From the signs, though, I rather think that his prey escaped him. With a little start they would be safe enough from him in the open."

There was nothing to do but continue on foot. The way led them across a low spur of the mountains, but the girl knew the trail as well as she did her mother's face. They walked in easy, swinging strides, Tarzan keeping a hand's breadth behind the girl's shoulder, that she might set the pace, and thus be less fatigued. As they walked they talked, occasionally stopping to listen for sounds of pursuit.

It was now a beautiful, moonlit night. The air was crisp and invigorating. Behind them lay the interminable vista of the desert, dotted here and there with an occasional oasis. The date palms of the little fertile spot they had just left, and the circle of goat-skin tents, stood out in sharp relief against the yellow sand—a phantom paradise upon a phantom sea. Before them rose the grim and silent mountains. Tarzan's blood leaped in his veins. This was life! He looked down upon the girl beside him—a daughter of the desert walking across the face of a dead world with a son of the jungle. He smiled at the thought. He wished that he had had a sister, and that she had been like this girl. What a bully chum she would have been!

They had entered the mountains now, and were progressing more slowly, for the trail was steeper and very rocky.

For a few minutes they had been silent. The girl was wondering if they would reach her father's *douar* before the pursuit had overtaken them. Tarzan was wishing that they might walk on thus forever. If the girl were only a man they might. He longed for a friend who loved the same wild life that he loved. He had learned to crave companionship, but it was his misfortune that most of the men he knew preferred immaculate linen and their clubs to nakedness and the jungle. It was, of course, difficult to understand, yet it was very evident that they did.

The two had just turned a projecting rock around which the trail ran when they were brought to a sudden stop. There, before them, directly in the middle of the path, stood Numa, *el adrea*, the black lion. His green eyes looked very wicked, and he bared his teeth, and lashed his bay-black sides with his angry tail. Then he roared—the fearsome, terror-inspiring roar of the hungry lion which is also angry.

"Your knife," said Tarzan to the girl, extending his hand. She slipped the hilt of the weapon into his waiting palm. As his fingers closed upon it he drew her back and pushed her behind him. "Walk back to the desert as rapidly as you can. If you hear me call you will know that all is well, and you may return."

"It is useless," she replied, resignedly. "This is the end."

"Do as I tell you," he commanded. "Quickly! He is about to charge." The girl dropped back a few paces, where she stood watching for the terrible sight that she knew she should soon witness.

The lion was advancing slowly toward Tarzan, his nose to the ground, like a challenging bull, his tail extended now and quivering as though with intense excitement.

The ape-man stood, half crouching, the long Arab knife glistening in the moonlight. Behind him the tense figure of the girl, motionless as a carven statue. She leaned slightly forward, her lips parted, her eyes wide. Her only conscious thought was wonder at the bravery of the man who dared face with a puny knife the lord with the large head. A man of her own blood would have knelt in prayer and gone down beneath those awful fangs without resistance. In either case the result would be the same—it was inevitable; but she could not repress a thrill of admiration as her eyes rested upon the heroic figure before her. Not a tremor in the whole giant frame—his attitude as menacing and defiant as that of *el adrea* himself.

The lion was quite close to him now—but a few paces intervened—he crouched, and then, with a deafening roar, he sprang.

XI

John Caldwell, London

s Numa *el adrea* launched himself with widespread paws and bared fangs he looked to find this puny man as easy prey as the score who had gone down beneath him in the past. To him man was a clumsy, slow-moving, defenseless creature—he had little respect for him.

But this time he found that he was pitted against a creature as agile and as quick as himself. When his mighty frame struck the spot where the man had been he was no longer there.

The watching girl was transfixed by astonishment at the ease with which the crouching man eluded the great paws. And now, O Allah! He had rushed in behind *el adrea*'s shoulder even before the beast could turn, and had grasped him by the mane. The lion reared upon his hind legs like a horse—Tarzan had known that he would do this, and he was ready. A giant arm encircled the black-maned throat, and once, twice, a dozen times a sharp blade darted in and out of the bay-black side behind the left shoulder.

Frantic were the leaps of Numa—awful his roars of rage and pain; but the giant upon his back could not be dislodged or brought within reach of fangs or talons in the brief interval of life that remained to the lord with the large head. He was quite dead when Tarzan of the Apes released his hold and arose. Then the daughter of the desert

398

witnessed a thing that terrified her even more than had the presence of *el adrea*. The man placed a foot upon the carcass of his kill, and, with his handsome face raised toward the full moon, gave voice to the most frightful cry that ever had smote upon her ears.

With a little cry of fear she shrank away from him—she thought that the fearful strain of the encounter had driven him mad. As the last note of that fiendish challenge died out in the diminishing echoes of the distance the man dropped his eyes until they rested upon the girl.

Instantly his face was lighted by the kindly smile that was ample assurance of his sanity, and the girl breathed freely once again, smiling in response.

"What manner of man are you?" she asked. "The thing you have done is unheard of. Even now I cannot believe that it is possible for a lone man armed only with a knife to have fought hand to hand with *el adrea* and conquered him, unscathed—to have conquered him at all. And that cry—it was not human. Why did you do that?"

Tarzan flushed. "It is because I forget," he said, "sometimes, that I am a civilized man. When I kill it must be that I am another creature." He did not try to explain further, for it always seemed to him that a woman must look with loathing upon one who was yet so nearly a beast.

Together they continued their journey. The sun was an hour high when they came out into the desert again beyond the mountains. Beside a little rivulet they found the girl's horses grazing. They had come this far on their way home, and with the cause of their fear no longer present had stopped to feed.

With little trouble Tarzan and the girl caught them, and, mounting, rode out into the desert toward the *douar* of Sheik Kadour ben Saden.

No sign of pursuit developed, and they came in safety about nine o'clock to their destination. The sheik had but just returned. He was frantic with grief at the absence of his daughter, whom he thought had been again abducted by the marauders. With fifty men he was already mounted to go in search of her when the two rode into the *douar*.

His joy at the safe return of his daughter was only equaled by his gratitude to Tarzan for bringing her safely to him through the dangers of the night, and his thankfulness that she had been in time to save the man who had once saved her.

No honor that Kadour ben Saden could heap upon the ape-man in acknowledgment of his esteem and friendship was neglected. When the girl had recited the story of the slaying of *el adrea* Tarzan was surrounded by a mob of worshiping Arabs—it was a sure road to their admiration and respect.

The old sheik insisted that Tarzan remain indefinitely as his guest. He even wished to adopt him as a member of the tribe, and there was for some time a half-formed resolution in the ape-man's mind to accept and remain forever with these wild people, whom he understood and who seemed to understand him. His friendship and liking for the girl were potent factors in urging him toward an affirmative decision.

Had she been a man, he argued, he should not have hesitated, for it would have meant a friend after his own heart, with whom he could ride and hunt at will; but as it was they would be hedged by the conventionalities that are even more strictly observed by the wild nomads of the desert than by their more civilized brothers and sisters. And in a little while she would be married to one of these swarthy warriors, and there would be an end to their friendship. So he decided against the sheik's proposal, though he remained a week as his guest.

When he left, Kadour ben Saden and fifty white-robed warriors rode with him to Bou Saada. While they were mounting in the *douar* of Kadour ben Saden the morning of their departure, the girl came to bid farewell to Tarzan.

"I have prayed that you would remain with us," she said simply, as he leaned from his saddle to clasp her hand in farewell, "and now I shall pray that you will return." There was an expression of wistfulness in her beautiful eyes, and a pathetic droop at the corners of her mouth. Tarzan was touched.

"Who knows?" and then he turned and rode after the departing Arabs.

Outside Bou Saada he bade Kadour ben Saden and his men good-by, for there were reasons which made him wish to make his entry into the town as secret as possible, and when he had explained them to the sheik the latter concurred in his decision. The Arabs were to enter Bou Saada ahead of him, saying nothing as to his presence with them. Later Tarzan would come in alone, and go directly to an obscure native inn.

Thus, making his entrance after dark, as he did, he was not seen by any one who knew him, and reached the inn unobserved. After dining with Kadour ben Saden as his guest, he went to his former hotel by a roundabout way, and, coming in by a rear entrance, sought the proprietor, who seemed much surprised to see him alive.

Yes, there was mail for monsieur; he would fetch it. No, he would mention monsieur's return to no one. Presently he returned with a packet of letters. One was an order from his superior to lay off on his present work, and hasten to Cape Town by the first steamer he could get. His further instructions would be awaiting him there in the hands of another agent whose name and address were given. That was all—brief but explicit. Tarzan arranged to leave Bou Saada early the next morning. Then he started for the garrison to see Captain Gerard, whom the hotel man had told him had returned with his detachment the previous day.

He found the officer in his quarters. He was filled with surprise and pleasure at seeing Tarzan alive and well.

"When Lieutenant Gernois returned and reported that he had

401

not found you at the spot that you had chosen to remain while the detachment was scouting, I was filled with alarm. We searched the mountain for days. Then came word that you had been killed and eaten by a lion. As proof your gun was brought to us. Your horse had returned to camp the second day after your disappearance. We could not doubt. Lieutenant Gernois was grief-stricken—he took all the blame upon himself. It was he who insisted on carrying on the search himself. It was he who found the Arab with your gun. He will be delighted to know that you are safe."

"Doubtless," said Tarzan, with a grim smile.

"He is down in the town now, or I should send for him," continued Captain Gerard. "I shall tell him as soon as he returns."

Tarzan let the officer think that he had been lost, wandering finally into the *douar* of Kadour ben Saden, who had escorted him back to Bou Saada. As soon as possible he bade the good officer adieu, and hastened back into the town. At the native inn he had learned through Kadour ben Saden a piece of interesting information. It told of a black-bearded white man who went always disguised as an Arab. For a time he had nursed a broken wrist. More recently he had been away from Bou Saada, but now he was back, and Tarzan knew his place of concealment. It was for there he headed.

Through narrow, stinking alleys, black as Erebus, he groped, and then up a rickety stairway, at the end of which was a closed door and a tiny, unglazed window. The window was high under the low eaves of the mud building. Tarzan could just reach the sill. He raised himself slowly until his eyes topped it. The room within was lighted, and at a table sat Rokoff and Gernois. Gernois was speaking.

"Rokoff, you are a devil!" he was saying. "You have hounded me until I have lost the last shred of my honor. You have driven me to murder, for the blood of that man Tarzan is on my hands. If it were not that that other devil's spawn, Paulvitch, still knew my secret, I should kill you here tonight with my bare hands."

Rokoff laughed. "You would not do that, my dear lieutenant," he said. "The moment I am reported dead by assassination that dear Alexis will forward to the minister of war full proof of the affair you so ardently long to conceal; and, further, will charge you with my murder. Come, be sensible. I am your best friend. Have I not protected your honor as though it were my own?"

Gernois sneered, and spat out an oath.

"Just one more little payment," continued Rokoff, "and the papers I wish, and you have my word of honor that I shall never ask another cent from you, or further information."

"And a good reason why," growled Gernois. "What you ask will take my last cent, and the only valuable military secret I hold. You ought to be paying me for the information, instead of taking both it and money, too."

"I am paying you by keeping a still tongue in my head," retorted Rokoff. "But let's have done. Will you, or will you not? I give you three minutes to decide. If you are not agreeable I shall send a note to your commandant tonight that will end in the degradation that Dreyfus suffered—the only difference being that he did not deserve it."

For a moment Gernois sat with bowed head. At length he arose. He drew two pieces of paper from his blouse.

"Here," he said hopelessly. "I had them ready, for I knew that there could be but one outcome." He held them toward the Russian.

Rokoff's cruel face lighted in malignant gloating. He seized the bits of paper.

"You have done well, Gernois," he said. "I shall not trouble you again—unless you happen to accumulate some more money or information," and he grinned.

"You never shall again, you dog!" hissed Gernois. "The next time I shall kill you. I came near doing it tonight. For an hour I sat with these two pieces of paper on my table before me ere I came here—beside them lay my loaded revolver. I was trying to decide which I should bring. Next time the choice shall be easier, for I already have decided. You had a close call tonight, Rokoff; do not tempt fate a second time."

Then Gernois rose to leave. Tarzan barely had time to drop to the landing and shrink back into the shadows on the far side of the door. Even then he scarcely hoped to elude detection. The landing was very small, and though he flattened himself against the wall at its far edge he was scarcely more than a foot from the doorway. Almost immediately it opened, and Gernois stepped out. Rokoff was behind him. Neither spoke. Gernois had taken perhaps three steps down the stairway when he halted and half turned, as though to retrace his steps.

Tarzan knew that discovery would be inevitable. Rokoff still stood on the threshold a foot from him, but he was looking in the opposite direction, toward Gernois. Then the officer evidently reconsidered his decision, and resumed his downward course. Tarzan could hear Rokoff's sigh of relief. A moment later the Russian went back into the room and closed the door.

Tarzan waited until Gernois had had time to get well out of hearing, then he pushed open the door and stepped into the room. He was on top of Rokoff before the man could rise from the chair where he sat scanning the paper Gernois had given him. As his eyes turned and fell upon the ape-man's face his own went livid.

"You!" he gasped.

"I," replied Tarzan.

"What do you want?" whispered Rokoff, for the look in the ape-man's eyes frightened him. "Have you come to kill me? You do not dare. They would guillotine you. You do not dare kill me."

"I dare kill you, Rokoff," replied Tarzan, "for no one knows that you are here or that I am here, and Paulvitch would tell them that it was Gernois. I heard you tell Gernois so. But that would not influence me, Rokoff. I would not care who knew that I had killed you; the pleasure of killing you would more than compensate for any punishment they might inflict upon me. You are the most despicable cur of a coward, Rokoff, I have ever heard of. You should be killed. I should love to kill you," and Tarzan approached closer to the man.

Rokoff's nerves were keyed to the breaking point. With a shriek he sprang toward an adjoining room, but the ape-man was upon his back while his leap was yet but half completed. Iron fingers sought his throat—the great coward squealed like a stuck pig, until Tarzan had shut off his wind. Then the ape-man dragged him to his feet, still choking him. The Russian struggled futilely—he was like a babe in the mighty grasp of Tarzan of the Apes.

Tarzan sat him in a chair, and long before there was danger of the man's dying he released his hold upon his throat. When the Russian's coughing spell had abated Tarzan spoke to him again.

"I have given you a taste of the suffering of death," he said. "But I shall not kill—this time. I am sparing you solely for the sake of a very good woman whose great misfortune it was to have been born of the same woman who gave birth to you. But I shall spare you only this once on her account. Should I ever learn that you have again annoyed her or her husband—should you ever annoy me again—should I hear that you have returned to France or to any French possession, I shall make it my sole business to hunt you down and complete the choking I commenced tonight." Then he turned to the table, on which the two pieces of paper still lay. As he picked them up Rokoff gasped in horror.

Tarzan examined both the check and the other. He was amazed at the information the latter contained. Rokoff had partially read it, but Tarzan knew that no one could remember the salient facts and figures it held which made it of real value to an enemy of France.

"These will interest the chief of staff," he said, as he slipped them into his pocket. Rokoff groaned. He did not dare curse aloud.

The next morning Tarzan rode north on his way to Bouira and Algiers. As he had ridden past the hotel Lieutenant Gernois was standing on the veranda. As his eyes discovered Tarzan he went white as chalk. The ape-man would have been glad had the meeting not occurred, but he could not avoid it. He saluted the officer as he rode past. Mechanically Gernois returned the salute, but those terrible, wide eyes followed the horseman, expressionless except for horror. It was as though a dead man looked upon a ghost.

At Sidi Aissa Tarzan met a French officer with whom he had become acquainted on the occasion of his recent sojourn in the town.

"You left Bou Saada early?" questioned the officer. "Then you have not heard about poor Gernois."

"He was the last man I saw as I rode away," replied Tarzan. "What about him?"

"He is dead. He shot himself about eight o'clock this morning."

Two days later Tarzan reached Algiers. There he found that he would have a two days' wait before he could catch a ship bound for Cape Town. He occupied his time in writing out a full report of his mission. The secret papers he had taken from Rokoff he did not inclose, for he did not dare trust them out of his own possession until he had been authorized to turn them over to another agent, or himself return to Paris with them.

As Tarzan boarded his ship after what seemed a most tedious wait to him, two men watched him from an upper deck. Both were fashionably dressed and smooth shaven. The taller of the two had sandy hair, but his eyebrows were very black. Later in the day they chanced to meet Tarzan on deck, but as one hurriedly called his companion's attention to something at sea their faces were turned from Tarzan as he passed, so that he did not notice their features. In fact, he had paid no attention to them at all.

Following the instructions of his chief, Tarzan had booked his passage under an assumed name—John Caldwell, London. He did not understand the necessity of this, and it caused him considerable speculation. He wondered what role he was to play in Cape Town.

"Well," he thought, "thank Heaven that I am rid of Rokoff. He was commencing to annoy me. I wonder if I am really becoming so civilized that presently I shall develop a set of nerves. He would give them to me if any one could, for he does not fight fair. One never knows through what new agency he is going to strike. It is as though Numa, the lion, had induced Tantor, the elephant, and Histah, the snake, to join him in attempting to kill me. I would then never have known what minute, or by whom, I was to be attacked next. But the brutes are more chivalrous than man—they do not stoop to cowardly intrigue."

At dinner that night Tarzan sat next to a young woman whose place was at the captain's left. The officer introduced them.

Miss Strong! Where had he heard the name before? It was very familiar. And then the girl's mother gave him the clew, for when she addressed her daughter she called her Hazel.

Hazel Strong! What memories the name inspired. It had been a letter to this girl, penned by the fair hand of Jane Porter, that had carried to him the first message from the woman he loved. How vividly he recalled the night he had stolen it from the desk in the cabin of his long-dead father, where Jane Porter had sat writing it late into the night, while he crouched in the darkness without. How terror-stricken she would have been that night had she known that the wild jungle beast squatted outside her window, watching her every move.

And this was Hazel Strong—Jane Porter's best friend!

XII

SHIPS THAT PASS

et us go back a few months to the little, wind-swept platform of a railway station in northern Wisconsin. The smoke of forest fires hangs low over the surrounding landscape, its acrid fumes smarting the eyes of a little party of six who stand waiting the coming of the train that is to bear them away toward the south.

Professor Archimedes Q. Porter, his hands clasped beneath the tails of his long coat, paces back and forth under the ever-watchful eye of his faithful secretary, Mr. Samuel T. Philander. Twice within the past few minutes he has started absent-mindedly across the tracks in the direction of a near-by swamp, only to be rescued and dragged back by the tireless Mr. Philander.

Jane Porter, the professor's daughter, is in strained and lifeless conversation with William Cecil Clayton and Tarzan of the Apes. Within the little waiting room, but a bare moment before, a confession of love and a renunciation had taken place that had blighted the lives and happiness of two of the party, but William Cecil Clayton, Lord Greystoke, was not one of them.

Behind Miss Porter hovered the motherly Esmeralda. She, too, was happy, for was she not returning to her beloved Maryland? Already she could see dimly through the fog of smoke the murky headlight of the oncoming engine. The men began to gather up the hand baggage. Suddenly Clayton exclaimed.

"By Jove! I've left my ulster in the waiting-room," and hastened off to fetch it.

"Good-bye, Jane," said Tarzan, extending his hand. "God bless you!"

"Good-bye," replied the girl faintly. "Try to forget me—no, not that—I could not bear to think that you had forgotten me."

"There is no danger of that, dear," he answered. "I wish to Heaven that I might forget. It would be so much easier than to go through life always remembering what might have been. You will be happy, though; I am sure you shall—you must be. You may tell the others of my decision to drive my car on to New York—I don't feel equal to bidding Clayton good-bye. I want always to remember him kindly, but I fear that I am too much of a wild beast yet to be trusted too long with the man who stands between me and the one person in all the world I want."

As Clayton stooped to pick up his coat in the waiting room his eyes fell on a telegraph blank lying face down upon the floor. He stooped to pick it up, thinking it might be a message of importance which some one had dropped. He glanced at it hastily, and then suddenly he forgot his coat, the approaching train—everything but that terrible little piece of yellow paper in his hand. He read it twice before he could fully grasp the terrific weight of meaning that it bore to him.

When he had picked it up he had been an English nobleman, the proud and wealthy possessor of vast estates—a moment later he had read it, and he knew that he was an untitled and penniless beggar. It was D'Arnot's cablegram to Tarzan, and it read:

Finger prints prove you Greystoke. Congratulations.

D'ARNOT.

He staggered as though he had received a mortal blow. Just then he heard the others calling to him to hurry—the train was coming

409

to a stop at the little platform. Like a man dazed he gathered up his ulster. He would tell them about the cablegram when they were all on board the train. Then he ran out upon the platform just as the engine whistled twice in the final warning that precedes the first rumbling jerk of coupling pins. The others were on board, leaning out from the platform of a Pullman, crying to him to hurry. Quite five minutes elapsed before they were settled in their seats, nor was it until then that Clayton discovered that Tarzan was not with them.

"Where is Tarzan?" he asked Jane Porter. "In another car?"

"No," she replied; "at the last minute he determined to drive his machine back to New York. He is anxious to see more of America than is possible from a car window. He is returning to France, you know."

Clayton did not reply. He was trying to find the right words to explain to Jane Porter the calamity that had befallen him—and her. He wondered just what the effect of his knowledge would be on her. Would she still wish to marry him—to be plain Mrs. Clayton? Suddenly the awful sacrifice which one of them must make loomed large before his imagination. Then came the question: Will Tarzan claim his own? The ape-man had known the contents of the message before he calmly denied knowledge of his parentage! He had admitted that Kala, the ape, was his mother! Could it have been for love of Jane Porter?

There was no other explanation which seemed reasonable. Then, having ignored the evidence of the message, was it not reasonable to assume that he meant never to claim his birthright? If this were so, what right had he, William Cecil Clayton, to thwart the wishes, to balk the self-sacrifice of this strange man? If Tarzan of the Apes could do this thing to save Jane Porter from unhappiness, why should he, to whose care she was intrusting her whole future, do aught to jeopardize her interests?

And so he reasoned until the first generous impulse to proclaim the truth and relinquish his titles and his estates to their rightful owner was forgotten beneath the mass of sophistries which self-interest had advanced. But during the balance of the trip, and for many days thereafter, he was moody and distraught. Occasionally the thought obtruded itself that possibly at some later day Tarzan would regret his magnanimity, and claim his rights.

Several days after they reached Baltimore Clayton broached the subject of an early marriage to Jane.

"What do you mean by early?" she asked.

"Within the next few days. I must return to England at once—I want you to return with me, dear."

"I can't get ready so soon as that," replied Jane. "It will take a whole month, at least."

She was glad, for she hoped that whatever called him to England might still further delay the wedding. She had made a bad bargain, but she intended carrying her part loyally to the bitter end—if she could manage to secure a temporary reprieve, though, she felt that she was warranted in doing so. His reply disconcerted her.

"Very well, Jane," he said. "I am disappointed, but I shall let my trip to England wait a month; then we can go back together."

But when the month was drawing to a close she found still another excuse upon which to hang a postponement, until at last, discouraged and doubting, Clayton was forced to go back to England alone.

The several letters that passed between them brought Clayton no nearer to a consummation of his hopes than he had been before, and so it was that he wrote directly to Professor Porter, and enlisted his services. The old man had always favored the match. He liked Clayton, and, being of an old southern family, he put rather an exaggerated value on the advantages of a title, which meant little or nothing to his daughter.

Clayton urged that the professor accept his invitation to be his guest in London, an invitation which included the professor's entire little family—Mr. Philander, Esmeralda, and all. The Englishman argued that once Jane was there, and home ties had been broken, she would not so dread the step which she had so long hesitated to take.

So the evening that he received Clayton's letter Professor Porter announced that they would leave for London the following week.

But once in London Jane Porter was no more tractable than she had been in Baltimore. She found one excuse after another, and when, finally, Lord Tennington invited the party to cruise around Africa in his yacht, she expressed the greatest delight in the idea, but absolutely refused to be married until they had returned to London. As the cruise was to consume a year at least, for they were to stop for indefinite periods at various points of interest, Clayton mentally anathematized Tennington for ever suggesting such a ridiculous trip.

It was Lord Tennington's plan to cruise through the Mediterranean, and the Red Sea to the Indian Ocean, and thus down the East Coast, putting in at every port that was worth the seeing.

And so it happened that on a certain day two vessels passed in the Strait of Gibraltar. The smaller, a trim white yacht, was speeding toward the east, and on her deck sat a young woman who gazed with sad eyes upon a diamond-studded locket which she idly fingered. Her thoughts were far away, in the dim, leafy fastness of a tropical jungle—and her heart was with her thoughts.

She wondered if the man who had given her the beautiful bauble, that had meant so much more to him than the intrinsic value which he had not even known could ever have meant to him, was back in his savage forest.

And upon the deck of the larger vessel, a passenger steamer passing toward the east, the man sat with another young woman, and the two idly speculated upon the identity of the dainty craft gliding so gracefully through the gentle swell of the lazy sea.

When the yacht had passed the man resumed the conversation that her appearance had broken off.

"Yes," he said, "I like America very much, and that means, of course, that I like Americans, for a country is only what its people make it. I met some very delightful people while I was there. I recall one family from your own city, Miss Strong, whom I liked particularly—Professor Porter and his daughter."

"Jane Porter!" exclaimed the girl. "Do you mean to tell me that you know Jane Porter? Why, she is the very best friend I have in the world. We were little children together—we have known each other for ages."

"Indeed!" he answered, smiling. "You would have difficulty in persuading any one of the fact who had seen either of you."

"I'll qualify the statement, then," she answered, with a laugh. "We have known each other for two ages—hers and mine. But seriously we are as dear to each other as sisters, and now that I am going to lose her I am almost heartbroken."

"Going to lose her?" exclaimed Tarzan. "Why, what do you mean? Oh, yes, I understand. You mean that now that she is married and living in England, you will seldom if ever see her."

"Yes," replied she; "and the saddest part of it all is that she is not marrying the man she loves. Oh, it is terrible. Marrying from a sense of duty! I think it is perfectly wicked, and I told her so. I have felt so strongly on the subject that although I was the only person outside of blood relations who was to have been asked to the wedding I would not let her invite me, for I should not have gone to witness the terrible mockery. But Jane Porter is peculiarly positive. She has convinced herself that she is doing the only honorable thing that she can do, and nothing in the world will ever prevent her from marrying Lord Greystoke except Greystoke himself, or death."

"I am sorry for her," said Tarzan.

"And I am sorry for the man she loves," said the girl, "for he loves her. I never met him, but from what Jane tells me he must be a very wonderful person. It seems that he was born in an African jungle, and brought up by fierce, anthropoid apes. He had never seen a white man or woman until Professor Porter and his party were marooned on the coast right at the threshold of his tiny cabin. He saved them from all manner of terrible beasts, and accomplished the most wonderful feats imaginable, and then to cap the climax he fell in love with Jane and she with him, though she never really knew it for sure until she had promised herself to Lord Greystoke."

"Most remarkable," murmured Tarzan, cudgeling his brain for some pretext upon which to turn the subject. He delighted in hearing Hazel Strong talk of Jane, but when he was the subject of the conversation he was bored and embarrassed. But he was soon given a respite, for the girl's mother joined them, and the talk became general.

The next few days passed uneventfully. The sea was quiet. The sky was clear. The steamer plowed steadily on toward the south without pause. Tarzan spent quite a little time with Miss Strong and her mother. They whiled away their hours on deck reading, talking, or taking pictures with Miss Strong's camera. When the sun had set they walked.

One day Tarzan found Miss Strong in conversation with a stranger, a man he had not seen on board before. As he approached the couple the man bowed to the girl and turned to walk away.

"Wait, Monsieur Thuran," said Miss Strong; "you must meet Mr. Caldwell. We are all fellow passengers, and should be acquainted."

The two men shook hands. As Tarzan looked into the eyes of Monsieur Thuran he was struck by the strange familiarity of their expression.

"I have had the honor of monsieur's acquaintance in the past, I am sure," said Tarzan, "though I cannot recall the circumstances."

Monsieur Thuran appeared ill at ease.

"I cannot say, monsieur," he replied. "It may be so. I have had that identical sensation myself when meeting a stranger."

"Monsieur Thuran has been explaining some of the mysteries of navigation to me," explained the girl.

Tarzan paid little heed to the conversation that ensued—he was attempting to recall where he had met Monsieur Thuran before. That it had been under peculiar circumstances he was positive. Presently the sun reached them, and the girl asked Monsieur Thuran to move her chair farther back into the shade. Tarzan happened to be watching the man at the time, and noticed the awkward manner in which he handled the chair—his left wrist was stiff. That clew was sufficient—a sudden train of associated ideas did the rest.

Monsieur Thuran had been trying to find an excuse to make a graceful departure. The lull in the conversation following the moving of their position gave him an opportunity to make his excuses. Bowing low to Miss Strong, and inclining his head to Tarzan, he turned to leave them.

"Just a moment," said Tarzan. "If Miss Strong will pardon me I will accompany you. I shall return in a moment, Miss Strong."

Monsieur Thuran looked uncomfortable. When the two men had passed out of the girl's sight, Tarzan stopped, laying a heavy hand on the other's shoulder.

"What is your game now, Rokoff?" he asked.

"I am leaving France as I promised you," replied the other, in a surly voice.

"I see you are," said Tarzan; "but I know you so well that I can scarcely believe that your being on the same boat with me is purely a coincidence. If I could believe it the fact that you are in disguise would immediately disabuse my mind of any such idea."

"Well," growled Rokoff, with a shrug, "I cannot see what you are going to do about it. This vessel flies the English flag. I have as much right on board her as you, and from the fact that you are booked under an assumed name I imagine that I have more right."

"We will not discuss it, Rokoff. All I wanted to say to you is that you must keep away from Miss Strong—she is a decent woman."

Rokoff turned scarlet.

"If you don't I shall pitch you overboard," continued Tarzan. "Do not forget that I am just waiting for some excuse." Then he turned on his heel, and left Rokoff standing there trembling with suppressed rage.

He did not see the man again for days, but Rokoff was not idle. In his stateroom with Paulvitch he fumed and swore, threatening the most terrible of revenges.

"I would throw him overboard tonight," he cried, "were I sure that those papers were not on his person. I cannot chance pitching them into the ocean with him. If you were not such a stupid coward, Alexis, you would find a way to enter his stateroom and search for the documents."

Paulvitch smiled. "You are supposed to be the brains of this partnership, my dear Nikolas," he replied. "Why do you not find the means to search Monsieur Caldwell's stateroom—eh?"

Two hours later fate was kind to them, for Paulvitch, who was ever on the watch, saw Tarzan leave his room without locking the door. Five minutes later Rokoff was stationed where he could give the alarm in case Tarzan returned, and Paulvitch was deftly searching the contents of the ape-man's luggage.

He was about to give up in despair when he saw a coat which Tarzan had just removed. A moment later he grasped an official envelope in his hand. A quick glance at its contents brought a broad smile to the Russian's face.

When he left the stateroom Tarzan himself could not have told that an article in it had been touched since he left it—Paulvitch was a past master in his chosen field. When he handed the packet to Rokoff in the seclusion of their stateroom the larger man rang for a steward, and ordered a pint of champagne.

"We must celebrate, my dear Alexis," he said.

"It was luck, Nikolas," explained Paulvitch. "It is evident that he carries these papers always upon his person—just by chance he neglected to transfer them when he changed coats a few minutes since. But there will be the deuce to pay when he discovers his loss. I am afraid that he will immediately connect you with it. Now that he knows that you are on board he will suspect you at once."

"It will make no difference whom he suspects—after to-night," said Rokoff, with a nasty grin.

After Miss Strong had gone below that night Tarzan stood leaning over the rail looking far out to sea. Every night he had done this since he had come on board—sometimes he stood thus for an hour. And the eyes that had been watching his every movement since he had boarded the ship at Algiers knew that this was his habit.

Even as he stood there this night those eyes were on him. Presently the last straggler had left the deck. It was a clear night, but there was no moon—objects on deck were barely discernible.

From the shadows of the cabin two figures crept stealthily upon the ape-man from behind. The lapping of the waves against the ship's sides, the whirring of the propeller, the throbbing of the engines, drowned the almost soundless approach of the two.

They were quite close to him now, and crouching low, like tacklers on a gridiron. One of them raised his hand and lowered it, as though counting off seconds—one—two—three! As one man the two leaped for their victim. Each grasped a leg, and before Tarzan of the Apes, lightning though he was, could turn to save himself he had been pitched over the low rail and was falling into the Atlantic.

Hazel Strong was looking from her darkened port across the dark sea. Suddenly a body shot past her eyes from the deck above. It dropped so quickly into the dark waters below that she could not be sure of what it was—it might have been a man, she could not say. She listened for some outcry from above—for the always-fearsome call, "Man overboard!" but it did not come. All was silence on the ship above—all was silence in the sea below.

The girl decided that she had but seen a bundle of refuse thrown overboard by one of the ship's crew, and a moment later sought her berth.

XIII

THE WRECK OF THE "LADY ALICE"

he next morning at breakfast Tarzan's place was vacant. Miss Strong was mildly curious, for Mr. Caldwell had always made it a point to wait that he might breakfast with her and her mother. As she was sitting on deck later Monsieur Thuran paused to exchange a half dozen pleasant words with her. He seemed in most excellent spirits—his manner was the extreme of affability. As he passed on Miss Strong thought what a very delightful man was Monsieur Thuran.

The day dragged heavily. She missed the quiet companionship of Mr. Caldwell—there had been something about him that had made the girl like him from the first; he had talked so entertainingly of the places he had seen—the peoples and their customs—the wild beasts; and he had always had a droll way of drawing striking comparisons between savage animals and civilized men that showed a considerable knowledge of the former, and a keen, though somewhat cynical, estimate of the latter.

When Monsieur Thuran stopped again to chat with her in the afternoon she welcomed the break in the day's monotony. But she had begun to become seriously concerned in Mr. Caldwell's continued absence; somehow she constantly associated it with the start she had had the night before, when the dark object fell past her port into the sea. Presently she broached the subject to Monsieur Thuran. Had he seen Mr. Caldwell today? He had not. Why?

"He was not at breakfast as usual, nor have I seen him once since yesterday," explained the girl.

Monsieur Thuran was extremely solicitous.

"I did not have the pleasure of intimate acquaintance with Mr. Caldwell," he said. "He seemed a most estimable gentleman, however. Can it be that he is indisposed, and has remained in his stateroom? It would not be strange."

"No," replied the girl, "it would not be strange, of course; but for some inexplicable reason I have one of those foolish feminine presentiments that all is not right with Mr. Caldwell. It is the strangest feeling—it is as though I knew that he was not on board the ship."

Monsieur Thuran laughed pleasantly. "Mercy, my dear Miss Strong," he said; "where in the world could he be then? We have not been within sight of land for days."

"Of course, it is ridiculous of me," she admitted. And then: "But I am not going to worry about it any longer; I am going to find out where Mr. Caldwell is," and she motioned to a passing steward.

"That may be more difficult than you imagine, my dear girl," thought Monsieur Thuran, but aloud he said: "By all means."

"Find Mr. Caldwell, please," she said to the steward, "and tell him that his friends are much worried by his continued absence."

"You are very fond of Mr. Caldwell?" suggested Monsieur Thuran.

"I think he is splendid," replied the girl. "And mamma is perfectly infatuated with him. He is the sort of man with whom one has a feeling of perfect security—no one could help but have confidence in Mr. Caldwell."

A moment later the steward returned to say that Mr. Caldwell was not in his stateroom. "I cannot find him, Miss Strong, and"—he hesitated—"I have learned that his berth was not occupied last night. I think that I had better report the matter to the captain."

"Most assuredly," exclaimed Miss Strong. "I shall go with you to the captain myself. It is terrible! I know that something awful has happened. My presentiments were not false, after all."

It was a very frightened young woman and an excited steward who presented themselves before the captain a few moments later. He listened to their stories in silence—a look of concern marking his expression as the steward assured him that he had sought for the missing passenger in every part of the ship that a passenger might be expected to frequent.

"And are you sure, Miss Strong, that you saw a body fall overboard last night?" he asked.

"There is not the slightest doubt about that," she answered. "I cannot say that it was a human body—there was no outcry. It might have been only what I thought it was—a bundle of refuse. But if Mr. Caldwell is not found on board I shall always be positive that it was he whom I saw fall past my port."

The captain ordered an immediate and thorough search of the entire ship from stem to stern—no nook or cranny was to be overlooked. Miss Strong remained in his cabin, waiting the outcome of the quest. The captain asked her many questions, but she could tell him nothing about the missing man other than what she had herself seen during their brief acquaintance on shipboard. For the first time she suddenly realized how very little indeed Mr. Caldwell had told her about himself or his past life. That he had been born in Africa and educated in Paris was about all she knew, and this meager information had been the result of her surprise that an Englishman should speak English with such a marked French accent.

"Did he ever speak of any enemies?" asked the captain.

"Never."

"Was he acquainted with any of the other passengers?"

"Only as he had been with me—through the circumstance of casual meeting as fellow shipmates."

"Er—was he, in your opinion, Miss Strong, a man who drank to excess?"

"I do not know that he drank at all—he certainly had not been drinking up to half an hour before I saw that body fall overboard," she answered, "for I was with him on deck up to that time."

"It is very strange," said the captain. "He did not look to me like a man who was subject to fainting spells, or anything of that sort. And even had he been it is scarcely credible that he should have fallen completely over the rail had he been taken with an attack while leaning upon it—he would rather have fallen inside, upon the deck. If he is not on board, Miss Strong, he was thrown overboard—and the fact that you heard no outcry would lead to the assumption that he was dead before he left the ship's deck—murdered."

The girl shuddered.

It was a full hour later that the first officer returned to report the outcome of the search.

"Mr. Caldwell is not on board, sir," he said.

"I fear that there is something more serious than accident here, Mr. Brently," said the captain. "I wish that you would make a personal and very careful examination of Mr. Caldwell's effects, to ascertain if there is any clew to a motive either for suicide or murder—sift the thing to the bottom."

"Aye, aye, sir!" responded Mr. Brently, and left to commence his investigation.

Hazel Strong was prostrated. For two days she did not leave her cabin, and when she finally ventured on deck she was very wan and white, with great, dark circles beneath her eyes. Waking or sleeping, it seemed that she constantly saw that dark body dropping, swift and silent, into the cold, grim sea.

Shortly after her first appearance on deck following the tragedy, Monsieur Thuran joined her with many expressions of kindly solicitude.

"Oh, but it is terrible, Miss Strong," he said. "I cannot rid my mind of it."

"Nor I," said the girl wearily. "I feel that he might have been saved had I but given the alarm."

"You must not reproach yourself, my dear Miss Strong," urged Monsieur Thuran. "It was in no way your fault. Another would have done as you did. Who would think that because something fell into the sea from a ship that it must necessarily be a man? Nor would the outcome have been different had you given an alarm. For a while they would have doubted your story, thinking it but the nervous hallucination of a woman—had you insisted it would have been too late to have rescued him by the time the ship could have been brought to a stop, and the boats lowered and rowed back miles in search of the unknown spot where the tragedy had occurred. No, you must not censure yourself. You have done more than any other of us for poor Mr. Caldwell—you were the only one to miss him. It was you who instituted the search."

The girl could not help but feel grateful to him for his kind and encouraging words. He was with her often—almost constantly for the remainder of the voyage—and she grew to like him very much indeed. Monsieur Thuran had learned that the beautiful Miss Strong, of Baltimore, was an American heiress—a very wealthy girl in her own right, and with future prospects that quite took his breath away when he contemplated them, and since he spent most of his time in that delectable pastime it is a wonder that he breathed at all.

It had been Monsieur Thuran's intention to leave the ship at the first port they touched after the disappearance of Tarzan. Did he not have in his coat pocket the thing he had taken passage upon this very boat to obtain? There was nothing more to detain him here. He could not return to the Continent fast enough, that he might board the first express for St. Petersburg.

But now another idea had obtruded itself, and was rapidly crowding his original intentions into the background. That American fortune was not to be sneezed at, nor was its possessor a whit less attractive.

"*Sapristi!* but she would cause a sensation in St. Petersburg." And he would, too, with the assistance of her inheritance.

After Monsieur Thuran had squandered a few million dollars, he discovered that the vocation was so entirely to his liking that he would continue on down to Cape Town, where he suddenly decided that he had pressing engagements that might detain him there for some time.

Miss Strong had told him that she and her mother were to visit the latter's brother there—they had not decided upon the duration of their stay, and it would probably run into months.

She was delighted when she found that Monsieur Thuran was to be there also.

"I hope that we shall be able to continue our acquaintance," she said. "You must call upon mamma and me as soon as we are settled."

Monsieur Thuran was delighted at the prospect, and lost no time in saying so. Mrs. Strong was not quite so favorably impressed by him as her daughter.

"I do not know why I should distrust him," she said to Hazel one day as they were discussing him. "He seems a perfect gentleman in every respect, but sometimes there is something about his eyes—a fleeting expression which I cannot describe, but which when I see it gives me a very uncanny feeling."

The girl laughed. "You are a silly dear, mamma," she said.

"I suppose so, but I am sorry that we have not poor Mr. Caldwell for company instead."

"And I, too," replied her daughter.

Monsieur Thuran became a frequent visitor at the home of Hazel Strong's uncle in Cape Town. His attentions were very marked, but they were so punctiliously arranged to meet the girl's every wish that she came to depend upon him more and more. Did she or her mother or a cousin require an escort—was there a little friendly service to be rendered, the genial and ubiquitous Monsieur Thuran was always available. Her uncle and his family grew to like him for his unfailing courtesy and willingness to be of service. Monsieur Thuran was becoming indispensable. At length, feeling the moment propitious, he proposed. Miss Strong was startled. She did not know what to say.

"I had never thought that you cared for me in any such way," she told him. "I have looked upon you always as a very dear friend. I shall not give you my answer now. Forget that you have asked me to be your wife. Let us go on as we have been—then I can consider you from an entirely different angle for a time. It may be that I shall discover that my feeling for you is more than friendship. I certainly have not thought for a moment that I loved you."

This arrangement was perfectly satisfactory to Monsieur Thuran. He deeply regretted that he had been hasty, but he had loved her for so long a time, and so devotedly, that he thought that every one must know it.

"From the first time I saw you, Hazel," he said, "I have loved you. I am willing to wait, for I am certain that so great and pure a love as mine will be rewarded. All that I care to know is that you do not love another. Will you tell me?"

"I have never been in love in my life," she replied, and he was quite satisfied. On the way home that night he purchased a steam yacht, and built a million-dollar villa on the Black Sea.

The next day Hazel Strong enjoyed one of the happiest surprises of her life—she ran face to face upon Jane Porter as she was coming out of a jeweler's shop.

"Why, Jane Porter!" she exclaimed. "Where in the world did you drop from? Why, I can't believe my own eyes."

"Well, of all things!" cried the equally astonished Jane. "And here I have been wasting whole reams of perfectly good imagination picturing you in Baltimore—the very idea!" And she threw her arms about her friend once more, and kissed her a dozen times.

By the time mutual explanations had been made Hazel knew that Lord Tennington's yacht had put in at Cape Town for at least a week's stay, and at the end of that time was to continue on her voyage—this time up the West Coast—and so back to England. "Where," concluded Jane, "I am to be married."

"Then you are not married yet?" asked Hazel.

"Not yet," replied Jane, and then, quite irrelevantly, "I wish England were a million miles from here."

Visits were exchanged between the yacht and Hazel's relatives. Dinners were arranged, and trips into the surrounding country to entertain the visitors. Monsieur Thuran was a welcome guest at every function. He gave a dinner himself to the men of the party, and managed to ingratiate himself in the good will of Lord Tennington by many little acts of hospitality.

Monsieur Thuran had heard dropped a hint of something which might result from this unexpected visit of Lord Tennington's yacht, and he wanted to be counted in on it. Once when he was alone with the Englishman he took occasion to make it quite plain that his engagement to Miss Strong was to be announced immediately upon their return to America. "But not a word of it, my dear Tennington—not a word of it."

"Certainly, I quite understand, my dear fellow," Tennington had replied. "But you are to be congratulated—ripping girl, don't you know—really."

The next day it came. Mrs. Strong, Hazel, and Monsieur Thuran were Lord Tennington's guests aboard his yacht. Mrs. Strong had been telling them how much she had enjoyed her visit at Cape Town, and that she regretted that a letter just received from her attorneys in Baltimore had necessitated her cutting her visit shorter than they had intended.

"When do you sail?" asked Tennington.

"The first of the week, I think," she replied. "Indeed?" exclaimed Monsieur Thuran. "I am very fortunate. I, too, have found that I must return at once, and now I shall have the honor of accompanying and serving you."

"That is nice of you, Monsieur Thuran," replied Mrs. Strong. "I am sure that we shall be glad to place ourselves under your protection." But in the bottom of her heart was the wish that they might escape him. Why, she could not have told.

"By Jove!" ejaculated Lord Tennington, a moment later. "Bully idea, by Jove!"

"Yes, Tennington, of course," ventured Clayton; "it must be a bully idea if you had it, but what the deuce is it? Goin' to steam to China via the south pole?"

"Oh, I say now, Clayton," returned Tennington, "you needn't be so rough on a fellow just because you didn't happen to suggest this trip yourself—you've acted a regular bounder ever since we sailed.

"No, sir," he continued, "it's a bully idea, and you'll all say so. It's to take Mrs. Strong and Miss Strong, and Thuran, too, if he'll come, as far as England with us on the yacht. Now, isn't that a corker?"

"Forgive me, Tenny, old boy," cried Clayton. "It certainly *is* a corking idea—I never should have suspected you of it. You're quite sure it's original, are you?"

"And we'll sail the first of the week, or any other time that suits your convenience, Mrs. Strong," concluded the big-hearted Englishman, as though the thing were all arranged except the sailing date.

"Mercy, Lord Tennington, you haven't even given us an opportunity to thank you, much less decide whether we shall be able to accept your generous invitation," said Mrs. Strong.

"Why, of course you'll come," responded Tennington. "We'll make as good time as any passenger boat, and you'll be fully as comfortable; and, anyway, we all want you, and won't take no for an answer."

And so it was settled that they should sail the following Monday.

Two days out the girls were sitting in Hazel's cabin, looking at some prints she had had finished in Cape Town. They represented all the pictures she had taken since she had left America, and the girls were both engrossed in them, Jane asking many questions, and Hazel keeping up a perfect torrent of comment and explanation of the various scenes and people.

"And here," she said suddenly, "here's a man you know. Poor fellow, I have so often intended asking you about him, but I never have been able to think of it when we were together." She was holding the little print so that Jane did not see the face of the man it portrayed.

"His name was John Caldwell," continued Hazel. "Do you recall him? He said that he met you in America. He is an Englishman."

"I do not recollect the name," replied Jane. "Let me see the picture." "The poor fellow was lost overboard on our trip down the coast," she said, as she handed the print to Jane.

"Lost over—Why, Hazel, Hazel—don't tell me that he is dead—drowned at sea! Hazel! Why don't you say that you are joking!" And before the astonished Miss Strong could catch her Jane Porter had slipped to the floor in a swoon.

After Hazel had restored her chum to consciousness she sat looking at her for a long time before either spoke.

"I did not know, Jane," said Hazel, in a constrained voice, "that you knew Mr. Caldwell so intimately that his death could prove such a shock to you."

"John Caldwell?" questioned Miss Porter. "You do not mean to tell me that you do not know who this man was, Hazel?"

"Why, yes, Jane; I know perfectly well who he was—his name was John Caldwell; he was from London."

"Oh, Hazel, I wish I could believe it," moaned the girl. "I wish I could believe it, but those features are burned so deep into my memory and my heart that I should recognize them anywhere in the world

THE RETURN OF TARZAN

from among a thousand others, who might appear identical to any one but me."

"What do you mean, Jane?" cried Hazel, now thoroughly alarmed. "Who do you think it is?"

"I don't think, Hazel. I know that that is a picture of Tarzan of the Apes."

"Jane!"

"I cannot be mistaken. Oh, Hazel, are you sure that he is dead? Can there be no mistake?"

"I am afraid not, dear," answered Hazel sadly. "I wish I could think that you are mistaken, but now a hundred and one little pieces of corroborative evidence occur to me that meant nothing to me while I thought that he was John Caldwell, of London. He said that he had been born in Africa, and educated in France."

"Yes, that would be true," murmured Jane Porter dully.

"The first officer, who searched his luggage, found nothing to identify John Caldwell, of London. Practically all his belongings had been made, or purchased, in Paris. Everything that bore an initial was marked either with a 'T' alone, or with 'J. C. T.' We thought that he was traveling incognito under his first two names—the J. C. standing for John Caldwell."

"Tarzan of the Apes took the name Jean C. Tarzan," said Jane, in the same lifeless monotone. "And he is dead! Oh! Hazel, it is horrible! He died all alone in this terrible ocean! It is unbelievable that that brave heart should have ceased to beat—that those mighty muscles are quiet and cold forever! That he who was the personification of life and health and manly strength should be the prey of slimy, crawling things, that—" But she could go no further, and with a little moan she buried her head in her arms, and sank sobbing to the floor.

For days Miss Porter was ill, and would see no one except Hazel and the faithful Esmeralda. When at last she came on deck all were struck by the sad change that had taken place in her. She was no longer the alert, vivacious American beauty who had charmed and delighted all who came in contact with her. Instead she was a very quiet and sad little girl—with an expression of hopeless wistfulness that none but Hazel Strong could interpret.

The entire party strove their utmost to cheer and amuse her, but all to no avail. Occasionally the jolly Lord Tennington would wring a wan smile from her, but for the most part she sat with wide eyes looking out across the sea.

With Jane Porter's illness one misfortune after another seemed to attack the yacht. First an engine broke down, and they drifted for two days while temporary repairs were being made. Then a squall struck them unaware, that carried overboard nearly everything above deck that was portable. Later two of the seamen fell to fighting in the forecastle, with the result that one of them was badly wounded with a knife, and the other had to be put in irons. Then, to cap the climax, the mate fell overboard at night, and was drowned before help could reach him. The yacht cruised about the spot for ten hours, but no sign of the man was seen after he disappeared from the deck into the sea.

Every member of the crew and guests was gloomy and depressed after these series of misfortunes. All were apprehensive of worse to come, and this was especially true of the seamen who recalled all sorts of terrible omens and warnings that had occurred during the early part of the voyage, and which they could now clearly translate into the precursors of some grim and terrible tragedy to come.

Nor did the croakers have long to wait. The second night after the drowning of the mate the little yacht was suddenly wracked from stem to stern. About one o'clock in the morning there was a terrific impact that threw the slumbering guests and crew from berth and bunk. A mighty shudder ran through the frail craft; she lay far over to starboard; the engines stopped. For a moment she hung there with her decks at an angle of forty-five degrees—then, with a sullen, rending sound, she slipped back into the sea and righted.

Instantly the men rushed upon deck, followed closely by the women. Though the night was cloudy, there was little wind or sea, nor was it so dark but that just off the port bow a black mass could be discerned floating low in the water.

"A derelict," was the terse explanation of the officer of the watch.

Presently the engineer hurried on deck in search of the captain.

"That patch we put on the cylinder head's blown out, sir," he reported, "and she's makin' water fast for'ard on the port bow."

An instant later a seaman rushed up from below.

"My Gawd!" he cried. "Her whole bleedin' bottom's ripped out. She can't float twenty minutes."

"Shut up!" roared Tennington. "Ladies, go below and get some of your things together. It may not be so bad as that, but we may have to take to the boats. It will be safer to be prepared. Go at once, please. And, Captain Jerrold, send some competent man below, please, to ascertain the exact extent of the damage. In the meantime I might suggest that you have the boats provisioned."

The calm, low voice of the owner did much to reassure the entire party, and a moment later all were occupied with the duties he had suggested. By the time the ladies had returned to the deck the rapid provisioning of the boats had been about completed, and a moment later the officer who had gone below had returned to report. But his opinion was scarcely needed to assure the huddled group of men and women that the end of the *Lady Alice* was at hand.

"Well, sir?" said the captain, as his officer hesitated.

"I dislike to frighten the ladies, sir," he said, "but she can't float a dozen minutes, in my opinion. There's a hole in her you could drive a bally cow through, sir."

For five minutes the *Lady Alice* had been settling rapidly by the bow. Already her stern loomed high in the air, and foothold on the deck was of the most precarious nature. She carried four boats, and these were all filled and lowered away in safety. As they pulled rapidly from the stricken little vessel Jane Porter turned to have one last look at her. Just then there came a loud crash and an ominous rumbling and pounding from the heart of the ship—her machinery had broken loose, and was dashing its way toward the bow, tearing out partitions and bulkheads as it went—the stern rose rapidly high above them; for a moment she seemed to pause there—a vertical shaft protruding from the bosom of the ocean, and then swiftly she dove headforemost beneath the waves.

In one of the boats the brave Lord Tennington wiped a tear from his eye—he had not seen a fortune in money go down forever into the sea, but a dear, beautiful friend whom he had loved.

At last the long night broke, and a tropical sun smote down upon the rolling water. Jane Porter had dropped into a fitful slumber—the fierce light of the sun upon her upturned face awoke her. She looked about her. In the boat with her were three sailors, Clayton, and Monsieur Thuran. Then she looked for the other boats, but as far as the eye could reach there was nothing to break the fearful monotony of that waste of waters—they were alone in a small boat upon the broad Atlantic.

XIV

BACK TO THE PRIMITIVE

s Tarzan struck the water, his first impulse was to swim clear of the ship and possible danger from her propellers. He knew whom to thank for his present predicament, and as he lay in the sea, just supporting himself by a gentle movement of his hands, his chief emotion was one of chagrin that he had been so easily bested by Rokoff.

He lay thus for some time, watching the receding and rapidly diminishing lights of the steamer without it ever once occurring to him to call for help. He never had called for help in his life, and so it is not strange that he did not think of it now. Always had he depended upon his own prowess and resourcefulness, nor had there ever been since the days of Kala any to answer an appeal for succor. When it did occur to him it was too late.

There was, thought Tarzan, a possible one chance in a hundred thousand that he might be picked up, and an even smaller chance that he would reach land, so he determined that to combine what slight chances there were, he would swim slowly in the direction of the coast—the ship might have been closer in than he had known.

His strokes were long and easy—it would be many hours before those giant muscles would commence to feel fatigue. As he swam, guided toward the east by the stars, he noticed that he felt the weight of his shoes, and so he removed them. His trousers went next, and he would have removed his coat at the same time but for the precious

432

papers in its pocket. To assure himself that he still had them he slipped his hand in to feel, but to his consternation they were gone.

Now he knew that something more than revenge had prompted Rokoff to pitch him overboard—the Russian had managed to obtain possession of the papers Tarzan had wrested from him at Bou Saada. The ape-man swore softly, and let his coat and shirt sink into the Atlantic. Before many hours he had divested himself of his remaining garments, and was swimming easily and unencumbered toward the east.

The first faint evidence of dawn was paling the stars ahead of him when the dim outlines of a low-lying black mass loomed up directly in his track. A few strong strokes brought him to its side—it was the bottom of a wave-washed derelict. Tarzan clambered upon it—he would rest there until daylight at least. He had no intention to remain there inactive—a prey to hunger and thirst. If he must die he preferred dying in action while making some semblance of an attempt to save himself.

The sea was quiet, so that the wreck had only a gently undulating motion, that was nothing to the swimmer who had had no sleep for twenty hours. Tarzan of the Apes curled up upon the slimy timbers, and was soon asleep.

The heat of the sun awoke him early in the forenoon. His first conscious sensation was of thirst, which grew almost to the proportions of suffering with full returning consciousness; but a moment later it was forgotten in the joy of two almost simultaneous discoveries. The first was a mass of wreckage floating beside the derelict in the midst of which, bottom up, rose and fell an overturned lifeboat; the other was the faint, dim line of a far-distant shore showing on the horizon in the east.

Tarzan dove into the water, and swam around the wreck to the lifeboat. The cool ocean refreshed him almost as much as would a draft of water, so that it was with renewed vigor that he brought the smaller boat alongside the derelict, and, after many herculean efforts, succeeded in dragging it onto the slimy ship's bottom. There he righted and examined it—the boat was quite sound, and a moment later floated upright alongside the wreck. Then Tarzan selected several pieces of wreckage that might answer him as paddles, and presently was making good headway toward the far-off shore.

It was late in the afternoon by the time he came close enough to distinguish objects on land, or to make out the contour of the shore line. Before him lay what appeared to be the entrance to a little, landlocked harbor. The wooded point to the north was strangely familiar. Could it be possible that fate had thrown him up at the very threshold of his own beloved jungle! But as the bow of his boat entered the mouth of the harbor the last shred of doubt was cleared away, for there before him upon the farther shore, under the shadows of his primeval forest, stood his own cabin—built before his birth by the hand of his long-dead father, John Clayton, Lord Greystoke.

With long sweeps of his giant muscles Tarzan sent the little craft speeding toward the beach. Its prow had scarcely touched when the ape-man leaped to shore—his heart beat fast in joy and exultation as each long-familiar object came beneath his roving eyes—the cabin, the beach, the little brook, the dense jungle, the black, impenetrable forest. The myriad birds in their brilliant plumage—the gorgeous tropical blooms upon the festooned creepers falling in great loops from the giant trees.

Tarzan of the Apes had come into his own again, and that all the world might know it he threw back his young head, and gave voice to the fierce, wild challenge of his tribe. For a moment silence reigned upon the jungle, and then, low and weird, came an answering challenge—it was the deep roar of Numa, the lion; and from a great distance, faintly, the fearsome answering bellow of a bull ape.

Tarzan went to the brook first, and slaked his thirst. Then he approached his cabin. The door was still closed and latched as he and D'Arnot had left it. He raised the latch and entered. Nothing had been disturbed; there were the table, the bed, and the little crib built by his father—the shelves and cupboards just as they had stood for ever twenty-three years—just as he had left them nearly two years before.

His eyes satisfied, Tarzan's stomach began to call aloud for attention—the pangs of hunger suggested a search for food. There was nothing in the cabin, nor had he any weapons; but upon a wall hung one of his old grass ropes. It had been many times broken and spliced, so that he had discarded it for a better one long before. Tarzan wished that he had a knife. Well, unless he was mistaken he should have that and a spear and bows and arrows before another sun had set—the rope would take care of that, and in the meantime it must be made to procure food for him. He coiled it carefully, and, throwing it about his shoulder, went out, closing the door behind him.

Close to the cabin the jungle commenced, and into it Tarzan of the Apes plunged, wary and noiseless—once more a savage beast hunting its food. For a time he kept to the ground, but finally, discovering no spoor indicative of nearby meat, he took to the trees. With the first dizzy swing from tree to tree all the old joy of living swept over him. Vain regrets and dull heartache were forgotten. Now was he living. Now, indeed, was the true happiness of perfect freedom his. Who would go back to the stifling, wicked cities of civilized man when the mighty reaches of the great jungle offered peace and liberty? Not he.

While it was yet light Tarzan came to a drinking place by the side of a jungle river. There was a ford there, and for countless ages the beasts of the forest had come down to drink at this spot. Here of a night might always be found either Sabor or Numa crouching in the dense foliage of the surrounding jungle awaiting an antelope or a water buck for their meal. Here came Horta, the boar, to water, and here came Tarzan of the Apes to make a kill, for he was very empty.

On a low branch he squatted above the trail. For an hour he waited. It was growing dark. A little to one side of the ford in the densest thicket he heard the faint sound of padded feet, and the brushing of a huge body against tall grasses and tangled creepers. None other than Tarzan might have heard it, but the ape-man heard and translated—it was Numa, the lion, on the same errand as himself. Tarzan smiled.

Presently he heard an animal approaching warily along the trail toward the drinking place. A moment more and it came in view—it was Horta, the boar. Here was delicious meat—and Tarzan's mouth watered. The grasses where Numa lay were very still now—ominously still. Horta passed beneath Tarzan—a few more steps and he would be within the radius of Numa's spring. Tarzan could imagine how old Numa's eyes were shining—how he was already sucking in his breath for the awful roar which would freeze his prey for the brief instant between the moment of the spring and the sinking of terrible fangs into splintering bones.

But as Numa gathered himself, a slender rope flew through the air from the low branches of a near-by tree. A noose settled about Horta's neck. There was a frightened grunt, a squeal, and then Numa saw his quarry dragged backward up the trail, and, as he sprang, Horta, the boar, soared upward beyond his clutches into the tree above, and a mocking face looked down and laughed into his own.

Then indeed did Numa roar. Angry, threatening, hungry, he paced back and forth beneath the taunting ape-man. Now he stopped, and, rising on his hind legs against the stem of the tree that held his enemy, sharpened his huge claws upon the bark, tearing out great pieces that laid bare the white wood beneath.

And in the meantime Tarzan had dragged the struggling Horta to the limb beside him. Sinewy fingers completed the work the choking noose had commenced. The ape-man had no knife, but nature had equipped him with the means of tearing his food from the quivering flank of his prey, and gleaming teeth sank into the succulent flesh while the raging lion looked on from below as another enjoyed the dinner that he had thought already his.

It was quite dark by the time Tarzan had gorged himself. Ah, but it had been delicious! Never had he quite accustomed himself to the ruined flesh that civilized men had served him, and in the bottom of his savage heart there had constantly been the craving for the warm meat of the fresh kill, and the rich, red blood.

He wiped his bloody hands upon a bunch of leaves, slung the remains of his kill across his shoulder, and swung off through the middle terrace of the forest toward his cabin, and at the same instant Jane Porter and William Cecil Clayton arose from a sumptuous dinner upon the *Lady Alice*, thousands of miles to the east, in the Indian Ocean.

Beneath Tarzan walked Numa, the lion, and when the ape-man deigned to glance downward he caught occasional glimpses of the baleful green eyes following through the darkness. Numa did not roar now—instead, he moved stealthily, like the shadow of a great cat; but yet he took no step that did not reach the sensitive ears of the ape-man.

Tarzan wondered if he would stalk him to his cabin door. He hoped not, for that would mean a night's sleep curled in the crotch of a tree, and he much preferred the bed of grasses within his own abode. But he knew just the tree and the most comfortable crotch, if necessity demanded that he sleep out. A hundred times in the past some great jungle cat had followed him home, and compelled him to seek shelter in this same tree, until another mood or the rising sun had sent his enemy away.

But presently Numa gave up the chase and, with a series of blood-curdling moans and roars, turned angrily back in search of another and an easier dinner. So Tarzan came to his cabin unattended, and a few moments later was curled up in the mildewed remnants of what had once been a bed of grasses. Thus easily did Monsieur Jean C. Tarzan slough the thin skin of his artificial civilization, and sink happy and contented into the deep sleep of the wild beast that has fed to repletion. Yet a woman's "yes" would have bound him to that other life forever, and made the thought of this savage existence repulsive.

Tarzan slept late into the following forenoon, for he had been very tired from the labors and exertion of the long night and day upon the ocean, and the jungle jaunt that had brought into play muscles that he had scarce used for nearly two years. When he awoke he ran to the brook first to drink. Then he took a plunge into the sea, swimming about for a quarter of an hour. Afterward he returned to his cabin, and breakfasted off the flesh of Horta. This done, he buried the balance of the carcass in the soft earth outside the cabin, for his evening meal.

Once more he took his rope and vanished into the jungle. This time he hunted nobler quarry—man; although had you asked him his own opinion he could have named a dozen other denizens of the jungle which he considered far the superiors in nobility of the men he hunted. Today Tarzan was in quest of weapons. He wondered if the women and children had remained in Mbonga's village after the punitive expedition from the French cruiser had massacred all the warriors in revenge for D'Arnot's supposed death. He hoped that he should find warriors there, for he knew not how long a quest he should have to make were the village deserted.

The ape-man traveled swiftly through the forest, and about noon came to the site of the village, but to his disappointment found that the jungle had overgrown the plantain fields and that the thatched huts had fallen in decay. There was no sign of man. He clambered

438

about among the ruins for half an hour, hoping that he might discover some forgotten weapon, but his search was without fruit, and so he took up his quest once more, following up the stream, which flowed from a southeasterly direction. He knew that near fresh water he would be most likely to find another settlement.

As he traveled he hunted as he had hunted with his ape people in the past, as Kala had taught him to hunt, turning over rotted logs to find some toothsome vermin, running high into the trees to rob a bird's nest, or pouncing upon a tiny rodent with the quickness of a cat. There were other things that he ate, too, but the less detailed the account of an ape's diet, the better—and Tarzan was again an ape, the same fierce, brutal anthropoid that Kala had taught him to be, and that he had been for the first twenty years of his life.

Occasionally he smiled as he recalled some friend who might even at the moment be sitting placid and immaculate within the precincts of his select Parisian club—just as Tarzan had sat but a few months before; and then he would stop, as though turned suddenly to stone as the gentle breeze carried to his trained nostrils the scent of some new prey or a formidable enemy.

That night he slept far inland from his cabin, securely wedged into the crotch of a giant tree, swaying a hundred feet above the ground. He had eaten heartily again—this time from the flesh of Bara, the deer, who had fallen prey to his quick noose.

Early the next morning he resumed his journey, always following the course of the stream. For three days he continued his quest, until he had come to a part of the jungle in which he never before had been. Occasionally upon the higher ground the forest was much thinner, and in the far distance through the trees he could see ranges of mighty mountains, with wide plains in the foreground. Here, in the open spaces, were new game—countless antelope and vast herds of zebra. Tarzan was entranced—he would make a long visit to this new world.

On the morning of the fourth day his nostrils were suddenly surprised by a faint new scent. It was the scent of man, but yet a long way off. The ape-man thrilled with pleasure. Every sense was on the alert as with crafty stealth he moved quickly through the trees, up-wind, in the direction of his prey. Presently he came upon it—a lone warrior treading softly through the jungle.

Tarzan followed close above his quarry, waiting for a clearer space in which to hurl his rope. As he stalked the unconscious man, new thoughts presented themselves to the ape-man—thoughts born of the refining influences of civilization, and of its cruelties. It came to him that seldom if ever did civilized man kill a fellow being without some pretext, however slight. It was true that Tarzan wished this man's weapons and ornaments, but was it necessary to take his life to obtain them?

The longer he thought about it, the more repugnant became the thought of taking human life needlessly; and thus it happened that while he was trying to decide just what to do, they had come to a little clearing, at the far side of which lay a palisaded village of bee-hive huts.

As the warrior emerged from the forest, Tarzan caught a fleeting glimpse of a tawny hide worming its way through the matted jungle grasses in his wake—it was Numa, the lion. He, too, was stalking the black man. With the instant that Tarzan realized the native's danger his attitude toward his erstwhile prey altered completely—now he was a fellow man threatened by a common enemy.

Numa was about to charge—there was little time in which to compare various methods or weigh the probable results of any. And then a number of things happened, almost simultaneously—the lion sprang from his ambush toward the retreating black—Tarzan cried out in warning—and the black turned just in time to see Numa halted in mid-flight by a slender strand of grass rope, the noosed end of which had fallen cleanly about his neck.

The ape-man had acted so quickly that he had been unable to prepare himself to withstand the strain and shock of Numa's great weight upon the rope, and so it was that though the rope stopped the beast before his mighty talons could fasten themselves in the flesh of the black, the strain overbalanced Tarzan, who came tumbling to the ground not six paces from the infuriated animal. Like lightning Numa turned upon this new enemy, and, defenseless as he was, Tarzan of the Apes was nearer to death that instant than he ever before had been. It was the black who saved him. The warrior realized in an instant that he owed his life to this strange white man, and he also saw that only a miracle could save his preserver from those fierce yellow fangs that had been so near to his own flesh.

With the quickness of thought his spear arm flew back, and then shot forward with all the force of the sinewy muscles that rolled beneath the shimmering ebon hide. True to its mark the iron-shod weapon flew, transfixing Numa's sleek carcass from the right groin to beneath the left shoulder. With a hideous scream of rage and pain the brute turned again upon the black. A dozen paces he had gone when Tarzan's rope brought him to a stand once more—then he wheeled again upon the ape-man, only to feel the painful prick of a barbed arrow as it sank half its length in his quivering flesh. Again he stopped, and by this time Tarzan had run twice around the stem of a great tree with his rope, and made the end fast.

The black saw the trick, and grinned, but Tarzan knew that Numa must be quickly finished before those mighty teeth had found and parted the slender cord that held him. It was a matter of but an instant to reach the black's side and drag his long knife from its scabbard. Then he signed the warrior to continue to shoot arrows into the great beast while he attempted to close in upon him with the knife; so as one tantalized upon one side, the other sneaked cautiously in upon the other. Numa was furious. He raised his voice in a perfect frenzy of shrieks, growls, and hideous moans, the while he reared upon his hind legs in futile attempt to reach first one and then the other of his tormentors.

But at length the agile ape-man saw his chance, and rushed in upon the beast's left side behind the mighty shoulder. A giant arm encircled the tawny throat, and a long blade sank once, true as a die, into the fierce heart. Then Tarzan arose, and the black man and the white looked into each other's eyes across the body of their kill—and the black made the sign of peace and friendship, and Tarzan of the Apes answered in kind.

XV

FROM APE TO SAVAGE

he noise of their battle with Numa had drawn an excited horde of savages from the nearby village, and a moment after the lion's death the two men were surrounded by lithe, ebon warriors, gesticulating and jabbering—a thousand questions that drowned each ventured reply.

And then the women came, and the children—eager, curious, and, at sight of Tarzan, more questioning than ever. The ape-man's new friend finally succeeded in making himself heard, and when he had done talking the men and women of the village vied with one another in doing honor to the strange creature who had saved their fellow and battled single-handed with fierce Numa.

At last they led him back to their village, where they brought him gifts of fowl, and goats, and cooked food. When he pointed to their weapons the warriors hastened to fetch spear, shield, arrows, and a bow. His friend of the encounter presented him with the knife with which he had killed Numa. There was nothing in all the village he could not have had for the asking.

How much easier this was, thought Tarzan, than murder and robbery to supply his wants. How close he had been to killing this man whom he never had seen before, and who now was manifesting by every primitive means at his command friendship and affection for his would-be slayer. Tarzan of the Apes was ashamed. Hereafter he would at least wait until he knew men deserved it before he thought of killing them.

The idea recalled Rokoff to his mind. He wished that he might have the Russian to himself in the dark jungle for a few minutes. There was a man who deserved killing if ever any one did. And if he could have seen Rokoff at that moment as he assiduously bent every endeavor to the pleasant task of ingratiating himself into the affections of the beautiful Miss Strong, he would have longed more than ever to mete out to the man the fate he deserved.

Tarzan's first night with the savages was devoted to a wild orgy in his honor. There was feasting, for the hunters had brought in an antelope and a zebra as trophies of their skill, and gallons of the weak native beer were consumed. As the warriors danced in the firelight, Tarzan was again impressed by the symmetry of their figures and the regularity of their features—the flat noses and thick lips of the typical West Coast savage were entirely missing. In repose the faces of the men were intelligent and dignified, those of the women ofttimes prepossessing.

It was during this dance that the ape-man first noticed that some of the men and many of the women wore ornaments of gold—principally anklets and armlets of great weight, apparently beaten out of the solid metal. When he expressed a wish to examine one of these, the owner removed it from her person and insisted, through the medium of signs, that Tarzan accept it as a gift. A close scrutiny of the bauble convinced the ape-man that the article was of virgin gold, and he was surprised, for it was the first time that he had ever seen golden ornaments among the savages of Africa, other than the trifling baubles those near the coast had purchased or stolen from Europeans. He tried to ask them from whence the metal came, but he could not make them understand.

When the dance was done Tarzan signified his intention to leave them, but they almost implored him to accept the hospitality of a great hut which the chief set apart for his sole use. He tried to explain that he would return in the morning, but they could not understand.

When he finally walked away from them toward the side of the village opposite the gate, they were still further mystified as to his intentions.

Tarzan, however, knew just what he was about. In the past he had had experience with the rodents and vermin that infest every native village, and, while he was not overscrupulous about such matters, he much preferred the fresh air of the swaying trees to the fetid atmosphere of a hut.

The natives followed him to where a great tree overhung the palisade, and as Tarzan leaped for a lower branch and disappeared into the foliage above, precisely after the manner of Manu, the monkey, there were loud exclamations of surprise and astonishment. For half an hour they called to him to return, but as he did not answer them they at last desisted, and sought the sleeping-mats within their huts.

Tarzan went back into the forest a short distance until he had found a tree suited to his primitive requirements, and then, curling himself in a great crotch, he fell immediately into a deep sleep.

The following morning he dropped into the village street as suddenly as he had disappeared the preceding night. For a moment the natives were startled and afraid, but when they recognized their guest of the night before they welcomed him with shouts and laughter. That day he accompanied a party of warriors to the nearby plains on a great hunt, and so dexterous did they find this white man with their own crude weapons that another bond of respect and admiration was thereby wrought.

For weeks Tarzan lived with his savage friends, hunting buffalo, antelope, and zebra for meat, and elephant for ivory. Quickly he learned their simple speech, their native customs, and the ethics of their wild, primitive tribal life. He found that they were not cannibals—that they looked with loathing and contempt upon men who ate men.

Busuli, the warrior whom he had stalked to the village, told him
many of the tribal legends—how, many years before, his people had
come many long marches from the north; how once they had been a
great and powerful tribe; and how the slave raiders had wrought such
havoc among them with their death-dealing guns that they had been
reduced to a mere remnant of their former numbers and power.

"They hunted us down as one hunts a fierce beast," said Busuli.
"There was no mercy in them. When it was not slaves they sought
it was ivory, but usually it was both. Our men were killed and our
women driven away like sheep. We fought against them for many
years, but our arrows and spears could not prevail against the sticks
which spit fire and lead and death to many times the distance that
our mightiest warrior could place an arrow. At last, when my father
was a young man, the Arabs came again, but our warriors saw them a
long way off, and Chowambi, who was chief then, told his people to
gather up their belongings and come away with him—that he would
lead them far to the south until they found a spot to which the Arab
raiders did not come.

"And they did as he bid, carrying all their belongings, including many tusks of ivory. For months they wandered, suffering untold
hardships and privations, for much of the way was through dense jungle, and across mighty mountains, but finally they came to this spot,
and although they sent parties farther on to search for an even better
location, none has ever been found."

"And the raiders have never found you here?" asked Tarzan.

"About a year ago a small party of Arabs and Manyuema stumbled upon us, but we drove them off, killing many. For days we followed them, stalking them for the wild beasts they are, picking them
off one by one, until but a handful remained, but these escaped us."

As Busuli talked he fingered a heavy gold armlet that encircled
the glossy hide of his left arm. Tarzan's eyes had been upon the
ornament, but his thoughts were elsewhere. Presently he recalled

the question he had tried to ask when he first came to the tribe—the question he could not at that time make them understand. For weeks he had forgotten so trivial a thing as gold, for he had been for the time a truly primeval man with no thought beyond today. But of a sudden the sight of gold awakened the sleeping civilization that was in him, and with it came the lust for wealth. That lesson Tarzan had learned well in his brief experience of the ways of civilized man. He knew that gold meant power and pleasure. He pointed to the bauble.

"From whence came the yellow metal, Busuli?" he asked.

The black pointed toward the southeast.

"A moon's march away—maybe more," he replied.

"Have you been there?" asked Tarzan.

"No, but some of our people were there years ago, when my father was yet a young man. One of the parties that searched farther for a location for the tribe when first they settled here came upon a strange people who wore many ornaments of yellow metal. Their spears were tipped with it, as were their arrows, and they cooked in vessels made all of solid metal like my armlet.

"They lived in a great village in huts that were built of stone and surrounded by a great wall. They were very fierce, rushing out and falling upon our warriors before ever they learned that their errand was a peaceful one. Our men were few in number, but they held their own at the top of a little rocky hill, until the fierce people went back at sunset into their wicked city. Then our warriors came down from their hill, and, after taking many ornaments of yellow metal from the bodies of those they had slain, they marched back out of the valley, nor have any of us ever returned.

"They are wicked people—neither white like you nor black like me, but covered with hair as is Bolgani, the gorilla. Yes, they are very bad people indeed, and Chowambi was glad to get out of their country."

"And are none of those alive who were with Chowambi, and saw these strange people and their wonderful city?" asked Tarzan.

"Waziri, our chief, was there," replied Busuli. "He was a very young man then, but he accompanied Chowambi, who was his father."

So that night Tarzan asked Waziri about it, and Waziri, who was now an old man, said that it was a long march, but that the way was not difficult to follow. He remembered it well.

"For ten days we followed this river which runs beside our village. Up toward its source we traveled until on the tenth day we came to a little spring far up upon the side of a lofty mountain range. In this little spring our river is born. The next day we crossed over the top of the mountain, and upon the other side we came to a tiny rivulet which we followed down into a great forest. For many days we traveled along the winding banks of the rivulet that had now become a river, until we came to a greater river, into which it emptied, and which ran down the center of a mighty valley.

"Then we followed this large river toward its source, hoping to come to more open land. After twenty days of marching from the time we had crossed the mountains and passed out of our own country we came again to another range of mountains. Up their side we followed the great river, that had now dwindled to a tiny rivulet, until we came to a little cave near the mountain-top. In this cave was the mother of the river.

"I remember that we camped there that night, and that it was very cold, for the mountains were high. The next day we decided to ascend to the top of the mountains, and see what the country upon the other side looked like, and if it seemed no better than that which we had so far traversed we would return to our village and tell them that they had already found the best place in all the world to live.

"And so we clambered up the face of the rocky cliffs until we reached the summit, and there from a flat mountain-top we saw, not far beneath us, a shallow valley, very narrow; and upon the far side of

448

it was a great village of stone, much of which had fallen and crumbled into decay."

The balance of Waziri's story was practically the same as that which Busuli had told.

"I should like to go there and see this strange city," said Tarzan, "and get some of their yellow metal from its fierce inhabitants."

"It is a long march," replied Waziri, "and I am an old man, but if you will wait until the rainy season is over and the rivers have gone down I will take some of my warriors and go with you."

And Tarzan had to be contented with that arrangement, though he would have liked it well enough to have set off the next morning—he was as impatient as a child. Really Tarzan of the Apes was but a child, or a primeval man, which is the same thing in a way.

The next day but one a small party of hunters returned to the village from the south to report a large herd of elephant some miles away. By climbing trees they had had a fairly good view of the herd, which they described as numbering several large tuskers, a great many cows and calves, and full-grown bulls whose ivory would be worth having.

The balance of the day and evening was filled with preparation for a great hunt—spears were overhauled, quivers were replenished, bows were restrung; and all the while the village witch doctor passed through the busy throngs disposing of various charms and amulets designed to protect the possessor from hurt, or bring him good fortune in the morrow's hunt.

At dawn the hunters were off. There were fifty sleek, black warriors, and in their midst, lithe and active as a young forest god, strode Tarzan of the Apes, his brown skin contrasting oddly with the ebony of his companions. Except for color he was one of them. His ornaments and weapons were the same as theirs—he spoke their language—he laughed and joked with them, and leaped and shouted in the brief wild dance that preceded their departure from the village, to all intent and purpose a savage among savages. Nor, had he questioned himself, is it to be doubted that he would have admitted that he was far more closely allied to these people and their life than to the Parisian friends whose ways, apelike, he had successfully mimicked for a few short months.

But he did think of D'Arnot, and a grin of amusement showed his strong white teeth as he pictured the immaculate Frenchman's expression could he by some means see Tarzan as he was that minute. Poor Paul, who had prided himself on having eradicated from his friend the last traces of wild savagery. "How quickly have I fallen!" thought Tarzan; but in his heart he did not consider it a fall—rather, he pitied the poor creatures of Paris, penned up like prisoners in their silly clothes, and watched by policemen all their poor lives, that they might do nothing that was not entirely artificial and tiresome.

A two hours' march brought them close to the vicinity in which the elephants had been seen the previous day. From there on they moved very quietly indeed searching for the spoor of the great beasts. At length they found the well-marked trail along which the herd had passed not many hours before. In single file they followed it for about half an hour. It was Tarzan who first raised his hand in signal that the quarry was at hand—his sensitive nose had warned him that the elephants were not far ahead of them.

The blacks were skeptical when he told them how he knew.

"Come with me," said Tarzan, "and we shall see."

With the agility of a squirrel he sprang into a tree and ran nimbly to the top. One of the blacks followed more slowly and carefully. When he had reached a lofty limb beside the ape-man the latter pointed to the south, and there, some few hundred yards away, the black saw a number of huge black backs swaying back and forth above the top of the lofty jungle grasses. He pointed the direction to the watchers below, indicating with his fingers the number of beasts he could count.

Immediately the hunters started toward the elephants. The black in the tree hastened down, but Tarzan stalked, after his own fashion, along the leafy way of the middle terrace.

It is no child's play to hunt wild elephants with the crude weapons of primitive man. Tarzan knew that few native tribes ever attempted it, and the fact that his tribe did so gave him no little pride—already he was commencing to think of himself as a member of the little community. As Tarzan moved silently through the trees he saw the warriors below creeping in a half circle upon the still unsuspecting elephants. Finally they were within sight of the great beasts. Now they singled out two large tuskers, and at a signal the fifty men rose from the ground where they had lain concealed, and hurled their heavy war spears at the two marked beasts. There was not a single miss; twenty-five spears were embedded in the sides of each of the giant animals. One never moved from the spot where it stood when the avalanche of spears struck it, for two, perfectly aimed, had penetrated its heart, and it lunged forward upon its knees, rolling to the ground without a struggle.

The other, standing nearly head-on toward the hunters, had not proved so good a mark, and though every spear struck not one entered the great heart. For a moment the huge bull stood trumpeting in rage and pain, casting about with its little eyes for the author of its hurt. The blacks had faded into the jungle before the weak eyes of the monster had fallen upon any of them, but now he caught the sound of their retreat, and, amid a terrific crashing of underbrush and branches, he charged in the direction of the noise.

It so happened that chance sent him in the direction of Busuli, whom he was overtaking so rapidly that it was as though the black were standing still instead of racing at full speed to escape the certain death which pursued him. Tarzan had witnessed the entire performance from the branches of a nearby tree, and now that he saw his friend's peril he raced toward the infuriated beast with loud cries, hoping to distract him.

But it had been as well had he saved his breath, for the brute was deaf and blind to all else save the particular object of his rage that raced futilely before him. And now Tarzan saw that only a miracle could save Busuli, and with the same unconcern with which he had once hunted this very man he hurled himself into the path of the elephant to save the black warrior's life.

He still grasped his spear, and while Tantor was yet six or eight paces behind his prey, a sinewy white warrior dropped as from the heavens, almost directly in his path. With a vicious lunge the elephant swerved to the right to dispose of this temerarious foeman who dared intervene between himself and his intended victim; but he had not reckoned on the lightning quickness that could galvanize those steel muscles into action so marvelously swift as to baffle even a keener eyesight than Tantor's.

And so it happened that before the elephant realized that his new enemy had leaped from his path Tarzan had driven his iron-shod spear from behind the massive shoulder straight into the fierce heart, and the colossal pachyderm had toppled to his death at the feet of the ape-man.

Busuli had not beheld the manner of his deliverance, but Waziri, the old chief, had seen, and several of the other warriors, and they hailed Tarzan with delight as they swarmed about him and his great kill. When he leaped upon the mighty carcass, and gave voice to the weird challenge with which he announced a great victory, the blacks shrank back in fear, for to them it marked the brutal Bolgani, whom they feared fully as much as they feared Numa, the lion; but with a fear with which was mixed a certain uncanny awe of the manlike thing to which they attributed supernatural powers.

But when Tarzan lowered his raised head and smiled upon them they were reassured, though they did not understand. Nor did they ever fully understand this strange creature who ran through the trees as quickly as Manu, yet was even more at home upon the ground than themselves; who was except as to color like unto themselves, yet as powerful as ten of them, and singlehanded a match for the fiercest denizens of the fierce jungle.

When the remainder of the warriors had gathered, the hunt was again taken up and the stalking of the retreating herd once more begun; but they had covered a bare hundred yards when from behind them, at a great distance, sounded faintly a strange popping.

For an instant they stood like a group of statuary, intently listening. Then Tarzan spoke.

"Guns!" he said. "The village is being attacked."

"Come!" cried Waziri. "The Arab raiders have returned with their cannibal slaves for our ivory and our women!"

XVI

THE IVORY RAIDERS

aziri's warriors marched at a rapid trot through the jungle in the direction of the village. For a few minutes, the sharp cracking of guns ahead warned them to haste, but finally the reports dwindled to an occasional shot, presently ceasing altogether. Nor was this less ominous than the rattle of musketry, for it suggested but a single solution to the little band of rescuers—that the illy garrisoned village had already succumbed to the onslaught of a superior force.

The returning hunters had covered a little more than three miles of the five that had separated them from the village when they met the first of the fugitives who had escaped the bullets and clutches of the foe. There were a dozen women, youths, and girls in the party, and so excited were they that they could scarce make themselves understood as they tried to relate to Waziri the calamity that had befallen his people.

"They are as many as the leaves of the forest," cried one of the women, in attempting to explain the enemy's force. "There are many Arabs and countless Manyuema, and they all have guns. They crept close to the village before we knew that they were about, and then, with many shouts, they rushed in upon us, shooting down men, and women, and children. Those of us who could fled in all directions into the jungle, but more were killed. I do not know whether they took any prisoners or not—they seemed only bent upon killing us all. The Manyuema called us many names, saying that they would eat us all before they left our country—that this was our punishment for killing their friends last year. I did not hear much, for I ran away quickly."

The march toward the village was now resumed, more slowly and with greater stealth, for Waziri knew that it was too late to rescue—their only mission could be one of revenge. Inside the next mile a hundred more fugitives were met. There were many men among these, and so the fighting strength of the party was augmented.

Now a dozen warriors were sent creeping ahead to reconnoiter. Waziri remained with the main body, which advanced in a thin line that spread in a great crescent through the forest. By the chief's side walked Tarzan.

Presently one of the scouts returned. He had come within sight of the village.

"They are all within the palisade," he whispered.

"Good!" said Waziri. "We shall rush in upon them and slay them all," and he made ready to send word along the line that they were to halt at the edge of the clearing until they saw him rush toward the village—then all were to follow.

"Wait!" cautioned Tarzan. "If there are even fifty guns within the palisade we shall be repulsed and slaughtered. Let me go alone through the trees, so that I may look down upon them from above, and see just how many there be, and what chance we might have were we to charge. It were foolish to lose a single man needlessly if there be no hope of success. I have an idea that we can accomplish more by cunning than by force. Will you wait, Waziri?"

"Yes," said the old chief. "Go!"

So Tarzan sprang into the trees and disappeared in the direction of the village. He moved more cautiously than was his wont, for he knew that men with guns could reach him quite as easily in the treetops as on the ground. And when Tarzan of the Apes elected to adopt stealth, no creature in all the jungle could move so silently or so completely efface himself from the sight of an enemy.

In five minutes he had wormed his way to the great tree that overhung the palisade at one end of the village, and from his point of vantage looked down upon the savage horde beneath. He counted fifty Arabs and estimated that there were five times as many Manyuema. The latter were gorging themselves upon food and, under the very noses of their white masters, preparing the gruesome feast which is the *piece de résistance* that follows a victory in which the bodies of their slain enemies fall into their horrid hands.

The ape-man saw that to charge that wild horde, armed as they were with guns, and barricaded behind the locked gates of the village, would be a futile task, and so he returned to Waziri and advised him to wait; that he, Tarzan, had a better plan.

But a moment before one of the fugitives had related to Waziri the story of the atrocious murder of the old chief's wife, and so crazed with rage was the old man that he cast discretion to the winds. Calling his warriors about him, he commanded them to charge, and, with brandishing spears and savage yells, the little force of scarcely more than a hundred dashed madly toward the village gates. Before the clearing had been half crossed the Arabs opened up a withering fire from behind the palisade.

With the first volley Waziri fell. The speed of the chargers slackened. Another volley brought down a half dozen more. A few reached the barred gates, only to be shot in their tracks, without the ghost of a chance to gain the inside of the palisade, and then the whole attack crumpled, and the remaining warriors scampered back into the forest. As they ran the raiders opened the gates, rushing after them, to complete the day's work with the utter extermination of the tribe. Tarzan had been among the last to turn back toward the forest, and now, as he ran slowly, he turned from time to time to speed a well-aimed arrow into the body of a pursuer.

Once within the jungle, he found a little knot of determined blacks waiting to give battle to the oncoming horde, but Tarzan cried to them to scatter, keeping out of harm's way until they could gather in force after dark.

"Do as I tell you," he urged, "and I will lead you to victory over these enemies of yours. Scatter through the forest, picking up as many stragglers as you can find, and at night, if you think that you have been followed, come by roundabout ways to the spot where we killed the elephants today. Then I will explain my plan, and you will find that it is good. You cannot hope to pit your puny strength and simple weapons against the numbers and the guns of the Arabs and the Manyuema."

They finally assented. "When you scatter," explained Tarzan, in conclusion, "your foes will have to scatter to follow you, and so it may happen that if you are watchful you can drop many a Manyuema with your arrows from behind some great trees."

They had barely time to hasten away farther into the forest before the first of the raiders had crossed the clearing and entered it in pursuit of them.

Tarzan ran a short distance along the ground before he took to the trees. Then he raced quickly to the upper terrace, there doubling on his tracks and making his way rapidly back toward the village. Here he found that every Arab and Manyuema had joined in the pursuit, leaving the village deserted except for the chained prisoners and a single guard.

The sentry stood at the open gate, looking in the direction of the forest, so that he did not see the agile giant that dropped to the ground at the far end of the village street. With drawn bow the ape-man crept stealthily toward his unsuspecting victim. The prisoners had already discovered him, and with wide eyes filled with wonder and with hope they watched their would-be rescuer. Now he halted not ten paces from the unconscious Manyuema. The shaft was drawn back its full length at the height of the keen gray eye that sighted along its polished surface. There was a sudden twang as the brown fingers released their hold, and without a sound the raider sank forward upon his face, a wooden shaft transfixing his heart and protruding a foot from his black chest.

Then Tarzan turned his attention to the fifty women and youths chained neck to neck on the long slave chain. There was no releasing of the ancient padlocks in the time that was left him, so the ape-man called to them to follow him as they were, and, snatching the gun and cartridge belt from the dead sentry, he led the now happy band out through the village gate and into the forest upon the far side of the clearing.

It was a slow and arduous march, for the slave chain was new to these people, and there were many delays as one of their number would stumble and fall, dragging others down with her. Then, too, Tarzan had been forced to make a wide detour to avoid any possibility of meeting with returning raiders. He was partially guided by occasional shots which indicated that the Arab horde was still in touch with the villagers; but he knew that if they would but follow his advice there would be but few casualties other than on the side of the marauders.

Toward dusk the firing ceased entirely, and Tarzan knew that the Arabs had all returned to the village. He could scarce repress a smile of triumph as he thought of their rage on discovering that their guard had been killed and their prisoners taken away. Tarzan had wished that he might have taken some of the great store of ivory the village contained, solely for the purpose of still further augmenting the wrath of his enemies; but he knew that that was not necessary for its salvation, since he already had a plan mapped out which would effectually prevent the Arabs leaving the country with a single tusk. And it would have been cruel to have needlessly burdened these poor, overwrought women with the extra weight of the heavy ivory.

It was after midnight when Tarzan, with his slow-moving caravan, approached the spot where the elephants lay. Long before they reached it they had been guided by the huge fire the natives had built in the center of a hastily improvised *boma*, partially for warmth and partially to keep off chance lions.

When they had come close to the encampment Tarzan called aloud to let them know that friends were coming. It was a joyous reception the little party received when the blacks within the *boma* saw the long file of fettered friends and relatives enter the firelight. These had all been given up as lost forever, as had Tarzan as well, so that the happy blacks would have remained awake all night to feast on elephant meat and celebrate the return of their fellows, had not Tarzan insisted that they take what sleep they could, against the work of the coming day.

At that, sleep was no easy matter, for the women who had lost their men or their children in the day's massacre and battle made night hideous with their continued wailing and howling. Finally, however, Tarzan succeeded in silencing them, on the plea that their noise would attract the Arabs to their hiding-place, when all would be slaughtered.

When dawn came Tarzan explained his plan of battle to the warriors, and without demur one and all agreed that it was the safest and surest way in which to rid themselves of their unwelcome visitors and be revenged for the murder of their fellows.

First the women and children, with a guard of some twenty old warriors and youths, were started southward, to be entirely out of the zone of danger. They had instructions to erect temporary shelter and construct a protecting *boma* of thorn bush; for the plan of campaign which Tarzan had chosen was one which might stretch out over many days, or even weeks, during which time the warriors would not return to the new camp.

Two hours after daylight a thin circle of black warriors surrounded the village. At intervals one was perched high in the branches of a tree which could overlook the palisade. Presently a Manyuema within the village fell, pierced by a single arrow. There had been no sound of attack—none of the hideous war-cries or vainglorious waving of menacing spears that ordinarily marks the attack of savages—just a silent messenger of death from out of the silent forest.

The Arabs and their followers were thrown into a fine rage at this unprecedented occurrence. They ran for the gates, to wreak dire vengeance upon the foolhardy perpetrator of the outrage; but they suddenly realized that they did not know which way to turn to find the foe. As they stood debating with many angry shouts and much gesticulating, one of the Arabs sank silently to the ground in their very midst—a thin arrow protruding from his heart.

Tarzan had placed the finest marksmen of the tribe in the surrounding trees, with directions never to reveal themselves while the enemy was faced in their direction. As a black released his messenger of death he would slink behind the sheltering stem of the tree he had selected, nor would he again aim until a watchful eye told him that none was looking toward his tree.

Three times the Arabs started across the clearing in the direction from which they thought the arrows came, but each time another arrow would come from behind to take its toll from among their number. Then they would turn and charge in a new direction. Finally they set out upon a determined search of the forest, but the blacks melted before them, so that they saw no sign of an enemy.

But above them lurked a grim figure in the dense foliage of the mighty trees—it was Tarzan of the Apes, hovering over them as if he had been the shadow of death. Presently a Manyuema forged ahead of his companions; there was none to see from what direction death came, and so it came quickly, and a moment later those behind stumbled over the dead body of their comrade—the inevitable arrow piercing the still heart.

It does not take a great deal of this manner of warfare to get upon the nerves of white men, and so it is little to be wondered at that the Manyuema were soon panic-stricken. Did one forge ahead an arrow found his heart; did one lag behind he never again was seen alive; did one stumble to one side, even for a bare moment from the sight of his fellows, he did not return—and always when they came upon the bodies of their dead they found those terrible arrows driven with the accuracy of superhuman power straight through the victim's heart. But worse than all else was the hideous fact that not once during the morning had they seen or heard the slightest sign of an enemy other than the pitiless arrows.

When finally they returned to the village it was no better. Every now and then, at varying intervals that were maddening in the terrible suspense they caused, a man would plunge forward dead. The blacks besought their masters to leave this terrible place, but the Arabs feared to take up the march through the grim and hostile forest beset by this new and terrible enemy while laden with the great store of ivory they had found within the village; but, worse yet, they hated to leave the ivory behind.

Finally the entire expedition took refuge within the thatched huts—here, at least, they would be free from the arrows. Tarzan, from the tree above the village, had marked the hut into which the chief Arabs had gone, and, balancing himself upon an overhanging limb, he drove his heavy spear with all the force of his giant muscles through the thatched roof. A howl of pain told him that it had found a mark. With this parting salute to convince them that there was no safety for them anywhere within the country, Tarzan returned to the forest, collected his warriors, and withdrew a mile to the south to rest and eat. He kept sentries in several trees that commanded a view of the trail toward the village, but there was no pursuit.

An inspection of his force showed not a single casualty—not even a minor wound; while rough estimates of the enemies' loss convinced the blacks that no fewer than twenty had fallen before their arrows. They were wild with elation, and were for finishing the day in one glorious rush upon the village, during which they would slaughter the last of their foemen. They were even picturing the various tortures they would inflict, and gloating over the suffering of the Manyuema, for whom they entertained a peculiar hatred, when Tarzan put his foot down flatly upon the plan.

"You are crazy!" he cried. "I have shown you the only way to fight these people. Already you have killed twenty of them without the loss of a single warrior, whereas, yesterday, following your own tactics, which you would now renew, you lost at least a dozen, and killed not a single Arab or Manyuema. You will fight just as I tell you to fight, or I shall leave you and go back to my own country."

They were frightened when he threatened this, and promised to obey him scrupulously if he would but promise not to desert them.

"Very well," he said. "We shall return to the elephant *boma* for the night. I have a plan to give the Arabs a little taste of what they may expect if they remain in our country, but I shall need no help. Come! If they suffer no more for the balance of the day they will feel reassured, and the relapse into fear will be even more nerve-racking than as though we continued to frighten them all afternoon."

So they marched back to their camp of the previous night, and, lighting great fires, ate and recounted the adventures of the day until long after dark. Tarzan slept until midnight, then he arose and crept into the Cimmerian blackness of the forest. An hour later he came to the edge of the clearing before the village. There was a camp-fire burning within the palisade. The ape-man crept across the clearing until he stood before the barred gates. Through the interstices he saw a lone sentry sitting before the fire.

Quietly Tarzan went to the tree at the end of the village street. He climbed softly to his place, and fitted an arrow to his bow. For several minutes he tried to sight fairly upon the sentry, but the waving branches and flickering firelight convinced him that the danger of a miss was too great—he must touch the heart full in the center to bring the quiet and sudden death his plan required.

He had brought, besides, his bow, arrows, and rope, the gun he had taken the previous day from the other sentry he had killed. Caching all these in a convenient crotch of the tree, he dropped lightly to the ground within the palisade, armed only with his long knife. The sentry's back was toward him. Like a cat Tarzan crept upon the dozing man. He was within two paces of him now—another instant and the knife would slide silently into the fellow's heart.

Tarzan crouched for a spring, for that is ever the quickest and surest attack of the jungle beast—when the man, warned, by some subtle sense, sprang to his feet and faced the ape-man.

XVII

THE WHITE CHIEF
OF THE WAZIRI

hen the eyes of the black Manyuema savage fell upon the strange apparition that confronted him with menacing knife they went wide in horror. He forgot the gun within his hands; he even forgot to cry out—his one thought was to escape this fearsome-looking white savage, this giant of a man upon whose massive rolling muscles and mighty chest the flickering firelight played.

But before he could turn Tarzan was upon him, and then the sentry thought to scream for aid, but it was too late. A great hand was upon his windpipe, and he was being borne to the earth. He battled furiously but futilely—with the grim tenacity of a bulldog those awful fingers were clinging to his throat. Swiftly and surely life was being choked from him. His eyes bulged, his tongue protruded, his face turned to a ghastly purplish hue—there was a convulsive tremor of the stiffening muscles, and the Manyuema sentry lay quite still.

The ape-man threw the body across one of his broad shoulders and, gathering up the fellow's gun, trotted silently up the sleeping village street toward the tree that gave him such easy ingress to the palisaded village. He bore the dead sentry into the midst of the leafy maze above.

First he stripped the body of cartridge belt and such ornaments as he craved, wedging it into a convenient crotch while his nimble fingers ran over it in search of the loot he could not plainly see in the dark. When he had finished he took the gun that had belonged to the man, and walked far out upon a limb, from the end of which he could obtain a better view of the huts. Drawing a careful bead on the beehive structure in which he knew the chief Arabs to be, he pulled the trigger. Almost instantly there was an answering groan. Tarzan smiled. He had made another lucky hit.

Following the shot there was a moment's silence in the camp, and then Manyuema and Arab came pouring from the huts like a swarm of angry hornets; but if the truth were known they were even more frightened than they were angry. The strain of the preceding day had wrought upon the fears of both black and white, and now this single shot in the night conjured all manner of terrible conjectures in their terrified minds.

When they discovered that their sentry had disappeared, their fears were in no way allayed, and as though to bolster their courage by warlike actions, they began to fire rapidly at the barred gates of the village, although no enemy was in sight. Tarzan took advantage of the deafening roar of this fusillade to fire into the mob beneath him.

No one heard his shot above the din of rattling musketry in the street, but some who were standing close saw one of their number crumple suddenly to the earth. When they leaned over him he was dead. They were panic-stricken, and it took all the brutal authority of the Arabs to keep the Manyuema from rushing helter-skelter into the jungle—anywhere to escape from this terrible village.

After a time they commenced to quiet down, and as no further mysterious deaths occurred among them they took heart again. But it was a short-lived respite, for just as they had concluded that they would not be disturbed again Tarzan gave voice to a weird moan, and as the raiders looked up in the direction from which the sound seemed to come, the ape-man, who stood swinging the dead body of the sentry gently to and fro, suddenly shot the corpse far out above their heads.

With howls of alarm the throng broke in all directions to escape this new and terrible creature who seemed to be springing upon them. To their fear-distorted imaginations the body of the sentry, falling with wide-sprawled arms and legs, assumed the likeness of a great beast of prey. In their anxiety to escape, many of the blacks scaled the palisade, while others tore down the bars from the gates and rushed madly across the clearing toward the jungle.

For a time no one turned back toward the thing that had frightened them, but Tarzan knew that they would in a moment, and when they discovered that it was but the dead body of their sentry, while they would doubtless be still further terrified, he had a rather definite idea as to what they would do, and so he faded silently away toward the south, taking the moonlit upper terrace back toward the camp of the Waziri.

Presently one of the Arabs turned and saw that the thing that had leaped from the tree upon them lay still and quiet where it had fallen in the center of the village street. Cautiously he crept back toward it until he saw that it was but a man. A moment later he was beside the figure, and in another had recognized it as the corpse of the Manyuema who had stood on guard at the village gate.

His companions rapidly gathered around at his call, and after a moment's excited conversation they did precisely what Tarzan had reasoned they would. Raising their guns to their shoulders, they poured volley after volley into the tree from which the corpse had been thrown—had Tarzan remained there he would have been riddled by a hundred bullets.

When the Arabs and Manyuema discovered that the only marks of violence upon the body of their dead comrade were giant finger prints upon his swollen throat they were again thrown into deeper apprehension and despair. That they were not even safe within a palisaded village at night came as a distinct shock to them. That an enemy could enter into the midst of their camp and kill their sentry with bare hands seemed outside the bounds of reason, and so the superstitious Manyuema commenced to attribute their ill luck to supernatural causes; nor were the Arabs able to offer any better explanation.

With at least fifty of their number flying through the black jungle, and without the slightest knowledge of when their uncanny foemen might resume the cold-blooded slaughter they had commenced, it was a desperate band of cut-throats that waited sleeplessly for the dawn. Only on the promise of the Arabs that they would leave the village at daybreak, and hasten onward toward their own land, would the remaining Manyuema consent to stay at the village a moment longer. Not even fear of their cruel masters was sufficient to overcome this new terror.

And so it was that when Tarzan and his warriors returned to the attack the next morning they found the raiders prepared to march out of the village. The Manyuema were laden with stolen ivory. As Tarzan saw it he grinned, for he knew that they would not carry it far. Then he saw something which caused him anxiety—a number of the Manyuema were lighting torches in the remnant of the camp-fire. They were about to fire the village.

Tarzan was perched in a tall tree some hundred yards from the palisade. Making a trumpet of his hands, he called loudly in the Arab tongue: "Do not fire the huts, or we shall kill you all! Do not fire the huts, or we shall kill you all!"

A dozen times he repeated it. The Manyuema hesitated, then one of them flung his torch into the campfire. The others were about to do the same when an Arab sprung upon them with a stick, beating them toward the huts. Tarzan could see that he was commanding them to fire the little thatched dwellings. Then he stood erect upon the swaying branch a hundred feet above the ground, and, raising one of the Arab guns to his shoulder, took careful aim and fired. With the report the Arab who was urging on his men to burn the village fell in his tracks, and the Manyuema threw away their torches and fled from the village. The last Tarzan saw of them they were racing toward the jungle, while their former masters knelt upon the ground and fired at them.

But however angry the Arabs might have been at the insubordination of their slaves, they were at least convinced that it would be the better part of wisdom to forego the pleasure of firing the village that had given them two such nasty receptions. In their hearts, however, they swore to return again with such force as would enable them to sweep the entire country for miles around, until no vestige of human life remained.

They had looked in vain for the owner of the voice which had frightened off the men who had been detailed to put the torch to the huts, but not even the keenest eye among them had been able to locate him. They had seen the puff of smoke from the tree following the shot that brought down the Arab, but, though a volley had immediately been loosed into its foliage, there had been no indication that it had been effective.

Tarzan was too intelligent to be caught in any such trap, and so the report of his shot had scarcely died away before the ape-man was on the ground and racing for another tree a hundred yards away. Here he again found a suitable perch from which he could watch the preparations of the raiders. It occurred to him that he might have considerable more fun with them, so again he called to them through his improvised trumpet.

"Leave the ivory!" he cried. "Leave the ivory! Dead men have no use for ivory!"

Some of the Manyuema started to lay down their loads, but this was altogether too much for the avaricious Arabs. With loud shouts and curses they aimed their guns full upon the bearers, threatening instant death to any who might lay down his load. They could give up firing the village, but the thought of abandoning this enormous fortune in ivory was quite beyond their conception—better death than that.

And so they marched out of the village of the Waziri, and on the shoulders of their slaves was the ivory ransom of a score of kings. Toward the north they marched, back toward their savage settlement in the wild and unknown country which lies back from the Kongo in the uttermost depths of The Great Forest, and on either side of them traveled an invisible and relentless foe.

Under Tarzan's guidance the black Waziri warriors stationed themselves along the trail on either side in the densest underbrush. They stood at far intervals, and, as the column passed, a single arrow or a heavy spear, well aimed, would pierce a Manyuema or an Arab. Then the Waziri would melt into the distance and run ahead to take his stand farther on. They did not strike unless success were sure and the danger of detection almost nothing, and so the arrows and the spears were few and far between, but so persistent and inevitable that the slow-moving column of heavy-laden raiders was in a constant state of panic—panic at the uncertainty of who the next would be to fall, and when.

It was with the greatest difficulty that the Arabs prevented their men a dozen times from throwing away their burdens and fleeing like frightened rabbits up the trail toward the north. And so the day wore on—a frightful nightmare of a day for the raiders—a day of weary but well-repaid work for the Waziri. At night the Arabs constructed a rude *boma* in a little clearing by a river, and went into camp.

At intervals during the night a rifle would bark close above their heads, and one of the dozen sentries which they now had posted would tumble to the ground. Such a condition was insupportable, for they saw that by means of these hideous tactics they would be completely wiped out, one by one, without inflicting a single death upon their enemy. But yet, with the persistent avariciousness of the white man, the Arabs clung to their loot, and when morning came forced the demoralized Manyuema to take up their burdens of death and stagger on into the jungle.

For three days the withering column kept up its frightful march. Each hour was marked by its deadly arrow or cruel spear. The nights were made hideous by the barking of the invisible gun that made sentry duty equivalent to a death sentence.

On the morning of the fourth day the Arabs were compelled to shoot two of their blacks before they could compel the balance to take up the hated ivory, and as they did so a voice rang out, clear and strong, from the jungle: "Today you die, oh, Manyuema, unless you lay down the ivory. Fall upon your cruel masters and kill them! You have guns, why do you not use them? Kill the Arabs, and we will not harm you. We will take you back to our village and feed you, and lead you out of our country in safety and in peace. Lay down the ivory, and fall upon your masters—we will help you. Else you die!"

As the voice died down the raiders stood as though turned to stone. The Arabs eyed their Manyuema slaves; the slaves looked first at one of their fellows, and then at another—they were but waiting for some one to take the initiative. There were some thirty Arabs left, and about one hundred and fifty blacks. All were armed—even those who were acting as porters had their rifles slung across their backs.

The Arabs drew together. The sheik ordered the Manyuema to take up the march, and as he spoke he cocked his rifle and raised it. But at the same instant one of the blacks threw down his load, and, snatching his rifle from his back, fired point-black at the group of Arabs. In an instant the camp was a cursing, howling mass of demons, fighting with guns and knives and pistols. The Arabs stood together, and defended their lives valiantly, but with the rain of lead that poured upon them from their own slaves, and the shower of arrows and spears which now leaped from the surrounding jungle aimed solely at them, there was little question from the first what the outcome would be. In ten minutes from the time the first porter had thrown down his load the last of the Arabs lay dead.

When the firing had ceased Tarzan spoke again to the Manyuema:

"Take up our ivory, and return it to our village, from whence you stole it. We shall not harm you."

For a moment the Manyuema hesitated. They had no stomach to retrace that difficult three days' trail. They talked together in low whispers, and one turned toward the jungle, calling aloud to the voice that had spoken to them from out of the foliage.

"How do we know that when you have us in your village you will not kill us all?" he asked.

"You do not know," replied Tarzan, "other than that we have promised not to harm you if you will return our ivory to us. But this you do know, that it lies within our power to kill you all if you do not return as we direct, and are we not more likely to do so if you anger us than if you do as we bid?"

"Who are you that speaks the tongue of our Arab masters?" cried the Manyuema spokesman. "Let us see you, and then we shall give you our answer."

Tarzan stepped out of the jungle a dozen paces from them.

"Look!" he said. When they saw that he was white they were filled with awe, for never had they seen a white savage before, and at his great muscles and giant frame they were struck with wonder and admiration.

"You may trust me," said Tarzan. "So long as you do as I tell you, and harm none of my people, we shall do you no hurt. Will you take up our ivory and return in peace to our village, or shall we follow along your trail toward the north as we have followed for the past three days?"

The recollection of the horrid days that had just passed was the thing that finally decided the Manyuema, and so, after a short conference, they took up their burdens and set off to retrace their steps toward the village of the Waziri. At the end of the third day they marched into the village gate, and were greeted by the survivors of the recent massacre, to whom Tarzan had sent a messenger in their temporary camp to the south on the day that the raiders had quitted the village, telling them that they might return in safety.

It took all the mastery and persuasion that Tarzan possessed to prevent the Waziri falling on the Manyuema tooth and nail, and tearing them to pieces, but when he had explained that he had given his word that they would not be molested if they carried the ivory back to the spot from which they had stolen it, and had further impressed upon his people that they owed their entire victory to him, they finally acceded to his demands, and allowed the cannibals to rest in peace within their palisade.

That night the village warriors held a big palaver to celebrate their victories, and to choose a new chief. Since old Waziri's death Tarzan had been directing the warriors in battle, and the temporary command had been tacitly conceded to him. There had been no time to choose a new chief from among their own number, and, in fact, so remarkably successful had they been under the ape-man's generalship that they had had no wish to delegate the supreme authority to another for fear that what they already had gained might be lost. They had so recently seen the results of running counter to this savage white man's advice in the disastrous charge ordered by Waziri, in which he himself had died, that it had not been difficult for them to accept Tarzan's authority as final.

The principal warriors sat in a circle about a small fire to discuss the relative merits of whomever might be suggested as old Waziri's successor. It was Busuli who spoke first:

"Since Waziri is dead, leaving no son, there is but one among us whom we know from experience is fitted to make us a good king. There is only one who has proved that he can successfully lead us against the guns of the white man, and bring us easy victory without the loss of a single life. There is only one, and that is the white man who has led us for the past few days," and Busuli sprang to his feet, and with uplifted spear and half-bent, crouching body commenced to dance slowly about Tarzan, chanting in time to his steps: "Waziri, king of the Waziri; Waziri, killer of Arabs; Waziri, king of the Waziri."

One by one the other warriors signified their acceptance of Tarzan as their king by joining in the solemn dance. The women came and squatted about the rim of the circle, beating upon tom-toms, clapping their hands in time to the steps of the dancers, and joining in the chant of the warriors. In the center of the circle sat Tarzan of the Apes—Waziri, king of the Waziri, for, like his predecessor, he was to take the name of his tribe as his own.

Faster and faster grew the pace of the dancers, louder and louder their wild and savage shouts. The women rose and fell in unison, shrieking now at the tops of their voices. The spears were brandishing fiercely, and as the dancers stooped down and beat their shields upon the hard-tramped earth of the village street the whole sight was as terribly primeval and savage as though it were being staged in the dim dawn of humanity, countless ages in the past.

As the excitement waxed the ape-man sprang to his feet and joined in the wild ceremony. In the center of the circle of glittering black bodies he leaped and roared and shook his heavy spear in the same mad abandon that enthralled his fellow savages. The last remnant of his civilization was forgotten—he was a primitive man to the fullest now; reveling in the freedom of the fierce, wild life he loved, gloating in his kingship among these wild blacks.

Ah, if Olga de Coude had but seen him then—could she have recognized the well-dressed, quiet young man whose well-bred face and irreproachable manners had so captivated her but a few short months ago? And Jane Porter! Would she have still loved this savage warrior chieftain, dancing naked among his naked savage subjects? And D'Arnot! Could D'Arnot have believed that this was the same man he had introduced into half a dozen of the most select clubs of

Paris? What would his fellow peers in the House of Lords have said had one pointed to this dancing giant, with his barbaric headdress and his metal ornaments, and said: "There, my lords, is John Clayton, Lord Greystoke."

And so Tarzan of the Apes came into a real kingship among men—slowly but surely was he following the evolution of his ancestors, for had he not started at the very bottom?

XVIII

THE LOTTERY OF DEATH

ane Porter had been the first of those in the lifeboat to awaken the morning after the wreck of the *Lady Alice*. The other members of the party were asleep upon the thwarts or huddled in cramped positions in the bottom of the boat.

When the girl realized that they had become separated from the other boats she was filled with alarm. The sense of utter loneliness and helplessness which the vast expanse of deserted ocean aroused in her was so depressing that, from the first, contemplation of the future held not the slightest ray of promise for her. She was confident that they were lost—lost beyond possibility of succor.

Presently Clayton awoke. It was several minutes before he could gather his senses sufficiently to realize where he was, or recall the disaster of the previous night. Finally his bewildered eyes fell upon the girl.

"Jane!" he cried. "Thank God that we are together!"

"Look," said the girl dully, indicating the horizon with an apathetic gesture. "We are all alone."

Clayton scanned the water in every direction.

"Where can they be?" he cried. "They cannot have gone down, for there has been no sea, and they were afloat after the yacht sank—I saw them all."

He awoke the other members of the party, and explained their plight.

"It is just as well that the boats are scattered, sir," said one of the sailors. "They are all provisioned, so that they do not need each other on that score, and should a storm blow up they could be of no service to one another even if they were together, but scattered about the ocean there is a much better chance that one at least will be picked up, and then a search will be at once started for the others. Were we together there would be but one chance of rescue, where now there may be four."

They saw the wisdom of his philosophy, and were cheered by it, but their joy was short-lived, for when it was decided that they should row steadily toward the east and the continent, it was discovered that the sailors who had been at the only two oars with which the boat had been provided had fallen asleep at their work, and allowed both to slip into the sea, nor were they in sight anywhere upon the water.

During the angry words and recriminations which followed the sailors nearly came to blows, but Clayton succeeded in quieting them; though a moment later Monsieur Thuran almost precipitated another row by making a nasty remark about the stupidity of all Englishmen, and especially English sailors.

"Come, come, mates," spoke up one of the men, Tompkins, who had taken no part in the altercation, "shootin' off our bloomin' mugs won't get us nothin'. As Spider 'ere said afore, we'll all bloody well be picked up, anyway, sez 'e, so wot's the use o' squabblin'? Let's eat, sez I."

"That's not a bad idea," said Monsieur Thuran, and then, turning to the third sailor, Wilson, he said: "Pass one of those tins aft, my good man."

"Fetch it yerself," retorted Wilson sullenly. "I ain't a-takin' no orders from no—furriner—you ain't captain o' this ship yet."

The result was that Clayton himself had to get the tin, and then another angry altercation ensued when one of the sailors accused Clayton and Monsieur Thuran of conspiring to control the provisions so that they could have the lion's share.

"Some one should take command of this boat," spoke up Jane Porter, thoroughly disgusted with the disgraceful wrangling that had marked the very opening of a forced companionship that might last for many days. "It is terrible enough to be alone in a frail boat on the Atlantic, without having the added misery and danger of constant bickering and brawling among the members of our party. You men should elect a leader, and then abide by his decisions in all matters. There is greater need for strict discipline here than there is upon a well-ordered ship."

She had hoped before she voiced her sentiments that it would not be necessary for her to enter into the transaction at all, for she believed that Clayton was amply able to cope with every emergency, but she had to admit that so far at least he had shown no greater promise of successfully handling the situation than any of the others, though he had at least refrained from adding in any way to the unpleasantness, even going so far as to give up the tin to the sailors when they objected to its being opened by him.

The girl's words temporarily quieted the men, and finally it was decided that the two kegs of water and the four tins of food should be divided into two parts, one-half going forward to the three sailors to do with as they saw best, and the balance aft to the three passengers.

Thus was the little company divided into two camps, and when the provisions had been apportioned each immediately set to work to open and distribute food and water. The sailors were the first to get one of the tins of "food" open, and their curses of rage and disappointment caused Clayton to ask what the trouble might be.

"Trouble!" shrieked Spider. "Trouble! It's worse than trouble—it's death! This—tin is full of coal oil!"

Hastily now Clayton and Monsieur Thuran tore open one of theirs, only to learn the hideous truth that it also contained, not food, but coal oil. One after another the four tins on board were opened.

And as the contents of each became known howls of anger announced the grim truth—there was not an ounce of food upon the boat.

"Well, thank Gawd it wasn't the water," cried Thompkins. "It's easier to get along without food than it is without water. We can eat our shoes if worse comes to worst, but we couldn't drink 'em."

As he spoke Wilson had been boring a hole in one of the water kegs, and as Spider held a tin cup he tilted the keg to pour a draft of the precious fluid. A thin stream of blackish, dry particles filtered slowly through the tiny aperture into the bottom of the cup. With a groan Wilson dropped the keg, and sat staring at the dry stuff in the cup, speechless with horror.

"The kegs are filled with gunpowder," said Spider, in a low tone, turning to those aft. And so it proved when the last had been opened.

"Coal oil and gunpowder!" cried Monsieur Thuran. "*Sapristi!* What a diet for shipwrecked mariners!"

With the full knowledge that there was neither food nor water on board, the pangs of hunger and thirst became immediately aggravated, and so on the first day of their tragic adventure real suffering commenced in grim earnest, and the full horrors of shipwreck were upon them.

As the days passed conditions became horrible. Aching eyes scanned the horizon day and night until the weak and weary watchers would sink exhausted to the bottom of the boat, and there wrest in dream-disturbed slumber a moment's respite from the horrors of the waking reality.

The sailors, goaded by the remorseless pangs of hunger, had eaten their leather belts, their shoes, the sweatbands from their caps, although both Clayton and Monsieur Thuran had done their best to convince them that these would only add to the suffering they were enduring.

Weak and hopeless, the entire party lay beneath the pitiless tropic sun, with parched lips and swollen tongues, waiting for the death they were beginning to crave. The intense suffering of the first few days had become deadened for the three passengers who had eaten nothing, but the agony of the sailors was pitiful, as their weak and impoverished stomachs attempted to cope with the bits of leather with which they had filled them. Tompkins was the first to succumb. Just a week from the day the *Lady Alice* went down the sailor died horribly in frightful convulsions.

For hours his contorted and hideous features lay grinning back at those in the stern of the little boat, until Jane Porter could endure the sight no longer. "Can you not drop his body overboard, William?" she asked.

Clayton rose and staggered toward the corpse. The two remaining sailors eyed him with a strange, baleful light in their sunken orbs. Futilely the Englishman tried to lift the corpse over the side of the boat, but his strength was not equal to the task.

"Lend me a hand here, please," he said to Wilson, who lay nearest him.

"Wot do you want to throw 'im over for?" questioned the sailor, in a querulous voice.

"We've got to before we're too weak to do it," replied Clayton. "He'd be awful by tomorrow, after a day under that broiling sun."

"Better leave well enough alone," grumbled Wilson. "We may need him before tomorrow."

Slowly the meaning of the man's words percolated into Clayton's understanding. At last he realized the fellow's reason for objecting to the disposal of the dead man.

"God!" whispered Clayton, in a horrified tone. "You don't mean—"

"W'y not?" growled Wilson. "Ain't we gotta live? He's dead," he added, jerking his thumb in the direction of the corpse. "He won't care."

"Come here, Thuran," said Clayton, turning toward the Russian.

"We'll have something worse than death aboard us if we don't get rid of this body before dark."

Wilson staggered up menacingly to prevent the contemplated act, but when his comrade, Spider, took sides with Clayton and Monsieur Thuran he gave up, and sat eying the corpse hungrily as the three men, by combining their efforts, succeeded in rolling it overboard.

All the balance of the day Wilson sat glaring at Clayton, in his eyes the gleam of insanity. Toward evening, as the sun was sinking into the sea, he commenced to chuckle and mumble to himself, but his eyes never left Clayton.

After it became quite dark Clayton could still feel those terrible eyes upon him. He dared not sleep, and yet so exhausted was he that it was a constant fight to retain consciousness. After what seemed an eternity of suffering his head dropped upon a thwart, and he slept. How long he was unconscious he did not know—he was awakened by a shuffling noise quite close to him. The moon had risen, and as he opened his startled eyes he saw Wilson creeping stealthily toward him, his mouth open and his swollen tongue hanging out.

The slight noise had awakened Jane Porter at the same time, and as she saw the hideous tableau she gave a shrill cry of alarm, and at the same instant the sailor lurched forward and fell upon Clayton. Like a wild beast his teeth sought the throat of his intended prey, but Clayton, weak though he was, still found sufficient strength to hold the maniac's mouth from him.

At Jane Porter's scream Monsieur Thuran and Spider awoke. On seeing the cause of her alarm, both men crawled to Clayton's rescue, and between the three of them were able to subdue Wilson and hurl him to the bottom of the boat. For a few minutes he lay there chattering and laughing, and then, with an awful scream, and before any of his companions could prevent, he staggered to his feet and leaped overboard.

The reaction from the terrific strain of excitement left the weak survivors trembling and prostrated. Spider broke down and wept; Jane Porter prayed; Clayton swore softly to himself; Monsieur Thuran sat with his head in his hands, thinking. The result of his cogitation developed the following morning in a proposition he made to Spider and Clayton.

"Gentlemen," said Monsieur Thuran, "you see the fate that awaits us all unless we are picked up within a day or two. That there is little hope of that is evidenced by the fact that during all the days we have drifted we have seen no sail, nor the faintest smudge of smoke upon the horizon.

"There might be a chance if we had food, but without food there is none. There remains for us, then, but one of two alternatives, and we must choose at once. Either we must all die together within a few days, or one must be sacrificed that the others may live. Do you quite clearly grasp my meaning?"

Jane Porter, who had overheard, was horrified. If the proposition had come from the poor, ignorant sailor, she might possibly have not been so surprised; but that it should come from one who posed as a man of culture and refinement, from a gentleman, she could scarcely credit.

"It is better that we die together, then," said Clayton.

"That is for the majority to decide," replied Monsieur Thuran. "As only one of us three will be the object of sacrifice, we shall decide. Miss Porter is not interested, since she will be in no danger."

"How shall we know who is to be first?" asked Spider.

"It may be fairly fixed by lot," replied Monsieur Thuran. "I have a number of franc pieces in my pocket. We can choose a certain date from among them—the one to draw this date first from beneath a piece of cloth will be the first."

"I shall have nothing to do with any such diabolical plan," muttered Clayton; "even yet land may be sighted or a ship appear—in time."

"You will do as the majority decide, or you will be 'the first' without the formality of drawing lots," said Monsieur Thuran threateningly. "Come, let us vote on the plan; I for one am in favor of it. How about you, Spider?"

"And I," replied the sailor.

"It is the will of the majority," announced Monsieur Thuran, "and now let us lose no time in drawing lots. It is as fair for one as for another. That three may live, one of us must die perhaps a few hours sooner than otherwise."

Then he began his preparation for the lottery of death, while Jane Porter sat wide-eyed and horrified at thought of the thing that she was about to witness. Monsieur Thuran spread his coat upon the bottom of the boat, and then from a handful of money he selected six franc pieces. The other two men bent close above him as he inspected them. Finally he handed them all to Clayton.

"Look at them carefully," he said. "The oldest date is eighteen-seventy-five, and there is only one of that year."

Clayton and the sailor inspected each coin. To them there seemed not the slightest difference that could be detected other than the dates. They were quite satisfied. Had they known that Monsieur Thuran's past experience as a card sharp had trained his sense of touch to so fine a point that he could almost differentiate between cards by the mere feel of them, they would scarcely have felt that the plan was so entirely fair. The 1875 piece was a hair thinner than the other coins, but neither Clayton nor Spider could have detected it without the aid of a micrometer.

"In what order shall we draw?" asked Monsieur Thuran, knowing from past experience that the majority of men always prefer last chance in a lottery where the single prize is some distasteful thing— there is always the chance and the hope that another will draw it first. Monsieur Thuran, for reasons of his own, preferred to draw first if the drawing should happen to require a second adventure beneath the coat.

THE LOTTERY OF DEATH

And so when Spider elected to draw last he graciously offered to take the first chance himself. His hand was under the coat for but a moment, yet those quick, deft fingers had felt of each coin, and found and discarded the fatal piece. When he brought forth his hand it contained an 1888 franc piece. Then Clayton drew. Jane Porter leaned forward with a tense and horrified expression on her face as the hand of the man she was to marry groped about beneath the coat. Presently he withdrew it, a franc piece lying in the palm. For an instant he dared not look, but Monsieur Thuran, who had leaned nearer to see the date, exclaimed that he was safe.

Jane Porter sank weak and trembling against the side of the boat. She felt sick and dizzy. And now, if Spider should not draw the 1875 piece she must endure the whole horrid thing again.

The sailor already had his hand beneath the coat. Great beads of sweat were standing upon his brow. He trembled as though with a fit of ague. Aloud he cursed himself for having taken the last draw, for now his chances for escape were but three to one, whereas Monsieur Thuran's had been five to one, and Clayton's four to one.

The Russian was very patient, and did not hurry the man, for he knew that he himself was quite safe whether the 1875 piece came out this time or not. When the sailor withdrew his hand and looked at the piece of money within, he dropped fainting to the bottom of the boat. Both Clayton and Monsieur Thuran hastened weakly to examine the coin, which had rolled from the man's hand and lay beside him. It was not dated 1875. The reaction from the state of fear he had been in had overcome Spider quite as effectually as though he had drawn the fated piece.

But now the whole proceeding must be gone through again. Once more the Russian drew forth a harmless coin. Jane Porter closed her eyes as Clayton reached beneath the coat. Spider bent, wide-eyed, toward the hand that was to decide his fate, for whatever luck was Clayton's on this last draw, the opposite would be Spider's.

Then William Cecil Clayton, Lord Greystoke, removed his hand from beneath the coat, and with a coin tight pressed within his palm where none might see it, he looked at Jane Porter. He did not dare open his hand.

"Quick!" hissed Spider. "My Gawd, let's see it."

Clayton opened his fingers. Spider was the first to see the date, and ere any knew what his intention was he raised himself to his feet, and lunged over the side of the boat, to disappear forever into the green depths beneath—the coin had not been the 1875 piece.

The strain had exhausted those who remained to such an extent that they lay half unconscious for the balance of the day, nor was the subject referred to again for several days. Horrible days of increasing weakness and hopelessness. At length Monsieur Thuran crawled to where Clayton lay.

"We must draw once more before we are too weak even to eat," he whispered.

Clayton was in such a state that he was scarcely master of his own will. Jane Porter had not spoken for three days. He knew that she was dying. Horrible as the thought was, he hoped that the sacrifice of either Thuran or himself might be the means of giving her renewed strength, and so he immediately agreed to the Russian's proposal.

They drew under the same plan as before, but there could be but one result—Clayton drew the 1875 piece.

"When shall it be?" he asked Thuran.

The Russian had already drawn a pocketknife from his trousers, and was weakly attempting to open it.

"Now," he muttered, and his greedy eyes gloated upon the Englishman.

"Can't you wait until dark?" asked Clayton. "Miss Porter must not see this thing done. We were to have been married, you know."

A look of disappointment came over Monsieur Thuran's face.

"Very well," he replied hesitatingly. "It will not be long until night. I have waited for many days—I can wait a few hours longer."

"Thank you, my friend," murmured Clayton. "Now I shall go to her side and remain with her until it is time. I would like to have an hour or two with her before I die."

When Clayton reached the girl's side she was unconscious—he knew that she was dying, and he was glad that she should not have to see or know the awful tragedy that was shortly to be enacted. He took her hand and raised it to his cracked and swollen lips. For a long time he lay caressing the emaciated, clawlike thing that had once been the beautiful, shapely white hand of the young Baltimore belle.

It was quite dark before he knew it, but he was recalled to himself by a voice out of the night. It was the Russian calling him to his doom.

"I am coming, Monsieur Thuran," he hastened to reply.

Thrice he attempted to turn himself upon his hands and knees, that he might crawl back to his death, but in the few hours that he had lain there he had become too weak to return to Thuran's side.

"You will have to come to me, monsieur," he called weakly. "I have not sufficient strength to gain my hands and knees."

"*Sapristi!*" muttered Monsieur Thuran. "You are attempting to cheat me out of my winnings."

Clayton heard the man shuffling about in the bottom of the boat. Finally there was a despairing groan. "I cannot crawl," he heard the Russian wail. "It is too late. You have tricked me, you dirty English dog."

"I have not tricked you, monsieur," replied Clayton. "I have done my best to rise, but I shall try again, and if you will try possibly each of us can crawl halfway, and then you shall have your 'winnings.'"

Again Clayton exerted his remaining strength to the utmost, and he heard Thuran apparently doing the same. Nearly an hour later the Englishman succeeded in raising himself to his hands and knees, but at the first forward movement he pitched upon his face.

485

A moment later he heard an exclamation of relief from Monsieur Thuran.

"I am coming," whispered the Russian.

Again Clayton essayed to stagger on to meet his fate, but once more he pitched headlong to the boat's bottom, nor, try as he would, could he again rise. His last effort caused him to roll over on his back, and there he lay looking up at the stars, while behind him, coming ever nearer and nearer, he could hear the laborious shuffling, and the stertorous breathing of the Russian.

It seemed that he must have lain thus an hour waiting for the thing to crawl out of the dark and end his misery. It was quite close now, but there were longer and longer pauses between its efforts to advance, and each forward movement seemed to the waiting Englishman to be almost imperceptible.

Finally he knew that Thuran was quite close beside him. He heard a cackling laugh, something touched his face, and he lost consciousness.

XIX

The City of Gold

he very night that Tarzan of the Apes became chief of the Waziri the woman he loved lay dying in a tiny boat two hundred miles west of him upon the Atlantic. As he danced among his naked fellow savages, the firelight gleaming against his great, rolling muscles, the personification of physical perfection and strength, the woman who loved him lay thin and emaciated in the last coma that precedes death by thirst and starvation.

The week following the induction of Tarzan into the kingship of the Waziri was occupied in escorting the Manyuema of the Arab raiders to the northern boundary of Waziri in accordance with the promise which Tarzan had made them. Before he left them he exacted a pledge from them that they would not lead any expeditions against the Waziri in the future, nor was it a difficult promise to obtain. They had had sufficient experience with the fighting tactics of the new Waziri chief not to have the slightest desire to accompany another predatory force within the boundaries of his domain.

Almost immediately upon his return to the village Tarzan commenced making preparations for leading an expedition in search of the ruined city of gold which old Waziri had described to him. He selected fifty of the sturdiest warriors of his tribe, choosing only men who seemed anxious to accompany him on the arduous march, and share the dangers of a new and hostile country.

The fabulous wealth of the fabled city had been almost constantly

487

in his mind since Waziri had recounted the strange adventures of the former expedition which had stumbled upon the vast ruins by chance. The lure of adventure may have been quite as powerful a factor in urging Tarzan of the Apes to undertake the journey as the lure of gold, but the lure of gold was there, too, for he had learned among civilized men something of the miracles that may be wrought by the possessor of the magic yellow metal. What he would do with a golden fortune in the heart of savage Africa it had not occurred to him to consider—it would be enough to possess the power to work wonders, even though he never had an opportunity to employ it.

So one glorious tropical morning Waziri, chief of the Waziri, set out at the head of fifty clean-limbed ebon warriors in quest of adventure and of riches. They followed the course which old Waziri had described to Tarzan. For days they marched—up one river, across a low divide; down another river; up a third, until at the end of the twenty-fifth day they camped upon a mountainside, from the summit of which they hoped to catch their first view of the marvelous city of treasure.

Early the next morning they were climbing the almost perpendicular crags which formed the last, but greatest, natural barrier between them and their destination. It was nearly noon before Tarzan, who headed the thin line of climbing warriors, scrambled over the top of the last cliff and stood upon the little flat table-land of the mountaintop.

On either hand towered mighty peaks thousands of feet higher than the pass through which they were entering the forbidden valley. Behind him stretched the wooded valley across which they had marched for many days, and at the opposite side the low range which marked the boundary of their own country.

But before him was the view that centered his attention. Here lay a desolate valley—a shallow, narrow valley dotted with stunted trees and covered with many great bowlders. And on the far side of the valley lay what appeared to be a mighty city, its great walls, its lofty spires, its turrets, minarets, and domes showing red and yellow in the sunlight. Tarzan was yet too far away to note the marks of ruin—to him it appeared a wonderful city of magnificent beauty, and in imagination he peopled its broad avenues and its huge temples with a throng of happy, active people.

For an hour the little expedition rested upon the mountain-top, and then Tarzan led them down into the valley below. There was no trail, but the way was less arduous than the ascent of the opposite face of the mountain had been. Once in the valley their progress was rapid, so that it was still light when they halted before the towering walls of the ancient city.

The outer wall was fifty feet in height where it had not fallen into ruin, but nowhere as far as they could see had more than ten or twenty feet of the upper courses fallen away. It was still a formidable defense. On several occasions Tarzan had thought that he discerned things moving behind the ruined portions of the wall near to them, as though creatures were watching them from behind the bulwarks of the ancient pile. And often he felt the sensation of unseen eyes upon him, but not once could he be sure that it was more than imagination.

That night they camped outside the city. Once, at midnight, they were awakened by a shrill scream from beyond the great wall. It was very high at first, descending gradually until it ended in a series of dismal moans. It had a strange effect upon the blacks, almost paralyzing them with terror while it lasted, and it was an hour before the camp settled down to sleep once more. In the morning the effects of it were still visible in the fearful, sidelong glances that the Waziri continually cast at the massive and forbidding structure which loomed above them.

It required considerable encouragement and urging on Tarzan's part to prevent the blacks from abandoning the venture on the spot and hastening back across the valley toward the cliffs they had scaled the day before. But at length, by dint of commands, and threats that he would enter the city alone, they agreed to accompany him.

For fifteen minutes they marched along the face of the wall before they discovered a means of ingress. Then they came to a narrow cleft about twenty inches wide. Within, a flight of concrete steps, worn hollow by centuries of use, rose before them, to disappear at a sharp turning of the passage a few yards ahead.

Into this narrow alley Tarzan made his way, turning his giant shoulders sideways that they might enter at all. Behind him trailed his black warriors. At the turn in the cleft the stairs ended, and the path was level; but it wound and twisted in a serpentine fashion, until suddenly at a sharp angle it debouched upon a narrow court, across which loomed an inner wall equally as high as the outer. This inner wall was set with little round towers alternating along its entire summit with pointed monoliths. In places these had fallen, and the wall was ruined, but it was in a much better state of preservation than the outer wall.

Another narrow passage led through this wall, and at its end Tarzan and his warriors found themselves in a broad avenue, on the opposite side of which crumbling edifices of hewn granite loomed dark and forbidding. Upon the crumbling debris along the face of the buildings trees had grown, and vines wound in and out of the hollow, staring windows; but the building directly opposite them seemed less overgrown than the others, and in a much better state of preservation. It was a massive pile, surmounted by an enormous dome. At either side of its great entrance stood rows of tall pillars, each capped by a huge, grotesque bird carved from the solid rock of the monoliths.

As the ape-man and his companions stood gazing in varying degrees of wonderment at this ancient city in the midst of savage Africa, several of them became aware of movement within the structure at which they were looking. Dim, shadowy shapes appeared to be moving about in the semi-darkness of the interior. There was nothing tangible that the eye could grasp—only an uncanny suggestion of life where it seemed that there should be no life, for living things seemed out of place in this weird, dead city of the long-dead past.

Tarzan recalled something that he had read in the library at Paris of a lost race of white men that native legend described as living in the heart of Africa. He wondered if he were not looking upon the ruins of the civilization that this strange people had wrought amid the savage surroundings of their strange and savage home. Could it be possible that even now a remnant of that lost race inhabited the ruined grandeur that had once been their progenitor? Again he became conscious of a stealthy movement within the great temple before him. "Come!" he said, to his Waziri. "Let us have a look at what lies behind those ruined walls."

His men were loath to follow him, but when they saw that he was bravely entering the frowning portal they trailed a few paces behind in a huddled group that seemed the personification of nervous terror. A single shriek such as they had heard the night before would have been sufficient to have sent them all racing madly for the narrow cleft that led through the great walls to the outer world.

As Tarzan entered the building he was distinctly aware of many eyes upon him. There was a rustling in the shadows of a near-by corridor, and he could have sworn that he saw a human hand withdrawn from an embrasure that opened above him into the domelike rotunda in which he found himself.

The floor of the chamber was of concrete, the walls of smooth granite, upon which strange figures of men and beasts were carved. In places tablets of yellow metal had been set in the solid masonry of the walls.

When he approached closer to one of these tablets he saw that it was of gold, and bore many hieroglyphics. Beyond this first chamber there were others, and back of them the building branched out into enormous wings. Tarzan passed through several of these chambers, finding many evidences of the fabulous wealth of the original builders. In one room were seven pillars of solid gold, and in another the floor itself was of the precious metal. And all the while that he explored, his blacks huddled close together at his back, and strange shapes hovered upon either hand and before them and behind, yet never close enough that any might say that they were not alone.

The strain, however, was telling upon the nerves of the Waziri. They begged Tarzan to return to the sunlight. They said that no good could come of such an expedition, for the ruins were haunted by the spirits of the dead who had once inhabited them.

"They are watching us, O king," whispered Busuli. "They are waiting until they have led us into the innermost recesses of their stronghold, and then they will fall upon us and tear us to pieces with their teeth. That is the way with spirits. My mother's uncle, who is a great witch doctor, has told me all about it many times."

Tarzan laughed. "Run back into the sunlight, my children," he said. "I will join you when I have searched this old ruin from top to bottom, and found the gold, or found that there is none. At least we may take the tablets from the walls, though the pillars are too heavy for us to handle; but there should be great storerooms filled with gold—gold that we can carry away upon our backs with ease. Run on now, out into the fresh air where you may breathe easier."

Some of the warriors started to obey their chief with alacrity, but Busuli and several others hesitated to leave him—hesitated between love and loyalty for their king, and superstitious fear of the unknown. And then, quite unexpectedly, that occurred which decided the question without the necessity for further discussion. Out of the silence of the ruined temple there rang, close to their ears, the same hideous shriek they had heard the previous night, and with horrified cries the black warriors turned and fled through the empty halls of the age-old edifice.

Behind them stood Tarzan of the Apes where they had left him,

492

a grim smile upon his lips—waiting for the enemy he fully expected was about to pounce upon him. But again silence reigned, except for the faint suggestion of the sound of naked feet moving stealthily in near-by places.

Then Tarzan wheeled and passed on into the depths of the temple. From room to room he went, until he came to one at which a rude, barred door still stood, and as he put his shoulder against it to push it in, again the shriek of warning rang out almost beside him. It was evident that he was being warned to refrain from desecrating this particular room. Or could it be that within lay the secret to the treasure stores?

At any rate, the very fact that the strange, invisible guardians of this weird place had some reason for wishing him not to enter this particular chamber was sufficient to treble Tarzan's desire to do so, and though the shrieking was repeated continuously, he kept his shoulder to the door until it gave before his giant strength to swing open upon creaking wooden hinges.

Within all was black as the tomb. There was no window to let in the faintest ray of light, and as the corridor upon which it opened was itself in semi-darkness, even the open door shed no relieving rays within. Feeling before him upon the floor with the butt of his spear, Tarzan entered the Stygian gloom. Suddenly the door behind him closed, and at the same time hands clutched him from every direction out of the darkness.

The ape-man fought with all the savage fury of self-preservation backed by the herculean strength that was his. But though he felt his blows land, and his teeth sink into soft flesh, there seemed always two new hands to take the place of those that he fought off. At last they dragged him down, and slowly, very slowly, they overcame him by the mere weight of their numbers. And then they bound him—his hands behind his back and his feet trussed up to meet them. He had heard no sound except the heavy breathing of his antagonists, and the noise of the battle. He knew not what manner of creatures had cap-tured him, but that they were human seemed evident from the fact that they had bound him.

Presently they lifted him from the floor, and half dragging, half pushing him, they brought him out of the black chamber through another doorway into an inner courtyard of the temple. Here he saw his captors. There must have been a hundred of them—short, stocky men, with great beards that covered their faces and fell upon their hairy breasts.

The thick, matted hair upon their heads grew low over their receding brows, and hung about their shoulders and their backs. Their crooked legs were short and heavy, their arms long and muscu-lar. About their loins they wore the skins of leopards and lions, and great necklaces of the claws of these same animals depended upon their breasts. Massive circlets of virgin gold adorned their arms and legs. For weapons they carried heavy, knotted bludgeons, and in the belts that confined their single garments each had a long, wicked-looking knife.

But the feature of them that made the most startling impres-sion upon their prisoner was their white skins—neither in color nor feature was there a trace of the negroid about them. Yet, with their receding foreheads, wicked little close-set eyes, and yellow fangs, they were far from prepossessing in appearance.

During the fight within the dark chamber, and while they had been dragging Tarzan to the inner court, no word had been spoken, but now several of them exchanged grunting, monosyllabic conversa-tion in a language unfamiliar to the ape-man, and presently they left him lying upon the concrete floor while they trooped off on their short legs into another part of the temple beyond the court.

As Tarzan lay there upon his back he saw that the temple entirely surrounded the little inclosure, and that on all sides its lofty walls rose high above him. At the top a little patch of blue sky was visible, and, in one direction, through an embrasure, he could see foliage, but whether it was beyond or within the temple he did not know.

About the court, from the ground to the top of the temple, were series of open galleries, and now and then the captive caught glimpses of bright eyes gleaming from beneath masses of tumbling hair, peering down upon him from above.

The ape-man gently tested the strength of the bonds that held him, and while he could not be sure it seemed that they were of insufficient strength to withstand the strain of his mighty muscles when the time came to make a break for freedom; but he did not dare to put them to the crucial test until darkness had fallen, or he felt that no spying eyes were upon him.

He had lain within the court for several hours before the first rays of sunlight penetrated the vertical shaft; almost simultaneously he heard the pattering of bare feet in the corridors about him, and a moment later saw the galleries above fill with crafty faces as a score or more entered the courtyard.

For a moment every eye was bent upon the noonday sun, and then in unison the people in the galleries and those in the court below took up the refrain of a low, weird chant. Presently those about Tarzan began to dance to the cadence of their solemn song. They circled him slowly, resembling in their manner of dancing a number of clumsy, shuffling bears; but as yet they did not look at him, keeping their little eyes fixed upon the sun.

For ten minutes or more they kept up their monotonous chant and steps, and then suddenly, and in perfect unison, they turned toward their victim with upraised bludgeons and emitting fearful howls, the while they contorted their features into the most diabolical expressions, they rushed upon him.

At the same instant a female figure dashed into the midst of the bloodthirsty horde, and, with a bludgeon similar to their own, except that it was wrought from gold, beat back the advancing men.

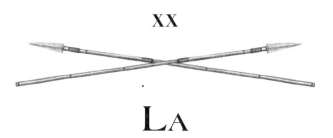

XX

LA

or a moment Tarzan thought that by some strange freak of fate a miracle had saved him, but when he realized the ease with which the girl had, single-handed, beaten off twenty gorilla-like males, and an instant later, as he saw them again take up their dance about him while she addressed them in a singsong monotone, which bore every evidence of rote, he came to the conclusion that it was all but a part of the ceremony of which he was the central figure.

After a moment or two the girl drew a knife from her girdle, and, leaning over Tarzan, cut the bonds from his legs. Then, as the men stopped their dance, and approached, she motioned to him to rise. Placing the rope that had been about his legs around his neck, she led him across the courtyard, the men following in twos.

Through winding corridors she led, farther and farther into the remoter precincts of the temple, until they came to a great chamber in the center of which stood an altar. Then it was that Tarzan translated the strange ceremony that had preceded his introduction into this holy of holies.

He had fallen into the hands of descendants of the ancient sun worshippers. His seeming rescue by a votaress of the high priestess of the sun had been but a part of the mimicry of their heathen ceremony—the sun looking down upon him through the opening at the top of the court had claimed him as his own, and the priestess had come from the inner temple to save him from the polluting hands of worldlings—to save him as a human offering to their flaming deity.

And had he needed further assurance as to the correctness of his theory he had only to cast his eyes upon the brownish-red stains that caked the stone altar and covered the floor in its immediate vicinity, or to the human skulls which grinned from countless niches in the towering walls.

The priestess led the victim to the altar steps. Again the galleries above filled with watchers, while from an arched doorway at the east end of the chamber a procession of females filed slowly into the room. They wore, like the men, only skins of wild animals caught about their waists with rawhide belts or chains of gold; but the black masses of their hair were incrusted with golden headgear composed of many circular and oval pieces of gold ingeniously held together to form a metal cap from which depended at each side of the head, long strings of oval pieces falling to the waist.

The females were more symmetrically proportioned than the males, their features were much more perfect, the shapes of their heads and their large, soft, black eyes denoting far greater intelligence and humanity than was possessed by their lords and masters.

Each priestess bore two golden cups, and as they formed in line along one side of the altar the men formed opposite them, advancing and taking each a cup from the female opposite. Then the chant began once more, and presently from a dark passageway beyond the altar another female emerged from the cavernous depths beneath the chamber.

The high priestess, thought Tarzan. She was a young woman with a rather intelligent and shapely face. Her ornaments were similar to those worn by her votaries, but much more elaborate, many being set with diamonds. Her bare arms and legs were almost concealed by the massive, bejeweled ornaments which covered them, while her single leopard skin was supported by a close-fitting girdle of golden rings set in strange designs with innumerable small diamonds. In the girdle she carried a long, jeweled knife, and in her hand a slender wand in lieu of a bludgeon.

As she advanced to the opposite side of the altar she halted, and the chanting ceased. The priests and priestesses knelt before her, while with wand extended above them she recited a long and tiresome prayer. Her voice was soft and musical—Tarzan could scarce realize that its possessor in a moment more would be transformed by the fanatical ecstasy of religious zeal into a wild-eyed and bloodthirsty executioner, who, with dripping knife, would be the first to drink her victim's red, warm blood from the little golden cup that stood upon the altar.

As she finished her prayer she let her eyes rest for the first time upon Tarzan. With every indication of considerable curiosity she examined him from head to foot. Then she addressed him, and when she had finished stood waiting, as though she expected a reply.

"I do not understand your language," said Tarzan. "Possibly we may speak together in another tongue?" But she could not understand him, though he tried French, English, Arab, Waziri, and, as a last resort, the mongrel tongue of the West Coast.

She shook her head, and it seemed that there was a note of weariness in her voice as she motioned to the priests to continue with the rites. These now circled in a repetition of their idiotic dance, which was terminated finally at a command from the priestess, who had stood throughout, still looking intently upon Tarzan.

At her signal the priests rushed upon the ape-man, and, lifting him bodily, laid him upon his back across the altar, his head hanging over one edge, his legs over the opposite. Then they and the priestesses formed in two lines, with their little golden cups in readiness to capture a share of the victim's lifeblood after the sacrificial knife had accomplished its work.

In the line of priests an altercation arose as to who should have first place. A burly brute with all the refined intelligence of a gorilla stamped upon his bestial face was attempting to push a smaller man to second place, but the smaller one appealed to the high priestess, who in a cold peremptory voice sent the larger to the extreme end of the line. Tarzan could hear him growling and rumbling as he went slowly to the inferior station.

Then the priestess, standing above him, began reciting what Tarzan took to be an invocation, the while she slowly raised her thin, sharp knife aloft. It seemed ages to the ape-man before her arm ceased its upward progress and the knife halted high above his unprotected breast.

Then it started downward, slowly at first, but as the incantation increased in rapidity, with greater speed. At the end of the line Tarzan could still hear the grumbling of the disgruntled priest. The man's voice rose louder and louder. A priestess near him spoke in sharp tones of rebuke. The knife was quite near to Tarzan's breast now, but it halted for an instant as the high priestess raised her eyes to shoot her swift displeasure at the instigator of this sacrilegious interruption.

There was a sudden commotion in the direction of the disputants, and Tarzan rolled his head in their direction in time to see the burly brute of a priest leap upon the woman opposite him, dashing out her brains with a single blow of his heavy cudgel. Then that happened which Tarzan had witnessed a hundred times before among the wild denizens of his own savage jungle. He had seen the thing fall upon Kerchak, and Tublat, and Terkoz; upon a dozen of the other mighty bull apes of his tribe; and upon Tantor, the elephant; there was scarce any of the males of the forest that did not at times fall prey to it. The priest went mad, and with his heavy bludgeon ran amuck among his fellows.

His screams of rage were frightful as he dashed hither and thither, dealing terrific blows with his giant weapon, or sinking his yellow fangs into the flesh of some luckless victim. And during it the priestess stood with poised knife above Tarzan, her eyes fixed in horror upon the maniacal thing that was dealing out death and destruction to her votaries.

Presently the room was emptied except for the dead and dying on the floor, the victim upon the altar, the high priestess, and the madman. As the cunning eyes of the latter fell upon the woman they lighted with a new and sudden lust. Slowly he crept toward her, and now he spoke; but this time there fell upon Tarzan's surprised ears a language he could understand; the last one that he would ever have thought of employing in attempting to converse with human beings—the low guttural barking of the tribe of great anthropoids— his own mother tongue. And the woman answered the man in the same language.

He was threatening—she attempting to reason with him, for it was quite evident that she saw that he was past her authority. The brute was quite close now—creeping with clawlike hands extended toward her around the end of the altar. Tarzan strained at the bonds which held his arms pinioned behind him. The woman did not see— she had forgotten her prey in the horror of the danger that threatened herself. As the brute leaped past Tarzan to clutch his victim, the apeman gave one superhuman wrench at the thongs that held him. The effort sent him rolling from the altar to the stone floor on the opposite side from that on which the priestess stood; but as he sprang to his feet the thongs dropped from his freed arms, and at the same time he realized that he was alone in the inner temple—the high priestess and the mad priest had disappeared.

And then a muffled scream came from the cavernous mouth of the dark hole beyond the sacrificial altar through which the priestess had entered the temple. Without even a thought for his own safety, or the possibility for escape which this rapid series of fortuitous circumstances had thrust upon him, Tarzan of the Apes answered the call of the woman in danger. With a little bound he was at the gaping entrance to the subterranean chamber, and a moment later was running down a flight of age-old concrete steps that led he knew not where.

The faint light that filtered in from above showed him a large, low-ceiled vault from which several doorways led off into inky darkness, but there was no need to thread an unknown way, for there before him lay the objects of his search—the mad brute had the girl upon the floor, and gorilla-like fingers were clutching frantically at her throat as she struggled to escape the fury of the awful thing upon her.

As Tarzan's heavy hand fell upon his shoulder the priest dropped his victim, and turned upon her would-be rescuer. With foam-flecked lips and bared fangs the mad sun-worshiper battled with the tenfold power of the maniac. In the blood lust of his fury the creature had undergone a sudden reversion to type, which left him a wild beast, forgetful of the dagger that projected from his belt—thinking only of nature's weapons with which his brute prototype had battled.

But if he could use his teeth and hands to advantage, he found one even better versed in the school of savage warfare to which he had reverted, for Tarzan of the Apes closed with him, and they fell to the floor tearing and rending at one another like two bull apes; while the primitive priestess stood flattened against the wall, watching with wide, fear-fascinated eyes the growing, snapping beasts at her feet.

At last she saw the stranger close one mighty hand upon the throat of his antagonist, and as he forced the bruteman's head far back rain blow after blow upon the upturned face. A moment later he threw the still thing from him, and, arising, shook himself like a lion. He placed a foot upon the carcass before him, and raised his head to give the victory cry of his kind, but as his eyes fell upon the opening above him leading into the temple of human sacrifice he thought better of his intended act.

The girl, who had been half paralyzed by fear as the two men fought, had just commenced to give thought to her probable fate now that, though released from the clutches of a madman, she had fallen into the hands of one whom but a moment before she had been upon the point of killing. She looked about for some means of escape. The black mouth of a diverging corridor was near at hand, but as she turned to dart into it the ape-man's eyes fell upon her, and with a quick leap he was at her side, and a restraining hand was laid upon her arm.

"Wait!" said Tarzan of the Apes, in the language of the tribe of Kerchak.

The girl looked at him in astonishment.

"Who are you," she whispered, "who speaks the language of the first man?"

"I am Tarzan of the Apes," he answered in the vernacular of the anthropoids.

"What do you want of me?" she continued. "For what purpose did you save me from Tha?"

"I could not see a woman murdered?" It was a half question that answered her.

"But what do you intend to do with me now?" she continued.

"Nothing," he replied, "but you can do something for me—you can lead me out of this place to freedom." He made the suggestion without the slightest thought that she would accede. He felt quite sure that the sacrifice would go on from the point where it had been interrupted if the high priestess had her way, though he was equally positive that they would find Tarzan of the Apes unbound and with a long dagger in his hand a much less tractable victim than Tarzan disarmed and bound.

The girl stood looking at him for a long moment before she spoke.

"You are a very wonderful man," she said. "You are such a man as I have seen in my daydreams ever since I was a little girl. You are such a man as I imagine the forbears of my people must have been—the great race of people who built this mighty city in the

502

heart of a savage world that they might wrest from the bowels of the earth the fabulous wealth for which they had sacrificed their far-distant civilization.

"I cannot understand why you came to my rescue in the first place, and now I cannot understand why, having me within your power, you do not wish to be revenged upon me for having sentenced you to death—for having almost put you to death with my own hand."

"I presume," replied the ape-man, "that you but followed the teachings of your religion. I cannot blame *you* for that, no matter what I may think of your creed. But who are you—what people have I fallen among?"

"I am La, high priestess of the Temple of the Sun, in the city of Opar. We are descendants of a people who came to this savage world more than ten thousand years ago in search of gold. Their cities stretched from a great sea under the rising sun to a great sea into which the sun descends at night to cool his flaming brow. They were very rich and very powerful, but they lived only a few months of the year in their magnificent palaces here; the rest of the time they spent in their native land, far, far to the north.

"Many ships went back and forth between this new world and the old. During the rainy season there were but few of the inhabitants remained here, only those who superintended the working of the mines by the black slaves, and the merchants who had to stay to supply their wants, and the soldiers who guarded the cities and the mines.

"It was at one of these times that the great calamity occurred. When the time came for the teeming thousands to return none came. For weeks the people waited. Then they sent out a great galley to learn why no one came from the mother country, but though they sailed about for many months, they were unable to find any trace of the mighty land that had for countless ages borne their ancient civilization—it had sunk into the sea.

"From that day dated the downfall of my people. Disheartened and unhappy, they soon became a prey to the black hordes of the north and the black hordes of the south. One by one the cities were deserted or overcome. The last remnant was finally forced to take shelter within this mighty mountain fortress. Slowly we have dwindled in power, in civilization, in intellect, in numbers, until now we are no more than a small tribe of savage apes.

"In fact, the apes live with us, and have for many ages. We call them the first men—we speak their language quite as much as we do our own; only in the rituals of the temple do we make any attempt to retain our mother tongue. In time it will be forgotten, and we will speak only the language of the apes; in time we will no longer banish those of our people who mate with apes, and so in time we shall descend to the very beasts from which ages ago our progenitors may have sprung."

"But why are you more human than the others?" asked the man.

"For some reason the women have not reverted to savagery so rapidly as the men. It may be because only the lower types of men remained here at the time of the great catastrophe, while the temples were filled with the noblest daughters of the race. My strain has remained clearer than the rest because for countless ages my foremothers were high priestesses—the sacred office descends from mother to daughter. Our husbands are chosen for us from the noblest in the land. The most perfect man, mentally and physically, is selected to be the husband of the high priestess."

"From what I saw of the gentlemen above," said Tarzan, with a grin, "there should be little trouble in choosing from among them."

The girl looked at him quizzically for a moment.

"Do not be sacrilegious," she said. "They are very holy men—they are priests."

"Then there are others who are better to look upon?" he asked.

"The others are all more ugly than the priests," she replied.

Tarzan shuddered at her fate, for even in the dim light of the vault he was impressed by her beauty.

"But how about myself?" he asked suddenly. "Are you going to lead me to liberty?"

"You have been chosen by The Flaming God as his own," she answered solemnly. "Not even I have the power to save you—should they find you again. But I do not intend that they shall find you. You risked your life to save mine. I may do no less for you. It will be no easy matter—it may require days; but in the end I think that I can lead you beyond the walls. Come, they will look here for me presently, and if they find us together we shall both be lost—they would kill me did they think that I had proved false to my god."

"You must not take the risk, then," he said quickly. "I will return to the temple, and if I can fight my way to freedom there will be no suspicion thrown upon you."

But she would not have it so, and finally persuaded him to follow her, saying that they had already remained in the vault too long to prevent suspicion from falling upon her even if they returned to the temple.

"I will hide you, and then return alone," she said, "telling them that I was long unconscious after you killed Tha, and that I do not know whither you escaped."

And so she led him through winding corridors of gloom, until finally they came to a small chamber into which a little light filtered through a stone grating in the ceiling.

"This is the Chamber of the Dead," she said. "None will think of searching here for you—they would not dare. I will return after it is dark. By that time I may have found a plan to effect your escape."

She was gone, and Tarzan of the Apes was left alone in the Chamber of the Dead, beneath the long-dead city of Opar.

XXI

THE CASTAWAYS

layton dreamed that he was drinking his fill of water, pure, delightful drafts of fresh water. With a start he gained consciousness to find himself wet through by torrents of rain that were falling upon his body and his upturned face. A heavy tropical shower was beating down upon them. He opened his mouth and drank. Presently he was so revived and strengthened that he was enabled to raise himself upon his hands. Across his legs lay Monsieur Thuran. A few feet aft Jane Porter was huddled in a pitiful little heap in the bottom of the boat—she was quite still. Clayton knew that she was dead.

After infinite labor he released himself from Thuran's pinioning body, and with renewed strength crawled toward the girl. He raised her head from the rough boards of the boat's bottom. There might be life in that poor, starved frame even yet. He could not quite abandon all hope, and so he seized a water-soaked rag and squeezed the precious drops between the swollen lips of the hideous thing that had but a few short days before glowed with the resplendent life of happy youth and glorious beauty.

For some time there was no sign of returning animation, but at last his efforts were rewarded by a slight tremor of the half-closed lids. He chafed the thin hands, and forced a few more drops of water into the parched throat. The girl opened her eyes, looking up at him for a long time before she could recall her surroundings.

"Water?" she whispered. "Are we saved?"

"It is raining," he explained. "We may at least drink. Already it has revived us both."

"Monsieur Thuran?" she asked. "He did not kill you. Is he dead?"

"I do not know," replied Clayton. "If he lives and this rain revives him—" But he stopped there, remembering too late that he must not add further to the horrors which the girl already had endured.

But she guessed what he would have said.

"Where is he?" she asked.

Clayton nodded his head toward the prostrate form of the Russian. For a time neither spoke.

"I will see if I can revive him," said Clayton at length.

"No," she whispered, extending a detaining hand toward him. "Do not do that—he will kill you when the water has given him strength. If he is dying, let him die. Do not leave me alone in this boat with that beast."

Clayton hesitated. His honor demanded that he attempt to revive Thuran, and there was the possibility, too, that the Russian was beyond human aid. It was not dishonorable to hope so. As he sat fighting out his battle he presently raised his eyes from the body of the man, and as they passed above the gunwale of the boat he staggered weakly to his feet with a little cry of joy.

"Land, Jane!" he almost shouted through his cracked lips. "Thank God, land!"

The girl looked, too, and there, not a hundred yards away, she saw a yellow beach, and, beyond, the luxurious foliage of a tropical jungle.

"Now you may revive him," said Jane Porter, for she, too, had been haunted with the pangs of conscience which had resulted from her decision to prevent Clayton from offering succor to their companion.

It required the better part of half an hour before the Russian evinced sufficient symptoms of returning consciousness to open his eyes, and it was some time later before they could bring him to a realization of their good fortune. By this time the boat was scraping gently upon the sandy bottom.

Between the refreshing water that he had drunk and the stimulus of renewed hope, Clayton found strength to stagger through the shallow water to the shore with a line made fast to the boat's bow. This he fastened to a small tree which grew at the top of a low bank, for the tide was at flood, and he feared that the boat might carry them all out to sea again with the ebb, since it was quite likely that it would be beyond his strength to get Jane Porter to the shore for several hours. Next he managed to stagger and crawl toward the near-by jungle, where he had seen evidences of profusion of tropical fruit. His former experience in the jungle of Tarzan of the Apes had taught him which of the many growing things were edible, and after nearly an hour of absence he returned to the beach with a little armful of food.

The rain had ceased, and the hot sun was beating down so mercilessly upon her that Jane Porter insisted on making an immediate attempt to gain the land. Still further invigorated by the food Clayton had brought, the three were able to reach the half shade of the small tree to which their boat was moored. Here, thoroughly exhausted, they threw themselves down to rest, sleeping until dark.

For a month they lived upon the beach in comparative safety. As their strength returned the two men constructed a rude shelter in the branches of a tree, high enough from the ground to insure safety from the larger beasts of prey. By day they gathered fruits and trapped small rodents; at night they lay cowering within their frail shelter while savage denizens of the jungle made hideous the hours of darkness.

They slept upon litters of jungle grasses, and for covering at night Jane Porter had only an old ulster that belonged to Clayton, the same garment that he had worn upon that memorable trip to the Wisconsin woods. Clayton had erected a frail partition of boughs to divide their arboreal shelter into two rooms—one for the girl and the other for Monsieur Thuran and himself.

From the first the Russian had exhibited every trait of his true character—selfishness, boorishness, arrogance, cowardice, and lust. Twice had he and Clayton come to blows because of Thuran's attitude toward the girl. Clayton dared not leave her alone with him for an instant. The existence of the Englishman and his fiancee was one continual nightmare of horror, and yet they lived on in hope of ultimate rescue.

Jane Porter's thoughts often reverted to her other experience on this savage shore. Ah, if the invincible forest god of that dead past were but with them now. No longer would there be aught to fear from prowling beasts, or from the bestial Russian. She could not well refrain from comparing the scant protection afforded her by Clayton with what she might have expected had Tarzan of the Apes been for a single instant confronted by the sinister and menacing attitude of Monsieur Thuran. Once, when Clayton had gone to the little stream for water, and Thuran had spoken coarsely to her, she voiced her thoughts.

"It is well for you, Monsieur Thuran," she said, "that the poor Monsieur Tarzan who was lost from the ship that brought you and Miss Strong to Cape Town is not here now."

"You knew the pig?" asked Thuran, with a sneer.

"I knew the man," she replied. "The only real man, I think, that I have ever known."

There was something in her tone of voice that led the Russian to attribute to her a deeper feeling for his enemy than friendship, and he grasped at the suggestion to be further revenged upon the man whom he supposed dead by besmirching his memory to the girl.

"He was worse than a pig," he cried. "He was a poltroon and a coward. To save himself from the righteous wrath of the husband of a woman he had wronged, he perjured his soul in an attempt to place the blame entirely upon her. Not succeeding in this, he ran away from France to escape meeting the husband upon the field of honor. That is why he was on board the ship that bore Miss Strong and myself to Cape Town. I know whereof I speak, for the woman in the case is my sister. Something more I know that I have never told another—your brave Monsieur Tarzan leaped overboard in an agony of fear because I recognized him, and insisted that he make reparation to me the following morning—we could have fought with knives in my stateroom."

Jane Porter laughed. "You do not for a moment imagine that one who has known both Monsieur Tarzan and you could ever believe such an impossible tale?"

"Then why did he travel under an assumed name?" asked Monsieur Thuran.

"I do not believe you," she cried, but nevertheless the seed of suspicion was sown, for she knew that Hazel Strong had known her forest god only as John Caldwell, of London.

A scant five miles north of their rude shelter, all unknown to them, and practically as remote as though separated by thousands of miles of impenetrable jungle, lay the snug little cabin of Tarzan of the Apes. While farther up the coast, a few miles beyond the cabin, in crude but well-built shelters, lived a little party of eighteen souls— the occupants of the three boats from the *Lady Alice* from which Clayton's boat had become separated.

Over a smooth sea they had rowed to the mainland in less than three days. None of the horrors of shipwreck had been theirs, and though depressed by sorrow, and suffering from the shock of the catastrophe and the unaccustomed hardships of their new existence there was none much the worse for the experience.

All were buoyed by the hope that the fourth boat had been picked up, and that a thorough search of the coast would be quickly made. As all the firearms and ammunition on the yacht had been placed in Lord Tennington's boat, the party was well equipped for defense, and for hunting the larger game for food.

Professor Archimedes Q. Porter was their only immediate anxiety. Fully assured in his own mind that his daughter had been picked up by a passing steamer, he gave over the last vestige of apprehension concerning her welfare, and devoted his giant intellect solely to the consideration of those momentous and abstruse scientific problems which he considered the only proper food for thought in one of his erudition. His mind appeared blank to the influence of all extraneous matters.

"Never," said the exhausted Mr. Samuel T. Philander, to Lord Tennington, "never has Professor Porter been more difficult—er—I might say, impossible. Why, only this morning, after I had been forced to relinquish my surveillance for a brief half hour he was entirely missing upon my return. And, bless me, sir, where do you imagine I discovered him? A half mile out in the ocean, sir, in one of the lifeboats, rowing away for dear life. I do not know how he attained even that magnificent distance from shore, for he had but a single oar, with which he was blissfully rowing about in circles.

"When one of the sailors had taken me out to him in another boat the professor became quite indignant at my suggestion that we return at once to land. 'Why, Mr. Philander,' he said, 'I am surprised that you, sir, a man of letters yourself, should have the temerity so to interrupt the progress of science. I had about deduced from certain astronomic phenomena I have had under minute observation during the past several tropic nights an entirely new nebular hypothesis which will unquestionably startle the scientific world. I wish to consult a very excellent monograph on Laplace's hypothesis, which I understand is in a certain private collection in New York City. Your interference, Mr. Philander, will result in an irreparable delay, for I was just rowing over to obtain this pamphlet.' And it was with the greatest difficulty that I persuaded him to return to shore, without resorting to force," concluded Mr. Philander.

Miss Strong and her mother were very brave under the strain of almost constant apprehension of the attacks of savage beasts. Nor were they quite able to accept so readily as the others the theory that Jane, Clayton, and Monsieur Thuran had been picked up safely.

Jane Porter's Esmeralda was in a constant state of tears at the cruel fate which had separated her from her "po, li'le honey."

Lord Tennington's great-hearted good nature never deserted him for a moment. He was still the jovial host, seeking always for the comfort and pleasure of his guests. With the men of his yacht he remained the just but firm commander—there was never any more question in the jungle than there had been on board the *Lady Alice* as to who was the final authority in all questions of importance, and in all emergencies requiring cool and intelligent leadership.

Could this well-organized and comparatively secure party of castaways have seen the ragged, fear-haunted trio a few miles south of them they would scarcely have recognized in them the formerly immaculate members of the little company that had laughed and played upon the *Lady Alice*. Clayton and Monsieur Thuran were almost naked, so torn had their clothes been by the thorn bushes and tangled vegetation of the matted jungle through which they had been compelled to force their way in search of their ever more difficult food supply.

Jane Porter had of course not been subjected to these strenuous expeditions, but her apparel was, nevertheless, in a sad state of disrepair.

Clayton, for lack of any better occupation, had carefully saved the skin of every animal they had killed. By stretching them upon the stems of trees, and diligently scraping them, he had managed to save them in a fair condition, and now that his clothes were threatening to cover his nakedness no longer, he commenced to fashion a rude garment of them, using a sharp thorn for a needle, and bits of tough grass and animal tendons in lieu of thread.

The result when completed was a sleeveless garment which fell nearly to his knees. As it was made up of numerous small pelts of different species of rodents, it presented a rather strange and wonderful appearance, which, together with the vile stench which permeated it, rendered it anything other than a desirable addition to a wardrobe. But the time came when for the sake of decency he was compelled to don it, and even the misery of their condition could not prevent Jane Porter from laughing heartily at sight of him.

Later, Thuran also found it necessary to construct a similar primitive garment, so that, with their bare legs and heavily bearded faces, they looked not unlike reincarnations of two prehistoric progenitors of the human race. Thuran acted like one.

Nearly two months of this existence had passed when the first great calamity befell them. It was prefaced by an adventure which came near terminating abruptly the sufferings of two of them—terminating them in the grim and horrible manner of the jungle, forever.

Thuran, down with an attack of jungle fever, lay in the shelter among the branches of their tree of refuge. Clayton had been into the jungle a few hundred yards in search of food. As he returned Jane Porter walked to meet him. Behind the man, cunning and crafty, crept an old and mangy lion. For three days his ancient thews and sinews had proved insufficient for the task of providing his cavernous belly with meat. For months he had eaten less and less frequently, and farther and farther had he roamed from his accustomed haunts in search of easier prey. At last he had found nature's weakest and most defenseless creature—in a moment more Numa would dine.

Clayton, all unconscious of the lurking death behind him, strode out into the open toward Jane. He had reached her side, a hundred feet from the tangled edge of jungle when past his shoulder the girl saw the tawny head and the wicked yellow eyes as the grasses parted, and the huge beast, nose to ground, stepped softly into view.

So frozen with horror was she that she could utter no sound, but the fixed and terrified gaze of her fear-widened eyes spoke as plainly to Clayton as words. A quick glance behind him revealed the hopelessness of their situation. The lion was scarce thirty paces from them, and they were equally as far from the shelter. The man was armed with a stout stick—as efficacious against a hungry lion, he realized, as a toy pop-gun charged with a tethered cork.

Numa, ravenous with hunger, had long since learned the futility of roaring and moaning as he searched for prey, but now that it was as surely his as though already he had felt the soft flesh beneath his still mighty paw, he opened his huge jaws, and gave vent to his long-pent rage in a series of deafening roars that made the air tremble.

"Run, Jane!" cried Clayton. "Quick! Run for the shelter!" But her paralyzed muscles refused to respond, and she stood mute and rigid, staring with ghastly countenance at the living death creeping toward them.

Thuran, at the sound of that awful roar, had come to the opening of the shelter, and as he saw the tableau below him he hopped up and down, shrieking to them in Russian.

"Run! Run!" he cried. "Run, or I shall be left all alone in this horrible place," and then he broke down and commenced to weep. For a moment this new voice distracted the attention of the lion, who halted to cast an inquiring glance in the direction of the tree. Clayton could endure the strain no longer. Turning his back upon the beast, he buried his head in his arms and waited.

The girl looked at him in horror. Why did he not do something? If he must die, why not die like a man—bravely; beating at that terrible face with his puny stick, no matter how futile it might be. Would Tarzan of the Apes have done thus? Would he not at least have gone down to his death fighting heroically to the last?

Now the lion was crouching for the spring that would end their young lives beneath cruel, rending, yellow fangs. Jane Porter sank to her knees in prayer, closing her eyes to shut out the last hideous instant. Thuran, weak from fever, fainted.

Seconds dragged into minutes, long minutes into an eternity, and yet the beast did not spring. Clayton was almost unconscious from the prolonged agony of fright—his knees trembled—a moment more and he would collapse.

Jane Porter could endure it no longer. She opened her eyes. Could she be dreaming?

"William," she whispered; "look!"

Clayton mastered himself sufficiently to raise his head and turn toward the lion. An ejaculation of surprise burst from his lips. At their very feet the beast lay crumpled in death. A heavy war spear protruded from the tawny hide. It had entered the great back above the right shoulder, and, passing entirely through the body, had pierced the savage heart.

Jane Porter had risen to her feet; as Clayton turned back to her she staggered in weakness. He put out his arms to save her from falling, and then drew her close to him—pressing her head against his shoulder, he stooped to kiss her in thanksgiving.

Gently the girl pushed him away.

"Please do not do that, William," she said. "I have lived a thousand years in the past brief moments. I have learned in the face of death how to live. I do not wish to hurt you more than is necessary; but I can no longer bear to live out the impossible position I have attempted because of a false sense of loyalty to an impulsive promise I made you.

"The last few seconds of my life have taught me that it would be hideous to attempt further to deceive myself and you, or to entertain for an instant longer the possibility of ever becoming your wife, should we regain civilization."

"Why, Jane," he cried, "what do you mean? What has our providential rescue to do with altering your feelings toward me? You are but unstrung—tomorrow you will be yourself again."

"I am more nearly myself this minute than I have been for over a year," she replied. "The thing that has just happened has again forced to my memory the fact that the bravest man that ever lived honored me with his love. Until it was too late I did not realize that I returned it, and so I sent him away. He is dead now, and I shall never marry. I certainly could not wed another less brave than he without harboring constantly a feeling of contempt for the relative cowardice of my husband. Do you understand me?"

"Yes," he answered, with bowed head, his face mantling with the flush of shame.

And it was the next day that the great calamity befell.

XXII

THE TREASURE VAULTS OF OPAR

t was quite dark before La, the high priestess, returned to the Chamber of the Dead with food and drink for Tarzan. She bore no light, feeling with her hands along the crumbling walls until she gained the chamber. Through the stone grating above, a tropic moon served dimly to illuminate the interior.

Tarzan, crouching in the shadows at the far side of the room as the first sound of approaching footsteps reached him, came forth to meet the girl as he recognized that it was she.

"They are furious," were her first words. "Never before has a human sacrifice escaped the altar. Already fifty have gone forth to track you down. They have searched the temple—all save this single room."

"Why do they fear to come here?" he asked.

"It is the Chamber of the Dead. Here the dead return to worship. See this ancient altar? It is here that the dead sacrifice the living—if they find a victim here. That is the reason our people shun this chamber. Were one to enter he knows that the waiting dead would seize him for their sacrifice."

"But you?" he asked.

"I am high priestess—I alone am safe from the dead. It is I who at rare intervals bring them a human sacrifice from the world above.

I alone may enter here in safety."

"Why have they not seized me?" he asked, humoring her gro-tesque belief.

She looked at him quizzically for a moment. Then she replied:

"It is the duty of a high priestess to instruct, to interpret—according to the creed that others, wiser than herself, have laid down; but there is nothing in the creed which says that she must believe. The more one knows of one's religion the less one believes—no one living knows more of mine than I."

"Then your only fear in aiding me to escape is that your fellow mortals may discover your duplicity?"

"That is all—the dead are dead; they cannot harm—or help. We must therefore depend entirely upon ourselves, and the sooner we act the better it will be. I had difficulty in eluding their vigilance but now in bringing you this morsel of food. To attempt to repeat the thing daily would be the height of folly. Come, let us see how far we may go toward liberty before I must return."

She led him back to the chamber beneath the altar room. Here she turned into one of the several corridors leading from it. In the darkness Tarzan could not see which one. For ten minutes they groped slowly along a winding passage, until at length they came to a closed door. Here he heard her fumbling with a key, and presently came the sound of a metal bolt grating against metal. The door swung in on scraping hinges, and they entered.

"You will be safe here until tomorrow night," she said.

Then she went out, and, closing the door, locked it behind her.

Where Tarzan stood it was dark as Erebus. Not even his trained eyes could penetrate the utter blackness. Cautiously he moved for-ward until his out-stretched hand touched a wall, then very slowly he traveled around the four walls of the chamber.

Apparently it was about twenty feet square. The floor was of concrete, the walls of the dry masonry that marked the method of construction above ground. Small pieces of granite of various sizes were ingeniously laid together without mortar to construct these ancient foundations.

The first time around the walls Tarzan thought he detected a strange phenomenon for a room with no windows but a single door. Again he crept carefully around close to the wall. No, he could not be mistaken! He paused before the center of the wall opposite the door. For a moment he stood quite motionless, then he moved a few feet to one side. Again he returned, only to move a few feet to the other side.

Once more he made the entire circuit of the room, feeling carefully every foot of the walls. Finally he stopped again before the particular section that had aroused his curiosity. There was no doubt of it! A distinct draft of fresh air was blowing into the chamber through the intersection of the masonry at that particular point—and nowhere else.

Tarzan tested several pieces of the granite which made up the wall at this spot, and finally was rewarded by finding one which lifted out readily. It was about ten inches wide, with a face some three by six inches showing within the chamber. One by one the ape-man lifted out similarly shaped stones. The wall at this point was constructed entirely, it seemed, of these almost perfect slabs. In a short time he had removed some dozen, when he reached in to test the next layer of masonry. To his surprise, he felt nothing behind the masonry he had removed as far as his long arm could reach.

It was a matter of but a few minutes to remove enough of the wall to permit his body to pass through the aperture. Directly ahead of him he thought he discerned a faint glow—scarcely more than a less impenetrable darkness. Cautiously he moved forward on hands and knees, until at about fifteen feet, or the average thickness of the foundation walls, the floor ended abruptly in a sudden drop. As far out as he could reach he felt nothing, nor could he find the bottom of the black abyss that yawned before him, though, clinging to the edge of the floor, he lowered his body into the darkness to its full length.

Finally it occurred to him to look up, and there above him he saw through a round opening a tiny circular patch of starry sky. Feeling up along the sides of the shaft as far as he could reach, the ape-man discovered that so much of the wall as he could feel converged toward the center of the shaft as it rose. This fact precluded possibility of escape in that direction.

As he sat speculating on the nature and uses of this strange passage and its terminal shaft, the moon topped the opening above, letting a flood of soft, silvery light into the shadowy place. Instantly the nature of the shaft became apparent to Tarzan, for far below him he saw the shimmering surface of water. He had come upon an ancient well—but what was the purpose of the connection between the well and the dungeon in which he had been hidden?

As the moon crossed the opening of the shaft its light flooded the whole interior, and then Tarzan saw directly across from him another opening in the opposite wall. He wondered if this might not be the mouth of a passage leading to possible escape. It would be worth investigating, at least, and this he determined to do.

Quickly returning to the wall he had demolished to explore what lay beyond it, he carried the stones into the passageway and replaced them from that side. The deep deposit of dust which he had noticed upon the blocks as he had first removed them from the wall had convinced him that even if the present occupants of the ancient pile had knowledge of this hidden passage they had made no use of it for perhaps generations.

The wall replaced, Tarzan turned to the shaft, which was some fifteen feet wide at this point. To leap across the intervening space was a small matter to the ape-man, and a moment later he was proceeding along a narrow tunnel, moving cautiously for fear of being precipitated into another shaft such as he had just crossed.

He had advanced some hundred feet when he came to a flight of steps leading downward into Stygian gloom. Some twenty feet below, the level floor of the tunnel recommenced, and shortly afterward his progress was stopped by a heavy wooden door which was secured by massive wooden bars upon the side of Tarzan's approach. This fact suggested to the ape-man that he might surely be in a passageway leading to the outer world, for the bolts, barring progress from the opposite side, tended to substantiate this hypothesis, unless it were merely a prison to which it led.

Along the tops of the bars were deep layers of dust—a further indication that the passage had lain long unused. As he pushed the massive obstacle aside, its great hinges shrieked out in weird protest against this unaccustomed disturbance. For a moment Tarzan paused to listen for any responsive note which might indicate that the unusual night noise had alarmed the inmates of the temple; but as he heard nothing he advanced beyond the doorway.

Carefully feeling about, he found himself within a large chamber, along the walls of which, and down the length of the floor, were piled many tiers of metal ingots of an odd though uniform shape. To his groping hands they felt not unlike double-headed bootjacks. The ingots were quite heavy, and but for the enormous number of them he would have been positive that they were gold; but the thought of the fabulous wealth these thousands of pounds of metal would have represented were they in reality gold, almost convinced him that they must be of some baser metal.

At the far end of the chamber he discovered another barred door, and again the bars upon the inside renewed the hope that he was traversing an ancient and forgotten passageway to liberty. Beyond the door the passage ran straight as a war spear, and it soon became evident to the ape-man that it had already led him beyond the outer walls of the temple. If he but knew the direction it was leading him! If toward the west, then he must also be beyond the city's outer walls.

With increasing hopes he forged ahead as rapidly as he dared, until at the end of half an hour he came to another flight of steps leading upward. At the bottom this flight was of concrete, but as he ascended his naked feet felt a sudden change in the substance they were treading. The steps of concrete had given place to steps of granite. Feeling with his hands, the ape-man discovered that these latter were evidently hewed from rock, for there was no crack to indicate a joint.

For a hundred feet the steps wound spirally up, until at a sudden turning Tarzan came into a narrow cleft between two rocky walls. Above him shone the starry sky, and before him a steep incline replaced the steps that had terminated at its foot. Up this pathway Tarzan hastened, and at its upper end came out upon the rough top of a huge granite bowlder.

A mile away lay the ruined city of Opar, its domes and turrets bathed in the soft light of the equatorial moon. Tarzan dropped his eyes to the ingot he had brought away with him. For a moment he examined it by the moon's bright rays, then he raised his head to look out upon the ancient piles of crumbling grandeur in the distance.

"Opar," he mused, "Opar, the enchanted city of a dead and forgotten past. The city of the beauties and the beasts. City of horrors and death; but—city of fabulous riches." The ingot was of virgin gold.

The bowlder on which Tarzan found himself lay well out in the plain between the city and the distant cliffs he and his black warriors had scaled the morning previous. To descend its rough and precipitous face was a task of infinite labor and considerable peril even to the ape-man; but at last he felt the soft soil of the valley beneath his feet, and without a backward glance at Opar he turned his face toward the guardian cliffs, and at a rapid trot set off across the valley.

The sun was just rising as he gained the summit of the flat mountain at the valley's western boundary. Far beneath him he saw smoke arising above the tree-tops of the forest at the base of the foothills.

"Man," he murmured. "And there were fifty who went forth to track me down. Can it be they?"

Swiftly he descended the face of the cliff, and, dropping into a narrow ravine which led down to the far forest, he hastened onward in the direction of the smoke. Striking the forest's edge about a quarter of a mile from the point at which the slender column arose into the still air, he took to the trees. Cautiously he approached until there suddenly burst upon his view a rude *boma*, in the center of which, squatted about their tiny fires, sat his fifty black Waziri. He called to them in their own tongue:

"Arise, my children, and greet thy king!"

With exclamations of surprise and fear the warriors leaped to their feet, scarcely knowing whether to flee or not. Then Tarzan dropped lightly from an overhanging branch into their midst. When they realized that it was indeed their chief in the flesh, and no materialized spirit, they went mad with joy.

"We were cowards, oh, Waziri," cried Busuli. "We ran away and left you to your fate; but when our panic was over we swore to return and save you, or at least take revenge upon your murderers. We were but now preparing to scale the heights once more and cross the desolate valley to the terrible city."

"Have you seen fifty frightful men pass down from the cliffs into this forest, my children?" asked Tarzan.

"Yes, Waziri," replied Busuli. "They passed us late yesterday, as we were about to turn back after you. They had no woodcraft. We heard them coming for a mile before we saw them, and as we had other business in hand we withdrew into the forest and let them pass. They were waddling rapidly along upon short legs, and now and then one would go upon all fours like Bolgani, the gorilla. They were indeed fifty frightful men, Waziri."

When Tarzan had related his adventures and told them of the yellow metal he had found, not one demurred when he outlined a plan to return by night and bring away what they could carry of the vast treasure; and so it was that as dusk fell across the desolate valley of Opar fifty ebon warriors trailed at a smart trot over the dry and dusty ground toward the giant bowlder that loomed before the city.

If it had seemed a difficult task to descend the face of the bowlder, Tarzan soon found that it would be next to impossible to get his fifty warriors to the summit. Finally the feat was accomplished by dint of herculean efforts upon the part of the ape-man. Ten spears were fastened end to end, and with one end of this remarkable chain attached to his waist, Tarzan at last succeeded in reaching the summit.

Once there, he drew up one of his blacks, and in this way the entire party was finally landed in safety upon the bowlder's top. Immediately Tarzan led them to the treasure chamber, where to each was allotted a load of two ingots, for each about eighty pounds.

By midnight the entire party stood once more at the foot of the bowlder, but with their heavy loads it was mid-forenoon ere they reached the summit of the cliffs. From there on the homeward journey was slow, as these proud fighting men were unaccustomed to the duties of porters. But they bore their burdens uncomplainingly, and at the end of thirty days entered their own country.

Here, instead of continuing on toward the northwest and their village, Tarzan guided them almost directly west, until on the morning of the thirty-third day he bade them break camp and return to their own village, leaving the gold where they had stacked it the previous night.

"And you, Waziri?" they asked.

"I shall remain here for a few days, my children," he replied. "Now hasten back to thy wives and children."

When they had gone Tarzan gathered up two of the ingots and, springing into a tree, ran lightly above the tangled and impenetrable mass of undergrowth for a couple of hundred yards, to emerge suddenly upon a circular clearing about which the giants of the jungle forest towered like a guardian host. In the center of this natural amphitheater, was a little flat-topped mound of hard earth.

Hundreds of times before had Tarzan been to this secluded spot, which was so densely surrounded by thorn bushes and tangled vines and creepers of huge girth that not even Sheeta, the leopard, could worm his sinuous way within, nor Tantor, with his giant strength, force the barriers which protected the council chamber of the great apes from all but the harmless denizens of the savage jungle.

Fifty trips Tarzan made before he had deposited all the ingots within the precincts of the amphitheater. Then from the hollow of an ancient, lightning-blasted tree he produced the very spade with which he had uncovered the chest of Professor Archimedes Q. Porter which he had once, apelike, buried in this selfsame spot. With this he dug a long trench, into which he laid the fortune that his blacks had carried from the forgotten treasure vaults of the city of Opar.

That night he slept within the amphitheater, and early the next morning set out to revisit his cabin before returning to his Waziri. Finding things as he had left them, he went forth into the jungle to hunt, intending to bring his prey to the cabin where he might feast in comfort, spending the night upon a comfortable couch.

For five miles toward the south he roamed, toward the banks of a fair-sized river that flowed into the sea about six miles from his cabin. He had gone inland about half a mile when there came suddenly to his trained nostrils the one scent that sets the whole savage jungle aquiver—Tarzan smelled man.

The wind was blowing off the ocean, so Tarzan knew that the authors of the scent were west of him. Mixed with the man scent was the scent of Numa. Man and lion. "I had better hasten," thought the ape-man, for he had recognized the scent of whites. "Numa may be a-hunting."

When he came through the trees to the edge of the jungle he saw a woman kneeling in prayer, and before her stood a wild, primitive-looking white man, his face buried in his arms. Behind the man a mangy lion was advancing slowly toward this easy prey. The man's face was averted; the woman's bowed in prayer. He could not see the features of either.

Already Numa was about to spring. There was not a second to spare. Tarzan could not even unsling his bow and fit an arrow in time to send one of his deadly poisoned shafts into the yellow hide. He was too far away to reach the beast in time with his knife. There was but a single hope—a lone alternative. And with the quickness of thought the ape-man acted.

A brawny arm flew back—for the briefest fraction of an instant a huge spear poised above the giant's shoulder—and then the mighty arm shot out, and swift death tore through the intervening leaves to bury itself in the heart of the leaping lion. Without a sound he rolled over at the very feet of his intended victims—dead.

For a moment neither the man nor the woman moved. Then the latter opened her eyes to look with wonder upon the dead beast behind her companion. As that beautiful head went up Tarzan of the Apes gave a gasp of incredulous astonishment. Was he mad? It could not be the woman he loved! But, indeed, it was none other.

And the woman rose, and the man took her in his arms to kiss her, and of a sudden the ape-man saw red through a bloody mist of murder, and the old scar upon his forehead burned scarlet against his brown hide.

There was a terrible expression upon his savage face as he fitted a poisoned shaft to his bow. An ugly light gleamed in those gray eyes as he sighted full at the back of the unsuspecting man beneath him.

For an instant he glanced along the polished shaft, drawing the bowstring far back, that the arrow might pierce through the heart for which it was aimed.

But he did not release the fatal messenger. Slowly the point of the arrow drooped; the scar upon the brown forehead faded; the bowstring relaxed; and Tarzan of the Apes, with bowed head, turned sadly into the jungle toward the village of the Waziri.

XXIII

THE FIFTY FRIGHTFUL MEN

or several long minutes Jane Porter and William Cecil Clayton stood silently looking at the dead body of the beast whose prey they had so narrowly escaped becoming.

The girl was the first to speak again after her outbreak of impulsive avowal.

"Who could it have been?" she whispered.

"God knows!" was the man's only reply.

"If it is a friend, why does he not show himself?" continued Jane. "Wouldn't it be well to call out to him, and at least thank him?"

Mechanically Clayton did her bidding, but there was no response.

Jane Porter shuddered. "The mysterious jungle," she murmured. "The terrible jungle. It renders even the manifestations of friendship terrifying."

"We had best return to the shelter," said Clayton. "You will be at least a little safer there. I am no protection whatever," he added bitterly.

"Do not say that, William," she hastened to urge, acutely sorry for the wound her words had caused. "You have done the best you could. You have been noble, and self-sacrificing, and brave. It is no fault of yours that you are not a superman. There is only one other man I have ever known who could have done more than you. My words were ill chosen in the excitement of the reaction—I did not wish to wound you. All that I wish is that we may both understand once and for all that I can never marry you—that such a marriage would be wicked."

"I think I understand," he replied. "Let us not speak of it again—at least until we are back in civilization."

The next day Thuran was worse. Almost constantly he was in a state of delirium. They could do nothing to relieve him, nor was Clayton over-anxious to attempt anything. On the girl's account he feared the Russian—in the bottom of his heart he hoped the man would die. The thought that something might befall him that would leave her entirely at the mercy of this beast caused him greater anxiety than the probability that almost certain death awaited her should she be left entirely alone upon the outskirts of the cruel forest.

The Englishman had extracted the heavy spear from the body of the lion, so that when he went into the forest to hunt that morning he had a feeling of much greater security than at any time since they had been cast upon the savage shore. The result was that he penetrated farther from the shelter than ever before.

To escape as far as possible from the mad ravings of the fever-stricken Russian, Jane Porter had descended from the shelter to the foot of the tree—she dared not venture farther. Here, beside the crude ladder Clayton had constructed for her, she sat looking out to sea, in the always surviving hope that a vessel might be sighted.

Her back was toward the jungle, and so she did not see the grasses part, or the savage face that peered from between. Little, bloodshot, close-set eyes scanned her intently, roving from time to time about the open beach for indications of the presence of others than herself. Presently another head appeared, and then another and another. The man in the shelter commenced to rave again, and the heads disappeared as silently and as suddenly as they had come. But soon they were thrust forth once more, as the girl gave no sign of perturbation at the continued wailing of the man above.

One by one grotesque forms emerged from the jungle to creep stealthily upon the unsuspecting woman. A faint rustling of the grasses attracted her attention. She turned, and at the sight that confronted her staggered to her feet with a little shriek of fear. Then they closed upon her with a rush. Lifting her bodily in his long, gorilla-like arms, one of the creatures turned and bore her into the jungle. A filthy paw covered her mouth to stifle her screams. Added to the weeks of torture she had already undergone, the shock was more than she could withstand. Shattered nerves collapsed, and she lost consciousness. When she regained her senses she found herself in the thick of the primeval forest. It was night. A huge fire burned brightly in the little clearing in which she lay. About it squatted fifty frightful men. Their heads and faces were covered with matted hair. Their long arms rested upon the bent knees of their short, crooked legs. They were gnawing, like beasts, upon unclean food. A pot boiled upon the edge of the fire, and out of it one of the creatures would occasionally drag a hunk of meat with a sharpened stick.

When they discovered that their captive had regained consciousness, a piece of this repulsive stew was tossed to her from the foul hand of a nearby feaster. It rolled close to her side, but she only closed her eyes as a qualm of nausea surged through her.

For many days they traveled through the dense forest. The girl, footsore and exhausted, was half dragged, half pushed through the long, hot, tedious days. Occasionally, when she would stumble and fall, she was cuffed and kicked by the nearest of the frightful men. Long before they reached their journey's end her shoes had been discarded—the soles entirely gone. Her clothes were torn to mere shreds and tatters, and through the pitiful rags her once white and tender skin showed raw and bleeding from contact with the thousand pitiless thorns and brambles through which she had been dragged.

The last two days of the journey found her in such utter exhaustion that no amount of kicking and abuse could force her to her poor, bleeding feet. Outraged nature had reached the limit of endurance, and the girl was physically powerless to raise herself even to her knees.

As the beasts surrounded her, chattering threateningly the while they goaded her with their cudgels and beat and kicked her with their fists and feet, she lay with closed eyes, praying for the merciful death that she knew alone could give her surcease from suffering; but it did not come, and presently the fifty frightful men realized that their victim was no longer able to walk, and so they picked her up and carried her the balance of the journey.

Late one afternoon she saw the ruined walls of a mighty city looming before them, but so weak and sick was she that it inspired not the faintest shadow of interest. Wherever they were bearing her, there could be but one end to her captivity among these fierce half brutes.

At last they passed through two great walls and came to the ruined city within. Into a crumbling pile they bore her, and here she was surrounded by hundreds more of the same creatures that had brought her; but among them were females who looked less horrible. At sight of them the first faint hope that she had entertained came to mitigate her misery. But it was short-lived, for the women offered her no sympathy, though, on the other hand, neither did they abuse her.

After she had been inspected to the entire satisfaction of the inmates of the building she was borne to a dark chamber in the vaults beneath, and here upon the bare floor she was left, with a metal bowl of water and another of food.

For a week she saw only some of the women whose duty it was to bring her food and water. Slowly her strength was returning—soon she would be in fit condition to offer as a sacrifice to The Flaming God. Fortunate indeed it was that she could not know the fate for which she was destined.

. . .

As Tarzan of the Apes moved slowly through the jungle after casting the spear that saved Clayton and Jane Porter from the fangs of Numa, his mind was filled with all the sorrow that belongs to a freshly opened heart wound.

He was glad that he had stayed his hand in time to prevent the consummation of the thing that in the first mad wave of jealous wrath he had contemplated. Only the fraction of a second had stood between Clayton and death at the hands of the ape-man. In the short moment that had elapsed after he had recognized the girl and her companion and the relaxing of the taut muscles that held the poisoned shaft directed at the Englishman's heart, Tarzan had been swayed by the swift and savage impulses of brute life.

He had seen the woman he craved—his woman—his mate—in the arms of another. There had been but one course open to him, according to the fierce jungle code that guided him in this other existence; but just before it had become too late the softer sentiments of his inherent chivalry had risen above the flaming fires of his passion and saved him. A thousand times he gave thanks that they had triumphed before his fingers had released that polished arrow.

As he contemplated his return to the Waziri the idea became repugnant. He did not wish to see a human being again. At least he would range alone through the jungle for a time, until the sharp edge of his sorrow had become blunted. Like his fellow beasts, he preferred to suffer in silence and alone.

That night he slept again in the amphitheater of the apes, and for several days he hunted from there, returning at night. On the afternoon of the third day he returned early. He had lain stretched upon the soft grass of the circular clearing for but a few moments when he heard far to the south a familiar sound. It was the passing through the jungle of a band of great apes—he could not mistake that. For several minutes he lay listening. They were coming in the direction of the amphitheater.

Tarzan arose lazily and stretched himself. His keen ears followed every movement of the advancing tribe. They were upwind, and presently he caught their scent, though he had not needed this added evidence to assure him that he was right.

As they came closer to the amphitheater Tarzan of the Apes melted into the branches upon the other side of the arena. There he waited to inspect the newcomers. Nor had he long to wait.

Presently a fierce, hairy face appeared among the lower branches opposite him. The cruel little eyes took in the clearing at a glance, then there was a chattered report returned to those behind. Tarzan could hear the words. The scout was telling the other members of the tribe that the coast was clear and that they might enter the amphitheater in safety.

First the leader dropped lightly upon the soft carpet of the grassy floor, and then, one by one, nearly a hundred anthropoids followed him. There were the huge adults and several young. A few nursing babes clung close to the shaggy necks of their savage mothers.

Tarzan recognized many members of the tribe. It was the same into which he had come as a tiny babe. Many of the adults had been little apes during his boyhood. He had frolicked and played about this very jungle with them during their brief childhood. He wondered if they would remember him—the memory of some apes is not overlong, and two years may be an eternity to them.

From the talk which he overheard he learned that they had come to choose a new king—their late chief had fallen a hundred feet beneath a broken limb to an untimely end.

Tarzan walked to the end of an overhanging limb in plain view of them. The quick eyes of a female caught sight of him first. With a barking guttural she called the attention of the others. Several huge bulls stood erect to get a better view of the intruder. With bared fangs and bristling necks they advanced slowly toward him, with deep-throated, ominous growls.

"Karnath, I am Tarzan of the Apes," said the ape-man in the vernacular of the tribe. "You remember me. Together we teased Numa when we were still little apes, throwing sticks and nuts at him from the safety of high branches."

The brute he had addressed stopped with a look of half-comprehending, dull wonderment upon his savage face.

"And Magor," continued Tarzan, addressing another, "do you not recall your former king—he who slew the mighty Kerchak? Look at me! Am I not the same Tarzan—mighty hunter—invincible fighter—that you all knew for many seasons?"

The apes all crowded forward now, but more in curiosity than threatening. They muttered among themselves for a few moments.

"What do you want among us now?" asked Karnath.

"Only peace," answered the ape-man.

Again the apes conferred. At length Karnath spoke again.

"Come in peace, then, Tarzan of the Apes," he said.

And so Tarzan of the Apes dropped lightly to the turf into the midst of the fierce and hideous horde—he had completed the cycle of evolution, and had returned to be once again a brute among brutes.

There were no greetings such as would have taken place among men after a separation of two years. The majority of the apes went on about the little activities that the advent of the ape-man had interrupted, paying no further attention to him than as though he had not been gone from the tribe at all.

One or two young bulls who had not been old enough to remember him sidled up on all fours to sniff at him, and one bared his fangs and growled threateningly—he wished to put Tarzan immediately into his proper place. Had Tarzan backed off, growling, the young bull would quite probably have been satisfied, but always after Tarzan's station among his fellow apes would have been beneath that of the bull which had made him step aside.

But Tarzan of the Apes did not back off. Instead, he swung his giant palm with all the force of his mighty muscles, and, catching the young bull alongside the head, sent him sprawling across the turf.

The ape was up and at him again in a second, and this time they closed with tearing fingers and rending fangs—or at least that had been the intention of the young bull; but scarcely had they gone down, growling and snapping, than the ape-man's fingers found the throat of his antagonist.

Presently the young bull ceased to struggle, and lay quite still. Then Tarzan released his hold and arose—he did not wish to kill, only to teach the young ape, and others who might be watching, that Tarzan of the Apes was still master.

The lesson served its purpose—the young apes kept out of his way, as young apes should when their betters were about, and the old bulls made no attempt to encroach upon his prerogatives. For several days the she-apes with young remained suspicious of him, and when he ventured too near rushed upon him with wide mouths and hideous roars. Then Tarzan discreetly skipped out of harm's way, for that also is a custom among the apes—only mad bulls will attack a mother. But after a while even they became accustomed to him.

He hunted with them as in days gone by, and when they found that his superior reason guided him to the best food sources, and that his cunning rope ensnared toothsome game that they seldom if ever tasted, they came again to look up to him as they had in the past after he had become their king. And so it was that before they left the amphitheater to return to their wanderings they had once more chosen him as their leader.

The ape-man felt quite contented with his new lot. He was not happy—that he never could be again, but he was at least as far from everything that might remind him of his past misery as he could be. Long since he had given up every intention of returning to civilization, and now he had decided to see no more his black friends of the Waziri. He had foresworn humanity forever. He had started life an ape—as an ape he would die.

He could not, however, erase from his memory the fact that the woman he loved was within a short journey of the stamping-ground of his tribe; nor could he banish the haunting fear that she might be constantly in danger. That she was illy protected he had seen in the brief instant that had witnessed Clayton's inefficiency. The more Tarzan thought of it, the more keenly his conscience pricked him.

Finally he came to loathe himself for permitting his own selfish sorrow and jealousy to stand between Jane Porter and safety. As the days passed the thing preyed more and more upon his mind, and he had about determined to return to the coast and place himself on guard over Jane Porter and Clayton, when news reached him that altered all his plans and sent him dashing madly toward the east in reckless disregard of accident and death.

Before Tarzan had returned to the tribe, a certain young bull, not being able to secure a mate from among his own people, had, according to custom, fared forth through the wild jungle, like some knight-errant of old, to win a fair lady from some neighboring community.

He had but just returned with his bride, and was narrating his adventures quickly before he should forget them. Among other things he told of seeing a great tribe of strange-looking apes.

"They were all hairy-faced bulls but one," he said, "and that one was a she, lighter in color even than this stranger," and he chucked a thumb at Tarzan.

The ape-man was all attention in an instant. He asked questions as rapidly as the slow-witted anthropoid could answer them.

"Were the bulls short, with crooked legs?"

"They were."

"Did they wear the skins of Numa and Sheeta about their loins, and carry sticks and knives?"

"They did."

"And were there many yellow rings about their arms and legs?"

"Yes."

"And the she one—was she small and slender, and very white?"

"Yes."

"Did she seem to be one of the tribe, or was she a prisoner?"

"They dragged her along—sometimes by an arm—sometimes by the long hair that grew upon her head; and always they kicked and beat her. Oh, but it was great fun to watch them."

"God!" muttered Tarzan.

"Where were they when you saw them, and which way were they going?" continued the ape-man.

"They were beside the second water back there," and he pointed to the south. "When they passed me they were going toward the morning, upward along the edge of the water."

"When was this?" asked Tarzan.

"Half a moon since."

Without another word the ape-man sprang into the trees and fled like a disembodied spirit eastward in the direction of the forgotten city of Opar.

XXIV

How Tarzan Came Again to Opar

hen Clayton returned to the shelter and found Jane Porter was missing, he became frantic with fear and grief. He found Monsieur Thuran quite rational, the fever having left him with the surprising suddenness which is one of its peculiarities. The Russian, weak and exhausted, still lay upon his bed of grasses within the shelter.

When Clayton asked him about the girl he seemed surprised to know that she was not there.

"I have heard nothing unusual," he said. "But then I have been unconscious much of the time."

Had it not been for the man's very evident weakness, Clayton should have suspected him of having sinister knowledge of the girl's whereabouts; but he could see that Thuran lacked sufficient vitality even to descend, unaided, from the shelter. He could not, in his present physical condition, have harmed the girl, nor could he have climbed the rude ladder back to the shelter.

Until dark the Englishman searched the nearby jungle for a trace of the missing one or a sign of the trail of her abductor. But though the spoor left by the fifty frightful men, unversed in woodcraft as they were, would have been as plain to the densest denizen of the jungle as a city street to the Englishman, yet he crossed and recrossed it twenty times without observing the slightest indication that many men had passed that way but a few short hours since.

As he searched, Clayton continued to call the girl's name aloud, but the only result of this was to attract Numa, the lion. Fortunately the man saw the shadowy form worming its way toward him in time to climb into the branches of a tree before the beast was close enough to reach him. This put an end to his search for the balance of the afternoon, as the lion paced back and forth beneath him until dark.

Even after the beast had left, Clayton dared not descend into the awful blackness beneath him, and so he spent a terrifying and hideous night in the tree. The next morning he returned to the beach, relinquishing the last hope of succoring Jane Porter.

During the week that followed, Monsieur Thuran rapidly regained his strength, lying in the shelter while Clayton hunted food for both. The men never spoke except as necessity demanded. Clayton now occupied the section of the shelter which had been reserved for Jane Porter, and only saw the Russian when he took food or water to him, or performed the other kindly offices which common humanity required.

When Thuran was again able to descend in search of food, Clayton was stricken with fever. For days he lay tossing in delirium and suffering, but not once did the Russian come near him. Food the Englishman could not have eaten, but his craving for water amounted practically to torture. Between the recurrent attacks of delirium, weak though he was, he managed to reach the brook once a day and fill a tiny can that had been among the few appointments of the lifeboat.

Thuran watched him on these occasions with an expression of malignant pleasure—he seemed really to enjoy the suffering of the man who, despite the just contempt in which he held him, had ministered to him to the best of his ability while he lay suffering the same agonies. At last Clayton became so weak that he was no longer able to descend from the shelter. For a day he suffered for water without appealing to the Russian, but finally, unable to endure it longer, he asked Thuran to fetch him a drink. The Russian came to the entrance to Clayton's room, a dish of water in his hand. A nasty grin contorted his features.

"Here is water," he said. "But first let me remind you that you maligned me before the girl—that you kept her to yourself, and would not share her with me——"

Clayton interrupted him. "Stop!" he cried. "Stop! What manner of cur are you that you traduce the character of a good woman whom we believe dead! God! I was a fool ever to let you live—you are not fit to live even in this vile land."

"Here is your water," said the Russian. "All you will get," and he raised the basin to his lips and drank; what was left he threw out upon the ground below. Then he turned and left the sick man.

Clayton rolled over, and, burying his face in his arms, gave up the battle.

The next day Thuran determined to set out toward the north along the coast, for he knew that eventually he must come to the habitations of civilized men—at least he could be no worse off than he was here, and, furthermore, the ravings of the dying Englishman were getting on his nerves. So he stole Clayton's spear and set off upon his journey. He would have killed the sick man before he left had it not occurred to him that it would really have been a kindness to do so.

That same day he came to a little cabin by the beach, and his heart filled with renewed hope as he saw this evidence of the proximity of civilization, for he thought it but the outpost of a nearby settlement. Had he known to whom it belonged, and that its owner was at that very moment but a few miles inland, Nikolas Rokoff would have fled the place as he would a pestilence. But he did not know, and so he remained for a few days to enjoy the security and comparative comforts of the cabin. Then he took up his northward journey once more.

In Lord Tennington's camp preparations were going forward to build permanent quarters, and then to send out an expedition of a few men to the north in search of relief.

As the days had passed without bringing the longed-for succor, hope that Jane Porter, Clayton, and Monsieur Thuran had been rescued began to die. No one spoke of the matter longer to Professor Porter, and he was so immersed in his scientific dreaming that he was not aware of the elapse of time.

Occasionally he would remark that within a few days they should certainly see a steamer drop anchor off their shore, and that then they should all be reunited happily. Sometimes he spoke of it as a train, and wondered if it were being delayed by snowstorms.

"If I didn't know the dear old fellow so well by now," Tennington remarked to Miss Strong, "I should be quite certain that he was— er—not quite right, don't you know." "If it were not so pathetic it would be ridiculous," said the girl, sadly. "I, who have known him all my life, know how he worships Jane; but to others it must seem that he is perfectly callous to her fate. It is only that he is so absolutely impractical that he cannot conceive of so real a thing as death unless nearly certain proof of it is thrust upon him."

"You'd never guess what he was about yesterday," continued Tennington. "I was coming in alone from a little hunt when I met him walking rapidly along the game trail that I was following back to camp. His hands were clasped beneath the tails of his long black coat, and his top hat was set firmly down upon his head, as with eyes bent upon the ground he hastened on, probably to some sudden death had I not intercepted him.

"'Why, where in the world are you bound, professor?' I asked him. 'I am going into town, Lord Tennington,' he said, as seriously as possible, 'to complain to the postmaster about the rural free delivery service we are suffering from here. Why, sir, I haven't had a piece of mail in weeks. There should be several letters for me from Jane. The matter must be reported to Washington at once.'

"And would you believe it, Miss Strong," continued Tennington, "I had the very deuce of a job to convince the old fellow that there was not only no rural free delivery, but no town, and that he was not even on the same continent as Washington, nor in the same hemisphere.

"When he did realize he commenced to worry about his daughter—I think it is the first time that he really has appreciated our position here, or the fact that Miss Porter may not have been rescued."

"I hate to think about it," said the girl, "and yet I can think of nothing else than the absent members of our party."

"Let us hope for the best," replied Tennington. "You yourself have set us each a splendid example of bravery, for in a way your loss has been the greatest."

"Yes," she replied; "I could have loved Jane Porter no more had she been my own sister."

Tennington did not show the surprise he felt. That was not at all what he meant. He had been much with this fair daughter of Maryland since the wreck of the *Lady Alice*, and it had recently come to him that he had grown much more fond of her than would prove good for the peace of his mind, for he recalled almost constantly now the confidence which Monsieur Thuran had imparted to him that he and Miss Strong were engaged. He wondered if, after all, Thuran had been quite accurate in his statement. He had never seen the slightest indication on the girl's part of more than ordinary friendship.

"And then in Monsieur Thuran's loss, if they are lost, you would suffer a severe bereavement," he ventured.

She looked up at him quickly. "Monsieur Thuran had become a very dear friend," she said. "I liked him very much, though I have known him but a short time."

"Then you were not engaged to marry him?" he blurted out.
"Heavens, no!" she cried. "I did not care for him at all in that way."

There was something that Lord Tennington wanted to say to
Hazel Strong—he wanted very badly to say it, and to say it at once;
but somehow the words stuck in his throat. He started lamely a couple
of times, cleared his throat, became red in the face, and finally ended
by remarking that he hoped the cabins would be finished before the
rainy season commenced.

But, though he did not know it, he had conveyed to the girl the
very message he intended, and it left her happy—happier than she
had ever before been in all her life.

Just then further conversation was interrupted by the sight of a
strange and terrible-looking figure which emerged from the jungle
just south of the camp. Tennington and the girl saw it at the same
time. The Englishman reached for his revolver, but when the half-
naked, bearded creature called his name aloud and came running
toward them he dropped his hand and advanced to meet it.

None would have recognized in the filthy, emaciated creature,
covered by a single garment of small skins, the immaculate Monsieur
Thuran the party had last seen upon the deck of the *Lady Alice*.

Before the other members of the little community were apprised
of his presence Tennington and Miss Strong questioned him regarding the other occupants of the missing boat.

"They are all dead," replied Thuran. "The three sailors died
before we made land. Miss Porter was carried off into the jungle by
some wild animal while I was lying delirious with fever. Clayton died
of the same fever but a few days since. And to think that all this time
we have been separated by but a few miles—scarcely a day's march.
It is terrible!"

. . .

How long Jane Porter lay in the darkness of the vault beneath the
temple in the ancient city of Opar she did not know. For a time she

was delirious with fever, but after this passed she commenced slowly to regain her strength. Every day the woman who brought her food beckoned to her to arise, but for many days the girl could only shake her head to indicate that she was too weak.

But eventually she was able to gain her feet, and then to stagger a few steps by supporting herself with one hand upon the wall. Her captors now watched her with increasing interest. The day was approaching, and the victim was gaining in strength.

Presently the day came, and a young woman whom Jane Porter had not seen before came with several others to her dungeon. Here some sort of ceremony was performed—that it was of a religious nature the girl was sure, and so she took new heart, and rejoiced that she had fallen among people upon whom the refining and softening influences of religion evidently had fallen. They would treat her humanely—of that she was now quite sure.

And so when they led her from her dungeon, through long, dark corridors, and up a flight of concrete steps to a brilliant courtyard, she went willingly, even gladly—for was she not among the servants of God? It might be, of course, that their interpretation of the supreme being differed from her own, but that they owned a god was sufficient evidence to her that they were kind and good.

But when she saw a stone altar in the center of the courtyard, and dark-brown stains upon it and the nearby concrete of the floor, she began to wonder and to doubt. And as they stooped and bound her ankles, and secured her wrists behind her, her doubts were turned to fear. A moment later, as she was lifted and placed supine across the altar's top, hope left her entirely, and she trembled in an agony of fright.

During the grotesque dance of the votaries which followed, she lay frozen in horror, nor did she require the sight of the thin blade in the hands of the high priestess as it rose slowly above her to enlighten her further as to her doom.

As the hand began its descent, Jane Porter closed her eyes and sent up a silent prayer to the Maker she was so soon to face—then she succumbed to the strain upon her tired nerves, and swooned.

· · ·

Day and night Tarzan of the Apes raced through the primeval forest toward the ruined city in which he was positive the woman he loved lay either a prisoner or dead.

In a day and a night he covered the same distance that the fifty frightful men had taken the better part of a week to traverse, for Tarzan of the Apes traveled along the middle terrace high above the tangled obstacles that impede progress upon the ground.

The story the young bull ape had told made it clear to him that the girl captive had been Jane Porter, for there was not another small white "she" in all the jungle. The "bulls" he had recognized from the ape's crude description as the grotesque parodies upon humanity who inhabit the ruins of Opar. And the girl's fate he could picture as plainly as though he were an eyewitness to it. When they would lay her across that trim altar he could not guess, but that her dear, frail body would eventually find its way there he was confident.

But, finally, after what seemed long ages to the impatient ape-man, he topped the barrier cliffs that hemmed the desolate valley, and below him lay the grim and awful ruins of the now hideous city of Opar. At a rapid trot he started across the dry and dusty, bowlder-strewn ground toward the goal of his desires.

Would he be in time to rescue? He hoped against hope. At least he could be revenged, and in his wrath it seemed to him that he was equal to the task of wiping out the entire population of that terrible city. It was nearly noon when he reached the great bowlder at the top of which terminated the secret passage to the pits beneath the city. Like a cat he scaled the precipitous sides of the frowning granite *kopje*. A moment later he was running through the darkness of the long, straight tunnel that led to the treasure vault. Through this he passed, then on and on until at last he came to the well-like shaft upon the opposite side of which lay the dungeon with the false wall.

As he paused a moment upon the brink of the well a faint sound came to him through the opening above. His quick ears caught and translated it—it was the dance of death that preceded a sacrifice, and the singsong ritual of the high priestess. He could even recognize the woman's voice. Could it be that the ceremony marked the very thing he had so hastened to prevent? A wave of horror swept over him. Was he, after all, to be just a moment too late? Like a frightened deer he leaped across the narrow chasm to the continuation of the passage beyond. At the false wall he tore like one possessed to demolish the barrier that confronted him—with giant muscles he forced the opening, thrusting his head and shoulders through the first small hole he made, and carrying the balance of the wall with him, to clatter resoundingly upon the cement floor of the dungeon.

With a single leap he cleared the length of the chamber and threw himself against the ancient door. But here he stopped. The mighty bars upon the other side were proof even against such muscles as his. It needed but a moment's effort to convince him of the futility of endeavoring to force that impregnable barrier. There was but one other way, and that led back through the long tunnels to the bowlder a mile beyond the city's walls, and then back across the open as he had come to the city first with his Waziri.

He realized that to retrace his steps and enter the city from above ground would mean that he would be too late to save the girl, if it were indeed she who lay upon the sacrificial altar above him. But there seemed no other way, and so he turned and ran swiftly back into the passageway beyond the broken wall. At the well he heard again the monotonous voice of the high priestess, and, as he glanced aloft, the opening, twenty feet above, seemed so near that he was tempted to leap for it in a mad endeavor to reach the inner courtyard that lay so near.

If he could but get one end of his grass rope caught upon some projection at the top of that tantalizing aperture! In the instant's pause and thought an idea occurred to him. He would attempt it. Turning back to the tumbled wall, he seized one of the large, flat slabs that had composed it. Hastily making one end of his rope fast to the piece of granite, he returned to the shaft, and, coiling the balance of the rope on the floor beside him, the ape-man took the heavy slab in both hands, and, swinging it several times to get the distance and the direction fixed, he let the weight fly up at a slight angle, so that, instead of falling straight back into the shaft again, it grazed the far edge, tumbling over into the court beyond.

Tarzan dragged for a moment upon the slack end of the rope until he felt that the stone was lodged with fair security at the shaft's top, then he swung out over the black depths beneath. The moment his full weight came upon the rope he felt it slip from above. He waited there in awful suspense as it dropped in little jerks, inch by inch. The stone was being dragged up the outside of the masonry surrounding the top of the shaft—would it catch at the very edge, or would his weight drag it over to fall upon him as he hurtled into the unknown depths below?

XXV

Through the Forest Primeval

 or a brief, sickening moment Tarzan felt the slipping of the rope to which he clung, and heard the scraping of the block of stone against the masonry above.

Then of a sudden the rope was still—the stone had caught at the very edge. Gingerly the ape-man clambered up the frail rope. In a moment his head was above the edge of the shaft. The court was empty. The inhabitants of Opar were viewing the sacrifice. Tarzan could hear the voice of La from the nearby sacrificial court. The dance had ceased. It must be almost time for the knife to fall; but even as he thought these things he was running rapidly toward the sound of the high priestess' voice.

Fate guided him to the very doorway of the great roofless chamber. Between him and the altar was the long row of priests and priestesses, awaiting with their golden cups the spilling of the warm blood of their victim. La's hand was descending slowly toward the bosom of the frail, quiet figure that lay stretched upon the hard stone. Tarzan gave a gasp that was almost a sob as he recognized the features of the girl he loved. And then the scar upon his forehead turned to a flaming band of scarlet, a red mist floated before his eyes, and, with the awful roar of the bull ape gone mad, he sprang like a huge lion into the midst of the votaries.

Seizing a cudgel from the nearest priest, he laid about him like a veritable demon as he forged his rapid way toward the altar. The hand of La had paused at the first noise of interruption. When she saw who the author of it was she went white. She had never been able to fathom the secret of the strange white man's escape from the dungeon in which she had locked him. She had not intended that he should ever leave Opar, for she had looked upon his giant frame and handsome face with the eyes of a woman and not those of a priestess.

In her clever mind she had concocted a story of wonderful revelation from the lips of the flaming god himself, in which she had been ordered to receive this white stranger as a messenger from him to his people on earth. That would satisfy the people of Opar, she knew. The man would be satisfied, she felt quite sure, to remain and be her husband rather than to return to the sacrificial altar.

But when she had gone to explain her plan to him he had disappeared, though the door had been tightly locked as she had left it. And now he had returned—materialized from thin air—and was killing her priests as though they had been sheep. For the moment she forgot her victim, and before she could gather her wits together again the huge white man was standing before her, the woman who had lain upon the altar in his arms.

"One side, La," he cried. "You saved me once, and so I would not harm you; but do not interfere or attempt to follow, or I shall have to kill you also."

As he spoke he stepped past her toward the entrance to the subterranean vaults.

"Who is she?" asked the high priestess, pointing at the unconscious woman.

"She is mine," said Tarzan of the Apes.

For a moment the girl of Opar stood wide-eyed and staring. Then a look of hopeless misery suffused her eyes—tears welled into them, and with a little cry she sank to the cold floor, just as a swarm of frightful men dashed past her to leap upon the ape-man.

But Tarzan of the Apes was not there when they reached out to seize him. With a light bound he had disappeared into the passage leading to the pits below, and when his pursuers came more cautiously after they found the chamber empty, they but laughed and jabbered to one another, for they knew that there was no exit from the pits other than the one through which he had entered. If he came out at all he must come this way, and they would wait and watch for him above.

And so Tarzan of the Apes, carrying the unconscious Jane Porter, came through the pits of Opar beneath the temple of The Flaming God without pursuit. But when the men of Opar had talked further about the matter, they recalled to mind that this very man had escaped once before into the pits, and, though they had watched the entrance he had not come forth; and yet today he had come upon them from the outside. They would again send fifty men out into the valley to find and capture this desecrater of their temple.

After Tarzan reached the shaft beyond the broken wall, he felt so positive of the successful issue of his flight that he stopped to replace the tumbled stones, for he was not anxious that any of the inmates should discover this forgotten passage, and through it come upon the treasure chamber. It was in his mind to return again to Opar and bear away a still greater fortune than he had already buried in the amphitheater of the apes.

On through the passageways he trotted, past the first door and through the treasure vault; past the second door and into the long, straight tunnel that led to the lofty hidden exit beyond the city. Jane Porter was still unconscious.

At the crest of the great bowlder he halted to cast a backward glance toward the city. Coming across the plain he saw a band of the hideous men of Opar. For a moment he hesitated. Should he descend and make a race for the distant cliffs, or should he hide here until night? And then a glance at the girl's white face determined him. He could not keep her here and permit her enemies to get between them and liberty. For aught he knew they might have been followed through the tunnels, and to have foes before and behind would result in almost certain capture, since he could not fight his way through the enemy burdened as he was with the unconscious girl.

To descend the steep face of the bowlder with Jane Porter was no easy task, but by binding her across his shoulders with the grass rope he succeeded in reaching the ground in safety before the Oparians arrived at the great rock. As the descent had been made upon the side away from the city, the searching party saw nothing of it, nor did they dream that their prey was so close before them.

By keeping the *kopje* between them and their pursuers, Tarzan of the Apes managed to cover nearly a mile before the men of Opar rounded the granite sentinel and saw the fugitive before them. With loud cries of savage delight, they broke into a mad run, thinking doubtless that they would soon overhaul the burdened runner; but they both underestimated the powers of the ape-man and overestimated the possibilities of their own short, crooked legs.

By maintaining an easy trot, Tarzan kept the distance between them always the same. Occasionally he would glance at the face so near his own. Had it not been for the faint beating of the heart pressed so close against his own, he would not have known that she was alive, so white and drawn was the poor, tired face.

And thus they came to the flat-topped mountain and the barrier cliffs. During the last mile Tarzan had let himself out, running like a deer that he might have ample time to descend the face of the cliffs before the Oparians could reach the summit and hurl rocks down upon them. And so it was that he was half a mile down the mountainside ere the fierce little men came panting to the edge.

With cries of rage and disappointment they ranged along the cliff top shaking their cudgels, and dancing up and down in a perfect passion of anger. But this time they did not pursue beyond the boundary of their own country. Whether it was because they recalled the futility of their former long and irksome search, or after witnessing the ease with which the ape-man swung along before them, and the last burst of speed, they realized the utter hopelessness of further pursuit, it is difficult to say; but as Tarzan reached the woods that began at the base of the foothills which skirted the barrier cliffs they turned their faces once more toward Opar.

Just within the forest's edge, where he could yet watch the cliff tops, Tarzan laid his burden upon the grass, and going to the near-by rivulet brought water with which he bathed her face and hands; but even this did not revive her, and, greatly worried, he gathered the girl into his strong arms once more and hurried on toward the west.

Late in the afternoon Jane Porter regained consciousness. She did not open her eyes at once—she was trying to recall the scenes that she had last witnessed. Ah, she remembered now. The altar, the terrible priestess, the descending knife. She gave a little shudder, for she thought that either this was death or that the knife had buried itself in her heart and she was experiencing the brief delirium preceding death. And when finally she mustered courage to open her eyes, the sight that met them confirmed her fears, for she saw that she was being borne through a leafy paradise in the arms of her dead love. "If this be death," she murmured, "thank God that I am dead."

"You spoke, Jane!" cried Tarzan. "You are regaining consciousness!"

"Yes, Tarzan of the Apes," she replied, and for the first time in months a smile of peace and happiness lighted her face.

"Thank God!" cried the ape-man, coming to the ground in a little grassy clearing beside the stream. "I was in time, after all."

"In time? What do you mean?" she questioned.

"In time to save you from death upon the altar, dear," he replied. "Do you not remember?"

"Save me from death?" she asked, in a puzzled tone. "Are we not both dead, my Tarzan?"

He had placed her upon the grass by now, her back resting against the stem of a huge tree. At her question he stepped back where he could the better see her face.

"Dead!" he repeated, and then he laughed. "You are not, Jane; and if you will return to the city of Opar and ask them who dwell there they will tell you that I was not dead a few short hours ago. No, dear, we are both very much alive."

"But both Hazel and Monsieur Thuran told me that you had fallen into the ocean many miles from land," she urged, as though trying to convince him that he must indeed be dead. "They said that there was no question but that it must have been you, and less that you could have survived or been picked up."

"How can I convince you that I am no spirit?" he asked, with a laugh. "It was I whom the delightful Monsieur Thuran pushed overboard, but I did not drown—I will tell you all about it after a while—and here I am very much the same wild man you first knew, Jane Porter."

The girl rose slowly to her feet and came toward him.

"I cannot even yet believe it," she murmured. "It cannot be that such happiness can be true after all the hideous things that I have passed through these awful months since the *Lady Alice* went down."

She came close to him and laid a hand, soft and trembling, upon his arm.

"It must be that I am dreaming, and that I shall awaken in a moment to see that awful knife descending toward my heart—kiss me, dear, just once before I lose my dream forever."

Tarzan of the Apes needed no second invitation. He took the girl he loved in his strong arms, and kissed her not once, but a hundred times, until she lay there panting for breath; yet when he stopped she put her arms about his neck and drew his lips down to hers once more.

"Am I alive and a reality, or am I but a dream?" he asked.

"If you are not alive, my man," she answered, "I pray that I may die thus before I awaken to the terrible realities of my last waking moments."

For a while both were silent—gazing into each others' eyes as though each still questioned the reality of the wonderful happiness that had come to them. The past, with all its hideous disappointments and horrors, was forgotten—the future did not belong to them; but the present—ah, it was theirs; none could take it from them. It was the girl who first broke the sweet silence.

"Where are we going, dear?" she asked. "What are we going to do?"

"Where would you like best to go?" he asked. "What would you like best to do?"

"To go where you go, my man; to do whatever seems best to you," she answered.

"But Clayton?" he asked. For a moment he had forgotten that there existed upon the earth other than they two. "We have forgotten your husband."

"I am not married, Tarzan of the Apes," she cried. "Nor am I longer promised in marriage. The day before those awful creatures captured me I spoke to Mr. Clayton of my love for you, and he understood then that I could not keep the wicked promise that I had made. It was after we had been miraculously saved from an attacking lion." She paused suddenly and looked up at him, a questioning light in her eyes. "Tarzan of the Apes," she cried, "it was you who did that thing? It could have been no other."

He dropped his eyes, for he was ashamed.

"How could you have gone away and left me?" she cried reproachfully.

"Don't, Jane!" he pleaded. "Please don't! You cannot know how I have suffered since for the cruelty of that act, or how I suffered then, first in jealous rage, and then in bitter resentment against the fate that I had not deserved. I went back to the apes after that, Jane, intending never again to see a human being." He told her then of his life since he had returned to the jungle—of how he had dropped like a plummet from a civilized Parisian to a savage Waziri warrior, and from there back to the brute that he had been raised.

She asked him many questions, and at last fearfully of the things that Monsieur Thuran had told her—of the woman in Paris. He narrated every detail of his civilized life to her, omitting nothing, for he felt no shame, since his heart always had been true to her. When he had finished he sat looking at her, as though waiting for her judgment, and his sentence.

"I knew that he was not speaking the truth," she said. "Oh, what a horrible creature he is!"

"You are not angry with me, then?" he asked.

And her reply, though apparently most irrelevant, was truly feminine.

"Is Olga de Coude very beautiful?" she asked.

And Tarzan laughed and kissed her again. "Not one-tenth so beautiful as you, dear," he said.

She gave a contented little sigh, and let her head rest against his shoulder. He knew that he was forgiven.

That night Tarzan built a snug little bower high among the swaying branches of a giant tree, and there the tired girl slept, while in a crotch beneath her the ape-man curled, ready, even in sleep, to protect her.

It took them many days to make the long journey to the coast. Where the way was easy they walked hand in hand beneath the arching boughs of the mighty forest, as might in a far-gone past have walked their primeval forbears. When the underbrush was tangled he took her in his great arms, and bore her lightly through the trees, and the days were all too short, for they were very happy. Had it not been for their anxiety to reach and succor Clayton they would have drawn out the sweet pleasure of that wonderful journey indefinitely.

On the last day before they reached the coast Tarzan caught the scent of men ahead of them—the scent of black men. He told the girl, and cautioned her to maintain silence. "There are few friends in the jungle," he remarked dryly.

In half an hour they came stealthily upon a small party of black warriors filing toward the west. As Tarzan saw them he gave a cry of delight—it was a band of his own Waziri. Busuli was there, and others who had accompanied him to Opar. At sight of him they danced and cried out in exuberant joy. For weeks they had been searching for him, they told him.

The blacks exhibited considerable wonderment at the presence of the white girl with him, and when they found that she was to be his woman they vied with one another to do her honor. With the happy Waziri laughing and dancing about them they came to the rude shelter by the shore.

There was no sign of life, and no response to their calls. Tarzan clambered quickly to the interior of the little tree hut, only to emerge a moment later with an empty tin. Throwing it down to Busuli, he told him to fetch water, and then he beckoned Jane Porter to come up.

Together they leaned over the emaciated thing that once had been an English nobleman. Tears came to the girl's eyes as she saw the poor, sunken cheeks and hollow eyes, and the lines of suffering upon the once young and handsome face.

"He still lives," said Tarzan. "We will do all that can be done for him, but I fear that we are too late."

When Busuli had brought the water Tarzan forced a few drops between the cracked and swollen lips. He wetted the hot forehead and bathed the pitiful limbs.

Presently Clayton opened his eyes. A faint, shadowy smile lighted his countenance as he saw the girl leaning over him. At sight of Tarzan the expression changed to one of wonderment.

"It's all right, old fellow," said the ape-man. "We've found you in time. Everything will be all right now, and we'll have you on your feet again before you know it."

The Englishman shook his head weakly. "It's too late," he whispered. "But it's just as well. I'd rather die."

"Where is Monsieur Thuran?" asked the girl.

"He left me after the fever got bad. He is a devil. When I begged for the water that I was too weak to get he drank before me, threw the rest out, and laughed in my face." At the thought of it the man was suddenly animated by a spark of vitality. He raised himself upon one elbow. "Yes," he almost shouted; "I will live. I will live long enough to find and kill that beast!" But the brief effort left him weaker than before, and he sank back again upon the rotting grasses that, with his old ulster, had been the bed of Jane Porter.

"Don't worry about Thuran," said Tarzan of the Apes, laying a reassuring hand on Clayton's forehead. "He belongs to me, and I shall get him in the end, never fear."

For a long time Clayton lay very still. Several times Tarzan had to put his ear quite close to the sunken chest to catch the faint beating of the worn-out heart. Toward evening he aroused again for a brief moment.

"Jane," he whispered. The girl bent her head closer to catch the faint message. "I have wronged you—and him," he nodded weakly toward the ape-man. "I loved you so—it is a poor excuse to offer for injuring you; but I could not bear to think of giving you up. I do not ask your forgiveness. I only wish to do now the thing I should have done over a year ago." He fumbled in the pocket of the ulster beneath him for something that he had discovered there while he lay between the paroxysms of fever. Presently he found it—a crumpled bit of yellow paper. He handed it to the girl, and as she took it his arm fell limply across his chest, his head dropped back, and with a little gasp he stiffened and was still. Then Tarzan of the Apes drew a fold of the ulster across the upturned face.

For a moment they remained kneeling there, the girl's lips moving in silent prayer, and as they rose and stood on either side of the now peaceful form, tears came to the ape-man's eyes, for through the anguish that his own heart had suffered he had learned compassion for the suffering of others.

Through her own tears the girl read the message upon the bit of faded yellow paper, and as she read her eyes went very wide. Twice she read those startling words before she could fully comprehend their meaning.

Finger prints prove you Greystoke. Congratulations.

D'ARNOT.

She handed the paper to Tarzan. "And he has known it all this time," she said, "and did not tell you?"

"I knew it first, Jane," replied the man. "I did not know that he knew it at all. I must have dropped this message that night in the waiting room. It was there that I received it."

"And afterward you told us that your mother was a she-ape, and that you had never known your father?" she asked incredulously.

"The title and the estates meant nothing to me without you, dear," he replied. "And if I had taken them away from him I should have been robbing the woman I love—don't you understand, Jane?" It was as though he attempted to excuse a fault.

She extended her arms toward him across the body of the dead man, and took his hands in hers.

"And I would have thrown away a love like that!" she said.

XXVI

THE PASSING OF
THE APE-MAN

he next morning they set out upon the short journey to Tarzan's cabin. Four Waziri bore the body of the dead Englishman. It had been the ape-man's suggestion that Clayton be buried beside the former Lord Greystoke near the edge of the jungle against the cabin that the older man had built.

Jane Porter was glad that it was to be so, and in her heart of hearts she wondered at the marvelous fineness of character of this wondrous man, who, though raised by brutes and among brutes, had the true chivalry and tenderness which only associates with the refinements of the highest civilization.

They had proceeded some three miles of the five that had separated them from Tarzan's own beach when the Waziri who were ahead stopped suddenly, pointing in amazement at a strange figure approaching them along the beach. It was a man with a shiny silk hat, who walked slowly with bent head, and hands clasped behind him underneath the tails of his long, black coat.

At sight of him Jane Porter uttered a little cry of surprise and joy, and ran quickly ahead to meet him. At the sound of her voice the old man looked up, and when he saw who it was confronting him he, too, cried out in relief and happiness. As Professor Archimedes Q. Porter folded his daughter in his arms tears streamed down his seamed old face, and it was several minutes before he could control himself sufficiently to speak.

When a moment later he recognized Tarzan it was with difficulty that they could convince him that his sorrow had not unbalanced his mind, for with the other members of the party he had been so thoroughly convinced that the ape-man was dead it was a problem to reconcile the conviction with the very lifelike appearance of Jane's "forest god." The old man was deeply touched at the news of Clayton's death.

"I cannot understand it," he said. "Monsieur Thuran assured us that Clayton passed away many days ago."

"Thuran is with you?" asked Tarzan.

"Yes; he but recently found us and led us to your cabin. We were camped but a short distance north of it. Bless me, but he will be delighted to see you both."

"And surprised," commented Tarzan.

A short time later the strange party came to the clearing in which stood the ape-man's cabin. It was filled with people coming and going, and almost the first whom Tarzan saw was D'Arnot.

"Paul!" he cried. "In the name of sanity what are you doing here? Or are we all insane?"

It was quickly explained, however, as were many other seemingly strange things. D'Arnot's ship had been cruising along the coast, on patrol duty, when at the lieutenant's suggestion they had anchored off the little landlocked harbor to have another look at the cabin and the jungle in which many of the officers and men had taken part in exciting adventures two years before. On landing they had found Lord Tennington's party, and arrangements were being made to take them all on board the following morning, and carry them back to civilization.

Hazel Strong and her mother, Esmeralda, and Mr. Samuel T. Philander were almost overcome by happiness at Jane Porter's safe return. Her escape seemed to them little short of miraculous, and it was the consensus of opinion that it could have been achieved by no other man than Tarzan of the Apes. They loaded the uncomfortable ape-man with eulogies and attentions until he wished himself back in the amphitheater of the apes.

All were interested in his savage Waziri, and many were the gifts the black men received from these friends of their king, but when they learned that he might sail away from them upon the great canoe that lay at anchor a mile off shore they became very sad.

As yet the newcomers had seen nothing of Lord Tennington and Monsieur Thuran. They had gone out for fresh meat early in the day, and had not yet returned.

"How surprised this man, whose name you say is Rokoff, will be to see you," said Jane Porter to Tarzan.

"His surprise will be short-lived," replied the ape-man grimly, and there was that in his tone that made her look up into his face in alarm. What she read there evidently confirmed her fears, for she put her hand upon his arm, and pleaded with him to leave the Russian to the laws of France.

"In the heart of the jungle, dear," she said, "with no other form of right or justice to appeal to other than your own mighty muscles, you would be warranted in executing upon this man the sentence he deserves; but with the strong arm of a civilized government at your disposal it would be murder to kill him now. Even your friends would have to submit to your arrest, or if you resisted it would plunge us all into misery and unhappiness again. I cannot bear to lose you again, my Tarzan. Promise me that you will but turn him over to Captain Dufranne, and let the law take its course—the beast is not worth risking our happiness for."

He saw the wisdom of her appeal, and promised. A half hour later Rokoff and Tennington emerged from the jungle. They were walking side by side. Tennington was the first to note the presence of strangers in the camp. He saw the black warriors palavering with the sailors from the cruiser, and then he saw a lithe, brown giant talking with Lieutenant D'Arnot and Captain Dufranne.

"Who is that, I wonder," said Tennington to Rokoff, and as the Russian raised his eyes and met those of the ape-man full upon him, he staggered and went white.

"*Sapristi!*" he cried, and before Tennington realized what he intended he had thrown his gun to his shoulder, and aiming point-blank at Tarzan pulled the trigger. But the Englishman was close to him—so close that his hand reached the leveled barrel a fraction of a second before the hammer fell upon the cartridge, and the bullet that was intended for Tarzan's heart whirred harmlessly above his head.

Before the Russian could fire again the ape-man was upon him and had wrested the firearm from his grasp. Captain Dufranne, Lieutenant D'Arnot, and a dozen sailors had rushed up at the sound of the shot, and now Tarzan turned the Russian over to them without a word. He had explained the matter to the French commander before Rokoff arrived, and the officer gave immediate orders to place the Russian in irons and confine him on board the cruiser.

Just before the guard escorted the prisoner into the small boat that was to transport him to his temporary prison Tarzan asked permission to search him, and to his delight found the stolen papers concealed upon his person.

The shot had brought Jane Porter and the others from the cabin, and a moment after the excitement had died down she greeted the surprised Lord Tennington. Tarzan joined them after he had taken the papers from Rokoff, and, as he approached, Jane Porter introduced him to Tennington.

"John Clayton, Lord Greystoke, my lord," she said.

The Englishman looked his astonishment in spite of his most her-culean efforts to appear courteous, and it required many repetitions of the strange story of the ape-man as told by himself, Jane Porter, and Lieutenant D'Arnot to convince Lord Tennington that they were not all quite mad.

At sunset they buried William Cecil Clayton beside the jungle graves of his uncle and his aunt, the former Lord and Lady Greystoke. And it was at Tarzan's request that three volleys were fired over the last resting place of "a brave man, who met his death bravely."

Professor Porter, who in his younger days had been ordained a minister, conducted the simple services for the dead. About the grave, with bowed heads, stood as strange a company of mourners as the sun ever looked down upon. There were French officers and sailors, two English lords, Americans, and a score of savage African braves.

Following the funeral Tarzan asked Captain Dufranne to delay the sailing of the cruiser a couple of days while he went inland a few miles to fetch his "belongings," and the officer gladly granted the favor.

Late the next afternoon Tarzan and his Waziri returned with the first load of "belongings," and when the party saw the ancient ingots of virgin gold they swarmed upon the ape-man with a thousand questions; but he was smilingly obdurate to their appeals—he declined to give them the slightest clew as to the source of his immense treasure. "There are a thousand that I left behind," he explained, "for every one that I brought away, and when these are spent I may wish to return for more."

The next day he returned to camp with the balance of his ingots, and when they were stored on board the cruiser Captain Dufranne said he felt like the commander of an old-time Spanish galleon returning from the treasure cities of the Aztecs. "I don't know what minute my crew will cut my throat, and take over the ship," he added.

The next morning, as they were preparing to embark upon the cruiser, Tarzan ventured a suggestion to Jane Porter.

"Wild beasts are supposed to be devoid of sentiment," he said, "but nevertheless I should like to be married in the cabin where I was born, beside the graves of my mother and my father, and surrounded by the savage jungle that always has been my home."

"Would it be quite regular, dear?" she asked. "For if it would I know of no other place in which I should rather be married to my forest god than beneath the shade of his primeval forest."

And when they spoke of it to the others they were assured that it would be quite regular, and a most splendid termination of a remarkable romance. So the entire party assembled within the little cabin and about the door to witness the second ceremony that Professor Porter was to solemnize within three days.

D'Arnot was to be best man, and Hazel Strong bridesmaid, until Tennington upset all the arrangements by another of his marvelous "ideas."

"If Mrs. Strong is agreeable," he said, taking the bridesmaid's hand in his, "Hazel and I think it would be ripping to make it a double wedding."

The next day they sailed, and as the cruiser steamed slowly out to sea a tall man, immaculate in white flannel, and a graceful girl leaned against her rail to watch the receding shore line upon which danced twenty naked, black warriors of the Waziri, waving their war spears above their savage heads, and shouting farewells to their departing king.

"I should hate to think that I am looking upon the jungle for the last time, dear," he said, "were it not that I know that I am going to a new world of happiness with you forever," and, bending down, Tarzan of the Apes kissed his mate upon her lips.

The Beasts of
TARZAN

The Adventures of Lord Greystoke:
Book Three

CONTENTS

to
JOAN BURROUGHS

I

KIDNAPPED

he entire affair is shrouded in mystery," said D'Arnot. "I have it on the best of authority that neither the police nor the special agents of the general staff have the faintest conception of how it was accomplished. All they know, all that anyone knows, is that Nikolas Rokoff has escaped."

John Clayton, Lord Greystoke—he who had been "Tarzan of the Apes"—sat in silence in the apartments of his friend, Lieutenant Paul D'Arnot, in Paris, gazing meditatively at the toe of his immaculate boot.

His mind revolved many memories, recalled by the escape of his arch-enemy from the French military prison to which he had been sentenced for life upon the testimony of the ape-man.

He thought of the lengths to which Rokoff had once gone to compass his death, and he realized that what the man had already done would doubtless be as nothing by comparison with what he would wish and plot to do now that he was again free.

Tarzan had recently brought his wife and infant son to London to escape the discomforts and dangers of the rainy season upon their vast estate in Uziri—the land of the savage Waziri warriors whose broad African domains the ape-man had once ruled.

He had run across the Channel for a brief visit with his old friend, but the news of the Russian's escape had already cast a shadow upon his outing, so that though he had but just arrived he was already contemplating an immediate return to London.

"It is not that I fear for myself, Paul," he said at last. "Many times in the past have I thwarted Rokoff's designs upon my life; but now there are others to consider. Unless I misjudge the man, he would more quickly strike at me through my wife or son than directly at me, for he doubtless realizes that in no other way could he inflict greater anguish upon me. I must go back to them at once, and remain with them until Rokoff is recaptured—or dead."

As these two talked in Paris, two other men were talking together in a little cottage upon the outskirts of London. Both were dark, sinister-looking men.

One was bearded, but the other, whose face wore the pallor of long confinement within doors, had but a few days' growth of black beard upon his face. It was he who was speaking.

"You must needs shave off that beard of yours, Alexis," he said to his companion. "With it he would recognize you on the instant. We must separate here in the hour, and when we meet again upon the deck of the *Kincaid*, let us hope that we shall have with us two honoured guests who little anticipate the pleasant voyage we have planned for them.

"In two hours I should be upon my way to Dover with one of them, and by tomorrow night, if you follow my instructions carefully, you should arrive with the other, provided, of course, that he returns to London as quickly as I presume he will.

"There should be both profit and pleasure as well as other good things to reward our efforts, my dear Alexis. Thanks to the stupidity of the French, they have gone to such lengths to conceal the fact of my escape for these many days that I have had ample opportunity to work out every detail of our little adventure so carefully that there is little chance of the slightest hitch occurring to mar our prospects. And now good-bye, and good luck!"

Three hours later a messenger mounted the steps to the apartment of Lieutenant D'Arnot.

"A telegram for Lord Greystoke," he said to the servant who answered his summons. "Is he here?"

The man answered in the affirmative, and, signing for the message, carried it within to Tarzan, who was already preparing to depart for London.

Tarzan tore open the envelope, and as he read his face went white.

"Read it, Paul," he said, handing the slip of paper to D'Arnot. "It has come already."

The Frenchman took the telegram and read:

"Jack stolen from the garden through complicity of new servant. Come at once.

—JANE."

As Tarzan leaped from the roadster that had met him at the station and ran up the steps to his London town house he was met at the door by a dry-eyed but almost frantic woman.

Quickly Jane Porter Clayton narrated all that she had been able to learn of the theft of the boy.

The baby's nurse had been wheeling him in the sunshine on the walk before the house when a closed taxicab drew up at the corner of the street. The woman had paid but passing attention to the vehicle, merely noting that it discharged no passenger, but stood at the kerb with the motor running as though waiting for a fare from the residence before which it had stopped.

Almost immediately the new houseman, Carl, had come running from the Greystoke house, saying that the girl's mistress wished to speak with her for a moment, and that she was to leave little Jack in his care until she returned.

The woman said that she entertained not the slightest suspicion of the man's motives until she had reached the doorway of the house, when it occurred to her to warn him not to turn the carriage so as to permit the sun to shine in the baby's eyes.

As she turned about to call this to him she was somewhat sur-prised to see that he was wheeling the carriage rapidly toward the corner, and at the same time she saw the door of the taxicab open and a swarthy face framed for a moment in the aperture.

Intuitively, the danger to the child flashed upon her, and with a shriek she dashed down the steps and up the walk toward the taxicab, into which Carl was now handing the baby to the swarthy one within.

Just before she reached the vehicle, Carl leaped in beside his con-federate, slamming the door behind him. At the same time the chauf-feur attempted to start his machine, but it was evident that something had gone wrong, as though the gears refused to mesh, and the delay caused by this, while he pushed the lever into reverse and backed the car a few inches before again attempting to go ahead, gave the nurse time to reach the side of the taxicab.

Leaping to the running-board, she had attempted to snatch the baby from the arms of the stranger, and here, screaming and fight-ing, she had clung to her position even after the taxicab had got under way; nor was it until the machine had passed the Greystoke residence at good speed that Carl, with a heavy blow to her face, had succeeded in knocking her to the pavement.

Her screams had attracted servants and members of the families from residences near by, as well as from the Greystoke home. Lady Greystoke had witnessed the girl's brave battle, and had herself tried to reach the rapidly passing vehicle, but had been too late.

That was all that anyone knew, nor did Lady Greystoke dream of the possible identity of the man at the bottom of the plot until her husband told her of the escape of Nikolas Rokoff from the French prison where they had hoped he was permanently confined.

As Tarzan and his wife stood planning the wisest course to pursue, the telephone bell rang in the library at their right. Tarzan quickly answered the call in person.

"Lord Greystoke?" asked a man's voice at the other end of the line.
"Yes."

"Your son has been stolen," continued the voice, "and I alone may help you to recover him. I am conversant with the plot of those who took him. In fact, I was a party to it, and was to share in the reward, but now they are trying to ditch me, and to be quits with them I will aid you to recover him on condition that you will not prosecute me for my part in the crime. What do you say?"

"If you lead me to where my son is hidden," replied the ape-man, "you need fear nothing from me."

"Good," replied the other. "But you must come alone to meet me, for it is enough that I must trust you. I cannot take the chance of permitting others to learn my identity."

"Where and when may I meet you?" asked Tarzan.

The other gave the name and location of a public-house on the water-front at Dover—a place frequented by sailors.

"Come," he concluded, "about ten o'clock tonight. It would do no good to arrive earlier. Your son will be safe enough in the meantime, and I can then lead you secretly to where he is hidden. But be sure to come alone, and under no circumstances notify Scotland Yard, for I know you well and shall be watching for you.

"Should any other accompany you, or should I see suspicious characters who might be agents of the police, I shall not meet you, and your last chance of recovering your son will be gone."

Without more words the man rang off.

Tarzan repeated the gist of the conversation to his wife. She begged to be allowed to accompany him, but he insisted that it might result in the man's carrying out his threat of refusing to aid them if Tarzan did not come alone, and so they parted, he to hasten to Dover, and she, ostensibly to wait at home until he should notify her of the outcome of his mission.

Little did either dream of what both were destined to pass

through before they should meet again, or the far-distant—but why anticipate?

For ten minutes after the ape-man had left her Jane Clayton walked restlessly back and forth across the silken rugs of the library. Her mother heart ached, bereft of its first-born. Her mind was in an anguish of hopes and fears.

Though her judgment told her that all would be well were her Tarzan to go alone in accordance with the mysterious stranger's summons, her intuition would not permit her to lay aside suspicion of the gravest dangers to both her husband and her son.

The more she thought of the matter, the more convinced she became that the recent telephone message might be but a ruse to keep them inactive until the boy was safely hidden away or spirited out of England. Or it might be that it had been simply a bait to lure Tarzan into the hands of the implacable Rokoff.

With the lodgment of this thought she stopped in wide-eyed terror. Instantly it became a conviction. She glanced at the great clock ticking the minutes in the corner of the library.

It was too late to catch the Dover train that Tarzan was to take. There was another, later, however, that would bring her to the Channel port in time to reach the address the stranger had given her husband before the appointed hour.

Summoning her maid and chauffeur, she issued instructions rapidly. Ten minutes later she was being whisked through the crowded streets toward the railway station.

It was nine-forty-five that night that Tarzan entered the squalid "pub" on the water-front in Dover. As he passed into the evil-smelling room a muffled figure brushed past him toward the street.

"Come, my lord!" whispered the stranger.

The ape-man wheeled about and followed the other into the ill-lit alley, which custom had dignified with the title of thoroughfare. Once outside, the fellow led the way into the darkness, nearer a wharf, where high-piled bales, boxes, and casks cast dense shadows. Here he halted.

"Where is the boy?" asked Greystoke.

"On that small steamer whose lights you can just see yonder," replied the other.

In the gloom Tarzan was trying to peer into the features of his companion, but he did not recognize the man as one whom he had ever before seen. Had he guessed that his guide was Alexis Paulvitch he would have realized that naught but treachery lay in the man's heart, and that danger lurked in the path of every move.

"He is unguarded now," continued the Russian. "Those who took him feel perfectly safe from detection, and with the exception of a couple of members of the crew, whom I have furnished with enough gin to silence them effectually for hours, there is none aboard the *Kincaid*. We can go aboard, get the child, and return without the slightest fear."

Tarzan nodded.

"Let's be about it, then," he said.

His guide led him to a small boat moored alongside the wharf. The two men entered, and Paulvitch pulled rapidly toward the steamer. The black smoke issuing from her funnel did not at the time make any suggestion to Tarzan's mind. All his thoughts were occupied with the hope that in a few moments he would again have his little son in his arms.

At the steamer's side they found a monkey-ladder dangling close above them, and up this the two men crept stealthily. Once on deck they hastened aft to where the Russian pointed to a hatch.

"The boy is hidden there," he said. "You had better go down after him, as there is less chance that he will cry in fright than should he find himself in the arms of a stranger. I will stand on guard here."

So anxious was Tarzan to rescue the child that he gave not the slightest thought to the strangeness of all the conditions surrounding the *Kincaid*. That her deck was deserted, though she had steam up, and from the volume of smoke pouring from her funnel was all ready to get under way made no impression upon him.

With the thought that in another instant he would fold that precious little bundle of humanity in his arms, the ape-man swung down into the darkness below. Scarcely had he released his hold upon the edge of the hatch than the heavy covering fell clattering above him.

Instantly he knew that he was the victim of a plot, and that far from rescuing his son he had himself fallen into the hands of his enemies. Though he immediately endeavoured to reach the hatch and lift the cover, he was unable to do so.

Striking a match, he explored his surroundings, finding that a little compartment had been partitioned off from the main hold, with the hatch above his head the only means of ingress or egress. It was evident that the room had been prepared for the very purpose of serving as a cell for himself.

There was nothing in the compartment, and no other occupant. If the child was on board the *Kincaid* he was confined elsewhere.

For over twenty years, from infancy to manhood, the ape-man had roamed his savage jungle haunts without human companionship of any nature. He had learned at the most impressionable period of his life to take his pleasures and his sorrows as the beasts take theirs.

So it was that he neither raved nor stormed against fate, but instead waited patiently for what might next befall him, though not by any means without an eye to doing the utmost to succour himself. To this end he examined his prison carefully, tested the heavy planking that formed its walls, and measured the distance of the hatch above him.

And while he was thus occupied there came suddenly to him the vibration of machinery and the throbbing of the propeller.

The ship was moving! Where to and to what fate was it carrying him?

And even as these thoughts passed through his mind there came to his ears above the din of the engines that which caused him to go cold with apprehension.

Clear and shrill from the deck above him rang the scream of a frightened woman.

II

MAROONED

s Tarzan and his guide had disappeared into the shadows upon the dark wharf the figure of a heavily veiled woman had hurried down the narrow alley to the entrance of the drinking-place the two men had just quitted.

Here she paused and looked about, and then as though satisfied that she had at last reached the place she sought, she pushed bravely into the interior of the vile den.

A score of half-drunken sailors and wharf-rats looked up at the unaccustomed sight of a richly gowned woman in their midst. Rapidly she approached the slovenly barmaid who stared half in envy, half in hate, at her more fortunate sister.

"Have you seen a tall, well-dressed man here, but a minute since," she asked, "who met another and went away with him?"

The girl answered in the affirmative, but could not tell which way the two had gone. A sailor who had approached to listen to the conversation vouchsafed the information that a moment before as he had been about to enter the "pub" he had seen two men leaving it who walked toward the wharf.

"Show me the direction they went," cried the woman, slipping a coin into the man's hand.

The fellow led her from the place, and together they walked quickly toward the wharf and along it until across the water they saw a small boat just pulling into the shadows of a near-by steamer.

"There they be," whispered the man.

"Ten pounds if you will find a boat and row me to that steamer," cried the woman.

"Quick, then," he replied, "for we gotta go it if we're goin' to catch the *Kincaid* afore she sails. She's had steam up for three hours an' jest been a-waitin' fer that one passenger. I was a-talkin' to one of her crew 'arf an hour ago."

As he spoke he led the way to the end of the wharf where he knew another boat lay moored, and, lowering the woman into it, he jumped in after and pushed off. The two were soon scudding over the water.

At the steamer's side the man demanded his pay and, without waiting to count out the exact amount, the woman thrust a handful of bank-notes into his outstretched hand. A single glance at them convinced the fellow that he had been more than well paid. Then he assisted her up the ladder, holding his skiff close to the ship's side against the chance that this profitable passenger might wish to be taken ashore later.

But presently the sound of the donkey engine and the rattle of a steel cable on the hoisting-drum proclaimed the fact that the *Kincaid*'s anchor was being raised, and a moment later the waiter heard the propellers revolving, and slowly the little steamer moved away from him out into the channel.

As he turned to row back to shore he heard a woman's shriek from the ship's deck.

"That's wot I calls rotten luck," he soliloquized. "I might jest as well of 'ad the whole bloomin' wad."

When Jane Clayton climbed to the deck of the *Kincaid* she found the ship apparently deserted. There was no sign of those she sought nor of any other aboard, and so she went about her search for her husband and the child she hoped against hope to find there without interruption.

Quickly she hastened to the cabin, which was half above and half below deck. As she hurried down the short companion-ladder into the main cabin, on either side of which were the smaller rooms occupied by the officers, she failed to note the quick closing of one of the doors before her. She passed the full length of the main room, and then retracing her steps stopped before each door to listen, furtively trying each latch.

All was silence, utter silence there, in which the throbbing of her own frightened heart seemed to her overwrought imagination to fill the ship with its thunderous alarm. One by one the doors opened before her touch, only to reveal empty interiors. In her absorption she did not note the sudden activity upon the vessel, the purring of the engines, the throbbing of the propeller. She had reached the last door upon the right now, and as she pushed it open she was seized from within by a powerful, dark-visaged man, and drawn hastily into the stuffy, ill-smelling interior.

The sudden shock of fright which the unexpected attack had upon her drew a single piercing scream from her throat; then the man clapped a hand roughly over the mouth.

"Not until we are farther from land, my dear," he said. "Then you may yell your pretty head off."

Lady Greystoke turned to look into the leering, bearded face so close to hers. The man relaxed the pressure of his fingers upon her lips, and with a little moan of terror as she recognized him the girl shrank away from her captor.

"Nikolas Rokoff! M. Thuran!" she exclaimed.

"Your devoted admirer," replied the Russian, with a low bow.

"My little boy," she said next, ignoring the terms of endearment—"where is he? Let me have him. How could you be so cruel—even as you—Nikolas Rokoff—cannot be entirely devoid of mercy and compassion? Tell me where he is. Is he aboard this ship? Oh, please, if such a thing as a heart beats within your breast, take me to my baby!"

"If you do as you are bid no harm will befall him," replied Rokoff. "But remember that it is your own fault that you are here. You came aboard voluntarily, and you may take the consequences. I little thought," he added to himself, "that any such good luck as this would come to me."

He went on deck then, locking the cabin-door upon his prisoner, and for several days she did not see him. The truth of the matter being that Nikolas Rokoff was so poor a sailor that the heavy seas the *Kincaid* encountered from the very beginning of her voyage sent the Russian to his berth with a bad attack of sea-sickness.

During this time her only visitor was an uncouth Swede, the *Kincaid's* unsavoury cook, who brought her meals to her. His name was Sven Anderssen, his one pride being that his patronymic was spelt with a double "s."

The man was tall and raw-boned, with a long yellow moustache, an unwholesome complexion, and filthy nails. The very sight of him with one grimy thumb buried deep in the lukewarm stew, that seemed, from the frequency of its repetition, to constitute the pride of his culinary art, was sufficient to take away the girl's appetite.

His small, blue, close-set eyes never met hers squarely. There was a shiftiness of his whole appearance that even found expression in the cat-like manner of his gait, and to it all a sinister suggestion was added by the long slim knife that always rested at his waist, slipped through the greasy cord that supported his soiled apron. Ostensibly it was but an implement of his calling; but the girl could never free herself of the conviction that it would require less provocation to witness it put to other and less harmless uses.

His manner toward her was surly, yet she never failed to meet him with a pleasant smile and a word of thanks when he brought her food to her, though more often than not she hurled the bulk of it through the tiny cabin port the moment that the door closed behind him.

During the days of anguish that followed Jane Clayton's imprisonment, but two questions were uppermost in her mind—the whereabouts of her husband and her son. She fully believed that the baby was aboard the *Kincaid*, provided that he still lived, but whether Tarzan had been permitted to live after having been lured aboard the evil craft she could not guess.

She knew, of course, the deep hatred that the Russian felt for the Englishman, and she could think of but one reason for having him brought aboard the ship—to dispatch him in comparative safety in revenge for his having thwarted Rokoff's pet schemes, and for having been at last the means of landing him in a French prison.

Tarzan, on his part, lay in the darkness of his cell, ignorant of the fact that his wife was a prisoner in the cabin almost above his head.

The same Swede that served Jane brought his meals to him, but, though on several occasions Tarzan had tried to draw the man into conversation, he had been unsuccessful. He had hoped to learn through this fellow whether his little son was aboard the *Kincaid*, but to every question upon this or kindred subjects the fellow returned but one reply, "Ay tank it blow purty soon purty hard." So after several attempts Tarzan gave it up.

For weeks that seemed months to the two prisoners the little steamer forged on they knew not where. Once the *Kincaid* stopped to coal, only immediately to take up the seemingly interminable voyage.

Rokoff had visited Jane Clayton but once since he had locked her in the tiny cabin. He had come gaunt and hollow-eyed from a long siege of sea-sickness. The object of his visit was to obtain from her her personal cheque for a large sum in return for a guarantee of her personal safety and return to England.

"When you set me down safely in any civilized port, together with my son and my husband," she replied, "I will pay you in gold twice the amount you ask; but until then you shall not have a cent, nor the promise of a cent under any other conditions."

"You will give me the cheque I ask," he replied with a snarl, "or neither you nor your child nor your husband will ever again set foot within any port, civilized or otherwise."

"I would not trust you," she replied. "What guarantee have I that you would not take my money and then do as you pleased with me and mine regardless of your promise?"

"I think you will do as I bid," he said, turning to leave the cabin. "Remember that I have your son—if you chance to hear the agonized wail of a tortured child it may console you to reflect that it is because of your stubbornness that the baby suffers—and that it is your baby."

"You would not do it!" cried the girl. "You would not—could not be so fiendishly cruel!"

"It is not I that am cruel, but you," he returned, "for you permit a paltry sum of money to stand between your baby and immunity from suffering."

The end of it was that Jane Clayton wrote out a cheque of large denomination and handed it to Nikolas Rokoff, who left her cabin with a grin of satisfaction upon his lips.

The following day the hatch was removed from Tarzan's cell, and as he looked up he saw Paulvitch's head framed in the square of light above him.

"Come up," commanded the Russian. "But bear in mind that you will be shot if you make a single move to attack me or any other aboard the ship."

The ape-man swung himself lightly to the deck. About him, but at a respectful distance, stood a half-dozen sailors armed with rifles and revolvers. Facing him was Paulvitch.

Tarzan looked about for Rokoff, who he felt sure must be aboard, but there was no sign of him.

"Lord Greystoke," commenced the Russian, "by your continued and wanton interference with M. Rokoff and his plans you have at last brought yourself and your family to this unfortunate extremity. You have only yourself to thank. As you may imagine, it has cost M. Rokoff a large amount of money to finance this expedition, and, as you are the sole cause of it, he naturally looks to you for reimbursement.

"Further, I may say that only by meeting M. Rokoff's just demands may you avert the most unpleasant consequences to your wife and child, and at the same time retain your own life and regain your liberty."

"What is the amount?" asked Tarzan. "And what assurance have I that you will live up to your end of the agreement? I have little reason to trust two such scoundrels as you and Rokoff, you know."

The Russian flushed.

"You are in no position to deliver insults," he said. "You have no assurance that we will live up to our agreement other than my word, but you have before you the assurance that we can make short work of you if you do not write out the cheque we demand.

"Unless you are a greater fool than I imagine, you should know that there is nothing that would give us greater pleasure than to order these men to fire. That we do not is because we have other plans for punishing you that would be entirely upset by your death."

"Answer one question," said Tarzan. "Is my son on board this ship?"

"No," replied Alexis Paulvitch, "your son is quite safe elsewhere; nor will he be killed until you refuse to accede to our fair demands. If it becomes necessary to kill you, there will be no reason for not killing the child, since with you gone the one whom we wish to punish through the boy will be gone, and he will then be to us only a constant source of danger and embarrassment. You see, therefore, that you may only save the life of your son by saving your own, and you can only save your own by giving us the cheque we ask."

"Very well," replied Tarzan, for he knew that he could trust them to carry out any sinister threat that Paulvitch had made, and there was a bare chance that by conceding their demands he might save the boy.

That they would permit him to live after he had appended his name to the cheque never occurred to him as being within the realms of probability. But he was determined to give them such a battle as they would never forget, and possibly to take Paulvitch with him into eternity. He was only sorry that it was not Rokoff.

He took his pocket cheque-book and fountain-pen from his pocket.

"What is the amount?" he asked.

Paulvitch named an enormous sum. Tarzan could scarce restrain a smile.

Their very cupidity was to prove the means of their undoing, in the matter of the ransom at least. Purposely he hesitated and haggled over the amount, but Paulvitch was obdurate. Finally the ape-man wrote out his cheque for a larger sum than stood to his credit at the bank.

As he turned to hand the worthless slip of paper to the Russian his glance chanced to pass across the starboard bow of the *Kincaid*. To his surprise he saw that the ship lay within a few hundred yards of land. Almost down to the water's edge ran a dense tropical jungle, and behind was higher land clothed in forest.

Paulvitch noted the direction of his gaze.

"You are to be set at liberty here," he said.

Tarzan's plan for immediate physical revenge upon the Russian vanished. He thought the land before him the mainland of Africa, and he knew that should they liberate him here he could doubtless find his way to civilization with comparative ease.

Paulvitch took the cheque.

"Remove your clothing," he said to the ape-man. "Here you will not need it."

Tarzan demurred.

Paulvitch pointed to the armed sailors. Then the Englishman slowly divested himself of his clothing.

A boat was lowered, and, still heavily guarded, the ape-man

was rowed ashore. Half an hour later the sailors had returned to the *Kincaid*, and the steamer was slowly getting under way.

As Tarzan stood upon the narrow strip of beach watching the departure of the vessel he saw a figure appear at the rail and call aloud to attract his attention.

The ape-man had been about to read a note that one of the sailors had handed him as the small boat that bore him to the shore was on the point of returning to the steamer, but at the hail from the vessel's deck he looked up.

He saw a black-bearded man who laughed at him in derision as he held high above his head the figure of a little child. Tarzan half started as though to rush through the surf and strike out for the already moving steamer; but realizing the futility of so rash an act he halted at the water's edge.

Thus he stood, his gaze riveted upon the *Kincaid* until it disappeared beyond a projecting promontory of the coast.

From the jungle at his back fierce bloodshot eyes glared from beneath shaggy overhanging brows upon him.

Little monkeys in the tree-tops chattered and scolded, and from the distance of the inland forest came the scream of a leopard.

But still John Clayton, Lord Greystoke, stood deaf and unseeing, suffering the pangs of keen regret for the opportunity that he had wasted because he had been so gullible as to place credence in a single statement of the first lieutenant of his arch-enemy.

"I have at least," he thought, "one consolation—the knowledge that Jane is safe in London. Thank Heaven she, too, did not fall into the clutches of those villains."

Behind him the hairy thing whose evil eyes had been watching his as a cat watches a mouse was creeping stealthily toward him.

Where were the trained senses of the savage ape-man?

Where the acute hearing?

Where the uncanny sense of scent?

III

BEASTS AT BAY

lowly Tarzan unfolded the note the sailor had thrust into his hand, and read it. At first it made little impression on his sorrow-numbed senses, but finally the full purport of the hideous plot of revenge unfolded itself before his imagination.

"This will explain to you" [the note read] *"the exact nature of my intentions relative to your offspring and to you.*

"You were born an ape. You lived naked in the jungles—to your own we have returned you; but your son shall rise a step above his sire. It is the immutable law of evolution.

"The father was a beast, but the son shall be a man—he shall take the next ascending step in the scale of progress. He shall be no naked beast of the jungle, but shall wear a loin-cloth and copper anklets, and, perchance, a ring in his nose, for he is to be reared by men—a tribe of savage cannibals.

"I might have killed you, but that would have curtailed the full measure of the punishment you have earned at my hands.

"Dead, you could not have suffered in the knowledge of your son's plight; but living and in a place from which you may not escape to seek or succour your child, you shall suffer worse than death for all the years of your life in contemplation of the horrors of your son's existence.

"This, then, is to be a part of your punishment for having dared to pit yourself against

N. R.

"P.S.—The balance of your punishment has to do with what shall presently befall your wife—that I shall leave to your imagination."

As he finished reading, a slight sound behind him brought him back with a start to the world of present realities.

Instantly his senses awoke, and he was again Tarzan of the Apes.

As he wheeled about, it was a beast at bay, vibrant with the instinct of self-preservation, that faced a huge bull-ape that was already charging down upon him.

The two years that had elapsed since Tarzan had come out of the savage forest with his rescued mate had witnessed slight diminution of the mighty powers that had made him the invincible lord of the jungle. His great estates in Uziri had claimed much of his time and attention, and there he had found ample field for the practical use and retention of his almost superhuman powers; but naked and unarmed to do battle with the shaggy, bull-necked beast that now confronted him was a test that the ape-man would scarce have welcomed at any period of his wild existence.

But there was no alternative other than to meet the rage-maddened creature with the weapons with which nature had endowed him.

Over the bull's shoulder Tarzan could see now the heads and shoulders of perhaps a dozen more of these mighty fore-runners of primitive man.

He knew, however, that there was little chance that they would attack him, since it is not within the reasoning powers of the anthropoid to be able to weigh or appreciate the value of concentrated action against an enemy—otherwise they would long since have become the dominant creatures of their haunts, so tremendous a power of destruction lies in their mighty thews and savage fangs.

With a low snarl the beast now hurled himself at Tarzan, but the ape-man had found, among other things in the haunts of civilized man, certain methods of scientific warfare that are unknown to the jungle folk.

Whereas, a few years since, he would have met the brute rush with brute force, he now sidestepped his antagonist's headlong charge, and as the brute hurtled past him swung a mighty right to the pit of the ape's stomach.

With a howl of mingled rage and anguish the great anthropoid bent double and sank to the ground, though almost instantly he was again struggling to his feet.

Before he could regain them, however, his white-skinned foe had wheeled and pounced upon him, and in the act there dropped from the shoulders of the English lord the last shred of his superficial mantle of civilization.

Once again he was the jungle beast revelling in bloody conflict with his kind. Once again he was Tarzan, son of Kala the she-ape.

His strong, white teeth sank into the hairy throat of his enemy as he sought the pulsing jugular.

Powerful fingers held the mighty fangs from his own flesh, or clenched and beat with the power of a steam-hammer upon the snarling, foam-flecked face of his adversary.

In a circle about them the balance of the tribe of apes stood watching and enjoying the struggle. They muttered low gutturals of approval as bits of white hide or hairy bloodstained skin were torn from one contestant or the other. But they were silent in amazement and expectation when they saw the mighty white ape wriggle upon the back of their king, and, with steel muscles tensed beneath the armpits of his antagonist, bear down mightily with his open palms upon the back of the thick bullneck, so that the king ape could but shriek in agony and flounder helplessly about upon the thick mat of jungle grass.

As Tarzan had overcome the huge Terkoz that time years before when he had been about to set out upon his quest for human beings of his own kind and colour, so now he overcame this other great ape with the same wrestling hold upon which he had stumbled by accident during that other combat. The little audience of fierce anthropoids heard the creaking of their king's neck mingling with his agonized shrieks and hideous roaring.

Then there came a sudden crack, like the breaking of a stout limb before the fury of the wind. The bullet-head crumpled forward upon its flaccid neck against the great hairy chest—the roaring and the shrieking ceased.

The little pig-eyes of the onlookers wandered from the still form of their leader to that of the white ape that was rising to its feet beside the vanquished, then back to their king as though in wonder that he did not arise and slay this presumptuous stranger.

They saw the new-comer place a foot upon the neck of the quiet figure at his feet and, throwing back his head, give vent to the wild, uncanny challenge of the bull-ape that has made a kill. Then they knew that their king was dead.

Across the jungle rolled the horrid notes of the victory cry. The little monkeys in the tree-tops ceased their chattering. The harsh-voiced, brilliant-plumed birds were still. From afar came the answering wail of a leopard and the deep roar of a lion.

It was the old Tarzan who turned questioning eyes upon the little knot of apes before him. It was the old Tarzan who shook his head as though to toss back a heavy mane that had fallen before his face—an old habit dating from the days that his great shock of thick, black hair had fallen about his shoulders, and often tumbled before his eyes when it had meant life or death to him to have his vision unobstructed.

The ape-man knew that he might expect an immediate attack on the part of that particular surviving bull-ape who felt himself best fitted to contend for the kingship of the tribe. Among his own apes he knew that it was not unusual for an entire stranger to enter a community and, after having dispatched the king, assume the leadership of the tribe himself, together with the fallen monarch's mates.

On the other hand, if he made no attempt to follow them, they might move slowly away from him, later to fight among themselves for the supremacy. That he could be king of them, if he so chose, he was confident; but he was not sure he cared to assume the sometimes irksome duties of that position, for he could see no particular advantage to be gained thereby.

One of the younger apes, a huge, splendidly muscled brute, was edging threateningly closer to the ape-man. Through his bared fighting fangs there issued a low, sullen growl. Tarzan watched his every move, standing rigid as a statue. To have fallen back a step would have been to precipitate an immediate charge; to have rushed forward to meet the other might have had the same result, or it might have put the bellicose one to flight—it all depended upon the young bull's stock of courage.

To stand perfectly still, waiting, was the middle course. In this event the bull would, according to custom, approach quite close to the object of his attention, growling hideously and baring slavering fangs. Slowly he would circle about the other, as though with a chip upon his shoulder; and this he did, even as Tarzan had foreseen.

It might be a bluff royal, or, on the other hand, so unstable is the mind of an ape, a passing impulse might hurl the hairy mass, tearing and rending, upon the man without an instant's warning.

As the brute circled him Tarzan turned slowly, keeping his eyes ever upon the eyes of his antagonist. He had appraised the young bull as one who had never quite felt equal to the task of overthrowing his former king, but who one day would have done so. Tarzan saw that the beast was of wondrous proportions, standing over seven feet upon his short, bowed legs.

His great, hairy arms reached almost to the ground even when he stood erect, and his fighting fangs, now quite close to Tarzan's face, were exceptionally long and sharp. Like the others of his tribe, he differed in several minor essentials from the apes of Tarzan's boyhood.

At first the ape-man had experienced a thrill of hope at sight of the shaggy bodies of the anthropoids—a hope that by some strange freak of fate he had been again returned to his own tribe; but a closer inspection had convinced him that these were another species.

As the threatening bull continued his stiff and jerky circling of the ape-man, much after the manner that you have noted among dogs when a strange canine comes among them, it occurred to Tarzan to discover if the language of his own tribe was identical with that of this other family, and so he addressed the brute in the language of the tribe of Kerchak.

"Who are you," he asked, "who threatens Tarzan of the Apes?"

The hairy brute looked his surprise.

"I am Akut," replied the other in the same simple, primal tongue which is so low in the scale of spoken languages that, as Tarzan had surmised, it was identical with that of the tribe in which the first twenty years of his life had been spent.

"I am Akut," said the ape. "Molak is dead. I am king. Go away or I shall kill you!"

"You saw how easily I killed Molak," replied Tarzan. "So I could kill you if I cared to be king. But Tarzan of the Apes would not be king of the tribe of Akut. All he wishes is to live in peace in this country. Let us be friends. Tarzan of the Apes can help you, and you can help Tarzan of the Apes."

"You cannot kill Akut," replied the other. "None is so great as Akut. Had you not killed Molak, Akut would have done so, for Akut was ready to be king."

For answer the ape-man hurled himself upon the great brute who during the conversation had slightly relaxed his vigilance.

In the twinkling of an eye the man had seized the wrist of the great ape, and before the other could grapple with him had whirled him about and leaped upon his broad back.

Down they went together, but so well had Tarzan's plan worked out that before ever they touched the ground he had gained the same hold upon Akut that had broken Molak's neck.

Slowly he brought the pressure to bear, and then as in days gone by he had given Kerchak the chance to surrender and live, so now he gave to Akut—in whom he saw a possible ally of great strength and resource—the option of living in amity with him or dying as he had just seen his savage and heretofore invincible king die.

"Ka-Goda?" whispered Tarzan to the ape beneath him.

It was the same question that he had whispered to Kerchak, and in the language of the apes it means, broadly, "Do you surrender?"

Akut thought of the creaking sound he had heard just before Molak's thick neck had snapped, and he shuddered.

He hated to give up the kingship, though, so again he struggled to free himself; but a sudden torturing pressure upon his vertebra brought an agonized "ka-goda!" from his lips.

Tarzan relaxed his grip a trifle.

"You may still be king, Akut," he said. "Tarzan told you that he did not wish to be king. If any question your right, Tarzan of the Apes will help you in your battles."

The ape-man rose, and Akut came slowly to his feet. Shaking his bullet head and growling angrily, he waddled toward his tribe, looking first at one and then at another of the larger bulls who might be expected to challenge his leadership.

But none did so; instead, they drew away as he approached, and presently the whole pack moved off into the jungle, and Tarzan was left alone once more upon the beach.

The ape-man was sore from the wounds that Molak had inflicted upon him, but he was inured to physical suffering and endured it with the calm and fortitude of the wild beasts that had taught him to lead the jungle life after the manner of all those that are born to it.

His first need, he realized, was for weapons of offence and defence, for his encounter with the apes, and the distant notes of the savage voices of Numa the lion, and Sheeta, the panther, warned him that his was to be no life of indolent ease and security.

It was but a return to the old existence of constant bloodshed and danger—to the hunting and the being hunted. Grim beasts would stalk him, as they had stalked him in the past, and never would there be a moment, by savage day or by cruel night, that he might not have instant need of such crude weapons as he could fashion from the materials at hand.

Upon the shore he found an out-cropping of brittle, igneous rock. By dint of much labour he managed to chip off a narrow sliver some twelve inches long by a quarter of an inch thick. One edge was quite thin for a few inches near the tip. It was the rudiment of a knife.

With it he went into the jungle, searching until he found a fallen tree of a certain species of hardwood with which he was familiar. From this he cut a small straight branch, which he pointed at one end.

Then he scooped a small, round hole in the surface of the prostrate trunk. Into this he crumbled a few bits of dry bark, minutely shredded, after which he inserted the tip of his pointed stick, and, sitting astride the bole of the tree, spun the slender rod rapidly between his palms.

After a time a thin smoke rose from the little mass of tinder, and a moment later the whole broke into flame. Heaping some larger twigs and sticks upon the tiny fire, Tarzan soon had quite a respectable blaze roaring in the enlarging cavity of the dead tree.

Into this he thrust the blade of his stone knife, and as it became superheated he would withdraw it, touching a spot near the thin edge with a drop of moisture. Beneath the wetted area a little flake of the glassy material would crack and scale away.

Thus, very slowly, the ape-man commenced the tedious operation of putting a thin edge upon his primitive hunting-knife.

He did not attempt to accomplish the feat all in one sitting. At first he was content to achieve a cutting edge of a couple of inches, with which he cut a long, pliable bow, a handle for his knife, a stout cudgel, and a goodly supply of arrows.

These he cached in a tall tree beside a little stream, and here also he constructed a platform with a roof of palm-leaves above it.

When all these things had been finished it was growing dusk, and Tarzan felt a strong desire to eat.

He had noted during the brief incursion he had made into the forest that a short distance up-stream from his tree there was a much-used watering place, where, from the trampled mud of either bank, it was evident beasts of all sorts and in great numbers came to drink. To this spot the hungry ape-man made his silent way.

Through the upper terrace of the tree-tops he swung with the grace and ease of a monkey. But for the heavy burden upon his heart he would have been happy in this return to the old free life of his boyhood.

Yet even with that burden he fell into the little habits and manners of his early life that were in reality more a part of him than the thin veneer of civilization that the past three years of his association with the white men of the outer world had spread lightly over him—a veneer that only hid the crudities of the beast that Tarzan of the Apes had been.

Could his fellow-peers of the House of Lords have seen him then they would have held up their noble hands in holy horror.

Silently he crouched in the lower branches of a great forest giant that overhung the trail, his keen eyes and sensitive ears strained into the distant jungle, from which he knew his dinner would presently emerge.

Nor had he long to wait.

Scarce had he settled himself to a comfortable position, his lithe, muscular legs drawn well up beneath him as the panther draws his hindquarters in preparation for the spring, than Bara, the deer, came daintily down to drink.

But more than Bara was coming. Behind the graceful buck came another which the deer could neither see nor scent, but whose movements were apparent to Tarzan of the Apes because of the elevated position of the ape-man's ambush.

He knew not yet exactly the nature of the thing that moved so stealthily through the jungle a few hundred yards behind the deer; but he was convinced that it was some great beast of prey stalking Bara for the selfsame purpose as that which prompted him to await the fleet animal. Numa, perhaps, or Sheeta, the panther.

In any event, Tarzan could see his repast slipping from his grasp unless Bara moved more rapidly toward the ford than at present.

Even as these thoughts passed through his mind some noise of the stalker in his rear must have come to the buck, for with a sudden start he paused for an instant, trembling, in his tracks, and then with a swift bound dashed straight for the river and Tarzan. It was his intention to flee through the shallow ford and escape upon the opposite side of the river.

Not a hundred yards behind him came Numa.

Tarzan could see him quite plainly now. Below the ape-man Bara was about to pass. Could he do it? But even as he asked himself the question the hungry man launched himself from his perch full upon the back of the startled buck.

In another instant Numa would be upon them both, so if the ape-man were to dine that night, or ever again, he must act quickly.

Scarcely had he touched the sleek hide of the deer with a momentum that sent the animal to its knees than he had grasped a horn in either hand, and with a single quick wrench twisted the animal's neck completely round, until he felt the vertebrae snap beneath his grip.

The lion was roaring in rage close behind him as he swung the deer across his shoulder, and, grasping a foreleg between his strong teeth, leaped for the nearest of the lower branches that swung above his head.

With both hands he grasped the limb, and, at the instant that Numa sprang, drew himself and his prey out of reach of the animal's cruel talons.

There was a thud below him as the baffled cat fell back to earth, and then Tarzan of the Apes, drawing his dinner farther up to the safety of a higher limb, looked down with grinning face into the gleaming yellow eyes of the other wild beast that glared up at him from beneath, and with taunting insults flaunted the tender carcass of his kill in the face of him whom he had cheated of it.

With his crude stone knife he cut a juicy steak from the hind-quarters, and while the great lion paced, growling, back and forth below him, Lord Greystoke filled his savage belly, nor ever in the choicest of his exclusive London clubs had a meal tasted more palat-able.

The warm blood of his kill smeared his hands and face and filled his nostrils with the scent that the savage carnivora love best.

And when he had finished he left the balance of the carcass in a high fork of the tree where he had dined, and with Numa trail-ing below him, still keen for revenge, he made his way back to his tree-top shelter, where he slept until the sun was high the following morning.

IV

SHEETA

he next few days were occupied by Tarzan in completing his weapons and exploring the jungle. He strung his bow with tendons from the buck upon which he had dined his first evening upon the new shore, and though he would have preferred the gut of Sheeta for the purpose, he was content to wait until opportunity permitted him to kill one of the great cats.

He also braided a long grass rope—such a rope as he had used so many years before to tantalize the ill-natured Tublat, and which later had developed into a wondrous effective weapon in the practised hands of the little ape-boy.

A sheath and handle for his hunting-knife he fashioned, and a quiver for arrows, and from the hide of Bara a belt and loin-cloth. Then he set out to learn something of the strange land in which he found himself. That it was not his old familiar west coast of the African continent he knew from the fact that it faced east—the rising sun came up out of the sea before the threshold of the jungle.

But that it was not the east coast of Africa he was equally positive, for he felt satisfied that the *Kincaid* had not passed through the Mediterranean, the Suez Canal, and the Red Sea, nor had she had time to round the Cape of Good Hope. So he was quite at a loss to know where he might be.

Sometimes he wondered if the ship had crossed the broad Atlantic to deposit him upon some wild South American shore; but the presence of Numa, the lion, decided him that such could not be the case.

As Tarzan made his lonely way through the jungle paralleling the shore, he felt strong upon him a desire for companionship, so that gradually he commenced to regret that he had not cast his lot with the apes. He had seen nothing of them since that first day, when the influences of civilization were still paramount within him.

Now he was more nearly returned to the Tarzan of old, and though he appreciated the fact that there could be little in common between himself and the great anthropoids, still they were better than no company at all.

Moving leisurely, sometimes upon the ground and again among the lower branches of the trees, gathering an occasional fruit or turning over a fallen log in search of the larger bugs, which he still found as palatable as of old, Tarzan had covered a mile or more when his attention was attracted by the scent of Sheeta up-wind ahead of him.

Now Sheeta, the panther, was one of whom Tarzan was exceptionally glad to fall in with, for he had it in mind not only to utilize the great cat's strong gut for his bow, but also to fashion a new quiver and loin-cloth from pieces of his hide. So, whereas the ape-man had gone carelessly before, he now became the personification of noiseless stealth.

Swiftly and silently he glided through the forest in the wake of the savage cat, nor was the pursuer, for all his noble birth, one whit less savage than the wild, fierce thing he stalked.

As he came closer to Sheeta he became aware that the panther on his part was stalking game of his own, and even as he realized this fact there came to his nostrils, wafted from his right by a vagrant breeze, the strong odour of a company of great apes.

The panther had taken to a large tree as Tarzan came within sight of him, and beyond and below him Tarzan saw the tribe of Akut lolling in a little, natural clearing. Some of them were dozing against the boles of trees, while others roamed about turning over bits of bark from beneath which they transferred the luscious grubs and beetles to their mouths.

Akut was the closest to Sheeta.

The great cat lay crouched upon a thick limb, hidden from the ape's view by dense foliage, waiting patiently until the anthropoid should come within range of his spring.

Tarzan cautiously gained a position in the same tree with the panther and a little above him. In his left hand he grasped his slim stone blade. He would have preferred to use his noose, but the foliage surrounding the huge cat precluded the possibility of an accurate throw with the rope.

Akut had now wandered quite close beneath the tree wherein lay the waiting death. Sheeta slowly edged his hind paws along the branch still further beneath him, and then with a hideous shriek he launched himself toward the great ape. The barest fraction of a second before his spring another beast of prey above him leaped, its weird and savage cry mingling with his.

As the startled Akut looked up he saw the panther almost above him, and already upon the panther's back the white ape that had bested him that day near the great water.

The teeth of the ape-man were buried in the back of Sheeta's neck and his right arm was round the fierce throat, while the left hand, grasping a slender piece of stone, rose and fell in mighty blows upon the panther's side behind the left shoulder.

Akut had just time to leap to one side to avoid being pinioned beneath these battling monsters of the jungle.

With a crash they came to earth at his feet. Sheeta was screaming, snarling, and roaring horribly; but the white ape clung tenaciously and in silence to the thrashing body of his quarry.

Steadily and remorselessly the stone knife was driven home through the glossy hide—time and again it drank deep, until with a final agonized lunge and shriek the great feline rolled over upon its side and, save for the spasmodic jerking of its muscles, lay quiet and still in death.

Then the ape-man raised his head, as he stood over the carcass of his kill, and once again through the jungle rang his wild and savage victory challenge.

Akut and the apes of Akut stood looking in startled wonder at the dead body of Sheeta and the lithe, straight figure of the man who had slain him.

Tarzan was the first to speak.

He had saved Akut's life for a purpose, and, knowing the limitations of the ape intellect, he also knew that he must make this purpose plain to the anthropoid if it were to serve him in the way he hoped.

"I am Tarzan of the Apes," he said, "Mighty hunter. Mighty fighter. By the great water I spared Akut's life when I might have taken it and become king of the tribe of Akut. Now I have saved Akut from death beneath the rending fangs of Sheeta.

"When Akut or the tribe of Akut is in danger, let them call to Tarzan thus"—and the ape-man raised the hideous cry with which the tribe of Kerchak had been wont to summon its absent members in times of peril.

"And," he continued, "when they hear Tarzan call to them, let them remember what he has done for Akut and come to him with great speed. Shall it be as Tarzan says?"

"*Huh!*" assented Akut, and from the members of his tribe there rose a unanimous "*Huh.*"

Then, presently, they went to feeding again as though nothing had happened, and with them fed John Clayton, Lord Greystoke.

He noticed, however, that Akut kept always close to him, and was often looking at him with a strange wonder in his little bloodshot eyes, and once he did a thing that Tarzan during all his long years among the apes had never before seen an ape do—he found a particularly tender morsel and handed it to Tarzan.

As the tribe hunted, the glistening body of the ape-man mingled with the brown, shaggy hides of his companions. Oftentimes they brushed together in passing, but the apes had already taken his presence for granted, so that he was as much one of them as Akut himself.

If he came too close to a she with a young baby, the former would bare her great fighting fangs and growl ominously, and occasionally a truculent young bull would snarl a warning if Tarzan approached while the former was eating. But in those things the treatment was no different from that which they accorded any other member of the tribe.

Tarzan on his part felt very much at home with these fierce, hairy progenitors of primitive man. He skipped nimbly out of reach of each threatening female—for such is the way of apes, if they be not in one of their occasional fits of bestial rage—and he growled back at the truculent young bulls, baring his canine teeth even as they. Thus easily he fell back into the way of his early life, nor did it seem that he had ever tasted association with creatures of his own kind.

For the better part of a week he roamed the jungle with his new friends, partly because of a desire for companionship and partially through a well-laid plan to impress himself indelibly upon their memories, which at best are none too long; for Tarzan from past experience knew that it might serve him in good stead to have a tribe of these powerful and terrible beasts at his call. When he was convinced that he had succeeded to some extent in fixing his identity upon them he decided to again take up his exploration. To this end he set out toward the north early one day, and, keeping parallel with the shore, travelled rapidly until almost nightfall.

When the sun rose the next morning he saw that it lay almost directly to his right as he stood upon the beach instead of straight out across the water as heretofore, and so he reasoned that the shore line had trended toward the west. All the second day he continued his rapid course, and when Tarzan of the Apes sought speed, he passed through the middle terrace of the forest with the rapidity of a squirrel.

That night the sun set straight out across the water opposite the land, and then the ape-man guessed at last the truth that he had been suspecting.

Rokoff had set him ashore upon an island.

He might have known it! If there was any plan that would render his position more harrowing he should have known that such would be the one adopted by the Russian, and what could be more terrible than to leave him to a lifetime of suspense upon an uninhabited island?

Rokoff doubtless had sailed directly to the mainland, where it would be a comparatively easy thing for him to find the means of delivering the infant Jack into the hands of the cruel and savage foster-parents, who, as his note had threatened, would have the upbringing of the child.

Tarzan shuddered as he thought of the cruel suffering the little one must endure in such a life, even though he might fall into the hands of individuals whose intentions toward him were of the kindest. The ape-man had had sufficient experience with the lower savages of Africa to know that even there may be found the cruder virtues of charity and humanity; but their lives were at best but a series of terrible privations, dangers, and sufferings.

Then there was the horrid after-fate that awaited the child as he grew to manhood. The horrible practices that would form a part of his life-training would alone be sufficient to bar him forever from association with those of his own race and station in life.

A cannibal! His little boy a savage man-eater! It was too horrible to contemplate.

The filed teeth, the slit nose, the little face painted hideously. Tarzan groaned. Could he but feel the throat of the Russ fiend beneath his steel fingers!

And Jane!

What tortures of doubt and fear and uncertainty she must be suffering. He felt that his position was infinitely less terrible than hers, for he at least knew that one of his loved ones was safe at home, while she had no idea of the whereabouts of either her husband or her son.

It is well for Tarzan that he did not guess the truth, for the knowledge would have but added a hundredfold to his suffering.

As he moved slowly through the jungle his mind absorbed by his gloomy thoughts, there presently came to his ears a strange scratching sound which he could not translate.

Cautiously he moved in the direction from which it emanated, presently coming upon a huge panther pinned beneath a fallen tree.

As Tarzan approached, the beast turned, snarling, toward him, struggling to extricate itself; but one great limb across its back and the smaller entangling branches pinioning its legs prevented it from moving but a few inches in any direction.

The ape-man stood before the helpless cat fitting an arrow to his bow that he might dispatch the beast that otherwise must die of starvation; but even as he drew back the shaft a sudden whim stayed his hand.

Why rob the poor creature of life and liberty, when it would be so easy a thing to restore both to it! He was sure from the fact that the panther moved all its limbs in its futile struggle for freedom that its spine was uninjured, and for the same reason he knew that none of its limbs were broken.

Relaxing his bowstring, he returned the arrow to the quiver and, throwing the bow about his shoulder, stepped closer to the pinioned beast.

On his lips was the soothing, purring sound that the great cats themselves made when contented and happy. It was the nearest approach to a friendly advance that Tarzan could make in the language of Sheeta.

The panther ceased his snarling and eyed the ape-man closely. To lift the tree's great weight from the animal it was necessary to come within reach of those long, strong talons, and when the tree had been removed the man would be totally at the mercy of the savage beast; but to Tarzan of the Apes fear was a thing unknown.

Having decided, he acted promptly.

Unhesitatingly, he stepped into the tangle of branches close to the panther's side, still voicing his friendly and conciliatory purr. The cat turned his head toward the man, eyeing him steadily—questioningly. The long fangs were bared, but more in preparedness than threat.

Tarzan put a broad shoulder beneath the bole of the tree, and as he did so his bare leg pressed against the cat's silken side, so close was the man to the great beast.

Slowly Tarzan extended his giant thews.

The great tree with its entangling branches rose gradually from the panther, who, feeling the encumbering weight diminish, quickly crawled from beneath. Tarzan let the tree fall back to earth, and the two beasts turned to look upon one another.

A grim smile lay upon the ape-man's lips, for he knew that he had taken his life in his hands to free this savage jungle fellow; nor would it have surprised him had the cat sprung upon him the instant that it had been released.

But it did not do so. Instead, it stood a few paces from the tree watching the ape-man clamber out of the maze of fallen branches.

Once outside, Tarzan was not three paces from the panther. He might have taken to the higher branches of the trees upon the opposite side, for Sheeta cannot climb to the heights to which the ape-man can go; but something, a spirit of bravado perhaps, prompted him to approach the panther as though to discover if any feeling of gratitude would prompt the beast to friendliness.

As he approached the mighty cat the creature stepped warily

to one side, and the ape-man brushed past him within a foot of the dripping jaws, and as he continued on through the forest the panther followed on behind him, as a hound follows at heel.

For a long time Tarzan could not tell whether the beast was following out of friendly feelings or merely stalking him against the time he should be hungry; but finally he was forced to believe that the former incentive it was that prompted the animal's action.

Later in the day the scent of a deer sent Tarzan into the trees, and when he had dropped his noose about the animal's neck he called to Sheeta, using a purr similar to that which he had utilized to pacify the brute's suspicions earlier in the day, but a trifle louder and more shrill.

It was similar to that which he had heard panthers use after a kill when they had been hunting in pairs.

Almost immediately there was a crashing of the underbrush close at hand, and the long, lithe body of his strange companion broke into view.

At sight of the body of Bara and the smell of blood the panther gave forth a shrill scream, and a moment later two beasts were feeding side by side upon the tender meat of the deer.

For several days this strangely assorted pair roamed the jungle together.

When one made a kill he called the other, and thus they fed well and often.

On one occasion as they were dining upon the carcass of a boar that Sheeta had dispatched, Numa, the lion, grim and terrible, broke through the tangled grasses close beside them.

With an angry, warning roar he sprang forward to chase them from their kill. Sheeta bounded into a near-by thicket, while Tarzan took to the low branches of an overhanging tree.

Here the ape-man unloosed his grass rope from about his neck, and as Numa stood above the body of the boar, challenging head erect, he dropped the sinuous noose about the maned neck, drawing the stout strands taut with a sudden jerk. At the same time he called shrilly to Sheeta, as he drew the struggling lion upward until only his hind feet touched the ground.

Quickly he made the rope fast to a stout branch, and as the panther, in answer to his summons, leaped into sight, Tarzan dropped to the earth beside the struggling and infuriated Numa, and with a long sharp knife sprang upon him at one side even as Sheeta did upon the other.

The panther tore and rent Numa upon the right, while the ape-man struck home with his stone knife upon the other, so that before the mighty clawing of the king of beasts had succeeded in parting the rope he hung quite dead and harmless in the noose.

And then upon the jungle air there rose in unison from two savage throats the victory cry of the bull-ape and the panther, blended into one frightful and uncanny scream.

As the last notes died away in a long-drawn, fearsome wail, a score of painted warriors, drawing their long war-canoe upon the beach, halted to stare in the direction of the jungle and to listen.

V

Mugambi

y the time that Tarzan had travelled entirely about the coast of the island, and made several trips inland from various points, he was sure that he was the only human being upon it.

Nowhere had he found any sign that men had stopped even temporarily upon this shore, though, of course, he knew that so quickly does the rank vegetation of the tropics erase all but the most permanent of human monuments that he might be in error in his deductions.

The day following the killing of Numa, Tarzan and Sheeta came upon the tribe of Akut. At sight of the panther the great apes took to flight, but after a time Tarzan succeeded in recalling them.

It had occurred to him that it would be at least an interesting experiment to attempt to reconcile these hereditary enemies. He welcomed anything that would occupy his time and his mind beyond the filling of his belly and the gloomy thoughts to which he fell prey the moment that he became idle.

To communicate his plan to the apes was not a particularly difficult matter, though their narrow and limited vocabulary was strained in the effort; but to impress upon the little, wicked brain of Sheeta that he was to hunt with and not for his legitimate prey proved a task almost beyond the powers of the ape-man.

Tarzan, among his other weapons, possessed a long, stout cudgel, and after fastening his rope about the panther's neck he used this instrument freely upon the snarling beast, endeavouring in this way to impress upon its memory that it must not attack the great, shaggy manlike creatures that had approached more closely once they had seen the purpose of the rope about Sheeta's neck.

That the cat did not turn and rend Tarzan is something of a miracle which may possibly be accounted for by the fact that twice when it turned growling upon the ape-man he had rapped it sharply upon its sensitive nose, inculcating in its mind thereby a most wholesome fear of the cudgel and the ape-beasts behind it.

It is a question if the original cause of his attachment for Tarzan was still at all clear in the mind of the panther, though doubtless some subconscious suggestion, superinduced by this primary reason and aided and abetted by the habit of the past few days, did much to compel the beast to tolerate treatment at his hands that would have sent it at the throat of any other creature.

Then, too, there was the compelling force of the manmind exerting its powerful influence over this creature of a lower order, and, after all, it may have been this that proved the most potent factor in Tarzan's supremacy over Sheeta and the other beasts of the jungle that had from time to time fallen under his domination.

Be that as it may, for days the man, the panther, and the great apes roamed their savage haunts side by side, making their kills together and sharing them with one another, and of all the fierce and savage band none was more terrible than the smooth-skinned, powerful beast that had been but a few short months before a familiar figure in many a London drawing room.

Sometimes the beasts separated to follow their own inclinations for an hour or a day, and it was upon one of these occasions when the ape-man had wandered through the tree-tops toward the beach, and was stretched in the hot sun upon the sand, that from the low summit of a near-by promontory a pair of keen eyes discovered him.

For a moment the owner of the eyes looked in astonishment at the figure of the savage white man basking in the rays of that hot, tropic sun; then he turned, making a sign to some one behind him. Presently another pair of eyes were looking down upon the ape-man, and then another and another, until a full score of hideously trapped, savage warriors were lying upon their bellies along the crest of the ridge watching the white-skinned stranger.

They were down wind from Tarzan, and so their scent was not carried to him, and as his back was turned half toward them he did not see their cautious advance over the edge of the promontory and down through the rank grass toward the sandy beach where he lay.

Big fellows they were, all of them, their barbaric headdresses and grotesquely painted faces, together with their many metal ornaments and gorgeously coloured feathers, adding to their wild, fierce appearance.

Once at the foot of the ridge, they came cautiously to their feet, and, bent half-double, advanced silently upon the unconscious white man, their heavy war-clubs swinging menacingly in their brawny hands.

The mental suffering that Tarzan's sorrowful thoughts induced had the effect of numbing his keen, perceptive faculties, so that the advancing savages were almost upon him before he became aware that he was no longer alone upon the beach.

So quickly, though, were his mind and muscles wont to react in unison to the slightest alarm that he was upon his feet and facing his enemies, even as he realized that something was behind him. As he sprang to his feet the warriors leaped toward him with raised clubs and savage yells, but the foremost went down to sudden death beneath the long, stout stick of the ape-man, and then the lithe, sinewy figure was among them, striking right and left with a fury, power, and precision that brought panic to the ranks of the blacks.

For a moment they withdrew, those that were left of them, and consulted together at a short distance from the ape-man, who stood with folded arms, a half-smile upon his handsome face, watching them. Presently they advanced upon him once more, this time wielding their heavy war-spears. They were between Tarzan and the jungle, in a little semicircle that closed in upon him as they advanced.

There seemed to the ape-man but slight chance to escape the final charge when all the great spears should be hurled simultaneously at him; but if he had desired to escape there was no way other than through the ranks of the savages except the open sea behind him.

His predicament was indeed most serious when an idea occurred to him that altered his smile to a broad grin. The warriors were still some little distance away, advancing slowly, making, after the manner of their kind, a frightful din with their savage yells and the pounding of their naked feet upon the ground as they leaped up and down in a fantastic war dance.

Then it was that the ape-man lifted his voice in a series of wild, weird screams that brought the blacks to a sudden, perplexed halt. They looked at one another questioningly, for here was a sound so hideous that their own frightful din faded into insignificance beside it. No human throat could have formed those bestial notes, they were sure, and yet with their own eyes they had seen this white man open his mouth to pour forth his awful cry.

But only for a moment they hesitated, and then with one accord they again took up their fantastic advance upon their prey; but even then a sudden crashing in the jungle behind them brought them once more to a halt, and as they turned to look in the direction of this new noise there broke upon their startled visions a sight that may well have frozen the blood of braver men than the Wagambi.

Leaping from the tangled vegetation of the jungle's rim came a huge panther, with blazing eyes and bared fangs, and in his wake a score of mighty, shaggy apes lumbering rapidly toward them, half erect upon their short, bowed legs, and with their long arms reaching to the ground, where their horny knuckles bore the weight of their ponderous bodies as they lurched from side to side in their grotesque advance.

The beasts of Tarzan had come in answer to his call.

Before the Wagambi could recover from their astonishment the frightful horde was upon them from one side and Tarzan of the Apes from the other. Heavy spears were hurled and mighty war-clubs wielded, and though apes went down never to rise, so, too, went down the men of Ugambi.

Sheeta's cruel fangs and tearing talons ripped and tore at the black hides. Akut's mighty yellow tusks found the jugular of more than one sleek-skinned savage, and Tarzan of the Apes was here and there and everywhere, urging on his fierce allies and taking a heavy toll with his long, slim knife.

In a moment the blacks had scattered for their lives, but of the score that had crept down the grassy sides of the promontory only a single warrior managed to escape the horde that had overwhelmed his people.

This one was Mugambi, chief of the Wagambi of Ugambi, and as he disappeared in the tangled luxuriousness of the rank growth upon the ridge's summit only the keen eyes of the ape-man saw the direction of his flight.

Leaving his pack to eat their fill upon the flesh of their victims— flesh that he could not touch—Tarzan of the Apes pursued the single survivor of the bloody fray. Just beyond the ridge he came within sight of the fleeing black, making with headlong leaps for a long war-canoe that was drawn well up upon the beach above the high tide surf.

Noiseless as the fellow's shadow, the ape-man raced after the terror-stricken black. In the white man's mind was a new plan, awakened by sight of the war-canoe. If these men had come to his island from another, or from the mainland, why not utilize their craft to make his way to the country from which they had come? Evidently it was an inhabited country, and no doubt had occasional intercourse with the mainland, if it were not itself upon the continent of Africa.

A heavy hand fell upon the shoulder of the escaping Mugambi before he was aware that he was being pursued, and as he turned to do battle with his assailant giant fingers closed about his wrists and he was hurled to earth with a giant astride him before he could strike a blow in his own defence.

In the language of the West Coast, Tarzan spoke to the prostrate man beneath him.

"Who are you?" he asked.

"Mugambi, chief of the Wagambi," replied the black.

"I will spare your life," said Tarzan, "if you will promise to help me to leave this island. What do you answer?"

"I will help you," replied Mugambi. "But now that you have killed all my warriors, I do not know that even I can leave your country, for there will be none to wield the paddles, and without paddlers we cannot cross the water."

Tarzan rose and allowed his prisoner to come to his feet. The fellow was a magnificent specimen of manhood—a black counterpart in physique of the splendid white man whom he faced.

"Come!" said the ape-man, and started back in the direction from which they could hear the snarling and growling of the feasting pack. Mugambi drew back.

"They will kill us," he said.

"I think not," replied Tarzan. "They are mine."

Still the black hesitated, fearful of the consequences of approaching the terrible creatures that were dining upon the bodies of his warriors; but Tarzan forced him to accompany him, and presently the two emerged from the jungle in full view of the grisly spectacle upon the beach. At sight of the men the beasts looked up with menacing

613

growls, but Tarzan strode in among them, dragging the trembling Wagambi with him.

As he had taught the apes to accept Sheeta, so he taught them to adopt Mugambi as well, and much more easily; but Sheeta seemed quite unable to understand that though he had been called upon to devour Mugambi's warriors he was not to be allowed to proceed after the same fashion with Mugambi. However, being well filled, he contented himself with walking round the terror-stricken savage, emitting low, menacing growls the while he kept his flaming, baleful eyes riveted upon the black. Mugambi, on his part, clung closely to Tarzan, so that the ape-man could scarce control his laughter at the pitiable condition to which the chief's fear had reduced him; but at length the white took the great cat by the scruff of the neck and, dragging it quite close to the Wagambi, slapped it sharply upon the nose each time that it growled at the stranger.

At the sight of the thing—a man mauling with his bare hands one of the most relentless and fierce of the jungle carnivora—Mugambi's eyes bulged from their sockets, and from entertaining a sullen respect for the giant white man who had made him prisoner, the black felt an almost worshipping awe of Tarzan.

The education of Sheeta progressed so well that in a short time Mugambi ceased to be the object of his hungry attention, and the black felt a degree more of safety in his society.

To say that Mugambi was entirely happy or at ease in his new environment would not be to adhere strictly to the truth. His eyes were constantly rolling apprehensively from side to side as now one and now another of the fierce pack chanced to wander near him, so that for the most of the time it was principally the whites that showed.

Together Tarzan and Mugambi, with Sheeta and Akut, lay in wait at the ford for a deer, and when at a word from the ape-man the four of them leaped out upon the affrighted animal the black was sure that the poor creature died of fright before ever one of the great beasts touched it.

Mugambi built a fire and cooked his portion of the kill; but Tarzan, Sheeta, and Akut tore theirs, raw, with their sharp teeth, growling among themselves when one ventured to encroach upon the share of another.

It was not, after all, strange that the white man's ways should have been so much more nearly related to those of the beasts than were the savage blacks. We are, all of us, creatures of habit, and when the seeming necessity for schooling ourselves in new ways ceases to exist, we fall naturally and easily into the manners and customs which long usage has implanted ineradicably within us.

Mugambi from childhood had eaten no meat until it had been cooked, while Tarzan, on the other hand, had never tasted cooked food of any sort until he had grown almost to manhood, and only within the past three or four years had he eaten cooked meat. Not only did the habit of a lifetime prompt him to eat it raw, but the craving of his palate as well; for to him cooked flesh was spoiled flesh when compared with the rich and juicy meat of a fresh, hot kill.

That he could, with relish, eat raw meat that had been buried by himself weeks before, and enjoy small rodents and disgusting grubs, seems to us who have been always "civilized" a revolting fact; but had we learned in childhood to eat these things, and had we seen all those about us eat them, they would seem no more sickening to us now than do many of our greatest dainties, at which a savage African cannibal would look with repugnance and turn up his nose.

For instance, there is a tribe in the vicinity of Lake Rudolph that will eat no sheep or cattle, though its next neighbors do so. Near by is another tribe that eats donkey-meat—a custom most revolting to the surrounding tribes that do not eat donkey. So who may say that it is nice to eat snails and frogs' legs and oysters, but disgusting to feed upon grubs and beetles, or that a raw oyster, hoof, horns, and tail, is less revolting than the sweet, clean meat of a fresh-killed buck?

The next few days Tarzan devoted to the weaving of a barkcloth sail with which to equip the canoe, for he despaired of being able to teach the apes to wield the paddles, though he did manage to get several of them to embark in the frail craft which he and Mugambi paddled about inside the reef where the water was quite smooth.

During these trips he had placed paddles in their hands, when they attempted to imitate the movements of him and Mugambi, but so difficult is it for them long to concentrate upon a thing that he soon saw that it would require weeks of patient training before they would be able to make any effective use of these new implements, if, in fact, they should ever do so.

There was one exception, however, and he was Akut. Almost from the first he showed an interest in this new sport that revealed a much higher plane of intelligence than that attained by any of his tribe. He seemed to grasp the purpose of the paddles, and when Tarzan saw that this was so he took much pains to explain in the meagre language of the anthropoid how they might be used to the best advantage.

From Mugambi Tarzan learned that the mainland lay but a short distance from the island. It seemed that the Wagambi warriors had ventured too far out in their frail craft, and when caught by a heavy tide and a high wind from off-shore they had been driven out of sight of land. After paddling for a whole night, thinking that they were headed for home, they had seen this land at sunrise, and, still taking it for the mainland, had hailed it with joy, nor had Mugambi been aware that it was an island until Tarzan had told him that this was the fact.

The Wagambi chief was quite dubious as to the sail, for he had never seen such a contrivance used. His country lay far up the broad Ugambi River, and this was the first occasion that any of his people had found their way to the ocean.

Tarzan, however, was confident that with a good west wind

he could navigate the little craft to the mainland. At any rate, he decided, it would be preferable to perish on the way than to remain indefinitely upon this evidently uncharted island to which no ships might ever be expected to come.

And so it was that when the first fair wind rose he embarked upon his cruise, and with him he took as strange and fearsome a crew as ever sailed under a savage master.

Mugambi and Akut went with him, and Sheeta, the panther, and a dozen great males of the tribe of Akut.

VI

A Hideous Crew

he war-canoe with its savage load moved slowly toward the break in the reef through which it must pass to gain the open sea. Tarzan, Mugambi, and Akut wielded the paddles, for the shore kept the west wind from the little sail.

Sheeta crouched in the bow at the ape-man's feet, for it had seemed best to Tarzan always to keep the wicked beast as far from the other members of the party as possible, since it would require little or no provocation to send him at the throat of any than the white man, whom he evidently now looked upon as his master.

In the stern was Mugambi, and just in front of him squatted Akut, while between Akut and Tarzan the twelve hairy apes sat upon their haunches, blinking dubiously this way and that, and now and then turning their eyes longingly back toward shore.

All went well until the canoe had passed beyond the reef. Here the breeze struck the sail, sending the rude craft lunging among the waves that ran higher and higher as they drew away from the shore.

With the tossing of the boat the apes became panic-stricken. They first moved uneasily about, and then commenced grumbling and whining. With difficulty Akut kept them in hand for a time; but when a particularly large wave struck the dugout simultaneously with a little squall of wind their terror broke all bounds, and, leaping to their feet, they all but overturned the boat before Akut and Tarzan together could quiet them. At last calm was restored, and eventually the apes became accustomed to the strange antics of their craft, after which no more trouble was experienced with them.

The trip was uneventful, the wind held, and after ten hours' steady sailing the black shadows of the coast loomed close before the straining eyes of the ape-man in the bow. It was far too dark to distinguish whether they had approached close to the mouth of the Ugambi or not, so Tarzan ran in through the surf at the closest point to await the dawn.

The dugout turned broadside the instant that its nose touched the sand, and immediately it rolled over, with all its crew scrambling madly for the shore. The next breaker rolled them over and over, but eventually they all succeeded in crawling to safety, and in a moment more their ungainly craft had been washed up beside them.

The balance of the night the apes sat huddled close to one another for warmth; while Mugambi built a fire close to them over which he crouched. Tarzan and Sheeta, however, were of a different mind, for neither of them feared the jungle night, and the insistent craving of their hunger sent them off into the Stygian blackness of the forest in search of prey.

Side by side they walked when there was room for two abreast. At other times in single file, first one and then the other in advance. It was Tarzan who first caught the scent of meat—a bull buffalo—and presently the two came stealthily upon the sleeping beast in the midst of a dense jungle of reeds close to a river.

Closer and closer they crept toward the unsuspecting beast, Sheeta upon his right side and Tarzan upon his left nearest the great heart. They had hunted together now for some time, so that they worked in unison, with only low, purring sounds as signals.

For a moment they lay quite silent near their prey, and then at a sign from the ape-man Sheeta sprang upon the great back, burying his strong teeth in the bull's neck. Instantly the brute sprang to his feet with a bellow of pain and rage, and at the same instant Tarzan rushed in upon his left side with the stone knife, striking repeatedly behind the shoulder.

One of the ape-man's hands clutched the thick mane, and as the bull raced madly through the reeds the thing striking at his life was dragged beside him. Sheeta but clung tenaciously to his hold upon the neck and back, biting deep in an effort to reach the spine.

For several hundred yards the bellowing bull carried his two savage antagonists, until at last the blade found his heart, when with a final bellow that was half-scream he plunged headlong to the earth. Then Tarzan and Sheeta feasted to repletion.

After the meal the two curled up together in a thicket, the man's black head pillowed upon the tawny side of the panther. Shortly after dawn they awoke and ate again, and then returned to the beach that Tarzan might lead the balance of the pack to the kill.

When the meal was done the brutes were for curling up to sleep, so Tarzan and Mugambi set off in search of the Ugambi River. They had proceeded scarce a hundred yards when they came suddenly upon a broad stream, which the Negro instantly recognized as that down which he and his warriors had paddled to the sea upon their ill-starred expedition.

The two now followed the stream down to the ocean, finding that it emptied into a bay not over a mile from the point upon the beach at which the canoe had been thrown the night before.

Tarzan was much elated by the discovery, as he knew that in the vicinity of a large watercourse he should find natives, and from some of these he had little doubt but that he should obtain news of Rokoff and the child, for he felt reasonably certain that the Russian would rid himself of the baby as quickly as possible after having disposed of Tarzan.

He and Mugambi now righted and launched the dugout, though it was a most difficult feat in the face of the surf which rolled continuously in upon the beach; but at last they were successful, and soon

after were paddling up the coast toward the mouth of the Ugambi.
Here they experienced considerable difficulty in making an entrance
against the combined current and ebb tide, but by taking advantage
of eddies close in to shore they came about dusk to a point nearly
opposite the spot where they had left the pack asleep.

Making the craft fast to an overhanging bough, the two made
their way into the jungle, presently coming upon some of the apes
feeding upon fruit a little beyond the reeds where the buffalo had
fallen. Sheeta was not anywhere to be seen, nor did he return that
night, so that Tarzan came to believe that he had wandered away in
search of his own kind.

Early the next morning the ape-man led his band down to the
river, and as he walked he gave vent to a series of shrill cries. Presently from a great distance and faintly there came an answering
scream, and a half-hour later the lithe form of Sheeta bounded into
view where the others of the pack were clambering gingerly into the
canoe.

The great beast, with arched back and purring like a contented tabby, rubbed his sides against the ape-man, and then at a
word from the latter sprang lightly to his former place in the bow
of the dugout.

When all were in place it was discovered that two of the apes
of Akut were missing, and though both the king ape and Tarzan
called to them for the better part of an hour, there was no response,
and finally the boat put off without them. As it happened that the
two missing ones were the very same who had evinced the least
desire to accompany the expedition from the island, and had suffered the most from fright during the voyage, Tarzan was quite sure
that they had absented themselves purposely rather than again enter
the canoe.

As the party were putting in for the shore shortly after noon to
search for food a slender, naked savage watched them for a moment

from behind the dense screen of verdure which lined the river's bank, then he melted away up-stream before any of those in the canoe discovered him.

Like a deer he bounded along the narrow trail until, filled with the excitement of his news, he burst into a native village several miles above the point at which Tarzan and his pack had stopped to hunt.

"Another white man is coming!" he cried to the chief who squatted before the entrance to his circular hut. "Another white man, and with him are many warriors. They come in a great war-canoe to kill and rob as did the black-bearded one who has just left us."

Kaviri leaped to his feet. He had but recently had a taste of the white man's medicine, and his savage heart was filled with bitterness and hate. In another moment the rumble of the war-drums rose from the village, calling in the hunters from the forest and the tillers from the fields.

Seven war-canoes were launched and manned by paint-daubed, befeathered warriors. Long spears bristled from the rude battle-ships, as they slid noiselessly over the bosom of the water, propelled by giant muscles rolling beneath glistening, ebony hides.

There was no beating of tom-toms now, nor blare of native horn, for Kaviri was a crafty warrior, and it was in his mind to take no chances, if they could be avoided. He would swoop noiselessly down with his seven canoes upon the single one of the white man, and before the guns of the latter could inflict much damage upon his people he would have overwhelmed the enemy by force of numbers.

Kaviri's own canoe went in advance of the others a short distance, and as it rounded a sharp bend in the river where the swift current bore it rapidly on its way it came suddenly upon the thing that Kaviri sought.

So close were the two canoes to one another that the black had only an opportunity to note the white face in the bow of the oncoming craft before the two touched and his own men were upon their feet, yelling like mad devils and thrusting their long spears at the occupants of the other canoe.

But a moment later, when Kaviri was able to realize the nature of the crew that manned the white man's dugout, he would have given all the beads and iron wire that he possessed to have been safely within his distant village. Scarcely had the two craft come together than the frightful apes of Akut rose, growling and barking, from the bottom of the canoe, and, with long, hairy arms far outstretched, grasped the menacing spears from the hands of Kaviri's warriors.

The blacks were overcome with terror, but there was nothing to do other than to fight. Now came the other war-canoes rapidly down upon the two craft. Their occupants were eager to join the battle, for they thought that their foes were white men and their native porters.

They swarmed about Tarzan's craft; but when they saw the nature of the enemy all but one turned and paddled swiftly up-river. That one came too close to the ape-man's craft before its occupants realized that their fellows were pitted against demons instead of men. As it touched Tarzan spoke a few low words to Sheeta and Akut, so that before the attacking warriors could draw away there sprang upon them with a blood-freezing scream a huge panther, and into the other end of their canoe clambered a great ape.

At one end the panther wrought fearful havoc with his mighty talons and long, sharp fangs, while Akut at the other buried his yellow canines in the necks of those that came within his reach, hurling the terror-stricken blacks overboard as he made his way toward the centre of the canoe.

Kaviri was so busily engaged with the demons that had entered his own craft that he could offer no assistance to his warriors in the other. A giant of a white devil had wrested his spear from him as though he, the mighty Kaviri, had been but a new-born babe. Hairy monsters were overcoming his fighting men, and a black chieftain like himself was fighting shoulder to shoulder with the hideous pack that opposed him.

Kaviri battled bravely against his antagonist, for he felt that death had already claimed him, and so the least that he could do would be to sell his life as dearly as possible; but it was soon evident that his best was quite futile when pitted against the superhuman brawn and agility of the creature that at last found his throat and bent him back into the bottom of the canoe.

Presently Kaviri's head began to whirl—objects became confused and dim before his eyes—there was a great pain in his chest as he struggled for the breath of life that the thing upon him was shutting off for ever. Then he lost consciousness.

When he opened his eyes once more he found, much to his surprise, that he was not dead. He lay, securely bound, in the bottom of his own canoe. A great panther sat upon its haunches, looking down upon him.

Kaviri shuddered and closed his eyes again, waiting for the ferocious creature to spring upon him and put him out of his misery of terror.

After a moment, no rending fangs having buried themselves in his trembling body, he again ventured to open his eyes. Beyond the panther kneeled the white giant who had overcome him.

The man was wielding a paddle, while directly behind him Kaviri saw some of his own warriors similarly engaged. Back of them again squatted several of the hairy apes.

Tarzan, seeing that the chief had regained consciousness, addressed him.

"Your warriors tell me that you are the chief of a numerous people, and that your name is Kaviri," he said.

"Yes," replied the black.

"Why did you attack me? I came in peace."

"Another white man 'came in peace' three moons ago," replied

Kaviri; "and after we had brought him presents of a goat and cassava and milk, he set upon us with his guns and killed many of my people, and then went on his way, taking all of our goats and many of our young men and women."

"I am not as this other white man," replied Tarzan. "I should not have harmed you had you not set upon me. Tell me, what was the face of this bad white man like? I am searching for one who has wronged me. Possibly this may be the very one."

"He was a man with a bad face, covered with a great, black beard, and he was very, very wicked—yes, very wicked indeed."

"Was there a little white child with him?" asked Tarzan, his heart almost stopped as he awaited the black's answer.

"No, *bwana*," replied Kaviri, "the white child was not with this man's party—it was with the other party."

"Other party!" exclaimed Tarzan. "What other party?"

"With the party that the very bad white man was pursuing. There was a white man, woman, and the child, with six Mosula porters. They passed up the river three days ahead of the very bad white man. I think that they were running away from him." A white man, woman, and child! Tarzan was puzzled. The child must be his little Jack; but who could the woman be—and the man? Was it possible that one of Rokoff's confederates had conspired with some woman—who had accompanied the Russian—to steal the baby from him?

If this was the case, they had doubtless purposed returning the child to civilization and there either claiming a reward or holding the little prisoner for ransom.

But now that Rokoff had succeeded in chasing them far inland, up the savage river, there could be little doubt but that he would eventually overhaul them, unless, as was still more probable, they should be captured and killed by the very cannibals farther up the Ugambi, to whom, Tarzan was now convinced, it had been Rokoff's intention to deliver the baby.

As he talked to Kaviri the canoes had been moving steadily up-river toward the chief's village. Kaviri's warriors plied the paddles in the three canoes, casting sidelong, terrified glances at their hideous passengers. Three of the apes of Akut had been killed in the encounter, but there were, with Akut, eight of the frightful beasts remaining, and there was Sheeta, the panther, and Tarzan and Mugambi.

Kaviri's warriors thought that they had never seen so terrible a crew in all their lives. Momentarily they expected to be pounced upon and torn asunder by some of their captors; and, in fact, it was all that Tarzan and Mugambi and Akut could do to keep the snarling, ill-natured brutes from snapping at the glistening, naked bodies that brushed against them now and then with the movements of the paddlers, whose very fear added incitement to the beasts.

At Kaviri's camp Tarzan paused only long enough to eat the food that the blacks furnished, and arrange with the chief for a dozen men to man the paddles of his canoe.

Kaviri was only too glad to comply with any demands that the ape-man might make if only such compliance would hasten the departure of the horrid pack; but it was easier, he discovered, to promise men than to furnish them, for when his people learned his intentions those that had not already fled into the jungle proceeded to do so without loss of time, so that when Kaviri turned to point out those who were to accompany Tarzan, he discovered that he was the only member of his tribe left within the village.

Tarzan could not repress a smile.

"They do not seem anxious to accompany us," he said; "but just remain quietly here, Kaviri, and presently you shall see your people flocking to your side."

Then the ape-man rose, and, calling his pack about him, commanded that Mugambi remain with Kaviri, and disappeared in the jungle with Sheeta and the apes at his heels.

For half an hour the silence of the grim forest was broken only

by the ordinary sounds of the teeming life that but adds to its lowering loneliness. Kaviri and Mugambi sat alone in the palisaded village,
waiting.

Presently from a great distance came a hideous sound. Mugambi
recognized the weird challenge of the ape-man. Immediately from different points of the compass rose a horrid semicircle of similar shrieks
and screams, punctuated now and again by the blood-curdling cry of
a hungry panther.

VII

BETRAYED

he two savages, Kaviri and Mugambi, squatting before the entrance to Kaviri's hut, looked at one another—Kaviri with ill-concealed alarm.

"What is it?" he whispered.

"It is Bwana Tarzan and his people," replied Mugambi. "But what they are doing I know not, unless it be that they are devouring your people who ran away."

Kaviri shuddered and rolled his eyes fearfully toward the jungle. In all his long life in the savage forest he had never heard such an awful, fearsome din.

Closer and closer came the sounds, and now with them were mingled the terrified shrieks of women and children and of men. For twenty long minutes the blood-curdling cries continued, until they seemed but a stone's throw from the palisade. Kaviri rose to flee, but Mugambi seized and held him, for such had been the command of Tarzan.

A moment later a horde of terrified natives burst from the jungle, racing toward the shelter of their huts. Like frightened sheep they ran, and behind them, driving them as sheep might be driven, came Tarzan and Sheeta and the hideous apes of Akut.

Presently Tarzan stood before Kaviri, the old quiet smile upon his lips.

"Your people have returned, my brother," he said, "and now you may select those who are to accompany me and paddle my canoe."

Tremblingly Kaviri tottered to his feet, calling to his people to come from their huts; but none responded to his summons.

"Tell them," suggested Tarzan, "that if they do not come I shall send my people in after them."

Kaviri did as he was bid, and in an instant the entire population of the village came forth, their wide and frightened eyes rolling from one to another of the savage creatures that wandered about the village street.

Quickly Kaviri designated a dozen warriors to accompany Tarzan. The poor fellows went almost white with terror at the prospect of close contact with the panther and the apes in the narrow confines of the canoes; but when Kaviri explained to them that there was no escape—that Bwana Tarzan would pursue them with his grim horde should they attempt to run away from the duty—they finally went gloomily down to the river and took their places in the canoe.

It was with a sigh of relief that their chieftain saw the party disappear about a headland a short distance up-river.

For three days the strange company continued farther and farther into the heart of the savage country that lies on either side of the almost unexplored Ugambi. Three of the twelve warriors deserted during that time; but as several of the apes had finally learned the secret of the paddles, Tarzan felt no dismay because of the loss.

As a matter of fact, he could have travelled much more rapidly on shore, but he believed that he could hold his own wild crew together to better advantage by keeping them to the boat as much as possible. Twice a day they landed to hunt and feed, and at night they slept upon the bank of the mainland or on one of the numerous little islands that dotted the river.

Before them the natives fled in alarm, so that they found only deserted villages in their path as they proceeded. Tarzan was anxious to get in touch with some of the savages who dwelt upon the river's banks, but so far he had been unable to do so.

Finally he decided to take to the land himself, leaving his company to follow after him by boat. He explained to Mugambi the thing that he had in mind, and told Akut to follow the directions of the black.

"I will join you again in a few days," he said. "Now I go ahead to learn what has become of the very bad white man whom I seek."

At the next halt Tarzan took to the shore, and was soon lost to the view of his people.

The first few villages he came to were deserted, showing that news of the coming of his pack had travelled rapidly; but toward evening he came upon a distant cluster of thatched huts surrounded by a rude palisade, within which were a couple of hundred natives.

The women were preparing the evening meal as Tarzan of the Apes poised above them in the branches of a giant tree which overhung the palisade at one point.

The ape-man was at a loss as to how he might enter into communication with these people without either frightening them or arousing their savage love of battle. He had no desire to fight now, for he was upon a much more important mission than that of battling with every chance tribe that he should happen to meet with.

At last he hit upon a plan, and after seeing that he was concealed from the view of those below, he gave a few hoarse grunts in imitation of a panther. All eyes immediately turned upward toward the foliage above.

It was growing dark, and they could not penetrate the leafy screen which shielded the ape-man from their view. The moment that he had won their attention he raised his voice to the shriller and more hideous scream of the beast he personated, and then, scarce stirring a leaf in his descent, dropped to the ground once again outside the palisade, and, with the speed of a deer, ran quickly round to the village gate.

Here he beat upon the fibre-bound saplings of which the barrier was constructed, shouting to the natives in their own tongue that he was a friend who wished food and shelter for the night.

Tarzan knew well the nature of the black man. He was aware that the grunting and screaming of Sheeta in the tree above them would set their nerves on edge, and that his pounding upon their gate after dark would still further add to their terror.

That they did not reply to his hail was no surprise, for natives are fearful of any voice that comes out of the night from beyond their palisades, attributing it always to some demon or other ghostly visitor; but still he continued to call.

"Let me in, my friends!" he cried. "I am a white man pursuing the very bad white man who passed this way a few days ago. I follow to punish him for the sins he has committed against you and me.

"If you doubt my friendship, I will prove it to you by going into the tree above your village and driving Sheeta back into the jungle before he leaps among you. If you will not promise to take me in and treat me as a friend I shall let Sheeta stay and devour you."

For a moment there was silence. Then the voice of an old man came out of the quiet of the village street.

"If you are indeed a white man and a friend, we will let you come in; but first you must drive Sheeta away."

"Very well," replied Tarzan. "Listen, and you shall hear Sheeta fleeing before me."

The ape-man returned quickly to the tree, and this time he made a great noise as he entered the branches, at the same time growling ominously after the manner of the panther, so that those below would believe that the great beast was still there.

When he reached a point well above the village street he made a great commotion, shaking the tree violently, crying aloud to the panther to flee or be killed, and punctuating his own voice with the screams and mouthings of an angry beast.

Presently he raced toward the opposite side of the tree and off into the jungle, pounding loudly against the boles of trees as he went, and voicing the panther's diminishing growls as he drew farther and farther away from the village.

A few minutes later he returned to the village gate, calling to the natives within.

"I have driven Sheeta away," he said. "Now come and admit me as you promised."

For a time there was the sound of excited discussion within the palisade, but at length a half-dozen warriors came and opened the gates, peering anxiously out in evident trepidation as to the nature of the creature which they should find waiting there. They were not much relieved at sight of an almost naked white man; but when Tarzan had reassured them in quiet tones, protesting his friendship for them, they opened the barrier a trifle farther and admitted him.

When the gates had been once more secured the self-confidence of the savages returned, and as Tarzan walked up the village street toward the chief's hut he was surrounded by a host of curious men, women, and children.

From the chief he learned that Rokoff had passed up the river a week previous, and that he had horns growing from his forehead, and was accompanied by a thousand devils. Later the chief said that the very bad white man had remained a month in his village.

Though none of these statements agreed with Kaviri's, that the Russian was but three days gone from the chieftain's village and that his following was much smaller than now stated, Tarzan was in no manner surprised at the discrepancies, for he was quite familiar with the savage mind's strange manner of functioning.

What he was most interested in knowing was that he was upon the right trail, and that it led toward the interior. In this circumstance he knew that Rokoff could never escape him.

After several hours of questioning and cross-questioning the ape-man learned that another party had preceded the Russian by several days—three whites—a man, a woman, and a little man-child, with several Mosulas.

Tarzan explained to the chief that his people would follow him in a canoe, probably the next day, and that though he might go on ahead of them the chief was to receive them kindly and have no fear of them, for Mugambi would see that they did not harm the chief's people, if they were accorded a friendly reception.

"And now," he concluded, "I shall lie down beneath this tree and sleep. I am very tired. Permit no one to disturb me."

The chief offered him a hut, but Tarzan, from past experience of native dwellings, preferred the open air, and, further, he had plans of his own that could be better carried out if he remained beneath the tree. He gave as his reason a desire to be close at hand should Sheeta return, and after this explanation the chief was very glad to permit him to sleep beneath the tree.

Tarzan had always found that it stood him in good stead to leave with natives the impression that he was to some extent possessed of more or less miraculous powers. He might easily have entered their village without recourse to the gates, but he believed that a sudden and unaccountable disappearance when he was ready to leave them would result in a more lasting impression upon their childlike minds, and so as soon as the village was quiet in sleep he rose, and, leaping into the branches of the tree above him, faded silently into the black mystery of the jungle night.

All the balance of that night the ape-man swung rapidly through the upper and middle terraces of the forest. When the going was good there he preferred the upper branches of the giant trees, for then his way was better lighted by the moon; but so accustomed were all his senses to the grim world of his birth that it was possible for him, even in the dense, black shadows near the ground, to move with ease and rapidity. You or I walking beneath the arcs of Main Street, or Broadway, or State Street, could not have moved more surely or with a tenth the speed of the agile ape-man through the gloomy mazes that would have baffled us entirely.

At dawn he stopped to feed, and then he slept for several hours, taking up the pursuit again toward noon.

Twice he came upon natives, and, though he had considerable difficulty in approaching them, he succeeded in each instance in quieting both their fears and bellicose intentions toward him, and learned from them that he was upon the trail of the Russian.

Two days later, still following up the Ugambi, he came upon a large village. The chief, a wicked-looking fellow with the sharp-filed teeth that often denote the cannibal, received him with apparent friendliness.

The ape-man was now thoroughly fatigued, and had determined to rest for eight or ten hours that he might be fresh and strong when he caught up with Rokoff, as he was sure he must do within a very short time.

The chief told him that the bearded white man had left his village only the morning before, and that doubtless he would be able to overtake him in a short time. The other party the chief had not seen or heard of, so he said.

Tarzan did not like the appearance or manner of the fellow, who seemed, though friendly enough, to harbour a certain contempt for this half-naked white man who came with no followers and offered no presents; but he needed the rest and food that the village would afford him with less effort than the jungle, and so, as he knew no fear of man, beast, or devil, he curled himself up in the shadow of a hut and was soon asleep.

Scarcely had he left the chief than the latter called two of his warriors, to whom he whispered a few instructions. A moment later the sleek, black bodies were racing along the river path, up-stream, toward the east.

In the village the chief maintained perfect quiet. He would

BETRAYED

permit no one to approach the sleeping visitor, nor any singing, nor loud talking. He was remarkably solicitous lest his guest be disturbed.

Three hours later several canoes came silently into view from up the Ugambi. They were being pushed ahead rapidly by the brawny muscles of their black crews. Upon the bank before the river stood the chief, his spear raised in a horizontal position above his head, as though in some manner of predetermined signal to those within the boats.

And such indeed was the purpose of his attitude—which meant that the white stranger within his village still slept peacefully.

In the bows of two of the canoes were the runners that the chief had sent forth three hours earlier. It was evident that they had been dispatched to follow and bring back this party, and that the signal from the bank was one that had been determined upon before they left the village.

In a few moments the dugouts drew up to the verdure-clad bank. The native warriors filed out, and with them a half-dozen white men. Sullen, ugly-looking customers they were, and none more so than the evil-faced, black-bearded man who commanded them.

"Where is the white man your messengers report to be with you?" he asked of the chief.

"This way, *bwana*," replied the native. "Carefully have I kept silence in the village that he might be still asleep when you returned. I do not know that he is one who seeks you to do you harm, but he questioned me closely about your coming and your going, and his appearance is as that of the one you described, but whom you believed safe in the country which you called Jungle Island.

"Had you not told me this tale I should not have recognized him, and then he might have gone after and slain you. If he is a friend and no enemy, then no harm has been done, *bwana*; but if he proves to be an enemy, I should like very much to have a rifle and some ammunition."

635

"You have done well," replied the white man, "and you shall have the rifle and ammunition whether he be a friend or enemy, provided that you stand with me."

"I shall stand with you, *bwana*," said the chief, "and now come and look upon the stranger, who sleeps within my village."

So saying, he turned and led the way toward the hut, in the shadow of which the unconscious Tarzan slept peacefully.

Behind the two men came the remaining whites and a score of warriors; but the raised forefingers of the chief and his companion held them all to perfect silence.

As they turned the corner of the hut, cautiously and upon tiptoe, an ugly smile touched the lips of the white as his eyes fell upon the giant figure of the sleeping ape-man.

The chief looked at the other inquiringly. The latter nodded his head, to signify that the chief had made no mistake in his suspicions. Then he turned to those behind him and, pointing to the sleeping man, motioned for them to seize and bind him.

A moment later a dozen brutes had leaped upon the surprised Tarzan, and so quickly did they work that he was securely bound before he could make half an effort to escape.

Then they threw him down upon his back, and as his eyes turned toward the crowd that stood near, they fell upon the malign face of Nikolas Rokoff.

A sneer curled the Russian's lips. He stepped quite close to Tarzan.

"Pig!" he cried. "Have you not learned sufficient wisdom to keep away from Nikolas Rokoff?"

Then he kicked the prostrate man full in the face.

"That for your welcome," he said.

"Tonight, before my Ethiop friends eat you, I shall tell you what has already befallen your wife and child, and what further plans I have for their futures."

VIII

THE DANCE OF DEATH

hrough the luxuriant, tangled vegetation of the Stygian jungle night a great lithe body made its way sinuously and in utter silence upon its soft padded feet. Only two blazing points of yellow-green flame shone occasionally with the reflected light of the equatorial moon that now and again pierced the softly sighing roof rustling in the night wind.

Occasionally the beast would stop with high-held nose, sniffing searchingly. At other times a quick, brief incursion into the branches above delayed it momentarily in its steady journey toward the east. To its sensitive nostrils came the subtle unseen spoor of many a tender four-footed creature, bringing the slaver of hunger to the cruel, drooping jowl.

But steadfastly it kept on its way, strangely ignoring the cravings of appetite that at another time would have sent the rolling, fur-clad muscles flying at some soft throat. All that night the creature pursued its lonely way, and the next day it halted only to make a single kill, which it tore to fragments and devoured with sullen, grumbling rumbles as though half famished for lack of food.

It was dusk when it approached the palisade that surrounded a large native village. Like the shadow of a swift and silent death it circled the village, nose to ground, halting at last close to the palisade, where it almost touched the backs of several huts. Here the beast sniffed for a moment, and then, turning its head upon one side, listened with up-pricked ears.

What it heard was no sound by the standards of human ears, yet to the highly attuned and delicate organs of the beast a message seemed to be borne to the savage brain. A wondrous transformation was wrought in the motionless mass of statuesque bone and muscle that had an instant before stood as though carved out of the living bronze.

As if it had been poised upon steel springs, suddenly released, it rose quickly and silently to the top of the palisade, disappearing, stealthily and cat-like, into the dark space between the wall and the back of an adjacent hut.

In the village street beyond women were preparing many little fires and fetching cooking-pots filled with water, for a great feast was to be celebrated ere the night was many hours older. About a stout stake near the centre of the circling fires a little knot of black warriors stood conversing, their bodies smeared with white and blue and ochre in broad and grotesque bands. Great circles of colour were drawn about their eyes and lips, their breasts and abdomens, and from their clay-plastered coiffures rose gay feathers and bits of long, straight wire.

The village was preparing for the feast, while in a hut at one side of the scene of the coming orgy the bound victim of their bestial appetites lay waiting for the end. And such an end!

Tarzan of the Apes, tensing his mighty muscles, strained at the bonds that pinioned him; but they had been re-enforced many times at the instigation of the Russian, so that not even the ape-man's giant brawn could budge them.

Death!

Tarzan had looked the Hideous Hunter in the face many a time, and smiled. And he would smile again tonight when he knew the end was coming quickly; but now his thoughts were not of himself, but of those others—the dear ones who must suffer most because of his passing.

Jane would never know the manner of it. For that he thanked Heaven; and he was thankful also that she at least was safe in the heart of the world's greatest city. Safe among kind and loving friends who would do their best to lighten her misery.

But the boy!

Tarzan writhed at the thought of him. His son! And now he— the mighty Lord of the Jungle—he, Tarzan, King of the Apes, the only one in all the world fitted to find and save the child from the horrors that Rokoff's evil mind had planned—had been trapped like a silly, dumb creature. He was to die in a few hours, and with him would go the child's last chance of succour.

Rokoff had been in to see and revile and abuse him several times during the afternoon; but he had been able to wring no word of remonstrance or murmur of pain from the lips of the giant captive.

So at last he had given up, reserving his particular bit of exquisite mental torture for the last moment, when, just before the savage spears of the cannibals should for ever make the object of his hatred immune to further suffering, the Russian planned to reveal to his enemy the true whereabouts of his wife whom he thought safe in England.

Dusk had fallen upon the village, and the ape-men could hear the preparations going forward for the torture and the feast. The dance of death he could picture in his mind's eye—for he had seen the thing many times in the past. Now he was to be the central figure, bound to the stake.

The torture of the slow death as the circling warriors cut him to bits with the fiendish skill, that mutilated without bringing unconsciousness, had no terrors for him. He was inured to suffering and to the sight of blood and to cruel death; but the desire to live was no less strong within him, and until the last spark of life should flicker and go out, his whole being would remain quick with hope and determination. Let them relax their watchfulness but for an instant, he knew that his cunning mind and giant muscles would find a way to escape—escape and revenge.

As he lay, thinking furiously on every possibility of self-salvation, there came to his sensitive nostrils a faint and a familiar scent. Instantly every faculty of his mind was upon the alert. Presently his trained ears caught the sound of the soundless presence without—behind the hut wherein he lay. His lips moved, and though no sound came forth that might have been appreciable to a human ear beyond the walls of his prison, yet he realized that the one beyond would hear. Already he knew who that one was, for his nostrils had told him as plainly as your eyes or mine tell us of the identity of an old friend whom we come upon in broad daylight.

An instant later he heard the soft sound of a fur-clad body and padded feet scaling the outer wall behind the hut and then a tearing at the poles which formed the wall. Presently through the hole thus made slunk a great beast, pressing its cold muzzle close to his neck.

It was Sheeta, the panther.

The beast snuffed round the prostrate man, whining a little. There was a limit to the interchange of ideas which could take place between these two, and so Tarzan could not be sure that Sheeta understood all that he attempted to communicate to him. That the man was tied and helpless Sheeta could, of course, see; but that to the mind of the panther this would carry any suggestion of harm in so far as his master was concerned, Tarzan could not guess.

What had brought the beast to him? The fact that he had come augured well for what he might accomplish; but when Tarzan tried to get Sheeta to gnaw his bonds asunder the great animal could not seem to understand what was expected of him, and, instead, but licked the wrists and arms of the prisoner.

Presently there came an interruption. Some one was approaching the hut. Sheeta gave a low growl and slunk into the blackness of a far corner. Evidently the visitor did not hear the warning sound, for almost immediately he entered the hut—a tall, naked, savage warrior.

He came to Tarzan's side and pricked him with a spear. From the lips of the ape-man came a weird, uncanny sound, and in answer to it there leaped from the blackness of the hut's farthermost corner a bolt of fur-clad death. Full upon the breast of the painted savage the great beast struck, burying sharp talons in the black flesh and sinking great yellow fangs in the ebon throat.

There was a fearful scream of anguish and terror from the black, and mingled with it was the hideous challenge of the killing panther. Then came silence—silence except for the rending of bloody flesh and the crunching of human bones between mighty jaws.

The noise had brought sudden quiet to the village without. Then there came the sound of voices in consultation.

High-pitched, fear-filled voices, and deep, low tones of authority, as the chief spoke. Tarzan and the panther heard the approaching footsteps of many men, and then, to Tarzan's surprise, the great cat rose from across the body of its kill, and slunk noiselessly from the hut through the aperture through which it had entered.

The man heard the soft scraping of the body as it passed over the top of the palisade, and then silence. From the opposite side of the hut he heard the savages approaching to investigate.

He had little hope that Sheeta would return, for had the great cat intended to defend him against all comers it would have remained by his side as it heard the approaching savages without.

Tarzan knew how strange were the workings of the brains of the mighty carnivora of the jungle—how fiendishly fearless they might be in the face of certain death, and again how timid upon the slightest provocation. There was doubt in his mind that some note of the approaching blacks vibrating with fear had struck an answering chord in the nervous system of the panther, sending him slinking through the jungle, his tail between his legs.

The man shrugged. Well, what of it? He had expected to die, and, after all, what might Sheeta have done for him other than to maul a couple of his enemies before a rifle in the hands of one of the whites should have dispatched him!

If the cat could have released him! Ah! that would have resulted in a very different story; but it had proved beyond the understanding of Sheeta, and now the beast was gone and Tarzan must definitely abandon hope.

The natives were at the entrance to the hut now, peering fearfully into the dark interior. Two in advance held lighted torches in their left hands and ready spears in their right. They held back timorously against those behind, who were pushing them forward.

The shrieks of the panther's victim, mingled with those of the great cat, had wrought mightily upon their poor nerves, and now the awful silence of the dark interior seemed even more terribly ominous than had the frightful screaming.

Presently one of those who was being forced unwillingly within hit upon a happy scheme for learning first the precise nature of the danger which menaced him from the silent interior. With a quick movement he flung his lighted torch into the centre of the hut. Instantly all within was illuminated for a brief second before the burning brand was dashed out against the earth floor.

There was the figure of the white prisoner still securely bound as they had last seen him, and in the centre of the hut another figure equally as motionless, its throat and breasts horribly torn and mangled.

The sight that met the eyes of the foremost savages inspired more terror within their superstitious breasts than would the presence of

Sheeta, for they saw only the result of a ferocious attack upon one of their fellows.

Not seeing the cause, their fear-ridden minds were free to attribute the ghastly work to supernatural causes, and with the thought they turned, screaming, from the hut, bowling over those who stood directly behind them in the exuberance of their terror.

For an hour Tarzan heard only the murmur of excited voices from the far end of the village. Evidently the savages were once more attempting to work up their flickering courage to a point that would permit them to make another invasion of the hut, for now and then came a savage yell, such as the warriors give to bolster up their bravery upon the field of battle.

But in the end it was two of the whites who first entered, carrying torches and guns. Tarzan was not surprised to discover that neither of them was Rokoff. He would have wagered his soul that no power on earth could have tempted that great coward to face the unknown menace of the hut.

When the natives saw that the white men were not attacked they, too, crowded into the interior, their voices hushed with terror as they looked upon the mutilated corpse of their comrade. The whites tried in vain to elicit an explanation from Tarzan; but to all their queries he but shook his head, a grim and knowing smile curving his lips.

At last Rokoff came.

His face grew very white as his eyes rested upon the bloody thing grinning up at him from the floor, the face set in a death mask of excruciating horror.

"Come!" he said to the chief. "Let us get to work and finish this demon before he has an opportunity to repeat this thing upon more of your people."

The chief gave orders that Tarzan should be lifted and carried to the stake; but it was several minutes before he could prevail upon any of his men to touch the prisoner.

At last, however, four of the younger warriors dragged Tarzan roughly from the hut, and once outside the pall of terror seemed lifted from the savage hearts.

A score of howling blacks pushed and buffeted the prisoner down the village street and bound him to the post in the centre of the circle of little fires and boiling cooking-pots.

When at last he was made fast and seemed quite helpless and beyond the faintest hope of succour, Rokoff's shrivelled wart of courage swelled to its usual proportions when danger was not present.

He stepped close to the ape-man, and, seizing a spear from the hands of one of the savages, was the first to prod the helpless victim. A little stream of blood trickled down the giant's smooth skin from the wound in his side; but no murmur of pain passed his lips.

The smile of contempt upon his face seemed to infuriate the Russian. With a volley of oaths he leaped at the helpless captive, beating him upon the face with his clenched fists and kicking him mercilessly about the legs.

Then he raised the heavy spear to drive it through the mighty heart, and still Tarzan of the Apes smiled contemptuously upon him.

Before Rokoff could drive the weapon home the chief sprang upon him and dragged him away from his intended victim.

"Stop, white man!" he cried. "Rob us of this prisoner and our death-dance, and you yourself may have to take his place."

The threat proved most effective in keeping the Russian from further assaults upon the prisoner, though he continued to stand a little apart and hurl taunts at his enemy. He told Tarzan that he himself was going to eat the ape-man's heart. He enlarged upon the horrors of the future life of Tarzan's son, and intimated that his vengeance would reach as well to Jane Clayton.

"You think your wife safe in England," said Rokoff. "Poor fool! She is even now in the hands of one not even of decent birth, and far from the safety of London and the protection of her friends. I had not meant to tell you this until I could bring to you upon Jungle Island proof of her fate.

"Now that you are about to die the most unthinkably horrid death that it is given a white man to die—let this word of the plight of your wife add to the torments that you must suffer before the last savage spear-thrust releases you from your torture."

The dance had commenced now, and the yells of the circling warriors drowned Rokoff's further attempts to distress his victim.

The leaping savages, the flickering firelight playing upon their painted bodies, circled about the victim at the stake.

To Tarzan's memory came a similar scene, when he had rescued D'Arnot from a like predicament at the last moment before the final spear-thrust should have ended his sufferings. Who was there now to rescue him? In all the world there was none able to save him from the torture and the death.

The thought that these human fiends would devour him when the dance was done caused him not a single qualm of horror or disgust. It did not add to his sufferings as it would have to those of an ordinary white man, for all his life Tarzan had seen the beasts of the jungle devour the flesh of their kills.

Had he not himself battled for the grisly forearm of a great ape at that long-gone Dum-Dum, when he had slain the fierce Tublat and won his niche in the respect of the Apes of Kerchak?

The dancers were leaping more closely to him now. The spears were commencing to find his body in the first torturing pricks that prefaced the more serious thrusts.

It would not be long now. The ape-man longed for the last savage lunge that would end his misery.

And then, far out in the mazes of the weird jungle, rose a shrill scream.

For an instant the dancers paused, and in the silence of the interval there rose from the lips of the fast-bound white man an answering shriek, more fearsome and more terrible than that of the jungle-beast that had roused it.

For several minutes the blacks hesitated; then, at the urging of Rokoff and their chief, they leaped in to finish the dance and the victim; but ere ever another spear touched the brown hide a tawny streak of green-eyed hate and ferocity bounded from the door of the hut in which Tarzan had been imprisoned, and Sheeta, the panther, stood snarling beside his master.

For an instant the blacks and the whites stood transfixed with terror. Their eyes were riveted upon the bared fangs of the jungle cat.

Only Tarzan of the Apes saw what else there was emerging from the dark interior of the hut.

IX

CHIVALRY OR VILLAINY

rom her cabin port upon the *Kincaid*, Jane Clayton had seen her husband rowed to the verdure-clad shore of Jungle Island, and then the ship once more proceeded upon its way.

For several days she saw no one other than Sven Anderssen, the *Kincaid*'s taciturn and repellent cook. She asked him the name of the shore upon which her husband had been set.

"Ay tank it blow purty soon purty hard," replied the Swede, and that was all that she could get out of him.

She had come to the conclusion that he spoke no other English, and so she ceased to importune him for information; but never did she forget to greet him pleasantly or to thank him for the hideous, nauseating meals he brought her.

Three days from the spot where Tarzan had been marooned the *Kincaid* came to anchor in the mouth of a great river, and presently Rokoff came to Jane Clayton's cabin.

"We have arrived, my dear," he said, with a sickening leer. "I have come to offer you safety, liberty, and ease. My heart has been softened toward you in your suffering, and I would make amends as best I may.

"Your husband was a brute—you know that best who found him naked in his native jungle, roaming wild with the savage beasts that were his fellows. Now I am a gentleman, not only born of noble blood, but raised gently as befits a man of quality.

"To you, dear Jane, I offer the love of a cultured man and association with one of culture and refinement, which you must have sorely missed in your relations with the poor ape that through your girlish infatuation you married so thoughtlessly. I love you, Jane. You have but to say the word and no further sorrows shall afflict you—even your baby shall be returned to you unharmed."

Outside the door Sven Anderssen paused with the noonday meal he had been carrying to Lady Greystoke. Upon the end of his long, stringy neck his little head was cocked to one side, his close-set eyes were half closed, his ears, so expressive was his whole attitude of stealthy eavesdropping, seemed truly to be cocked forward—even his long, yellow, straggly moustache appeared to assume a sly droop.

As Rokoff closed his appeal, awaiting the reply he invited, the look of surprise upon Jane Clayton's face turned to one of disgust. She fairly shuddered in the fellow's face.

"I would not have been surprised, M. Rokoff," she said, "had you attempted to force me to submit to your evil desires, but that you should be so fatuous as to believe that I, wife of John Clayton, would come to you willingly, even to save my life, I should never have imagined. I have known you for a scoundrel, M. Rokoff; but until now I had not taken you for a fool."

Rokoff's eyes narrowed, and the red of mortification flushed out the pallor of his face. He took a step toward the girl, threateningly.

"We shall see who is the fool at last," he hissed, "when I have broken you to my will and your plebeian Yankee stubbornness has cost you all that you hold dear—even the life of your baby—for, by the bones of St. Peter, I'll forego all that I had planned for the brat and cut its heart out before your very eyes. You'll learn what it means to insult Nikolas Rokoff."

Jane Clayton turned wearily away.

"What is the use," she said, "of expatiating upon the depths to which your vengeful nature can sink? You cannot move me either by threats or deeds. My baby cannot judge yet for himself, but I, his mother, can foresee that should it have been given him to survive to man's estate he would willingly sacrifice his life for the honour of his mother. Love him as I do, I would not purchase his life at such a price. Did I, he would execrate my memory to the day of his death." Rokoff was now thoroughly angered because of his failure to reduce the girl to terror. He felt only hate for her, but it had come to his diseased mind that if he could force her to accede to his demands as the price of her life and her child's, the cup of his revenge would be filled to brimming when he could flaunt the wife of Lord Greystoke in the capitals of Europe as his mistress.

Again he stepped closer to her. His evil face was convulsed with rage and desire. Like a wild beast he sprang upon her, and with his strong fingers at her throat forced her backward upon the berth.

At the same instant the door of the cabin opened noisily. Rokoff leaped to his feet, and, turning, faced the Swede cook.

Into the fellow's usually foxy eyes had come an expression of utter stupidity. His lower jaw drooped in vacuous harmony. He busied himself in arranging Lady Greystoke's meal upon the tiny table at one side of her cabin.

The Russian glared at him.

"What do you mean," he cried, "by entering here without permission? Get out!"

The cook turned his watery blue eyes upon Rokoff and smiled vacuously.

"Ay tank it blow purty soon purty hard," he said, and then he began rearranging the few dishes upon the little table.

"Get out of here, or I'll throw you out, you miserable blockhead!" roared Rokoff, taking a threatening step toward the Swede.

Anderssen continued to smile foolishly in his direction, but one ham-like paw slid stealthily to the handle of the long, slim knife that protruded from the greasy cord supporting his soiled apron.

649

Rokoff saw the move and stopped short in his advance. Then he turned toward Jane Clayton.

"I will give you until tomorrow," he said, "to reconsider your answer to my offer. All will be sent ashore upon one pretext or another except you and the child, Paulvitch and myself. Then without interruption you will be able to witness the death of the baby."

He spoke in French that the cook might not understand the sinister portent of his words. When he had done he banged out of the cabin without another look at the man who had interrupted him in his sorry work.

When he had gone, Sven Anderssen turned toward Lady Greystoke—the idiotic expression that had masked his thoughts had fallen away, and in its place was one of craft and cunning.

"Hay tank Ay ban a fool," he said. "Hay ben the fool. Ay savvy Franch."

Jane Clayton looked at him in surprise.

"You understood all that he said, then?"

Anderssen grinned.

"You bat," he said.

"And you heard what was going on in here and came to protect me?"

"You bane good to me," explained the Swede. "Hay treat me like darty dog. Ay help you, lady. You yust vait—Ay help you. Ay ban Vast Coast lots times."

"But how can you help me, Sven," she asked, "when all these men will be against us?"

"Ay tank," said Sven Anderssen, "it blow purty soon purty hard," and then he turned and left the cabin.

Though Jane Clayton doubted the cook's ability to be of any material service to her, she was nevertheless deeply grateful to him for what he already had done. The feeling that among these enemies she had one friend brought the first ray of comfort that had come to lighten the burden of her miserable apprehensions throughout the long voyage of the *Kincaid*.

She saw no more of Rokoff that day, nor of any other until Sven came with her evening meal. She tried to draw him into conversation relative to his plans to aid her, but all that she could get from him was his stereotyped prophecy as to the future state of the wind. He seemed suddenly to have relapsed into his wonted state of dense stupidity.

However, when he was leaving her cabin a little later with the empty dishes he whispered very low, "Leave on your clothes an' roll up your blankets. Ay come back after you purty soon."

He would have slipped from the room at once, but Jane laid her hand upon his sleeve.

"My baby?" she asked. "I cannot go without him."

"You do wot Ay tal you," said Anderssen, scowling. "Ay ban halpin' you, so don't you gat too fonny."

When he had gone Jane Clayton sank down upon her berth in utter bewilderment. What was she to do? Suspicions as to the intentions of the Swede swarmed her brain. Might she not be infinitely worse off if she gave herself into his power than she already was?

No, she could be no worse off in company with the devil himself than with Nikolas Rokoff, for the devil at least bore the reputation of being a gentleman.

She swore a dozen times that she would not leave the *Kincaid* without her baby, and yet she remained clothed long past her usual hour for retiring, and her blankets were neatly rolled and bound with stout cord, when about midnight there came a stealthy scratching upon the panels of her door.

Swiftly she crossed the room and drew the bolt. Softly the door swung open to admit the muffled figure of the Swede. On one arm he carried a bundle, evidently his blankets. His other hand was raised in a gesture commanding silence, a grimy forefinger upon his lips.

He came quite close to her.

"Carry this," he said. "Do not make some noise when you see it. It ban you kid."

Quick hands snatched the bundle from the cook, and hungry mother arms folded the sleeping infant to her breast, while hot tears of joy ran down her cheeks and her whole frame shook with the emotion of the moment.

"Come!" said Anderssen. "We got no time to vaste."

He snatched up her bundle of blankets, and outside the cabin door his own as well. Then he led her to the ship's side, steadied her descent of the monkey-ladder, holding the child for her as she climbed to the waiting boat below. A moment later he had cut the rope that held the small boat to the steamer's side, and, bending silently to the muffled oars, was pulling toward the black shadows up the Ugambi River.

Anderssen rowed on as though quite sure of his ground, and when after half an hour the moon broke through the clouds there was revealed upon their left the mouth of a tributary running into the Ugambi. Up this narrow channel the Swede turned the prow of the small boat.

Jane Clayton wondered if the man knew where he was bound. She did not know that in his capacity as cook he had that day been rowed up this very stream to a little village where he had bartered with the natives for such provisions as they had for sale, and that he had there arranged the details of his plan for the adventure upon which they were now setting forth.

Even though the moon was full, the surface of the small river was quite dark. The giant trees overhung its narrow banks, meeting in a great arch above the centre of the river. Spanish moss dropped from the gracefully bending limbs, and enormous creepers clambered in riotous profusion from the ground to the loftiest branch, falling in curving loops almost to the water's placid breast.

Now and then the river's surface would be suddenly broken ahead of them by a huge crocodile, startled by the splashing of the oars, or, snorting and blowing, a family of hippos would dive from a sandy bar to the cool, safe depths of the bottom.

From the dense jungles upon either side came the weird night cries of the carnivora—the maniacal voice of the hyena, the coughing grunt of the panther, the deep and awful roar of the lion. And with them strange, uncanny notes that the girl could not ascribe to any particular night prowler—more terrible because of their mystery.

Huddled in the stern of the boat she sat with her baby strained close to her bosom, and because of that little tender, helpless thing she was happier tonight than she had been for many a sorrow-ridden day.

Even though she knew not to what fate she was going, or how soon that fate might overtake her, still was she happy and thankful for the moment, however brief, that she might press her baby tightly in her arms. She could scarce wait for the coming of the day that she might look again upon the bright face of her little, black-eyed Jack.

Again and again she tried to strain her eyes through the blackness of the jungle night to have but a tiny peep at those beloved features, but only the dim outline of the baby face rewarded her efforts. Then once more she would cuddle the warm, little bundle close to her throbbing heart.

It must have been close to three o'clock in the morning that Anderssen brought the boat's nose to the shore before a clearing where could be dimly seen in the waning moonlight a cluster of native huts encircled by a thorn *boma*.

At the village gate they were admitted by a native woman, the wife of the chief whom Anderssen had paid to assist him. She took them to the chief's hut, but Anderssen said that they would sleep without upon the ground, and so, her duty having been completed, she left them to their own devices.

The Swede, after explaining in his gruff way that the huts were doubtless filthy and vermin-ridden, spread Jane's blankets on the ground for her, and at a little distance unrolled his own and lay down to sleep.

It was some time before the girl could find a comfortable position upon the hard ground, but at last, the baby in the hollow of her arm, she dropped asleep from utter exhaustion. When she awoke it was broad daylight.

About her were clustered a score of curious natives—mostly men, for among the aborigines it is the male who owns this characteristic in its most exaggerated form. Instinctively Jane Clayton drew the baby more closely to her, though she soon saw that the blacks were far from intending her or the child any harm.

In fact, one of them offered her a gourd of milk—a filthy, smoke-begrimed gourd, with the ancient rind of long-curdled milk caked in layers within its neck; but the spirit of the giver touched her deeply, and her face lightened for a moment with one of those almost forgotten smiles of radiance that had helped to make her beauty famous both in Baltimore and London.

She took the gourd in one hand, and rather than cause the giver pain raised it to her lips, though for the life of her she could scarce restrain the qualm of nausea that surged through her as the malodorous thing approached her nostrils.

It was Anderssen who came to her rescue, and taking the gourd from her, drank a portion himself, and then returned it to the native with a gift of blue beads.

The sun was shining brightly now, and though the baby still slept, Jane could scarce restrain her impatient desire to have at least a brief glance at the beloved face. The natives had withdrawn at a command from their chief, who now stood talking with Anderssen, a little apart from her.

As she debated the wisdom of risking disturbing the child's

slumber by lifting the blanket that now protected its face from the sun, she noted that the cook conversed with the chief in the language of the Negro.

What a remarkable man the fellow was, indeed! She had thought him ignorant and stupid but a short day before, and now, within the past twenty-four hours, she had learned that he spoke not only English but French as well, and the primitive dialect of the West Coast.

She had thought him shifty, cruel, and untrustworthy, yet in so far as she had reason to believe he had proved himself in every way the contrary since the day before. It scarce seemed credible that he could be serving her from motives purely chivalrous. There must be something deeper in his intentions and plans than he had yet disclosed.

She wondered, and when she looked at him—at his close-set, shifty eyes and repulsive features, she shuddered, for she was convinced that no lofty characteristics could be hid behind so foul an exterior.

As she was thinking of these things the while she debated the wisdom of uncovering the baby's face, there came a little grunt from the wee bundle in her lap, and then a gurgling coo that set her heart in raptures.

The baby was awake! Now she might feast her eyes upon him.

Quickly she snatched the blanket from before the infant's face; Anderssen was looking at her as she did so.

He saw her stagger to her feet, holding the baby at arm's length from her, her eyes glued in horror upon the little chubby face and twinkling eyes.

Then he heard her piteous cry as her knees gave beneath her, and she sank to the ground in a swoon.

X

THE SWEDE

s the warriors, clustered thick about Tarzan and Sheeta, realized that it was a flesh-and-blood panther that had interrupted their dance of death, they took heart a trifle, for in the face of all those circling spears even the mighty Sheeta would be doomed.

Rokoff was urging the chief to have his spearmen launch their missiles, and the black was upon the instant of issuing the command, when his eyes strayed beyond Tarzan, following the gaze of the ape-man.

With a yell of terror the chief turned and fled toward the village gate, and as his people looked to see the cause of his fright, they too took to their heels—for there, lumbering down upon them, their huge forms exaggerated by the play of moonlight and camp fire, came the hideous apes of Akut.

The instant the natives turned to flee the ape-man's savage cry rang out above the shrieks of the blacks, and in answer to it Sheeta and the apes leaped growling after the fugitives. Some of the warriors turned to battle with their enraged antagonists, but before the fiendish ferocity of the fierce beasts they went down to bloody death.

Others were dragged down in their flight, and it was not until the village was empty and the last of the blacks had disappeared into the bush that Tarzan was able to recall his savage pack to his side. Then it was that he discovered to his chagrin that he could not make one of them, not even the comparatively intelligent Akut, understand that he wished to be freed from the bonds that held him to the stake.

In time, of course, the idea would filter through their thick skulls, but in the meanwhile many things might happen—the blacks might return in force to regain their village; the whites might readily pick them all off with their rifles from the surrounding trees; he might even starve to death before the dull-witted apes realized that he wished them to gnaw through his bonds.

As for Sheeta—the great cat understood even less than the apes; but yet Tarzan could not but marvel at the remarkable characteristics this beast had evidenced. That it felt real affection for him there seemed little doubt, for now that the blacks were disposed of it walked slowly back and forth about the stake, rubbing its sides against the ape-man's legs and purring like a contented tabby. That it had gone of its own volition to bring the balance of the pack to his rescue, Tarzan could not doubt. His Sheeta was indeed a jewel among beasts.

Mugambi's absence worried the ape-man not a little. He attempted to learn from Akut what had become of the black, fearing that the beasts, freed from the restraint of Tarzan's presence, might have fallen upon the man and devoured him; but to all his questions the great ape but pointed back in the direction from which they had come out of the jungle.

The night passed with Tarzan still fast bound to the stake, and shortly after dawn his fears were realized in the discovery of naked black figures moving stealthily just within the edge of the jungle about the village. The blacks were returning.

With daylight their courage would be equal to the demands of a charge upon the handful of beasts that had routed them from their rightful abodes. The result of the encounter seemed foregone if the savages could curb their superstitious terror, for against their overwhelming numbers, their long spears and poisoned arrows, the panther and the apes could not be expected to survive a really determined attack.

657

That the blacks were preparing for a charge became apparent a few moments later, when they commenced to show themselves in force upon the edge of the clearing, dancing and jumping about as they waved their spears and shouted taunts and fierce warcries toward the village.

These manoeuvres Tarzan knew would continue until the blacks had worked themselves into a state of hysterical courage sufficient to sustain them for a short charge toward the village, and even though he doubted that they would reach it at the first attempt, he believed that at the second or the third they would swarm through the gateway, when the outcome could not be aught than the extermination of Tarzan's bold, but unarmed and undisciplined, defenders.

Even as he had guessed, the first charge carried the howling warriors but a short distance into the open—a shrill, weird challenge from the ape-man being all that was necessary to send them scurrying back to the bush. For half an hour they pranced and yelled their courage to the sticking-point, and again essayed a charge.

This time they came quite to the village gate, but when Sheeta and the hideous apes leaped among them they turned screaming in terror, and again fled to the jungle.

Again was the dancing and shouting repeated. This time Tarzan felt no doubt they would enter the village and complete the work that a handful of determined white men would have carried to a successful conclusion at the first attempt.

To have rescue come so close only to be thwarted because he could not make his poor, savage friends understand precisely what he wanted of them was most irritating, but he could not find it in his heart to place blame upon them. They had done their best, and now he was sure they would doubtless remain to die with him in a fruitless effort to defend him.

The blacks were already preparing for the charge. A few individuals had advanced a short distance toward the village and were exhorting the others to follow them. In a moment the whole savage horde would be racing across the clearing.

Tarzan thought only of the little child somewhere in this cruel, relentless wilderness. His heart ached for the son that he might no longer seek to save—that and the realization of Jane's suffering were all that weighed upon his brave spirit in these that he thought his last moments of life. Succour, all that he could hope for, had come to him in the instant of his extremity—and failed. There was nothing further for which to hope.

The blacks were half-way across the clearing when Tarzan's attention was attracted by the actions of one of the apes. The beast was glaring toward one of the huts. Tarzan followed his gaze. To his infinite relief and delight he saw the stalwart form of Mugambi racing toward him.

The huge black was panting heavily as though from strenuous physical exertion and nervous excitement. He rushed to Tarzan's side, and as the first of the savages reached the village gate the native's knife severed the last of the cords that bound Tarzan to the stake.

In the street lay the corpses of the savages that had fallen before the pack the night before. From one of these Tarzan seized a spear and knob stick, and with Mugambi at his side and the snarling pack about him, he met the natives as they poured through the gate.

Fierce and terrible was the battle that ensued, but at last the savages were routed, more by terror, perhaps, at sight of a black man and a white fighting in company with a panther and the huge fierce apes of Akut, than because of their inability to overcome the relatively small force that opposed them.

One prisoner fell into the hands of Tarzan, and him the ape-man questioned in an effort to learn what had become of Rokoff and his party. Promised his liberty in return for the information, the black told all he knew concerning the movements of the Russian.

It seemed that early in the morning their chief had attempted to prevail upon the whites to return with him to the village and with their guns destroy the ferocious pack that had taken possession of it, but Rokoff appeared to entertain even more fears of the giant white man and his strange companions than even the blacks themselves.

Upon no conditions would he consent to returning even within sight of the village. Instead, he took his party hurriedly to the river, where they stole a number of canoes the blacks had hidden there. The last that had been seen of them they had been paddling strongly up-stream, their porters from Kaviri's village wielding the blades. So once more Tarzan of the Apes with his hideous pack took up his search for the ape-man's son and the pursuit of his abductor.

For weary days they followed through an almost uninhabited country, only to learn at last that they were upon the wrong trail. The little band had been reduced by three, for three of Akut's apes had fallen in the fighting at the village. Now, with Akut, there were five great apes, and Sheeta was there—and Mugambi and Tarzan.

The ape-man no longer heard rumors even of the three who had preceded Rokoff—the white man and woman and the child. Who the man and woman were he could not guess, but that the child was his was enough to keep him hot upon the trail. He was sure that Rokoff would be following this trio, and so he felt confident that so long as he could keep upon the Russian's trail he would be winning so much nearer to the time he might snatch his son from the dangers and horrors that menaced him.

In retracing their way after losing Rokoff's trail Tarzan picked it up again at a point where the Russian had left the river and taken to the brush in a northerly direction. He could only account for this change on the ground that the child had been carried away from the river by the two who now had possession of it.

Nowhere along the way, however, could he gain definite information that might assure him positively that the child was ahead of him. Not a single native they questioned had seen or heard of this other party, though nearly all had had direct experience with the Russian or had talked with others who had.

It was with difficulty that Tarzan could find means to communicate with the natives, as the moment their eyes fell upon his companions they fled precipitately into the bush. His only alternative was to go ahead of his pack and waylay an occasional warrior whom he found alone in the jungle.

One day as he was thus engaged, tracking an unsuspecting savage, he came upon the fellow in the act of hurling a spear at a wounded white man who crouched in a clump of bush at the trail's side. The white was one whom Tarzan had often seen, and whom he recognized at once.

Deep in his memory was implanted those repulsive features—the close-set eyes, the shifty expression, the drooping yellow moustache.

Instantly it occurred to the ape-man that this fellow had not been among those who had accompanied Rokoff at the village where Tarzan had been a prisoner. He had seen them all, and this fellow had not been there. There could be but one explanation—he it was who had fled ahead of the Russian with the woman and the child—and the woman had been Jane Clayton. He was sure now of the meaning of Rokoff's words.

The ape-man's face went white as he looked upon the pasty, vice-marked countenance of the Swede. Across Tarzan's forehead stood out the broad band of scarlet that marked the scar where, years before, Terkoz had torn a great strip of the ape-man's scalp from his skull in the fierce battle in which Tarzan had sustained his fitness to the kingship of the apes of Kerchak.

The man was his prey—the black should not have him, and with the thought he leaped upon the warrior, striking down the spear before it could reach its mark. The black, whipping out his knife, turned to do battle with this new enemy, while the Swede, lying in the bush, witnessed a duel, the like of which he had never dreamed to see—a half-naked white man battling with a half-naked black, hand to hand with the crude weapons of primeval man at first, and then with hands and teeth like the primordial brutes from whose loins their forebears sprung.

For a time Anderssen did not recognize the white, and when at last it dawned upon him that he had seen this giant before, his eyes went wide in surprise that this growling, rending beast could ever have been the well-groomed English gentleman who had been a prisoner aboard the *Kincaid*.

An English nobleman! He had learned the identity of the *Kincaid's* prisoners from Lady Greystoke during their flight up the Ugambi. Before, in common with the other members of the crew of the steamer, he had not known who the two might be.

The fight was over. Tarzan had been compelled to kill his antagonist, as the fellow would not surrender.

The Swede saw the white man leap to his feet beside the corpse of his foe, and placing one foot upon the broken neck lift his voice in the hideous challenge of the victorious bull-ape.

Anderssen shuddered. Then Tarzan turned toward him. His face was cold and cruel, and in the grey eyes the Swede read murder.

"Where is my wife?" growled the ape-man. "Where is the child?"

Anderssen tried to reply, but a sudden fit of coughing choked him. There was an arrow entirely through his chest, and as he coughed the blood from his wounded lung poured suddenly from his mouth and nostrils.

Tarzan stood waiting for the paroxysm to pass. Like a bronze image—cold, hard, and relentless—he stood over the helpless man, waiting to wring such information from him as he needed, and then to kill.

Presently the coughing and haemorrhage ceased, and again the wounded man tried to speak. Tarzan knelt near the faintly moving lips.

"The wife and child!" he repeated. "Where are they?"

Anderssen pointed up the trail.

"The Russian—he got them," he whispered.

"How did you come here?" continued Tarzan. "Why are you not with Rokoff?"

"They catch us," replied Anderssen, in a voice so low that the ape-man could just distinguish the words. "They catch us. Ay fight, but my men they all run away. Then they get me when Ay ban vounded. Rokoff he say leave me here for the hyenas. That vas vorse than to kill. He tak your vife and kid."

"What were you doing with them—where were you taking them?" asked Tarzan, and then fiercely, leaping close to the fellow with fierce eyes blazing with the passion of hate and vengeance that he had with difficulty controlled, "What harm did you do to my wife or child? Speak quick before I kill you! Make your peace with God! Tell me the worst, or I will tear you to pieces with my hands and teeth. You have seen that I can do it!"

A look of wide-eyed surprise overspread Anderssen's face.

"Why," he whispered, "Ay did not hurt them. Ay tried to save them from that Russian. Your vife was kind to me on the *Kincaid*, and Ay hear that little baby cry sometimes. Ay got a vife an' kid for my own by Christiania an' Ay couldn't bear for to see them separated an' in Rokoff's hands any more. That vas all. Do Ay look like Ay ban here to hurt them?" he continued after a pause, pointing to the arrow protruding from his breast.

There was something in the man's tone and expression that convinced Tarzan of the truth of his assertions. More weighty than anything else was the fact that Anderssen evidently seemed more hurt than frightened. He knew he was going to die, so Tarzan's threats had little effect upon him; but it was quite apparent that he wished the Englishman to know the truth and not to wrong him by harbouring the belief that his words and manner indicated that he had entertained.

The ape-man instantly dropped to his knees beside the Swede.

"I am sorry," he said very simply. "I had looked for none but knaves in company with Rokoff. I see that I was wrong. That is past now, and we will drop it for the more important matter of getting you to a place of comfort and looking after your wounds. We must have you on your feet again as soon as possible."

The Swede, smiling, shook his head.

"You go on an' look for the vife an' kid," he said. "Ay ban as gude as dead already; but"—he hesitated—"Ay hate to think of the hyenas. Von't you finish up this job?"

Tarzan shuddered. A moment ago he had been upon the point of killing this man. Now he could no more have taken his life than he could have taken the life of any of his best friends.

He lifted the Swede's head in his arms to change and ease his position.

Again came a fit of coughing and the terrible haemorrhage. After it was over Anderssen lay with closed eyes.

Tarzan thought that he was dead, until he suddenly raised his eyes to those of the ape-man, sighed, and spoke—in a very low, weak whisper.

"Ay tank it blow purty soon purty hard!" he said, and died.

XI

TAMBUDZA

arzan scooped a shallow grave for the *Kincaid*'s cook, beneath whose repulsive exterior had beaten the heart of a chivalrous gentleman. That was all he could do in the cruel jungle for the man who had given his life in the service of his little son and his wife.

Then Tarzan took up again the pursuit of Rokoff. Now that he was positive that the woman ahead of him was indeed Jane, and that she had again fallen into the hands of the Russian, it seemed that with all the incredible speed of his fleet and agile muscles he moved at but a snail's pace.

It was with difficulty that he kept the trail, for there were many paths through the jungle at this point—crossing and crisscrossing, forking and branching in all directions, and over them all had passed natives innumerable, coming and going. The spoor of the white men was obliterated by that of the native carriers who had followed them, and over all was the spoor of other natives and of wild beasts.

It was most perplexing; yet Tarzan kept on assiduously, checking his sense of sight against his sense of smell, that he might more surely keep to the right trail. But, with all his care, night found him at a point where he was positive that he was on the wrong trail entirely.

He knew that the pack would follow his spoor, and so he had been careful to make it as distinct as possible, brushing often against the vines and creepers that walled the jungle-path, and in other ways leaving his scent-spoor plainly discernible.

As darkness settled a heavy rain set in, and there was nothing for the baffled ape-man to do but wait in the partial shelter of a huge tree until morning; but the coming of dawn brought no cessation of the torrential downpour.

For a week the sun was obscured by heavy clouds, while violent rain and wind storms obliterated the last remnants of the spoor Tarzan constantly though vainly sought.

During all this time he saw no signs of natives, nor of his own pack, the members of which he feared had lost his trail during the terrific storm. As the country was strange to him, he had been unable to judge his course accurately, since he had had neither sun by day nor moon nor stars by night to guide him.

When the sun at last broke through the clouds in the fore-noon of the seventh day, it looked down upon an almost frantic ape-man.

For the first time in his life, Tarzan of the Apes had been lost in the jungle. That the experience should have befallen him at such a time seemed cruel beyond expression. Somewhere in this savage land his wife and son lay in the clutches of the arch-fiend Rokoff.

What hideous trials might they not have undergone during those seven awful days that nature had thwarted him in his endeavours to locate them? Tarzan knew the Russian, in whose power they were, so well that he could not doubt but that the man, filled with rage that Jane had once escaped him, and knowing that Tarzan might be close upon his trail, would wreak without further loss of time whatever vengeance his polluted mind might be able to conceive.

But now that the sun shone once more, the ape-man was still at a loss as to what direction to take. He knew that Rokoff had left the river in pursuit of Anderssen, but whether he would continue inland or return to the Ugambi was a question.

The ape-man had seen that the river at the point he had left it was growing narrow and swift, so that he judged that it could not be navigable even for canoes to any great distance farther toward its source. However, if Rokoff had not returned to the river, in what direction had he proceeded?

From the direction of Anderssen's flight with Jane and the child Tarzan was convinced that the man had purposed attempting the tremendous feat of crossing the continent to Zanzibar; but whether Rokoff would dare so dangerous a journey or not was a question.

Fear might drive him to the attempt now that he knew the manner of horrible pack that was upon his trail, and that Tarzan of the Apes was following him to wreak upon him the vengeance that he deserved.

At last the ape-man determined to continue toward the northeast in the general direction of German East Africa until he came upon natives from whom he might gain information as to Rokoff's whereabouts.

The second day following the cessation of the rain Tarzan came upon a native village the inhabitants of which fled into the bush the instant their eyes fell upon him. Tarzan, not to be thwarted in any such manner as this, pursued them, and after a brief chase caught up with a young warrior. The fellow was so badly frightened that he was unable to defend himself, dropping his weapons and falling upon the ground, wide-eyed and screaming as he gazed on his captor.

It was with considerable difficulty that the ape-man quieted the fellow's fears sufficiently to obtain a coherent statement from him as to the cause of his uncalled-for terror.

From him Tarzan learned, by dint of much coaxing, that a party of whites had passed through the village several days before. These men had told them of a terrible white devil that pursued them, warning the natives against it and the frightful pack of demons that accompanied it.

The black had recognized Tarzan as the white devil from the descriptions given by the whites and their black servants. Behind him he had expected to see a horde of demons disguised as apes and panthers.

In this Tarzan saw the cunning hand of Rokoff. The Russian was attempting to make travel as difficult as possible for him by turning the natives against him in superstitious fear.

The native further told Tarzan that the white man who had led the recent expedition had promised them a fabulous reward if they would kill the white devil. This they had fully intended doing should the opportunity present itself; but the moment they had seen Tarzan their blood had turned to water, as the porters of the white men had told them would be the case.

Finding the ape-man made no attempt to harm him, the native at last recovered his grasp upon his courage, and, at Tarzan's suggestion, accompanied the white devil back to the village, calling as he went for his fellows to return also, as "the white devil has promised to do you no harm if you come back right away and answer his questions."

One by one the blacks straggled into the village, but that their fears were not entirely allayed was evident from the amount of white that showed about the eyes of the majority of them as they cast constant and apprehensive sidelong glances at the ape-man.

The chief was among the first to return to the village, and as it was he that Tarzan was most anxious to interview, he lost no time in entering into a palaver with the black.

The fellow was short and stout, with an unusually low and degraded countenance and apelike arms. His whole expression denoted deceitfulness.

Only the superstitious terror engendered in him by the stories poured into his ears by the whites and blacks of the Russian's party kept him from leaping upon Tarzan with his warriors and slaying him forthwith, for he and his people were inveterate maneaters. But the fear that he might indeed be a devil, and that out there in the jungle behind him his fierce demons waited to do his bidding, kept M'ganwazam from putting his desires into action.

Tarzan questioned the fellow closely, and by comparing his statements with those of the young warrior he had first talked with he learned that Rokoff and his *safari* were in terror-stricken retreat in the direction of the far East Coast.

Many of the Russian's porters had already deserted him. In that very village he had hanged five for theft and attempted desertion. Judging, however, from what the Waganwazam had learned from those of the Russian's blacks who were not too far gone in terror of the brutal Rokoff to fear even to speak of their plans, it was apparent that he would not travel any great distance before the last of his porters, cooks, tent-boys, gun-bearers, *askari*, and even his headman, would have turned back into the bush, leaving him to the mercy of the merciless jungle.

M'ganwazam denied that there had been any white woman or child with the party of whites; but even as he spoke Tarzan was convinced that he lied. Several times the ape-man approached the subject from different angles, but never was he successful in surprising the wily cannibal into a direct contradiction of his original statement that there had been no women or children with the party.

Tarzan demanded food of the chief, and after considerable haggling on the part of the monarch succeeded in obtaining a meal. He then tried to draw out others of the tribe, especially the young man whom he had captured in the bush, but M'ganwazam's presence sealed their lips.

At last, convinced that these people knew a great deal more than they had told him concerning the whereabouts of the Russian and the fate of Jane and the child, Tarzan determined to remain overnight among them in the hope of discovering something further of importance.

When he had stated his decision to the chief he was rather surprised to note the sudden change in the fellow's attitude toward him.

From apparent dislike and suspicion M'ganwazam became a most eager and solicitous host.

Nothing would do but that the ape-man should occupy the best hut in the village, from which M'ganwazam's oldest wife was forthwith summarily ejected, while the chief took up his temporary abode in the hut of one of his younger consorts.

Had Tarzan chanced to recall the fact that a princely reward had been offered the blacks if they should succeed in killing him, he might have more quickly interpreted M'ganwazam's sudden change in front.

To have the white giant sleeping peacefully in one of his own huts would greatly facilitate the matter of earning the reward, and so the chief was urgent in his suggestions that Tarzan, doubtless being very much fatigued after his travels, should retire early to the comforts of the anything but inviting palace.

As much as the ape-man detested the thought of sleeping within a native hut, he had determined to do so this night, on the chance that he might be able to induce one of the younger men to sit and chat with him before the fire that burned in the centre of the smoke-filled dwelling, and from him draw the truths he sought. So Tarzan accepted the invitation of old M'ganwazam, insisting, however, that he much preferred sharing a hut with some of the younger men rather than driving the chief's old wife out in the cold.

The toothless old hag grinned her appreciation of this suggestion, and as the plan still better suited the chief's scheme, in that it would permit him to surround Tarzan with a gang of picked assassins, he readily assented, so that presently Tarzan had been installed in a hut close to the village gate.

As there was to be a dance that night in honour of a band of recently returned hunters, Tarzan was left alone in the hut, the young men, as M'ganwazam explained, having to take part in the festivities.

As soon as the ape-man was safely installed in the trap,

M'ganwazam called about him the young warriors whom he had selected to spend the night with the white devil!

None of them was overly enthusiastic about the plan, since deep in their superstitious hearts lay an exaggerated fear of the strange white giant; but the word of M'ganwazam was law among his people, so not one dared refuse the duty he was called upon to perform.

As M'ganwazam unfolded his plan in whispers to the savages squatting about him the old, toothless hag, to whom Tarzan had saved her hut for the night, hovered about the conspirators ostensibly to replenish the supply of firewood for the blaze about which the men sat, but really to drink in as much of their conversation as possible.

Tarzan had slept for perhaps an hour or two despite the savage din of the revellers when his keen senses came suddenly alert to a suspiciously stealthy movement in the hut in which he lay. The fire had died down to a little heap of glowing embers, which accentuated rather than relieved the darkness that shrouded the interior of the evil-smelling dwelling, yet the trained senses of the ape-man warned him of another presence creeping almost silently toward him through the gloom. He doubted that it was one of his hut mates returning from the festivities, for he still heard the wild cries of the dancers and the din of the tom-toms in the village street without. Who could it be that took such pains to conceal his approach?

As the presence came within reach of him the ape-man bounded lightly to the opposite side of the hut, his spear poised ready at his side.

"Who is it," he asked, "that creeps upon Tarzan of the Apes, like a hungry lion out of the darkness?"

"Silence, *bwana!*" replied an old cracked voice. "It is Tambudza— she whose hut you would not take, and thus drive an old woman out into the cold night."

"What does Tambudza want of Tarzan of the Apes?" asked the ape-man.

"You were kind to me to whom none is now kind, and I have come to warn you in payment of your kindness," answered the old hag.

"Warn me of what?"

"M'ganwazam has chosen the young men who are to sleep in the hut with you," replied Tambudza. "I was near as he talked with them, and heard him issuing his instructions to them. When the dance is run well into the morning they are to come to the hut.

"If you are awake they are to pretend that they have come to sleep, but if you sleep it is M'ganwazam's command that you be killed. If you are not then asleep they will wait quietly beside you until you do sleep, and then they will all fall upon you together and slay you. M'ganwazam is determined to win the reward the white man has offered."

"I had forgotten the reward," said Tarzan, half to himself, and then he added, "How may M'ganwazam hope to collect the reward now that the white men who are my enemies have left his country and gone he knows not where?"

"Oh, they have not gone far," replied Tambudza. "M'ganwazam knows where they camp. His runners could quickly overtake them—they move slowly."

"Where are they?" asked Tarzan.

"Do you wish to come to them?" asked Tambudza in way of reply. Tarzan nodded.

"I cannot tell you where they lie so that you could come to the place yourself, but I could lead you to them, *bwana*."

In their interest in the conversation neither of the speakers had noticed the little figure which crept into the darkness of the hut behind them, nor did they see it when it slunk noiselessly out again.

It was little Buulaoo, the chief's son by one of his younger wives—a vindictive, degenerate little rascal who hated Tambudza, and was ever seeking opportunities to spy upon her and report her slightest breach of custom to his father.

"Come, then," said Tarzan quickly, "let us be on our way."

This Buulaoo did not hear, for he was already legging it up the village street to where his hideous sire guzzled native beer, and watched the evolutions of the frantic dancers leaping high in the air and cavorting wildly in their hysterical capers.

So it happened that as Tarzan and Tambudza sneaked warily from the village and melted into the Stygian darkness of the jungle two lithe runners took their way in the same direction, though by another trail.

When they had come sufficiently far from the village to make it safe for them to speak above a whisper, Tarzan asked the old woman if she had seen aught of a white woman and a little child.

"Yes, *bwana*," replied Tambudza, "there was a woman with them and a little child—a little white piccaninny. It died here in our village of the fever and they buried it!"

XII

A BLACK SCOUNDREL

 hen Jane Clayton regained consciousness she saw Anderssen standing over her, holding the baby in his arms. As her eyes rested upon them an expression of misery and horror overspread her countenance.

"What is the matter?" he asked. "You ban sick?"

"Where is my baby?" she cried, ignoring his questions.

Anderssen held out the chubby infant, but she shook her head.

"It is not mine," she said. "You knew that it was not mine. You are a devil like the Russian."

Anderssen's blue eyes stretched in surprise.

"Not yours!" he exclaimed. "You tole me the kid aboard the *Kincaid* ban your kid."

"Not this one," replied Jane dully. "The other. Where is the other? There must have been two. I did not know about this one."

"There vasn't no other kid. Ay tank this ban yours. Ay am very sorry."

Anderssen fidgeted about, standing first on one foot and then upon the other. It was perfectly evident to Jane that he was honest in his protestations of ignorance of the true identity of the child.

Presently the baby commenced to crow, and bounce up and down in the Swede's arms, at the same time leaning forward with little hands out-reaching toward the young woman.

She could not withstand the appeal, and with a low cry she

674

sprang to her feet and gathered the baby to her breast.

For a few minutes she wept silently, her face buried in the baby's soiled little dress. The first shock of disappointment that the tiny thing had not been her beloved Jack was giving way to a great hope that after all some miracle had occurred to snatch her baby from Rokoff's hands at the last instant before the *Kincaid* sailed from England.

Then, too, there was the mute appeal of this wee waif alone and unloved in the midst of the horrors of the savage jungle. It was this thought more than any other that had sent her mother's heart out to the innocent babe, while still she suffered from disappointment that she had been deceived in its identity.

"Have you no idea whose child this is?" she asked Anderssen.

The man shook his head.

"Not now," he said. "If he ain't ban your kid, Ay don' know whose kid he do ban. Rokoff said it was yours. Ay tank he tank so, too.

"What do we do with it now? Ay can't go back to the *Kincaid*. Rokoff would have me shot; but you can go back. Ay take you to the sea, and then some of these black men they take you to the ship—eh?"

"No! no!" cried Jane. "Not for the world. I would rather die than fall into the hands of that man again. No, let us go on and take this poor little creature with us. If God is willing we shall be saved in one way or another."

So they again took up their flight through the wilderness, taking with them a half-dozen of the Mosulas to carry provisions and the tents that Anderssen had smuggled aboard the small boat in preparation for the attempted escape.

The days and nights of torture that the young woman suffered were so merged into one long, unbroken nightmare of hideousness that she soon lost all track of time. Whether they had been wandering for days or years she could not tell. The one bright spot in that eternity of fear and suffering was the little child whose tiny hands had long since fastened their softly groping fingers firmly about her heart.

In a way the little thing took the place and filled the aching void that the theft of her own baby had left. It could never be the same, of course, but yet, day by day, she found her mother-love, enveloping the waif more closely until she sometimes sat with closed eyes lost in the sweet imagining that the little bundle of humanity at her breast was truly her own.

For some time their progress inland was extremely slow. Word came to them from time to time through natives passing from the coast on hunting excursions that Rokoff had not yet guessed the direction of their flight. This, and the desire to make the journey as light as possible for the gently bred woman, kept Anderssen to a slow advance of short and easy marches with many rests.

The Swede insisted upon carrying the child while they travelled, and in countless other ways did what he could to help Jane Clayton conserve her strength. He had been terribly chagrined on discovering the mistake he had made in the identity of the baby, but once the young woman became convinced that his motives were truly chivalrous she would not permit him longer to upbraid himself for the error that he could not by any means have avoided.

At the close of each day's march Anderssen saw to the erection of a comfortable shelter for Jane and the child. Her tent was always pitched in the most favourable location. The thorn *boma* round it was the strongest and most impregnable that the Mosula could construct.

Her food was the best that their limited stores and the rifle of the Swede could provide, but the thing that touched her heart the closest was the gentle consideration and courtesy which the man always accorded her.

That such nobility of character could lie beneath so repulsive an exterior never ceased to be a source of wonder and amazement to her, until at last the innate chivalry of the man, and his unfailing kindliness and sympathy transformed his appearance in so far as Jane was concerned until she saw only the sweetness of his character mirrored in his countenance.

They had commenced to make a little better progress when word reached them that Rokoff was but a few marches behind them, and that he had at last discovered the direction of their flight. It was then that Anderssen took to the river, purchasing a canoe from a chief whose village lay a short distance from the Ugambi upon the bank of a tributary.

Thereafter the little party of fugitives fled up the broad Ugambi, and so rapid had their flight become that they no longer received word of their pursuers. At the end of canoe navigation upon the river, they abandoned their canoe and took to the jungle. Here progress became at once arduous, slow, and dangerous.

The second day after leaving the Ugambi the baby fell ill with fever. Anderssen knew what the outcome must be, but he had not the heart to tell Jane Clayton the truth, for he had seen that the young woman had come to love the child almost as passionately as though it had been her own flesh and blood.

As the baby's condition precluded farther advance, Anderssen withdrew a little from the main trail he had been following and built a camp in a natural clearing on the bank of a little river.

Here Jane devoted her every moment to caring for the tiny sufferer, and as though her sorrow and anxiety were not all that she could bear, a further blow came with the sudden announcement of one of the Mosula porters who had been foraging in the jungle adjacent that Rokoff and his party were camped quite close to them, and were evidently upon their trail to this little nook which all had thought so excellent a hiding-place.

This information could mean but one thing, and that they must break camp and fly onward regardless of the baby's condition. Jane Clayton knew the traits of the Russian well enough to be positive that he would separate her from the child the moment that he recaptured them, and she knew that separation would mean the immediate death of the baby.

As they stumbled forward through the tangled vegetation along an old and almost overgrown game trail the Mosula porters deserted them one by one.

The men had been staunch enough in their devotion and loyalty as long as they were in no danger of being overtaken by the Russian and his party. They had heard, however, so much of the atrocious disposition of Rokoff that they had grown to hold him in mortal terror, and now that they knew he was close upon them their timid hearts would fortify them no longer, and as quickly as possible they deserted the three whites.

Yet on and on went Anderssen and the girl. The Swede went ahead, to hew a way through the brush where the path was entirely overgrown, so that on this march it was necessary that the young woman carry the child.

All day they marched. Late in the afternoon they realized that they had failed. Close behind them they heard the noise of a large *safari* advancing along the trail which they had cleared for their pursuers.

When it became quite evident that they must be overtaken in a short time Anderssen hid Jane behind a large tree, covering her and the child with brush.

"There is a village about a mile farther on," he said to her. "The Mosula told me its location before they deserted us. Ay try to lead the Russian off your trail, then you go on to the village. Ay tank the chief ban friendly to white men—the Mosula tal me he ban. Anyhow, that was all we can do.

"After while you get chief to tak you down by the Mosula village at the sea again, an' after a while a ship is sure to put into the mouth of the Ugambi. Then you be all right. Gude-by an' gude luck to you, lady!"

"But where are you going, Sven?" asked Jane. "Why can't you hide here and go back to the sea with me?"

"Ay gotta tal the Russian you ban dead, so that he don't luke for you no more," and Anderssen grinned.

"Why can't you join me then after you have told him that?" insisted the girl.

Anderssen shook his head.

"Ay don't tank Ay join anybody any more after Ay tal the Russian you ban dead," he said.

"You don't mean that you think he will kill you?" asked Jane, and yet in her heart she knew that that was exactly what the great scoundrel would do in revenge for his having been thwarted by the Swede. Anderssen did not reply, other than to warn her to silence and point toward the path along which they had just come.

"I don't care," whispered Jane Clayton. "I shall not let you die to save me if I can prevent it in any way. Give me your revolver. I can use that, and together we may be able to hold them off until we can find some means of escape."

"It won't work, lady," replied Anderssen. "They would only get us both, and then Ay couldn't do you no good at all. Think of the kid, lady, and what it would be for you both to fall into Rokoff's hands again. For his sake you must do what Ay say. Here, take my rifle and ammunition; you may need them."

He shoved the gun and bandoleer into the shelter beside Jane. Then he was gone.

She watched him as he returned along the path to meet the oncoming *safari* of the Russian. Soon a turn in the trail hid him from view.

Her first impulse was to follow. With the rifle she might be of assistance to him, and, further, she could not bear the terrible thought of being left alone at the mercy of the fearful jungle without a single friend to aid her.

She started to crawl from her shelter with the intention of running after Anderssen as fast as she could. As she drew the baby close to her she glanced down into its little face.

How red it was! How unnatural the little thing looked. She raised the cheek to hers. It was fiery hot with fever!

With a little gasp of terror Jane Clayton rose to her feet in the jungle path. The rifle and bandoleer lay forgotten in the shelter beside her. Anderssen was forgotten, and Rokoff, and her great peril.

All that rioted through her fear-mad brain was the fearful fact that this little, helpless child was stricken with the terrible jungle-fever, and that she was helpless to do aught to allay its sufferings— sufferings that were sure to coming during ensuing intervals of partial consciousness.

Her one thought was to find some one who could help her— some woman who had had children of her own—and with the thought came recollection of the friendly village of which Anderssen had spoken. If she could but reach it—in time!

There was no time to be lost. Like a startled antelope she turned and fled up the trail in the direction Anderssen had indicated.

From far behind came the sudden shouting of men, the sound of shots, and then silence. She knew that Anderssen had met the Russian.

A half-hour later she stumbled, exhausted, into a little thatched village. Instantly she was surrounded by men, women, and children. Eager, curious, excited natives plied her with a hundred questions, no one of which she could understand or answer.

All that she could do was to point tearfully at the baby, now wailing piteously in her arms, and repeat over and over, "Fever— fever—fever."

The blacks did not understand her words, but they saw the cause of her trouble, and soon a young woman had pulled her into a hut and with several others was doing her poor best to quiet the child and allay its agony.

The witch doctor came and built a little fire before the infant, upon which he boiled some strange concoction in a small earthen pot, making weird passes above it and mumbling strange, monotonous chants. Presently he dipped a zebra's tail into the brew, and with further mutterings and incantations sprinkled a few drops of the liquid over the baby's face.

After he had gone the women sat about and moaned and wailed until Jane thought that she should go mad; but, knowing that they were doing it all out of the kindness of their hearts, she endured the frightful waking nightmare of those awful hours in dumb and patient suffering.

It must have been well toward midnight that she became conscious of a sudden commotion in the village. She heard the voices of the natives raised in controversy, but she could not understand the words.

Presently she heard footsteps approaching the hut in which she squatted before a bright fire with the baby on her lap. The little thing lay very still now, its lids, half-raised, showed the pupils horribly upturned.

Jane Clayton looked into the little face with fear-haunted eyes. It was not her baby—not her flesh and blood—but how close, how dear the tiny, helpless thing had become to her. Her heart, bereft of its own, had gone out to this poor, little, nameless waif, and lavished upon it all the love that had been denied her during the long, bitter weeks of her captivity aboard the *Kincaid*.

She saw that the end was near, and though she was terrified at contemplation of her loss, still she hoped that it would come quickly now and end the sufferings of the little victim.

The footsteps she had heard without the hut now halted before the door. There was a whispered colloquy, and a moment later M'ganwazam, chief of the tribe, entered. She had seen but little of him, as the women had taken her in hand almost as soon as she had entered the village.

681

M'ganwazam, she now saw, was an evil-appearing savage with every mark of brutal degeneracy writ large upon his bestial countenance. To Jane Clayton he looked more gorilla than human. He tried to converse with her, but without success, and finally he called to some one without.

In answer to his summons another Negro entered—a man of very different appearance from M'ganwazam—so different, in fact, that Jane Clayton immediately decided that he was of another tribe. This man acted as interpreter, and almost from the first question that M'ganwazam put to her, Jane felt an intuitive conviction that the savage was attempting to draw information from her for some ulterior motive.

She thought it strange that the fellow should so suddenly have become interested in her plans, and especially in her intended destination when her journey had been interrupted at his village.

Seeing no reason for withholding the information, she told him the truth; but when he asked if she expected to meet her husband at the end of the trip, she shook her head negatively.

Then he told her the purpose of his visit, talking through the interpreter.

"I have just learned," he said, "from some men who live by the side of the great water, that your husband followed you up the Ugambi for several marches, when he was at last set upon by natives and killed. Therefore I have told you this that you might not waste your time in a long journey if you expected to meet your husband at the end of it; but instead could turn and retrace your steps to the coast."

Jane thanked M'ganwazam for his kindness, though her heart was numb with suffering at this new blow. She who had suffered so much was at last beyond reach of the keenest of misery's pangs, for her senses were numbed and calloused.

With bowed head she sat staring with unseeing eyes upon the face of the baby in her lap. M'ganwazam had left the hut. Sometime later she heard a noise at the entrance—another had entered. One of the women sitting opposite her threw a faggot upon the dying embers of the fire between them.

With a sudden flare it burst into renewed flame, lighting up the hut's interior as though by magic.

The flame disclosed to Jane Clayton's horrified gaze that the baby was quite dead. How long it had been so she could not guess.

A choking lump rose to her throat, her head drooped in silent misery upon the little bundle that she had caught suddenly to her breast. For a moment the silence of the hut was unbroken. Then the native woman broke into a hideous wail.

A man coughed close before Jane Clayton and spoke her name.

With a start she raised her eyes to look into the sardonic countenance of Nikolas Rokoff.

XIII

ESCAPE

or a moment Rokoff stood sneering down upon Jane Clayton, then his eyes fell to the little bundle in her lap. Jane had drawn one corner of the blanket over the child's face, so that to one who did not know the truth it seemed but to be sleeping.

"You have gone to a great deal of unnecessary trouble," said Rokoff, "to bring the child to this village. If you had attended to your own affairs I should have brought it here myself.

"You would have been spared the dangers and fatigue of the journey. But I suppose I must thank you for relieving me of the inconvenience of having to care for a young infant on the march.

"This is the village to which the child was destined from the first. M'ganwazam will rear him carefully, making a good cannibal of him, and if you ever chance to return to civilization it will doubtless afford you much food for thought as you compare the luxuries and comforts of your life with the details of the life your son is living in the village of the Waganwazam.

"Again I thank you for bringing him here for me, and now I must ask you to surrender him to me, that I may turn him over to his foster parents." As he concluded Rokoff held out his hands for the child, a nasty grin of vindictiveness upon his lips.

To his surprise Jane Clayton rose and, without a word of protest, laid the little bundle in his arms.

684

"Here is the child," she said. "Thank God he is beyond your power to harm."

Grasping the import of her words, Rokoff snatched the blanket from the child's face to seek confirmation of his fears. Jane Clayton watched his expression closely.

She had been puzzled for days for an answer to the question of Rokoff's knowledge of the child's identity. If she had been in doubt before the last shred of that doubt was wiped away as she witnessed the terrible anger of the Russian as he looked upon the dead face of the baby and realized that at the last moment his dearest wish for vengeance had been thwarted by a higher power.

Almost throwing the body of the child back into Jane Clayton's arms, Rokoff stamped up and down the hut, pounding the air with his clenched fists and cursing terribly. At last he halted in front of the young woman, bringing his face down close to hers.

"You are laughing at me," he shrieked. "You think that you have beaten me—eh? I'll show you, as I have shown the miserable ape you call 'husband,' what it means to interfere with the plans of Nikolas Rokoff.

"You have robbed me of the child. I cannot make him the son of a cannibal chief, but"—and he paused as though to let the full meaning of his threat sink deep—"I can make the mother the wife of a cannibal, and that I shall do—after I have finished with her myself."

If he had thought to wring from Jane Clayton any sign of terror he failed miserably. She was beyond that. Her brain and nerves were numb to suffering and shock.

To his surprise a faint, almost happy smile touched her lips. She was thinking with thankful heart that this poor little corpse was not that of her own wee Jack, and that—best of all—Rokoff evidently did not know the truth.

She would have liked to have flaunted the fact in his face, but she dared not. If he continued to believe that the child had been hers, so much safer would be the real Jack wherever he might be. She had, of course, no knowledge of the whereabouts of her little son—she did not know, even, that he still lived, and yet there was the chance that he might.

It was more than possible that without Rokoff's knowledge this child had been substituted for hers by one of the Russian's confederates, and that even now her son might be safe with friends in London, where there were many, both able and willing, to have paid any ransom which the traitorous conspirator might have asked for the safe release of Lord Greystoke's son.

She had thought it all out a hundred times since she had discovered that the baby which Anderssen had placed in her arms that night upon the *Kincaid* was not her own, and it had been a constant and gnawing source of happiness to her to dream the whole fantasy through in its every detail.

No, the Russian must never know that this was not her baby. She realized that her position was hopeless—with Anderssen and her husband dead there was no one in all the world with a desire to succour her who knew where she might be found.

Rokoff's threat, she realized, was no idle one. That he would do, or attempt to do, all that he had promised, she was perfectly sure; but at the worst it meant but a little earlier release from the hideous anguish that she had been enduring. She must find some way to take her own life before the Russian could harm her further.

Just now she wanted time—time to think and prepare herself for the end. She felt that she could not take the last, awful step until she had exhausted every possibility of escape. She did not care to live unless she might find her way back to her own child, but slight as such a hope appeared she would not admit its impossibility until the last moment had come, and she faced the fearful reality of choosing between the final alternatives—Nikolas Rokoff on one hand and self-destruction upon the other.

"Go away!" she said to the Russian. "Go away and leave me in peace with my dead. Have you not brought sufficient misery and anguish upon me without attempting to harm me further? What wrong have I ever done you that you should persist in persecuting me?"

"You are suffering for the sins of the monkey you chose when you might have had the love of a gentleman—of Nikolas Rokoff," he replied. "But where is the use in discussing the matter? We shall bury the child here, and you will return with me at once to my own camp. Tomorrow I shall bring you back and turn you over to your new husband—the lovely M'ganwazam. Come!"

He reached out for the child. Jane, who was on her feet now, turned away from him.

"I shall bury the body," she said. "Send some men to dig a grave outside the village."

Rokoff was anxious to have the thing over and get back to his camp with his victim. He thought he saw in her apathy a resignation to her fate. Stepping outside the hut, he motioned her to follow him, and a moment later, with his men, he escorted Jane beyond the village, where beneath a great tree the blacks scooped a shallow grave.

Wrapping the tiny body in a blanket, Jane laid it tenderly in the black hole, and, turning her head that she might not see the mouldy earth falling upon the pitiful little bundle, she breathed a prayer beside the grave of the nameless waif that had won its way to the innermost recesses of her heart.

Then, dry-eyed but suffering, she rose and followed the Russian through the Stygian blackness of the jungle, along the winding, leafy corridor that led from the village of M'ganwazam, the black cannibal, to the camp of Nikolas Rokoff, the white fiend.

Beside them, in the impenetrable thickets that fringed the path, rising to arch above it and shut out the moon, the girl could hear the stealthy, muffled footfalls of great beasts, and ever round about them rose the deafening roars of hunting lions, until the earth trembled to the mighty sound.

The porters lighted torches now and waved them upon either hand to frighten off the beasts of prey. Rokoff urged them to greater speed, and from the quavering note in his voice Jane Clayton knew that he was weak from terror.

The sounds of the jungle night recalled most vividly the days and nights that she had spent in a similar jungle with her forest god—with the fearless and unconquerable Tarzan of the Apes. Then there had been no thoughts of terror, though the jungle noises were new to her, and the roar of a lion had seemed the most awe-inspiring sound upon the great earth.

How different would it be now if she knew that he was somewhere there in the wilderness, seeking her! Then, indeed, would there be that for which to live, and every reason to believe that succour was close at hand—but he was dead! It was incredible that it should be so.

There seemed no place in death for that great body and those mighty thews. Had Rokoff been the one to tell her of her lord's passing she would have known that he lied. There could be no reason, she thought, why M'ganwazam should have deceived her. She did not know that the Russian had talked with the savage a few minutes before the chief had come to her with his tale.

At last they reached the rude *boma* that Rokoff's porters had thrown up round the Russian's camp. Here they found all in turmoil. She did not know what it was all about, but she saw that Rokoff was very angry, and from bits of conversation which she could translate she gleaned that there had been further desertions while he had been absent, and that the deserters had taken the bulk of his food and ammunition.

When he had done venting his rage upon those who remained he returned to where Jane stood under guard of a couple of his white sailors. He grasped her roughly by the arm and started to drag her toward his tent. The girl struggled and fought to free herself, while the two sailors stood by, laughing at the rare treat.

Rokoff did not hesitate to use rough methods when he found that he was to have difficulty in carrying out his designs. Repeatedly he struck Jane Clayton in the face, until at last, half-conscious, she was dragged within his tent.

Rokoff's boy had lighted the Russian's lamp, and now at a word from his master he made himself scarce. Jane had sunk to the floor in the middle of the enclosure. Slowly her numbed senses were returning to her and she was commencing to think very fast indeed. Quickly her eyes ran round the interior of the tent, taking in every detail of its equipment and contents.

Now the Russian was lifting her to her feet and attempting to drag her to the camp cot that stood at one side of the tent. At his belt hung a heavy revolver. Jane Clayton's eyes riveted themselves upon it. Her palm itched to grasp the huge butt. She feigned again to swoon, but through her half-closed lids she waited her opportunity.

It came just as Rokoff was lifting her upon the cot. A noise at the tent door behind him brought his head quickly about and away from the girl. The butt of the gun was not an inch from her hand. With a single, lightning-like move she snatched the weapon from its holster, and at the same instant Rokoff turned back toward her, realizing his peril.

She did not dare fire for fear the shot would bring his people about him, and with Rokoff dead she would fall into hands no better than his and to a fate probably even worse than he alone could have imagined. The memory of the two brutes who stood and laughed as Rokoff struck her was still vivid.

As the rage and fear-filled countenance of the Slav turned toward her Jane Clayton raised the heavy revolver high above the pasty face and with all her strength dealt the man a terrific blow between the eyes.

Without a sound he sank, limp and unconscious, to the ground.

A moment later the girl stood beside him—for a moment at least free from the menace of his lust.

Outside the tent she again heard the noise that had distracted Rokoff's attention. What it was she did not know, but, fearing the return of the servant and the discovery of her deed, she stepped quickly to the camp table upon which burned the oil lamp and extinguished the smudgy, evil-smelling flame.

In the total darkness of the interior she paused for a moment to collect her wits and plan for the next step in her venture for freedom.

About her was a camp of enemies. Beyond these foes a black wilderness of savage jungle peopled by hideous beasts of prey and still more hideous human beasts.

There was little or no chance that she could survive even a few days of the constant dangers that would confront her there; but the knowledge that she had already passed through so many perils unscathed, and that somewhere out in the faraway world a little child was doubtless at that very moment crying for her, filled her with determination to make the effort to accomplish the seemingly impossible and cross that awful land of horror in search of the sea and the remote chance of succour she might find there.

Rokoff's tent stood almost exactly in the centre of the *boma*. Surrounding it were the tents and shelters of his white companions and the natives of his *safari*. To pass through these and find egress through the *boma* seemed a task too fraught with insurmountable obstacles to warrant even the slightest consideration, and yet there was no other way.

To remain in the tent until she should be discovered would be to set at naught all that she had risked to gain her freedom, and so with stealthy step and every sense alert she approached the back of the tent to set out upon the first stage of her adventure.

Groping along the rear of the canvas wall, she found that there was no opening there. Quickly she returned to the side of the unconscious Russian. In his belt her groping fingers came upon the hilt of a long hunting-knife, and with this she cut a hole in the back wall of the tent.

Silently she stepped without. To her immense relief she saw that the camp was apparently asleep. In the dim and flickering light of the dying fires she saw but a single sentry, and he was dozing upon his haunches at the opposite side of the enclosure.

Keeping the tent between him and herself, she crossed between the small shelters of the native porters to the *boma* wall beyond.

Outside, in the darkness of the tangled jungle, she could hear the roaring of lions, the laughing of hyenas, and the countless, nameless noises of the midnight jungle.

For a moment she hesitated, trembling. The thought of the prowling beasts out there in the darkness was appalling. Then, with a sudden brave toss of her head, she attacked the thorny *boma* wall with her delicate hands. Torn and bleeding though they were, she worked on breathlessly until she had made an opening through which she could worm her body, and at last she stood outside the enclosure.

Behind her lay a fate worse than death, at the hands of human beings.

Before her lay an almost certain fate—but it was only death— sudden, merciful, and honourable death.

Without a tremor and without regret she darted away from the camp, and a moment later the mysterious jungle had closed about her.

XIV

Alone in the Jungle

ambudza, leading Tarzan of the Apes toward the camp of the Russian, moved very slowly along the winding jungle path, for she was old and her legs stiff with rheumatism.

So it was that the runners dispatched by M'ganwazam to warn Rokoff that the white giant was in his village and that he would be slain that night reached the Russian's camp before Tarzan and his ancient guide had covered half the distance.

The guides found the white man's camp in a turmoil. Rokoff had that morning been discovered stunned and bleeding within his tent. When he had recovered his senses and realized that Jane Clayton had escaped, his rage was boundless.

Rushing about the camp with his rifle, he had sought to shoot down the native sentries who had allowed the young woman to elude their vigilance, but several of the other whites, realizing that they were already in a precarious position owing to the numerous desertions that Rokoff's cruelty had brought about, seized and disarmed him.

Then came the messengers from M'ganwazam, but scarce had they told their story and Rokoff was preparing to depart with them for their village when other runners, panting from the exertions of their swift flight through the jungle, rushed breathless into the firelight, crying that the great white giant had escaped from M'ganwazam and was already on his way to wreak vengeance against his enemies.

Instantly confusion reigned within the encircling *boma*. The blacks belonging to Rokoff's *safari* were terror-stricken at the thought of the proximity of the white giant who hunted through the jungle with a fierce pack of apes and panthers at his heels.

Before the whites realized what had happened the superstitious fears of the natives had sent them scurrying into the bush—their own carriers as well as the messengers from M'ganwazam—but even in their haste they had not neglected to take with them every article of value upon which they could lay their hands.

Thus Rokoff and the seven white sailors found themselves deserted and robbed in the midst of a wilderness.

The Russian, following his usual custom, berated his companions, laying all the blame upon their shoulders for the events which had led up to the almost hopeless condition in which they now found themselves; but the sailors were in no mood to brook his insults and his cursing.

In the midst of this tirade one of them drew a revolver and fired point-blank at the Russian. The fellow's aim was poor, but his act so terrified Rokoff that he turned and fled for his tent.

As he ran his eyes chanced to pass beyond the *boma* to the edge of the forest, and there he caught a glimpse of that which sent his craven heart cold with a fear that almost expunged his terror of the seven men at his back, who by this time were all firing in hate and revenge at his retreating figure.

What he saw was the giant figure of an almost naked white man emerging from the bush.

Darting into his tent, the Russian did not halt in his flight, but kept right on through the rear wall, taking advantage of the long slit that Jane Clayton had made the night before.

The terror-stricken Muscovite scurried like a hunted rabbit through the hole that still gaped in the *boma's* wall at the point where his own prey had escaped, and as Tarzan approached the camp upon the opposite side Rokoff disappeared into the jungle in the wake of Jane Clayton.

As the ape-man entered the *boma* with old Tambudza at his elbow the seven sailors, recognizing him, turned and fled in the opposite direction. Tarzan saw that Rokoff was not among them, and so he let them go their way—his business was with the Russian, whom he expected to find in his tent. As to the sailors, he was sure that the jungle would exact from them expiation for their villainies, nor, doubtless, was he wrong, for his were the last white man's eyes to rest upon any of them.

Finding Rokoff's tent empty, Tarzan was about to set out in search of the Russian when Tambudza suggested to him that the departure of the white man could only have resulted from word reaching him from M'ganwazam that Tarzan was in his village.

"He has doubtless hastened there," argued the old woman. "If you would find him let us return at once."

Tarzan himself thought that this would probably prove to be the fact, so he did not waste time in an endeavour to locate the Russian's trail, but, instead, set out briskly for the village of M'ganwazam, leaving Tambudza to plod slowly in his wake.

His one hope was that Jane was still safe and with Rokoff. If this was the case, it would be but a matter of an hour or more before he should be able to wrest her from the Russian.

He knew now that M'ganwazam was treacherous and that he might have to fight to regain possession of his wife. He wished that Mugambi, Sheeta, Akut, and the balance of the pack were with him, for he realized that single-handed it would be no child's play to bring Jane safely from the clutches of two such scoundrels as Rokoff and the wily M'ganwazam.

To his surprise he found no sign of either Rokoff or Jane in the village, and as he could not trust the word of the chief, he wasted no time in futile inquiry. So sudden and unexpected had been his

return, and so quickly had he vanished into the jungle after learning that those he sought were not among the Waganwazam, that old
M'ganwazam had no time to prevent his going.

Swinging through the trees, he hastened back to the deserted
camp he had so recently left, for here, he knew, was the logical place
to take up the trail of Rokoff and Jane.

Arrived at the *boma*, he circled carefully about the outside of the
enclosure until, opposite a break in the thorny wall, he came to indications that something had recently passed into the jungle. His acute
sense of smell told him that both of those he sought had fled from the
camp in this direction, and a moment later he had taken up the trail
and was following the faint spoor. Far ahead of him a terror-stricken
young woman was slinking along a narrow game-trail, fearful that
the next moment would bring her face to face with some savage beast
or equally savage man. As she ran on, hoping against hope that she
had hit upon the direction that would lead her eventually to the great
river, she came suddenly upon a familiar spot.

At one side of the trail, beneath a giant tree, lay a little heap of
loosely piled brush—to her dying day that little spot of jungle would
be indelibly impressed upon her memory. It was where Anderssen
had hidden her—where he had given up his life in the vain effort to
save her from Rokoff.

At sight of it she recalled the rifle and ammunition that the man
had thrust upon her at the last moment. Until now she had forgotten them entirely. Still clutched in her hand was the revolver she had
snatched from Rokoff's belt, but that could contain at most not over
six cartridges—not enough to furnish her with food and protection
both on the long journey to the sea.

With bated breath she groped beneath the little mound, scarce
daring to hope that the treasure remained where she had left it; but,
to her infinite relief and joy, her hand came at once upon the barrel of
the heavy weapon and then upon the bandoleer of cartridges.

As she threw the latter about her shoulder and felt the weight of the big game-gun in her hand a sudden sense of security suffused her. It was with new hope and a feeling almost of assured success that she again set forward upon her journey.

That night she slept in the crotch of a tree, as Tarzan had so often told her that he was accustomed to doing, and early the next morning was upon her way again. Late in the afternoon, as she was about to cross a little clearing, she was startled at the sight of a huge ape coming from the jungle upon the opposite side.

The wind was blowing directly across the clearing between them, and Jane lost no time in putting herself downwind from the huge creature. Then she hid in a clump of heavy bush and watched, holding the rifle ready for instant use.

To her consternation she saw that the apes were pausing in the centre of the clearing. They came together in a little knot, where they stood looking backward, as though in expectation of the coming of others of their tribe. Jane wished that they would go on, for she knew that at any moment some little, eddying gust of wind might carry her scent down to their nostrils, and then what would the protection of her rifle amount to in the face of those gigantic muscles and mighty fangs?

Her eyes moved back and forth between the apes and the edge of the jungle toward which they were gazing until at last she perceived the object of their halt and the thing that they awaited. They were being stalked.

Of this she was positive, as she saw the lithe, sinewy form of a panther glide noiselessly from the jungle at the point at which the apes had emerged but a moment before.

Quickly the beast trotted across the clearing toward the anthropoids. Jane wondered at their apparent apathy, and a moment later her wonder turned to amazement as she saw the great cat come quite close to the apes, who appeared entirely unconcerned by its presence, and, squatting down in their midst, fell assiduously to the business of preening, which occupies most of the waking hours of the cat family.

If the young woman was surprised by the sight of these natural enemies fraternizing, it was with emotions little short of fear for her own sanity that she presently saw a tall, muscular warrior enter the clearing and join the group of savage beasts assembled there.

At first sight of the man she had been positive that he would be torn to pieces, and she had half risen from her shelter, raising her rifle to her shoulder to do what she could to avert the man's terrible fate.

Now she saw that he seemed actually conversing with the beasts—issuing orders to them.

Presently the entire company filed on across the clearing and disappeared in the jungle upon the opposite side.

With a gasp of mingled incredulity and relief Jane Clayton staggered to her feet and fled on away from the terrible horde that had just passed her, while a half-mile behind her another individual, following the same trail as she, lay frozen with terror behind an ant-hill as the hideous band passed quite close to him.

This one was Rokoff; but he had recognized the members of the awful aggregation as allies of Tarzan of the Apes. No sooner, therefore, had the beasts passed him than he rose and raced through the jungle as fast as he could go, in order that he might put as much distance as possible between himself and these frightful beasts.

So it happened that as Jane Clayton came to the bank of the river, down which she hoped to float to the ocean and eventual rescue, Nikolas Rokoff was but a short distance in her rear.

Upon the bank the girl saw a great dugout drawn half-way from the water and tied securely to a near-by tree.

This, she felt, would solve the question of transportation to the sea could she but launch the huge, unwieldy craft. Unfastening the rope that had moored it to the tree, Jane pushed frantically upon the bow of the heavy canoe, but for all the results that were apparent she might as well have been attempting to shove the earth out of its orbit.

She was about winded when it occurred to her to try working the dugout into the stream by loading the stern with ballast and then rocking the bow back and forth along the bank until the craft eventually worked itself into the river.

There were no stones or rocks available, but along the shore she found quantities of driftwood deposited by the river at a slightly higher stage. These she gathered and piled far in the stern of the boat, until at last, to her immense relief, she saw the bow rise gently from the mud of the bank and the stern drift slowly with the current until it again lodged a few feet farther down-stream.

Jane found that by running back and forth between the bow and stern she could alternately raise and lower each end of the boat as she shifted her weight from one end to the other, with the result that each time she leaped to the stern the canoe moved a few inches farther into the river.

As the success of her plan approached more closely to fruition she became so wrapped in her efforts that she failed to note the figure of a man standing beneath a huge tree at the edge of the jungle from which he had just emerged.

He watched her and her labours with a cruel and malicious grin upon his swarthy countenance.

The boat at last became so nearly free of the retarding mud and of the bank that Jane felt positive that she could pole it off into deeper water with one of the paddles which lay in the bottom of the rude craft. With this end in view she seized upon one of these implements and had just plunged it into the river bottom close to the shore when her eyes happened to rise to the edge of the jungle.

As her gaze fell upon the figure of the man a little cry of terror rose to her lips. It was Rokoff.

He was running toward her now and shouting to her to wait or he would shoot—though he was entirely unarmed it was difficult to discover just how he intended making good his threat.

Jane Clayton knew nothing of the various misfortunes that had befallen the Russian since she had escaped from his tent, so she believed that his followers must be close at hand.

However, she had no intention of falling again into the man's clutches. She would rather die at once than that that should happen to her. Another minute and the boat would be free.

Once in the current of the river she would be beyond Rokoff's power to stop her, for there was no other boat upon the shore, and no man, and certainly not the cowardly Rokoff, would dare to attempt to swim the crocodile-infested water in an effort to overtake her.

Rokoff, on his part, was bent more upon escape than aught else. He would gladly have forgone any designs he might have had upon Jane Clayton would she but permit him to share this means of escape that she had discovered. He would promise anything if she would let him come aboard the dugout, but he did not think that it was necessary to do so.

He saw that he could easily reach the bow of the boat before it cleared the shore, and then it would not be necessary to make promises of any sort. Not that Rokoff would have felt the slightest compunction in ignoring any promises he might have made the girl, but he disliked the idea of having to sue for favour with one who had so recently assaulted and escaped him.

Already he was gloating over the days and nights of revenge that would be his while the heavy dugout drifted its slow way to the ocean.

Jane Clayton, working furiously to shove the boat beyond his reach, suddenly realized that she was to be successful, for with a little lurch the dugout swung quickly into the current, just as the Russian reached out to place his hand upon its bow.

His fingers did not miss their goal by a half-dozen inches. The girl almost collapsed with the reaction from the terrific mental, physical, and nervous strain under which she had been labouring for the past few minutes. But, thank Heaven, at last she was safe!

Even as she breathed a silent prayer of thanksgiving, she saw a sudden expression of triumph lighten the features of the cursing Russian, and at the same instant he dropped suddenly to the ground, grasping firmly upon something which wriggled through the mud toward the water.

Jane Clayton crouched, wide-eyed and horror-stricken, in the bottom of the boat as she realized that at the last instant success had been turned to failure, and that she was indeed again in the power of the malignant Rokoff.

For the thing that the man had seen and grasped was the end of the trailing rope with which the dugout had been moored to the tree.

XV

DOWN THE UGAMBI

 alfway between the Ugambi and the village of the Waganwazam, Tarzan came upon the pack moving slowly along his old spoor. Mugambi could scarce believe that the trail of the Russian and the mate of his savage master had passed so close to that of the pack.

It seemed incredible that two human beings should have come so close to them without having been detected by some of the marvellously keen and alert beasts; but Tarzan pointed out the spoor of the two he trailed, and at certain points the black could see that the man and the woman must have been in hiding as the pack passed them, watching every move of the ferocious creatures.

It had been apparent to Tarzan from the first that Jane and Rokoff were not travelling together. The spoor showed distinctly that the young woman had been a considerable distance ahead of the Russian at first, though the farther the ape-man continued along the trail the more obvious it became that the man was rapidly overhauling his quarry.

At first there had been the spoor of wild beasts over the footprints of Jane Clayton, while upon the top of all Rokoff's spoor showed that he had passed over the trail after the animals had left their records upon the ground. But later there were fewer and fewer animal imprints occurring between those of Jane's and the Russian's feet, until as he approached the river the ape-man became aware that

Rokoff could not have been more than a few hundred yards behind the girl.

He felt they must be close ahead of him now, and, with a little thrill of expectation, he leaped rapidly forward ahead of the pack. Swinging swiftly through the trees, he came out upon the river-bank at the very point at which Rokoff had overhauled Jane as she endeavoured to launch the cumbersome dugout.

In the mud along the bank the ape-man saw the footprints of the two he sought, but there was neither boat nor people there when he arrived, nor, at first glance, any sign of their whereabouts.

It was plain that they had shoved off a native canoe and embarked upon the bosom of the stream, and as the ape-man's eye ran swiftly down the course of the river beneath the shadows of the overarching trees he saw in the distance, just as it rounded a bend that shut it off from his view, a drifting dugout in the stern of which was the figure of a man.

Just as the pack came in sight of the river they saw their agile leader racing down the river's bank, leaping from hummock to hummock of the swampy ground that spread between them and a little promontory which rose just where the river curved inward from their sight.

To follow him it was necessary for the heavy, cumbersome apes to make a wide detour, and Sheeta, too, who hated water. Mugambi followed after them as rapidly as he could in the wake of the great white master.

A half-hour of rapid travelling across the swampy neck of land and over the rising promontory brought Tarzan, by a short cut, to the inward bend of the winding river, and there before him upon the bosom of the stream he saw the dugout, and in its stern Nikolas Rokoff.

Jane was not with the Russian.

At sight of his enemy the broad scar upon the ape-man's brow burned scarlet, and there rose to his lips the hideous, bestial challenge of the bull-ape.

Rokoff shuddered as the weird and terrible alarm fell upon his ears. Cowering in the bottom of the boat, his teeth chattering in terror, he watched the man he feared above all other creatures upon the face of the earth as he ran quickly to the edge of the water.

Even though the Russian knew that he was safe from his enemy, the very sight of him threw him into a frenzy of trembling cowardice, which became frantic hysteria as he saw the white giant dive fearlessly into the forbidding waters of the tropical river.

With steady, powerful strokes the ape-man forged out into the stream toward the drifting dugout. Now Rokoff seized one of the paddles lying in the bottom of the craft, and, with terrorwide eyes still glued upon the living death that pursued him, struck out madly in an effort to augment the speed of the unwieldy canoe.

And from the opposite bank a sinister ripple, unseen by either man, moving steadily toward the half-naked swimmer.

Tarzan had reached the stern of the craft at last. One hand upstretched grasped the gunwale. Rokoff sat frozen with fear, unable to move a hand or foot, his eyes riveted upon the face of his Nemesis.

Then a sudden commotion in the water behind the swimmer caught his attention. He saw the ripple, and he knew what caused it.

At the same instant Tarzan felt mighty jaws close upon his right leg. He tried to struggle free and raise himself over the side of the boat. His efforts would have succeeded had not this unexpected interruption galvanized the malign brain of the Russian into instant action with its sudden promise of deliverance and revenge.

Like a venomous snake the man leaped toward the stern of the boat, and with a single swift blow struck Tarzan across the head with the heavy paddle. The ape-man's fingers slipped from their hold upon the gunwale.

There was a short struggle at the surface, and then a swirl of waters, a little eddy, and a burst of bubbles soon smoothed out by the flowing current marked for the instant the spot where Tarzan of the Apes, Lord of the Jungle, disappeared from the sight of men beneath the gloomy waters of the dark and forbidding Ugambi.

Weak from terror, Rokoff sank shuddering into the bottom of the dugout. For a moment he could not realize the good fortune that had befallen him—all that he could see was the figure of a silent, struggling white man disappearing beneath the surface of the river to unthinkable death in the slimy mud of the bottom.

Slowly all that it meant to him filtered into the mind of the Russian, and then a cruel smile of relief and triumph touched his lips; but it was short-lived, for just as he was congratulating himself that he was now comparatively safe to proceed upon his way to the coast unmolested, a mighty pandemonium rose from the river-bank close by.

As his eyes sought the authors of the frightful sound he saw standing upon the shore, glaring at him with hate-filled eyes, a devil-faced panther surrounded by the hideous apes of Akut, and in the forefront of them a giant black warrior who shook his fist at him, threatening him with terrible death.

The nightmare of that flight down the Ugambi with the hideous horde racing after him by day and by night, now abreast of him, now lost in the mazes of the jungle far behind for hours and once for a whole day, only to reappear again upon his trail grim, relentless, and terrible, reduced the Russian from a strong and robust man to an emaciated, white-haired, fear-gibbering thing before ever the bay and the ocean broke upon his hopeless vision.

Past populous villages he had fled. Time and again warriors had put out in their canoes to intercept him, but each time the hideous horde had swept into view to send the terrified natives shrieking back to the shore to lose themselves in the jungle.

Nowhere in his flight had he seen aught of Jane Clayton. Not once had his eyes rested upon her since that moment at the river's brim his hand had closed upon the rope attached to the bow of her dugout and he had believed her safely in his power again, only to be thwarted an instant later as the girl snatched up a heavy express rifle from the bottom of the craft and levelled it full at his breast.

Quickly he had dropped the rope then and seen her float away beyond his reach, but a moment later he had been racing up-stream toward a little tributary in the mouth of which was hidden the canoe in which he and his party had come thus far upon their journey in pursuit of the girl and Anderssen.

What had become of her?

There seemed little doubt in the Russian's mind, however, but that she had been captured by warriors from one of the several villages she would have been compelled to pass on her way down to the sea. Well, he was at least rid of most of his human enemies.

But at that he would gladly have had them all back in the land of the living could he thus have been freed from the menace of the frightful creatures who pursued him with awful relentlessness, screaming and growling at him every time they came within sight of him. The one that filled him with the greatest terror was the panther—the flaming-eyed, devil-faced panther whose grinning jaws gaped wide at him by day, and whose fiery orbs gleamed wickedly out across the water from the Cimmerian blackness of the jungle nights.

The sight of the mouth of the Ugambi filled Rokoff with renewed hope, for there, upon the yellow waters of the bay, floated the *Kincaid* at anchor. He had sent the little steamer away to coal while he had gone up the river, leaving Paulvitch in charge of her, and he could have cried aloud in his relief as he saw that she had returned in time to save him.

Frantically he alternately paddled furiously toward her and rose to his feet waving his paddle and crying aloud in an attempt to attract the attention of those on board. But loud as he screamed his cries awakened no answering challenge from the deck of the silent craft.

Upon the shore behind him a hurried backward glance revealed the presence of the snarling pack. Even now, he thought, these man-like devils might yet find a way to reach him even upon the deck of the steamer unless there were those there to repel them with firearms.

What could have happened to those he had left upon the *Kincaid?* Where was Paulvitch? Could it be that the vessel was deserted, and that, after all, he was doomed to be overtaken by the terrible fate that he had been flying from through all these hideous days and nights? He shivered as might one upon whose brow death has already laid his clammy finger.

Yet he did not cease to paddle frantically toward the steamer, and at last, after what seemed an eternity, the bow of the dugout bumped against the timbers of the *Kincaid.* Over the ship's side hung a monkey-ladder, but as the Russian grasped it to ascend to the deck he heard a warning challenge from above, and, looking up, gazed into the cold, relentless muzzle of a rifle.

After Jane Clayton, with rifle levelled at the breast of Rokoff, had succeeded in holding him off until the dugout in which she had taken refuge had drifted out upon the bosom of the Ugambi beyond the man's reach, she had lost no time in paddling to the swiftest sweep of the channel, nor did she for long days and weary nights cease to hold her craft to the most rapidly moving part of the river, except when during the hottest hours of the day she had been wont to drift as the current would take her, lying prone in the bottom of the canoe, her face sheltered from the sun with a great palm leaf. Thus only did she gain rest upon the voyage; at other times she continually sought to augment the movement of the craft by wielding the heavy paddle.

Rokoff, on the other hand, had used little or no intelligence in his flight along the Ugambi, so that more often than not his craft had drifted in the slow-going eddies, for he habitually hugged the bank farthest from that along which the hideous horde pursued and menaced him.

Thus it was that, though he had put out upon the river but a short time subsequent to the girl, yet she had reached the bay fully two hours ahead of him. When she had first seen the anchored ship upon the quiet water, Jane Clayton's heart had beat fast with hope and thanksgiving, but as she drew closer to the craft and saw that it was the *Kincaid*, her pleasure gave place to the gravest misgivings.

It was too late, however, to turn back, for the current that carried her toward the ship was much too strong for her muscles. She could not have forced the heavy dugout up-stream against it, and all that was left her was to attempt either to make the shore without being seen by those upon the deck of the *Kincaid*, or to throw herself upon their mercy—otherwise she must be swept out to sea.

She knew that the shore held little hope of life for her, as she had no knowledge of the location of the friendly Mosula village to which Anderssen had taken her through the darkness of the night of their escape from the *Kincaid*.

With Rokoff away from the steamer it might be possible that by offering those in charge a large reward they could be induced to carry her to the nearest civilized port. It was worth risking—if she could make the steamer at all.

The current was bearing her swiftly down the river, and she found that only by dint of the utmost exertion could she direct the awkward craft toward the vicinity of the *Kincaid*. Having reached the decision to board the steamer, she now looked to it for aid, but to her surprise the decks appeared to be empty and she saw no sign of life aboard the ship.

The dugout was drawing closer and closer to the bow of the vessel, and yet no hail came over the side from any lookout aboard. In a moment more, Jane realized, she would be swept beyond the steamer, and then, unless they lowered a boat to rescue her, she would be carried far out to sea by the current and the swift ebb tide that was running.

The young woman called loudly for assistance, but there was no reply other than the shrill scream of some savage beast upon the jungle-shrouded shore. Frantically Jane wielded the paddle in an effort to carry her craft close alongside the steamer.

For a moment it seemed that she should miss her goal by but a few feet, but at the last moment the canoe swung close beneath the steamer's bow and Jane barely managed to grasp the anchor chain.

Heroically she clung to the heavy iron links, almost dragged from the canoe by the strain of the current upon her craft. Beyond her she saw a monkey-ladder dangling over the steamer's side. To release her hold upon the chain and chance clambering to the ladder as her canoe was swept beneath it seemed beyond the pale of possibility, yet to remain clinging to the anchor chain appeared equally as futile.

Finally her glance chanced to fall upon the rope in the bow of the dugout, and, making one end of this fast to the chain, she succeeded in drifting the canoe slowly down until it lay directly beneath the ladder. A moment later, her rifle slung about her shoulders, she had clambered safely to the deserted deck.

Her first task was to explore the ship, and this she did, her rifle ready for instant use should she meet with any human menace aboard the *Kincaid*. She was not long in discovering the cause of the apparently deserted condition of the steamer, for in the forecastle she found the sailors, who had evidently been left to guard the ship, deep in drunken slumber.

With a shudder of disgust she clambered above, and to the best of her ability closed and made fast the hatch above the heads of the sleeping guard. Next she sought the galley and food, and, having appeased her hunger, she took her place on deck, determined that none should board the *Kincaid* without first having agreed to her demands.

For an hour or so nothing appeared upon the surface of the river to cause her alarm, but then, about a bend up-stream, she saw a canoe appear in which sat a single figure. It had not proceeded far in her direction before she recognized the occupant as Rokoff, and when the fellow attempted to board he found a rifle staring him in the face.

When the Russian discovered who it was that repelled his advance he became furious, cursing and threatening in a most horrible manner; but, finding that these tactics failed to frighten or move the girl, he at last fell to pleading and promising.

Jane had but a single reply for his every proposition, and that was that nothing would ever persuade her to permit Rokoff upon the same vessel with her. That she would put her threats into action and shoot him should he persist in his endeavour to board the ship he was convinced.

So, as there was no other alternative, the great coward dropped back into his dugout and, at imminent risk of being swept to sea, finally succeeded in making the shore far down the bay and upon the opposite side from that on which the horde of beasts stood snarling and roaring.

Jane Clayton knew that the fellow could not alone and unaided bring his heavy craft back up-stream to the *Kincaid*, and so she had no further fear of an attack by him. The hideous crew upon the shore she thought she recognized as the same that had passed her in the jungle far up the Ugambi several days before, for it seemed quite beyond reason that there should be more than one such a strangely assorted pack; but what had brought them down-stream to the mouth of the river she could not imagine.

Toward the day's close the girl was suddenly alarmed by the shouting of the Russian from the opposite bank of the stream, and a moment later, following the direction of his gaze, she was terrified to see a ship's boat approaching from up-stream, in which, she felt assured, there could be only members of the *Kincaid's* missing crew—only heartless ruffians and enemies.

XVI

In the Darkness of the Night

hen Tarzan of the Apes realized that he was in the grip of the great jaws of a crocodile he did not, as an ordinary man might have done, give up all hope and resign himself to his fate.

Instead, he filled his lungs with air before the huge reptile dragged him beneath the surface, and then, with all the might of his great muscles, fought bitterly for freedom. But out of his native element the ape-man was too greatly handicapped to do more than excite the monster to greater speed as it dragged its prey swiftly through the water.

Tarzan's lungs were bursting for a breath of pure fresh air. He knew that he could survive but a moment more, and in the last paroxysm of his suffering he did what he could to avenge his own death.

His body trailed out beside the slimy carcass of his captor, and into the tough armour the ape-man attempted to plunge his stone knife as he was borne to the creature's horrid den.

His efforts but served to accelerate the speed of the crocodile, and just as the ape-man realized that he had reached the limit of his endurance he felt his body dragged to a muddy bed and his nostrils rise above the water's surface. All about him was the blackness of the pit—the silence of the grave.

For a moment Tarzan of the Apes lay gasping for breath upon the slimy, evil-smelling bed to which the animal had borne him. Close at his side he could feel the cold, hard plates of the creature's coat rising and falling as though with spasmodic efforts to breathe.

For several minutes the two lay thus, and then a sudden convulsion of the giant carcass at the man's side, a tremor, and a stiffening brought Tarzan to his knees beside the crocodile. To his utter amazement he found that the beast was dead. The slim knife had found a vulnerable spot in the scaly armour.

Staggering to his feet, the ape-man groped about the reeking, oozy den. He found that he was imprisoned in a subterranean chamber amply large enough to have accommodated a dozen or more of the huge animals such as the one that had dragged him thither.

He realized that he was in the creature's hidden nest far under the bank of the stream, and that doubtless the only means of ingress or egress lay through the submerged opening through which the crocodile had brought him.

His first thought, of course, was of escape, but that he could make his way to the surface of the river beyond and then to the shore seemed highly improbable. There might be turns and windings in the neck of the passage, or, most to be feared, he might meet another of the slimy inhabitants of the retreat upon his journey outward.

Even should he reach the river in safety, there was still the danger of his being again attacked before he could effect a safe landing. Still there was no alternative, and, filling his lungs with the close and reeking air of the chamber, Tarzan of the Apes dived into the dark and watery hole which he could not see but had felt out and found with his feet and legs.

The leg which had been held within the jaws of the crocodile was badly lacerated, but the bone had not been broken, nor were the muscles or tendons sufficiently injured to render it useless. It gave him excruciating pain, that was all.

But Tarzan of the Apes was accustomed to pain, and gave it no further thought when he found that the use of his legs was not greatly impaired by the sharp teeth of the monster.

Rapidly he crawled and swam through the passage which inclined downward and finally upward to open at last into the river bottom but a few feet from the shore line. As the ape-man reached the surface he saw the heads of two great crocodiles but a short distance from him. They were making rapidly in his direction, and with a super-human effort the man struck out for the overhanging branches of a near-by tree.

Nor was he a moment too soon, for scarcely had he drawn him-self to the safety of the limb than two gaping mouths snapped venom-ously below him. For a few minutes Tarzan rested in the tree that had proved the means of his salvation. His eyes scanned the river as far down-stream as the tortuous channel would permit, but there was no sign of the Russian or his dugout.

When he had rested and bound up his wounded leg he started on in pursuit of the drifting canoe. He found himself upon the opposite of the river to that at which he had entered the stream, but as his quarry was upon the bosom of the water it made little difference to the ape-man upon which side he took up the pursuit.

To his intense chagrin he soon found that his leg was more badly injured than he had thought, and that its condition seriously impeded his progress. It was only with the greatest difficulty that he could proceed faster than a walk upon the ground, and in the trees he dis-covered that it not only impeded his progress, but rendered travelling distinctly dangerous.

From the old negress, Tambudza, Tarzan had gathered a sugges-tion that now filled his mind with doubts and misgivings. When the old woman had told him of the child's death she had also added that the white woman, though grief-stricken, had confided to her that the baby was not hers.

Tarzan could see no reason for believing that Jane could have found it advisable to deny her identity or that of the child; the only explanation that he could put upon the matter was that, after all, the white woman who had accompanied his son and the Swede into the jungle fastness of the interior had not been Jane at all.

The more he gave thought to the problem, the more firmly convinced he became that his son was dead and his wife still safe in London, and in ignorance of the terrible fate that had overtaken her first-born.

After all, then, his interpretation of Rokoff's sinister taunt had been erroneous, and he had been bearing the burden of a double apprehension needlessly—at least so thought the ape-man. From this belief he garnered some slight surcease from the numbing grief that the death of his little son had thrust upon him.

And such a death! Even the savage beast that was the real Tarzan, inured to the sufferings and horrors of the grim jungle, shuddered as he contemplated the hideous fate that had overtaken the innocent child.

As he made his way painfully towards the coast, he let his mind dwell so constantly upon the frightful crimes which the Russian had perpetrated against his loved ones that the great scar upon his forehead stood out almost continuously in the vivid scarlet that marked the man's most relentless and bestial moods of rage. At times he startled even himself and sent the lesser creatures of the wild jungle scampering to their hiding places as involuntary roars and growls rumbled from his throat.

Could he but lay his hand upon the Russian!

Twice upon the way to the coast bellicose natives ran threateningly from their villages to bar his further progress, but when the awful cry of the bull-ape thundered upon their affrighted ears, and the great white giant charged bellowing upon them, they had turned and fled into the bush, nor ventured thence until he had safely passed.

Though his progress seemed tantalizingly slow to the ape-man whose idea of speed had been gained by such standards as the lesser apes attain, he made, as a matter of fact, almost as rapid progress as the drifting canoe that bore Rokoff on ahead of him, so that he came to the bay and within sight of the ocean just after darkness had fallen upon the same day that Jane Clayton and the Russian ended their flights from the interior.

The darkness lowered so heavily upon the black river and the encircling jungle that Tarzan, even with eyes accustomed to much use after dark, could make out nothing a few yards from him. His idea was to search the shore that night for signs of the Russian and the woman who he was certain must have preceded Rokoff down the Ugambi. That the *Kincaid* or other ship lay at anchor but a hundred yards from him he did not dream, for no light showed on board the steamer.

Even as he commenced his search his attention was suddenly attracted by a noise that he had not at first perceived—the stealthy dip of paddles in the water some distance from the shore, and about opposite the point at which he stood. Motionless as a statue he stood listening to the faint sound.

Presently it ceased, to be followed by a shuffling noise that the ape-man's trained ears could interpret as resulting from but a single cause—the scraping of leather-shod feet upon the rounds of a ship's monkey-ladder. And yet, as far as he could see, there was no ship there—nor might there be one within a thousand miles.

As he stood thus, peering out into the darkness of the cloud-enshrouded night, there came to him from across the water, like a slap in the face, so sudden and unexpected was it, the sharp staccato of an exchange of shots and then the scream of a woman.

Wounded though he was, and with the memory of his recent horrible experience still strong upon him, Tarzan of the Apes did not hesitate as the notes of that frightened cry rose shrill and piercing upon the still night air. With a bound he cleared the intervening bush—there was a splash as the water closed about him—and then, with powerful strokes, he swam out into the impenetrable night with no guide save the memory of an illusive cry, and for company the hideous denizens of an equatorial river.

The boat that had attracted Jane's attention as she stood guard upon the deck of the *Kincaid* had been perceived by Rokoff upon one bank and Mugambi and the horde upon the other. The cries of the Russian had brought the dugout first to him, and then, after a conference, it had been turned toward the *Kincaid*, but before ever it covered half the distance between the shore and the steamer a rifle had spoken from the latter's deck and one of the sailors in the bow of the canoe had crumpled and fallen into the water.

After that they went more slowly, and presently, when Jane's rifle had found another member of the party, the canoe withdrew to the shore, where it lay as long as daylight lasted.

The savage, snarling pack upon the opposite shore had been directed in their pursuit by the black warrior, Mugambi, chief of the Wagambi. Only he knew which might be foe and which friend of their lost master.

Could they have reached either the canoe or the *Kincaid* they would have made short work of any whom they found there, but the gulf of black water intervening shut them off from farther advance as effectually as though it had been the broad ocean that separated them from their prey.

Mugambi knew something of the occurrences which had led up to the landing of Tarzan upon Jungle Island and the pursuit of the whites up the Ugambi. He knew that his savage master sought his wife and child who had been stolen by the wicked white man whom they had followed far into the interior and now back to the sea.

He believed also that this same man had killed the great white giant whom he had come to respect and love as he had never loved the greatest chiefs of his own people. And so in the wild breast of Mugambi burned an iron resolve to win to the side of the wicked one and wreak vengeance upon him for the murder of the ape-man.

But when he saw the canoe come down the river and take in Rokoff, when he saw it make for the *Kincaid*, he realized that only by possessing himself of a canoe could he hope to transport the beasts of the pack within striking distance of the enemy.

So it happened that even before Jane Clayton fired the first shot into Rokoff's canoe the beasts of Tarzan had disappeared into the jungle.

After the Russian and his party, which consisted of Paulvitch and the several men he had left upon the *Kincaid* to attend to the matter of coaling, had retreated before her fire, Jane realized that it would be but a temporary respite from their attentions which she had gained, and with the conviction came a determination to make a bold and final stroke for freedom from the menacing threat of Rokoff's evil purpose.

With this idea in view she opened negotiations with the two sailors she had imprisoned in the forecastle, and having forced their consent to her plans, upon pain of death should they attempt disloyalty, she released them just as darkness closed about the ship.

With ready revolver to compel obedience, she let them up one by one, searching them carefully for concealed weapons as they stood with hands elevated above their heads. Once satisfied that they were unarmed, she set them to work cutting the cable which held the *Kincaid* to her anchorage, for her bold plan was nothing less than to set the steamer adrift and float with her out into the open sea, there to trust to the mercy of the elements, which she was confident would be no more merciless than Nikolas Rokoff should he again capture her.

There was, too, the chance that the *Kincaid* might be sighted by some passing ship, and as she was well stocked with provisions and water—the men had assured her of this fact—and as the season of storm was well over, she had every reason to hope for the eventual success of her plan.

The night was deeply overcast, heavy clouds riding low above the jungle and the water—only to the west, where the broad ocean spread beyond the river's mouth, was there a suggestion of lessening gloom.

It was a perfect night for the purposes of the work in hand.

Her enemies could not see the activity aboard the ship nor mark her course as the swift current bore her outward into the ocean. Before daylight broke the ebb-tide would have carried the *Kincaid* well into the Benguela current which flows northward along the coast of Africa, and, as a south wind was prevailing, Jane hoped to be out of sight of the mouth of the Ugambi before Rokoff could become aware of the departure of the steamer.

Standing over the labouring seamen, the young woman breathed a sigh of relief as the last strand of the cable parted and she knew that the vessel was on its way out of the maw of the savage Ugambi. With her two prisoners still beneath the coercing influence of her rifle, she ordered them upon deck with the intention of again imprisoning them in the forecastle; but at length she permitted herself to be influenced by their promises of loyalty and the arguments which they put forth that they could be of service to her, and permitted them to remain above.

For a few minutes the *Kincaid* drifted rapidly with the current, and then, with a grinding jar, she stopped in midstream. The ship had run upon a low-lying bar that splits the channel about a quarter of a mile from the sea.

For a moment she hung there, and then, swinging round until her bow pointed toward the shore, she broke adrift once more.

At the same instant, just as Jane Clayton was congratulating herself that the ship was once more free, there fell upon her ears from a point up the river about where the *Kincaid* had been anchored the rattle of musketry and a woman's scream—shrill, piercing, fear-laden.

The sailors heard the shots with certain conviction that they announced the coming of their employer, and as they had no relish for the plan that would consign them to the deck of a drifting derelict, they whispered together a hurried plan to overcome the young woman and hail Rokoff and their companions to their rescue.

It seemed that fate would play into their hands, for with the reports of the guns Jane Clayton's attention had been distracted from her unwilling assistants, and instead of keeping one eye upon them as she had intended doing, she ran to the bow of the *Kincaid* to peer through the darkness toward the source of the disturbance upon the river's bosom.

Seeing that she was off her guard, the two sailors crept stealthily upon her from behind.

The scraping upon the deck of the shoes of one of them startled the girl to a sudden appreciation of her danger, but the warning had come too late.

As she turned, both men leaped upon her and bore her to the deck, and as she went down beneath them she saw, outlined against the lesser gloom of the ocean, the figure of another man clamber over the side of the *Kincaid*.

After all her pains her heroic struggle for freedom had failed. With a stifled sob she gave up the unequal battle.

XVII

ON THE DECK
OF THE "KINCAID"

hen Mugambi had turned back into the jungle with the pack he had a definite purpose in view. It was to obtain a dugout wherewith to transport the beasts of Tarzan to the side of the *Kincaid.* Nor was he long in coming upon the object which he sought.

Just at dusk he found a canoe moored to the bank of a small tributary of the Ugambi at a point where he had felt certain that he should find one.

Without loss of time he piled his hideous fellows into the craft and shoved out into the stream. So quickly had they taken possession of the canoe that the warrior had not noticed that it was already occupied. The huddled figure sleeping in the bottom had entirely escaped his observation in the darkness of the night that had now fallen.

But no sooner were they afloat than a savage growling from one of the apes directly ahead of him in the dugout attracted his attention to a shivering and cowering figure that trembled between him and the great anthropoid. To Mugambi's astonishment he saw that it was a native woman. With difficulty he kept the ape from her throat, and after a time succeeded in quelling her fears.

It seemed that she had been fleeing from marriage with an old man she loathed and had taken refuge for the night in the canoe she had found upon the river's edge.

Mugambi did not wish her presence, but there she was, and rather than lose time by returning her to the shore the black permitted her to remain on board the canoe.

As quickly as his awkward companions could paddle the dugout down-stream toward the Ugambi and the *Kincaid* they moved through the darkness. It was with difficulty that Mugambi could make out the shadowy form of the steamer, but as he had it between himself and the ocean it was much more apparent than to one upon either shore of the river.

As he approached it he was amazed to note that it seemed to be receding from him, and finally he was convinced that the vessel was moving down-stream. Just as he was about to urge his creatures to renewed efforts to overtake the steamer the outline of another canoe burst suddenly into view not three yards from the bow of his own craft.

At the same instant the occupants of the stranger discovered the proximity of Mugambi's horde, but they did not at first recognize the nature of the fearful crew. A man in the bow of the oncoming boat challenged them just as the two dugouts were about to touch.

For answer came the menacing growl of a panther, and the fellow found himself gazing into the flaming eyes of Sheeta, who had raised himself with his forepaws upon the bow of the boat, ready to leap in upon the occupants of the other craft.

Instantly Rokoff realized the peril that confronted him and his fellows. He gave a quick command to fire upon the occupants of the other canoe, and it was this volley and the scream of the terrified native woman in the canoe with Mugambi that both Tarzan and Jane had heard.

Before the slower and less skilled paddlers in Mugambi's canoe could press their advantage and effect a boarding of the enemy the latter had turned swiftly down-stream and were paddling for their lives in the direction of the *Kincaid*, which was now visible to them.

The vessel after striking upon the bar had swung loose again into a slow-moving eddy, which returns up-stream close to the southern shore of the Ugambi only to circle out once more and join the down-ward flow a hundred yards or so farther up. Thus the *Kincaid* was returning Jane Clayton directly into the hands of her enemies.

It so happened that as Tarzan sprang into the river the vessel was not visible to him, and as he swam out into the night he had no idea that a ship drifted so close at hand. He was guided by the sounds which he could hear coming from the two canoes.

As he swam he had vivid recollections of the last occasion upon which he had swum in the waters of the Ugambi, and with them a sudden shudder shook the frame of the giant.

But, though he twice felt something brush his legs from the slimy depths below him, nothing seized him, and of a sudden he quite forgot about crocodiles in the astonishment of seeing a dark mass loom suddenly before him where he had still expected to find the open river.

So close was it that a few strokes brought him up to the thing, when to his amazement his outstretched hand came in contact with a ship's side.

As the agile ape-man clambered over the vessel's rail there came to his sensitive ears the sound of a struggle at the opposite side of the deck.

Noiselessly he sped across the intervening space.

The moon had risen now, and, though the sky was still banked with clouds, a lesser darkness enveloped the scene than that which had blotted out all sight earlier in the night. His keen eyes, therefore, saw the figures of two men grappling with a woman.

That it was the woman who had accompanied Anderssen toward the interior he did not know, though he suspected as much, as he was now quite certain that this was the deck of the *Kincaid* upon which chance had led him.

But he wasted little time in idle speculation. There was a woman in danger of harm from two ruffians, which was enough excuse for the ape-man to project his giant thews into the conflict without further investigation.

The first that either of the sailors knew that there was a new force at work upon the ship was the falling of a mighty hand upon a shoulder of each. As if they had been in the grip of a fly-wheel, they were jerked suddenly from their prey.

"What means this?" asked a low voice in their ears.

They were given no time to reply, however, for at the sound of that voice the young woman had sprung to her feet and with a little cry of joy leaped toward their assailant.

"Tarzan!" she cried.

The ape-man hurled the two sailors across the deck, where they rolled, stunned and terrified, into the scuppers upon the opposite side, and with an exclamation of incredulity gathered the girl into his arms.

Brief, however, were the moments for their greeting.

Scarcely had they recognized one another than the clouds above them parted to show the figures of a half-dozen men clambering over the side of the *Kincaid* to the steamer's deck.

Foremost among them was the Russian. As the brilliant rays of the equatorial moon lighted the deck, and he realized that the man before him was Lord Greystoke, he screamed hysterical commands to his followers to fire upon the two.

Tarzan pushed Jane behind the cabin near which they had been standing, and with a quick bound started for Rokoff. The men behind the Russian, at least two of them, raised their rifles and fired at the charging ape-man; but those behind them were otherwise engaged—for up the monkey-ladder in their rear was thronging a hideous horde.

First came five snarling apes, huge, manlike beasts, with bared fangs and slavering jaws; and after them a giant black warrior, his long spear gleaming in the moonlight.

Behind him again scrambled another creature, and of all the horrid horde it was this they most feared—Sheeta, the panther, with gleaming jaws agape and fiery eyes blazing at them in the mightiness of his hate and of his blood lust.

The shots that had been fired at Tarzan missed him, and he would have been upon Rokoff in another instant had not the great coward dodged backward between his two henchmen, and, screaming in hysterical terror, bolted forward toward the forecastle.

For the moment Tarzan's attention was distracted by the two men before him, so that he could not at the time pursue the Russian. About him the apes and Mugambi were battling with the balance of the Russian's party.

Beneath the terrible ferocity of the beasts the men were soon scampering in all directions—those who still lived to scamper, for the great fangs of the apes of Akut and the tearing talons of Sheeta already had found more than a single victim.

Four, however, escaped and disappeared into the forecastle, where they hoped to barricade themselves against further assault. Here they found Rokoff, and, enraged at his desertion of them in their moment of peril, no less than at the uniformly brutal treatment it had been his wont to accord them, they gloated upon the opportunity now offered them to revenge themselves in part upon their hated employer.

Despite his prayers and grovelling pleas, therefore, they hurled him bodily out upon the deck, delivering him to the mercy of the fearful things from which they had themselves just escaped.

Tarzan saw the man emerge from the forecastle—saw and recognized his enemy; but another saw him even as soon.

It was Sheeta, and with grinning jaws the mighty beast slunk silently toward the terror-stricken man.

When Rokoff saw what it was that stalked him his shrieks for help filled the air, as with trembling knees he stood, as one paralyzed, before the hideous death that was creeping upon him.

Tarzan took a step toward the Russian, his brain burning with a raging fire of vengeance. At last he had the murderer of his son at his mercy. His was the right to avenge.

Once Jane had stayed his hand that time that he sought to take the law into his own power and mete to Rokoff the death that he had so long merited; but this time none should stay him.

His fingers clenched and unclenched spasmodically as he approached the trembling Russ, beastlike and ominous as a brute of prey.

Presently he saw that Sheeta was about to forestall him, robbing him of the fruits of his great hate.

He called sharply to the panther, and the words, as if they had broken a hideous spell that had held the Russian, galvanized him into sudden action. With a scream he turned and fled toward the bridge.

After him pounced Sheeta the panther, unmindful of his master's warning voice.

Tarzan was about to leap after the two when he felt a light touch upon his arm. Turning, he found Jane at his elbow.

"Do not leave me," she whispered. "I am afraid."

Tarzan glanced behind her.

All about were the hideous apes of Akut. Some, even, were approaching the young woman with bared fangs and menacing guttural warnings.

The ape-man warned them back. He had forgotten for the moment that these were but beasts, unable to differentiate his friends and his foes. Their savage natures were roused by their recent battle with the sailors, and now all flesh outside the pack was meat to them.

Tarzan turned again toward the Russian, chagrined that he should have to forgo the pleasure of personal revenge—unless the man should escape Sheeta. But as he looked he saw that there could be no hope of that. The fellow had retreated to the end of the bridge, where he now stood trembling and wide-eyed, facing the beast that moved slowly toward him.

The panther crawled with belly to the planking, uttering uncanny mouthings. Rokoff stood as though petrified, his eyes protruding from their sockets, his mouth agape, and the cold sweat of terror clammy upon his brow.

Below him, upon the deck, he had seen the great anthropoids, and so had not dared to seek escape in that direction. In fact, even now one of the brutes was leaping to seize the bridge-rail and draw himself up to the Russian's side.

Before him was the panther, silent and crouched.

Rokoff could not move. His knees trembled. His voice broke in inarticulate shrieks. With a last piercing wail he sank to his knees—and then Sheeta sprang.

Full upon the man's breast the tawny body hurtled, tumbling the Russian to his back.

As the great fangs tore at the throat and chest, Jane Clayton turned away in horror; but not so Tarzan of the Apes. A cold smile of satisfaction touched his lips. The scar upon his forehead that had burned scarlet faded to the normal hue of his tanned skin and disappeared.

Rokoff fought furiously but futilely against the growling, rending fate that had overtaken him. For all his countless crimes he was punished in the brief moment of the hideous death that claimed him at the last.

After his struggles ceased Tarzan approached, at Jane's suggestion, to wrest the body from the panther and give what remained of
it decent human burial; but the great cat rose snarling above its kill,
threatening even the master it loved in its savage way, so that rather
than kill his friend of the jungle, Tarzan was forced to relinquish his
intentions.

All that night Sheeta, the panther, crouched upon the grisly thing
that had been Nikolas Rokoff. The bridge of the *Kincaid* was slippery
with blood. Beneath the brilliant tropic moon the great beast feasted
until, when the sun rose the following morning, there remained of
Tarzan's great enemy only gnawed and broken bones.

Of the Russian's party, all were accounted for except Paulvitch.
Four were prisoners in the *Kincaid*'s forecastle. The rest were dead.

With these men Tarzan got up steam upon the vessel, and with
the knowledge of the mate, who happened to be one of those surviving, he planned to set out in quest of Jungle Island; but as the morning
dawned there came with it a heavy gale from the west which raised a
sea into which the mate of the *Kincaid* dared not venture. All that day
the ship lay within the shelter of the mouth of the river; for, though
night witnessed a lessening of the wind, it was thought safer to wait
for daylight before attempting the navigation of the winding channel
to the sea.

Upon the deck of the steamer the pack wandered without let
or hindrance by day, for they had soon learned through Tarzan and
Mugambi that they must harm no one upon the *Kincaid*; but at night
they were confined below.

Tarzan's joy had been unbounded when he learned from his wife
that the little child who had died in the village of M'ganwazam was
not their son. Who the baby could have been, or what had become of
their own, they could not imagine, and as both Rokoff and Paulvitch
were gone, there was no way of discovering.

There was, however, a certain sense of relief in the knowledge that they might yet hope. Until positive proof of the baby's death reached them there was always that to buoy them up.

It seemed quite evident that their little Jack had not been brought aboard the *Kincaid*. Anderssen would have known of it had such been the case, but he had assured Jane time and time again that the little one he had brought to her cabin the night he aided her to escape was the only one that had been aboard the *Kincaid* since she lay at Dover.

XVIII

PAULVITCH
PLOTS REVENGE

s Jane and Tarzan stood upon the vessel's deck recounting to one another the details of the various adventures through which each had passed since they had parted in their London home, there glared at them from beneath scowling brows a hidden watcher upon the shore.

Through the man's brain passed plan after plan whereby he might thwart the escape of the Englishman and his wife, for so long as the vital spark remained within the vindictive brain of Alexander Paulvitch none who had aroused the enmity of the Russian might be entirely safe.

Plan after plan he formed only to discard each either as impracticable, or unworthy the vengeance his wrongs demanded. So warped by faulty reasoning was the criminal mind of Rokoff's lieutenant that he could not grasp the real truth of that which lay between himself and the ape-man and see that always the fault had been, not with the English lord, but with himself and his confederate.

And at the rejection of each new scheme Paulvitch arrived always at the same conclusion—that he could accomplish naught while half the breadth of the Ugambi separated him from the object of his hatred.

But how was he to span the crocodile-infested waters? There was no canoe nearer than the Mosula village, and Paulvitch was none

728

too sure that the *Kincaid* would still be at anchor in the river when he returned should he take the time to traverse the jungle to the distant village and return with a canoe. Yet there was no other way, and so, convinced that thus alone might he hope to reach his prey, Paulvitch, with a parting scowl at the two figures upon the *Kincaid*'s deck, turned away from the river.

Hastening through the dense jungle, his mind centred upon his one fetich—revenge—the Russian forgot even his terror of the savage world through which he moved.

Baffled and beaten at every turn of Fortune's wheel, reacted upon time after time by his own malign plotting, the principal victim of his own criminality, Paulvitch was yet so blind as to imagine that his greatest happiness lay in a continuation of the plottings and schemings which had ever brought him and Rokoff to disaster, and the latter finally to a hideous death.

As the Russian stumbled on through the jungle toward the Mosula village there presently crystallized within his brain a plan which seemed more feasible than any that he had as yet considered.

He would come by night to the side of the *Kincaid*, and once aboard, would search out the members of the ship's original crew who had survived the terrors of this frightful expedition, and enlist them in an attempt to wrest the vessel from Tarzan and his beasts.

In the cabin were arms and ammunition, and hidden in a secret receptacle in the cabin table was one of those infernal machines, the construction of which had occupied much of Paulvitch's spare time when he had stood high in the confidence of the Nihilists of his native land.

That was before he had sold them out for immunity and gold to the police of Petrograd. Paulvitch winced as he recalled the denunciation of him that had fallen from the lips of one of his former comrades ere the poor devil expiated his political sins at the end of a hempen rope.

But the infernal machine was the thing to think of now. He could do much with that if he could but get his hands upon it. Within the little hardwood case hidden in the cabin table rested sufficient potential destructiveness to wipe out in the fraction of a second every enemy aboard the *Kincaid*. Paulvitch licked his lips in anticipatory joy, and urged his tired legs to greater speed that he might not be too late to the ship's anchorage to carry out his designs.

All depended, of course, upon when the *Kincaid* departed. The Russian realized that nothing could be accomplished beneath the light of day. Darkness must shroud his approach to the ship's side, for should he be sighted by Tarzan or Lady Greystoke he would have no chance to board the vessel.

The gale that was blowing was, he believed, the cause of the delay in getting the *Kincaid* under way, and if it continued to blow until night then the chances were all in his favour, for he knew that there was little likelihood of the ape-man attempting to navigate the tortuous channel of the Ugambi while darkness lay upon the surface of the water, hiding the many bars and the numerous small islands which are scattered over the expanse of the river's mouth.

It was well after noon when Paulvitch came to the Mosula village upon the bank of the tributary of the Ugambi. Here he was received with suspicion and unfriendliness by the native chief, who, like all those who came in contact with Rokoff or Paulvitch, had suffered in some manner from the greed, the cruelty, or the lust of the two Muscovites.

When Paulvitch demanded the use of a canoe the chief grumbled a surly refusal and ordered the white man from the village. Surrounded by angry, muttering warriors who seemed to be but waiting some slight pretext to transfix him with their menacing spears the Russian could do naught else than withdraw.

A dozen fighting men led him to the edge of the clearing, leaving him with a warning never to show himself again in the vicinity of their village.

Stifling his anger, Paulvitch slunk into the jungle; but once beyond the sight of the warriors he paused and listened intently. He could hear the voices of his escort as the men returned to the village, and when he was sure that they were not following him he wormed his way through the bushes to the edge of the river, still determined some way to obtain a canoe.

Life itself depended upon his reaching the *Kincaid* and enlisting the survivors of the ship's crew in his service, for to be abandoned here amidst the dangers of the African jungle where he had won the enmity of the natives was, he well knew, practically equivalent to a sentence of death.

A desire for revenge acted as an almost equally powerful incentive to spur him into the face of danger to accomplish his design, so that it was a desperate man that lay hidden in the foliage beside the little river searching with eager eyes for some sign of a small canoe which might be easily handled by a single paddle.

Nor had the Russian long to wait before one of the awkward little skiffs which the Mosula fashion came in sight upon the bosom of the river. A youth was paddling lazily out into midstream from a point beside the village. When he reached the channel he allowed the sluggish current to carry him slowly along while he lolled indolently in the bottom of his crude canoe.

All ignorant of the unseen enemy upon the river's bank the lad floated slowly down the stream while Paulvitch followed along the jungle path a few yards behind him.

A mile below the village the black boy dipped his paddle into the water and forced his skiff toward the bank. Paulvitch, elated by the chance which had drawn the youth to the same side of the river as that along which he followed rather than to the opposite side where he would have been beyond the stalker's reach, hid in the brush close beside the point at which it was evident the skiff would touch the bank of the slow-moving stream, which seemed jealous of each fleeting instant which drew it nearer to the broad and muddy Ugambi where it must for ever lose its identity in the larger stream that would presently cast its waters into the great ocean.

Equally indolent were the motions of the Mosula youth as he drew his skiff beneath an overhanging limb of a great tree that leaned down to implant a farewell kiss upon the bosom of the departing water, caressing with green fronds the soft breast of its languorous love.

And, snake-like, amidst the concealing foliage lay the malevolent Russ. Cruel, shifty eyes gloated upon the outlines of the coveted canoe, and measured the stature of its owner, while the crafty brain weighed the chances of the white man should physical encounter with the black become necessary.

Only direct necessity could drive Alexander Paulvitch to personal conflict; but it was indeed dire necessity which goaded him on to action now.

There was time, just time enough, to reach the *Kincaid* by nightfall. Would the black fool never quit his skiff? Paulvitch squirmed and fidgeted. The lad yawned and stretched. With exasperating deliberateness he examined the arrows in his quiver, tested his bow, and looked to the edge upon the hunting-knife in his loin-cloth.

Again he stretched and yawned, glanced up at the river-bank, shrugged his shoulders, and lay down in the bottom of his canoe for a little nap before he plunged into the jungle after the prey he had come forth to hunt.

Paulvitch half rose, and with tensed muscles stood glaring down upon his unsuspecting victim. The boy's lids drooped and closed. Presently his breast rose and fell to the deep breaths of slumber. The time had come!

The Russian crept stealthily nearer. A branch rustled beneath his weight and the lad stirred in his sleep. Paulvitch drew his revolver and levelled it upon the black. For a moment he remained in rigid quiet, and then again the youth relapsed into undisturbed slumber.

The white man crept closer. He could not chance a shot until there was no risk of missing. Presently he leaned close above the Mosula. The cold steel of the revolver in his hand insinuated itself nearer and nearer to the breast of the unconscious lad. Now it stopped but a few inches above the strongly beating heart.

But the pressure of a finger lay between the harmless boy and eternity. The soft bloom of youth still lay upon the brown cheek, a smile half parted the beardless lips. Did any qualm of conscience point its disquieting finger of reproach at the murderer?

To all such was Alexander Paulvitch immune. A sneer curled his bearded lip as his forefinger closed upon the trigger of his revolver. There was a loud report. A little hole appeared above the heart of the sleeping boy, a little hole about which lay a blackened rim of powder-burned flesh.

The youthful body half rose to a sitting posture. The smiling lips tensed to the nervous shock of a momentary agony which the conscious mind never apprehended, and then the dead sank limply back into that deepest of slumbers from which there is no awakening.

The killer dropped quickly into the skiff beside the killed. Ruthless hands seized the dead boy heartlessly and raised him to the low gunwale. A little shove, a splash, some widening ripples broken by the sudden surge of a dark, hidden body from the slimy depths, and the coveted canoe was in the sole possession of the white man—more savage than the youth whose life he had taken.

Casting off the tie rope and seizing the paddle, Paulvitch bent feverishly to the task of driving the skiff downward toward the Ugambi at top speed.

Night had fallen when the prow of the bloodstained craft shot out into the current of the larger stream. Constantly the Russian strained his eyes into the increasing darkness ahead in vain endeavour to pierce the black shadows which lay between him and the anchorage of the *Kincaid*.

Was the ship still riding there upon the waters of the Ugambi, or had the ape-man at last persuaded himself of the safety of venturing forth into the abating storm? As Paulvitch forged ahead with the current he asked himself these questions, and many more beside, not the least disquieting of which were those which related to his future should it chance that the *Kincaid* had already steamed away, leaving him to the merciless horrors of the savage wilderness.

In the darkness it seemed to the paddler that he was fairly flying over the water, and he had become convinced that the ship had left her moorings and that he had already passed the spot at which she had lain earlier in the day, when there appeared before him beyond a projecting point which he had but just rounded the flickering light from a ship's lantern.

Alexander Paulvitch could scarce restrain an exclamation of triumph. The *Kincaid* had not departed! Life and vengeance were not to elude him after all.

He stopped paddling the moment that he descried the gleaming beacon of hope ahead of him. Silently he drifted down the muddy waters of the Ugambi, occasionally dipping his paddle's blade gently into the current that he might guide his primitive craft to the vessel's side.

As he approached more closely the dark bulk of a ship loomed before him out of the blackness of the night. No sound came from the vessel's deck. Paulvitch drifted, unseen, close to the *Kincaid*'s side. Only the momentary scraping of his canoe's nose against the ship's planking broke the silence of the night.

Trembling with nervous excitement, the Russian remained motionless for several minutes; but there was no sound from the great bulk above him to indicate that his coming had been noted.

Stealthily he worked his craft forward until the stays of the bowsprit were directly above him. He could just reach them. To make his canoe fast there was the work of but a minute or two, and then the man raised himself quietly aloft.

A moment later he dropped softly to the deck. Thoughts of the hideous pack which tenanted the ship induced cold tremors along the spine of the cowardly prowler; but life itself depended upon the success of his venture, and so he was enabled to steel himself to the frightful chances which lay before him.

No sound or sign of watch appeared upon the ship's deck. Paulvitch crept stealthily toward the forecastle. All was silence. The hatch was raised, and as the man peered downward he saw one of the *Kincaid*'s crew reading by the light of the smoky lantern depending from the ceiling of the crew's quarters.

Paulvitch knew the man well, a surly cut-throat upon whom he figured strongly in the carrying out of the plan which he had conceived. Gently the Russ lowered himself through the aperture to the rounds of the ladder which led into the forecastle.

He kept his eyes turned upon the reading man, ready to warn him to silence the moment that the fellow discovered him; but so deeply immersed was the sailor in the magazine that the Russian came, unobserved, to the forecastle floor.

There he turned and whispered the reader's name. The man raised his eyes from the magazine—eyes that went wide for a moment as they fell upon the familiar countenance of Rokoff's lieutenant, only to narrow instantly in a scowl of disapproval.

"The devil!" he ejaculated. "Where did you come from? We all thought you were done for and gone where you ought to have gone a long time ago. His lordship will be mighty pleased to see you."

Paulvitch crossed to the sailor's side. A friendly smile lay on the Russian's lips, and his right hand was extended in greeting, as though the other might have been a dear and long lost friend. The sailor ignored the proffered hand, nor did he return the other's smile.

"I've come to help you," explained Paulvitch. "I'm going to help you get rid of the Englishman and his beasts—then there will be no danger from the law when we get back to civilization. We can sneak in on them while they sleep—that is Greystoke, his wife, and that black scoundrel, Mugambi. Afterward it will be a simple matter to clean up the beasts. Where are they?"

"They're below," replied the sailor; "but just let me tell you something, Paulvitch. You haven't got no more show to turn us men against the Englishman than nothing. We had all we wanted of you and that other beast. He's dead, an' if I don't miss my guess a whole lot you'll be dead too before long. You two treated us like dogs, and if you think we got any love for you you better forget it."

"You mean to say that you're going to turn against me?" demanded Paulvitch.

The other nodded, and then after a momentary pause, during which an idea seemed to have occurred to him, he spoke again.

"Unless," he said, "you can make it worth my while to let you go before the Englishman finds you here."

"You wouldn't turn me away in the jungle, would you?" asked Paulvitch. "Why, I'd die there in a week."

"You'd have a chance there," replied the sailor. "Here, you wouldn't have no chance. Why, if I woke up my maties here they'd probably cut your heart out of you before the Englishman got a chance at you at all. It's mighty lucky for you that I'm the one to be awake now and not none of the others."

"You're crazy," cried Paulvitch. "Don't you know that the Englishman will have you all hanged when he gets you back where the law can get hold of you?"

"No, he won't do nothing of the kind," replied the sailor. "He's told us as much, for he says that there wasn't nobody to blame but you and Rokoff—the rest of us was just tools. See?"

For half an hour the Russian pleaded or threatened as the mood seized him. Sometimes he was upon the verge of tears, and again he was promising his listener either fabulous rewards or condign punishment; but the other was obdurate.

He made it plain to the Russian that there were but two plans open to him—either he must consent to being turned over immediately to Lord Greystoke, or he must pay to the sailor, as a price for permission to quit the *Kincaid* unmolested, every cent of money and article of value upon his person and in his cabin.

"And you'll have to make up your mind mighty quick," growled the man, "for I want to turn in. Come now, choose—his lordship or the jungle?"

"You'll be sorry for this," grumbled the Russian.

"Shut up," admonished the sailor. "If you get funny I may change my mind, and keep you here after all."

Now Paulvitch had no intention of permitting himself to fall into the hands of Tarzan of the Apes if he could possibly avoid it, and while the terrors of the jungle appalled him they were, to his mind, infinitely preferable to the certain death which he knew he merited and for which he might look at the hands of the ape-man.

"Is anyone sleeping in my cabin?" he asked.

The sailor shook his head. "No," he said; "Lord and Lady Greystoke have the captain's cabin. The mate is in his own, and there ain't no one in yours."

"I'll go and get my valuables for you," said Paulvitch.

"I'll go with you to see that you don't try any funny business," said the sailor, and he followed the Russian up the ladder to the deck.

At the cabin entrance the sailor halted to watch, permitting Paulvitch to go alone to his cabin. Here he gathered together his few belongings that were to buy him the uncertain safety of escape, and as he stood for a moment beside the little table on which he had piled them he searched his brain for some feasible plan either to ensure his safety or to bring revenge upon his enemies.

And presently as he thought there recurred to his memory the little black box which lay hidden in a secret receptacle beneath a false top upon the table where his hand rested.

The Russian's face lighted to a sinister gleam of malevolent satisfaction as he stooped and felt beneath the table top. A moment later he withdrew from its hiding-place the thing he sought. He had lighted the lantern swinging from the beams overhead that he might see to collect his belongings, and now he held the black box well in the rays of the lamplight, while he fingered at the clasp that fastened its lid.

The lifted cover revealed two compartments within the box. In one was a mechanism which resembled the works of a small clock. There also was a little battery of two dry cells. A wire ran from the clockwork to one of the poles of the battery, and from the other pole through the partition into the other compartment, a second wire returning directly to the clockwork.

Whatever lay within the second compartment was not visible, for a cover lay over it and appeared to be sealed in place by asphaltum. In the bottom of the box, beside the clockwork, lay a key, and this Paulvitch now withdrew and fitted to the winding stem.

Gently he turned the key, muffling the noise of the winding operation by throwing a couple of articles of clothing over the box. All the time he listened intently for any sound which might indicate that the sailor or another were approaching his cabin; but none came to interrupt his work.

When the winding was completed the Russian set a pointer upon a small dial at the side of the clockwork, then he replaced the cover upon the black box, and returned the entire machine to its hiding-place in the table.

A sinister smile curled the man's bearded lips as he gathered up his valuables, blew out the lamp, and stepped from his cabin to the side of the waiting sailor.

"Here are my things," said the Russian; "now let me go."

"I'll first take a look in your pockets," replied the sailor. "You might have overlooked some trifling thing that won't be of no use to you in the jungle, but that'll come in mighty handy to a poor sailor-man in London. Ah! just as I feared," he ejaculated an instant later as he withdrew a roll of bank-notes from Paulvitch's inside coat pocket.

The Russian scowled, muttering an imprecation; but nothing could be gained by argument, and so he did his best to reconcile himself to his loss in the knowledge that the sailor would never reach London to enjoy the fruits of his thievery.

It was with difficulty that Paulvitch restrained a consuming desire to taunt the man with a suggestion of the fate that would presently overtake him and the other members of the *Kincaid*'s company; but fearing to arouse the fellow's suspicions, he crossed the deck and lowered himself in silence into his canoe.

A minute or two later he was paddling toward the shore to be swallowed up in the darkness of the jungle night, and the terrors of a hideous existence from which, could he have had even a slight fore-knowledge of what awaited him in the long years to come, he would have fled to the certain death of the open sea rather than endure it.

The sailor, having made sure that Paulvitch had departed, returned to the forecastle, where he hid away his booty and turned into his bunk, while in the cabin that had belonged to the Russian there ticked on and on through the silences of the night the little mechanism in the small black box which held for the unconscious sleepers upon the ill-starred *Kincaid* the coming vengeance of the thwarted Russian.

XIX

THE LAST
OF THE "KINCAID"

hortly after the break of day Tarzan was on deck noting the condition of the weather. The wind had abated. The sky was cloudless. Every condition seemed ideal for the commencement of the return voyage to Jungle Island, where the beasts were to be left. And then—home!

The ape-man aroused the mate and gave instructions that the *Kincaid* sail at the earliest possible moment. The remaining members of the crew, safe in Lord Greystoke's assurance that they would not be prosecuted for their share in the villainies of the two Russians, hastened with cheerful alacrity to their several duties.

The beasts, liberated from the confinement of the hold, wandered about the deck, not a little to the discomfiture of the crew in whose minds there remained a still vivid picture of the savagery of the beasts in conflict with those who had gone to their deaths beneath the fangs and talons which even now seemed itching for the soft flesh of further prey.

Beneath the watchful eyes of Tarzan and Mugambi, however, Sheeta and the apes of Akut curbed their desires, so that the men worked about the deck amongst them in far greater security than they imagined.

At last the *Kincaid* slipped down the Ugambi and ran out upon the shimmering waters of the Atlantic. Tarzan and Jane Clayton watched the verdure-clad shore-line receding in the ship's wake, and for once the ape-man left his native soil without one single pang of regret. No ship that sailed the seven seas could have borne him away from Africa to resume his search for his lost boy with half the speed that the Englishman would have desired, and the slow-moving *Kincaid* seemed scarce to move at all to the impatient mind of the bereaved father.

Yet the vessel made progress even when she seemed to be standing still, and presently the low hills of Jungle Island became distinctly visible upon the western horizon ahead.

In the cabin of Alexander Paulvitch the thing within the black box ticked, ticked, ticked, with apparently unending monotony; but yet, second by second, a little arm which protruded from the periphery of one of its wheels came nearer and nearer to another little arm which projected from the hand which Paulvitch had set at a certain point upon the dial beside the clockwork. When those two arms touched one another the ticking of the mechanism would cease—for ever.

Jane and Tarzan stood upon the bridge looking out toward Jungle Island. The men were forward, also watching the land grow upward out of the ocean. The beasts had sought the shade of the galley, where they were curled up in sleep. All was quiet and peace upon the ship, and upon the waters.

Suddenly, without warning, the cabin roof shot up into the air, a cloud of dense smoke puffed far above the *Kincaid*, there was a terrific explosion which shook the vessel from stem to stern.

Instantly pandemonium broke loose upon the deck. The apes of Akut, terrified by the sound, ran hither and thither, snarling and growling. Sheeta leaped here and there, screaming out his startled terror in hideous cries that sent the ice of fear straight to the hearts of the *Kincaid*'s crew.

Mugambi, too, was trembling. Only Tarzan of the Apes and his wife retained their composure. Scarce had the debris settled than the ape-man was among the beasts, quieting their fears, talking to them in low, pacific tones, stroking their shaggy bodies, and assuring them, as only he could, that the immediate danger was over.

An examination of the wreckage showed that their greatest danger, now, lay in fire, for the flames were licking hungrily at the splintered wood of the wrecked cabin, and had already found a foothold upon the lower deck through a great jagged hole which the explosion had opened.

By a miracle no member of the ship's company had been injured by the blast, the origin of which remained for ever a total mystery to all but one—the sailor who knew that Paulvitch had been aboard the *Kincaid* and in his cabin the previous night. He guessed the truth; but discretion sealed his lips. It would, doubtless, fare none too well for the man who had permitted the arch enemy of them all aboard the ship in the watches of the night, where later he might set an infernal machine to blow them all to kingdom come. No, the man decided that he would keep this knowledge to himself.

As the flames gained headway it became apparent to Tarzan that whatever had caused the explosion had scattered some highly inflammable substance upon the surrounding woodwork, for the water which they poured in from the pump seemed rather to spread than to extinguish the blaze.

Fifteen minutes after the explosion great, black clouds of smoke were rising from the hold of the doomed vessel. The flames had reached the engine-room, and the ship no longer moved toward the shore. Her fate was as certain as though the waters had already closed above her charred and smoking remains.

"It is useless to remain aboard her longer," remarked the ape-man to the mate. "There is no telling but there may be other explosions, and as we cannot hope to save her, the safest thing which we can do is to take to the boats without further loss of time and make land."

Nor was there other alternative. Only the sailors could bring away any belongings, for the fire, which had not yet reached the forecastle, had consumed all in the vicinity of the cabin which the explosion had not destroyed.

Two boats were lowered, and as there was no sea the landing was made with infinite ease. Eager and anxious, the beasts of Tarzan sniffed the familiar air of their native island as the small boats drew in toward the beach, and scarce had their keels grated upon the sand than Sheeta and the apes of Akut were over the bows and racing swiftly toward the jungle. A half-sad smile curved the lips of the ape-man as he watched them go.

"Good-bye, my friends," he murmured. "You have been good and faithful allies, and I shall miss you."

"They will return, will they not, dear?" asked Jane Clayton, at his side.

"They may and they may not," replied the ape-man. "They have been ill at ease since they were forced to accept so many human beings into their confidence. Mugambi and I alone affected them less, for he and I are, at best, but half human. You, however, and the members of the crew are far too civilized for my beasts—it is you whom they are fleeing. Doubtless they feel that they cannot trust themselves in the close vicinity of so much perfectly good food without the danger that they may help themselves to a mouthful some time by mistake."

Jane laughed. "I think they are just trying to escape you," she retorted. "You are always making them stop something which they see no reason why they should not do. Like little children they are doubtless delighted at this opportunity to flee from the zone of parental discipline. If they come back, though, I hope they won't come by night."

"Or come hungry, eh?" laughed Tarzan.

For two hours after landing the little party stood watching the burning ship which they had abandoned. Then there came faintly to them from across the water the sound of a second explosion. The *Kincaid* settled rapidly almost immediately thereafter, and sank within a few minutes.

The cause of the second explosion was less a mystery than that of the first, the mate attributing it to the bursting of the boilers when the flames had finally reached them; but what had caused the first explosion was a subject of considerable speculation among the stranded company.

XX

JUNGLE ISLAND AGAIN

he first consideration of the party was to locate fresh water and make camp, for all knew that their term of existence upon Jungle Island might be drawn out to months, or even years.

Tarzan knew the nearest water, and to this he immediately led the party. Here the men fell to work to construct shelters and rude furniture while Tarzan went into the jungle after meat, leaving the faithful Mugambi and the Mosula woman to guard Jane, whose safety he would never trust to any member of the *Kincaid*'s cut-throat crew.

Lady Greystoke suffered far greater anguish than any other of the castaways, for the blow to her hopes and her already cruelly lacerated mother-heart lay not in her own privations but in the knowledge that she might now never be able to learn the fate of her first-born or do aught to discover his whereabouts, or ameliorate his condition—a condition which imagination naturally pictured in the most frightful forms.

For two weeks the party divided the time amongst the various duties which had been allotted to each. A daylight watch was maintained from sunrise to sunset upon a bluff near the camp—a jutting shoulder of rock which overlooked the sea. Here, ready for instant lighting, was gathered a huge pile of dry branches, while from a lofty pole which they had set in the ground there floated an improvised distress signal fashioned from a red undershirt which belonged to the mate of the *Kincaid*.

But never a speck upon the horizon that might be sail or smoke rewarded the tired eyes that in their endless, hopeless vigil strained daily out across the vast expanse of ocean.

It was Tarzan who suggested, finally, that they attempt to construct a vessel that would bear them back to the mainland. He alone could show them how to fashion rude tools, and when the idea had taken root in the minds of the men they were eager to commence their labours.

But as time went on and the Herculean nature of their task became more and more apparent they fell to grumbling, and to quarrelling among themselves, so that to the other dangers were now added dissension and suspicion.

More than before did Tarzan now fear to leave Jane among the half brutes of the *Kincaid*'s crew; but hunting he must do, for none other could so surely go forth and return with meat as he. Sometimes Mugambi spelled him at the hunting; but the black's spear and arrows were never so sure of results as the rope and knife of the ape-man.

Finally the men shirked their work, going off into the jungle by twos to explore and to hunt. All this time the camp had had no sight of Sheeta, or Akut and the other great apes, though Tarzan had sometimes met them in the jungle as he hunted.

And as matters tended from bad to worse in the camp of the castaways upon the east coast of Jungle Island, another camp came into being upon the north coast.

Here, in a little cove, lay a small schooner, the *Cowrie*, whose decks had but a few days since run red with the blood of her officers and the loyal members of her crew, for the *Cowrie* had fallen upon bad days when it had shipped such men as Gust and Momulla the Maori and that arch-fiend Kai Shang of Fachan.

There were others, too, ten of them all told, the scum of the South Sea ports; but Gust and Momulla and Kai Shang were the brains and cunning of the company. It was they who had instigated the mutiny that they might seize and divide the catch of pearls which constituted the wealth of the *Cowrie's* cargo.

It was Kai Shang who had murdered the captain as he lay asleep in his berth, and it had been Momulla the Maori who had led the attack upon the officer of the watch.

Gust, after his own peculiar habit, had found means to delegate to the others the actual taking of life. Not that Gust entertained any scruples on the subject, other than those which induced in him a rare regard for his own personal safety. There is always a certain element of risk to the assassin, for victims of deadly assault are seldom prone to die quietly and considerately. There is always a certain element of risk to go so far as to dispute the issue with the murderer. It was this chance of dispute which Gust preferred to forgo.

But now that the work was done the Swede aspired to the position of highest command among the mutineers. He had even gone so far as to appropriate and wear certain articles belonging to the murdered captain of the *Cowrie*—articles of apparel which bore upon them the badges and insignia of authority.

Kai Shang was peeved. He had no love for authority, and certainly not the slightest intention of submitting to the domination of an ordinary Swede sailor.

The seeds of discontent were, therefore, already planted in the camp of the mutineers of the *Cowrie* at the north edge of Jungle Island. But Kai Shang realized that he must act with circumspection, for Gust alone of the motley horde possessed sufficient knowledge of navigation to get them out of the South Atlantic and around the cape into more congenial waters where they might find a market for their ill-gotten wealth, and no questions asked.

The day before they sighted Jungle Island and discovered the little land-locked harbour upon the bosom of which the *Cowrie* now rode quietly at anchor, the watch had discovered the smoke and funnels of a warship upon the southern horizon.

The chance of being spoken to and investigated by a man-of-war appealed not at all to any of them, so they put into hiding for a few days until the danger should have passed.

And now Gust did not wish to venture out to sea again. There was no telling, he insisted, but that the ship they had seen was actually searching for them. Kai Shang pointed out that such could not be the case since it was impossible for any human being other than themselves to have knowledge of what had transpired aboard the *Cowrie*.

But Gust was not to be persuaded. In his wicked heart he nursed a scheme whereby he might increase his share of the booty by something like one hundred per cent. He alone could sail the *Cowrie*, therefore the others could not leave Jungle Island without him; but what was there to prevent Gust, with just sufficient men to man the schooner, slipping away from Kai Shang, Momulla the Maori, and some half of the crew when opportunity presented?

It was for this opportunity that Gust waited. Some day there would come a moment when Kai Shang, Momulla, and three or four of the others would be absent from camp, exploring or hunting. The Swede racked his brain for some plan whereby he might successfully lure from the sight of the anchored ship those whom he had determined to abandon.

To this end he organized hunting party after hunting party, but always the devil of perversity seemed to enter the soul of Kai Shang, so that wily celestial would never hunt except in the company of Gust himself.

One day Kai Shang spoke secretly with Momulla the Maori, pouring into the brown ear of his companion the suspicions which he harboured concerning the Swede. Momulla was for going immediately and running a long knife through the heart of the traitor.

It is true that Kai Shang had no other evidence than the natural cunning of his own knavish soul—but he imagined in the intentions of Gust what he himself would have been glad to accomplish had the means lain at hand.

But he dared not let Momulla slay the Swede, upon whom they depended to guide them to their destination. They decided, however, that it would do no harm to attempt to frighten Gust into acceding to their demands, and with this purpose in mind the Maori sought out the self-constituted commander of the party.

When he broached the subject of immediate departure Gust again raised his former objection—that the warship might very probably be patrolling the sea directly in their southern path, waiting for them to make the attempt to reach other waters.

Momulla scoffed at the fears of his fellow, pointing out that as no one aboard any warship knew of their mutiny there could be no reason why they should be suspected.

"Ah!" exclaimed Gust, "there is where you are wrong. There is where you are lucky that you have an educated man like me to tell you what to do. You are an ignorant savage, Momulla, and so you know nothing of wireless."

The Maori leaped to his feet and laid his hand upon the hilt of his knife.

"I am no savage," he shouted.

"I was only joking," the Swede hastened to explain. "We are old friends, Momulla; we cannot afford to quarrel, at least not while old Kai Shang is plotting to steal all the pearls from us. If he could find a man to navigate the *Cowrie* he would leave us in a minute. All his talk about getting away from here is just because he has some scheme in his head to get rid of us."

"But the wireless," asked Momulla. "What has the wireless to do with our remaining here?"

"Oh yes," replied Gust, scratching his head. He was wondering if the Maori were really so ignorant as to believe the preposterous lie he was about to unload upon him. "Oh yes! You see every warship is equipped with what they call a wireless apparatus. It lets them talk to other ships hundreds of miles away, and it lets them listen to all that is said on these other ships. Now, you see, when you fellows were shooting up the *Cowrie* you did a whole lot of loud talking, and there isn't any doubt but that that warship was a-lyin' off south of us listenin' to it all. Of course they might not have learned the name of the ship, but they heard enough to know that the crew of some ship was mutinying and killin' her officers. So you see they'll be waiting to search every ship they sight for a long time to come, and they may not be far away now."

When he had ceased speaking the Swede strove to assume an air of composure that his listener might not have his suspicions aroused as to the truth of the statements that had just been made.

Momulla sat for some time in silence, eyeing Gust. At last he rose.

"You are a great liar," he said. "If you don't get us on our way by tomorrow you'll never have another chance to lie, for I heard two of the men saying that they'd like to run a knife into you and that if you kept them in this hole any longer they'd do it."

"Go and ask Kai Shang if there is not a wireless," replied Gust. "He will tell you that there is such a thing and that vessels can talk to one another across hundreds of miles of water. Then say to the two men who wish to kill me that if they do so they will never live to spend their share of the swag, for only I can get you safely to any port."

So Momulla went to Kai Shang and asked him if there was such an apparatus as a wireless by means of which ships could talk with each other at great distances, and Kai Shang told him that there was.

Momulla was puzzled; but still he wished to leave the island, and was willing to take his chances on the open sea rather than to remain longer in the monotony of the camp.

"If we only had someone else who could navigate a ship!" wailed Kai Shang.

That afternoon Momulla went hunting with two other Maoris. They hunted toward the south, and had not gone far from camp when they were surprised by the sound of voices ahead of them in the jungle.

They knew that none of their own men had preceded them, and as all were convinced that the island was uninhabited, they were inclined to flee in terror on the hypothesis that the place was haunted—possibly by the ghosts of the murdered officers and men of the *Cowrie*.

But Momulla was even more curious than he was superstitious, and so he quelled his natural desire to flee from the supernatural. Motioning his companions to follow his example, he dropped to his hands and knees, crawling forward stealthily and with quakings of heart through the jungle in the direction from which came the voices of the unseen speakers.

Presently, at the edge of a little clearing, he halted, and there he breathed a deep sigh of relief, for plainly before him he saw two flesh-and-blood men sitting upon a fallen log and talking earnestly together.

One was Schneider, mate of the *Kincaid,* and the other was a seaman named Schmidt.

"I think we can do it, Schmidt," Schneider was saying. "A good canoe wouldn't be hard to build, and three of us could paddle it to the mainland in a day if the wind was right and the sea reasonably calm. There ain't no use waiting for the men to build a big enough boat to take the whole party, for they're sore now and sick of working like slaves all day long. It ain't none of our business anyway to save the Englishman. Let him look out for himself, says I." He paused for a moment, and then eyeing the other to note the effect of his next words, he continued, "But we might take the woman. It would be a shame to leave a nice-lookin' piece like she is in such a Gott-forsaken hole as this here island."

Schmidt looked up and grinned.

"So that's how she's blowin', is it?" he asked. "Why didn't you say so in the first place? Wot's in it for me if I help you?"

"She ought to pay us well to get her back to civilization," explained Schneider, "an' I tell you what I'll do. I'll just whack up with the two men that helps me. I'll take half an' they can divide the other half—you an' whoever the other bloke is. I'm sick of this place, an' the sooner I get out of it the better I'll like it. What do you say?"

"Suits me," replied Schmidt. "I wouldn't know how to reach the mainland myself, an' know that none o' the other fellows would, so's you're the only one that knows anything of navigation you're the fellow I'll tie to."

Momulla the Maori pricked up his ears. He had a smattering of every tongue that is spoken upon the seas, and more than a few times had he sailed on English ships, so that he understood fairly well all that had passed between Schneider and Schmidt since he had stumbled upon them.

He rose to his feet and stepped into the clearing. Schneider and his companion started as nervously as though a ghost had risen before them. Schneider reached for his revolver. Momulla raised his right hand, palm forward, as a sign of his pacific intentions.

"I am a friend," he said. "I heard you; but do not fear that I will reveal what you have said. I can help you, and you can help me." He was addressing Schneider. "You can navigate a ship, but you have no ship. We have a ship, but no one to navigate it. If you will come with us and ask no questions we will let you take the ship where you will after you have landed us at a certain port, the name of which we will give you later. You can take the woman of whom you speak, and we will ask no questions either. Is it a bargain?" Schneider desired more information, and got as much as Momulla thought best to give him. Then the Maori suggested that they speak with Kai Shang. The two members of the *Kincaid*'s company followed Momulla and his fellows to a point in the jungle close by the camp of the mutineers. Here Momulla hid them while he went in search of Kai Shang, first admonishing his Maori companions to stand guard over the two sailors lest they change their minds and attempt to escape. Schneider and Schmidt were virtually prisoners, though they did not know it.

Presently Momulla returned with Kai Shang, to whom he had briefly narrated the details of the stroke of good fortune that had come to them. The Chinaman spoke at length with Schneider, until, notwithstanding his natural suspicion of the sincerity of all men, he became quite convinced that Schneider was quite as much a rogue as himself and that the fellow was anxious to leave the island.

These two premises accepted there could be little doubt that Schneider would prove trustworthy in so far as accepting the command of the *Cowrie* was concerned; after that Kai Shang knew that he could find means to coerce the man into submission to his further wishes.

When Schneider and Schmidt left them and set out in the direction of their own camp, it was with feelings of far greater relief than they had experienced in many a day. Now at last they saw a feasible plan for leaving the island upon a seaworthy craft. There would be no more hard labour at ship-building, and no risking their lives upon a crudely built makeshift that would be quite as likely to go to the bottom as it would to reach the mainland.

Also, they were to have assistance in capturing the woman, or rather women, for when Momulla had learned that there was a black woman in the other camp he had insisted that she be brought along as well as the white woman.

As Kai Shang and Momulla entered their camp, it was with a realization that they no longer needed Gust. They marched straight to the tent in which they might expect to find him at that hour of the day, for though it would have been more comfortable for the entire party to remain aboard the ship, they had mutually decided that it would be safer for all concerned were they to pitch their camp ashore.

Each knew that in the heart of the others was sufficient treachery to make it unsafe for any member of the party to go ashore leaving the others in possession of the *Cowrie*, so not more than two or three men at a time were ever permitted aboard the vessel unless all the balance of the company was there too.

As the two crossed toward Gust's tent the Maori felt the edge of his long knife with one grimy, calloused thumb. The Swede would have felt far from comfortable could he have seen this significant action, or read what was passing amid the convolutions of the brown man's cruel brain.

Now it happened that Gust was at that moment in the tent occupied by the cook, and this tent stood but a few feet from his own. So that he heard the approach of Kai Shang and Momulla, though he did not, of course, dream that it had any special significance for him.

Chance had it, though, that he glanced out of the doorway of the cook's tent at the very moment that Kai Shang and Momulla approached the entrance to his, and he thought that he noted a stealthiness in their movements that comported poorly with amicable or friendly intentions, and then, just as they two slunk within the interior, Gust caught a glimpse of the long knife which Momulla the Maori was then carrying behind his back.

The Swede's eyes opened wide, and a funny little sensation assailed the roots of his hairs. Also he turned almost white beneath his tan. Quite precipitately he left the cook's tent. He was not one who required a detailed exposition of intentions that were quite all too obvious.

As surely as though he had heard them plotting, he knew that Kai Shang and Momulla had come to take his life. The knowledge that he alone could navigate the *Cowrie* had, up to now, been sufficient assurance of his safety; but quite evidently something had occurred of which he had no knowledge that would make it quite worth the while of his co-conspirators to eliminate him.

Without a pause Gust darted across the beach and into the jungle. He was afraid of the jungle; uncanny noises that were indeed frightful came forth from its recesses—the tangled mazes of the mysterious country back of the beach.

But if Gust was afraid of the jungle he was far more afraid of Kai Shang and Momulla. The dangers of the jungle were more or less problematical, while the danger that menaced him at the hands of his companions was a perfectly well-known quantity, which might be expressed in terms of a few inches of cold steel, or the coil of a light rope. He had seen Kai Shang garrotte a man at Pai-sha in a dark alleyway back of Loo Kotai's place. He feared the rope, therefore, more than he did the knife of the Maori; but he feared them both too much to remain within reach of either. Therefore he chose the pitiless jungle.

XXI

The Law of the Jungle

I n Tarzan's camp, by dint of threats and promised rewards, the ape-man had finally succeeded in getting the hull of a large skiff almost completed. Much of the work he and Mugambi had done with their own hands in addition to furnishing the camp with meat.

Schneider, the mate, had been doing considerable grumbling, and had at last openly deserted the work and gone off into the jungle with Schmidt to hunt. He said that he wanted a rest, and Tarzan, rather than add to the unpleasantness which already made camp life almost unendurable, had permitted the two men to depart without a remonstrance.

Upon the following day, however, Schneider affected a feeling of remorse for his action, and set to work with a will upon the skiff. Schmidt also worked good-naturedly, and Lord Greystoke congratulated himself that at last the men had awakened to the necessity for the labour which was being asked of them and to their obligations to the balance of the party.

It was with a feeling of greater relief than he had experienced for many a day that he set out that noon to hunt deep in the jungle for a herd of small deer which Schneider reported that he and Schmidt had seen there the day before.

The direction in which Schneider had reported seeing the deer was toward the south-west, and to that point the ape-man swung easily through the tangled verdure of the forest.

And as he went there approached from the north a half-dozen ill-featured men who went stealthily through the jungle as go men bent upon the commission of a wicked act.

They thought that they travelled unseen; but behind them, almost from the moment they quitted their own camp, a tall man crept upon their trail. In the man's eyes were hate and fear, and a great curiosity. Why went Kai Shang and Momulla and the others thus stealthily toward the south? What did they expect to find there? Gust shook his low-browed head in perplexity. But he would know. He would follow them and learn their plans, and then if he could thwart them he would—that went without question.

At first he had thought that they searched for him; but finally his better judgment assured him that such could not be the case, since they had accomplished all they really desired by chasing him out of camp. Never would Kai Shang or Momulla go to such pains to slay him or another unless it would put money into their pockets, and as Gust had no money it was evident that they were searching for some-one else.

Presently the party he trailed came to a halt. Its members concealed themselves in the foliage bordering the game trail along which they had come. Gust, that he might the better observe, clambered into the branches of a tree to the rear of them, being careful that the leafy fronds hid him from the view of his erstwhile mates.

He had not long to wait before he saw a strange white man approach carefully along the trail from the south.

At sight of the new-comer Momulla and Kai Shang arose from their places of concealment and greeted him. Gust could not overhear what passed between them. Then the man returned in the direction from which he had come.

He was Schneider. Nearing his camp he circled to the opposite side of it, and presently came running in breathlessly. Excitedly he hastened to Mugambi.

"Quick!" he cried. "Those apes of yours have caught Schmidt and will kill him if we do not hasten to his aid. You alone can call them off. Take Jones and Sullivan—you may need help—and get to him as quick as you can. Follow the game trail south for about a mile. I will remain here. I am too spent with running to go back with you," and the mate of the *Kincaid* threw himself upon the ground, panting as though he was almost done for.

Mugambi hesitated. He had been left to guard the two women. He did not know what to do, and then Jane Clayton, who had heard Schneider's story, added her pleas to those of the mate.

"Do not delay," she urged. "We shall be all right here. Mr. Schneider will remain with us. Go, Mugambi. The poor fellow must be saved."

Schmidt, who lay hidden in a bush at the edge of the camp, grinned. Mugambi, heeding the commands of his mistress, though still doubtful of the wisdom of his action, started off toward the south, with Jones and Sullivan at his heels.

No sooner had he disappeared than Schmidt rose and darted north into the jungle, and a few minutes later the face of Kai Shang of Fachan appeared at the edge of the clearing. Schneider saw the China-man, and motioned to him that the coast was clear.

Jane Clayton and the Mosula woman were sitting at the opening of the former's tent, their backs toward the approaching ruffians. The first intimation that either had of the presence of strangers in camp was the sudden appearance of a half-dozen ragged villains about them.

"Come!" said Kai Shang, motioning that the two arise and follow him.

Jane Clayton sprang to her feet and looked about for Schneider, only to see him standing behind the newcomers, a grin upon his face. At his side stood Schmidt. Instantly she saw that she had been made the victim of a plot.

"What is the meaning of this?" she asked, addressing the mate.

"It means that we have found a ship and that we can now escape from Jungle Island," replied the man.

"Why did you send Mugambi and the others into the jungle?" she inquired.

"They are not coming with us—only you and I, and the Mosula woman."

"Come!" repeated Kai Shang, and seized Jane Clayton's wrist.

One of the Maoris grasped the black woman by the arm, and when she would have screamed struck her across the mouth.

Mugambi raced through the jungle toward the south. Jones and Sullivan trailed far behind. For a mile he continued upon his way to the relief of Schmidt, but no signs saw he of the missing man or of any of the apes of Akut.

At last he halted and called aloud the summons which he and Tarzan had used to hail the great anthropoids. There was no response. Jones and Sullivan came up with the black warrior as the latter stood voicing his weird call. For another half-mile the black searched, calling occasionally.

Finally the truth flashed upon him, and then, like a frightened deer, he wheeled and dashed back toward camp. Arriving there, it was but a moment before full confirmation of his fears was impressed upon him. Lady Greystoke and the Mosula woman were gone. So, likewise, was Schneider.

When Jones and Sullivan joined Mugambi he would have killed them in his anger, thinking them parties to the plot; but they finally succeeded in partially convincing him that they had known nothing of it.

As they stood speculating upon the probable whereabouts of the women and their abductor, and the purpose which Schneider had in mind in taking them from camp, Tarzan of the Apes swung from the branches of a tree and crossed the clearing toward them.

His keen eyes detected at once that something was radically wrong, and when he had heard Mugambi's story his jaws clicked angrily together as he knitted his brows in thought.

What could the mate hope to accomplish by taking Jane Clayton from a camp upon a small island from which there was no escape from the vengeance of Tarzan? The ape-man could not believe the fellow such a fool, and then a slight realization of the truth dawned upon him.

Schneider would not have committed such an act unless he had been reasonably sure that there was a way by which he could quit Jungle Island with his prisoners. But why had he taken the black woman as well? There must have been others, one of whom wanted the dusky female.

"Come," said Tarzan, "there is but one thing to do now, and that is to follow the trail."

As he finished speaking a tall, ungainly figure emerged from the jungle north of the camp. He came straight toward the four men. He was an entire stranger to all of them, not one of whom had dreamed that another human being than those of their own camp dwelt upon the unfriendly shores of Jungle Island.

It was Gust. He came directly to the point.

"Your women were stolen," he said. "If you want ever to see them again, come quickly and follow me. If we do not hurry the *Cowrie* will be standing out to sea by the time we reach her anchorage."

"Who are you?" asked Tarzan. "What do you know of the theft of my wife and the black woman?"

"I heard Kai Shang and Momulla the Maori plot with two men of your camp. They had chased me from our camp, and would have killed me. Now I will get even with them. Come!"

Gust led the four men of the *Kincaid's* camp at a rapid trot through the jungle toward the north. Would they come to the sea in time? But a few more minutes would answer the question.

And when at last the little party did break through the last of the screening foliage, and the harbour and the ocean lay before them, they realized that fate had been most cruelly unkind, for the *Cowrie* was already under sail and moving slowly out of the mouth of the harbour into the open sea.

What were they to do? Tarzan's broad chest rose and fell to the force of his pent emotions. The last blow seemed to have fallen, and if ever in all his life Tarzan of the Apes had had occasion to abandon hope it was now that he saw the ship bearing his wife to some frightful fate moving gracefully over the rippling water, so very near and yet so hideously far away.

In silence he stood watching the vessel. He saw it turn toward the east and finally disappear around a headland on its way he knew not whither. Then he dropped upon his haunches and buried his face in his hands.

It was after dark that the five men returned to the camp on the east shore. The night was hot and sultry. No slightest breeze ruffled the foliage of the trees or rippled the mirror-like surface of the ocean. Only a gentle swell rolled softly in upon the beach.

Never had Tarzan seen the great Atlantic so ominously at peace. He was standing at the edge of the beach gazing out to sea in the direction of the mainland, his mind filled with sorrow and hopelessness, when from the jungle close behind the camp came the uncanny wail of a panther.

There was a familiar note in the weird cry, and almost mechanically Tarzan turned his head and answered. A moment later the tawny figure of Sheeta slunk out into the half-light of the beach. There was no moon, but the sky was brilliant with stars. Silently the savage brute came to the side of the man. It had been long since Tarzan had seen his old fighting companion, but the soft purr was sufficient to assure him that the animal still recalled the bonds which had united them in the past.

The ape-man let his fingers fall upon the beast's coat, and as Sheeta pressed close against his leg he caressed and fondled the wicked head while his eyes continued to search the blackness of the waters.

Presently he started. What was that? He strained his eyes into the night. Then he turned and called aloud to the men smoking upon their blankets in the camp. They came running to his side; but Gust hesitated when he saw the nature of Tarzan's companion.

"Look!" cried Tarzan. "A light! A ship's light! It must be the *Cowrie*. They are becalmed." And then with an exclamation of renewed hope, "We can reach them! The skiff will carry us easily."

Gust demurred. "They are well armed," he warned. "We could not take the ship—just five of us."

"There are six now," replied Tarzan, pointing to Sheeta, "and we can have more still in a half-hour. Sheeta is the equivalent of twenty men, and the few others I can bring will add full a hundred to our fighting strength. You do not know them."

The ape-man turned and raised his head toward the jungle, while there pealed from his lips, time after time, the fearsome cry of the bull-ape who would summon his fellows.

Presently from the jungle came an answering cry, and then another and another. Gust shuddered. Among what sort of creatures had fate thrown him? Were not Kai Shang and Momulla to be preferred to this great white giant who stroked a panther and called to the beasts of the jungle?

In a few minutes the apes of Akut came crashing through the underbrush and out upon the beach, while in the meantime the five men had been struggling with the unwieldy bulk of the skiff's hull.

By dint of Herculean efforts they had managed to get it to the water's edge. The oars from the two small boats of the *Kincaid*, which had been washed away by an off-shore wind the very night that the party had landed, had been in use to support the canvas of the sailcloth tents. These were hastily requisitioned, and by the time Akut and his followers came down to the water all was ready for embarkation.

Once again the hideous crew entered the service of their master, and without question took up their places in the skiff. The four men, for Gust could not be prevailed upon to accompany the party, fell to the oars, using them paddle-wise, while some of the apes followed their example, and presently the ungainly skiff was moving quietly out to sea in the direction of the light which rose and fell gently with the swell.

A sleepy sailor kept a poor vigil upon the *Cowrie's* deck, while in the cabin below Schneider paced up and down arguing with Jane Clayton. The woman had found a revolver in a table drawer in the room in which she had been locked, and now she kept the mate of the *Kincaid* at bay with the weapon.

The Mosula woman kneeled behind her, while Schneider paced up and down before the door, threatening and pleading and promising, but all to no avail. Presently from the deck above came a shout of warning and a shot. For an instant Jane Clayton relaxed her vigilance, and turned her eyes toward the cabin skylight. Simultaneously Schneider was upon her.

The first intimation the watch had that there was another craft within a thousand miles of the *Cowrie* came when he saw the head and shoulders of a man poked over the ship's side. Instantly the fellow sprang to his feet with a cry and levelled his revolver at the intruder. It was his cry and the subsequent report of the revolver which threw Jane Clayton off her guard.

Upon deck the quiet of fancied security soon gave place to the wildest pandemonium. The crew of the *Cowrie* rushed above armed with revolvers, cutlasses, and the long knives that many of them habitually wore; but the alarm had come too late. Already the beasts of Tarzan were upon the ship's deck, with Tarzan and the two men of the *Kincaid's* crew.

In the face of the frightful beasts the courage of the mutineers wavered and broke. Those with revolvers fired a few scattering shots and then raced for some place of supposed safety. Into the shrouds went some; but the apes of Akut were more at home there than they.

Screaming with terror the Maoris were dragged from their lofty perches. The beasts, uncontrolled by Tarzan who had gone in search of Jane, loosed in the full fury of their savage natures upon the unhappy wretches who fell into their clutches.

Sheeta, in the meanwhile, had felt his great fangs sink into but a singular jugular. For a moment he mauled the corpse, and then he spied Kai Shang darting down the companionway toward his cabin.

With a shrill scream Sheeta was after him—a scream which awoke an almost equally uncanny cry in the throat of the terror-stricken Chinaman. But Kai Shang reached his cabin a fraction of a second ahead of the panther, and leaping within slammed the door— just too late. Sheeta's great body hurtled against it before the catch engaged, and a moment later Kai Shang was gibbering and shrieking in the back of an upper berth.

Lightly Sheeta sprang after his victim, and presently the wicked days of Kai Shang of Fachan were ended, and Sheeta was gorging himself upon tough and stringy flesh.

A moment scarcely had elapsed after Schneider leaped upon Jane Clayton and wrenched the revolver from her hand, when the door of the cabin opened and a tall and half-naked white man stood framed within the portal.

Silently he leaped across the cabin. Schneider felt sinewy fingers at his throat. He turned his head to see who had attacked him, and his eyes went wide when he saw the face of the ape-man close above his own.

Grimly the fingers tightened upon the mate's throat. He tried to scream, to plead, but no sound came forth. His eyes protruded as he struggled for freedom, for breath, for life.

Jane Clayton seized her husband's hands and tried to drag them from the throat of the dying man; but Tarzan only shook his head.

"Not again," he said quietly. "Before have I permitted scoundrels to live, only to suffer and to have you suffer for my mercy. This time we shall make sure of one scoundrel—sure that he will never again harm us or another," and with a sudden wrench he twisted the neck of the perfidious mate until there was a sharp crack, and the man's body lay limp and motionless in the ape-man's grasp. With a gesture of disgust Tarzan tossed the corpse aside. Then he returned to the deck, followed by Jane and the Mosula woman.

The battle there was over. Schmidt and Momulla and two others alone remained alive of all the company of the *Cowrie*, for they had found sanctuary in the forecastle. The others had died, horribly, and as they deserved, beneath the fangs and talons of the beasts of Tarzan, and in the morning the sun rose on a grisly sight upon the deck of the unhappy *Cowrie*; but this time the blood which stained her white planking was the blood of the guilty and not of the innocent.

Tarzan brought forth the men who had hidden in the forecastle, and without promises of immunity from punishment forced them to help work the vessel—the only alternative was immediate death.

A stiff breeze had risen with the sun, and with canvas spread the *Cowrie* set in toward Jungle Island, where a few hours later, Tarzan picked up Gust and bid farewell to Sheeta and the apes of Akut, for here he set the beasts ashore to pursue the wild and natural life they loved so well; nor did they lose a moment's time in disappearing into the cool depths of their beloved jungle.

That they knew that Tarzan was to leave them may be doubted— except possibly in the case of the more intelligent Akut, who alone of all the others remained upon the beach as the small boat drew away toward the schooner, carrying his savage lord and master from him.

And as long as their eyes could span the distance, Jane and Tarzan, standing upon the deck, saw the lonely figure of the shaggy anthropoid motionless upon the surf-beaten sands of Jungle Island.

It was three days later that the *Cowrie* fell in with H.M. sloop-of-war *Shorewater*, through whose wireless Lord Greystoke soon got in communication with London. Thus he learned that which filled his and his wife's heart with joy and thanksgiving—little Jack was safe at Lord Greystoke's town house.

It was not until they reached London that they learned the details of the remarkable chain of circumstances that had preserved the infant unharmed.

It developed that Rokoff, fearing to take the child aboard the *Kincaid* by day, had hidden it in a low den where nameless infants were harboured, intending to carry it to the steamer after dark.

His confederate and chief lieutenant, Paulvitch, true to the long years of teaching of his wily master, had at last succumbed to the treachery and greed that had always marked his superior, and, lured by the thoughts of the immense ransom that he might win by returning the child unharmed, had divulged the secret of its parentage to the woman who maintained the foundling asylum. Through her he had arranged for the substitution of another infant, knowing full well that never until it was too late would Rokoff suspect the trick that had been played upon him.

The woman had promised to keep the child until Paulvitch returned to England; but she, in turn, had been tempted to betray her trust by the lure of gold, and so had opened negotiations with Lord Greystoke's solicitors for the return of the child.

Esmeralda, the old Negro nurse whose absence on a vacation in America at the time of the abduction of little Jack had been attributed by her as the cause of the calamity, had returned and positively identified the infant.

The ransom had been paid, and within ten days of the date of his kidnapping the future Lord Greystoke, none the worse for his experience, had been returned to his father's home.

And so that last and greatest of Nikolas Rokoff's many rascalities had not only miserably miscarried through the treachery he had taught his only friend, but it had resulted in the arch-villain's death, and given to Lord and Lady Greystoke a peace of mind that neither could ever have felt so long as the vital spark remained in the body of the Russian and his malign mind was free to formulate new atrocities against them.

Rokoff was dead, and while the fate of Paulvitch was unknown, they had every reason to believe that he had succumbed to the dangers of the jungle where last they had seen him—the malicious tool of his master.

And thus, in so far as they might know, they were to be freed for ever from the menace of these two men—the only enemies which Tarzan of the Apes ever had had occasion to fear, because they struck at him cowardly blows, through those he loved.

It was a happy family party that were reunited in Greystoke House the day that Lord Greystoke and his lady landed upon English soil from the deck of the *Shorewater*.

Accompanying them were Mugambi and the Mosula woman whom he had found in the bottom of the canoe that night upon the bank of the little tributary of the Ugambi.

The woman had preferred to cling to her new lord and master rather than return to the marriage she had tried to escape.

Tarzan had proposed to them that they might find a home upon his vast African estates in the land of the Waziri, where they were to be sent as soon as opportunity presented itself.

Possibly we shall see them all there amid the savage romance of the grim jungle and the great plains where Tarzan of the Apes loves best to be.

Who knows?

ABOUT THE AUTHOR

 orn on September 1, 1875, into a well-to-do-family in Chicago, Edgar Rice Burroughs enjoyed a privileged upbringing and education. He tried his hand at several business ventures, but found himself drawn more to an itinerant life of adventure than to a life in the boardroom.

In 1912, after many failed business ventures, the thirty-six-year-old Burroughs published his first story, "Under the Moons of Mars," in the pulp magazine *All-Story*. It was so successful that he turned soon thereafter to writing full time. He would write nearly 70 novels and numerous short stories before his death in 1950. Although best known for his immensely popular *Tarzan* novels—he later bought an estate near where the films were shot in Southern California that he named Tarzana—Burroughs didn't confine himself to a single genre, and also wrote medieval romances, westerns, and mainstream novels.

Among his many science-fiction works, Burroughs wrote eleven novels in the John Carter of Mars series, the titular final installment of which was published fourteen years after his death.